HIGH PRAISE FOR DAVID ZINDELL

NEVERNESS

"Excellent hard science fiction . . . Ideas splash out of Zindell's mind and flow across the pages of this book."—Orson Scott Card

"A first novel that has the power to renew one's faith in the genre."—*Booklist*

"[Zindell's] feat of universe crafting propels him instantly into the big leagues with the likes of Frank Herbert and Ursula K. LeGuin."—Edward Bryant

"Talented, ambitious . . . thoughtful philosophic concepts and challenging writing, recalling early John Barth."—*Publishers Weekly*

THE BROKEN GOD

"Science fiction as it ought to be: challenging, imaginative, thought-provoking—and well written. Zindell has placed himself at the forefront of literary SF."—*Times Literary Supplement*, London

"Rich and rewarding . . . Zindell's come into his maturity, and science fiction is the better for it."—*Locus*

"Perhaps the most ambitious cosmology opera yet . . . rich and skillful."—Paul McAuley

"One of the greatest series of an imagined world."
—*The Denver Post*

THE WILD

"Magnificently written . . . science meets art, mysticism, ecstasy, terror, and one's first reaction is likely to be WOW!"—*Locus*

"Sweeping and poetic."—*The Denver Post*

BOOKS BY DAVID ZINDELL

The Broken God
Neverness
The Wild

DAVID ZINDELL

WAR
IN
HEAVEN

BANTAM BOOKS
NEW YORK · TORONTO · LONDON · SYDNEY · AUCKLAND

THE WAR IN HEAVEN

A Bantam Spectra Book / January 1998

ISBN 0-553-28967-5

Published simultaneously in the United States and Canada

Bantam Books are published by Bantam Books, a division of Bantam Double-
day Dell Publishing Group, Inc. Its trademark, consisting of the words ''Bantam Books'' and the portrayal of a rooster, is Registered in U.S. Patent and
Trademark Office and in other countries. Marca Registrada. Bantam Books,
1540 Broadway, New York, New York 10036.

PRINTED IN THE UNITED STATES OF AMERICA

WCD   10 9 8 7 6 5 4 3 2 1

WAR IN HEAVEN

IN THE HALL OF
THE LORDS

Everything is God.
God is the wild white thallow alone in the sky;
God is the snowworm dreaming in his icy burrow;
God is the silence out in the great loneliness of the sea;
God is the scream of a mother giving birth to her child.
Who has beheld the world through God's shimmering
  eyes?
God can see all things but cannot see himself.
God is a baby blind to his own terrible beauty.
Someday God will be a man who has learned how to
  see.

—from the Devaki *Song of Life*

I know little of God, but all too much of that godly race of beings that some call man. As gods we are destined to be—so teach the scryers and prophets of religions new and old. And yet few understand what is required to be a god, much less a true man. There are those who view the gods of the galaxy—the Degula Trinity, Iamme, the Silicon God, and all the rest—as perfect beings beyond pain or strife or death. But it is not so. The gods, though they be made of a million crystalline spheres as large as a moon, can die: the murder of Ede the God gives proof of the ultimate doom awaiting all beings whether made of diamond circuitry or flesh and blood. The gods, too, make war upon each other. Two million years ago, it is said, the Ieldra defeated the Dark God and thus saved the Milky Way from the fate of Dichali and the Aud Spiral and other galaxies that have disappeared down the black hole of the gods' lust for the infinite.

It is also said that the Ieldra have fused their souls into the light streaming out of the core of our galaxy, but other gods have evolved to replace them. There is Ai and Pure Mind and the April Colonial Intelligence and the One. And, of course, the greatest god of all, the Solid State Entity, She who had once been a woman named Kalinda of the Flowers. Compared to Her love of the stars and the life born in their fiery, hydrogen wombs, the ardor of a man and a woman for each other is only as a flaming match held up to the sun. And compared to Her hatred of the Silicon God, the passion of all the human beings who have ever lived is less than a drop of water in a boiling sea. And yet the human urge to destroy is no small thing. Human beings, as well as gods, can make war. They can destroy the stars. And yet they can say yes to the unfolding of new forms throughout the universe and create, too. This is the story of a man who was both creator and destroyer, my son, Danlo wi Soli Ringess—a simple pilot wise in the ways of peace who brought war to the heavens of many worlds.

One day as the galaxy turned slowly about its celestial center, a lightship fell out into the near space above a watery world named Thiells. The *Snowy Owl* was a long, graceful sweep of spun diamond, and it had carried Danlo across the galaxy from the Star of Neverness to lost Tannahill. His journey across the stars, and through the wild spaces of the manifold that lies *beneath* the stars, had been dangerous and long. Nine other pilots in their individual ships had set out on his quest to talk with a goddess, but only he had survived to fall on to the far reaches of the galaxy's Perseus Arm. He had crossed the entire Vild, that hellish region of fractured space and dust and stars blown into dazzling supernovas. And then he had returned coreward across many light years to Thiells at the other edge of the Vild. Although he had fallen farther than any pilot in history, he was not the only one to have made a great journey.

His order—the Order of Mystic Mathematicians—had begun the great Second Vild Mission to save the stars. Other pilots on other quests had flung their lightships into the Vild like so many grains of sand cast into a raging sea. They were Peter Eyota and Henrios li Radman and the great Edreiya Chu, she of the *Golden Lotus* and the golden eyes that could see deeper into the manifold than could most pilots. Still others—Helena Charbo, Aja, and Alark of Urradeth—had already found their way back to Thiells or were returning to the safety of the Order only now, even as Danlo returned. Of course, no place in the Vild (or the universe) was truly safe, for even such a peaceful world as Thiells must turn its soft, round face to the killing radiation of the stars. These great white blisters of light erupted from the black heavens all about Danlo's ship. All were old supernovas, and distant—too weak to burn the trees or birds or flowers of Thiells. But no one knew when a more murderous light might suddenly devour the sky and put an end to the new academy that the lords of Danlo's order had decided to build on this world. It was, in part, to tell of one such supernova that Danlo had come to Thiells.

And so he took his shimmering ship down through the sky's cold ozone into the lower and warmer layers of the atmosphere. It was a perfect, blue inside blue day of sunlight and clarity. Flying was a joy—falling and gliding down through space on wings of diamond toward the Order's new city, which the Lord Pilot had named, simply, Lightstone. As with Neverness, whom the pilots and other ordermen had abandoned a few years before, this was to be a City of Light—a great, gleaming city upon a hill that would bring the Order's cold enlightenment to all the peoples of the Vild.

Actually, Lightstone was built across three hills, on a peninsula of a large island surrounded by ocean. And it shimmered in the noonday sun, for all its buildings were wrought of white granite or organic stone. As Danlo fell down to earth, he looked out the windows of the *Snowy Owl* and caught the glint of rose and amethyst and a thousand other colors scattered from street to street and hill to hill. Soon his ship swooped down to one of the many runs crossing the city's light field. There, a mile from a neighborhood of little stone cottages, out on a plain covered with flowering bushes and rocks, the *Snowy Owl* at last came to rest. And for the first time in many days, Danlo felt the long, heavy pull of gravity deep within his bones. It took him little time to gather his things together into the plain wooden chest that he had been given as a novice years ago. He dressed himself in his formal, black pilot's robe before breaking the seal to the pit of his ship. And then he climbed down to the run's hard surface. For the first time in more than a year, he stood squinting at the bright light of a real and open sky.

"Hello, Pilot," a voice called out to him. "You've fallen far and well, haven't you?"

Danlo stood holding his wooden chest while he turned to look toward the end of the run and the great sweeping buildings beyond. There waited the usual cadre of programmers, tinkers and other professionals who attended the arrival of any light ship. He recognized a red-robed horologe named Ian Hedeon, but it was a pilot who had spoken to him. This was the Sonderval, an impossibly tall man dressed in black silks even as was Danlo. He was as straight and imposing as a yu tree, and as proud—in truth he was prouder of his brilliance than any other man whom Danlo had ever known.

"Master Pilot," Danlo said, "it is good to see you again."

"You may address me as 'Lord Pilot,' " the Sonderval said, stepping closer. "I've been elevated since last we met."

"Lord . . . Pilot, then," Danlo said. He remembered very well the evening that he and the Sonderval had talked beneath the twilight sky of Farfara some few years ago. It had been a night of the new supernova—the last night before the Second Vild Mission had left the last of the Civilized Worlds for Thiells. "Lord Pilot . . . can you tell me the date?"

"The date on this planet or on Neverness?"

"The date on Neverness, if you please."

The Sonderval looked off at the sky, making a quick calculation. "It's the 65th of midwinter spring."

"Yes," Danlo said, "but what year is it?"

"The year is 2959," the Sonderval said. "Almost three thousand years since the founding of the Old Order."

Danlo closed his eyes a moment in remembrance. It had been almost five years since he had set out with the Second Vild Mission from Neverness, and he suddenly realized that he must be twenty-seven years old.

"So long," Danlo said. Then he opened his eyes and smiled at the Sonderval. "But you look well, sir."

"You look well, too," the Sonderval said. "But there's something strange about you—you look different, I think. Gentler, almost. Wiser and even wilder, if that can be believed."

In truth, Danlo wi Soli Ringess was the wildest of men. In the time since Neverness, his hair had grown long and free so that it fell almost to his waist. In this thick black hair, shot with strands of red, he had fastened a white feather that his grandfather had given him years before. Once, as a young man, he had made a blood-offering to the spirits of his dead family, and he had slashed his forehead with a sharp stone. A lightning-bolt scar still marked him to remind others that here was an uncommon man, a fierce man of deep purposes who would listen for his fate calling in the wind or look inside the secret fires of his heart. It was his greatest joy to gaze without fear upon the terrible beauties of the world. His marvellous eyes were like the deepest, bluest cobalt glass, and they held light as a chalice does water. And more, they shone like stars, and it was this mysterious deepening of his gaze that the Sonderval had remarked, the way that light seemed to pour out of him as if fed by some wild and infinite source.

"You look sadder, too," the Sonderval continued. "And yet you've returned to your Order as a pilot should, having made discoveries."

"Yes, truly, I have made . . . discoveries."

Danlo looked past the field's other runs, noisy with rocket fire of light ships and jammers and other craft. Toward the ocean to the west, the city of Lightstone spread out over its three hills in lovely crystalline buildings, each house or tower giving shelter to human beings who had risked their lives to come to the Vild. Whenever Danlo pondered the fate of his bloody but blessed race, his face fell full of sadness. He always felt the pain of others too easily, just as the men and women whom he met almost always sensed his essential gentleness. Once, when he was only fourteen, he had taken a vow of ahimsa never to kill or harm any animal or man. And yet he was not *only* kind and compassionate, but strong and fierce as a thallow. With his quick, bold, wild face, he even looked something like that most noble of all creatures. Like the thallows of Icefall—the blue and the silver and the rare white thallows—his long, graceful body fairly rippled with *animajii,* a wild joy of life. That was his gift (and curse), that like a man holding fire in one hand and black ice in the other, he could always contain the most violent of opposites within himself. Even when he was saddest, he could hear the golden notes of a deeper and more universal song. Once, he had been told that he had been born laughing, and even now, as a man who had witnessed the death of stars and people whom he loved, he liked to laugh whenever he could.

"*Important* discoveries, I think," the Sonderval said. "You've called for the entire College of Lords to convene—no pilot has done that since your father returned from the Solid State Entity."

"Yes, I have much to tell of, sir."

"Have you succeeded in *your* quest to speak to the Entity?"

Danlo smiled as he looked up at the Sonderval's long, stern face. Although Danlo was a tall man, the Sonderval stood more than a foot and a half taller.

"Can any man *truly* speak with a goddess?" Danlo asked, remembering.

"It's been some years since we last met, and still you like to answer my questions with questions."

"I . . . am sorry, Lord Pilot."

"At least you're not *wholly* changed," the Sonderval said.

Danlo laughed and said, "I am still always I—who else could I be?"

"Your father asked the same question—and arrived at a different answer."

"Because he was fated to become a god?"

"I still won't believe that Mallory Ringess became a god," the Sonderval said. "He was Lord Pilot of the Order, a powerful and brilliant man—I'll allow that. But a god? Simply because half his brain was replaced with biological computers and he could think faster than most other men? No, no—I think not."

"It . . . can be hard to know who is a god and who is not."

"Have you found your father?" the Sonderval demanded. "Is this why you've asked the lords' college to convene?"

"Well, I've found *a* god," Danlo said, almost laughing. "Shall I show you, sir?"

Without waiting for the Lord Pilot's response, Danlo set down his wooden chest. He bent and opened the heavy lid. A moment later he drew out a cubical box covered along its six faces with many jewelled computer eyes. In the bright sunlight, they glittered like hundreds of diamonds. Just above the box, in truth projected *out* of it into the clear air, floated a ghostlike hologram of a little dark-skinned man.

"This is a devotionary computer," Danlo said. "The Architects of some of the Cybernetic Churches carry them about wherever they go."

"I've seen suchlike before," the Sonderval said as he pointed his long finger at the hologram. "And this is the likeness of Nikolos Daru Ede, isn't it?"

"Yes," Danlo said, smiling with amusement. "His . . . likeness."

The Sonderval studied Ede's soft lips and sensuous black eyes, and he declared, "I've never understood why the Architects worshipped such a small man. He looks like a merchant, doesn't he?"

"But Ede the Man became Ede the God, and it is upon this miracle that the Architects have built their church."

"Have you found Ede the God, then? Is this what you've discovered?"

"This *is* Ede the God," Danlo said. "What is left of him."

The Sonderval thought that Danlo was making a joke, for he laughed impatiently and waved his long hand at the Ede hologram as if he wanted to sweep it back into its box. The Sonderval was staring at Danlo, so he didn't see the Ede hologram wink at Danlo and flash him a quick burst of finger signs.

"A god, indeed!" the Sonderval said. "But you *have* spoken to a goddess, I'm sure. At least, that monstrous computer floating in space that men call a goddess. The son of Mallory Ringess wouldn't return to call the lords together if he hadn't completed his quest to find the Entity."

"Truly? Would he not?" Danlo asked. For the first time, he was more vexed than amused by the Sonderval's overweening manner.

"Please, Pilot—questions I have in abundance; it's answers that I desire."

"I . . . am sorry," Danlo said. He supposed that he should have been honored that the Lord Pilot himself had chosen to meet him at the light field. But the Sonderval was always a man of multiple purposes.

"It might help us prepare for the lords' conclave if you would tell me what you've discovered."

Yes, Danlo thought, and it would certainly help the Sonderval if he were privy to information in advance of Lord Nikolos. Everyone knew that the Sonderval thought that he should have been made Lord of the Order on Thiells in Lord Nikolos' place.

"Have you found a cure for the Great Plague?" the Sonderval asked. "Have you found a group of lost Architects who knew the cure?"

Danlo closed his eyes as he remembered the faces of Haidar and Chandra and Choclo and others of his adoptive tribe who had died of a *shaida* disease that he called the slow evil. For the ten-thousandth time, he beheld the terrible colors of the plague: the white froth upon their screaming lips, the red blood pouring from their ears, the flesh around their eyes blackened in death. The many other tribes of Alaloi on Icefall were also infected with this plague virus, which might yet wait many years before falling into its active phase—or might be killing his whole people at that very moment.

"I . . . almost found a cure," Danlo said as he clasped his hand to his forehead.

"Well, what *have* you discovered, Pilot?"

Danlo waited a moment as he breathed deeply the scent of flowers and rocket fire filling the air. He swallowed to moisten his throat; he had a warm and melodious voice but he was unused to speaking. "If you'd like, I will tell you a thing," he said.

"Well, then?"

"I have found Tannahill, sir. I . . . have been with the Architects of the Old Church."

At this astonishing news, the Sonderval stood as still as a tree and stared at Danlo. The Lord Pilot was the coolest of men and seldom betrayed any emotions other than pride in himself or loathing for his fellow man. But on that day, under the hot, high sun, with a crowd of people watching him from the end of the run, he punched his fist into his open hand and shouted out in envy, joy, and disbelief, "It can't be true!"

And then, noticing that a couple of olive-robed programmers were staring at him, he motioned for Danlo to follow him away from the run. He led him down a little walkway leading to one of the run's access streets. Danlo looked over his shoulder to see the cadre of professionals converge upon his ship like hungry wolves around a beached seal. Then he walked with the Sonderval up to the gleaming black sled which would take them into the city of Lightstone.

"We'll talk as we ride," the Sonderval said. He opened the sled's doors and invited Danlo to sit inside. He explained that this long, wheeled vehicle should have been named differently but for the Lord Akashic's nostalgia for Neverness and sleek sleds that rocket down her icy streets.

"On Tannahill, I have been inside such vehicles before," Danlo said. "They call them *choches.*"

While the Sonderval piloted the sled along the streets leading from the field into Lightstone, Danlo told of another city far across the Vild—and of hard plastic *choches* armored against bombs and ancient religious disputes and war.

"You amaze me," the Sonderval said. "We've sent two hundred pilots into the Vild. And no one has returned with a breath of a hint as to where Tannahill might be found."

"Truly?"

"I, myself, have searched for this world. From Perdido Luz to the Shatarei Void. I, myself, Pilot."

"I . . . am sorry."

"Why is it that some men have so much luck? You and your father—both born under the same lucky star."

Just then, as Danlo gazed at the colors of the city looming up beyond him, an old pain stabbed through his head. He thought of the sudden death of the entire Devaki tribe: his found-father and mother and sisters who had raised him until he was fourteen years old; he remembered the betrayal of his deepest friend, Hanuman li Tosh, and the loss of Tamara Ten Ashtoreth, she of the golden hair and golden soul—the woman whom he had loved almost more than life itself. With the hurt of his head pressing deeply into him like an iron fist, he recalled the very recent War of Terror on Tannahill, the eye tlolts and burning lasers and hydrogen bombs.

In a way, he himself had brought this war upon the Architects of the Old Church. In a way, although a kind of victory had been achieved, this war was not yet done.

"I . . . have not always been lucky," Danlo said. He pressed his palm against his left eye, which seemed to be the source of his terrible headaches. "In my life there has been much light, yes, and I have always sought its source, its center. But sometimes I am afraid that I am only like a moth circling closer to the flames of what you call my star. Sometimes I have wondered if I am only being pulled toward a terrible fate."

For a while, as they moved down a sunlit boulevard toward the three hills gleaming with new buildings, they talked about fate: the fate of the Order, the fate of the Civilized Worlds, the fate of pilots on desperate quests to the Vild's deadly stars. The Sonderval told of pilots who had returned to Thiells having made significant discoveries. Helena Charbo, out by the great Ilias Double, had found a world of lost Architects who had been sundered from the Old Church for almost two thousand years. And the fabulous Aja had befriended another group of lost Architects whose only means of journeying across the stars was to destroy them one by one: to cause a star to explode into a supernova, thereby tearing open great rents in the manifold into which their vast ships might fall and emerge light-years away into the sundrenched vacuum of realspace. All these lost Architects longed for reunion with their Mother Church, but they didn't even know of Tannahill's existence, much less where it might be found. They longed to interface the Old Church's sacred computers and let the High Holy Ivi guide them through wondrous cybernetic realms straight to the mysterious face of Ede the God. It was the Order's hope that if they could find Tannahill and win the Holy Ivi to their purpose, then the Church might re-establish its authority over the lost Architects and command them to stop destroying the stars. This was the essence of the Order's mission to the Vild. And so the Order on Neverness had sent its finest pilots and professionals to Thiells to build a city. The ancient Order had divided in two, weakening itself, so that the new Order might flourish and grow.

"The city will be complete in another year," the Sonderval said, pointing out the sled's window. "Of course, there's enough space if needed to expand over the next fifty years—or fifty thousand."

Danlo looked behind them, past the light field to the open plains covered with flowering bushes and little trees hung with red *ritsa* fruits. Truly, the city *could* expand almost infinitely down the mountainous peninsula and into the interior of this island continent that was as yet unnamed. But the heart of Lightstone would always be the three hills overlooking the ocean. There, to the west, on the gentle slopes of the centermost hill, the Order had almost finished building its new Academy. There were the new dormitories to house novice pilots, and the new library, and the Soli Pavilion, and the great Cetic's Tower rising up from the top of the hill like a massive white pillar holding up the sky. Just below it, on a little shelf of land overlooking the sea a few miles away, stood the circular Hall of the Lords. And all these buildings swept skyward with the grace of organic stone, a marvelously strong substance flecked with bits of tisander and diamond.

Everywhere Danlo looked, down the side streets of the great boulevard and behind him, new houses and hospices and apartments and shops were arising almost magically like crystals exploding out of the earth. But it was no magic that made these lovely structures. Over the faces of every unfinished building swarmed billions of little black robots, layering down the lacy organic stone as efficiently as spiders spinning out the silk of their webs. In the hold of their deep ships, the Order had brought some of these robots to Thiells, and had brought still other robots programmed to make yet more robots: disassemblers to mine minerals from every square foot of the rocky soil, and assemblers to put these elements together in beautiful new ways. The result of this outlawed technology (outlawed on Neverness and most of the Civilized Worlds), was that a city *could* almost be built overnight. The only thing Lightstone lacked was people, for the Order had sent scarcely more than ten thousand men and women into the Vild. But many of the peoples of the Vild, perhaps excited that a new power had arisen to save them from the fury of the stars, were pouring into the city.

From the nearby worlds of Caraghar, Asherah, Eshte, Kimmit and Skalla they came to be part of this glorious undertaking. And on more distant worlds further along the Orion Arm where the stars glittered like diamonds, the Order's pilots spread the news of their great mission, and invited programmers and priests, artists and arhats and aliens to join them on Thiells. And so these people came to Lightstone, and the sky day and night shook with the thunder of rocket fire, and the new city grew. The Sonderval estimated its population at a hundred thousand. In another year, he said, more than a million human beings (and perhaps a few thousand aliens) would call her home.

"We must train some of these to be pilots," the Sonderval

said. "Now that you've been so lucky as to have found Tannahill, we'll need many more pilots, won't we?"

Soon the Sonderval's sled rolled onto the hilly grounds of the new Academy. Danlo, who knew every spire, stone and tree of Neverness' Academy, immediately felt like a stranger come calling on an alien world. Everything about this Academy was different from the old, from the lawns of green grass to the sleds rolling down the Academy's stone streets. In truth, there were only a few of these gleaming black monstrosities, for only the Lords of the Order or a few illuminati from the rest of the city were permitted to take a sled down the Academy's tree-lined streets. But the Sonderval, after all, was the Lord Pilot of the Order, and it was with great pride that he guided his sled through a maze of unfamiliar streets and arrived in front of the Hall of the Lords.

"The Lords are waiting for you to address them," the Sonderval said. "I thank you for telling me of Tannahill, as little as that was."

"I . . . am sorry," Danlo said. "Sometimes it is difficult for me to talk very much, now. But soon you will hear the whole story of my journey."

The Sonderval climbed out of the sled, and his face was set with a strange smile. "Yes, I will sit at table with a hundred other lords and listen to how the son of Mallory Ringess, alone of all pilots, accomplished his Order's mission. Well, I *am* proud of you, Pilot. I'm proud that I tested you to be a novice and tutored you in toplogy—I suppose I knew that if anyone found Tannahill, it would be you."

So saying, the Sonderval strode up the white steps of the Hall of the Lords. Danlo, bearing the large wooden chest of his possessions in his arms, hurried to follow him. Though far from the largest of the Academy's buildings, it was one of the most beautiful, with its circles of delicate stone sweeping into the air and suspended in space almost as if its makers had discovered the secret of cancelling gravity. The sunlight poured down its walls like liquid fire, and the organic stone seemed to gleam from within as if burning with billions of living jewels.

Splendid it was, and Danlo, who had spent too many days in the darkened pit of his ship, squinted against its dazzling light. Inside the doorway—in the curving entrance corridor filled with paintings and sculptures of some of the Order's greatest Lords—the intense brightness softened to a warm radiance of colors. After the dull white and green plastics of Tannahill, Danlo was as thirsty for color as a newly hatched thallow chick drinking in his first glimpse of the sky. And then the Sonderval led him through a set of doors opening into the Hall's main chamber, and Danlo filled his eyes with many colors.

High above, surmounting the bright, open spaces of the hall, was a dome of clear organic stone. Its millions of tiny facets scattered the sunlight like so many diamond prisms so that the whole of the Hall danced with streamers of red and green and violet and blue. Lower down, there were yet more colors, not only the amethyst and golden flecks of the white floor, but all the colors of Danlo's Order.

At circular tables curving around the room waited all the Lords of the Order, each of the hundred and twelve men and women wearing a uniquely hued silken robe. At the center table sat Lord Nikolos, *the* Lord of the Order, in his bright yellow akashic's robe. And next to him the ever-plump Morena Sung filled out the folds of an eschatologist's blue silks. At this same table was the Lord Holist, Sul Estarei, wearing a robe of deep cobalt, and the mysterious Mithuna, the eyeless Lord Scryer, dressed all in white. Behind them were other lords: the Lord Horologe, Historian, Semanticist, Cetic, Programmer and all the other princes of the Order. As they sat close together whispering and wondering why a mere pilot had called them together, they formed a sea of colors from purple and pink to indigo and brown and orange and tens of others.

The last lord to take his place that day was the Sonderval. He sat in the empty chair to the right of Lord Nikolos, and his black pilot's robe almost overshadowed Lord Nikolos' yellow. Black, as Danlo had been taught, was the color of deep space and infinite possibilities, for out of the universe's primeval blackness comes light and form and all things. For three thousand years, the pilots of the Order had always worn black, and now Danlo in his formal black robe took his place in front of the assembled lords as his father had before him.

"We will now hear from the pilot, Danlo wi Soli Ringess," Lord Nikolos said as he stood to address his fellow lords. That was all the introduction that Danlo received. Lord Nikolos was a small but energetic man always eager to accomplish whatever task lay before him. He hated wasting words as a merchant does coins, and so he sat back down in his chair and studied Danlo cooly with his bright, blue eyes.

"My lords," Danlo began. He took a deep breath, relieved to have put his heavy wooden chest down on the floor. He stood at the center of the chamber where a circle of black diamond had been set into the floor's white stone. According to tradition, no pilot or anyone else who had taken vows could tell any untruth while standing in this circle.

Behind him, at the tables along the wall of the chamber's southern half, he recognized the master pilots Helena Charbo, Alark of Urradeth, Lara Jesusa, and the devout Aja, who lived for her pilot's art as a mother does her child. And also in this lesser place of honor there were other masters from other professions: Morasha li Estar, the master fabulist, and Bodaway Smye and Yamuna Chu, and anyone else whom the lords had deemed important enough to listen to Danlo's story. "My lords, and Master Pilots and Master Academicians," Danlo continued, "I would like to tell you of my journey. I . . . have found Tannahill."

For a moment no one moved as more than a hundred faces stared straight at Danlo in wonderment. And then Danlo began to speak, and the men and women of his order sat entranced while they listened to the story of a lone pilot who had possibly accomplished more than any other—more even than Dario the Bold or Danlo's own grandfather, Leopold Soli, who had penetrated almost to the galaxy's core and learned of the gods' mysterious secret wisdom known as the Elder Eddas. Danlo began his story with an account of his journey to the Solid State Entity. He told of the great chaos storm near the heart of the Entity that had killed Dolores Nun and Leander of Darkmoon and his seven other fellow pilots as they fell through swirling black spaces as deadly as any danger of the manifold. He had found his way through this storm, he said, only to fall out above an earthlike world upon which the Entity had imprisoned him for many days while She tested him. He spoke little of these tests. He had no liking for fame or glory, and so he stood breathing deeply under the watchful eyes of the lords as he tried to convey the essence of what he had learned from the Entity with as little focus as possible upon himself. But neither was he falsely modest, for he prized truth as some do gold. And the truth was that the Entity had entrusted him with great knowledge because he had shown great virtue in surviving the chaos space as well as Her tests.

"There is war in heaven," Danlo told the assembled masters and lords. Hillel Astoret, the brown-robed Lord Historian sitting behind Lord Nikolos, would later remark this as a great moment when the knowledge of universe-shaking events first came into the halls of the Order. "It is truly a terrible, *shaida* war. The Silicon God has made war upon the Solid State Entity. He has allies, other gods of the galaxy: they are Chimene, Maralah, Hsi

Wang Mu, Iamme and what we call the Degula Trinity. And the Entity is not alone, either. I believe that Pure Mind and the One are allied with Her. And possibly even the April Colonial Intelligence. And my father, Mallory Ringess, if he truly became a god, then somehow he is involved with the Entity's design. Somewhere among the stars. I . . . was not able to find out where.''

Usually the Lords of the Order are as polite as women and men can be. But that day, despite the rule that anyone standing in the circle be allowed to speak without interruption except by the Lord of the Order himself, a dozen different lords turned their faces close to each other and began whispering urgently.

''I would like to ask for silence, please,'' Lord Nikolos said as he stood and held up his hand. Although he was physically smaller than almost anyone in the room, his calm, clear voice seemed to fill the Hall and to sober the excited lords. Even the Sonderval, who was talking with Kolenya Mor, heard the call to obediance and immediately fell silent. ''Let's allow the pilot to finish his story.''

Danlo went on to tell of a crucial battle in this cosmic war between the gods: It seemed that the Silicon God had found a way to destroy Ede the God. This had been no small feat. Ede, as a man, as a human being living in the flesh, had been almost as small as Lord Nikolos. But after his great vastening, when he had carked his consciousness into a computer and become a god, he had grown. As a seed ice crystal may build into a hailstone many billion times larger than itself, this computer that was Ede had added neurologics and circuitry until Ede the God's body was vaster than whole worlds and filled the spaces of many star systems.

''The Entity told me where I might find Ede the God,'' Danlo said. ''It was deeper into the Vild. There were many stars: Berura, Gauri, Ahira, as I named them. There were many old supernovas. And I found the Star of Ede: it is a blue-white hotstar. And Ede himself, what was left of this god. It, he, was all wreckage. Fused neurologics and dead assemblers and hydrogen clouds spread out over light-years of space. Ede must have been . . . truly vast. And now he was dead. The Entity had said that he was dead, but that it might be that he was also somewhat alive.''

Danlo paused to stare down at his wooden chest where it rested just outside the black diamond circle. Its top was carved with a great sunburst, and he closed his eyes for a moment as he dwelt in the remembrance of all the suns and light he had ever beheld.

''Pilot!'' a voice called as if from far away. Danlo opened his eyes to see Lord Nikolos addressing him. "Pilot, the Entity is famous for speaking in paradoxes and riddles—did you ever discover what She meant?"

"Yes," Danlo said. "I did."

"Will you please share your discovery with us, then?"

"If you'd like," Danlo said, smiling. Then he stepped over to the wooden chest and opened it. He drew out the devotionary computer and held it up so that all the assembled lords could see the little glowing hologram of Nikolos Daru Ede.

"What is this?" Lord Nikolos demanded.

Hillel Astoret and several of the lords behind Lord Nikolos began talking all at once, pointing at the computer's jeweled eyes and shaking their heads in disapproval. Then Lord Nikolos turned his head in disapproval of this interruption and caught the lords with his icy eyes until they fell silent.

"This," Danlo said, "is Nikolos Daru Ede. Ede the God—what is left of him."

The Ede hologram, with its seductive face and bright, black eyes, seemed to stare straight at Lord Nikolos.

"Pilot, please remember where you are—this is no place for jokes!"

"But I am not joking."

"This," said Lord Nikolos, pointing at the glittering box that Danlo held in his hands, "is nothing more than a *religious* artifact."

The cooly logical Lord Nikolos was well-known for despising man's irrational or mystical impulses, which was one reason he had been chosen to lead the Mission to the Old Church. He continued, "The Architects carry these *idols* around in order to worship an image of Ede, don't they? Aren't these devotionary computers programmed to speak Ede's blessings and other such nonsense?"

"Yes," Danlo said. "But it is possible . . . for them to be programmed otherwise."

"Please explain yourself."

Danlo glanced at the Ede imago, and he almost smiled to see the eyes of the hologram flick sideways to catch his gaze.

"The Silicon God," he said, "did not slay Ede in a moment. The battle lasted many seconds. And at the end, a whole nebula of stars was destroyed. And Ede's brains were all destroyed—almost all. At the very end, Ede wrote a program compressing and encoding his essential selfness. It is this program that this devotionary computer now runs."

"Impossible!"

"Not . . . impossible," Danlo said. He turned to see Lara Jesusa and some of the other master pilots smiling to give him encouragement in the face of Lord Nikolos' intense skepticism. "Ede the God is dead, truly. But it may be . . . that he is also somewhat alive."

"This *machine?*" Lord Nikolos asked in his quiet but steely voice. "And where did you find this dead god that might be alive?"

"On an earth that Ede had made."

From far in the back of the hall came the sound of muffled laughter, perhaps from Sanura Snowden, the Lord Semanticist, or the Lord Imprimatur who sat nearby. At times, Lord Nikolos was capable of a dry sense of humor, but he would not tolerate anyone making jokes at his expense.

"Please watch your words," Lord Nikolos chided Danlo. "You're a full pilot of the Order, and you've been taught to speak precisely. We do not refer to engineered worlds, no matter how earthlike their biospheres, as 'earths.' "

"Neither do I, sir," Danlo said, and his dark blue eyes shone with amusement at Lord Nikolos' doubt. "The gods make earths. Truly. The Solid State Entity, and especially Ede the God—from the elements of dead stars, they have built these earths. Whole continents and oceans, forests and mountains and rocks, in exact duplication of Old Earth."

Danlo went on to describe a succession of blue-white earths that he had discovered around the stars of Ede the God. Now all the lords in the Hall had fallen very quiet, and even Lord Nikolos sat back down in his chair and regarded Danlo with something like awe.

"I didn't know the gods had such power to remake the universe," Lord Nikolos said quietly.

Danlo looked boldly at Lord Nikolos and said, "But this is just what it *means* to be a god, yes? They make war upon each other . . . in order to remake the universe according to their different visions of what must be."

"But why *earths,* Pilot?"

"I . . . do not know." Danlo closed his eyes as he remembered the sandy beach and dark green forest of the earth upon which the Entity had imprisoned him. The Entity, at least, had certainly made Her earth as a laboratory for experimenting with the evolution of human beings. From images stolen from his mind, She had created a slel of Tamara Ten Astoreth, an almost perfect copy of the woman whom he had loved. The slel was meant to be a perfect woman—or rather a creation of a perfected humanity as it might someday be. "The Architects of the Cybernetic Churches have a doctrine. They call it the Program of the Second Creation. At the end of time, when Ede has grown to absorb the whole of the universe, then a miracle will occur. From his own infinite body, Ede will make an infinite number of earths. And all the Architects who have ever lived will be reincarnated into new bodies. Perfect bodies that will live forever in these paradises."

At this piece of nonsense, Lord Nikolos pressed his lips together as if someone were trying to force a piece of rotten meat into his mouth. "But Ede the God is dead, you say."

"Yes."

"Do you really believe that Ede was making his earths as a home for the souls of dead Architects?"

"I . . . do not like to believe anything."

"Nor I," Lord Nikolos said. "It's too bad that we can't simply ask the Ede of your devotionary computer what his original plan was."

Danlo smiled because he had asked the Ede exactly this question—and many others—to no avail.

"And now," Lord Nikolos went on, looking at Danlo, "I suppose I should ask you to give this devotionary to the Lord Tinker and Lord Programmer. They will take it down and disassemble it to discover the source of any programs that it might run."

In a moment—in the time it took for the devotionary computer to modulate the coherent light beams of its hologram—the glowing face of Nikolos Daru Ede fell into a mask of panic. And then a loud, almost whiny voice issued into the Hall as Ede cried out, "No, please don't take me down!"

At this startling event, Lord Sung pointed her plump finger at the devotionary and gasped. Sanura Snowden and several other lords cried out, "What? What's this?"

Lord Nikolos just stared at the hologram of Nikolos Daru Ede while he sat blinking his icy blue eyes. And then he said, simply, "It speaks."

"Oh, indeed, I do speak," the Ede said. "I see and hear, as well. The jewels on the devotionary's sides are computer eyes and—"

"We're familiar with such technolgies," Lord Nikolos said. He, too, had been bred to politeness, but he had no compunction against interrupting the word flow of a machine."

"I think, as well," the Ede said, "and therefore I am, as are you, self-aware, and I am—"

"A clever program, nothing more," Lord Nikolos said. "We're also familiar with Ai programs, though it may be that this one is more sophisticated than any our Order has seen. The Lord Programmer will be able to determine—"

"No, I must ask you not to take me down!" the Ede cried out again. Lord Nikolos and 120 other Lords gaped at the Ede hologram. No one had ever exerienced an Ai program interrupting a human being.

Ede turned his frightened face to Danlo, who met eyes with this little hologram projected out of the computer that he held in his hands. "Lord Nikolos," Danlo said, "I have borne this devotionary halfway across the Vild. I have valued its . . . information."

"Are you asking to keep it for yourself?"

"Yes."

"But a pilot may not keep *any* discovery to himself. You know our rule."

"Truly, I do. But this devotionary, this Ede, has aided me on my journey. I . . . have made promises to him."

For a moment, nobody spoke. Then Lord Nikolos asked, "You made *promises* to an idol programmed out of a machine?"

"Yes. In return for helping me find Tannahill, I promised not to take him down. I promised to help him . . . accomplish a thing."

"What thing?"

"His . . . purpose."

"And do I dare ask what purpose you might think this machine could be programmed to achieve?"

Again, Danlo looked at the Ede hologram. He looked at Lord Nikolos and the Sonderval, and at the many other lords and masters. He felt his heart beating hard up through his throat and his face burning as if he had stood all day in the sun. He did not want to tell these cold-eyed men and women of Ede's purpose.

"Well, Pilot?"

"He, this Ede, wants to. . . ."

The Ede flashed Danlo a hand sign, and Danlo suddenly stopped talking. And then Ede addressed Lord Nikolos and the other lords, and said, "I want to be a man again."

Lord Nikolos stared at the glowing hologram as if he couldn't understand the simple sounds of human (or artificial) speech.

None of the lords in the hall seemed to know what Ede might mean.

"The pilot, Danlo wi Soli Ringess, promised to help me recover my body, if that is possible. To help me live as a man again."

Seeing Lord Nikolos' bewilderment, Danlo smiled and said, "I must tell you of his body."

"Please do," Lord Nikolos said with a sigh.

Danlo bowed his head, and then told the Lords of the Order of the body of Nikolos Daru Ede, which the Architects had kept frozen in a clary crypt for three thousand years. He explained how the entire crypt had been stolen from Ede's Tomb on Tannahill. The Ede hologram hoped that his body might someday be recovered; he prayed that the Order's cryologists might be able to revive this body after reconfiguring the damaged neurons and synapses of its brain to instantiate the program of the devotionary computer. And thus to raise the dead. "We . . . were going to ask the Architects for the return of this body," Danlo said.

"I see," Lord Nikolos said. "You didn't by chance bear this body across the Vild in the hold of your ship?"

"No, there were terrible events. I . . . was unable to recover it."

Again Lord Nikolos sighed as if a weight had been taken from his shoulders. "Why don't you finish your story, Pilot, and tell us of this body."

And so Danlo stood within his circle of black diamond and continued the story of his journey. He told of dead worlds burnt black in the fire of supernovas and ruined alien civilizations. And stars, millions of red or yellow or blue stars burning like flame globes in the long black reaches of space. Around a star named *Gelasalia* he had come across a great rainbow system of seventeen ringworlds from which the resident human beings had vanished in the most mysterious of ways, seemingly transcending their bodies, perhaps to live as beings of pure information (or light) as the Ieldra had done two million years before. He had followed this trail of transcendence deeper into the Vild where the radiations of exploded stars grew thick and deadly. On the world of Alumit Bridge just inside the galaxy's Perseus Arm, he had found a civilization of people who lived for the transcendence of the glittering cybernetic spaces inside their computers. They called themselves the Narain. They were, he said, a pale and wormlike people who wanted to be as gods. In truth, they were Architects in their lineage, heretics who had left Tannahill some two hundred years before in a bitter schism with their mother Church. "I . . . made friends with the Narain," Danlo said. "They feared war with the Old Church and asked me to speak for them to the Holy Ivi. To journey to Tannahill—it was the Narain who pointed out Tannahill's star."

And so finally after having crossed thirty thousand light years of blazing and broken stars, Danlo had come to lost Tannahill. There he had won the favor and friendship of Harrah Ivi en li Ede, the High Holy Ivi of the Cybernetic Universal Church. Because of him, she had installed new programs for her church, completely reversing the Architects mandate to procreate wantonly and destroy the stars. There, too, he had won the enmity of the Elder Bertram Jaspari, Harrah's rival for the architectcy and a man who would kill for power like a mad sleekit ravening through a nest of its own family. Bertram Jaspari was also the leader of the Iviomils, a fanatical sect who preached religious purity and called for religious war. Bertram Jaspari would carry the burning torches of this *facifah* to other sects of Architects on Tannahill, and to the Narain on Alumit Bridge—and even out to the peoples of the Vild and beyond. "The Iviomils fought a war with the other Architects," Danlo said. "I . . . became involved in this war."

He stared up at the brilliant colors of the dome, and he did not explain how Harrah Ivi en li Ede—and billions of other Architcects across Tannahill—had come to regard him as the Lightbringer foretold by their prophecies.

Lord Morena Sung, sitting next to Lord Nikolos, turned to the Sonderval and sadly shook her head. Both these lords had known Danlo since his novice years on Neverness, and it was obvious to them that Danlo's involvement in this war had been neither accidental nor slight. Now Sul Estarei was searching Danlo's face for truth, too, and many, many other lords. The Hall of the Lords, so bright with dancing shards of light, suddenly seemed gloomy and grim, as if the mood of 120 women and men could darken the air itself with their dread. No one liked all this talk of war. No one liked the pain they saw on Danlo's face or the presentiment of death burning in his deep blue eyes. Many remembered his mother, Katharine the Scryer, and they wondered if he, too, was gifted with visions of terrible moments yet to be.

"Please tell us about this war," Lord Nikolos said gently.

Danlo stood at the center of his circle as he looked out upon many faces falling heavy with fear. He remembered that once, as a young man, he had wanted to journey to the center of the universe so that he might finally see the true nature of all things just as it really was. Although he had long since abandoned this quest as hopeless, he knew that it was his fate to bring *a* truth to the Lords of the Order. He was like a pilot unlocking a window to the dark and depthless spaces of the manifold, only the opening he now showed these anxious lords was into his own soul. And from the bright, black centers of his eyes and the deeper center of himself came the memory of all that he had sensed and seen. Like the long, dark roar of a stellar wind it blew through the hall carrying the scent of hydrogen bombs and burnt flesh and stars exploding into light. And so Danlo told of how the Iviomils had slaughtered their fellow Architects, only to be utterly defeated in the end. Bertram Jaspari had assembled a fleet of the surviving Iviomils and had fled Tannahill into the stars. But before his disappearance into the galaxy's wastelands, he had completed two acts. The first was the theft of Ede's body and clary crypt in the great tomb. And the second was the destruction of a star.

"The Iviomils hated the Narain people," Danlo said. "They called them heretics, apostates. They . . . had called for a *facifah* against the Narain. A holy war to cleanse the Church of anyone who had betrayed it. So Bertram Jaspari led his Iviomils to Alumit Bridge. To the star that lights the Narain's world. And they . . . destroyed it."

Because Danlo's mouth was dry, he stopped speaking for a moment. He bent over to place the devotionary computer on top of his wooden chest. Then, from a pocket sewn into the pants leg of his robe, he drew out a long bamboo flute. It was an ancient shakuhachi that his teacher had once given him. It smelled of woodsmoke and wind and wild dreams, and of all his possessions, it was the most beloved. In silence he pressed its ivory mouthpiece to his lips and tongue, but he played no music. He let the soft coolness of the ivory touch off the flow of water in his mouth, and suddenly he found that he could finish his story.

"In one of their ships, the Iviomils have a machine," he said. "A . . . *morrashar,* they call it. A star-killer—the Architects are masters of this technology, yes? They have at least one star-killer. Bertram Jaspari used it to destroy the Narain people. Their whole world. I . . . confirmed this crime. After I left Tannahill, I journeyed to where the Star of Alumit Bridge should have been. But there was only the remnant of a supernova, radiation, hydrogen, glowing gases, light. And of Alumit Bridge, itself, almost nothing remained. Only dust."

Again, Danlo placed his shakuhachi to his lips, and he closed his eyes in remembrance of Shahar and Abraxax and all the people and the great beings whom he had known among the Narain.

"This is a terrible story," Lord Nikolos said as he stared at Danlo. Behind him, too, almost every face in the hall was turned toward this pilot who had brought such tragic news. For a while, he and the other lords talked about another supernova, called Merripen's Star, which had exploded near Neverness some thirty years before. At the end of the year 2960, less than two years hence, the radiation of the supernova was due to fall upon Neverness. It seemed that only the growth of the Golden Ring—a mysterious ecology of gases and new, golden life that had appeared in the sky above the city—might protect the peoples of Neverness from death. Supernovas everywhere blossomed among the stars like flowers of evil, Lord Sung observed, but on many worlds, ever since the disappearance of Mallory Ringess, these rings had mysteriously appeared in the heavens like protective bands of gold.

"These are terrible times in which we live," Lord Nikolos observed. And then he turned back toward Danlo. "But it's also a time of great hope, as well. You, Danlo wi Soli Ringess, have found Tannahill. And the Architects of the Old Church. And this man, Bertram Jaspari, of whom you speak, has been defeated. The Iviomils whom he leads, as well. And, it would seem, the Architect's Holy Ivi whom you befriended awaits the arrival of our Order's emmissaries. Your accomplishment, Pilot, is of a magnitude beyond any—"

"Please, Lord Nikolos," Danlo broke in. "There . . . is more."

Lord Nikolos was unused to being interrupted by young pilots, no less than a hologram out of a devotionary computer, but so great was the pain in Danlo's voice that he did not chastise him. Silently—but kindly—he bowed his head to Danlo inviting him to continue. And he and all the other lords and masters in the Hall sat in their chairs as they waited for Danlo to tell of some other dreadful event that they could only imagine.

"I . . . made enemies of Bertram Jaspari," Danlo said. "I believe that he blames me and our Order for his defeat in the war. I believe that he wishes for revenge."

Now Lord Nikolos sat as still as stone, and it seemed that he had forgotten how to breathe. Next to him the Sonderval did not move, nor Kolenya Mor, nor anyone else at their table.

Then Lord Nikolos asked, "It's not possible, is it, that Bertram Jaspari might have learned the fixed-points of *our* star?"

Danlo would rather have cut off his own hand than give away such a secret, and so he smiled in grim amusement and then said, "No, I do not think that it is possible. But it is not only our Order here on Thiells that Bertram Jaspari blames and hates. It is the Order on Neverness. Neverness herself. I believe . . . that the Iviomils would bring their *facifah* to the Civilized Worlds and destroy the Star of Neverness."

And they would do this *shaida* thing, Danlo said, out of reasons other than mere vengeance. Danlo recounted how on Neverness only a few years before, a new religion had arisen to teach that men and women could become gods. They dreamed of following the example of Danlo's own father, Mallory wi Soli Ringess, and thus they called their faith the Way of Ringess. Bertram Jaspari had learned of this new Way. For any Iviomil—in truth for any Architect of the Old Church—the teaching that any human being other than Ede could become a god was the worst of blasphemies. Any person who aspired to such transcendence was called a *hakra,* and it was the Old Church's duty to cleanse them totally of such hubris. Or to annihilate them. This, especially, was the program of the Iviomils, to annihilate the Ringists of Neverness before they spread their poisonous teachings to the rest of the Civilized Worlds and to the stars beyond.

"I believe that Bertram Jaspari might want to become a *power* among the Civilized Worlds," Danlo said. He listened to his voice carry out over the tables of the lords and fill the sun-streaked spaces of the Hall. "He has a star-killer. He has deepships full of missionaries. He has dreams. He has . . . much hatred."

Lord Nikolos stared unblinking at Danlo, and then said, "What you've told us is terrible. But I think we need not fear that these Iviomils could ever find the Star of Neverness. Even though its fixed-points be known, they could never find their way across the Vild. Thirty thousand light-years! Even our finest pilots have failed in attempting such a crossing."

"But some . . . have succeeded," Danlo said softly.

"Only you, Pilot, and it's not—"

"*Not* only I," Danlo said. He gripped his hard bamboo flute. "On Farfara, before we entered the Vild, I met a man. In Mer Tadeo's garden just before the supernova lit the sky. Malaclypse Redring of Qallar—that was his name. A warrior-poet. He . . . wore a red ring on each hand. He, too, sought Tannahill. It was his intention to follow our Mission into the Vild."

"A warrior-poet, by himself?"

"He was not alone. A ronin pilot had brought him to Farfara. Sivan wi Mawi Sarkissian, in his ship, the *Red Dragon.*"

Just then the Sonderval rapped his black diamond ring against the tabletop. He told the lords, "I knew Sivan well before he became a renegade during the Pilots' War. Other than myself, and perhaps Mallory Ringess, he had no equal as a pilot."

The Sonderval's arrogant observation did not please Aja, or Helena Charbo—or any of the other master pilots sitting by the wall. It did not please Lord Nikolos, who bowed to Danlo and grimly said, "Continue your story."

Danlo returned his bow and said, "Malaclypse and Sivan followed me into the Solid State Entity. Across the entire Vild. They . . . pursued my ship to Tannahill. They became involved with the Architects' war, too."

"It seems that this was a popular war," Lord Nikolos said dryly.

"Malaclypse Redring allied himself with Bertram Jaspari," Danlo said. "Truly, it was he who enabled the Iviomils to fight as long as they did."

"Warrior-poets allied with Architects," Lord Nikolos said, shaking his head. "This is not good."

"It is Sivan in his *Red Dragon* who leads the Iviomil ships. Sivan and Malaclypse."

"This is bad," Lord Nikolos said.

"The Entity believes that the Silicon God is using both the warrior-poets and the Architects in *His* war," Danlo said. "She believes that the Silicon God would destroy the whole galaxy, if He could."

Or possibly the whole universe, Danlo thought.

He went on to speak of Bertram Jaspari's dream of establishing his Iviomils in a new church somewhere among the stars coreward from Neverness. Like the fanatical Architects they were, they would continue destroying the stars in their God-given Program to remake the universe.

"I am afraid . . . that they could eventually create another Vild," Danlo said. "Or worse."

And what could possibly be worse than the creation of a new region of dead and dying stars? As Ti Sen Sarojin, the Lord Astronomer, observed, if the Iviomils began destroying stars among the densely packed stars of the core, they might possibly set off a chain-reaction of supernovas that would explode outward star by star and consume the galaxy in a vast ball of fire and light.

"This is very bad," Lord Nikolos said quietly. Throughout the hall the lords sat at their tables in deathly silence. Never in living memory had the calm and cool Lord Nikolos used the words "very" and "bad" together.

"I am sorry," Danlo said.

"Religious fanatics and *facifahs* and star killers and renegade pilots and gods! What a story you bring us, Pilot! Well, we can do nothing about the wars of gods, but it is upon us to—"

"Lord Nikolos," Danlo interrupted.

Lord Nikolos took a a quick breath and said, "What is it, then?"

"There is something that the Entity told me about the Silicon God. About all the gods."

"Please, do tell us as well."

Danlo looked around the hall to see Lord Berebir and Lord Lado and all the others fairly hanging on his words. "The Entity believes that we ourselves hold the secret of defeating the Silicon God. We human beings."

"But how can this be?" Morena Sung, the Lord Eschatologist broke in.

"Because this secret is part of the Elder Eddas," Danlo said. "And the Eddas are believed to be encoded only in human DNA."

In truth, no one knew what the Elder Eddas really were. Supposedly, some fifty thousand years ago on Old Earth, the mythical Ieldra had written all their godly wisdom into the human genome. Now, millenia later, trillions of men and women on countless worlds carried these sleeping memories in every cell of their bodies. And it was through the art of remembrancing alone (or so the remembrancers claimed) that the Elder Eddas could be awakened and called up before the mind's eye like living paintings and understood.

Some experienced the Eddas as a clear and mystical light. Some believed that this wisdom was nothing less than instructions on becoming gods—and possibly much more. Danlo, who had once had a great remembrance and apprehension of the One Memory, sensed that the Eddas might contain all consciousness, perhaps even all possible memory itself. If true, then it would certainly be possible for a man—or perhaps even a child—to remember how the Ieldra long ago had defeated the Dark God and saved the Milky Way from annihilation. This was the grail that the Solid State Entity sought in Her war against the Silicon God, and it was possible that Danlo and the Sonderval and Lord Nikolos in his bright yellow robe—and everyone else sitting in the hall that day—carried this secret inside them.

"I haven't heard our remembrancers speak of any war secrets contained in the Elder Eddas," Lord Nikolos said. Here he turned to exchange looks with Mensah Ashtoreth, the silver-robed Lord Remembrancer who sat at a table nearby shaking his head. "As for the Neverness remembrancers, who knows what they have discovered in the years since the Order divided and our mission came here to Thiells?"

He did not add that the many thousands of converts to the new religion of Ringism sought remembrance of the Elder Eddas as well. Lord Nikolos could scarcely countenance an information so mysterious as the Elder Eddas, much less the possibility that some wild-eyed religionary on Neverness might uncover secrets unknown to his finest academicians.

"And yet," Danlo said, "the Entity hopes that some day some woman or man will remember this secret."

"But not," Lord Nikolos said, "some god?"

"Possibly some god," Danlo said. "Possibly my father. But most of the gods are nothing more than vast computers. Neurologics and opticals and diamond circuitry. They . . . do not live as a man lives. They cannot remember as we remember."

"And do you believe that the Solid State Entity would have us remember for Her?"

"Yes."

"Then She would use us—our Order—as the Silicon God uses the Architects and the warrior-poets?"

"My father," Danlo said, smiling, "once wrote that the Entity referred to man as the *instrumentum vocale*. The tool with a voice."

"And you find this amusing?"

"Truly, I do," Danlo said, looking down at the flute he held in his hand. "Because these tools that we are also have free will. And our lives are the songs that sing the universe into existence."

"What songs will we sing, I wonder, if we become involved in the gods' wars?" Lord Nikolos asked.

"I do not know," Danlo said. "But if we could remember this secret of the Eddas, then in a way it would be we human beings who used the Entity to destroy the Silicon God, yes?"

"Is this what you advise, Pilot? That the Order use its resources in helping the Entity fight Her war?"

Danlo suddenly fell into silence, and he gripped his flute so hard that the holes along the shaft cut into his skin. He said, "I

. . . do not believe in war at all. The Lord Akashic must know that I have taken a vow of ahimsa.''

Never to harm any living thing, Danlo thought. *Even at the cost of one's own life, never to dishonor another life, never to harm, never to kill.*

"Well, I don't believe in war either," Lord Nikolos said from his chair. "War is the stupidest of human activities, with the possible exception of religion. And as for the kind of *religious war* of which you've spoken today . . ."

Lord Nikolos let his voice die for a moment as he turned to catch the eyes of the Sonderval and Mornena Sung and the other lords sitting near him. He shook his head sadly as if all agreed that religious war was by its very nature insane. Then he continued: "Nevertheless, it is upon us to consider this war that the Architects fought among themselves and would bring to other worlds. Perhaps we must also consider the wars of the gods."

Danlo looked at Lord Nikolos then, and quickly bowed his head.

"Pilot," Lord Nikolos asked, "have you finished your story?"

"Yes."

"Then I must ask you to wait outside while we consider these stupidities and crimes that you have brought to our attention."

Danlo bowed his head again and said, "If you'd like, sir." He knew of the rule that only lords and masters may attend the most serious deliberations of the Order. He stepped out of the black diamond circle and moved to pick up his wooden chest where it sat on the floor.

"A moment," the Sonderval suddenly said. He slowly stood away from his chair and stretched himself up to his full eight feet of height. "I would like to applaud the Pilot's accomplishment in discovering so much and falling so far."

So saying he rapped his diamond pilots' ring against the table. Helena Charbo and Aja, sitting across the room at the master pilots' table, knocked diamond against wood, as did Lara Jesusa and Alark of Urradeth. But none of the other lords and masters in the hall that day wore rings, and so they had to content themselves with clapping their hands together and bowing their heads in honor of Danlo's great feat.

"And now," the Sonderval said, "I would like to ask Danlo wi Soli Ringess to remain here with us today."

At this unexpected presumption, Lord Nikolos turned abruptly and shot the Sonderval a puzzled and offended look.

"I would like to ask him to remain as a *master* pilot," the

Sonderval explained. "Can anyone doubt that his accomplishments merit his elevation to a mastership? I think not. And therefore as Lord Pilot, I welcome him to the rank of master. We will hold the ceremony later in the Pilots' Hall."

For a long time Lord Nikolos and the Sonderval stared at each other like two cats preparing to spring at each other's throat. True, as Lord Pilot, the Sonderval had the power to make new masters as he chose. But he was supposed to put the names of all candidates before a board of master pilots who would make their recommendations according to each candidate's prowess and worthiness. And then by tradition, if not rule, the Lord of the Order himself would approve the elevation and make the first welcoming of the new master. Precipitous times often require precipitous decisions, but the Sonderval usurped Lord Nikolos' prerogatives less from need than pure arrogance. Since the Sonderval thought that he himself should have been made the Lord of the Order on Thiells, he exulted in acting in Lord Nikolos' place whenever he could.

"Very well," Lord Nikolos finally said, forcing the words from his tight, thin lips. He turned to Danlo, who still stood at the center of the hall waiting and watching this little drama between the most powerful lords of his Order. "Very well, Master Pilot, would you please remain here while we make our decision as to what must be done?"

Danlo bowed formally, then smiled and said, "Yes." Then he carried his wooden chest over to the table where the master pilots sat and took his place on a chair between Lara Jesusa and Alark of Urradeth. Alark, a quick, hot-tempered man who had once crossed the Detheshaloon solely as the result of a dare, embraced Danlo and whispered his welcome as he rapped his ring against the table.

"And now," Lord Nikolos said, standing to address the lords, "we must reconsider our mission in light of all that Danlo wi Soli Ringess has told us."

So began the great war debate in the Hall of the Lords. At first, however, it was more a personal argument between the Sonderval and Lord Nikolos. Although no one favored full war, the Sonderval wanted to lead a group of lightships to the Civilized Worlds, there to intercept and destroy Bertram Jaspari's fleet along the stellar Fallaways before they could reach Neverness. Lord Nikolos, however, a frugal man always concerned to husband his resources, pointed out that the New Order's lightships were few in number, and every ship would be needed now that

Tannahill had been found. For the Order's mission, Lord Nikolos suggested, was still to the Architects of the Old Church. An embassy would have to be sent to Tannahill. The Order would have to provide the Architects with ships and pilots so that the Church's missionaries could spread their new programs to every corner of the Vild. Architects everywhere must know that they were no longer permitted (or encouraged) to blow up the stars.

"We must not become involved in these wars between religions and their sects," he told the assembled lords. And here he turned to smile at Danlo. "And as for the wars between the gods, unless one of us suddenly remembrances these war secrets of the Elder Eddas, then we *cannot* become involved, for there is nothing we can do to touch the gods or influence them in any way."

Most of the lords accepted the logic of Lord Nikolos, for they sat in their chairs whispering to each other and nodding their heads. But the Sonderval, waiting impatiently next to Lord Nikolos, turned to him and asked, "But what of the Iviomil fleet that the warrior-poet and the renegade lead toward Neverness? Are we simply to abandon the world from which we came?"

"Have you heard me speak of abandonment?" Lord Nikolos asked.

"I haven't heard you speak of protecting our brothers and sisters on Neverness!" the Sonderval said with great passion. Once, years before, he had lost his beloved when a comet struck her planet, and since that time he had never been with another woman. "I would hope this isn't because you're afraid of risking a few tens of lightships."

"There are always risks no matter what course of action we choose," Lord Nikolos said. "But risks must be calculated. Costs must be assessed."

"Calculations and costs!" the Sonderval mocked. "Thus do the merchant-pilots of Tria speak."

"Thus does any sane man speak who must accomplish difficult things with limited means."

"As Lord Pilot of our Order," the Sonderval said with great pride, "it's my charge to encourage my pilots to attempt impossible things beyond what we conceive as our limitations."

Here he bowed to Danlo, honoring him as an exemplar of the pilots' greatest traditions. Many of the lords suddenly looked his way, and Danlo freely met their eyes even though he hated such public attention.

"As Lord Pilot of the Order nothing more could be asked of you," Lord Nikolos said to the Sonderval. "But as *Lord* of the

Order, I must constrain the heroics of my pilots, even such a great pilot as yourself.''

This mixture of compliment and veiled criticism momentarily flustered the Sonderval, who sat glaring at Lord Nikolos. Lord Nikolos seized this opportunity to deliver his crowning jewel of logic in avoidance of conflict. ''I propose that we send three pilots to Neverness. Three of our finest pilots in our swiftest ships. They will warn the Lords of Neverness of Bertram Jaspari's Iviomils and this star-killer that their fleet brings with them. The Old Order has more pilots than we—let the pilots of Neverness fight this war with the Iviomils, if indeed any war is to be fought.''

Danlo watched as Lara Jesusa traded a quick look with Alark of Urradeth, and the brilliant Aja turned her dark eyes to meet Danlo's. Already, it seemed, the master pilots had accepted Lord Nikolos' plan and were vying to see who might be selected to journey home to Neverness. The lords, too, could find nothing to argue with. They sat silently in their seats, looking back and forth between Lord Nikolos and the Sonderval. For a moment, it seemed that the lords would make the obvious decision and that war thus had been averted.

But the universe is a strange place always alive with irony and cosmic dramas. Sometimes the play of chance and impossible coincidence may persuade us that we are part of a larger game whose purpose is as infinite as it is mysterious. Sometimes, in a moment, a woman might act or a man might speak, and history will be changed forever. As Lord Nikolos called for a formal vote as to his plan, such a moment came to the Hall of the Lords. The great golden door through which Danlo had passed scarcely an hour earlier swung suddenly open, and three men made their way into the hall. Two of these were novice horologes, young men in tight red robes who had volunteered to guard the hall and act as guides for any ambassador or luminary who had business there. The third was an uncommonly large man dressed all in black. He had a thick black beard and blackish eyes and purple-black skin, and his mood at the moment was pure black because the horologes were harrying him, clutching at his arms and trying to prevent him from entering the hall. ''Let go of me, goddammit!'' he shouted as he swung his great arms and flung off the two small novices as if they were insects. ''Let go—haven't I explained that I've important news for your lords and masters that won't wait? What's wrong with you? I'm no assassin, by God! I'm a pilot!''

Although a score of lords had risen out of their chairs in alarm, Danlo smiled and his eyes filled with light because he knew this man. He looked across the hall and exchanged smiles with him. He was Pesheval Sarojin Vishnu-Shiva Lal, commonly known as Bardo, a former pilot of the Order and one of Danlo's oldest friends.

"Please restrain yourselves!" Lord Nikolos commanded in his steely voice, speaking to his fellow lords no less Bardo. "Please sit down."

"Yes, sit down before your knees buckle and you fall down," Bardo said as he strode to the black diamond circle at the center of the hall. "I've much to tell, and you'll need all your courage to hear it."

"You," Lord Nikolos said pointing at Bardo, "are no longer a pilot of the Order."

Twelve years before, in the hall of the Lords on Neverness, Lord Nikolos and many other of the lords (and Danlo) had watched as Bardo had flung his pilots' ring against a granite pillar, shattering it and abjuring his vows as a pilot. And then, after drinking the sacred remembrancers' drug and preaching the return of his best friend, Mallory Ringess, he had gone on to found the religion known as the Way of Ringess.

"No," Bardo said. "I'm no longer of the Order. But I'm still a *pilot,* by God! And I've crossed half the galaxy to tell you what I must tell you."

"And what is that?"

Bardo took a moment to fill his huge lungs with air. He looked at the Sonderval, with whom he had shared his journeyman years at the Pilots' College, Resa. He looked at Lord Nikolos and Morena Sung and Sul Estarei, and lastly, he looked at Danlo wi Soli Ringess. "There will soon be war in Neverness," his great voice boomed out into the hall. "And war among the Civilized Worlds. For the first time in two thousand years, a bloody, stupid war. I've journeyed twenty thousand light-years to tell you how this tragedy has happened and what we must do."

Although Bardo had blustered his way into a place where he was neither expected nor welcome, no one voiced objection to his presence. Lord Nikolos sat rigidly as if his chair had been electrified, and the eyes of every lord and master were fixed straight ahead on this huge man who commanded their attention. And so it happened that in the Hall of the Lords, a former pilot of the Order brought them news of a war that would change each of their lives and perhaps the face of the universe itself.

FATE

There is a war that opens the doors of heaven;
Glad are the warriors whose fate is to fight such a war.
—from the Bhagavad Gita 2.32

At the center of the floor of the the Hall of the Lords was a circle of inlaid black diamond. It might be thought that Bardo, standing in this circle with his black skin and black garments, would almost disappear into this purest of colors. But Bardo was not a man to be overshadowed, neither by man nor woman nor events nor the onstreaming black neverness of the universe itself. Like a hot giant star floating in the middle of the intergalactic void, he demanded attention. He had been born a prince of Summerworld, and he still thought of himself as a luminary among lesser lights, even though his innate nobility (and compassion) obliged him to help others rather than scorning them as beneath his concern, as did the Sonderval.

He was a natural dramatist. His huge voice filled the hall and fired the imagination of every master and lord. His whole manner touched others deeply, and yet little of this display resulted from conscious calculation, but was rather an expression of his deepest self. For instance, his clothing that day was as eye-catching as it was strange. Although the color of his clothing was pure black, he wore neither wool kamelaika nor formal black silks, as did Danlo—and Lara Jesusa and the other master pilots sitting at their table. A suit of spun nall, a fiber both exquisite and rare, covered his body from neck to ankle. Spun nall, of course, is harder and stronger than diamond, proof against lasers or knives or exploding projectiles. And to guard against blows, the suit's upper piece had been reinforced with sheets of plate nall molded to conform to his muscles. Between his legs he wore a huge nall codpiece to safeguard the most vulnerable and valuable of organs. A huge shimmering cape of shesheen, in which he might swaddle himself in the event of radiation bursts or plasma bombs, completed his raiment. And all this grandiloquent battle armor was of Bardo's own design. Having once been killed in defense of his best friend's life and subsequently resurrected, he placed great value on his own flesh and spared no expense in protecting it. As he told the assembled lords, he had gone off to war, and he entertained no illusions as to the terrors that he—and they—must soon face.

"There's already been a battle in Neverness," he said. "Oh, it was a small enough battle, and some will call it no more than a skirmish, with only three pilots killed, but it's a harbinger of worse to come, soon enough, all too soon—I don't have to be a goddamned scryer to tell you that."

Bardo went on to describe the events leading up to this battle. What had occurred on Neverness since the Vild Mission departed almost five years before was complicated, of course, as all such history truly is. But here, briefly, is what Bardo told the lords: That he had originally founded the religion known as the Way of Ringess to honor the life and discoveries of his best friend, Mallory Ringess. Mallory Ringess had shown the Order—and all humankind—that any man or woman could become a god through remembrance of the Elder Eddas. Bardo had brought this teaching to Neverness, and more, in his joyances and ceremonies where the sacred remembrancers' drug, kalla, was drunk, he had made the *experience* of the One Memory available to the Order's academicians and the swarms of seekers who peopled the city. But Bardo, as Bardo said, was better at beginning great works than completing them. And he was no prophet, but only a man with a few uncommon talents, a former pilot of the Order who simply wanted to help his friends and followers toward the infinite possibilities that awaited them. From almost the very beginning of the founding of Ringism, he had become involved with the cetic, Hanuman li Tosh.

"Ah, you all know of Hanuman," Bardo said. He paused to exchange a quick look with Danlo. Once, before they had become enemies, Danlo and Hanuman had been the deepest of friends. "But how many of you really *know* Hanuman?"

He went on to admit that Hanuman li Tosh was a brilliant and charismatic young man—and also a religious genius who had shaped the explosive expansion of Ringism in the city of Neverness and throughout the Civilized Worlds. But Hanuman was secretly cruel and vain, Bardo said, and monstrously ambitious. Hanuman, Bardo said, had been like a cancer in the belly of his church: making secret alliances with other luminaries within the Way; devising and leading new ceremonies to directly control their followers' minds; and worst of all, spreading lies about

Bardo and undermining Bardo's leadership in any way that he
could. As Ringism grew and grew and spread its tentacles (this
was Bardo's word) into the halls of the Order and the cities of the
Civilized Worlds, the new religion was sick at its center, with
Hanuman robbing it of true life in his terrible hunger for power.
Finally, on a day that Bardo would never forget, Hanuman had
challenged his authority directly and ousted him as Lord of the
Way of Ringess.

"He stole my goddamned church!" Bardo thundered at the
astonished lords. His face was enpurpled with rage, and he
stamped his black, nall-skin boot against the black diamond circle. "My lovely, blessed, beautiful church!"

For a moment no one spoke. Then Lord Nikolos fixed his icy
eyes on Bardo and asked, "Do you refer to the cathedral which
your cult purchased from one of the Kristian sects, or the organi-
zation of believers whom you gulled into following you?"

Bardo, who knew very well what Lord Nikolos thought about
religions, decided to take no offense from this. He simply said,
"Both. At first, it was the cathedral, and then Hanuman poisoned
the Ringists' minds against me. Ah, too bad! Too bad."

"And how does one steal a cathedral?" Lord Nikolos asked.

Bardo looked straight at Lord Nikolos and sighed. "Do you
remember how the cathedral was financed?"

"I'm not sure I ever cared to know."

"Well, it was an expensive building," Bardo said. "Hideously
expensive—but the grandest building in all the city. I had to have
it. That is we had to have it, we Ringists who followed the Way.
We needed a structure in which to honor and remembrance Mallory Ringess' great accomplishment. So we decided to buy it in
condominium. The money for it came from the pockets of each
Ringist. There was a problem, of course, with some of the
Ringists owning a share in such a building."

"Because these Ringists were also ordermen?"

"Exactly. Since the Order's canons forbade ownership of
property, they had to turn their shares over to others outside the
Order who held it in trust for them. Hanuman, in secret, began to
win these trustees to his confidence—and many other Ringists as
well. And then one day, on the fourteenth of deep winter, he—"

"He called for a vote setting rules as to who was permitted
entrance to the cathedral," Lord Nikolos said.

"How did you know that?" Bardo called out, less suspicious
than amazed.

"It seems an obvious enough strategem," Lord Nikolos said. "How is it that you didn't foresee it?"

"Ah, well, at first I did. Is Bardo a stupid man? No, indeed I'm not, and I thought that I was full aware of who among the trustees was loyal to me and who was not. But I'm afraid I miscounted. I was, ah, busy with other concerns. It's no simple thing, you know, founding a goddamned religion."

Here Danlo looked at Bardo across the hall and smiled. It was a shameful admission for a pilot steeped in the art of mathematics to admit that he had miscounted. But Bardo, for all his cunning, could be the most careless of men. Most likely his "other concerns" were the seduction and sexing of the many beautiful young women who sought to serve the Way of Ringess in any way they could.

"It seems," Lord Nikolos said, "that Hanuman has his own concerns."

"He barred me from my own church, by God! He installed himself as Lord of the Way!"

"And the Ringists followed him?"

"Too many did, too many," Bardo admitted. "Ah, they were sheep anyway—who else would have originally followed such an ill-fated man as I? Oh, at first I tried to lead the remembrancing ceremonies from my own house. For half a year, there were *two* Ways of Ringess in Neverness. But I no longer had the heart for it. For religion, that is. I saw what Hanuman was doing with *my* church, and it made me want to cry."

And what Hanuman was doing, Bardo said, was the total suborning of the Order—not for the sake of remembrancing the Elder Eddas and honoring Mallory Ringess' journey into godhood, but solely for the sake of power. Years before, Hanuman had made a secret pact with the Lord Cetic, Audric Pall, whom he had helped become Lord of the Order. Lord Pall had manuevered to have the Order's canons ammended, and for the first time in history, the lords and masters and academicians of Neverness were permitted formal association with a religion. Indeed, they were encouraged, even pressured, to profess their faith in the Three Pillars of Ringism and interface Hanuman's computers, in which the remembrance of the Elder Eddas had supposedly been stored as compelling images and vivid surrealities. Lord Pall gained for the stale, old Order the energies of an explosive new religion. And Hanuman gained alliance with the Order's many pilots who might set forth in their sparkling lightships and bring the Way of Ringess to the Civilized Worlds and to the stars beyond. Soon,

Bardo said, the Way of Ringess and the Order would be as one: a single religio-scientific entity whose power would be without constraint or bound.

When Bardo had finished speaking, all the lords sat motionless in stunned silence. Then Lord Nikolos blinked his eyes in disbelief and said, "This is very, very bad."

In truth neither he nor any other lord could have foreseen that this would-be universal religion called Ringism, like a ravenous beast, would gobble up the Order and many of the Civilized Worlds in only five years.

"I've always mistrusted the religious impulse," Lord Nikolos said, pointing his small finger at Bardo. "But I never understood the true nature of my mistrust. Now I do. I offer my apology to every lord, master, and orderman. Had I known the danger that this man and his cult posed, I never would have allowed the Order to divide in two. We should have remained in Neverness to oppose this abomination with all our will."

He didn't add that Lord Pall had originally chosen many members of the Second Vild Mission precisely *because* they opposed the Way of Ringess. Danlo wi Soli Ringess, who had spoken out against the Way and was now Hanuman's mortal enemy, had seen his name placed at the top of Lord Pall's list of exiles. And as for Lord Nikolos himself, he had been only too happy to flee what he now called an "abomination," to take his place as Lord of the New Order far from Neverness.

"Ah, well, no one can know how the future will unfold," Bardo told him. "If I had known that a little worm of a cetic named Hanuman li Tosh would steal my church and pervert my golden teachings into sleekit dung, I never would have held my first remembrancing ceremony."

"But like any prophet," Lord Nikolos said, "you thought you had seen the secret of the universe and had to share it with everyone."

This snide remark wounded and angered Bardo, who said, "I've seen what I've seen, by God! I've remembranced what I've remembranced. The Elder Eddas are real. I'm not the only one here today who has apprehended this knowledge. Morena has drunk kalla with me in my house, and Sul Estarei, and Alark of Urradeth. The Lord Remembrancer himself has had his own experience of the Eddas, and Danlo wi Soli Ringess is famous for his remembrance of the One Memory. The truth is the truth! You can't fault the religious impulse that drives us towards it. It's only what we make of our *religions* that is so wrong. Somehow, whenever men organize the pursuit of the divine, all that's most blessed and numinous is ruined like picked apples rotting in the sun. As I, Bardo, of all men should know.''

And I, too, Danlo thought as he sat staring at Bardo and remembering his own involvement with the Way of Ringess.

"I won't argue with you," Lord Nikolos said, and in his voice there was cold steel.

"Ah, well, I didn't fall across the stars to argue."

"Whatever the impulse that initially drove you, the Way of Ringess is what it is. And you've made what you've made."

"By God, do you think I don't know that!" Bardo roared. "Why do you think I've risked my goddamned life to tell you what's happened on Neverness?"

"Why, indeed? We'd all like to know that, wouldn't we?"

"I must undo what I have done."

"I see."

"I've helped create a wildly growing cancer. Now I would ask for help in cutting it out before it's too late."

With a bow toward Lord Nikolos then, Bardo finished his story. After losing his beautiful cathedral and abandoning his attempt to run an opposing church from his house, Bardo had fallen into a terrible melancholy. For five days he shut himself in his room, amazingly (for Bardo) refusing the food and drink that his many loyal friends tried to bring him. He sat alone in an immense bejewelled chair as he contemplated killing himself. But Bardo was no suicide. Even as the days of deep winter darkened and the weather grew as cold as death, his rage turned outward. It was Hanuman li Tosh whom he should kill, he thought, or Lord Pall, or even his cousin, Surya Surata Lal, an ugly little woman who had once been his most faithful confidant before Hanuman had charmed her into betraying Bardo. He should kill *somebody,* and in dark and wild days of deep winter the year before, such murderous intentions were not impossible to fulfill, for the entire city of Neverness had fallen into evil times.

At least ten of the Order's lords and masters died mysteriously, some said of poison or unknown and undetectable viruses. The Order issued oppressive new laws and regulations. For the first time since the Dark Year when the Great Plague had ravaged Neverness, there was a nightly curfew in the city. The sacred drug, kalla, was forbidden to everyone except the remembrancers—and even these silver-robed masters of the mind had to apply to Lord Pall for permission to hold their time-honored ceremonies in the confinement of the remembrancers' tower. Various sects such as the autists found themselves suddenly persecuted. Lord Pall himself announced his intention to break the harijan sect, which had challenged the Order's authority for at least three centuries.

During the almost lightless days of midwinter spring, the Order had begun a program of great works, building new churches across the city and even planning a great new cathedral within the walls of the Academy itself. Lord Pall planned to compel all ordermen to make daily attendence at these churches' remembrancing ceremonies. There they would place the sacred remembrancing heaumes upon their heads, and open themselves to visions of the Elder Eddas—or so it was said. But in truth, they would only open themselves, their very brains, to whatever dogma, images, secret messages, or propaganda that Hanuman li Tosh or Lord Pall wished them to believe.

Of course, the rise of this tyranny in such a historically free and illuminated city as Neverness did not go unopposed. All the aliens—led by the Fravashi—spoke out against the Order's favoring this potentially totalitarian new religion. Ambassadors from the worlds of Larondissement and Yarkona made formal objections and threatened to sever relations with the Order. The numerous astriers, most of whom counted themselves as members of one of the Cybernetic Universal Churches, shunned Ringism as they might poisoned wine, and they kept to their houses and churches in the Farsiders' Quarter. At this time, perhaps no more than a tenth of the city's residents outside the Order were willing to embrace the Three Pillars of Ringism. But, in the fierce struggle for power occurring in Neverness, it was the lords and masters and adepts *within* the Order who really mattered.

Many there were who would never countenance Ringism or their Order's association with it. Lord Pall had not managed to banish *all* his potential enemies to the Vild. Especially among the returning pilots—and in Neverness there were always pilots returning in their lightships from years-long journeys to the stars— there were brave men and women inured to the terrors of the manifold. They were far too proud to allow themselves terror of Lord Pall or the cetic assassins which he was rumored to command. Indeed, some of them such as Alesar Esterei and Cristobel, had fought with Mallory Ringess and distinguished themselves in the Pilots' War years before. Inevitably, as Bardo told the story, Bardo had made connection with these pilots. They formed a cadre perhaps fifty strong, and they began meeting nightly at Bardo's grand house in the Old City. They called themselves the

Fellowship of Free Pilots. They planned to form a nucleus around which anyone who opposed Ringism, inside the Order or out, might gather to talk and encourage each other. And to plot revolt.

For Bardo, it was his fifth career. Having begun life as a Summerworld prince, he had journeyed to Neverness to become a famous pilot, and later, Master of Novices. Then, after abjuring his vows and leaving the Order, he had gained fabulous wealth as a merchant, before returning to Neverness as the prophet of a new religion. And now at last, as he told the lords of the New Order, after having been rich and poor, famous and scorned, enlightened and despairing, (and alive and dead), he had come into his true calling as a warrior.

"We must fight them, by God!" Bardo said. "What else can we do?"

Bardo told of how Lord Pall—or perhaps Hanuman—had sent an assassin to kill him. The assassin had caught Bardo on the street one evening returning home, and it was only because of the incredible courage of a man named Minowara ni Kei, who was one of Bardo's followers, that Bardo was still alive. Just as the black-robed assassin had fired a spikhaxo at Bardo, Minowara had thrown his body in front of Bardo, taking the naitarre-poisoned dart in his shoulder and dying a hideous, spasming death. This had given Bardo time to overpower the assassin, in truth to club him to death with his huge hand as a bear might slay a child. Upon realizing how vulnerable his flesh was to such deadly needles, he had gone down to the Farsiders' Quarter the next day and ordered his suit of nall armor.

After this naked attempt to murder Bardo, the Fellowship of Free Pilots decided that their continued existence in Neverness was doubtful. Cristobel believed that their best hope to oppose the Ringists would be for each pilot to journey to as many of the Civilized Worlds as possible and bring the blazing torch of resistance to all who loved their freedom. Bardo himself was to make the perilous journey to Thiells. The only problem with this plan was that Lord Pall knew the names of every pilot in the Fellowship. He forbade them to leave the city.

And so one gloomy day near the begining of midwinter spring, Bardo and his fellow pilots stormed the Cavern of the Thousand Lightships, surprising the Ringists that Lord Pall had set to guard the Order's most glorious vessels. This was the battle that Bardo had spoken of earlier. In the flash of laser fire and fierce fighting along the steel walkways deep below the earth, Vamana Chu and

Marrim Danladi and Oriana of Darkmoon had been killed. But the rest of the pilots escaped with their ships.

Since Bardo was no longer formally a pilot of the Order, he of course had no ship. But this lack did not daunt him. After obtaining the entrance codes from a terrified programmer whose jaw Bardo threatened to tear off with his naked hands, Bardo appropriated the Lord Pilot's very own ship: a stately expanse of black diamond that Lord Salmalin had named the *Silver Lotus*. Upon breaking free into deep space above Neverness and falling into the shimmering manifold that underlies all space and time, Bardo had immediately renamed his ship the *Sword of Shiva*.

Thus had he crossed the stellar Fallaways and entered the unmapped spaces of the Vild. He, who had always considered himself a potentially finer pilot than even the Sonderval, had found his way past the manifold's infinite trees and the countless supernovas blighting the galaxy's Orion Arm. From Cristobel he had learned the fixed-points of Thiells, and so after many days he came to this faraway world and to the New Order with a mission of his own. Upon taking the *Sword of Shiva* down to the very same light field where Danlo had come to earth only a few hours earlier, he discovered that the Lords of the New Order were meeting at that very moment in a conclave. He had tried to send word of his arrival to Lord Nikolos, but a rather self-important young horologe had informed him that the lords were discussing matters of the greatest importance and could not be disturbed.

And so Bardo, in Bardo's inimitable way, had raced across Thiells in a sled, charmed his way past the Academy's gatekeeper (whom he had once known as Master of Novices years ago), and had stormed into the Hall of the Lords. And now he stood before them, a towering and impassioned man clad in a suit of armored clothing, a great pilot and would-be warrior who called all the pilots of the New Order to a grand and glorious fate.

"On the 60th of false winter, Neverness time, there will be a gathering on Sheydveg," he said. "The Fellowship of Free Pilots is calling each of the Civilized Worlds to send ships and men and women unafraid to fight. We'll gather a fleet and fall against Neverness like a thousand silver swords—against the goddamned Ringists, against Hanuman li Tosh and Lord Pall. All the New Order's pilots and lightships will be needed in this war."

At the center table in the Hall of the Lords, Lord Nikolos Sar Petrosian sat fingering the silken folds of his yellow robe. He liked to believe that he was the most self-controlled of men, and he usually disdained such fidgeting, preferring to keep his body motions precisely directed at all times. But Bardo's story clearly had shaken him; despite himself, he reverted to nervous habits that he had thought he had long since overcome.

"Is there anything more that you need to tell us?" Lord Nikolos asked.

"Ah, well, there *is* one more thing," Bardo said. "The Order—under Hanuman's direction—is building something. In the near space at the first Lagrange point above the city. Hanuman calls it his Universal Computer. It's a huge thing, and ugly, like a great, goddamned black moon. And someday, if the Ringists have their way, it will be as big as a moon. Even now, the Ringists are using disassemblers to mine the moons above Neverness for elements with which to build this hideous machine."

He did not add that the Old Order's eschatologists were afraid that the making of the Universal Computer, in using elements from Icefall's moons, might inhibit and retard the growth of the Golden Ring.

Lord Nikolos gasped in outrage, then, and his face fell red with blood. What Hanuman—and the Ringists—had done in using assembler technology to mine the moons above Neverness and build a possibly godlike computer violated the Law of the Civilized Worlds. After managing to get his breathing under control, he looked at Lord Morena Sung sitting next to him as she tapped her plump lips. Even the Sonderval seemed taken aback by this news, for he forgot all protocol and spoke in Lord Nikolos' place. "Will you inform us, Pilot, as to what the Ringists might be doing with this computer?"

Although Bardo was no longer of the Order, it pleased him to be called Pilot, especially by his former rival and the greatest pilot of the Order, New or Old. He said, "I know what Hanuman has told the Ringists. Ah, you all know how damnably difficult the Elder Eddas are to remembrance. Few have had a clear memory of them. I, myself, almost, and Hanuman li Tosh much more so, and Thomas Rane. And, of course, Danlo wi Soli Ringess, who's had perhaps the clearest and greatest memory of all."

Bardo turned in his circle to bow to Danlo, and suddenly Danlo became aware of a hundred lords looking at him.

"Because only a few geniuses could remembrance the Eddas fully," Bardo said, "we were forced to copy our experiences of them and store them in the remembrancing computers. In the heaumes that we placed on our heads. How else could we share this wisdom with the multitudes of Ringists who knew nothing of the remembrancers' art?"

To counterfeit the experience of remembrance, Danlo thought. He held himself very still, gazing at Bardo as he touched his flute to his lips and recalled how Bardo had once asked him to make a copy of his great remembrance. But such an act would only mock true remembrance, and Danlo had refused, thus straining his friendship with Bardo and making enemies of Hanuman li Tosh altogether.

Despite all that Bardo has said, he is still angry with me for not supporting his cybernetic illusions and lies.

As if Bardo had a private window into Danlo's mind, he stared into Danlo's dark, blue eyes and suddenly snapped his fist into the palm of his hand. And then he called out, "The Eddas should be for everyone, by God! For anyone. And anyone can put a goddamned computer on his head and interface a simulation of the Eddas. Ah, it's not *exactly* remembrancing, too bad, but it's as close as most will ever come. And Hanuman always said that as we made better and better simulations of the Eddas, the experience would more closely approach that of true remembrance. And if the simulation could be made detailed enough, as well as deep and profound, well, then even the One Memory might be faced by all. This is the reason for Hanuman's computer. A universal computer—he's promised that it will hold a whole universe of memories. If it's vast enough, the simulation of the Eddas can be made infinitely refined. Ah, infinitely powerful. When it's finished, if you believe Hanuman, every Ringist on Neverness will be able to look up at this goddamned machine floating in the sky and fall into a rapture of the One Memory."

Truly, Hanuman would almost die to interface such a computer, Danlo thought. *The power of it would be almost as if he were a god.*

After a long pause in which the attention of the lords was drawn back to Bardo, Lord Nikolos stared at this huge, harbinger of doom, and asked him, "Are you finished, now?"

"I am finished," Bardo said with a bow.

Lord Nikolos drew in a slow breath, then said, "What you've told us is beyond bad. This is the worst thing I've ever heard."

"Ah, well, it *is* too, too terribly bad, which is why we must decide—"

"That is true," Lord Nikolos interrupted. He looked at the lords and masters of the New Order all around him, and said, *"We* must decide what is to be done."

At this implied rebuke of Bardo's abandonment of the Order, Bardo ground the toe of his nall-skin boot against the floor. As nall is almost the hardest thing there is, it left scratches in the smooth black diamond. But Lord Nikolos was devoid of neither compassion nor good sense, and so he said, "You know that it's our way to decide such questions among ourselves. But since you were once a master pilot and are clearly involved in this nightmare which has befallen us, I'd like to ask you to remain."

So saying, Lord Nikolos indicated that Bardo should take a seat at the master pilots' table.

"Thank you, Lord Nikolos," Bardo said. He stepped out of the circle and strode across the room. He found an empty chair across from Danlo, and with much huffing and sighing, sat down.

"This has been a strange day," Lord Nikolos said. For Bardo's benefit, he quickly summarized what Danlo had told the lords about his journey and the war fought between the Architects, and then said, "First Danlo wi Soli Ringess falls out of the stars to tell us that Tannahill has been found and a madman is loose among the galaxy with a star-killing machine. And two hours later, his father's best friend arrives to tell us that the whole city of Neverness has fallen mad. What are we to make of such strangenesses?"

This was the first anyone had remarked the incredible coincidence of Bardo and Danlo meeting each other on a faraway planet in the Vild after so many years apart. But fate itself is strange, and as Danlo looked at Bardo looking at him in astonishment across a few feet of swirling air, he felt something wild and irresitable pulling Bardo and himself (and all the other pilots in the hall) toward a singular point in time not very far in the future.

"And *now* we must decide which course of action to pursue," Lord Nikolos said. "I would like to ask the lords for their wisdom."

Sul Estarei, the clear-thinking and cautious Lord Holist sitting at the end of Lord Nikolos' table, suddenly found his voice and said, "The Bardo has called us to a gathering on Sheydveg in only ninety-five more days. And what will be the result of this gathering? War—a civil war on a vast scale, for I think it's clear that many of the Civilized Worlds have already been overwhelmed with this Ringism madness and will support the Old Order. And many more will remain loyal out of habit. We must ask ourselves if we're prepared to be part of such an inconceivable war?"

"Are we prepared *not* to be?" the Sonderval asked.

"That's surely the correct question," Lord Morena Sung said. For all the softness of her face and soul, she was a fearless woman driven by a desire to view the truth of any situation no matter how terrible. "If we don't send our pilots to Sheydveg, what will happen?"

"But *our* mission is to the Vild," said an old lord named Demothi Bede from a table at the rear of the hall. "What will come of what Danlo wi Soli Ringess has gained on Tannahill if we send all our pilots to Sheydveg?"

"Are we just to abandon the Civilized Worlds?" Morena Sung asked. "Neverness, herself, where I was born?"

"Are we to abandon the Vild and let the supernovas consume the entire galaxy?" Demothi Bede countered. "I'd rather see every one of the Civilized Worlds converted to Ringism than even one of worlds in the Vild destroyed because its star had exploded."

At this Morena Sung pursed her plump lips and asked, "Do you mean, as the star of the Narain people whom Danlo told us about was exploded?"

"The Lord Sung reminds us," the Sonderval said, "of what we shouldn't have forgotten. What of Bertram Jaspari and his Iviomils with their star-killer? How can we let these fanatics loose among the Civilized Worlds?"

For a while, as the sun fell towards the ocean outside and sent rays of light streaming through the hall's dome in a brilliant display of colors, the lords of the New Order debated war. During a moment of silence after Lord Fatima Paz recited the names of all the men and women killed during the Pilots' War, Danlo closed his eyes and whispered a prayer for the spirits of each of these pilots. And then he slowly stood away from his table, squeezed his flute tightly in his hand, and said, "Lord Nikolos, there is something I would like to say."

Lord Nikolos bowed to him and said, "Then please speak, if you will."

Danlo, whose Fravashi teacher had once bestowed upon him the title of "Peacewise" for his devotion to ahimsa, politely returned the bow. Then he looked out over the tables of men and women in all their brightly hued robes, and he said, "You lords . . . have spoken of war in abstractions such as 'abandonment' of political entities or 'support' of causes or of our Order's 'mission' to the Vild. But war is as real as a child screaming in the night. I know. On Tannahill, in my arms, I held a young girl whose face had been burned away by a plastic bomb. On Tannahill I saw . . . many things. Tannahill is far from here, thousands of light-years, and so is Neverness. But war is not something that happens only to people far away. When a man goes over bleeding his life away, for him it is always *here*. There is always such a terrible *hereness* about dying, yes? And for each of us, we are always here, too, wherever we are. Who can say that this war of which you have spoken so abstractly will not come here to Thiells? Who here today, at this moment, is prepared to face the fire of a hydrogen bomb and die? Who is prepared to watch us pilots die, as pilots do die, falling into the hearts of suns and cooking like meat or falling mad lost in the manifold or exploding from the inside out and freezing into blood crystals in the vacuum of space? Why . . . has no one asked if there must be war at all? What of peace, then? Is there no hope of constraining the Ringists without killing? Or even the Iviomils? I must believe . . . that peace is always a possibility."

After Danlo had finished speaking, he met eyes with the Sonderval and Demothi Bede and Angelina Maria Zorete, and many other lords. Then he sat down and looked at Bardo. Bardo, he knew, had immense powers of visualization (and a keen memory), and obviously had no difficulty imagining how terrible a full war would be, for his huge face fell soft and compassionate, and he muttered, "The poor pilots, the poor children, all the poor people, too bad. Ah, what have I started? Poor Bardo—too, too bad."

Lord Nikolos, sitting across the room, couldn't have made out Bardo's words, but he seemed disquieted even so. And then, to Danlo, he said, "Thank you for reminding us that peace is always a possibility. At this moment, unfortunately, it seems a very far possibility. Nevertheless, we must consider every chance. War *is* real, as you say, and in making our plan, we must consider limiting this war or forestalling it altogether. If you've no more to add—or anyone else—here is what I believe our course should be."

Lord Nikolos' plan was clear and straightforward. In a reversal of what he had originally proposed, he would send a few pilots to escort ambassadors to Tannahill. But most of the New Order's pilots would journey in their light ships to the gathering on Sheydveg, either to forestall war if possible or wage it with all their power.

"I'll also send ambassadors to Neverness," Lord Nikolos said. "It's possible that we still might reason with Lord Pall and Hanuman li Tosh. Since this will be a very dangerous journey, I'll ask only those of you who really wish to make such a mission to offer your services. I, of course, will lead this embassy and—"

Here Lord Morena Sung shook her head and asked to speak.

She smoothed over the folds of her blue eschatologists' robe, then said, "Lord Nikolos, you must *not* go to Neverness. Your place, as you surely must know, is here on Thiells. But I would like to make this mission, if I could."

All at once, ten other Lords, including Sul Estarei and Demothi Bede, called out that they, too, were willing to journey to Neverness. Then Morena Sung said, "There is one present today who knows Hanuman li Tosh's mind more deeply than any other. Although he's only a master, he and Hanuman were once deepest—"

"Are you speaking of Danlo wi Soli Ringess?" the Sonderval demanded.

"I am."

The Sonderval, who would lead the pilots to Sheydveg and thence most likely to war, shook his head, then told her, "I'm loathe to lose such a fine pilot to what will probably be a futile mission. Danlo and Hanuman were once deep friends, this is true, but they also parted enemies. What kind of ambassador do you think he'd really make?"

"One who won't be fooled by Hanuman's deceits or lies," Lord Sung said.

"But we don't even know if Danlo would wish to make such a mission," the Sonderval said.

At this, almost every lord and master in the hall turned to look at Danlo, who gripped his flute and drew in a deep breath. Just as he was about to tell the lords that he would serve the New Order in any way he could, Lord Nikolos smiled at him and said, "I had thought to send Danlo back to Tannahill as ambassador. He's already won Harrah Ivi en li Ede's confidence—this Holy Ivi has already changed the doctrines of the Old Church because of him. Who better to send on such a mission?"

"But Lord Nikolos," Morena Sung said, "surely that is the point? The greatest part of our mission to Tannahill is already accomplished. Thanks to Danlo. Wouldn't his talents be better used elsewhere?"

"And his greatest talent," the Sonderval said, "is as a pilot. I'll need all my pilots if war comes and we fall against the Ringists."

At this mention of war, Danlo continued to hold his breath, and he felt his heart beating like a drum at the center of his chest.

"To send Danlo to Sheydveg would be cruel," Lord Nikolos said to the Sonderval. "Have you forgotten his vow of ahimsa? How can one sworn to peace go to war?"

Never to kill, Danlo thought. *Never to harm any living being.*

"If I thought about it at all," the Sonderval said, staring at Danlo, "I had supposed his duty to the Order would overcome his commitment to some private and unworkable ideal."

Lord Nikolos slowly shook his head, then turned slightly so that his words carried more forcefully out into the Hall. "We mustn't forget that Danlo's vow preceded the vows he made when he entered the Order. At the time, no one foresaw that his vow of ahimsa might ever pose a conflict. I don't believe we should ask him to abjure this vow simply because the circumstances have changed."

Danlo looked down at his hands which had once held the bloody head of a dying friend named Thomas Ivieehl, and he thought, *But I would never abandon ahimsa.*

"Even to send Danlo to Neverness on a mission of peace might prove problematic," Lord Nikolos continued. "If this embassy fails and war falls upon the Civilized Worlds, bad chance might pose him terrible conflicts. The waves of war might overcome him and sweep him away."

"But killing always poses conflicts, and war might sweep any of us away," the Sonderval countered. "Who among us can escape his own fate?"

"And who can make another's journey towards his own fate?" Lord Nikolos asked. "I won't make Danlo journey to Sheydveg."

At this news, Danlo sighed and looked at Lord Nikolos eye to eye.

"I believe," Lord Nikolos said, "that it would best suit Danlo to be sent back to Tannahill. But it would best suit the Order for him to be one of our ambassadors to Neverness."

Now Danlo held his flute tightly in his hands and held his breath in his lungs. Lord Nikolos' gaze was cold but not unkind, and it seemed that he was searching Danlo's face for some sign of what the future might unfold.

"It's unusual for the Lord of the Order to leave such a decision to a pilot," Lord Nikolos said. "But this is an unusual situation."

All the lords in the hall looked at Danlo to see what he might say. Bardo smiled at him, and a part of his great strength seemed to flow out of his soft brown eyes and into Danlo.

"I would ask you to choose between the ambassadorships to Tannahill or Neverness," Lord Nikolos said to Danlo. "If you need more time to—"

"No," Danlo suddenly said, letting go his breath. "I will choose now."

He closed his eyes as his listened to the wind beating against the hall's crystal dome and to the sound of his own deep breath. Fate, he thought, was calling him to the future with all the force of a star pulling a lightship towards its fiery center. All people had a fate—or at least a golden path toward the realization of life's deepest possibilities. Some refused to hear the call or ignored it when it cried out within them. Some fled their fate like a snowhare leaping in zigs and zags away from a diving thallow. Too often a man or a woman lived in a dull, defeated acceptance of the inevitable, all the while hating themselves and bewailing the unfairness of the universe. Only a few rare beings embraced the terrible beauty of life. And only the rarest of the rare loved their fate whether or not their lives were drenched in sunshine and honey or filled with fire, flashing swords, nightmare and death.

In all of Danlo's journeys, he thought that he had found only one such, and that was his onetime friend, Hanuman li Tosh. And now it seemed that Hanuman had made an irreversible crossing of some dark, inner ocean, perhaps towards godly power, perhaps only towards madness—it was hard to know. And now Hanuman waited for him in the icy, shimmering City of Light, just as across the room, in the Hall of the Lords sparkling with so many colors, Bardo and Lord Nikolos and a hundred other lords watched his face for signs of weakness and waited to see which path he might choose.

For in the end we choose our futures, he remembered.

He closed his eyes tightly then, and time opened like a window onto a deep blue sky, and he beheld the shape and shimmer of moments yet to be. Everything waited for him in Neverness. High in the tower of a great cathedral, beneath a clear dome, a pale and beautiful man stood watching the stars for Danlo's lightship to fall out of the night. On the ice-locked islands hundreds of miles from Neverness, men and women in white furs looked for Danlo to bring them a cure to a disease that lay coiled in their blood waiting to explode into life. A child waited for him, too. He saw this child lying in his arms, helpless, trusting, gazing up at him with eyes as wild and deeply blue as his own. He saw himself waiting for himself: his future self who was fiercer, wiser, nobler and marked down to his soul with a terrible love of life. The universe itself, from the Edge galaxies to the stars of the Vild, waited for him—waited for him to decide if he would go to Neverness, yes or no.

That is always the deepest question, the only true question— yes or no.

Once, the goddess known as the Solid State Entity had told him that he would someday go to war, and he saw that *that* terror awaited him in Neverness as well. But what kind of war? Would it be battles of lasers and exploding bombs or a struggle of a deeper and more universal nature? This he could not see. But he knew that even if war should sweep him away in the maneuvers of lightships, armies and men firing eye tlolts at each other, even if his own flesh was opened with a nerve knife, he would keep his vow of ahimsa; always he would keep true to the calling of his own soul.

I would never kill another, even though I and everyone I love must die.

When he opened his eyes, it was as he had only blinked and almost no time had passed. Lord Nikolos and everyone else still waited for his answer. Danlo sat gripping his flute, and he remembered another thing that the Entity had once told him: that he would find his father at his journey's end. Perhaps his father, too, waited for him in Neverness. He could almost hear his father's voice carrying along the stellar winds from far across the galaxy, calling him home to his fate.

"I . . . will go to Neverness," he finally said. He looked at Lord Nikolos and tried to smile as a fierce pain stabbed through his left eye.

"Very well, then," Lord Nikolos said. "And now I must decide who the other ambassadors will be. There's much to be decided, for all of us, but not now. Since the hour is late, we'll adjourn for dinner. And tomorrow meet again."

Lord Nikolos suddenly stood away from his table. The other lords followed his lead, and some began talking in groups of two or ten, while others filed out of the hall. Bardo and the master pilots sitting at Danlo's table immediately began to discuss the forcing of an enemy's lightship into the fiery center of a star and other battle strategems, and for the moment Danlo was left sitting alone to marvel at the terrible energies unleashed by the mere talk of war. He rubbed his aching eye, all the while breathing deeply against the terrible soaring anticipation in the center of his belly.

I, too, love my fate, he thought. *My terrible, beautiful fate.*

And then he stood up to greet Bardo and tell the other pilots of new strategems of mastering the manifold, and the first waves of war swept him under as well.

THE TWO HUNDRED LIGHTSHIPS

Only the dead have seen an end to war.
—Plato

During the next few days, Lord Nikolos and the College of Lords made many decisions. All the pilots on Thiells were told to prepare their light ships and make their farewells. Thomas Sonderval, the Lord Pilot, in his gleaming ship the *Cardinal Virtue*, would lead two hundred others across the Vild's dangerous stars to Sheydveg. Should death befall this great pilot—if a supernova should catch him in wild blast of photons or the manifold devour his ship—Helena Charbo would act as Lord Pilot in his place. And if Helena and her *Infinite Pearl* were to meet a similar fate, Sabri Dur li Kadir would succeed her, and then Aja, Charl Rappaporth and Veronika Menchik, all masters of great renown who had once fought with Mallory Ringess in the Pilot's War. The flashing battles they had once waged through the Fallways had taught them that war consumes human lives as quickly as a flame held to dry sticks.

Two hundred pilots seemed almost too few to send to the gathering on Sheydveg, but in truth the Order was lucky to muster so many. The pilots had journeyed twenty thousand light years from Neverness not to wait planet-bound for war, but to make great quests into the Vild. Almost fifty pilots still fell among the wild stars toward the galaxy's Perseus Arm, searching for Tannahill or exploring rainbow star systems or discovering dead, burnt-out alien worlds. Peter Eyota, in his *Akashara,* Henrios li Radman, Paloma the Elder—none could say when these pilots might return.

By sheer good chance (or perhaps ill), on the day before the pilots were to set forth to the stars, Edreiya Chu *did* return, falling down to Thiells' only light field and bringing her ship to rest along with all the others. There, on a long, broad run, the *Golden Lotus* joined the *August Moon,* the *Flame of God,* the *Ibi Ibis* and other needles of black diamond formed up in twenty rows. There too gleamed the *Sword of Shiva,* which Bardo had stolen in Neverness, and Danlo's ship, the *Snowy Owl,* she of the long, sweeping hull and graceful wings. In less time than it took for Old Earth to turn its face in revolution once to the sun, the pilots would climb inside these two hundred ships and point their way towards Sheydveg's great red sun. In preparation for this journey, they were supposed to be resting or practicing the pilots' mental art of hallning or praying or saying goodbye to beloved friends.

At least two pilots, however, on this long night of cool sea winds and blazing stars, did not spend their time with goodbyes. Rather they arranged a rendezvous to say hello. Because Danlo had been very busy the last few days describing his discoveries to the cetics and eschatologists (and talking in private with Lord Nikolos), he hadn't had the chance to greet Bardo properly. And so when they had broken free from their duties, these two old friends met on a grassy lawn outside the glittering stone halls of the Pilots' College. Beneath tall, alien trees overlooking the sea, they called out in gladness and hurried to embrace each other.

"Little Fellow, Little Fellow!" Bardo said as he threw his arms around Danlo and thumped his back. "I thought I'd never have the chance to talk with you."

Although Danlo was taller and stronger than most men, embracing Bardo was like trying to clasp a mountain to himself. With a gasp of air (Bardo's huge arms had nearly cracked his ribs), Danlo stepped away and smiled at Bardo. He said, simply, "I . . . missed you."

"Did you? Did you? Well, I missed you, too. It's been too, too long."

Bardo turned his huge head right and left, looking for a chair or bench. But Danlo, who had always hated sitting on any kind of furniture, had already dropped down to the soft grass. With a sigh and much groaning, Bardo carefully lowered his huge body until he sat face to face with Danlo. Although there was no need for such precautions within the safety of the Academy, Bardo still wore his suit of battle armor, and the stiff plates of nall reinforcing his garments impeded his motions.

"By God, it's a miracle to find you here!" Bardo said, wiping drops of water from his forehead. Despite the coolness of the night, he was sweating in his layers of black nall. "To find that you and I have fallen out of the goddammned stars almost at the same hour—the same fateful hour—after having crossed the galaxy from opposite ends!"

As ever, Danlo smiled at Bardo's enthusiasm, no less his choice of words. "Some might call it only an extraordinary coincidence."

"A miracle, I said! A goddamned miracle! What more proof do we need that you and I share a miraculous fate?"

"These last few days . . . I have often thought about fate."

"Can you feel it, Little Fellow?" Bardo's eyes, in the light of the flame globes around the lawn, were pools of burning ink. "It's like a star pulling at a comet. It's like a beautiful woman calling to her man. It's like . . . ah, well, it's each cell in your body coming awake and singing the same song, and that song roaring outward until it touches every rock on every planet and sets the whole goddamned universe humming."

"I have always loved listening to you speak," Danlo said, as amused as he was truly delighted.

"Can you doubt it? You and I—we've been chosen to do great things, and this is the moment for the doing."

"Perhaps. Or perhaps it is only that we have chosen. Out of all the chances life offers, and out of our pride, Bardo . . . perhaps we have only chosen the most desperate of chances."

Bardo shook his head so hard that drops of sweat spun off his thick, black beard into the night. He said, "There's a line from a poem your father once told me: 'Fate and chance, the same glad dance.' "

For a long moment, Danlo sat gazing at Bardo. He thought that he had never seen this huge man so animated, not even during the first breathtaking days of false winter six years ago when he (and Danlo and Hanuman li Tosh) had been busy founding the Way of Ringess and all things seemed possible. Danlo reflected on all that Bardo had said in the Hall of the Lords concerning the corruption of the church and Hanuman's ousting him as Lord of the Way. Although Bardo was the most sincere of men, the full truth of his life often escaped him because he was wont to fool himself. He liked to believe that he acted from the purest of purposes, usually to serve others, but all too often Bardo served only Bardo.

Danlo thought that his true motive in journeying to Thiells was not to save the Civilized Worlds from the cancerous new religion that he had made, but rather revenge and glory. Bardo had always had a sense of his own inborn greatness, and he knew that great men must do great things. But it was the tragedy of his life that he'd never quite found the way to realize his deepest possibilities. At various periods he had sought exaltation through mathematics, women, wealth, drugs and religion. And now war was to be the vessel carrying him toward his glorious fate, and this was perhaps the greatest tragedy of all.

"Did you know," Danlo finally mused, "that the Architects of the Old Church—at least the Iviomils—believe that Ede himself has written the program for the universe? And that all we do is part of this program?"

"Ah, no, I didn't know that."

"Truly, on Tannahill, the very mention of chance is a *talaw* punishable by a cleansing of the mind."

"Barbarians!" Bardo muttered. "It's a miracle you survived your mission there."

"Yes, I know."

"It's a miracle, of course, but something much more. I've heard the full story of your journey from the Sonderval. How you walked with the dead and went deeper into your own mind than any cetic. There's something about you now that I've never seen before. A fire and light: it's as if your goddamned eyes are windows to the stars."

Danlo looked up at the heavens, and a strange look fell over his face. And then Bardo continued to extoll his accomplishments. "And how you plunged into the goddamned chaos space in the heart of the Entity! You're a braver pilot than the Sonderval, Little Fellow, and a finer. By God, you're the finest since Mallory Ringess, and he was a goddamned god!"

"*Was,* Bardo?"

"Ah, I mean he was a divine pilot, a god of a pilot who could take his ship anywhere in the universe."

Danlo smiled at this exaggeration, for no pilot, not even Mallory Ringess who had proved it was possible for a lightship to fenester instantly between any two stars, had ever fallen from the Milky Way to one of the universe's other galaxies.

"Have you had news of my father?" Danlo asked.

The so-called First Pillar of the creed of Ringism stated that one day Mallory Ringess would return to Neverness. Although Danlo now rejected the beliefs of all religions, he had always wondered at his father's fate and waited for the moment of the Return—as had many thousands of others.

"No, I haven't, Little Fellow—I'm sorry. In all the journeys of all the pilots, no one has come back telling of anyone who has seen him."

Danlo ran his fingers through the cool grass next to his crossed legs and listened to the sound of the ocean moving far below the academy. Although it was near midnight, various pilots and professionals, in twos and threes, crossed the walks leading to the dormitories all around them. Their low voices fell across the lawn where Danlo and Bardo sat, and for a moment Danlo was silent.

"Once, before he left Neverness," Bardo said, "your father told me that he would journey yet again to the Entity. There was to be, ah, a kind of mystical union between them. Something that they must create together."

At this, Danlo smiled strangely and said, "Truly, the Entity is a passionate goddess—She's all fire and tears and dreams. It may be that She desires union with our kind."

He did not tell Bardo that the Entity had tried to capture him on an earth that She had made. Nor that She had tried to seduce him by creating an incarnation of Tamara Ten Ashtoreth from sea water and earth elements and memories stolen from deep in his mind.

"When the Sonderval told me that you'd spent much time with the Entity, I wondered if you might have learned anything about your father."

"She said only that I would find him at my journey's end."

"In Neverness?"

"I . . . do not know. The Entity always speaks so mysteriously."

"*I* still believe your father will return to Neverness. It's where his fate lies, not out in the stars with some capricious goddess."

For a moment, Danlo looked west at the strange, shimmering stars just over the rim of the sea, but he said nothing.

"And when he *does* return, by God, there will be an accounting! He'll open his eyes to every barbaric thing that Hanuman li Tosh has done in his name, and fall across the city in wrath. He'll chastise him, perhaps even slay him—your father, despite his compassion, was always such a murderous man."

"But, Bardo, don't you believe he is now a god?"

"Do you think the gods don't slay human beings as easily as flies—or even each other?"

Danlo thought of the Silicon God's destruction of Ede the God, and he said, "I know that they do."

For a while, beneath their tree's silvery leaves rustling in the wind, they gazed out at the stars and talked about the galaxy's gods—and fate and war and other cosmic things. Then Danlo turned to look at Bardo, and asked him about something closer to his heart.

"Have you seen her, Bardo?"

"Tamara?"

Danlo held his head still in total silence, but his eyes gleaming in the half-light like liquid jewels, spoke for him.

"Well, no, I haven't seen her," Bardo said. "You know I'd heard that she had left the city—I never heard that she returned."

"But where did she go?"

"I don't know. Perhaps it's only a rumor."

"Did Hanuman ever speak of what he did to her? Did he ever say that there might be a way to restore her?"

Bardo sighed and laid a heavy hand on Danlo's shoulder. "Ah, Little Fellow—he never said anything, too bad. You still hate him, don't you?"

Lightning flashed in Danlo's eyes, then, and he said, "He raped her mind! He destroyed her memories, Bardo! All her memories of us together, everything blessed."

"Little Fellow, Little Fellow."

Danlo chose that moment to take out his flute and press the hard ivory mouthpiece against his forehead. He drew in a deep breath, then said, "But I . . . must not hate. I try so hard not to hate."

"And I love you for such nobility," Bardo said, "but as for myself, I try to let all my hatred for that worm of a man fill my belly like firewine. It will make it easier to destroy him when the time comes."

Slowly Danlo shook his head. "You know that I would not wish to see any harm come to him."

"Well, perhaps you should. Perhaps it would be best if you'd forswear your vow and find a way to move close to him. And then . . ."

"Yes?"

"And then kill him, by God! Slip a knife into his treacherous heart or squeeze the breath from his lying throat!"

At the mere invocation of such terrible images, Danlo's own breath caught in his chest. He gripped his flute as tightly as a drowning man being offered a stick to pull him out of icy, black waters. And then, as he realized the impossibility of what Bardo had suggested, he slowly relaxed and smiled in deep amusement. "You know that I could never harm him," he said.

"Well, I *do* know that, too bad. And that is why, short of war, there's little hope of stopping him."

"But there is still our mission, yes? Our hope for peace."

Bardo laughed softly, then said, "I remember that your Fravashi teacher once gave you the title of 'Peacewise.' But it takes two to make a peace, you know."

"But all people long for peace."

"There speaks your hope," Bardo said. "There speaks your will to make reality conform to the dreams of your lovely heart."

"But Hanuman has a heart, too. He is still just a man, yes?"

"I'm not so sure. Sometimes I think he's a demon from hell."

As Danlo thought of Hanuman's hellish ice-blue eyes, he smiled gravely in remembrance. And then he said, "In a strange way, I think he was the most compassionate man I have ever met."

"Hanuman li Tosh?"

"You did not know him as I did, Bardo. Once upon a time, as a boy, and before, he was so innocent. Truly . . . he was born with such a gentle soul."

"What changed him, then?"

"The world changed him," Danlo said. "His religion, the way his father would read negative programs in his littlest misdoings and force a cleansing heaume on his head to rape his mind—that changed him, too. And he changed himself. I have never met anyone with such a terrible will to change himself."

"Well, you never knew your father, Little Fellow."

Danlo stared down at the dark holes along the shaft of his flute, and waited for Bardo to say more.

"But your father finally found his compassion, while Hanuman has lost his. And where your father became a light for the whole damn universe, Hanuman has embraced the darkness—like a slel necker sucking at a corpse."

"I would still like to believe that, somehow, there is infinite hope for everyone."

Infinite possibilities, Danlo remembered as he closed his eyes. *Inside everyone, everything, this infinite light.*

"Well," Bardo said, "Hanuman's hope for himself is certainly infinite."

"Because he speaks of becoming a god?"

The Second Pillar of Ringism was that each man and woman could become a god by following the way of Mallory Ringess, and in this ambition, Hanuman was no different than a million others.

"But he has done much more than speak of this," Bardo said. "Why do you think he has torn apart most of a moon to build that goddamned computer that floats in space like a death mask?"

"But you yourself once taught that the way to godhood was only in remembrance of the Elder Eddas."

"I did? Ah, I suppose I did. Well, there are different ways of becoming gods, aren't there?"

"I . . . would not know."

"When his universal computer is finally assembled and Hanuman interfaces it, he'll have power as godly as any god. He'll be like the Entity, only smaller—for a while."

The Solid State Entity, Danlo remembered, had once been a warrior-poet named Kalinda who had added neurologics to her human brain, component by component, until She grew to encompass whole star systems.

"He would not be the first to attempt such a thing."

"But he'd be the first in the history of the Civilized Worlds!" Bardo said. "And the last. I think he wouldn't care if he destroyed every world from Solsken to Farfara."

Danlo brought his flute closer to his lips as he brooded over everything Bardo had told him. Truly, he thought, the danger of Ringism corrupting the Civilized Worlds was the least of what Hanuman might accomplish.

"Hanuman always had a dream," Danlo said softly. "A beautiful and terrible dream."

"What kind of dream?"

"I . . . do not know. Not wholly. Once, like city lights glittering through a snowstorm, I thought I saw the shape of it. The colors. He has dreams of a better universe, truly. And something more. I am afraid . . . that he would become more than a god, if he could."

"Ha! What could be more than a goddamned god?"

But now Danlo closed his eyes and played a long, low note upon his flute as he lost himself in memories of the past and future. In the center of some inner darkness bloomed a tiny flower of light that grew and grew until it filled all possible space within the universe of his mind.

"Well, *I* say he'll never even become a god," Bardo growled. "We won't let that happen."

Danlo suddenly put aside his flute and looked at Bardo. "No?"

"We'll stop him. Of course, it's really too bad that the Ringists themselves won't stop him, but they've been gulled into believeing that the Universal Computer is only a tool to help them remembrance the Eddas."

Danlo sighed, then breathed deeply of the cool night air. He said, "You believe in the power of war to change the face of the universe. And truly, war is a refining fire that can touch almost anything. But what if it is our own faces that are burnt to char, Bardo? What if we lose this war?''

"Lose? By God, we won't lose, what are you saying?''

"But along with the Old Order, the Ringists will have more lightships than we.''

"Well, even if chance spat on us and we *did* lose, Hanuman would still be stopped, eventually. Do you think the Entity and Chimene and all the galaxy's other gods would just let Hanuman's computer gobble up the Civilized Worlds?''

"But the gods have their own war,'' Danlo said. "Do they note our actions any more than we would worms in the belly of a dog?''

"Ah, I suppose you're right not to hope for the help of the gods. Now is the time for rocket fire and lasers, boldness and valor.''

"Bardo, Bardo, no, there must be a—''

"Do you think you'll stop Hanuman with *that?*'' Bardo blurted out as he pointed to Danlo's flute. "He always hated the goddamned mystical music that you played, didn't he?''

Danlo made no reply to this, but simply sat watching the starlight play upon his flute's golden length.

"You're really a prideful man, like your father,'' Bardo said. "You still hope to touch Hanuman's heart, don't you?''

"Yes.''

"And Tamara, if she could be found—you still believe there's a way to restore her to her memories.''

To heal the wound that cannot be healed, Danlo thought. *To light the light that never goes out.*

And then he said, "The remembrancers say that memory can be created but not destroyed.''

Bardo looked at Danlo with his big brown eyes and sighed. Then he said, "It's *dangerous* for you to return to Neverness, Little Fellow. I think the Sonderval is right: you should abjure your vow and come with us to Sheydveg. You'll be safer in battle than in the tower of Hanuman's goddamned cathedral. Fight with us! Your father was such a formidable fighter, and his father—all your bloody line. Can't you feel it inside yourself, the holy fire? By God, why don't you do what you were born to do?''

"I . . . will go to Neverness,'' Danlo finally said.

"Ah, well, I think I knew you would.'' Bardo yawned hugely and turned to watch the stars setting over the ocean to the west.

"It is far past midnight,'' Danlo said. "Perhaps we should sleep before tomorrow.''

"Sleep? I'll sleep when I die. There's still too much to do tonight to waste time sleeping."

Danlo caught a strange, sad gleam in Bardo's eyes, and he said, "Yes?"

"Well, I've sworn not to drink beer anymore, so I suppose I should find a woman. Someone plump and fertile—it's been too, too long, and who knows if this will be the last time."

Danlo waited for Bardo to stand up, but the huge man remained like a rock almost stuck to the earth.

"Ah, the truth is, I don't want to leave you now, Little Fellow. Who knows if this will be the last time I see you?"

As tears began to flow freely in Bardo's eyes, Danlo smiled and laughed softly. He jumped up, then practically pulled Bardo to his feet. "I shall miss you," he said as he embraced him.

"Ah, Little Fellow, Little Fellow."

"But of course we'll see each other again," Danlo said. "Even though a million stars and all the lightships of Neverness lie between us."

"Do you really think so?"

"Yes. It . . . is our fate."

With that, Bardo thumped Danlo's back one last time, bowed, and ambled off towards the acamedicians' apartments to find his woman—probably some young journeyman whom he had met during the last few days. Danlo watched him disappear into the shadows; then he turned and waited for the sun to rise over the plains and the light field to the east.

That morning most of the New Order on Thiells assembled at the light field to bid the pilots farewell. Some nine thousand ordermen lined the field's main run for a mile on either side. Their formal silk robes, in colors of amber, red, indigo, cobalt and violet, rippled like banners in the wind. Akashics, horologes, historians, cetics and remembrancers—it was their pride to honor the two hundred pilots who would risk war to protect them. And to protect the Order's ancient dream of awakening a star-flung humanity to the light of reason and truth's bright, ineffable flame. No one knew when these brave pilots might return. No one knew what might befall them—and the New Order—if they *never* returned, but it was also their pride to match the pilots' bravery with their own, and so almost every face was smiling and bright with cheer.

Much of the city of Lightstone, as well, turned out to watch the

spectacle of the pilots' departure. There were some eighty-nine
thousand of these people, mostly farsiders from the worlds of
Asherah, Eshte and Nahele, but also arhats and artists from the
Silvain Estates, and even a handful of aliens. All of them crowded
the run behind the Order's academicians; they were dressed in
every conceivable garment from kaftans to korrebebs, and with
much jostling and vying for position, they craned their necks for a
better view of the two hundred light ships shimmering in the early
sun.

At precisely the first hour after first light, Lord Nikolos arrived
at the field in a gleaming red sled and took his place on the
middle of the run. There, in front of their rows of lightships, the
pilots had been called together to receive his final charge and
blessings. The Sonderval, as Lord Pilot, stood foremost among
them, a great tree of a man nearly eight feet tall dressed in his
formal black robe. The master pilots waited near him in order of
precedence of the date on which they had taken vows. Helena
Charbo, with her great shock of silver hair and her fearless face,
was the first of these, followed by Charl Rappaporth, Aja and
Sabri Dur li Kadir. Fifty other masters were arrayed in line, Veronika Menchik, Ona Tetsu, Edreiya Chu, Richardess, and others,
as well as Peter Eyota and Henrios li Radman who had recently
returned from the deepest part of the Vild. The last of the master
pilots, of course, was Danlo wi Soli Ringess. He stood watching
the sky with his deep blue eyes—and watching Lord Nikolos and
all the thousands of men and women pressing up against the run
from the east and west. He might have traded a few last words
with Lara Jesusa and other full pilots drawn up behind him, but
Lord Nikolos had called out to speak and was waiting only for the
throngs of farsiders to stop talking and cheering and fall into a
proper silence.

Two other people standing on the run off to the side were not
pilots of the Order. These were Demothi Bede, the Lord Neologician robed in ocher and of course, Pesheval Lal, whom Danlo
and everyone else always called Bardo. Once, this huge man
might have stood in the Sonderval's place, or not far behind, but
no one had forgotten how he had abjured his vows and abandoned
the Order. But he was still a great pilot, if now a ronin, and his
stolen ship, the *Sword of Shiva*, was lined up last with all the
others. He too wore black, the dreadful black of nall armor and
his swirling shesheen cape. If he had accomplished his purpose of
the previous night, he gave no sign, for his face was as stern and
serious as any other. He traded serious looks with Demothi Bede,

who would soon set forth as an ambassador and passenger in Danlo's ship. In only a few more moments they would both leave this soft and beautiful world—Bardo to go to war and Demothi to journey to Neverness to prevent it.

"Silence, it's time!" a red-robed horologe called out from a crowd of academicians waiting not far from Lord Nikolos. Others picked up the cry, and passed voice to voice for a mile down the run: "Silence, it's time."

Then, in the sudden quiet, Lord Nikolos spoke to the pilots in his calm, clear voice. He began by discussing the meaning of being a pilot and reminding them of their vows, especially their fourth vow, that of restraint. For in the coming days, he said, they would need restraint above all other virtues, even courage and faith. "The Order was founded to illuminate the peoples of all worlds, not to make war upon them. We keepers of the ineffable flame are no warriors, nor shall we ever be. Nevertheless, it may be that we must *act* as warriors for a time. Therefore we must act in clear conscience of what is permitted and what is not."

He then enjoined them above all else to avoid war if they could. Danlo, along with the Lord Bede, was to be given a chance to reason with Hanuman li Tosh. If a display of virtuosity and threat might bring peace, they were to use their lightships towards this end only. And if battle came to them howling on an ill-wind of fate, pilots were to fall in violence only against other pilots and ships of war. They were not to attack merchant ships, nor any world or peoples supporting Hanuman and the Way of Ringess.

Specifically, Lord Nikolos charged them with upholding the Laws of the Civilized Worlds. They were not to arm their lightships with hydrogen bombs or other weapons of genocide. They were not to infect planetary communications' systems with information viruses or disable them with logic bombs. The purpose of the war must be as clear to them as a diamond crystal: First, they were to stop Hanuman from using the Old Order to spread Ringism to the Civilized Worlds. If possible, they were to restore the Old Order to its original vision and age-old injunction against associating with any religion. And last, he said, at any cost to themselves in wounds or death, Hanuman's Universal Computer must be destroyed. To this end, he asked them to pledge their honor and lives.

After they had made their vows, he reminded them that the meaning of the ancient word for pilot was 'steersman.' He told them that they must always find their way between the hard rocks of pride and the whirlpool of self-deception to the truth shining always beyond. And so he led them in a prayer for the most essential of all the pilot's arts, which was vision. And then he said, "I wish I could go with you, but since I cannot, I wish you well. Fall far, fall well, and return."

He bowed to them, deeply, and the pilots returned his bow. Led by the Sonderval, they each walked up to their ships and climbed inside. It took some little time for Demothi Bede to enter the passenger room of Danlo's ship and prepare for his journey. But when he had shut himself inside his sleeping cell and Lord Nikolos and everyone else had moved to safety, the Master of the Fields gave the signal for the pilots to depart. One by one, the lightships began rocketing down the run, where the swarms of the city formed a gauntlet on either side of them.

Of course, the lights ships, having no wheels, did not need to use the run to gain the blueness of the sky beyond. But the pilots wanted to make a show of their art, and so the Sonderval took his silver-black *Cardinal Virtue* roaring into the air. Helena Charbo, in the *Infinite Pearl,* followed his line of ascent only seconds behind, and then came the other ships, the *Montsalvat,* the *Blue Rose* and the *Bright Moon,* and the *August Moon,* the *Sagittarius Bridge,* and all the others strung out like diamonds on a necklace connecting earth to the heavens.

The *Snowy Owl,* with its long, graceful lines and sweeping wings, was only one ship among two hundred of these jewels. Although Danlo would soon enough leave his brother and sister pilots behind, he felt in his pounding blood the sense of shared purpose that connected him to all other pilots. And then, when the world of Thiells lay spinning beneath him like a great blue ball, the manifold opened before him. He entered into the raging deeps of the universe, and then he, as with all the pilots in their two hundred lights ships, had only his vision and his heart to guide him.

SHEYDVEG

> We call our region of the galaxy the Civilized Worlds. We
> believe that we seek for ourselves an ideal state of human
> culture beyond barbarism or war. If this be true, however,
> how are we to think of Summerworld, with its silver mines
> and slaves, as civilized? Or Catava where the Architects of
> the Reformed Churches use their holy cleansing computers
> to mutilate their own children's minds? Or Simoom, or
> Urradeth, and so on, and so on? The truth is that we have
> come to define civilization very narrowly: We are civilized
> who honor and keep the Three Laws. And what is the
> essence of these laws? Very simply, that we agree to limit
> our technology. To be civilized is to make a choice to live
> as careful and natural human beings in harmony with our
> environments. The Civilized Worlds, then, are nothing
> more than those three thousand spheres of water and earth
> where man has chosen to remain as man.
>
> —from *A Requiem for Homo Sapiens*, by Horthy Hosthoh

And so the pilots of the New Order returned across the stars as
they had come only a few years before. Although this part of their
journey from Thiells to Farfara was much the shortest, in distance, as measured in time it took many days to fall even a few
hundred light-years between such stars as Natal and Acayib the
Brilliant, for the manifold underlying the Vild was as changeable
as quicksand and mappings made one moment might prove
worthless the next. The Sonderval, though, led the lightships with
panache and good order past Kefira and Cho Chumu, and Rhea
Luz, all hot and swollen with its angry red light.

Perhaps it was good chance—or only fate—that no pilots were
lost during this first fenestration of window to window giving out
on the treacherous stars. Once, when they fell through a Danladi
fold caused by the explosion of some recent supernova, Ona
Tetsu's *Ibi Ibis* almost vanished into an infinite series of infold-
ings. But with great presence of mind characteristic of all her

famous line, that wily pilot found a mapping that took her through a window to the Birdella Double, which was the next star pair in the sequence of stars that the Sonderval had set. There she waited for the two hundred lightships to rejoin her—waited with great coolness as if she hadn't almost lost her life like a child smothered in sheets of wildly flapping plastic.

Most of the pilots, of course, would have liked to prove their virtue by finding mappings independent of the others, but accidents such as Ona's befell few of them, and the Sonderval had ordered them to stay together. And so they moved through the Vild as one body of ships, remaining always within the same neighborhood of stars. They passed Ishvara, Stirrit and Seio Luz, a cool yellow sun almost identical in shape and color to the Star of Neverness. And Kalkin and Vaishnara, and others, and finally they came to Sattva Luz, a brilliant white ball of light just within the inner envelope of the Vild. From here, their mappings would carry them only a few more stars to Renenet and Akar, and thus to Shoka and Savona, where they would break free from the Vild's outer envelope and look out on Farfara and the stars of the Civilized Worlds.

It was here, just beyond Sattva Luz's intense gravity field, that they came upon a quite deadly phase space. Or rather this menace of the manifold came upon them. Some of the surviving pilots were to describe it as like an earthquake; others spoke of boiling oil or point-set correspondences that shattered like a dropped cup. For Danlo wi Soli Ringess, caught in the worst part of the phase space, it was as if one moment he were floating on a calm blue sea, and the next, a tidal wave of every color from ruby to violet were breaking over him. He had almost no time to find a mapping to a small white dwarf near Renenet. Others, however, were not so lucky. (Or skillful.) Three pilots died that day: Ricardo Dor, Lais Blackstone, and Midori Astoret in her famous *Rose of Neverness*. None will ever know how the manifold appeared to them in the last moment before they were crushed into oblivion. But all the survivors agreed that they had lived through one of the worst mathematical spaces ever encountered and were very glad when the Sonderval called a halt near Shoka to speak the dead pilots' names in remembrance.

When the pilots finally reached Farfara many days later, many desired to make planetfall as they had done on their way into the Vild. They wanted to feel earth beneath their boots again, to stand in Mer Tadeo's garden beneath the stars drinking firewine and talking of brave deeds. But the Sonderval would not allow this.

They had reached the Civilized Worlds, he said, and though it might be unlikely, it was always possible that pilots from Neverness might fall out of the manifold like birds of prey at night and destroy their ships while they were on the ground.

"We must begin thinking strategically," he told them. "We must not regard ourselves as wayfarers needing a little comfort, but as warriors going to war."

That there truly might be a war was no news to Mer Tadeo dur li Marar or any of the other merchant princes of Farfara. As Bardo had promised, his friends of the Fellowship of Free Pilots had journeyed to the most important Civilized Worlds to tell of the gathering at Sheydveg. They had called for ships, robots, water and food—and men and women armed with lasers, eye tlolts, or even knives. The Farfarans, of course, had no experience of war. But then almost none of the peoples of the Civilized Worlds did. Farfara was a rich planet whose merchant elite opposed the spread of Ringism. And so they decided to send their own contribution to the gathering on Sheydveg: food and firewine, but also twenty deepships each carrying ten thousand hastily trained soldiers and secretly armed with lasers and neutron bombs. And they provided seventy-two blackships, which were really much like the Order's lightships except that they were clumsier and duller, with hulls wrought of black nall and pilots who had only enough mathematics to take them along the well-established mappings of the Fallaways. In battle against the Order's sleek, gleaming lightships, they might prove more of a hindrance than a help, but the Sonderval reluctantly thanked the Farfarans and quite peremptorily commanded their pilots to follow the two hundred lightships into the manifold as best they could.

From Farfara they fell on to Freeport, where they gained ten more deepships and thirty-eight blackships. And at Vesper their fleet increased similarly, and so at Wakanda. Their journey took them through the most ancient part of the Fallaways, Kittery and Rollo's Rock and Nwarth, worlds colonized well before the Lost Centuries when the First Wave of the Swarming had reached its crest. Only some of these worlds supported the New Order's mission to Farfara. Many, such as Ituha and Makis, chose to remain as neutrals in the coming strife. And many more favored the Old Order out of age-long loyalties or welcomed Ringism as a force that would save them from millennia of stagnation. Some unfortunate worlds were divided against themselves, half their people embracing Ringism, while their brothers and sisters fought to oppose this wild and criminal religion. By the time the lightships passed their way, Zesiro and Redstone had nearly fallen into civil war.

The peoples of Fostora, too, were close to killing each other. The Fostorans, of course, were famous throughout the Civilized Worlds for creating the Silicon God. They well remembered this great crime against the Three Laws, and many Fostorans, in their undying shame, were ready to give their lives that such an abomination would never come into being again. But others on this dark, cold world had more ancient dreams. Like their forefathers five thousand years before, they chafed at the limitations of the Three Laws. While they were not willing to make another god-computer that might threaten the Civilized Worlds and perhaps all the galaxy's stars, they fell into love with the idea that they might make themselves as gods. And so they became Ringists, mind, body and soul. They fought to nullify the Three Laws and remake the Civilized Worlds as a paradise where men and women might move toward godhood. How this miracle of evolution might occur, no one quite knew. But they believed the words of Hanuman li Tosh's missionaries, that for them to blaze like stars, they must be willing to endure fire, burning, and ultimately, war.

Each man and woman is a star. Even as the New Order's fleet fell through the manifold after gathering another fifty blackships on Monteer, Danlo floated inside his ship and fell into remembrance. Once, on a long night years ago on Neverness, he had stood in the bitter cold listening to Hanuman deliver these words to thousands of cheering people. *How could you wish to become new unless you had first become ashes?*

He remembered that over the millennia, there had been other attempts to break away from the Laws of the Civilized Worlds and shape a new face for humanity. As the Fifth Mentality of Man reached its limits, anarchists from Fostora had founded Alumit as a world where all things might be possible. It was no mistake, Danlo thought, that Nikolos Daru Ede had been born on Alumit, and there carked his consciousness into a computer that had grown to be almost the greatest of the galaxy's gods.

And the Warrior-Poets of Qallar, after perfecting the art of using computer neurologics to replace parts of the human brain, had begun a campaign of terror and extreme proselytization to convert others to their way. They would have rewritten the Three Laws to allow for terrible mutilations of the bodysoul, but the Order of Scientists, as the Order had then been called, under the implacable Timekeeper, had opposed them. The first war fought with the Warrior-Poets had nearly destroyed the Order, but the

Order's superior command of lightships and the manifold allowed them to impose a peace upon Qallar. The Warrior-Poets agreed to many hated limits to their technologies of the mind—and over the seven thousand years since the Third Dark Age, they had broken their agreement many times.

This, Danlo thought in the quiet of his ship, had been the deepest tension on every Civilized World almost for-ever: that human beings were always secretly dying to break out of their old ways and turn their faces to something new. And human beings *needed* newness as a hungry thallow chick does meat, but the Third Law was right to proclaim that man may not stare too long at the face of the computer and still remain as man. How then should they turn? If women and men were not to fall as cold and mechanical as silicon computers, in what direction might they look to take on a *new* face, one truly human and yet beyond the fearful yearning and pride that had marked man's visage for so long? No one knew. No one had ever known, neither the first *Homo sapiens* who had looked up at the stars in longing for the infinite lights, nor the Warrior-Poets, nor the god-men of Agathange.

But many were the prophets who had understood that the pressure to evolve was the deepest, most terrible of all man's drives. Hanuman li Tosh was only the most recent of these firebrands. But he was a religious genius, and more, a man with a terrible will to fate. And perhaps most importantly, he brought his Way of Ringess to the stars at a fateful time in history when people were prepared to burn worlds and turn a whole civilization to ashes if only they might create themselves anew.

Terrible pressure, Danlo thought as he fell deeper into the Civilized Worlds. *The terrible light—people do not know what is inside them.*

At last the lightships—and deepships and blackships—came to Madeus Luz at the edge of the galaxy's Orion Arm. This blue-white giant was like a signpost lighting their way into the darker spaces into which they soon must pass. Only a score of stars lay along their pathway now to Sheydveg, itself one of the few stars to brighten this part of the Fallaways. The pilots fell on to Jonah's Star Far Group, where the world of Shatoreth added to their numbers, and then they made a series of mappings toward Sheydveg.

For Danlo, floating in the pit of the *Snowy Owl*, this was the longest and most uneventful segment of his journey. According to Lord Nikolos' orders, at Sheydveg he would say goodbye to his fellow pilots and fall on alone to the dense stars of the Sagittarius

Arm and then to Neverness, but now there was almost nothing outside his ship to occupy his attentions. The manifold between these two arms of the galaxy flattened out like a sheet of burnished gold. To enlighten himself, he might have taken conversation with Demothi Bede, but this lord of the Order stayed in his passenger cell, either sleeping or interfaced into quicktime, where the ship-computer slowed his mind as cold does tree sap so that time for him passed much more quickly.

Danlo did speak with his devotionary computer. The hologram of Nikolos Daru Ede, with its bald head and black, mystic's eyes, floated like a glowing ghost in the ship's omnipresent darkness. Danlo had long since tired of Ede's warnings as to the manifold's dangers and his continually-voiced desire to get his body back and incarnate again as a human being. But he did not know the word that would take this annoying computer down, and in truth, he had been alone in stars so long that he welcomed almost any form of companionship. And rarely, Ede might even amuse him. Once, when they had just fenestered past a fiery, white double, Ede reminded him for the thousandth time that the fleet of Bertram Jaspari's Iviomils was likely falling among similar stars on their way to Neverness to destroy it.

"And they have my body, Pilot. If the Iviomils destroy the Star of Neverness and flee into the core stars, how will I ever recover my body?"

"We will not let them destroy the Star of Neverness," Danlo said for the thousandth time.

"I should like only to feel the world through my body once more."

"And then?" Danlo asked yet one more time. "What will you do with this resurrected body?"

The expression on Ede's face froze into a kind of mechanical wistfulness. "I shall drink the finest firewine; I shall bask in the sunlight on the sands of the Astaret Sea; I shall smell roses; I shall suffer and weep and play with children; I should like to fall into love with a woman."

Usually this conversation went no further, but because Danlo was in a playful mood, he asked, "But what if your body no longer has the passion to be a body?"

For a moment Ede seemed lost in computation (or thought), and then he asked, "What do you mean?"

"Your body has been frozen for three thousand years, yes?"

"Only 2,745 years."

Danlo smiled and said, "My friend Bardo once died and was

frozen in preservation for only a few days. When the cryologists thawed him, he found that he had lost certain of his powers."

"What powers?"

"He found it impossible . . . to be with a woman."

"But I always found it so easy to be with women."

In truth, Nikolos Daru Ede, the man, had always been too absorbed with his computers and his journey godward to love any woman deeply. But as for swiving them, he had been the founder of humanity's greatest religion, and as with most such charismatic leaders, his bed had rarely been empty.

"Bardo always had an easy way with women, too," Danlo said. "But after he was restored to himself, his spear would not rise."

"Then in the thawing of *my* body, I shall have to take precautions that my spear remains risen."

"Remains?"

"Have I never told you the story of my vastening?" Ede asked.

"Yes, truly you have—you told me that after your brain had been copied in an eternal computer, your body was frozen."

"Of course, but what was I doing in the hours *before* I carked my consciousness into the computer and became a god?"

"How . . . would I know?" Danlo asked. But then he immediately smiled because a vivid image came flashing into his mind: the plump, naked Nikolos Daru Ede sexing with three beautiful women whom he had married that morning in honor of the great vastening to occur that afternoon.

"Before I was vastened, I wanted to be a *man* one last time," Ede said. "So I took my three new wives to bed for the day. But I became overstimulated—I think due to the *kuri* drink that Amaris mixed to fortify me. When it came time for my vastening, I'm afraid I was still tumescent."

Danlo was now struggling hard not to laugh. "You went to your vastening with your spear pointing toward the heavens, yes?"

"Well, I wore a kimono, Pilot. It was voluminous. No one could see."

"But after you had died . . . . that is, after the programmers had torn apart your brain and scanned and copied its pattern, after this *vastening* into what you believe is a greater life, could it be that your body returned to a less excited state?"

"My vastening lasted only nine and a half seconds, Pilot."

"I had thought it took much longer."

"Of course, the ceremonies lasted for hours—a great event requires great pageantry, don't you think?"

"Yes—truly."

"I had ordered the cryologists to freeze me the moment that my vastening was accomplished. Nine and a half seconds—not enough time for my spear to fall."

"And thus the Cybernetic Universal Church has preserved you through the ages?"

"They froze me in my kimono. It was all quite dignified."

Now Danlo laughed openly, deep from his belly in waves of sound that filled the pit of his ship. Then he said, "There is something funny about religions, yes? Something strange, the way men worship other men—even a fat little bald man who went into his crypt swollen between the legs like a satyr."

"You insult me, Pilot."

"I am sorry."

"Of course, the Architects of the Cybernetic Churches don't worship me as a man. They worship the miracle of my becoming a god."

"I see."

"But it would be an even greater miracle if we could recover my body and restore me to a life in the flesh."

"Truly, it would."

"You will help me recover my body, won't you, Pilot?"

"I have promised I would."

"Even if my spear no longer rises, I would still like to hold a woman again."

Danlo closed his eyes, then, as he remembered holding Tamara Ten Ashtoreth in morning sun and the intense fire of their love. "I . . . understand," he said.

The Ede imago seemed to respect this sudden silence, for it was many moments before he asked, "Pilot?"

"Yes?"

"Whatever happened with Bardo's spear? Did he ever regain his powers?"

"Yes, truly he did. He . . . found a cure. Bardo is more Bardo than ever."

"I'm happy for him. It's bad to be without a woman."

Now Danlo opened his eyes and stared at Ede's sad, shining face. It was the first time he had ever heard this flickering hologram express any concern for a human being. "I would like to believe . . . that we will recover your body," he said. "Somehow, at the end of our journey, you will look upon your blessed body."

Other conversations with Ede were of more immediate moment. This little ghost of a god proved to know much about war. When he computed how quickly the fleet was adding ships, he observed that the Sonderval would soon face the problem of how to coordinate and command them. And then at Skamander they received an unexpected boon of fifty-five deepships and ninety-two blackships, and the Sonderval's command problem became critical. It was hard enough for the Order's finest pilots to move through the manifold as a single, coordinated body of ships.

It was harder still for the Sonderval, as the lone Lord Pilot, to aid the blackships' pilots in mapping through the swirling spaces of the manifold. In his overweening arrogance, the Sonderval's first impulse was simply to abandon this huge fleet and let them find their own way to Sheydveg. Time was pressing upon him like the overpressures of an approaching winter storm. And he doubted the blackships' and deepships' worthiness in battle. He might actually have left them with a few lightships as escorts, but then an event occurred that made this strategy unthinkable.

It was just after they had fallen out into realspace around a red-orange giant named Ulladulla. The lightships had kept in good order, gathering as a group near point-exits only a few million miles from Ulladulla's flaming corona. But the blackships and deepships, as they fell-out from the manifold's point-exits, scattered themselves through space like hundreds of dice cast onto black felt. As always, the Sonderval, in his brilliant *Cardinal Virtue*, would have to wait for them to make their corrective mappings and rejoin the lightships. This always took time, and the Sonderval always counted the moments like a merchant begrudgingly fingering over golden coins to a tax collector. And *this* time, the regrouping was to take more than a few moments because further in toward the sun, half-concealed by Ulladulla's fierce radiance, five lightships from the Order on Neverness waited to ambush them.

So blindingly quick was their attack that neither the Sonderval nor any other pilot save one identified the names of their ships. But it was certain that they were Neverness lightships which had journeyed to this star to terrorize the blackships and their pilots. Any ship, of course, as it opens windows in and out of realspace will perturb the manifold like a stone cast into a quiet pool of water. A skillful pilot, if she has maneuvered close enough to another, can read these faint ripples and actually predict another ship's mappings through the manifold. But if many ships are moving as one towards point-exits around a fixed star, it requires much less skill to make a probability mapping, for the perturbations merge like a streaming river and are easy to perceive.

If the pilots of Neverness had known of the gathering on Sheydveg—as they *must* have known—then it would be a simple thing for them to divide their forces and lie in wait along the many probable pathways leading to Sheydveg. In time, one of their attack groups would be almost certain to detect the raging river of the Sonderval's fleet. It would be a simple strategem, yes, but a foolish one, or so the Sonderval had calculated when he had weighed the risks of various approaches to Sheydveg. For there were many pathways through the manifold, as many as sleekit tunnels through a forest, and whoever led the Neverness pilots would have to divide his ships too thinly.

If the purpose of this attack had been to vanquish the New Order's fleet, then the Sonderval's reasoning would have proved sound. But the five light ships' purpose was only terror. In truth, the lightships of the Sonderval's fleet were never in danger, nor were the main body of blackships and deepships. But a few of the most scattered of these were in deadly danger. The Old Order's lightships fell out of the sun upon them like hawks among a flock of *kitikeesha* birds. Using a tactic devised in the Pilots' War, they maneuvered close to their target ships and fixed a point-source into the manifold. In essence, they made mappings *for* their victims. Death-mappings: their spacetime engines opened windows into the manifold and forced a deepship or blackship to fall along a pathway leading straight into the heart of the nearest star. These mappings only took moments. And so in less than nine and half seconds, the pilots from Neverness darted in and out of realspace like needles of light. They sent two deepships and thirteen blackships spinning to their fiery deaths inside Ulladulla. And then as quickly as they had appeared, they were gone, five wraithlike ships vanishing into the manifold toward other stars far away.

This lightning raid stunned the Sonderval's fleet. Almost no one had expected such a disaster, for the two Orders were not yet at war. Only one pilot had the presence of mind (or courage) to act in vengeance. This was Bardo, who had long since proved his prowess in the Pilot's War. When he looked out into deep space and saw how easily the Neverness pilots had destroyed fifteen ships, he cried out after them, "You're barbarians, by God! They were as helpless as babes—oh, all the poor men and women, too bad."

So saying, he used his *Sword of Shiva* to slice open a window from the black fabric of realspace, and then he and his great diamond ship fell into the burning pathways of the manifold.

When he returned to the spaces of Ulladulla three hundred seconds later, he found that the Sonderval had drawn his shaken fleet together. He gave a quick account of his pursuit of the Neverness ships. By light radio he told the Sonderval and all the pilots of the lightships (and only these) what had happened during the brief time he had been gone. In the pit of the *Snowy Owl*, a glowing hologram of Bardo fairly popped out of the air, and this is what Danlo heard the huge man say: "Five ships, and they scattered in five different directions. So I had to choose one pathway, one ship. I was lucky, by God! I was still within a well-defined region of one of them, and was able to close the radius of convergence quickly. I came upon him by a blue hotstar five light-years from Ulladulla. When I fell out into realspace, I saw that it was Marrim Masala in the *Golden Rhomb*. He has the ugliest little ship with it ugly straight wings and ugly tail. *Had*, that is—I sent him and his goddamned ship to hell inside the star, too bad. But I've no regrets, for he slaughtered innocents. And in the Pilot's War he killed Lahela Shatareh, and who could forgive him for that?"

The battle that Bardo had fought with Marrim Masala had been much like any contest between two lightships: nerve-shattering, fierce and quick. Like two swords flashing in the night, Bardo's and Marrim's ships slipped in and out of the manifold seeking an advantageous probability mapping. Bardo, the more mathematical and cunning of the two pilots, in some hundred and ten seconds of these lightning maneuvers, had finally prevailed. He predicted which point-exit the *Golden Rhomb* would take into realspace, and he made a forced mapping. And then the *Sword of Shiva* swept forward and sliced open a window into the manifold. And the *Golden Rhomb* instantly fell through this window into the hotstar's terrible fires.

And so one pilot of the Old Order had been slain against fifteen pilots of the Civilized Worlds—and twenty thousand soldiers helpless in the holds of the two deepships. Helpless, yes, but they were not innocents as Bardo had said, but rather full men and women armed for war. Still, no one had thought war would come to them so soon. With the loss of the *Kaliska* and the *El-lama Tueth*, both deepships from Vesper, terror did spread among the Sonderval's fleet. The fifty-five deepships and ninety-two blackships recently gained at Skamander might have immediately deserted for that rich world, but their pilots were afraid that the Neverness lightships might intercept them on their way home. To quell the fears of these soft, too-civilized pilots—and to protect them—the Sonderval immediately reorganized his command. Henceforth the lightships would not move as a separate body from the hundreds of deepships and blackships. (After the Old Order's ambush, there were now some 1,268 of these.) The Sonderval divided his two hundred light ships into ten battle groups, each to be led by a master pilot who would act as captain and commander of the twenty pilots beneath him—as well as the tens of blackship and deepship pilots assigned to his group. In effect, the lightship pilots would act as shepherd dogs keeping the deepships and blackships together and protecting them against wolves.

For these ten pilot-captains the Sonderval chose masters who had fought with him in the Pilot's War: Helena Charbo and Aja, of course, and Charl Rappaporth and Veronika Menchik. He elevated as well Richardess, Edreiya Chu, Ona Tetsu, Sabri dur li Kadir, and Alark of Urradeth in his famous ship, the *Crossing Maker*. For the tenth pilot-captain, the Sonderval might have favored Matteth Jons or Paloma the Younger or a score of others. But he astonished almost everyone by naming Bardo to command the Tenth Battle Group. By light radio, he told the assembled pilots of his reasons for this strange decision: although no longer of the Order, Bardo was perhaps the master pilot with the most talent for war. And next to the Sonderval, as the Sonderval said, he was the finest of tacticians, and quick-minded and valorous, as his recent pursuit of the five Neverness light ships had proved. Although no one disputed Bardo's prowess as a pilot, Peter Eyota and Zapata Karek doubted his ability to lead other pilots and their ships to war. And Dario Ashtoreth stridently denied a ronin pilot's right even to associate with other pilots, much less command them. But the Sonderval was a practical and imperious man. He brooked no argument with his decisions. He had said that Bardo would act as pilot-captain of the Tenth Battle Group, and so it came to be.

After this the Sonderval's fleet fell on without incident to Sheydveg. This was the name of a cool, orange star shining almost exactly halfway between two arms of the galaxy. Its name meant "crossing of the roads," not only for its physical location at the center of the Civilized Worlds but because of its famous thickspace where millions of pathways through the manifold converged. Before Rollo Gallivare had discovered the great thickspace near the Star of Neverness, it had been the topological nexus of the Fallaways, the one star to which pilots might fall and easily find a series of pathways leading to any other. Sheydveg was also the star's single world, a fat blue-white sphere of deep oceans and broad, mountainous continents. It was an old world well-settled by its two billion human beings. With its many light fields and vast robot factories, it was the perfect world to host the gathering that Bardo had spoken of so many days before in the Hall of the Lords.

"Well, Pilot, it seems that there really *will* be war after all," the Ede imago said in the darkness of the *Snowy Owl.* "I've never seen so many ships."

When Danlo looked out the diamond-paned windows of his lightship, out into the black swirls of space, he saw what others saw: the Sonderval's thousand ships merging with the vast fleet already gathered there. There were deepships from Darkmoon and Silvaplana, and blackships from nearly a thousand worlds. Solsken had sent twenty longships, and these glorious, monstrous engines of destruction spun slowly in the silence of the night. From Ultima had come a hundred fireships, and the Rainbow Double had contributed sixty similar vessels. Even as Danlo watched, more ships arrived, falling out of the manifold like snowflakes from a shaken cloak. These thousands of ships came from Fiesole and Avalon, as well as the carked worlds of Anya, Hoshi, and Newvannia, and many others. Altogether, Danlo counted some thirty thousand ships gathered above Sheydveg in a vast, shimmering swath of diamond and black nall.

Only a few of these, however, were lightships. Two hundred lightships had set forth from Thiells, and these (less the five already lost) were now joined by a hundred and ten others rebelling against the madness on Neverness. The Fellowship of Free Pilots, they called themselves—and some of these were the very pilots whom Bardo had led in the storming of the Lightship Caverns and thereafter sent to the Civilized Worlds to call them to war. Cristobel, in his beautiful *Diamond Lotus,* commanded them, along with the master pilots Alesar Estarei and Salome wu wei Chu. Although they politely greeted their brother and sister pilots of the New Order, there was an immediate coolness between these two groups. Cristobel, a quick-eyed lion of a man, told the Sonderval that the Fellowship of Free Pilots was the soul of the opposition to the Old Order and the Way of Ringess.

"It is we of the Fellowship who have suffered to watch the evils of Ringism spread across the stars," Cristobel explained when the pilots of both Neverness and Thiells held a conclave by light radio. "It is we who have journeyed far among the Civilized Worlds, and we who have called all these ships and warriors here today. And we have given our name to those who would fight against Hanuman li Tosh and the Ringists: we have gathered here the *Fellowship of Free Worlds,* and it is we who should lead them."

And as to who should lead the Fellowship of Free Pilots, Cristobel didn't hesitate to put forth himself, although it had been Bardo who had organized the Fellowship. Upon hearing Cristobel speak thusly, Bardo fell wroth.

"By God, you're a treacherous little worm of a man!" Bardo's voice thundered in the pits of a three hundred lightships as he instantiated as a blazing hologram. His face was purple-black, his fist like a club pounding against his hand. Although Cristobel was in truth a large man, next to Bardo, whether by hologram or actual presence in the body, he did seem rather small. "Who was it who called the Fellowship of Free Pilots together at his house when everyone was quaking at Lord Pall's goddamned edicts against assemblage? Who gave them their name? Who led the attack on the Lightship Caverns? It was Bardo, by God!" Bardo said. "It was Bardo, too bad."

"We honor you for your efforts," Cristobel said with a sneer. "But it seems you've already found your place beneath the Sonderval."

Here the Sonderval's hologram appeared in the pits of the lightships. His handsome face had fallen as hard as the granite of Icefall's mountains. To Cristobel, he said, "He is pilot-captain of twenty lightships and a hundred and twenty other vessels beneath the Lord Pilot of the New Order."

"But he's still only a ronin pilot, after all," Cristobel said.

Now, as if regarding a wormrunner or some loathsome species of alien, the Sonderval slowly shook his head. "When you speak to me, Cristobel, you may address me as 'Lord Pilot.' "

"But you are not *my* Lord Pilot, after all."

"No—is that Salmalin the Prudent, then?" the Sonderval asked, naming the Old Order's present Lord Pilot.

"I have no Lord Pilot."

"Then if you've left the Order and are without a Lord Pilot, you are as much of a ronin as Bardo."

"Not so," Cristobel said. "We of the Fellowship carry the spirit of the Order with us. The true Order, before Ringism corrupted it."

"And I honor your spirit," the Sonderval said. "But is it your intention to appoint yourself Lord Pilot of the Fellowship?"

Here several pilots of the Fellowship—Vadin Steele, Rohana of Urradeth, and Keleman the Wise—began speaking in favor of Cristobel becoming Lord Pilot of the Fellowship. It was obvious to Danlo, as it must have been to others, that they had planned this power play immediately upon learning that Bardo had been successful in reaching the New Order on Thiells.

"By God, if anyone is to be Lord Pilot of the Fellowship, it's Bardo!" Bardo roared.

"Why should the Fellowship have a Lord Pilot at all?" Richardess quietly asked when Bardo's voice had faded to a hum. In his body and face, he was as delicate as Yarkona glass, but he was the only pilot ever to have dared the deadly spaces of Chimene. "We already have a great Lord Pilot in the Sonderval. Why don't you pilots of the Fellowship simply join us?"

"Why don't you pilots of the New Order join *us?*" Cristobel countered.

"Because you're ronins!" Zapata Karek said.

"And you're ignorant of what is really occurring in Neverness," Vadin Steele said.

"Ignorant! Well you're as power-hungry as a Scutari shahzadi."

For a long time, the pilots argued among themselves like novices unable to choose captains for a game of hokkee. Danlo listened to their words grow wilder and more belligerent with every pilot who spoke. Their childishness might have amused him, but a great many lives hung on the slender thread of their reaching an understanding. Although Danlo felt time slipping away like sands on a windswept beach and was eager to complete his journey, he felt that he should be sure of who led the Fellowship of Free Worlds before acting on their behalf as an ambassador to Neverness. And Demothi Bede, when Danlo roused him from the half-sleep of quicktime, agreed with him. Lord Bede seemed particularly shocked at the unforseen play of events.

"But this is madness!" the thin, reedy Demothi Bede said in his thin, old voice. He crowded with Danlo into the pit of the *Snowy Owl*. "If we don't do something, we'll be at war with each other instead of the Ringists."

"Truly, we should do *something,*" Danlo said as he floated in his formal black robes. "Since we're supposed to be ambassadors and peacemakers."

"It's obvious that the ronin pilots must join us," Lord Bede said. He was very much a traditionalist, and his face fell dour and smug. "They should take vows to the New Order."

Now Danlo did smile, for although a thousand Cilivized Worlds were represented in the ships sailing through space all around them, Cristobel and the Sonderval—and Lord Bede—acted as if only the pilots of the two Orders mattered. But what right did they have, Danlo wondered, to choose the fates of thirty thousand ships and millions of men and women? These lords and masters of his Order obviously assumed that after they had decided upon a Lord Pilot, they would parcel out the other ships to their command like colorfully-wrapped presents given at Year's End—or rather as the Sonderval had already done with the black-ships and deepships he had escorted to Sheydveg. Or if the Sonderval and Cristobel could not decide who should lead whom, then the two hundred pilots from Thiells and the Fellowship of Free Pilots might fight independently of each other—after first fighting each other for the prize of the vast fleet waiting in the light of a cool, orange star.

"I must speak to the pilots," Danlo told Demothi Bede. For the moment, he was faced away from his fellow pilots' arguments, and the pit of his lightship was quiet. "This fighting among ourselves, this arrogance of ours . . . is *shaida.*"

"Do you have a plan, then, Pilot?" Demothi Bede asked.

Danlo nodded his head, then told him his plan.

"Very well," Demothi said, smiling his approval. "If you're to try to stop a war, you might as well begin now."

And so Danlo added his voice to the cacophony filling the pits of three hundred and five light ships. As a master pilot he had as much right to speak as anyone, and he too instantiated as a hologram among them. Because of his renown at mastering a chaos space and crossing the entire Vild—or perhaps because of his blazing blue eyes—the other pilots fell silent and listened to him.

"We pilots," he said, "have thought of ourselves as the spirit of the Civilized Worlds. But we have never been their rulers. The Fellowship of Free Worlds—but where is our fellowship when we call each other names like barbarians? And where is the freedom of these worlds if they must simply wait for us to order them to war? Do they, who have homes and children, risk less than we? If we cannot stop this war, they will die like snowworms caught in the sun, perhaps a thousand or a million of them for every pilot who loses his ship. Truly. Where is their freedom, then, to choose their own fate? We are pilots of three hundred and five lightships. Outside my window I have counted . . . a hundred times as many other ships. Shouldn't we let *their* pilots choose who will lead them to war?''

Most of the lightship pilots, upon listening to Danlo, immediately saw the sense of what he said. In truth, few of them really wanted to wage war as two separate Orders of ships, and they dreaded the uncertainties of Cristobel's dispute with the Sonderval. The Sonderval, for his part, was loathe to surrender any important decision to such inferior beings as the pilots and peoples of the Civilized Worlds. But he was at heart a shrewd man whose farsightedness overshadowed even his arrogance. And so, with carefully feigned reluctance, after trading knowing looks with Danlo, he approved his proposal. Only Cristobel, really, and a few of his closest friends such as Alesar Estarei, argued against Danlo. But the tide of passion—the tide of history—had already turned against him. In the pits of their ships, two hundred and fifty pilots struck their diamond rings against whatever hard surface they could find, and called out that the Fellowship of Free Worlds should decide its own fate.

Of course, there was never any real doubt as to what the Fellowship would decide—if indeed they could decide anything at all. More than thirty thousand ships now orbited Sheydveg, and these held at least five million men and women representing a thousand Civilized Worlds. Many of these were princes or gurus, exemplars or elders or arhats. Many there were who might have wished to command the fleet themselves, but except for Markoman of Solsken and Prince Henrios li Ashtoreth, no one was so deluded as to imagine that he could match the skills with even the youngest of lightship pilots. Their debate, then, centered around *how* they should choose between the Sonderval and Cristobel as Lord Pilot of the Fellowship. (Or if they should favor Helena Charbo or some other master pilot less vainglorious.) Some held that each man and woman of the Fellowship should cast a vote for whomever he believed to be the greatest pilot. Some thought this unfair since a few worlds had sent more than fifty deepships carrying thousands of soldiers in each, while many worlds had sent only a few score of blackships; each individual *world*, it was argued, should cast a single vote.

There isn't space here to describe the tortuous pathways by which these many people of many worlds came to a decision. It took them sixteen days to agree that each world would indeed have one vote. It took them much less time to cast these votes in favor of allowing the pilots of both Orders to lead them; as Danlo had hoped, they chose the Sonderval as Lord Pilot of the Fellow-

ship of Free Worlds. But the Sonderval was *not* to be their autarch
or ruler; his power was as a warlord only, to command them in
battle if they should decide on war. This crucial decision—and
many others relating to grand strategy—they would make for
themselves. And if they should win against the Ringists and force
a peace upon Neverness, it was they who would decide its terms.

The effect of allowing the Civilized Worlds a greater part in
wielding power was profound. Although it limited the Sonderval's
freedom to impose his will upon those he led, it actually strengthened his leadership, for it strengthened the feeling of fellowship
just beginning to flower among these many worlds like a delicate,
new bud. Among those who would die together in war, between
leader and led, there can never be too much fellowship. This, too,
was part of Danlo's plan. Many thanked him for his part in ending
the stalemate between Cristobel and the Sonderval and playing
midwife to the birth of the true Fellowship of Free Worlds. But
when Lord Demothi Bede congratulated him on a fine work of
diplomacy, his response was strange.

"Truly, I have helped close the rift between our two Orders of
pilots," he said in the quiet of his ship's pit. As he spoke to
Demothi Bede (and to the Ede imago), he touched the lightning-
bolt scar cut deeply into his forehead.

"Even Cristobel has accepted the inevitable," the Ede imago
said with a programmed smile.

"As well he should," Demothi Bede said, "considering the
Sonderval's graciousness."

The Sonderval, after being chosen to lead the fleet, had invited
Cristobel and the other ronin pilots to take vows as pilots of the
New Order. As an incentive, he had offered to make Cristobel and
Alesar Estarei pilot-captains of the newly formed Eleventh and
Twelfth Battle Groups—and even named Cristobel as his counsel-
lor in all matters of tactics and strategy. Given the Sonderval's
private ways, this would prove an empty honor, but it seemed to
cool the fiery Cristobel nevertheless.

"All has fallen out as you'd hoped," Demothi Bede said to
Danlo as he played with a mole on the side of his face. "Even
Prince Henrios has agreed to lead his ships under Alesar Estarei's
command—a prince of Tolikna Tak under orders from a simple
master pilot!"

"Yes," Danlo agreed, "there is peace among the Fellowship,
now."

"Then why do you seem so sad?"

Danlo stared out of his lightship's window at the flashing

lights of thirty-thousand other ships spread out through near space above Sheydveg. His eyes fell grave and deep, and he said, "What if I have brought a peace to the Fellowship . . . only to have created a better engine for the waging of war?"

"That's posssible, Pilot. But what if you've helped create a stronger Fellowship dedicated to avoiding war? Isn't it possible that there will be no war?"

But the Fellowship was already at war, or so Sabri dur li Kadir and many others argued during the days that followed. The Ringists' ambush and destruction of fifteen ships certainly constituted an act of war, so why should the Fellowship pretend that there still might be peace? Could they trust the Ringists *not* to fall against them in full strength out of the howling black forest of the manifold? Should they themselves avoid destroying the Ringists ships if offered such a chance?

"We must fall against them before they fall against us," Sabri dur li Kadir said in full conclave with all thirty thousand ships of the Fellowship. His face was as black as obsidian and as sharp. "We must lay our plans as soon as possible and then attack."

There were, however, voices of peace as well. Danlo and Lord Bede argued that the Fellowship should use its power to discourage the Ringists from war, while Makara of Newvannia, a well-known arhat, suggested that the Ringists' raid might be overlooked as an unfortunate accident. And one of the Vesper exemplars, Onan Nayati, who was either a coward or a very wise man, told everyone that they would be mad to make war upon the Ringists for they would be as a hawk attacking an eagle. This led to a measuring of their respective strengths.

The Fellowship comprised 1,091 worlds opposed to Ringism—and four more if the alien worlds of Darghin, Fravashing, Elidin and Scutarix could be counted, which of course they couldn't because they would never send ships to fight in a human war. Perhaps four hundred worlds had decided to remain neutral, and an equal number warred with themselves as to whom they would support. That left some 1,202 worlds as fervently Ringist: Urradeth, Yarkona, Askling, Heavens' Gate, Arcite, and many others of the richest and most powerful Civilized Worlds. Onan Nayati estimated that they could gather a fleet of at least 35,000 deepships and blackships. And as for the lightships of Neverness, the shining swords of the night, Cristobel said that Lord Salmalin would command 451.

The odds, then, had fallen against the Fellowship, especially considering that in battle one lightship would be worth twenty blackships—or possibly more. The pilots and princes of the Fellowship might very well have decided to wait upon war, but then something happened that broadened their field of vision and reminded them that stars burned with a terrible purpose far beyond their own.

On the 83rd day of false winter, as time is measured in Neverness, a single lightship fell out to join the others in orbit above Sheydveg. This was the *Infinite Rose,* piloted by Arrio Verjin, a master pilot of the Old Order. That is, he *had* been of the Order before returning to Neverness from a journey lasting several years. But when he had seen how Ringism had ruined his beloved Order and made virtual slaves out of pilots whom he had respected all his life, he had fled across the stars to the gathering at Sheydveg. And he brought with him the most astonishing news: he had witnessed with his own eyes a battle fought among the gods. In the spaces further in toward the core—beyond the Morbio Inferiore where the stars blaze as densely as exploding fireworks—the god known as Pure Mind had been slain. The moon-sized lobes of his great brain had been pulverized into a glowing dust. Arrio told of the destruction of a whole region of stars, impossibly intense lights erupting out of blackness, the detonation of the zero-point energies of the spacetime continuum itself.

The radiations from this apocalypse were vaster than that of a hundred supernovas. Only the gods, he said, could wield such technologies. He did not know why one god would wish to slay another. When Danlo told him of the Solid State Entity and the war among the gods, Arrio said, "Perhaps it was the Silicon God, then, who did this terrible thing. Or perhaps one of his allies, Chimene or the Degula Trinity. How will we ever know? But the effects of what has happened will run deep."

And the first and most terrible effect, Arrio said, was that these explosions out near the Morbio Inferiore had created huge distortions beneath spacetime, a kind of deadly bubbling known as a Danladi-set expansion. The Order's cantors, who had only hypothesized such a nightmare, sometimes referred to it as a Danladi wave. For these purest of mathematicians it was no more (or no less) real than a torison space or an infinite tree, but for Arrio Verjin it had been like a tidal wave sweeping toward his ship. He had barely escaped in his all too fragile *Infinite Rose.* But the Danladi wave was still spreading through the manifold like a wall of white water, expanding outward toward the stars of the Sagittarius Arm. Soon it would reach Neverness and other worlds of the Fallaways, and then the manifold there might prove as treacherous as the spaces of the Vild.

"We must prepare ourselves for tremendous distortions," Arrio told the assembled fleet. "The Danladi wave will perturb the entire manifold until it dies out toward the edge stars."

The second effect of Pure Mind's destruction was to quicken the Fellowship's move toward war. It reminded even the lightship pilots that their power was nothing compared to the fire and lightning of the gods. The galaxy's gods—Iamme or Maralah or Chimene—could destroy whole constellations of stars as easily as the Architects of the Old Church could blow up a single sun. If the gods were provoked, their wrath might fall upon any of the Civilized Worlds: Summerworld or Clarity or Lechoix or Larondissement. Or Neverness. As Cristobel pointed out, the gods might regard Hanuman li Tosh's building of his Universal Computer as a bid for godhood.

The eschatologists have a word for this kind of break-out from human being into something much vaster: *hakariad*. Throughout the galaxy over the past ten thousand years, there had been many hakariads, and perhaps many wars fought to stop such transcendent events. The gods, it is said, are jealous and do not like company. If the Silicon God saw Hanuman's acts as a hakariad, then he might destroy the Star of Neverness—and a hundred others nearby such as Avalon, Qallar and Silvaplana. Therefore, Cristobel said, the Fellowship must destroy Hanuman's Universal Computer before the gods did. This must be the first of their purposes, and to accomplish it, they must fall against Neverness in full war.

Almost all the warriors of the worlds represented in the Sonderval's fleet saw the logic of Cristobel's argument. It took the Fellowship, casting votes world by world, only two days to make a formal declaration of war. And so on the 85th of false winter in the year 2959 since the founding of Neverness, the War of the Gods, as it would be called, began.

That night, as Danlo prepared the *Snowy Owl* for his journey to Neverness, the Sonderval summoned him to a meeting. While their ships orbited Sheydveg, they maneuvered these sleek diamond needles so that they touched side to side. And then Danlo broke the seal of his ship and entered the *Cardinal Virtue,* the first pilot that the privacy-loving Lord Pilot had honored in this way. Danlo floated in the darkness, and he looked about the rather large interior of the Sonderval's lightship, taking note of the design of the neurologics which surrounded both the Sonderval and himself like a soft, purple cocoon. The Sonderval, stern and serious in his formal black robe, waited in the center of his ship's pit. He greeted Danlo warmly. "Welcome, Pilot," he said, "I'm glad you could join me."

"Thank you for asking me here tonight."

"It is I who should thank you," the Sonderval said. He began to play with a rather large diamond broach pinned to his black silk robe just over his heart. "If not for your foresight, we might have lost Cristobel and the others. And I might have been Lord Pilot over a much smaller fleet."

Here Danlo smiled and said, "But no one could have known how the Fellowship would decide. There was always a chance . . . that Cristobel would have been chosen Lord Pilot, and not you."

"Chance favors the bold—as you've proved, Danlo wi Soli Ringess."

Danlo bowed his head quickly, then studied the Sonderval's wide smile and the wide, white, perfect teeth. He said, "Your fleet . . . is small enough as it is."

"We've slightly fewer deepships and blackships than the Ringists," the Sonderval said. "But I believe that we'll have a more coherent command of them."

"And the lightships?"

"True, they've half again as many as we," the Sonderval said. "But don't forget that the best pilots went with us to the Vild. The best and the boldest, Pilot."

"You seem so confident," Danlo said.

"Well, I was born for war—I think it's my fate."

"But in war . . . there are so many terrible chances."

"This is also true, which is why I would still stop this war if I could."

"There . . . must be a way to stop it," Danlo said.

"Unfortunately," the Sonderval said, "it's easier to forestall a war than to stop one once it's begun. Your mission won't be easy."

"No."

"It might be difficult for you even to reach Neverness."

Danlo nodded his head that this was so, then said, "But I *will* return there. I . . . will speak with Hanuman once again. My fate, Lord Pilot. Only I must ask you for time. Hanuman burns like a thallow flying too close to the sun, and it will take time to cool his soul."

"I can't promise that. We'll fall against Neverness as soon as possible."

"How . . . soon?"

"I'm not sure," the Sonderval said. "We won't be able to approach Neverness directly, and the ships will require some time before they're able to perform the maneuvers I'll require of them. But soon enough, Pilot. You must make your journey as quickly as you can."

"I see."

For a long time the Sonderval regarded Danlo with his hard, calm eyes. Then he said, "I don't envy you your mission, you know. I wouldn't like to be there when you tell Hanuman that he must dismantle his Universal Computer."

At this Danlo smiled gravely but said nothing.

"Perhaps," the Sonderval said, "it would be best if Lord Bede presented the Fellowship's demands."

"If you'd like, Lord Pilot."

"And if by some miracle you're successful and Hanuman sees the light of reason, you must bring me word as soon as you can."

"But once the fleet has left Sheydveg, how will I find you?"

"That's a problem, isn't it?" Again the Sonderval fingered the brooch that adorned his robe, then sighed. "I could give you the fixed-points of the stars along the pathway I've chosen toward Neverness."

Danlo waited silently through the count of ten heartbeats for the Sonderval to say more.

"I *could* do that, Pilot, but it might not prove wise. The chances of war might cause us to choose different pathways. Then, too . . ."

"Yes?"

"Well, the chances of your reasoning with Hanuman aren't very great. Why should I burden you with information you'll probably never need?"

"I . . . see."

"*Vital* information," the Sonderval said. "If Lord Salmalin knew our pathway, he could lie in wait for our fleet and destroy it."

Danlo watched the Sonderval squeezing the diamond brooch between his long fingers; he watched and waited, saying nothing.

"Nevertheless, I've decided to give you this information—it might possibly keep us from a battle for which there's no need. And I must give you something else as well."

So saying, the Sonderval unpinned the brooch with infinite

care and closed it safely before giving it to Danlo. For the count of twenty heartbeats, Danlo stared at this piece of jewelry waiting like a scorpion in his open hand.

"Thank you, Lord Pilot," Danlo said politely. But his voice was full of irony and amusement—and with dread.

"If your mission fails and you're imprisoned, you mustn't let the akashics read your mind. And you mustn't let the Ringists torture you."

"Do you truly think that Hanuman would—"

"Some chances would be foolish to take," the Sonderval said. "The brooch's pin is tipped with matrikax. If pushed into a vein, it kills instantly."

"I see."

"Your vow of ahimsa doesn't prevent you from taking your own life, does it?"

Never killing or harming another, not even in one's own thoughts, Danlo remembered. And then he said, "Some would say that it does."

"And what do *you* say, then?"

"I . . . . will never tell anyone the stars along your pathway."

"Very well," the Sonderval said.

He moved closer to Danlo and bent his long neck down as might a swan. For a few moments, he whispered in Danlo's ear. Then he backed away as if he couldn't bear such closeness with another human being.

"Before you leave, I'll meet with Lord Bede by imago," the Sonderval said. "But I won't tell him what I've just told you."

"But is he not a lord of the New Order?"

"He is not a *pilot.* There are some things only pilots should know."

Danlo bowed, then fixed his deep, burning eyes on the Sonderval. For a time, in the deep silence of space, the two men held each other's gaze and looked into each other's heart. And then finally the Sonderval had to turn away.

"I was both wrong and right about you," the Sonderval said. "Wrong, because you'll serve us very well as an ambassador. But you would have made a great warrior, too. As I know you secretly are. The fire, Pilot, the light. Hanuman would do well to fear you."

"But it is I . . . . who will be at his mercy."

"Perhaps, perhaps."

For a moment, the Sonderval looked at Danlo strangely before bowing to him. Perhaps some presentiment of doom came flooding into him like an ocean wave then, for his eyes misted and his perfectly shaped chin trembled slightly. Considering that he was *the* Sonderval, the most perfect and aloof of all men, this was one of the most remarkable things Danlo had ever seen.

"I wish you well, Lord Pilot."

"And I wish you well. I hope I see you again."

Danlo smiled and said, "When we have stopped the war—when the war is done."

"When the war is done," the Sonderval repeated. And then he said, "Fall far and fall well, Pilot."

With a final bow, Danlo returned to his ship. It took only moments for the two pilots to disengage the *Cardinal Virtue* and the *Snowy Owl*. These beautiful lightships orbited above Sheydveg while Lord Demothi Bede spoke with the Sonderval and received his final instructions. And then the *Snowy Owl* rocketed away from the thirty thousand other ships toward Sheydveg's orange-red sun. Danlo opened a window into the manifold, and so he began the last part of his journey to return home and to bring an end to war.

THE GOLDEN RING

Life is light trapped in matter.
—saying of the gnostics

Life is the ability of matter to trap light.
—saying of the eschatologists

In mapping his pathways from Sheydveg to Neverness, Danlo had a choice between two conflicting purposes. Since his mission cried out for speed, he might have fallen from star to star by the shortest pathway, which would have taken him to Arcite, Darkmoon and Darghin, and thence to Fravashing and Silvaplana before falling on to Qallar and Neverness. But his safety—and Demothi Bede's—was important, too; dead ambassadors stop no wars. Since the Ringists were already at war, a lone lightship such as the *Snowy Owl,* falling suddenly out of the manifold near some hostile world such as Arcite, might find itself attacked by ten others. Certainly, therefore, Danlo would best avoid Arcite and Qallar. Perhaps, he thought, he should avoid those other worlds as well, for Ringist pilots might be lying in wait along such an obvious pathway. It would be safest for him to make a great circle through the Fallaways, past the great red sun of the Elidi and then on to Flewelling, the Nave, Simoom and Catava. Safest, truly, but such a journey would take long, long. In the end, he decided upon the shorter pathway. Once, his friends and fellow pilots had called him Danlo the Wild. But he was not wild beyond the cooling draughts of reason, and so he began his journey with a falling off toward Agathange instead of Arcite and planned to approach Neverness by way of Kenshin or Tyr.

His journey across the stars was both the easiest and hardest he had ever made. Easy, because he fenestered through the most ancient and well-mapped part of the Fallaways, and the spaces he crossed were almost as familiar to him as the snowy islands of his childhood. If Arrio Verjin was right and a Danladi wave would soon rip through the Fallaways and turn the manifold into a raging black sea, Danlo saw no sign of this. The manifold before him—the emerald invarient spaces and Gallivare sets—were no more dangerous than a forest brook. He passed well-known stars, Baran Luz and Pilisi, a red giant almost as lovely to look upon as the Eye of Ursola. As always, he marveled at the colors, the hot blue stars, the red and orange, and those loveliest of lights whose tones shone more as pale rose or golden yellow. This, he thought, was the glory of being a pilot. To behold a star with such closeness as if it were a bright red apple hanging from a tree was very different from standing on an icy world and looking up at the sky. Then, at night, the stars hung from the heavens like a million tiny jewels. And they were almost all white. From far away, the stars were like white diamonds because the human eye's faint-light nerve cells couldn't respond to color, while the color receptors couldn't feel the faint touch of starlight. Once, as a child, as might a snowy owl circling closer to the sun, he had hoped to see the stars just as they really were. And someday, he thought, he still might look out at the galaxies with his eyes truly open and naked to the universe. But now it was very good just to gaze at the colors of Cohila Luz or Tur Tupeng through the clearness of his lightship's windows.

The hard part of this journey came from his continual surveillance of the manifold. For many days, he studied this space beneath space with the intensity of a tyard bird watching a snow field for the slightest sign of a worm. Always, within a well-defined region about him known as a Lavi neighborhood, the manifold rippled with undulations, most as faint as a whisper of wind upon a starlit sea. These he ignored, indeed, scarcely even noticed. What he sought—and hoped not to find—were the tells of a lightship, those violet traceries and luminous streaks made when a ship such as the *Diamond Lotus* perturbed the manifold. Just as he passed by a spinning thickspace near the Valeska Double, he thought that he descryed such tells. For the count of ten heartbeats, he didn't breathe. But upon deeper scrutiny, it proved to be only the reflection of the *Snowy Owl's* own tells, an unusual but not unheard-of phenomenon when the manifold flattens out like a clear mountain lake. Four more times between Darkmoon and Silvaplana, Danlo was to detect such reflections (and two similar mirages), and each time he felt his heart in his throat and the blood pounding behind his eyes.

"If you continue like this, Pilot, you'll kill yourself."

This came from Demothi Bede, who temporily crowded into the pit of the *Snowy Owl*. No pilot, of course, while falling through the manifold would permit such a violation of his sacred space by another. And very few would share this sanctum of the soul at any time. But in order to rest, Danlo had fallen out into the quiet of realspace near Andulka. And because he loved company—sometimes—he didn't mind talking with Demothi Bede. And so after he had finished sleeping, he had invited this crusty old lord inside the very brain of his ship.

"But I have just slept . . . so deeply," Danlo said with a yawn.

"But not long. Six hours of sleep you've had in the last sixty, by my count."

"I did not know . . . that you were keeping count."

"There's little else for me to do," Demothi said. Although his face was as old and forbidding-looking as a cratered moon, when he spoke there was a flash of good white teeth and true compassion that Danlo thought endearing.

"I cannot sleep safely in the manifold," Danlo said. "And I cannot risk too many exits into realspace."

In truth, the most dangerous part of their journey, as far as being detected by other ships, lay in opening windows to and from realspace. Then, when the *Snowy Owl*'s spacetime engines tore through the luminous tapestry of the manifold, there was always a release of light. Through telescopes or the naked human eye, other pilots could watch the blackness for flashes of light and so mark the coming or passing of a lightship.

"But you could sleep longer," Demothi said.

"If only I did not have to sleep at all."

As Danlo said this, he glanced at the Ede hologram floating in the darkness. Nikolos Daru Ede, as a program running inside his devotionary computer, never slept. And he never kept silent, either, if he perceived any threat to his continued existence.

"The Lord Demothi is right, you know," the Ede imago said. "If you exhaust yourself, you might map us into a collapsing torison space."

Danlo smiled at this because the Ede program had learned enough mathematics of the manifold to speak almost as if he were a pilot or a real human being.

"And what will you do if we cross pathways with another lightship? If you're too tired to think?"

"I have never been that tired," Danlo said. Once, as a boy out hunting in the wild, he had stood awake for three days by a hole cut into the sea's ice—awake and waiting with his harpoon for a seal to appear.

"This machine asks a good question, though," Demothi Bede

said pointing at the imago. "What will we do if we cross pathways with a Neverness lightship?"

"Or ten ships?" the Ede imago asked.

"How . . . could I know?"

"You don't know what you'd *do* if ten light ships fell upon us?"

"No, truly I do not," Danlo said. And then he smiled because sometimes he liked playing games with the Ede imago. "But part of the pilots' art is knowing what to do . . . when you do not know what to do."

"But shouldn't we at least agree upon a strategy?" Demothi Bede broke in. "It seems that if we're discovered, we'll have only two choices: to flee into the stars, or to declare ourselves as ambassadors and trust we'll be escorted to Neverness."

"Have you so great a trust of others, then?" Danlo asked.

"We're speaking of pilots of the Order, not barbarians."

"But these pilots are also Ringists," Danlo said. "And they are at war with the Fellowship."

Here Demothi Bede sucked in a breath with such force that his lungs fairly rattled. He said, "We don't know that with certainty. It might be that the ambush near Ulladulla was an accident or only the belligerence of those five pilots who committed this massacre."

"No," Danlo said, closing his eyes. "It was no accident."

"Then you've decided to flee?"

"I have decided nothing."

"But how will you make your decision?"

"That will depend on many things: the configuration of the stars, how many ships we meet and who their pilots are." And, Danlo thought, on the pattern of the N-set waves rippling through the manifold or the whispers that he heard in the solar wind if they had fallen out near a star.

Now the Ede imago spoke again, and it was his turn to play with Danlo. "Do you really think you could escape ten lightships?"

"Why not?"

"On your journey to Tannahill, Sivan wi Mawi Sarkissian pursued you across the entire Vild."

"That is true," Danlo said. He remembered how Sivan, in his ship the *Red Dragon,* for a distance of twenty thousand lightyears, had hovered ghostlike always just at the radius of convergence in the same neighborhood of space as the *Snowy Owl.* He remembered, too, Sivan's passenger (and master), Malaclypse Redring of Qallar, the warrior-poet who had hoped that Danlo would lead him to his father. The warrior-poets had a new rule, which was to kill all potential gods, and so Malaclypse had fallen halfway across the galaxy to find Mallory Ringess.

"Well, Pilot?"

"There is no pilot in Neverness the equal of Sivan wi Mawi Sarkissian," Danlo said.

"Are you certain of that?"

Danlo, of course, was not certain, but to reassure the Ede imago, he said, "The best pilots went with the Sonderval to the Vild."

"And the very best of these is here before you," Demothi Bede said to the Ede imago. One of the old lord's virtues was that he would defend a pilot of his Order against anyone, especially a glowing hologram projected out of a computer. "And isn't it possible, Pilot, that you learned new aspects of your art in being pursued by Sivan?"

"It is possible," Danlo said with a smile.

"Then it's clear that if the Ringists should surprise us, we'll have to trust to your judgement and your art. But now, we should leave you alone so that you may take a few hours more sleep."

"No," Danlo said. "Now we must open a window and journey on—and pray that Arrio Verjin's Danladi wave doesn't smash through the manifold just as we are making a mapping."

And so the *Snowy Owl* fell on past Aquene, all aflame like a plamsa torch, and then entered into the spaces of the alien worlds of Darghin and Fravashing. During this time of haste and sleeplessness, Danlo saw no sign of an approaching Danladi wave or another lightship. But he never ceased the searching of his eyes or his deeper mathematical senses. And deeper still burned memories that lent urgency to his return to Neverness. He could never forget his people, the Alaloi, and how they were slowly dying from an incurable disease. Incurable, truly, by any known medicines or technologies, and yet it might be that Danlo carried the cure inside himself like an elixir of light. It would be terrible, he thought, if he found the secret of this cure only to arrive home too late.

Of course the *shaida* disease called the slow evil was not the only threat to the Alaloi tribes' survival, nor were they the only people on Icefall exposed to sudden doom. If war came to Neverness, the entire city—and much of the planet—might be destroyed by hydrogen bombs. And Bertram Jaspari and his fleet of Iviomil fanatics might be falling towards Neverness at that very moment.

On Tannahill, this prince of the Old Church Architects had subtly threatened to end the Ringism abomination and cleanse the galaxy of all would-be gods. With their great star-killing engine called a *morrashar*, the Iviomils certainly wielded the means to destroy the Star of Neverness—as they already had the great red sun of the Narain people far across the Vild.

The gods, too, might destroy all space itself in the stars near Neverness, by design or perhaps only by accident of the vast war that they waged across the heavens. It was said that the Silicon God's deep programs prevented him from directly harming human beings. But Danlo took little solace from this fact. The Silicon God, like any other god, was certainly clever enough to find a thousand ways to menace humanity *indirectly*. And even if no god or bomb or star-killing machine ever touched Neverness, there was always the terror of Merripen's Star. Its malignant light was very real. This supernova had exploded out near the Abelian Group nearly thirty years before, and for all that time a wavefront of radiation had fallen outward across the galaxy. Soon its terrible energies would fall upon Neverness and bathe all of Icefall in a shower of death. Or life. In truth, no one knew how intense its radiation would be, nor if the Golden Ring growing above Icefall's atmosphere would simply absorb this cosmic light and burst into a new phase of its evolution.

Sometimes, in the darkest wormholes of the manifold, Danlo prayed for this new life, just as he prayed for his people. But sometimes his words seemed only words, no more potent against the forces of the universe than a whisper cast into a winter wind.

As Danlo continued along his pathway toward Silvaplana, Tyr and then Neverness, he fell out around a worldless star named Shoshange. It was a subdwarf, small but of very high density, and hot and blue much like the central star of the Ring Nebula in Lyra. He might have spent many moments gazing at this rare star, but immediately upon exiting the manifold, he found that seven lightships were waiting for him. Through his telescopes he made out the lines of the *Cantor's Dream*, with its curving diamond wings, and the *Fire Drinker*, and each of the others.

Once, as a journeyman, Danlo had memorized the silhouettes and design of every lightship of the Order; he knew these ships' names and those of the pilots who belonged to them. These seven pilots must have seen the *Snowy Owl* fall out of the manifold; their names were Sigurd Narvarian, Timothy Wolf, the Shammara, Marja Valasquez, Femi wi Matana, Taras Moswen and Tukuli li Chu. Their names, unfortunately, were almost all that Danlo knew

of these seven, for he had never met any of them. Only two—
Sigurd Narvarian and Tukuli li Chu—were master pilots. And
certainly Marja Valasquez deserved a mastership, but her famous
evil temperment had alienated every elder pilot who might have
helped to elevate her. It was said that in the Pilot's War, she had
destroyed the ship of Sevilin Ordando, who had surrendered to
her, but this slander had never been confirmed.

It took Danlo only a moment to decide to flee. He closed his
eyes envisioning the colors and contours of the manifold in this
neighborhood of space; he listened to the whispers of his heart,
and then he reached out with his mind to his ship-computer to
make interface. And then he was gone. The *Snowy Owl* plunged
into the manifold like a diamond needle falling into the ocean. He
knew that the other ships would follow him. Very well, he
thought, then let them follow him into the darkest part of the
manifold, where the spaces fell deep and wild and strange. In the
gentle topology of the Fallaways, few such spaces existed, but
there were always Flowtow bubbles and torison tubes and decision
trees. And, of course, the rare but bewildering paradox tunnels.
No pilot would willingly seek out such a deranged space—unless
he were being pursued by seven others determined to destroy him.

By chance (or fate), such a tunnel could be found beneath the
blazing fires of Shoshange. From a journey that the Sonderval had
once described making as a young pilot, Danlo remembered the
fixed-points of this tunnel. And so he made a difficult mapping.
He found the paradox tunnel all infolded among itself like a nest
of snakes. His ship disappeared into the opening of the tunnel—
and to any ship pursuing him, it would seem as if the *Snowy Owl*
had been swallowed by twenty dark, yawning, serpentine mouths,
all at once.

"We're in danger, aren't we, Pilot? We've been discovered,
haven't we? Shouldn't you alert the Lord Bede?"

As always, Danlo's devotionary computer floated in the pit of
his ship near his side. And the Ede imago floated in the dark air,
talking, always talking. But when Danlo was fully faced into his
ship-computer and his mind opened to the terrors and beauties of
the manifold, he scarcely noticed this noisy hologram. Only
rarely, when he had need of making mathematics at lightning
speed in order to survive, did he ask for complete silence. And so
when the *Snowy Owl* began to phase in and out of existence like a
single firefly winking on and off from a dozen cave mouths all at
once, Danlo lifted his little finger, a sign that Ede should be quiet.
Unfortunately, it was also a sign that they were in deadly danger,

and Ede must have found it paradoxical that just when he needed to talk the most, he must keep as silent as a stone.

As for rousing Demothi Bede from quicktime, Danlo never considered this. He was too busy making mappings and applying Gallivare's Point Theorem in order to find his way out of this bizarre space. Danlo always perceived the manifold both mathematically and sensually, as a vast tapestry of shimmering colors. Always, there was a logic and sensibility to these colors, the way that the intense carmine of a Lavi space might break apart into maroon, rose and auburn as one approached the first bounded interval. But here, in this disturbing paradox tunnel, there seemed to be little logic. One moment a deep violet might stain his entire field of vision, while in the next, a shocking yellow might spread before him like an artist's spilled paint. And then there were moments of no color, or colors such as smalt or chlorine which somehow seemed so drained of their essence that they appeared almost black or white.

And too often white would darken to black, and black mutate into white like the figure and ground in a painting shifting back and forth, in and out. Twice Danlo thought that he had escaped into a flatter, brighter part of the manifold only to find himself falling through a part of the tunnel as dark and twisting as the bowels of a bear. How long he remained in this cavern-like place he could never say. But at last he made a mapping and fell free into a simple Lavi neighborhood; his relief must have been as that of an oyster miraculously coughed out of a seagull's throat.

"We're free, aren't we, Pilot?" On his journey toward Tannahill, Danlo had programmed his ship-computer to project a simulation of the manifold for Ede to study. With its geometric and too-literal representations of the most sublime mathematics, this hologram wasn't really like the way that Danlo perceived this space beneath space. But it allowed Ede a certain intake of information, and more than once, Ede had pointed out dangers that Danlo himself might have overlooked. "We've lost the other ships, haven't we? I can't find a trace of a tell."

At that very moment, Danlo was scanning the neighborhood about him with all the intensity of a hunter searching a snowfield for signs of a great white bear.

"We're alone now, aren't we? There's no other ship within the radius of convergence."

Once, Danlo had explained that past the boundaries of a Lavi neighborhood, the radius of convergence shoots off toward infinity and it becomes almost impossible to read the tells of another lightship.

"You escaped that strange space, whatever it was, and now we're alone."

For a moment, Danlo thought that they *had* lost the other ships. With his mind's eye and his mathematics he delved the aquamarine depths all about him searching for the slighest streak of light. He held his breath, counting his heatbeats: one, two, three. . . . And then, in a low, soft voice, he said, "No, we are not alone."

Outward in the direction of the paradox tunnel, at the very boundary of this neighborhood of space, two tiny sparks lit the manifold. They were two lightships floating like luminous linfey seeds just at the radius of convergence.

"Where, Pilot? Oh, there—now I see them. Which ships are they?"

It is, of course, impossible to identify a lightship solely from tells it makes in the manifold. But when Danlo closed his eyes, he saw two ships spinning towards him like drillworms: the *Cantor's Dream* and the *Fire Drinker* piloted by the bloodthirsty Marja Valasquez.

"What shall we do—shall we flee?"

Even as the *Snowy Owl* fell deeper into the manifold towards the core stars, Danlo searched this neighborhood's flickering boundary, waiting to see if any more ships pursued him. After he had counted ten more heartbeats, he said, "Yes, we shall flee."

And so Danlo took his ship into other spaces, the blue-black invariant spaces and segmented spaces and klein tubes that bent back upon themselves like a snake swallowing its tail. For four days this pursuit lasted. When Danlo grew so tired that his eyes burned and his head ached as if pressed by the slow grind of glacier ice, the Ede imago reminded him that he couldn't go forever without sleep. Danlo's reply, when he finally managed to force the words from his cracked, bleeding lips, was simple and to the point: "Neither can the other pilots."

Somewhere beyond the double star known as the Almira Twins, Danlo lost one of the other ships. For half a day he fell through a Zeeman space as flat and green as a field of grass, and he descried the tells of only one other ship. After he had mapped through a short but particularly tortuous point-set tunnel and only a single spark emerged from its black, empty mouth, he felt certain that only a single ship followed him.

"Must we still flee?" the Ede imago asked Danlo. "You're so tired you can scarcely keep your eyes open."

Danlo *was* tired, so dreadfully tired that he felt it as a burning sickness deep in his belly. The one reason that he kept his eyes open at all was to look at the glowing Ede hologram. To pilot the *Snowy Owl* he need only reach out to his ship with the seeing center of his brain, and its computer would infuse mathematical images directly into him. To pilot his ship with elegance and grace, he thus most often kept his eyes closed. In truth, when he interfaced the manifold and the beauty of the number storm swept over him like ten thousand interwoven rainbows, his eyes fell as blind to the sights around him as a newborn child's.

"I can *lose* this ship," Danlo said. At the boundary of this neighborhood of space, a glimmering ripple now told of another ship. He was certain that it was the *Fire Drinker*. He remembered what the Sonderval had once said about her pilot, Marja Valasquez: that as ferocious and bold as she was, she had a peculiar dread of phase spaces.

For a while, as the manifold began curving into a blueness as gentle as the watery world of Agathange, Danlo searched for a phase space. But he never found one. He kept well-distanced from the *Fire Drinker*, however; always this other lightship remained just at the boundary of whatever neighborhood of space that Danlo passed through.

"This Marja Valasquez," Ede said, "seems almost as good a pilot as Sivan wi Mawi Sarkissian. He, too, followed you at the boundary for almost your entire journey into the Vild."

Danlo smiled grimly at this, and rubbed his burning, bloodshot eyes. He wiped the blood from his lips, then said, "Many times I tried to lose Sivan but never could. Even in the inversion spaces of the Vild. I always thought . . . that he could have closed the radius and caught me whenever he wanted."

"But not Marja Valasquez?"

"No. I think that she follows me only with the greatest difficulty."

"Then you still hope to lose her?"

"I . . . *will* lose her. Even if I must stay awake for ten days."

"But perhaps she was better rested than you before this ordeal began. Or perhaps she uses forbidden drugs to give her a greater wakefulness."

"Then I will lose her in a phase space, if I can find one," Danlo said. "Or perhaps a Soli tree."

"But if you enter these spaces, might not the probability mappings fall against you? Aren't you at a terrible disadvantage in letting her pursue you?"

"Do I have another choice?"

"You might fall out into realspace and signal for a parlay."

"No, I will not do that. Floating in space, waiting in the star's light like a dove with a broken wing . . . we would be so helpless."

"Then why not pursue *her?*"

At this suggestion a sudden pain stabbed through Danlo's eye, and he asked, "Toward what end?"

"Towards destroying her, of course! As you pilots do with your ships, dancing the dance of light and death."

For a moment, Danlo's deep blue eyes filled with a terrible radiance, and he stared at Ede in silence.

"At least your chances would be even. Much more than even, if you're the better pilot, as I'm sure you are."

"I will not fall against her," Danlo said.

The program running the projection of Ede must have called for pursuasion, for now his dark, plump face glowed with all the craftiness of a merchant selling firestones of uncertain virtue. "You've made your vow, of course. But isn't the spirit of this vow to serve life? You'd never harm another's life—but consider the great harm that might come to many lives if you let Marja destroy you. Wouldn't you best serve your vow by ensuring that you reach Neverness however you can?"

"No," Danlo said.

"But, Pilot, this one time—who would ever know?"

"No."

"But think of it! You've let this other pilot follow you across four thousand light years. It would be so easy to take her into a Klein tube. To quickly Klein back across your pathway and fall against her, she might never suspect such a—"

"No, I will not!"

"But if you—"

"Please do not speak of this any more."

For a moment, the Ede program caused his countenance to fall into the appearance of contrition. And then he asked, "But, Pilot, what will you *do?*"

"I will stay awake," Danlo said. "I . . . will fall on."

And so Danlo fell, taking the *Snowy Owl* through the manifold as fast as he could. He made his mappings and artfully arrayed the windows upon the Fallaways, and he fenestered from star to star with a rare grace. And still Marja Valasquez in her *Fire Drinker* followed him. Soon, if he continued on this pathway, he must make a final sequence of mappings that would cause him to fall out near the Star of Neverness. And Marja would fall out too, and if he didn't want to confront her ship to ship in realspace, then he must find some way to lose her before then.

He was wondering how he might accomplish this purpose when he entered an unusually flat null space. The manifold fell very calm; its colors quieted from quicksilver to emerald and then to a gentle turquoise without flaw or variegation of tone. Other than the *Snowy Owl*'s perturbations and the faint tells of Marja's ship, no other ripples touched the almost deathly stillness of this space. Something was wrong here, he thought, something that he had never encountered before, not even in the endless null spaces of the Vild. There was a strangeness all about him and inside him, a waiting for some terrible event to occur; it was almost like standing on the sea's ice on a clear winter day and watching the horizon for the whitish-blue clouds of a storm. He sensed such a storm. How this could be he did not know, for his mathematics told him that the manifold was as peaceful as a tropical sea—even if he extended his search outside the boundary of this neighborhood to other neighborhoods within a rather vast and ill-defined region.

He might have sought the tells of this topological event forever, for outside the radius of convergence, the perturbations of the manifold become infinitely faint. But he was keen of vision, both in his eyes and in his deeper mathematical senses; something like a shimmer of light caused him to look deep into the manifold, inward toward the fixed-points of the Morbio Inferiore. And then, from far away, after his heart had beat nineteen times, he saw it. There was, in truth, a swelling whiteness like that of a storm. Or a wave—a tidal wave of the manifold. As his heart beat more quickly, he knew that the Danladi wave told of by Arrio Verjin would soon sweep through the manifold and fall over any ship caught in its path.

"Pilot, what is it?" the Ede imago asked. "What do you see—my simulation shows nothing."

"I see a wave, far off, toward the core singularity. It . . . builds. It is a Danladi wave."

"A Danladi wave! Are you sure? Then soon it will sweep through this neighborhood and twist the topology beyond calculation."

"Yes."

"If we're caught here, it will sweep us under and destroy us."

"Possibly."

"Then we must flee immediately! We must fall out into real-space where we'll be safe."

"We will flee," Danlo said strangely. His voice was low and yet strong like a building wind; suddenly the weariness seemed to melt from him, and his eyes grew as bright as double stars.

"What do you wait for, then?"

"We will flee, but not into realspace, not yet," Danlo said. "We will flee into the Danladi wave."

"Are you mad, Pilot? Would you destroy us for the sake of your willfulness?"

"I pray . . . that I will not destroy us."

Then with a flick of his hand for Ede to be silent, he made a mapping and pointed the *Snowy Owl* toward the Danladi wave. He began falling from window to window as quickly as he could and still maintain a sense of interfenestration. Because he knew that Marja Valasquez would follow him, he spared not a moment searching for the tells of the *Fire Drinker* behind him. His whole awareness concentrated on what lay ahead. He fell through the manifold like a streak of light, and yet the Danladi wave swept toward him even more quickly. For it did not "move" as he moved, but rather deformed the manifold almost instantaneously in all directions. In a way, it was the essence of motion itself. Danlo could scarcely believe at how quickly it built. One moment it was no more significant than the hump of a snow hut on the frozen sea. But in the next, it began to brighten and swell as if a flat plain of ice had suddenly heaved itself up into the highest of mountains. Soon, in moments, it would fall upon him, and then he must make the choice either to look for a mapping and dive under this impossibly monstrous wave, or to escape into realspace as Ede had advised.

Ahira, Ahira—what shall I do? For a moment, Danlo prayed to the name of the snowy owl, his spirit animal whom he had once believed held half his soul. *Ahira, Ahira.*

By now, Danlo thought, Marja Valasquez must have descried the shape of the Danladi wave. But so fast did they race towards its boiling center—and it towards them—that she might have had too little time to understand its true nature. Arrio Verjin, after all, would not have warned the Order's pilots of its coming. She might perceive it as only a Wimund wave or even the much simpler N-set waves of a Gallivare inversion. She must assume that he would try to use its topological complexities to escape her, perhaps diving beneath the wave into calmer regions of the manifold at the last moment. But for many moments, Danlo had been making lightning calculations and going through every known theorem pertaining to Danladi waves; he felt almost certain that there could be no escaping such a wave simply by "diving" beneath it. Its perturbations were too powerful, and it propagated much too quickly for that. Already, as the wave began to crest, rising, rising, he descried an astonishing density of zero-points, like trillions of bacteria churned into a huge, black sucking mass. The wave itself began to suck at him now as he crossed the last bounded interval; now, in less than a moment, he must either make a mapping into real space or prepare to die.

Ahira, Ahira—give me me the courage to do what I must do.

He waited as long as he could, waited until the *Fire Drinker* crossed the last bounded interval, too. And then, in the terrible toplogical distortions of the wave that was almost upon them, all possible windows into realspace suddenly closed, and there could be no escape in that direction. There could be only pathways downward into the swirling blackness beneath the wave. Or pathways *into* the wave. Since the moment that Danlo had first sighted the wave far across the shimmering manifold, he had contemplated this other possibility. It would be seeming-madness to take his ship into the wave itself, but all his mathematics told him that diving under it would be suicide. Marja Valasquez, however, obviously hadn't had the chance to make such calculations, for she made a mapping at the last moment and found a pathway beneath the wave. Danlo watched the *Fire Drinker* disappear like a diamond pin dropped into a cauldron of molten steel. And then he pointed the *Snowy Owl* straight into the bore of the wave, and it fell upon him with a terrible weight, breaking into colors of cobalt and rose and foaming violet.

Ahira, Ahira—give me your golden eyes that I might see.

Almost immediately he lost his mappings. Supposedly, no pilot could survive such a disaster, for without a map from point to point within the swirling complexities of the manifold, one became hopelessly lost. But once before, when he had entered the chaos space in the heart of the Entity, he had found a way out of what should have been a fatal topological trap. New mappings always existed if a pilot were artful enough to discover them. Even as the wave swept the *Snowy Owl* along at a tremendous speed, he searched for such mappings.

If he had had endless time, he might have found a mapping very quickly, for the greatest of his mathematical skills lay in seeing the pattern that connects. But he had almost no time. In truth, he was fighting to stay alive. The wave broke all around him in colors of jade and viridian; only the lightning rush of its momentum outward balanced the almost impossible suck of its dark emerald weight. He lived in this balance. He piloted the *Snowy Owl* into a pocket along the wavefront, and there he remained perfectly poised within its hideously complex dynamics. He called upon the three deepest virtues of a pilot: fearlessness, flawlessness, and flowingness. If he let himself be afraid, even for a moment, he might try to flee the wave in the wrong direction and be swept under like a piece of driftwood in a raging sea. And if his piloting were anything less than flawless, he would lose the flow of his perfect balance, and the wave's terrible energies would crush his ship to pieces as if it were only a clam shell.

Ahira, Ahira—I must not be afraid.

There was a moment. For Danlo in his *Snowy Owl* riding the crest of an almost impossible topological wave far beneath space and time, as for everyone, always only a moment between life and death. It was a moment of intense awareness. Colors swirled all around him and broke into bands of magenta and brilliant blue, into flaming scarlet traceries and thousands of other patterns. There were always patterns, always a hidden order beneath the surface chaos. As the Danladi wave propagated through the manifold, Danlo perceived subtle, silvered reflections at each encounter with the various topological structures it swept across. There were refractions, too, the way that the wave continually broke upon itself in intense showers of light and reformed into a vast moving mountain only a moment later. The wave orthogonals appeared as parallel lines of silver-blue. After a while he noticed something about these orthogonals: although they changed direction from moment to moment as the wave distorted the very substance of the manifold, making the discovery of a mapping into realspace almost impossible, there was a pattern to these changes.

He tried to find a mathematical model to fit this pattern. He tried Q-sets and Gallivare fields and a hundred others before he found that orthogonals' spinning motions could be best represented by a simple Soli set. If his timing were almost perfect, he might predict the exact moment when the orthogonals would line up away from the wave and point towards an exit into realspace. If his piloting were flawless, he might make a mapping in this moment and accomplish what only the maddest (or wildest) of pilots would ever have dared to attempt.

One, two, three, four, five, six, seven . . .

At exactly halfway through the seventh beat of his heart, he made a mapping. And instantaneously, the vast Danladi wave disappeared, and the *Snowy Owl* fell out around a cool white star. In the emptiness of space, it was quiet around this star. It showered the *Snowy Owl* with its lovely white light. Danlo floated in the quiet, looking out at the star as he gasped for breath and continued counting his heartbeats: *thirteen, fourteen, fifteen* . . .

"Pilot, we're free!" This came from the Ede imago, floating near Danlo who was looking out the ship's diamond window. "We're free, and we've lost the other ship, haven't we?"

"Yes," Danlo said. He pressed his hand against the scar above his eye and grimaced in pain. "We . . . have lost her."

"How did you lose her, then? I'm afraid that in the distortions of the wave, my simulation showed little."

Danlo felt his heartbeats in the throbbing of his eye, and then he told Ede exactly how he had lost Marja Valasquez and the *Fire Drinker*.

"That was very clever of you," Ede said. "To slay her that way."

"I did not slay her!"

"You lured her to her death."

"No, she had choices. Before she crossed the last interval, she might have escaped into realspace."

"But you knew that she would follow you."

"I knew . . . only that she would want to follow me."

"And you knew that she would dive beneath the wave and be destroyed, didn't you?"

"How could I truly know which pathway she would choose?"

"How could you *not* know?"

"But she might have tried to ride the wave out, as I did."

"Oh, Pilot."

"Truly, she always had a choice. And she dove beneath the wave. *Her* will, not mine."

The Ede imago glowed softly as it regarded Danlo. Then it said, "How was it that you once defined this vow of ahimsa that you've made? Never harming another, not even in one's own thoughts."

"I . . . never wished Marja dead. I only wanted to lose her."

"And yet you led her to lose her life."

"Yes."

"It would seem that the practice of ahimsa can be difficult and subtle."

"Yes."

Ede continued staring at Danlo, then said, "I'm sorry—this must be hard for you."

At this, a sudden pain shot through Danlo's eye and filled his head like an explosive tlolt. His eye began to water, and the other one, too, and he blinked hard against the cool but hurtful light of the star outside his ship.

"I . . . am sorry, too," he said.

Then he closed his eyes and whispered a prayer for Marja's spirit, "Marja Evangelina wi Eshte Valasquez, *mi alasharia la shantih*."

Some time later he roused Demothi Bede from the sleep of quicktime and invited him into the pit of his ship. The sleepy-eyed Demothi took a long look at the star outside the pit's window, yawned and said, "It looks like the Star of Neverness—are we home, then?"

"No," Danlo said, smiling despite his aching head. "The color of this star is white, not yellow-white. We are still far from Neverness."

"How far, then? What is this star's name?"

"It has no name that I know," Danlo said. "But it lies close to Kalkin."

"Kalkin!" Demothi exclaimed. He may have had poor eyes for stellar spectra, but he remembered his astronomy lessons. "Kalkin is only ten light-years distance from Summerworld!"

"Yes," Danlo said. "We . . . have departed from our pathway."

After wiping away the salt crusts from corners of his eyes, he told Demothi of Marja Valasquez and the *Fire Drinker* and their long pursuit through the manifold. He tried to describe the vastness of the Danladi wave, its terrible beauty, but he found that his words failed him. He said only that the wave had swept them far along the galaxy's Sagittarius Arm almost to the stars of the Jovim Cluster.

"Why didn't you wake me, Pilot? Would you have had me go to my death half-asleep?"

Again Danlo smiled because he remembered something that his Fravashi teacher had once said: that the manswarms of the human race went about their whole lives half-asleep and stumbling towards death.

"I did not want to alarm you," Danlo said.

"What will we do now?"

"Continue our journey."

"How much longer has our journey become, then? The wave has caused us such a vast dislocation."

"As measured in light-years this is true," Danlo said. "But the pathways between Kalkin and Neverness are well-known. The mappings are very easy. Our journey will not have grown much more difficult or tiresome."

"But what if the wave has changed or broken the old pathways? Aren't such permanent distortions of the manifold possible?"

"Yes—truly this is possible."

"Well, then?"

"It is possible, too, that the pathways remain unbroken."

"You must be eager to discover if this is so."

"Truly, I am," Danlo said, yawning. He closed his eyes for a moment, and the rising swells of unconsciousness swept towards him in black, rolling waves. Then with a sudden snap of his head, he looked at Demothi and smiled. "But I am even more eager for sleep. I will sleep now. When my computer wakes me in two more hours, then we shall see if we can find an easy pathway towards Neverness."

With that he closed his eyes again and fell instantly into a deep and peaceful sleep. So total was his exhaustion that when his ship-computer touched his brain with soft musics two hours later, he did not awaken. Nor twenty hours later. Both Demothi Bede and the Ede hologram seemed astonished to discover how long Danlo could sleep when he was really tired—in this instance, for most of three days. When he finally broke back into consciousness and looked out on the stars, he realized that he had slept too long.

"We will fall on, now," he said, angry with himself though well rested. "I only hope that war hasn't come to Neverness while I was dreaming."

And so they fell. Danlo took the *Snowy Owl* back into the manifold, and they fell on past Kalkin and Skibbereen and the great red giant star known as Daru Luz. Although the Danladi wave had slightly flattened these familiar spaces and broken a few of the familiar Fallaways as a windstorm might snap a tree's twigs, most of the pathways through the manifold remained untouched. He made a mapping to a little star near Summerworld, and then on past Tria, Larondissement and Avalon. All these stars lay along the rather roundabout pathway towards Neverness that he had once rejected as too lengthy. But the Danladi wave had made it so that this journey required little more time than his original and more straightforward approach. And it required much less risk.

Even in the spaces near Larondissement, one of the Civilized Worlds most devoted to the new religion of Ringism, he descryed no tells of any Ringist ship which might be lying in wait for him. On this last segment of his surprisingly peaceful journey, he encountered no other ships at all, not even the vast deepships of the Trian merchant-pilots which usually plied the Fallaways filled with cargoes of gossilk, neurologics, firestones, firewine, Gilada pearls, sulki grids, bloodfruits, jook, jambool, blacking oil, and a million other things grown or manufactured on the worlds of man.

When he reached Avalon, a pretty blue star so close to the star of his birth, he made a final mapping. It was the famous Ashtoreth mapping, named for the pilot Villiama li Ashtoreth who had discovered it at the beginning of the Order's Golden Age in the year 681. It carried the *Snowy Owl* across three hundred light-years of space in a single fold, where it fell out in the thickspace near the Star of Neverness.

"Home," Danlo whispered as he looked out at the soft, yellow star that had lit all the days of his childhood. *"O, Sawel, miralando mi kalabara, kareeska."*

In truth, however, he wasn't *quite* home, not yet. He looked out with his telescopes across seventy million miles of vacuum where he spied the planet Icefall spinning like a white and blue jewel in the blackness of space. He might have instantly made a mapping to a point-exit only a few hundred miles above Icefall's atmosphere, but such a rash act would have set-off the planetary defense systems, and he and his ship would surely have been destroyed. As it was, his peril was still great. The *Snowy Owl* gleamed in the radiance of the Star of Neverness like a dove with a broken wing. Its opening of a window from the manifold had surely created tells that any lightship in this neighborhood of stars would detect. And surely, with war so near, the Lord Pilot, Salmalin the Prudent, would have deployed many ships to protect Neverness from surprise attack.

Danlo waited for the arrival of these ships. It was almost all that he could do. But first he aimed a radio signal at the city of Neverness informing the lords of the Order of the *Snowy Owl*'s mission. He did not think that the Old Order's Ringists had sunk so far into barbarism that they would simply murder two ambassadors out of hand. The danger was that one of the arriving lightships might act without waiting for instructions from Neverness. Some reckless young pilot such as Ciro Dalibar might perceive the *Snowy Owl* as only the vanguard of an invasion fleet and fall immediately against him. Even with the *Snowy Owl* gently rocking its wings as a signal for a parlay, Ciro or the ruthless Riesa Eshte, perhaps, might first destroy him and then claim Danlo's peaceful intention was only a ruse.

And so Danlo waited in the pit of the *Snowy Owl*, counting heartbeats as he searched for the tells of other lightships. He began counting the 714 seconds that his radio signal would take to cross seventy million miles of realspace and be returned as a command to all the Order's lightships that Danlo and Demothi Bede were not to be harmed. He waited exactly eighty-eight seconds, and then a lightship fell out of the thickspace near him, followed only a few seconds later by four more of these deathly diamond needles.

He recognized these ships. There was the *Infinite Dactyl*, piloted by Dario of Urradeth, and the *Blue Lotus* and the *Bell of Time*. And Nicabar Blackstone's *Ark of the Angels*, with its lovely, curving wings. The fifth ship he knew well because he had been at Resa with its pilot, Ciro Dalibar, as chance would fall. He had even helped Ciro design the heuristics for this uniquely pointed ship, which Ciro had named the *Diamond Arrow*. "Ahira, Ahira," Danlo prayed, and he beamed a radio signal to each of these ships. And now he waited for the five pilots either to accept his parlay or to destroy him. That was the true terror of war, that often one had to accept danger and simply wait to live or die.

Much later he would learn that these five pilots, floating in the dazzling void near the Star of Neverness, had held a conclave among themselves. Ciro Dalibar, with his cruel, thin lips and jealousy of Danlo, had argued that as a pilot of the Order of the Vild—and thus of the Fellowship—he should be slain as a just act of war. But Cham Estarei of the *Blue Lotus* had spoken against such bloodthirstiness, as had Nicabar Blackstone. Nicabar, a master pilot and eldest of the five, told the others that it would do no harm to wait to hear from the lords on Neverness. If they wished to accept Danlo's and Demothi's embassy, well and good. If they did not, then the *Snowy Owl* could be sent back to Sheydveg or wherever the Order of the Vild's fleet might be. Or they could send Danlo into the Star of Neverness. The five ships, acting together, could open a window into this blazing star whenever they wished and send Danlo's ship into the fires of hell.

"We'll wait for the wishes of the lords," Nicabar Blackstone told Danlo and Demothi. Nicabar's imago, with its glowing green eyes and deathly white countenance, had appeared in the pit of the

Snowy Owl. "We must ask that you attempt no motion in real-space nor open any windows into the manifold. If you do, we'll fall against you and destroy you."

And so, with the noses of five ships pointing at him across only a few miles of space, Danlo waited. It took more than two thousand seconds for the Lords of Neverness' message to arrive. Neither Danlo nor Demothi Bede were to be harmed. Danlo wi Soli Ringess was instructed to make a mapping to a certain point-exit above Neverness. The five lightships were to ensure that the *Snowy Owl* fell out into near space exactly where it should. Then they were to escort the ambassadors down through the atmosphere to the Hollow Fields, where a sled would carry them to an emergency session of the Lord's College.

"I'd advise caution," the Ede hologram said in the privacy of the *Snowy Owl.* "The Ringists might wish to trap you."

"Yes," Danlo said. "Of course they will—we will be as prisoners the moment we touch the ice of Neverness."

Demothi Bede drew his hand across his old, wrinkled face and said, "Still, it will be good to see the city again. And my old friends. I never thought I would."

"To see old friends," Danlo repeated softly. His eyes were grave yet full of light. He felt a terrible burning behind his eyes, and terrible images began streaming into his mind as if he were looking far across space and time. "To see the city again—and what lies above."

A few moments later, at Nicabar Blackstone's command, Danlo made a mapping to the point-exit above Neverness. The *Snowy Owl* fell out exactly as arranged, and Danlo gasped at the changes that only a few years had wrought in the once-empty reaches of space encircling Icefall. To begin with, the sky above his world's sky was swarming with ships. There were deepships and longships, fireships and goldships and many, many blackships armed for war.

He counted more than forty-eight thousand ships spread out below him in a vast moving carpet of steel and diamond and black nall. He counted two hundred and ten lightships, too. He knew the names of all of these, most notably Riesa Eshte's *Cube of Space,* and the *Caduceus,* and the famous *Golden Butterfly* piloted by Salome wi Maya Hastari. There was the *Silver Snake,* orbiting among a pack of blackships, and the *Ouroboros,* and Charl Odissan's *Phoenix Rising.* And perhaps most notable of all, the triangular-winged *Alpha Omega.* This was the Lord Pilot Salmalin the Prudent's new ship, which he had designed to replace the one that

Bardo had stolen. It held a central position in the fleet that he commanded.

Truly, it was a much larger fleet than that of the Fellowship of Free Worlds, even though all the Ringist lightships were not present. Some of these 231 missing ships would be off on raiding missions such as the one that had surprised the Sonderval's ships near Ulladulla. Others would try to detect the movements of the Fellowship's fleet when it finally fell away from Sheydveg on its unknown pathway toward Neverness. Surely, in this neighborhood of space, waiting near such stars as Songfire and Keahi, Salmalin would have positioned more than a few lightships in a protective cordon around the Star of Neverness. And at least twenty of these lightships protected something else, something more precious to the Ringists than firestones or pearls or even the icy ground beneath their feet.

This was Hanuman li Tosh's Universal Computer, floating many miles above Neverness like a dazzling, black moon. In a way, it *was* a moon, for it was huge and made from the elements of Kasotat, Vierge and Varvara, three of the six moons that Danlo had beheld shining in the sky since the year of his birth. With his ship's telescope he looked out at these nearby moons. The surface of each one swarmed with robots and disassemblers smaller than bacteria. These infinitesimal engines of destruction were tearing apart dirt and rocks even as he watched, reducing layer after layer of the moons into their constituent elements. Their once silvery surfaces were grey and pitted as a hibakusha's face.

Truly, as Bardo had said, Hanuman and the Ringists had ordered the mining of these moons, this *shaida* act that was a crime against the laws of the Civilized Worlds. At any moment, from any of the three moons, there might issue a flash of light as a deep ship filled with silicon or carbon or gold would disappear into the manifold only to fall out an instant later at a point-exit above the Universal Computer. There, in vast floating factories, its cargo would be assembled into diamond chips and neurologics and opticals—the very substance and circuitry of the Universal Computer. More robots assembled these parts into an ungodly (or perhaps just the opposite) machine. One day, if nothing were done to halt this monument to one man's hubris, it would grow to the size of a moon.

Ahira, Ahira, ki los shaida, shaida neti shaida.

"If you're ready, Pilot, we'll make our planetfall now." This was Nicabar Blackstone's voice, spilling into the pit of the *Snowy Owl* like an overturned goblet of honey-wine. He was a master pilot whose sweet-rich voice almost belied his innate ruthlessness. "We'll make a straight fall for the Fields. I'll lead the way, and you must follow—and then Dario of Urradeth, Cham Estarei, Ciro Dalibar and the Visolela will follow you."

With that, the *Ark of the Angels* dipped its diamond nose toward the planet below them, followed in line by the *Snowy Owl*, the *Infinite Dactyl*, the *Golden Lotus*, the *Diamond Arrow* and the *Bell of Time*. The six ships slowly fell toward Icefall. And now, even as they passed through the ships of the fleet like needles through a thick carpet, Danlo had a moment to gaze upon the most profound of the changes that had come to his world. This was the Golden Ring. Ahead of him, and below, enveloping all of Icefall in a sphere of living gold, was this miracle of evolution that had taken root in the uppermost atmospheres of many worlds throughout the galaxy.

Many believed the Ring to be the Entity's handiwork, or rather the child of her vast stellar womb. For the Ring was life itself, newly created to flourish in the harsh environment of near space. A few hundred miles below Danlo's ship floated the Ring organisms, the nektons and triptons and sestons, the vacuum flowers and pipal trees and fritillaries. And of course, the little makers. These were the fundament of the Ring, the trillions of trillions of single-celled plants drifting in the faint solar wind that blew down upon Icefall. Each of the little makers was a tiny sphere of thin diamond membranes encasing the cellular machinery of enzymes and acids and red chlorophyll. The little makers would breathe the exhalations of the stars, absorbing light and transforming this most universal of energies into food that would feed the other life of the Ring.

It was the red chlorphyll that gave the Ring its color, for when the light of the sun fell through the tissues of the uncountable little makers and refracted from diamond sphere to diamond sphere, it appeared to the naked eye in hues of ruby-amber and gold. The whole of the world below was enswathed in a tapestry of shimmering gold as lovely and diaphanous as a courtesan's silks. Through this living veil, Danlo could make out the jagged coastline of Neverness Island far below him and the deep blue sheen of the sea. Someday, perhaps, the Ring would grow more opaque to light, and it might grow difficult to see the mountains of Neverness from near space or the six moons of Icefall from the surface of the planet. But it would be sad beyond tears, Danlo thought, if the Ring ever grew to obscure the light of the stars themselves.

Fara gelstei, he whispered, speaking the name of the Golden Ring that he had learned as a child. *Loshisha shona, loshisha halla—sawisha halla neti shaida.*

Soon the *Snowy Owl* entered the Ring with less moment than if it had fallen through a cloud. The Ring itself was much more tenuous than any cloud, and Danlo had no trouble seeing his way through the faint tinge of gold staining the sky. He looked for the largest Ring organisms, the predatory goswhales whose nerves were woven of neurologics, a kind of biological lightship that could swim through the cold currents of space.

The Order's eschatologists believed the goswhales to be more intelligent than human beings; some called them godwhales in honor of their considerable powers. But however one named them, they were very rare; in all his life, Danlo would never lay eyes upon one. But through this diamond window he did see a swarm of fritillaries, with their huge silver wings like solar sails to catch the light of the sun and drive them across space. They were lovely creatures but also strange; they had telescopic eyes which could pick out a vacuum flower across two hundred miles of space, and long, graceful metallic antennae for receiving and transmitting radio signals.

Once, as a boy looking up from the sea's ice to the gold-streaked sky, Danlo had wondered about the rapidly evolving life of the Ring. He had wanted to journey to the heavens, to ask such creatures as the fritillary their true names and to give them his own. "Ahira, Ahira," he said, whispering the name of his other-self, the snowy owl. He would have liked to stay here falling slowly through this ocean of gold for a long time, but the *Ark of the Angels* pointed down toward Neverness, and he had to follow her. *"Lokelani miralando la shantih."*

As the lightships fell down toward the white-capped mountains of Neverness Island, the Ring began to thicken. The little makers fed on sunlight like any plant, but they also breathed carbon dioxide, hydrogen and nitrogen, and other nutrients of Icefall's upper atmosphere. Some eschatologists believed that the rarity of these gases would place a severe upper limit on the Ring's potential for growth. Others thought that the sestons and nektons would eventually evolve into something like robot disassemblers and learn how to mine the six moons for their vast store of elements. It might be thought that the Ring would simply grow *lower* through the troposphere and begin colonizing Icefall's islands and oceans like some alien invasion of wild, new life. But it seemed that this would never happen. On no known world had the Ring grown in this direction. Indeed, the Ring seemed designed to grow outward like a sunflower opening into darkness, perhaps into the deep space as far as the Star of Neverness' ten other planets. Already, Larissa the Bold had sighted a goswhale orbiting Berural as if in contemplation of the brilliant swirling reds and violets of that gaseous world. Someday, perhaps the Ring would find a way to thrive in interstellar vacuum or even in the great loneliness between the galaxies themselves.

"It's beautiful, isn't it, Pilot?" Demothi Bede, still sharing the pit of Danlo's ship, gazed out the window at the Ring shimmering like gold dust in the light of the sun. "Who would have thought I'd live to see such miracles?"

Truly, Danlo thought, the Ring *was* a miracle—but perhaps no more miraculous than snowworms or human beings or any other kind of life. The miraculous thing was life itself, the way that matter had moved itself from the beginning of time, moved and evolved and reached out into ever more complex and conscious forms. And now life everywhere was moving off planets made of water and rocks out towards the stars. In a way, this astonishing event should have astonished no one. For space is cold, and low temperatures favor order. And what was life except matter organized into the highest degrees of order? As Danlo looked out at the little makers of the Ring, he remembered something that a master biologist had once told him:

The rate of metabolism of energy varies according to the square of the temperature.

This was true for the fritillaries and jewel-like nektons floating above Icefall no less than the bears he had once hunted as a child or the mosquitoes that had drunk his blood. In the vast coldness of deep space, a pipal tree or a golden, glittering goswhale could be very thrifty in its use of energy. That was a grace of the Ring, its thriftiness. The little makers, for example, utilized almost every molecule of carbon dioxide and other nutrient that floated up from the lower atmosphere. As with a tropical ecosystem, the Ring concentrated these nutrients within the individual plants and organisms themselves. They excreted little waste into the stratosphere, mostly oxygen in its diatomic state which would quickly react with the sun, break down and then recombine into ozone. It was this building blanket of pale blue ozone miles above Icefall that would shield its forests and oceans from the worst of the Vild's radiations. Soon, in less than two years, the light of the supernova that had once been Merripen's Star would fall over Danlo's world with a terrible intensity of illumination. Whether or not this wavefront of hard light would be mostly reflected or absorbed by the Ring and its life-protecting ozone, not even the eschatologists could say.

The Ring is not growing as it should, Danlo thought. How he knew this was a mystery, but he was as certain of its truth as his next breath of air. *It is Hanuman's Universal Computer—it is keeping the Ring from growing.*

"It's a miracle," Demothi Bede repeated. "A miracle that this creation of the gods will keep Neverness safe from the supernova."

For a moment Danlo closed his eyes and listened to the silence of the deep sky. It was almost as if he could hear the ping of each of the millions of diamond-like little makers striking the diamond hull of his ship and spinning off into the air like tiny, ringing bells. Almost as if the Golden Ring itself could speak to him. It was possible, he knew, that this miracle of new life *would* protect his world from the supernova. But which one? There was the radiation of Merripen's Star which had crossed some thirty light-years of space on its journey towards Neverness. Perhaps if the Universal Computer were unmade, through war or the grace of Hanuman himself, the Ring would shield against this killing light. But if Bertram Jaspari and his Iviomils ever succeeded in exploding the Star of Neverness, neither the Ring nor the greatest god of the galaxy could save his world from being vaporized.

"Don't you think it's a miracle, Pilot?"

"A miracle—yes," Danlo said.

With that he pointed his ship down a steep angle of descent, following the *Ark of the Angels* into the thick air of the lower atmosphere. He fell down toward Neverness, the City of Light, where he sensed that the greatest of miracles still awaited him.

THE LORDS
OF NEVERNESS

Where are we really going? Always home.
— Novalis, Holocaust century poet

The poets say that there are only two ways to come to Neverness for the first time. A child might arrive through the bloody gate between his mother's legs, gasping his first breath of air and crying at the dazzling light of the City of Pain. Or a man might fall down from space in a lightship or ferry and step out onto an icy run of the Hollow Fields where a friend might greet him with smiles, embraces and perhaps a mug of peppermint tea steaming in the cold air.

Among the singularities of the life of Danlo wi Soli Ringess was the miracle that he had first come to the city otherwise. When only fourteen years old, he had left the island of his birth and crossed six hundred miles of the frozen ocean with his dogsled and skis. In the middle of a storm so fierce that he could hardly see his frozen feet through the wind-whipped snow, he had stumbled onto the sands of North Beach half-dead and alone. Alone and yet not alone: strangely, by chance or fate, a white-furred alien called Old Father had been waiting there to greet him and give him the bamboo flute that would become his most cherished possession. As Danlo now stepped from the pit of the *Snowy Owl,* he reflected on the irony of his homecoming. Although many must have heard the news of his arrival, neither Old Father nor any friend awaited him with musical instruments or mugs of tea. Almost the moment that his boots touched the hard surface of his world, twenty journeymen dressed in variously colored robes— but each sporting an armband of gold—converged upon him. Unbelievably, Danlo thought, the journeymen wore lasers holstered in sheaths of black leather at their sides.

"Danlo wi Soli Ringess, have you fallen well?" One of the journeymen, a rather haughty young man in the green robe of a mechanic, greeted him formally. He stared at Danlo's black robe and the diamond brooch pinned above his heart. And then he turned to Danlo's fellow ambassador. "Lord Demothi Bede, have you fallen well?"

That was the only welcome they received. Quickly, with a cold manner that bordered on rudeness, the journeymen ushered Danlo and Lord Bede into a large sled waiting on one of the nearby glidderies. One of the journeymen sat at the front of this black-shelled sled to pilot it while two others sat beside Danlo and Lord Bede in the passenger seat. The remaining seventeen journeymen took their places in the seventeen other sleds lining the gliddery. Although they extended no friendship towards these two enemy ambassadors of their Order, they would escort them through the streets of Neverness in safety and great style.

Before they began their short journey through the city, however, five pilots dressed in light wool kamelaikas approached the open sled. They stepped carefully across the gliddery's slick, red ice. Each of these five, too, wore a golden band around the upper arm—gold against midnight black, the very symbol of Ringism.

"Hello, Pilot," the first of them said to Danlo. This was Nicabar Blackstone, a hard-faced man with hard gray eyes and a shock of precisely cut gray hair. His lightship, the *Ark of the Angels,* lay ready on the run for a return to near space. Lined up behind it like long silver beads on a strand of wire were the *Infinite Dactyl,* the *Blue Lotus,* the *Diamond Arrow* and the *Bell of Time.* Behind Nicabar stood Dario of Urradeth, Cham Estarei, Ciro Dalibar and the Visolela. Each of them greeted Danlo and Demothi Bede in turn. And then Nicabar said, "Word has arrived that the Second Vild Mission has been successful. It's said that Tannahill has been found, and that Danlo wi Soli Ringess was the pilot who found it. That he crossed the entire Vild into the Perseus Arm. Thirty thousand light-years through the Vild! Is that true, Danlo wi Soli Ringess?"

"Yes," Danlo said, and then bowed his head slightly. "It is true."

"Then you are to be honored."

"Thank you . . . for honoring me," Danlo said.

Nicabar Blackstone bowed deeply to Danlo, as did Cham Estarei, Dario of Urradeth and even the Visolela, with her thin, old body and stiff joints. Only Ciro Dalibar held back, snapping his little head at Danlo in a quick mockery of a bow as if he were a turtle. His little eyes regarded Danlo coolly and jealously, but when Danlo tried to look at him, he turned his face down toward the gliddery as if he were a newcomer to Neverness marveling that the streets of the city were made of colored ice.

"But I won't honor your embassy to our Order," Nicabar said. "It isn't worthy of a pilot who has mastered the Vild—and the son of Mallory Ringess himself!"

"We seek only to stop this war," Danlo said. "Is this so dishonorable?"

"You *bring* war to our city—to all the Civilized Worlds. You who have betrayed our Order to join what you call a Fellowship of Free Worlds."

"No—we would bring peace. There must be a way towards peace."

"Peace on *your* terms," Nicabar said. "Such a peace can only inflame the desire for war."

Until now Demothi Bede had remained silent, letting the two pilots argue among themselves as pilots are wont to do. But then he looked at Ciro Dalibar who was staring at Danlo openly with a silent, burning rage. "It would seem," Demothi said, "that there are those of your Order who desire war merely for the sake of war."

Ciro scowled at this, looking back and forth between Demothi and Danlo. In his high, angry voice, he said, "It's too bad that you *ambassadors* will be safe in the city while we *pilots* risk our lives in space to protect you from your own Fellowship when it attacks us."

"And as for that," Nicabar broke in, "you should be aware that things are very different in Neverness than when you deserted her five years ago. We'll try to ensure your safety, but there are many who won't welcome you, either as ambassadors or as wayless."

"I am sorry, but I am not familiar with that word," Danlo said.

Ciro Dalibar shot Danlo a quick, cruel look, and he was only too happy to explain this term in Nicabar's place. "There are those who follow the way of Mallory Ringess into godhood. And there are those who refuse to realize the truths of Ringism and turn their faces from the way. These are the wayless."

"I see."

"Some, of course, have never heard the truth so it's our glory to bring it to them."

"I see," Danlo said in a voice as deep and calm as a tropical sea.

But his equipoise seemed only to enrage Ciro further, for he stared at Danlo and half-shouted, "And you—you're the worst of the wayless! You helped make Ringism into a force for truth, and then you just betrayed us! You betrayed your own father and everything he lived for."

Danlo had no answer for this, in words. He only looked at Ciro, and suddenly his dark blue eyes deepened like liquid jewels alive with an intense inner light. Because Ciro couldn't bear the sheer wildness and truth of this gaze, he muttered something about traitors and then stared down at the ice in silence.

"We'll say farewell, now," Nicabar Blackstone said. "The lords are waiting for you and we must return to the stars. I'm only sorry that in the coming battles, I won't have the chance to test myself against the pilot who mastered the Vild."

With that he bowed to Danlo with perfect punctilio and led the other pilots back across the gliddery's ice to their ships. It took them only a moment to fire their rockets and a few moments more to shoot off into the deep blue sky.

The tall, serious journeyman who had his hand on the throttle of Danlo's and Demothi's sled, turned to look at his two passengers. "Are you ready, Pilot? Lord Ambassador?"

"Yes," Danlo said. "Please."

"Very well. My name is Yemon Astoret, if you should need to address me."

All at once the seventeen sleds fired their own rockets, and eight of these thundered down the gliddery ahead of Danlo's sled. Then, with a jolt, he felt his sled begin to move, sliding across the red ice on its gleaming chromium runners. The remaining eight sleds followed them across the Hollow Fields northward into the city that had once been his home.

"So this is Neverness." The Ede hologram, projected out of the devotionary computer that Danlo carried on his lap, seemed to be drinking in the splendor of the city as if he were as alive as Demothi Bede or Danlo. "The City of Man."

Many call Neverness by many names, but all call her beautiful. Once, Danlo had thought of this beauty as *shona-manse*, the beauty that men and woman make with their hands. But there is always beauty inside beauty, and Neverness had been built inside a half-ring of three of the most beautiful mountains in the world. Adjoining the Hollow Fields, almost so close that Danlo could have reached his out his hand into the cold air and touched it, was Urkel, a great cone of basalt and granite and fir trees gleaming in the sun. And to the north, Attakel the Infinite, with its jagged, white-capped peak pointing the way toward the heavens for all to see. Just below Attakel, where the city rises up against the mountain, Danlo could make out the stunning rock formations of the Elf Garden where he had once gone to meditate as a journeyman. And far across the city to the northwest—across a narrow sound of the ocean which froze hard and fast in winter—he saw his favorite of the three mountains, Waaskel. It was Waaskel, this shining, white horn, that had guided him when he had first come to Neverness from a very different direction so many years before.

Losas shona, he thought. *Shona eth halla.*

Halla was the beauty of nature, and the glory of Neverness as a city was to mirror the natural beauty of Neverness Island itself. As Danlo rocketed slowly along the broad orange sliddery connecting the Hollow Fields to the Academy, he marveled at the great gleaming spires built of white granite or diamond or organic stone. There were the spires of the Old City, numerous, lovely and ancient, and the more recently built spires such as those named for Tadeo Ashtoreth and Ada Zenimura. And the most recent of all, Soli's Spire, named for Danlo's grandfather. This needle of pink granite was the tallest in the city. At the end of the Pilot's War, when a hydrogen bomb had destroyed much of the Hollow Fields and the surrounding neighborhoods, Mallory Ringess had ordered it raised up as part of his rebuilding program. This newly-made part of the city he called, simply, the New City, and it was these well-ordered blocks and graceful buildings through which the procession of sleds escorting Danlo now passed.

"I was in the Timekeeper's Tower when the bomb exploded," Demothi told Danlo above the wind whipping through the open sled. "I saw the mushroom cloud rise over this part of the city. And after, the utter ruin of streets that I had skated as a child. Every tower of the Fields broken, blown down. Almost every building. And look at it now! There's no sign of the war, is there?"

Danlo looked out at the shopfronts and the many people coming and going from the various apartments giving out onto the street. Many of these buildings, with their pink granite and sweeping garlands of icevine flowers, reminded him of similar architecture he had seen all throughout the Old City. All kinds of people thronged the sliddery itself, making travel slow. He saw wormrunners, courtesans, astriers, harijan, hibakusha and of course many ordermen skating in the lanes to the side of them.

The Academy Sliddery, as this street had been called for three thousand years, was one of the oldest in the city and usually one of the busiest. And now, on this 98th day of false winter in the year 2959 since the founding of Neverness, it seemed much as it always had at this time of day in this fairest of seasons. The air had fallen warm enough to melt the sliddery's orange ice, and a sheen of water slickened its smooth surface. Songbirds warbled from their roosts in the elaborate stonework of the buildings while frittilaries swarmed the icevine flowers or the snow dahlia bursting from the planters in front of many restaurants. These were *real* fritillaries, insects with their lovely violet wings, not the organisms of Golden Ring named for them. They added to the brightness and gaiety of the street; looking at them fluttering about in their thousands, it was almost impossible not to feel a certain peace.

And yet beneath the surface serenity of a typical false winter day, Danlo saw signs of war. *Not* the Pilot's War that had befallen Neverness when he was still a child, but the coming war, the one he must stop even if it cost him his life. To begin with, too many people were wearing gold. Wormrunners and astriers and even harijan in their billowing pantaloons—many of them wore at least one garment that had been dyed a golden hue.

All the courtesans, he saw, in their two or three-piece silken pyjamas, were dressed wholly in gold, a clear sign that their Society had wholly converted to Ringism. And all the ordermen wore bands of gold, often sewn into the very fabric of their robes. Five times he saw ordermen actually wearing golden robes, and these were not grammarians as their color once would have shown, but rather a horologe, a librarian, a cantor, a notationist and a holist. *These* five women and men wore armbands colored red, brown, gray, maroon and cobalt to distinguish their respective professions. The most devoted of the Order's Ringists, who called themselves godlings, prided themselves on beginning a trend which they hoped would spread throughout the halls of the Academy; soon, it was said, even the Lord of the Order himself, Audric Pall, would take off his cetic's orange robe and don one of purest gold.

Even the bustle of the street heralded the opposite of peace. Danlo saw too many sleds laden with furs or foodstuffs or other goods that people might hoard if the times grew violent. With the sliddery so crowded, it was the slowest journey he ever remembered making between the Fields and the Academy. At the intersection of the great East-West sliddery, the second longest street in the city, a sled had run out of hydrogen and stood blocking traffic. There was a snarl of stalled sleds and frustrated skaters backed up along both slidderies; many people were shouting and pushing their way through the manswarms as if they had forgotten every social grace.

A fight broke out between two wormrunners. One of these, a large, black-bearded man bedecked in black sable furs and diamonds, whipped out a laser from a hidden holster and fairly shoved it in the other wormrunner's face. He threatened to burn through his eyes and boil his brains. And then, realizing that the penalty for the crime of keeping a laser would be banishment from the city, he put away this vicious weapon and quickly skulked off into the crowd. That wormrunners might now carry lasers instead of their usual knives alarmed Danlo; that no one tried to chastise the wormrunner or seemed to regard his open display of outlawed technology as unusual alarmed him even more.

But they traversed the remaining seven long blocks to the Academy without further incident. And then they came to the scorched steel doors of the Wounded Wall, which surrounded the Academy to the south, west and north. The gates to this high granite barrier stood open awaiting their arrival. Danlo remembered that when he had been a journeyman, they always closed at night, making it necessary for him and Hanuman li Tosh and other friends to climb its rough stone blocks in their forbidden forays into the Farsider's Quarter. Now, Yemon Astoret said, the gates were often closed during the day—for the first time since the Dark Year when the Order's schools on eight hundred worlds had been burned in the Architect religious riots and the Great Plague had come to Neverness. Now, Yemon said as if addressing two novices, the Lords of the Order feared that the astrier and harijan sects might riot under intense pressure to convert to Ringism. Or warrior-poets might try to storm through the gates on a mission of assassination. There were too many warrior-poets in the city; over the last year, these bringers of death in their rainbow robes had flocked to Neverness like goshawks gathering for a killing frenzy.

As the procession of sleds passed through the South Gate and threaded through the Academy's narrow red glidderies, Danlo filled with memories as if he were drinking an ocean. He gazed at the beloved Morning Towers of Resa, the Pilot's College where he had spent his early manhood learning the mathematics of the manifold. Almost in the shadow of these twin pillars of the sun were the Rose Womb Cloisters, the buildings housing the salt water tanks where he had floated and practiced his arts of hallning, adagio and zazen.

He saw many journeyman pilots in their black kamelaikas skating the glidderies leading to the Cloisters or to Resa Commons. He couldn't help but feel a camaraderie and compassion for them; many of them, he supposed, would be pressed into piloting lightships in the coming war before they had quite mastered their art. He wanted to stop his sled, to skate over to a group of these young pilots and tell them that he, too, had been elevated to a full pilotship at a very young age and had taken a lightship into the Vild before he was quite ready. But in their flashing eyes and anxious faces, he saw no welcome. They well knew who he was and why he had returned to Neverness. One of them, a burly man who was said to be the secret son of Lord Burgos Harsha, actually spat at the ice as Danlo's sled moved past, and in a rather loud, braying voice called out, "The wayless return." Several of his friends, who all wore golden armbands, picked up the cue and cried out the newly popular saying, "Wayless, godless, hopeless."

As they passed beneath the great old yu trees lining the streets and gracing the Academy's lawns, other ordermen—akashics, tinkers, mechanics, and imprimaturs—greeted them in a similar manner. Danlo could only imagine what insults might await him in the College of the Lords. He didn't have to wait long. Soon the sleds rounded the gliddery that runs past the Timekeeper's Tower, and in a few more moments glided to a rest outside a square building faced with huge slabs of white granite.

The College of the Lords was nestled between the Academy's cemetary to the south and the lovely Shih Grove just to the north; to the east, the grounds gave way to the rising slopes of the Hill of Sorrows, still covered with purple and white wildflowers, late in the season though it was. Danlo and Demothi thanked Yemon Astoret and the other journeymen for their accompaniment, but, of course, their little mission was not finished. They insisted on escorting them up the steps and into an anteroom off the College's main council chamber. There, a red-robed horologe named Ivar Luan bowed to them and immediately led them through a pair of sliding wooden doors into a circular chamber where the Lords of the Order had gathered.

Once before Danlo had been invited into this place of history and great moment. With its circular walls of polished white granite and the great clary dome high above, it was a dazzlingly bright room but also drafty and always cold. He remembered how he had once knelt on the cold black floor stones before some of these very men and women (one of whom had been Demothi Bede).

But now, since he and Demothi were no longer of the Old Order, they were not bidden to kneel on a Fravashi carpet according to tradition, but rather provided chairs on which to sit before the watchful eyes of a hundred and twenty lords. These tense men and women waited at their little crescent tables arrayed in a half-circle around four chairs in the center of the room.

Danlo, who had always hated sitting in chairs, took his seat with great disquiet, and he wondered at the two empty chairs next to him. As before, he smelled jewood polished with lemon oil and the reek of many old people's fear. The greatest lords sat directly across from him at the two center tables. Danlo knew many of them quite well, especially Kolenya Mor, the Lord Eschatologist who played with the silken folds of her new golden robe. Kolenya was plump, moon-faced, intelligent and kind—and utterly beguiled by this new religion called Ringism. She was a bold women and also the first lord to trade in her traditional robe for a new one of gold. Also at her table were Jonath Parsons, Rodrigo Diaz, Mahavira Netis and Burgos Harsha with his plain brown robe and glass-pocked face.

At the other center table sat Ian Kutikoff, the Lord Semanticist, and Eva Zarifa in a purple robe displaying not one but two golden armbands. Next to her, old Vishnu Suso shifted about in his chair, all the while staring at Danlo and fingering his armband as if he suddenly found it too tight. He seemed uncomfortable sharing so close a physical space with the other lord at the end of the table, Audric Pall, the Lord of the Order himself.

And no wonder, for Danlo had never seen a more horrible human being in all his life. It almost hurt him even to look at Lord Pall, with his pink, albino's eyes and skin as white as bleached bone. This rare genetic deformity was accentuated by his black teeth, revealed whenever he spoke or smiled, which was not often. Lord Pall liked to communicate only by using his hands and fingers, making the little cetic signs which the journeyman cetic sitting by his side like a parratock bird translated into spoken language. He was as silent as a cetic, as the saying goes, and also cynical, subtle and wholly corrupt in his spirit.

Eli los shaida, Danlo thought. *Shaida eth shaida.*

Lord Pall lifted his finger slightly, and the cetic sitting at his side—a handsome young man with the blond hair and ferocious blue eyes of a Thorskaller—spoke in his place: "Have you fallen well, Lord Demothi Bede? Danlo wi Soli Ringess? We wish you well. We accept you as the legitimate ambassadors of the Fellowship of Free Worlds, though you should know that we do not accept the legitimacy of the Fellowship itself.''

"Perhaps in time that will change,'' Demothi said.

"Perhaps,'' Lord Pall said through his mouthpiece. But his little pink eyes betrayed no sign that he thought this might be possible. "Time is strange, isn't it? We have so little of it. At this moment, the wavefront from the supernova is falling toward us at the speed of light. And perhaps the fleet of your Fellowship approaches even more quickly. And these aren't even the most immediate dangers that we face.''

"Of what dangers do you speak, my Lord?'' Demothi asked.

"That you will soon know,'' Lord Pall replied. He turned to look at a journeyman horologe standing by the doors to a second anteroom across the chamber. The horologe bowed his head, then drew the laser that he wore in a holster at his hip. He very warily opened the anteroom's doors. Two men were waiting for him there, and, with a wave of his laser, he escorted them into the chamber toward Danlo and Demothi Bede and the two empty chairs.

"No!'' Danlo suddenly said, forgetting all restraint. Then, realizing that he had spoken out of place, he held his head as still as a thallow as he locked eyes on these two men whom he knew too well.

"I see that you're acquainted,'' Lord Pall said. "But allow me to present our guests to the rest of the College: Malaclypse Redring of Qallar, and Bertram Jaspari of Tannahill.''

At the saying of this name, a hundred lords gasped as if sharing a single breath. From lost Tannahill, thirty thousand lightyears across the stars, Bertram Jaspari had come to Neverness even as Danlo had come. With his pointed, bald head and skin discolored blue from the *mehalis* disease common to Tannahill, he was an ugly man—perhaps the ugliest whom Danlo had ever known. His mouth was as small and puckered as a dried bloodfruit and his eyes cold and dead-gray like rotting seal flesh. His whole face seemed set with a permanent sneer. And all these eyecatching physical features bespoke only the work of his surface self; his true ugliness went much deeper. Danlo knew him to be devious, vain, stingy, cruel and utterly lacking in grace. And worse, he had no care for any human being other than himself, and worse still, he liked using others in his lust to grab power. And perhaps worst of all, he was small in his spirit, small and twisted like a plant deformed by lack of water and sunlight. If he had competed with Lord Pall to see which one of them could best embody pure *shaida,* it would have been hard to judge the winner.

"You are a liar and a murderer," Danlo whispered as Bertram Jaspari let himself down into the chair next to him. "A murderer of a planet and a whole people."

Bertram Jaspari pretended that he hadn't heard these soft yet fierce words of Danlo. He seemed afraid to meet Danlo's blazing blue eyes. He just sat in his jewood chair, adjusting the folds of his kimono, the traditional garment of the Architects of the Infinite Intelligence of the Cybernetic Universal Church. Scarcely a year earlier, in the War of Terror which he had inflicted upon Tannahill, he had dyed his kimono a bright red as a sign of his willingness to shed blood. (Though as far as Danlo knew, he had shed only the blood of his fellow Architects and never his own.) All of the fanatical sect called the Iviomils now wore these same, ugly kimonos. Somewhere in space, perhaps hiding behind a nearby star, Bertram's fleet of Iviomils would be waiting to shed more blood or to accomplish a much more *shaida* purpose.

Next to him, above the remaining empty chair, stood a man who seemed his opposite. He wore a dazzling, rainbow-colored robe and a single red ring on the little finger of either hand. Like all warrior-poets, Malaclypse Redring was physically beautiful. His skin was like burnished copper; his hair was black and shiny as a sable's fur. Everything about him rippled with an intense aliveness, especially his eyes, all violet and deep and quick. He, at least, dared to meet Danlo face to face. While the eyes of every lord in the chamber nervously regarded him and wondered why he remained standing, he turned his head to look at Danlo and seek out his fierce gaze. As they had twice before, they locked eyes and stared at each other for a long time. The light streaming deep in Danlo's eyes seemed to draw him like a fritillary to a star, and yet something he saw there must have unnerved him, too, for without warning he suddenly looked away. No one, it is said, can stare down a warrior-poet, especially only the second one in history to wear two red rings, and the hundred and twenty lords sitting safely behind their tables looked back and forth between Danlo and Malaclypse, afraid to believe the truth of what they had just seen.

Malaclypse Redring, too, was afraid, though he had no qualms about letting his fear be known. Once more he looked at Danlo, and told him, "You've changed, Pilot. Again. Every time I see you, you grow closer to who you really are. And what is that? I don't know. It's something almost too bright. I look at you, and I see a terrible beauty. I'm afraid of you, and I don't know why."

It is said that warrior-poets fear nothing in the universe, especially death, which they seek with all the concentration and joy of a tiger stalking his prey. For all Malaclypse Redring's words about being afraid of Danlo, he was still very much like a tiger: beautiful and dangerous. In truth, he was no less a murderer than Bertram Jaspari. The horologe who had escorted him into the chamber waited only a few paces away with his laser targeting the back of his neck. He never took his eyes off this deadly warrior-poet; if Malaclypse should suddenly decide to assassinate Danlo or Demothi Bede—or even Lord Pall—the horologe stood ready to execute him instantly.

"Won't you please take your seat?" Lord Pall said to him.

Slowly, with exquisite control of every nerve and muscle, Malaclypse sat down next to Bertram Jaspari. But he ignored Lord Pall and everyone else in the room. Again, he locked eyes with Danlo, and this time he held his gaze for the count of twenty heartbeats.

"I must apologize," Lord Pall said, "for not informing the College of these men's arrival. But you must understand: a warrior-poet who wears two red rings and the leader of the Iviomil Architects who—"

Here, Bertram Jaspari silenced the cetic who spoke for Lord Pall, saying, "You may address me as the Holy Ivi of the Cybernetic Universal Church."

Lord Pall hated to be interrupted, but he showed little sign of his emotions. As he stared at Bertram Jaspari, his face remained as silent as a cetic's. Only the artery of his throat, which Danlo could see jumping beneath his white, withered skin across thirty feet, betrayed his sudden and secret wrath.

"Holy Iviii, as you say," Lord Pall said, speaking in his own voice, which hissed with venom like that of a Scutari seneschal. "The Holy Ivi has led a fleet of ships from Tannahill, and around which star they wait, no one knows. The Holy Ivi must soon send word of his safety to this fleet; if he does not—or can not—he threatens terrible things. To ensure his safety, I have withheld the fact of his arrival from the College until now. Again, my apologies, my fellow lords."

Burgos Harsha, who had never supported Lord Pall's rise to the Lordship of the Order, called out in his raspy voice, "What things does he threaten, then? Why weren't we told of this threat?"

"That you will soon know," Lord Pall said—this time through the mouth of his interpreter.

"How soon, then?" Burgos Harsha bellowed out with all the forbearance of a shagshay bull in rut.

"Soon, soon," Lord Pall said. He began drumming his bony white fingers against the resonant jewood of the tabletop. This might have been a secret communication to the cetic attending him—or merely a sign that he was as impatient as Burgos Harsha.

"What do we wait for?"

"For Hanuman li Tosh to arrive," Lord Pall said. "I've asked him to attend this meeting."

This news, while exciting the hopes of Kolenya Mor and other lords who fairly worshipped Hanuman as the Lord of the Way of Ringess, did not please everyone. Vishnu Suso sat quite close to Lord Pall, and he eyed him suspiciously as he fingered the folds of his old, black skin. "Is this wise?" he asked. "Is this a precedent we wish to set?"

And Burgos Harsha quickly added, "He's Lord of the Way, but no lord of the Order."

Eva Zarifa, an elegant woman with a rather quick and sardonic smile, reminded the lords, "Having abjured his vows five years ago, Hanuman li Tosh is no longer even *of* the Order."

For some time, the lords debated the proper relationship between the Way of Ringess (and Hanuman li Tosh) and the Order. Some lords, such as Burgos Harsha, argued for a strict separation between these two powers; while the Order might change its ancient rule against allowing its members any sort of religiosity and actually encourage the following of the Way, it would be wrong to identify the Order's purpose too closely with this new religion. Others, however, pointed out that most ordermen had already become Ringists. Their purpose was to become gods, and therefore the Order must evolve toward an exploration of how this great purpose might be achieved. They favored an *evolution* of the Order to include the tenets of Ringism and a cooperation with Hanuman and his godlings in bringing word of the Way to the stars. But the Order, they said, must always remain the Order; and the power to decide the Order's fate must remain in the hands of the College of Lords.

Still a third group of these exalted men and women—led by Kolenya Mor—believed that the Order and the Way of Ringess were destined to merge as a single and gloriously powerful entity. Already, most of the peoples of the Civilized Worlds saw the Order as merely an arm of Ringism—or Ringism as a tool of the ancient and still mighty Order. Kolenya Mor told her peers that the sooner they exchanged their colored robes for ones of gold, the easier would be the inevitable transition of the Order into a truly irresistible power.

"We should all accept Hanuman li Tosh's vision and leadership," she said. "Even if he isn't technically a lord, he has earned the right to be called Lord Hanuman—no one more so. We should welcome him here today as if he is still of the Order. He never abjured his vows, as some believe. After all, he was forced to leave us only because of the injunction against the holding of religious office. This was the Timekeeper's rule and has since been changed. Indeed, I propose that all such as Hanuman who have been unjustly driven from the Order should be allowed to renew their vows and—"

"This isn't the time for such a discussion," Lord Pall interrupted through the young cetic next to him. "I've asked Hanuman here today because events have moved to threaten all our lives. And Hanuman is involved in deciding how this threat must be met."

As if Lord Pall had given a cue, at that moment the doors to the first anteroom slid open and Hanuman li Tosh strode into view. Molded to his shaved head was a diamond clearface, a glittering computer that enabled him almost continually to interface other and greater computers, perhaps, Danlo thought, even the Universal Computer itself. This symbol of his secret powers riveted the stares of Lord Pall and everyone else sitting at their little tables.

Although Hanuman had grown no taller since he and Danlo had last parted, he seemed mysteriously to have gained in stature. Dressed as he was in a long and perfectly fitted robe of gold, with his dazzling smile, he was like a sun filling up the room. But it wasn't just his charisma or otherworldly beauty that transfixed the lords. There was something deeper, an intense inner fire connecting him to the suffering of his own soul—and to the secret suffering of all those who came close to him. He seemed always to be looking inside himself at a fiery and terrible place that others refused to see. It was his pride that he could bear a burning that would destroy a lesser being. And burn he did, not only in his spirit, but in his body which moved as if each cell were being heated by a separate, tiny, red-hot flame. Danlo felt certain that if he could have touched Hanuman's forehead, the skin would have been hot as with fever; watching Hanuman as he glided over the black floorstones, it was almost as if his eyes could see into the

infrared and thus descry the waves of heat emanating from Hanuman's hands, his heart, his nobly-shaped head. Strangely, little of
this inner fire communicated itself through his eyes. Hanuman
had cold eyes, hellish eyes, ice-blue like a sled dog's. *Shaida eyes,*
Danlo thought for the ten thousandth time. In Hanuman's eyes
were impossible dreams and cold, crystalline worlds devoid of
love or true life—as well as a cold, terrible, beautiful will towards
perfection. It was his will, above all else, that marked him as
different than others. It was why even Lord Pall feared him. In all
Hanuman's life, he had met only one other man whose will
matched his own, and that was Danlo wi Soli Ringess. Once, he
had loved Danlo as his deepest friend, but now the hatred was
there for all to see, filling up his eyes with a pale, cold fury.

"Hello, Danlo," Hanuman said as he paused before his chair
at the center of the room. He spoke fluidly and easily as if he had
happened to meet an acquaintance on the street. He took little
notice of Bertram Jaspari or Malaclypse Redring and none at all
of the hundred and twenty lords waiting for him to sit down. "I
didn't think that I'd ever see you again—but somehow I knew I
would."

"Hello, Hanuman. I am glad to see you."

"Are you? Are you?"

Danlo tried to smiled at Hanuman but could not; he touched
eyes with him, and it was as if two blue icicles were being driven
into his brain.

I must not hate him, he thought. *I must not hate.*

"I am glad to see . . . for myself what you have become,"
Danlo said. He gazed into Hanuman's eyes, and he disappeared
into a world of memory and pain.

"You shouldn't have returned, you know. But you always had
to follow your fate, didn't you?"

"But, Hanu, it was you who always spoke of the need to love
one's fate."

"And you who wanted to love one's life."

"Truly, to love life, itself . . . yes."

"Is that why you've returned, then, out of love?"

The strange turn of this conversation amused Danlo, but it also
disturbed him deeply. He felt the eyes of a hundred lords searching his face for falsity or truth. From the chair next to him, Malaclypse Redring watched like a tiger for any sign of hesitation or
weakness, and Bertram Jaspari stared at him as well. It was unseemly to hold such an intimate discussion with all the Lords of
Neverness and the whole universe watching and waiting. But if

his fate had truly led him to such a strange moment, then he would embrace it, wildly, with all the force of his will.

"I still love you," he said to Hanuman without shame. In his marvelous voice there was an utter openness and truth. "I always will."

This simple statement fairly astonished the lords. It astonished Hanuman, too. He looked at Danlo, and for a moment all the hurts and betrayals of the past years evaporated like ice crystals beneath a hot sun, and there was nothing between them except the truth of who they really were. For a moment, there was love. But then there was the other thing, too. Hanuman couldn't bear the light in Danlo's dark, wild eyes, and he wanted to look away. It was his hell that he could not. It was both their hells that Danlo always reminded him of the one thing in the universe that he feared above all else.

How he fears, how he hates, Danlo thought. *And I have made him hate; I have made him who he is.*

Without another word, Hanuman bowed to Danlo and then stepped over to the table nearest Lord Pall's. He took his seat in an empty chair between Alesar Druze and the elegant Okalani wi Nori Chu. From this central position he could easily observe the faces of Danlo and the others sitting near him, or turn to exchange meaningful looks with Lord Pall.

"We will now hear from the Holy Ivi Bertram Jaspari, as he calls himself," Lord Pall said. "And then I will ask the warrior-poet to speak. And lastly, the ambassadors from the Fellowship. I invite any lord to interrupt with questions as necessary. This may seem an unprecedented barbarism, I know, but these are unprecedented times. Never in our history have we held a conclave with so many different powers. And never—not even during the War of the Faces—has the potential for power to destroy us all been so grave. So then, Holy Ivi, if you please."

Bertram Jaspari, sitting in his chair next to Danlo, smoothed out the folds of his clumsily dyed red kimono. He opened his little mouth to speak, but precisely at that moment, Danlo interrupted him before he could give voice to his first word.

"The Holy Ivi of the Cybernetic Universal Church," Danlo said, "is Harrah Ivi en li Ede. This man tried to murder her and take her place."

At this, Bertram Jaspari glared hatred at Danlo for a moment, but said nothing.

"That may be true," Lord Pall said. "But he comes to us as the leader of the Iviomils whose fleet of ships has set forth among the stars. For the time, we'll respect whatever title he chooses to bestow upon himself. So then, Holy Ivi, if you please.''

Bertram Jaspari adjusted the padded brown dobra covering the pointed bones of his head. Again he began to speak, and for the time no one gainsaid him.

''My Lords of the Order of Mystic Mathematicians and Other Seekers of the Ineffable Flame,'' he said with grave formality. ''You must know that we Iviomils are the true Architects of the Infinite Intelligence of the Cybernetic Universal Church. You must know that the name of this Intelligence is Ede, the God, the Infinite—the Master Architect of the Universe.''

At the saying of this name, the Ede hologram glowing above Danlo's devotionary computer flashed Danlo a knowing look and actually winked at him. Danlo had set the computer on the arm of his chair in plain sight of Bertram Jaspari, who had seen millions of such computers on Tannahill. But he had never seen a hologram of Nikolos Daru Ede programmed to act in such an intimate—and irreligious—manner. For the moment he seemed affronted and deeply suspicious. And then he returned to his speech.

''In our holy *Algorithm* it is written that, 'No god is there but God; God is one, and there can be only one God.' You must know that it is the gravest of errors for any man or woman to try to become a god in emulation of Nikolos Daru Ede. To become an accursed *hakra* and challenge the divinity of God, Himself— could there be a worse negative program than this? However, it is an error all too easy to fall into, which is why our Church has taught compassion for any and all who might become *hakras*. Is it not written that, 'It is a thousand times easier to stop a thousand men from becoming *hakras* than to stop one *hakra* from poisoning the minds of a million men'? This is why we of the Church have come to the Civilized Worlds, to help you through this difficult time when many are tempted to write their own programs and become *hakras*.''

Bertram Jaspari delivered these devious words smoothly, devoutly, and with great energy. Having learned the Language of the Civilized Worlds only on his journey from Tannahill, he spoke with a heavy accent, but he had no trouble communicating his meaning to the Lords of Neverness or to Danlo or Demothi Bede. To these two ambassadors he implied that the Iviomils would make natural allies with the Fellowship if the Order should fail to restrain the greater ambitions and hubris of Ringism. And, as slippery as a water snake, at the same time, he appealed to the

Lords of Neverness, promising that the Iviomils could help the Ringists temper their doctrines to bring their new religion in line with Ede's Program for the Universe.

But beneath his seeming congeniality and reasonableness coiled the threat of naked power. At first he was loathe to show this power for what it was. He didn't wish to shock anyone into an unreasoning opposition. He spoke only in promises and platitudes, telling the assembled lords of his hope of returning the peoples of the Civilized Worlds to Ede. As he reminded Lord Pall and everyone else, Nikolos Daru Ede had been born on Alumit, and all peoples everywhere must return to truth which He had first shown the Architects of Alumit—and Newvannia and Cilehe and all the other Civilized Worlds.

When he had finished speaking, the lords sat muttering and looking at each other, not quite wanting to believe this Holy Ivi's immense effrontery. And then Danlo, in his clear, strong voice, said, "On Tannahill, during the war that the Iviomils inflicted upon their families and friends, the Iviomils often talked of returning people to Ede. This meant . . . murdering them."

At this, Lord Pall flashed Hanuman a quick look and then sucked in a quick breath between his black teeth. He looked at Danlo and said, "If you please, will you tell us what you know about this war?"

And so Danlo told the Lords of Neverness about the War of Terror and his part in this latest schism of the Cybernetic Universal Church in which Architect had murdered Architect. He described his friendship with Harrah Ivi en li Ede; it was this remarkable woman, he said, who had found the courage to redefine the Program of Increase and the Program of Totality, the two doctrines which had led the Architects to destroy the stars of the Vild.

"Bertram Jaspari never accepted Harrah's New Program," Danlo said. "And so he began a *facifah* and brought this war to every part of Tannahill. He . . . destroyed the city of Montellivi. With a hydrogen bomb, he murdered ten million people."

Just then a pain shot through Danlo's head as if his eyes were still open to the light-flash of this bomb. Lord Pall watched as Danlo pressed his palm to his forehead, and told him, "Please go on."

"But Bertram Jaspari . . . couldn't kill every Architect who fell against him by exploding bombs," Danlo said. "When he saw that the war was lost, he fled Tannahill. All the Iviomils fled. He assembled a fleet of ships and disappeared into the stars. But before the Iviomils left the Vild, they did one more thing. A . . . truly *shaida* thing. There was a star. Thirty-seven light-years from Tannahill, the star that shined upon the planet of the Narain people. The Narain were Architects, too. Once, they were Architects. Only, they had left Tannahill to find their own way towards Ede. Heretics, Bertram Jaspari called them. And so he brought his *facifah* to the Narain. He returned them to Ede. In one of his ships, the Iviomils carry a *morrashar*. A star-killer. Bertram Jaspari ordered his Iviomils to to use this machine to destroy this star. To destroy a whole planet, a whole people. I . . . know he did. I saw the star explode. On my return through the Vild, I found the remnants of this star, the gases and radioactive dust. But there was nothing left of the Narain people."

Almost the moment that Danlo had finished speaking, Burgos Harsha slapped his hand against the top of his table so that a loud crack rang out into the room. He glared at Lord Pall and asked, "Is what the pilot says true?"

Cetics—the Lord Cetic above all others—are supposed to be able to read falsity or truth from the tells that mark a man's face. Lord Pall looked at Hanuman, who had been looking at Danlo. Hanuman softly tapped his knuckles together and held his eyes unblinking. It seeemed that he was passing secret knowledge to Lord Pall and controlling him in a secret and subtle way. After a moment, Lord Pall made a sign to his interpreter, who said, "Danlo wi Soli Ringess has always been the most truthful of men—as far as he can see what is true and what is not. But we needn't accept his word only. Look at this Holy Ivi, Bertram Jaspari! One doesn't have to be a cetic to see what is written on his face."

In truth, Bertram Jaspari, far from denying the murder of the Narain people, now fairly exulted in this terrible act. Danlo had shown him for who he really was; very well, then, he would pretend to friendship no longer. His bluish face fell through the shallow emotions of sanctity and ambition, perhaps touched with an underlying sadism. In truth, it was much to his purpose that his power be known. He looked at Lord Pall, smiled at Danlo, and then quoted from his holy *Algorithm:* "The Iviomils are those vastened in God who shall wield the light of the stars like swords."

Most of the lords sitting at their tables that day were old but far from senile. No one supposed that Bertram Jaspari was speaking metaphorically, in a spiritual sense. Lord Nitara Tan of Urradeth, Alesar Druze, Sasha Chu—they each looked at Bertram Jaspari (and at each other), and no one doubted that this ugly man meant to rule the Civilized Worlds through the threat of destroying them.

"Harrah en li Ede had fallen into negative programs," Bertram Jaspari explained. "The *Algorithm* tells us that anyone who has so fallen must be cleansed—by the fire of a *facifah,* if necessary. All peoples who deny Ede's Program for the Universe must be cleansed."

At this, Morasha the Bright, a white-haired exemplar from Veda Luz, pointed a bony finger at Bertram and asked the lords, "If this man holds the power to destroy stars, why didn't he use this *morrashar* against Tannahill's star before he fled the Vild?"

Bertram Jaspari smiled at this obvious question, then explained, "Despite what the pilot has told you, we Iviomils are not murderers. Most of our fellow Architects on Tannahill know Harrah's redefinitions of the Programs of Increase and Totality to be in error. Would you have us cleanse an entire planet merely for the negative programs of an old woman and those who support the oppression of her architectcy?"

He hopes to return to Tannahill, Danlo suddenly knew. *Someday, after regaining power, he hopes to return and rule Tannahill as the Church's Holy Ivi.*

Lord Pall watched Hanuman pursing his thin lips, and then, with a flick of his fingers, he said, "I'm afraid we must assume that Bertram Jaspari is willing and able to use this *morrashar* to destroy the Star of Neverness."

For a moment, no one spoke and no one moved. Bertram Jaspari sat staring at the lords, and his face had fallen implacable with his purpose.

Burgos Harsha, whose face had been scarred when a hydrogen bomb had blown in the windows of the Timekeeper's Tower, had a particular hatred of any man willing to explode hydrogen into light. He glared at Bertram, and in his growly old voice, he said, "It may be that this 'Holy Ivi' possesses the means to destroy our star. I've often warned against the tolerance of the forbidden technologies. But how is he to *use* this technology, this *morrashar* of which Danlo wi Soli Ringess has spoken? Wouldn't his fleet have to maneuver close to the Star of Neverness if he wishes to destroy her? And aren't our pilots adept enough to detect the Iviomil ships the moment they fall out of the manifold and destroy *them?*"

This touched off a wild round of argument as the lords broke into groups of three or four and debated the strategies that the Iviomils might use to explode their star. Finally, Lord Pall waved his hand, blinked his little pink eyes, and said, "I see that Danlo wi Soli Ringess has more to tell us."

"I do," Danlo said. He squeezed the black diamond pilot's ring that he wore around his little finger, and then said, "There is a ronin pilot who followed me into the Vild. He provided passage for Malaclypse Redring, who hoped that I would lead him to my father. Both these men followed me through the stars, all the way to Tannahill. I could not lose them."

"What was this pilot's name?" Lord Pall asked.

The lords had now fallen deathly silent, and the room was so quiet that Danlo could hear his heart beating like a drum.

"It was Sivan wi Mawi Sarkissian in the *Red Dragon*," Danlo said. "I believe that he pilots the deep ship containing the Iviomil's *morrashar*."

Again Bertram Jaspari smiled, affirming what Danlo knew to be true.

"Sivan wi Mawi Sarkissian!" Rodrigo Diaz said. Many of the lords sighed and groaned at this name, but most just continued staring at Bertram Jaspari as if they wished their vows permitted them the indulgence of murder.

"Before Sivan left the Order," Jonath Parsons said, "he was a pilot of the first rank. Perhaps the equal of Salmalin or even Mallory Ringess."

"But why would he serve a sect of star-killing fanatics?"

None of the lords had an answer to this question, not even Lord Pall who could read most men's minds as easily as he might a map of the city's streets. Hanuman's face was silent as he closed his eyes and disappeared for a moment into a private, interior world illuminated by the clearface that covered his head. And then Malaclypse Redring, who flashed Danlo a quick, almost secret smile, said, "He serves me; he serves the Order of Warrior-Poets."

"Traitor!" twenty lords shouted at once. And then fifty other voices: "Ronin! Wayless! Renegade!"

Malaclypse held up his red-ringed hands for the lords to regain their restraint and compose themselves. Then he told them, "You might do better to ask why my order has allied itself with these Iviomils of the Cybernetic Universal Church."

"Well, why have you?" Burgos Harsha asked.

"That's no mystery," Kolenya Mor said. "The warrior-poets have been trying to destroy our Order for seven thousand years."

"It . . . is more than that," Danlo said. He paused to see Hanuman eyeing him coolly, then told the lords a secret that he had shared with no one except Bardo for more than ten years. "I learned this from the warrior-poet Marek in the library—it was the day that he tried to kill Hanuman li Tosh."

Now Hanuman's eyes were as hard and cold as frozen pools of water. He must have well remembered how Marek had threatened to push his killing knife slowly up the optic nerve of his eye. Certainly he remembered the pain of his torture at Marck's hand for Marek had touched him with a dart tipped with ekkana: a drug that continued to poison him and would cause the nerves of his body to burn like fire for the rest of his life.

"Please go on," Lord Pall said to Danlo.

Danlo bowed his head to Hanuman in honor of the terrible pain that he would have to bear moment by moment forever—or until the cold hand of death fell upon his face and relieved him of his agony. Then he said, "The warrior-poets have a new rule. They would slay all potential gods. This is why Malaclypse followed me across the Vild. He hoped that I would lead him to my father. He . . . hopes to slay him."

"But your father is Mallory Ringess!" Kolenya Mor said. "He's a god!"

"How can a warrior-poet slay a god?" Nitara Tan wanted to know.

"Perhaps Mallory Ringess will return to Neverness and slay *him*," Kolenya Mor said. And then, quite pleased for the chance to affirm her faith in the First Pillar of Ringism, she went on, "One day, he will return to help show us the way towards godhood. We *will* become gods one day. If the Order of Warrior-Poets' new rule is to slay all potential gods, they should be prepared to slay half the peoples of the Civilized Worlds."

The Warrior-Poets, who believe that the universe eternally recurs in endless cycles of death and rebirth, eagerly await the supreme Moment of the Possible when all things return to their divine source. If indeed the universe had evolved close to this Moment of fire and light, then, Danlo thought, the Warrior-Poets might well be prepared to see everyone and everything slain in order to fulfill this terrible fate.

The light pouring down through the dome found the colors of Malaclypse's robe and enveloped him in a rainbow of fire. He smiled and said, "We don't seek to slay everyone who professes a wish to move godward—only those such as Mallory Ringess who may already have done so."

But why slay gods at all? As Danlo lost himself in Malaclypse's marvelous violet eyes, he wondered about the deeper purposes of the Warrior-Poets. Once, they had sought mental powers very like personal godhood, but now it was almost as if the gods themselves restrained them from this dream. *If there truly is a moment for the universe when all things become possible, if they accept the limitations of their humanity and seek this moment, why not let the gods hasten its coming?*

It was strange, he thought, that the Warrior-Poets should share a similar eschatology with the Architects. *The Algorithm* of all the Cybernetic Churches taught that there would come the Last Days at the end of time when Ede the God would grow to absorb the entire universe and, as Master Architect, make it anew in what they called the Second Creation. To test the Warrior-Poets' purposes, Danlo caught Malaclypse's gaze and then pointed at the devotionary computer sitting on the arm of his chair. "Did you know that Ede is dead? The program that runs this devotionary is all that remains of him."

Danlo then went on to recount his journey to the Solid State Entity and then to the spaces out near Gilada Luz where he had discovered the wreckage of the god that had been Ede. Ede, he said, had fought a terrible war with the Silicon God. In the last moments of their last battle, Ede had encoded the program of his selfness into a radio signal that had been received by this very devotionary computer. Now the program ran the circuitry of this little jeweled box instead of a vast machine the size of many star systems.

"Liar!" Bertram Jaspari suddenly called out. His usually blue face had reddened to a livid purple. Whatever Malaclypse thought of Danlo's story, the effects of this news on Bertram were immediate and profound. *"Naman,* liar—all *namans* are liars because they don't accept the truth of Ede's divinity. But I must tell you, Pilot, that Ede *is* God. The only God, the Infinite, the Inevitable, the Eternal. Whatever *god* you found dead in the galaxy's wastelands must have been a *hakra* slain by Ede for his hubris."

He believes his Church's myths literally, Danlo suddenly realized. Until this moment, he had supposed that Bertram had only played at devoutness, mostly for the purpose of gaining power. *This is his true danger, that he truly believes.*

"And if your father ever does return," Bertram said, "it won't be necessary for the Warrior-Poets to slay him. Ede, Himself, will slay him."

He stared straight at Danlo, then, and quoted from one of the books of *The Algorithm*: **And so Ede faced the universe, and he was vastened, and he saw that the face of God was his own.**

Then the would-be gods, who are the *hakra* devils of the darkest depths of space, from the farthest reaches of time, saw what Ede had done, and they were jealous. And so they turned their eyes godward in jealousy and lust for the infinite lights, but in their countenances God read hubris, and he struck them blind. For here is the oldest of teachings, here is wisdom: No god is there but God; God is one, and there can be only one God.

As Bertram Jaspari finished speaking with a flourish of pomposity and false reverence, Danlo looked down at the Ede hologram floating above the devotionary computer. Ede's large sensuous lips were set with determination, and his black eyes shone brightly. He flashed Danlo the cetics' finger signs that Danlo had taught him. Many of the lords in the room, of course, knew how to read such signs, but they sat too far away and their eyes were too old to descry what passed between Danlo and Ede. Hanuman, though, sat close and his vision was nearly as keen as Danlo's. So it must have mystified him to read Ede's secret communication: "I suppose this isn't the best moment to tell Bertram Jaspari that Ede, the Infinite, the Inevitable, the Eternal, asks for the return of his human body."

Danlo smiled as he stared at this representation of Nikolos Daru Ede. Ede's coffee-colored skin fairly glowed with hope and humor; once again Danlo wondered if a bit of program running a box-like computer could possibly be conscious in the same way as a man.

Finally, for the first time that day in the College of the Lords, Hanuman li Tosh spoke to the lords. He had a silver tongue and a beautiful, golden voice; his voice was his sword, and through his cetic's art he had polished and honed it until it cut to the heart of people's dreams and deepest fears.

"Of course Mallory Ringess will return to Neverness," he said. He closed his eyes suddenly, and the clearface covering his head glowed and glittered for all to see. When he turned to stare at Bertram Jaspari a moment later, he seemed to blaze with renewed energy. "Of course Mallory Ringess won't let a warrior-poet slay him. He, the greatest pilot in the history of the Order, will return to lead our ships to victory. Or he will return after Salmalin has destroyed the Fellowship's fleet. But return he will, as he promised before he left Neverness to become a god."

He turned to address Lord Pall with his hypnotic voice while his face flickered with eye shadings and little movements that only Lord Pall would understand. There were two cetic sign languages, as Danlo knew. There was the secret language of the hands and fingers, and then there was the truly secret system in which a tightening of the jaw muscles combined with a slight pause in breathing, for example, might convey light-streams of information. But only from one cetic to another. And only some cetics, those of the higher grades, ever learned this second sign system, and so it was something of a mystery how Hanuman li Tosh had acquired this knowledge. But Danlo saw that he truly had—just as he saw Hanuman's subtle and sinister power over Lord Pall.

"My Lord Cetic," he said to his former teacher and master, "something should be done with the warrior-poet."

"What do you mean?" Lord Pall asked, although he knew precisely what Hanuman meant.

"We shouldn't live in fear that he'll try to assassinate Mallory Ringess when he returns."

"No," Lord Pall agreed.

"We shouldn't live in fear of him, now, as he sits before us free to move as a tiger."

Malaclypse sat lightly in his chair and stared at Hanuman as if he were a predator intent on his prey. The muscles beneath his rainbow robe fairly trembled with tension as if he might at any moment spring into motion.

"But he *is* restrained," Burgos Harsha observed, bowing to the horologe behind Malaclypse. The horologe, whose red robe showed dark sweat-stains beneath his arms, still pointed his laser at the back of Malaclypse's neck.

"It's impossible to restrain a warrior-poet thusly," Hanuman said. "Having no fear of death, the warrior-poet could slay as he wishes. You should know, he could stick a poison needle in one of our ambassadors' necks before the horologe even realized that he had moved."

Danlo, who remembered how blindingly quick a warrior-poet could move, simply sat next to Malaclypse looking at him deeply. Demothi Bede looked at him, too; but his were the eyes of a hunted animal, and he nervously fingered the collar of his robe as if he suddenly found it too tight.

"And how would *you* restrain him, then?" Burgos Harsha asked Hanuman. "Since you think our Order's precautions insufficient?"

Hanuman smiled then, and turned to Lord Pall. He said, "With my Lord's permission, I've arranged other precautions."

Lord Pall, caught in the freeze of Hanuman's ice-blue eyes, fluttered his fingers for a moment and said, "We can't be too cautious with the warrior-poets. What arrangements have you made, Lord Hanuman?''

This was the first time that Danlo had heard Hanuman addressed as ''Lord,'' and he saw that Hanuman accepted this title as a warlord might tribute from a defeated enemy.

''*These* arrangements,'' Hanuman said in his golden voice that filled the Lords' College like sunlight. He nodded to another horologe who stood outside the door to one of the room's antechambers. The horologe opened the door, carved with the figures of some of the Order's most famous lords. And then a cadre of Ringists—six strong-looking men wearing the golden robes identical to Hanuman's—strode across the black floor and surrounded the chair where Malaclypse sat waiting for them.

''This is uncalled for!'' Burgos Harsha protested. ''These men aren't of the Order, and they have no place here!''

''No, it's just the opposite,'' Hanuman said. ''*I* have called them here—they're my personal guard. My godlings. And their place is by my side.''

So saying, he nodded at the first of the Ringists, a hard and cruel-looking man who had once been a warrior-poet before he had deserted his order to turn ronin. His eyes, perhaps destroyed in some private war or torture among his violent kind, had been replaced with jeweled eyes: cold, glittering, mechanical orbs that were horrible to look upon. And yet Malaclypse Redring, who sat so close to where this fearsome man stood, looked at him easily and penetratingly as if he could see through these twin computers straight into the man's soul. In truth, it was the ronin warrior-poet who had difficulty looking at Malaclypse. With great wariness, he removed a spinneret from a pocket of his robe. He thumbed the trigger, causing a fine jet of liquid proteins to squirt out of the nozzle. Upon contact with the room's cool air, the proteins immediately hardened into an incredibly tough filament known as acid wire. It took the ronin warrior-poet only a few moments to make many circles with the spinneret about Malaclypse, binding his arms and legs to the chair. Now, if Malaclypse made the slightest motion, the glittering wire would cut into him and touch his nerves like acid.

''This is really too much!'' Burgos Harsha protested again. He, like every other lord in the room, must have wondered (and feared) how Hanuman had managed to convert a former warrior-poet to the Way of Ringess.

And Hanuman replied, ''No, Lord Historian, again, it's just the opposite. It's really not enough.''

Hanuman nodded at the ronin, whose name was Jaroslav Bulba. Jaroslav—and one of the other golden-robed godlings—immediately began searching Malaclypse for weapons.

"But surely Malaclypse Redring has already been well-searched!"

"No, Lord Historian," Hanuman said. "He's a warrior-poet, and so surely he hasn't been searched well enough."

While the second godling, who was also a ronin warrior-poet, ran a scanner over Malaclypse's arms, torso and legs, Jaroslav Bulba dared to pick through his thick, shiny hair. Hanuman had chosen Jaroslav as leader of his personal guard for his loyalty and courage (and cruelty), and Jaroslav could scarcely wait to inflict his rage at his former order upon a warrior-poet who wore two red rings. Because he secretly feared this man who might well be able to kill him as easily as he might a furfly, he sought to face his fear in the crudest of ways. Courageously—but stupidly and for no good reason—he clamped his fingers in Malaclypse's hair and jerked his head to the right and left. It must have emboldened him to manhandle Malaclypse so, for his jeweled eyes glowed red like plasma lights. And then, as he examined the black and white curls above Malaclypse's temples, suddenly, without warning, Malaclypse opened his mouth—like a serpent about to strike with venomed fangs, or so Jaroslav must have perceived. For he immediately jumped back and knocked into the other godling, nearly causing him to drop his scanner. But Malaclypse had neither drug darts to spit at Jaroslav nor venom, but only words. "I'll remember you," he said. "When your moment of the possible comes, I'll remember who you really are."

After that, Jaroslav completed his search with the greatest circumspection if not gentleness. As did the other ronin warrior-poet. In little time, they had amassed a truly astonishing cache of weapons: red-tipped needles sewn into fabric of Malaclypse's robe; acid wire sewn *as* the fabric of his robe; plastic explosive molded into the lining of his boots; two poison teeth; a heat tlolt; two finger knives; three flesh pockets containing biologicals, most likely programmed bacteria or some sort of murderous virus; and perhaps most astonishing of all, the warrior-poet's killing knife: a long blade of diamond-steel set into a black nall haft. Surely, Danlo thought, even the most cursory of searches would have uncovered this most revered of all a warrior-poet's weapons. How Malaclypse had smuggled it into the College of Lords remained a mystery.

"It's done, Lord Hanuman," Jaroslav said. He held the

double-edged killing knife in his sweaty hand and pointed it at Malaclypse. "This warrior-poet is no danger now."

Now completely unarmed though he was, Malaclypse's eyes cut into Jaroslav like violet knives. "It's said that whoever touches a warrior-poet's knife, that knife shall touch him."

"I'll remember that," Jaroslav said, as he slipped the long knife through the black belt he wore around his robe. "I'll keep your knife, should it ever be necessary for me to touch *you.*"

Hanuman looked at Lord Pall, and he raised one eyebrow, slightly. And Lord Pall said, "It's time that we heard from the ambassadors of the Fellowship. Lord Bede, Danlo wi Soli Ringess—if you please."

"My Lords of the Order," Demothi Bede began. As eldest, both he and Danlo thought it seemly that he should speak first. "My Lords, Lord Hanuman li Tosh, we've been charged with a mission to end this war before the worst of it begins. We've been charged with the power to negotiate a peace acceptable to both the Fellowship and the Order. Danlo wi Soli Ringess and I are to remain on Neverness as long as is needed to conclude these negotiations."

He went on to make a fine little speech as to the great traditions of the Order in bringing the light of reason and the ineffable flame of truth to the Civilized Worlds. It was his hope, he said—and the hope of everyone—that reason and truth would eventually prevail.

When he had finished speaking, Hanuman glanced in Lord Pall's direction and tapped his thumbs together as he rolled his left shoulder forward slightly. And Lord Pall said, "We, too, hope that truth will prevail. In the service of truth, then, we invite you to state your demands."

"My Lord Pall, I should hardly like to begin negotiations by characterizing the Fellowship's concerns as—"

"State your demands," Lord Pall fairly snapped. Because he chafed at Hanuman's intimidation and control of him, he now sought to intimidate and control others. "We've little time for the niceties of diplomacy. With every word we waste, your fleet falls nearer to Neverness."

And so without further superfluosities, Demothi Bede was forced to tell the College of Lords the Fellowship's purpose in waging war. He accused the Order of violating the Law of the Civilized Worlds in using assembler technology to mine the moons of Neverness and construct Hanuman's Universal Computer. The Fellowship's foremost "demand," he said, must be that the Order cease the mining of these moons and disassemble the Universal Computer before the wrath of some jealous god fell upon the Civilized Worlds and destroyed them.

"Of course, the Order would be free to pursue the religion of Ringism—any person on any of the Civilized Worlds will be," Demothi said. "But the Law of the Civilized Worlds must be inviolate. We're here, in part, to negotiate a set of agreements that will ensure that Ringism doesn't lead any person or world into the black whirlpools of chaos outside the Law."

With a sigh at what he saw in the stony faces of a hundred and twenty lords staring at him, Lord Demothi Bede bowed to Danlo to indicate that he had no more to say. And then Danlo touched the poison pearl brooch pinned to his silken robes; he drew in a deep breath and began, "My Lords, there must be a way toward peace. Truly, peace is—"

But he got no further than this before Bertram Jaspari interrupted him. "This *naman,*" he said, pointing at Danlo, "has called us Iviomils terrorists and murderers. We call him a hypocrite. He speaks of peace, and of stopping war. But how does he think to bring this peace? By threatening war. By threatening Neverness with the armed terror of the Fellowship's fleet if you lords refuse to accede to his demands. Danlo wi Soli Ringess has been called Peacewise and Lightbringer, but we call him murderer: for surely the deaths of those murdered in this war will be upon his hands as much as any pilot of any lightship."

Bertram Jaspari was a sadistic and shallow man, but he was also quite shrewd in his way. He knew Danlo well enough to hurt him—or at least to cause him the gravest of doubts.

Truly, the Fellowship threatens violence no less than do the Iviomils, he thought. *And I am of the Fellowship as a hand is part of an arm.*

For a moment, it seemed that Bertram had shamed Danlo into silence. And then Danlo drew in another deep breath and said, "The Fellowship has murdered no one. I . . . have come to Neverness so that no one murders anyone. There must be a way for men and women beyond murder."

Although this was the essence of all that he had to tell the lords, he might have said still more, but just then one of Hanuman's most devoted lords, an old woman named Tirza Wen, called out from the rear of the room, "The Wayless dares to tell *us* of a way!"

And the Lord Phantast, Pedar Sulkin, said, "There *is* a way for man, of course. The Way of Ringess."

"A way for *woman*," Kolenya Mor said, eyeing Lord Sulkin with a smile. "A way for women and men to become gods. A new way for humankind."

"A new way," Hanuman said in his golden voice. He spoke with compassion and grace, but with fire, too. He looked to his right and to his left to draw the attention of all the lords in the room. "We must remember that the Way of Ringess is new. *We* must be new. We must be as godlings breaking out of the shells of the old thoughtways that have kept us from our destiny. We must fly on golden wings as we were meant to fly. Which is why we need a new law. The Law of the Civilized Worlds was made for human beings. In truth, it was made precisely to *keep* human beings human—all too human. And why? Because its makers feared our infinite possibilities. They were cowards but who can blame them? The greater the height, the greater the fall, or so it's said. But a time comes for any race when it must dare to soar beyond its deepest dreams—either that or become mired in the mudsands of evolutionary failure. This is our time. We must choose the clouds and the Golden Rings of the universe or else the mud. And haven't we already chosen? Half of the Civilized Worlds have chosen the Way of Ringess. We who wear the gold would never seek to tell the Wayless which way they must choose. But neither will we be told what our law must be. A new law—isn't it time we made a new law for the new beings we are becoming? A law for gods."

He paused a moment and then said, "But I'm only Lord of the Way of Ringess. I would never think to tell the Lords of the Order how they should respond to these ambassadors who demand such a blind adherence to the old laws."

Now, as he looked at Lord Pall, his eyes flicked to the right and to the left, and then he blinked twice, slowly. And Lord Pall, controlled by these nearly invisible strings of light, said, "It would be silly to pretend that the Order isn't involved in the Way of Ringess. Therefore, I think it appropriate that we of the Order ask Lord Hanuman's advice."

Burgos Harsha opened his mouth as if to protest Lord Pall's suggestion. But before he could speak, quicker than a silver knife flashing in the sun, Hanuman slid his voice into the room.

"These are dangerous times, and there's danger in whichever way we choose," he said. He bowed his head to Bertram Jaspari and the warrior-poet bound in gleaming filaments of acid wire. And then he bowed to Demothi Bede and finally to Danlo. "The representatives of two powers sit before us. The Fellowship demands that we disassemble the greatest of our works and obey their law. The Iviomils demand even more: that they should rule the Civilized Worlds and we become their slaves. You should know, this is what they really desire. But who can become a slave who has almost become a god? For myself, I would choose death rather than submission to another's power. But even if I were willing to be a slave—even if we all were—there's no safety in such cravenness.

"We live in dangerous times—I can't say that often enough. The gods make war upon each other, and if Danlo wi Soli Ringess can be believed, even Ede the God has been destroyed. And then there are the Iviomils. With their *morrashar,* the Iviomils destroy the stars. They threaten to destroy *our* star. Are we to face such power with the weakness of slaves? Or with the glory of gods? This I know; this I've seen: it's only in becoming gods that we shall ever be safe from the gods. And safe from those such as the Iviomils and the warrior-poets who would slay all godlings. It's a paradox, I know, but the way of the greatest danger is also the safest. We are millions of millions; we are stardust; we are golden—can even the greatest of gods stop us from exploding across the universe?"

Few of the lords sitting at their tables that day had any wish to become anyone's slave. For three thousand years, the Order had been the greatest power among the Civilized Worlds, and the Lords of the Order had grown as sure of their power as a wealthy man is of a never-ending supply of wine and food. But at this critical moment in history, they feared losing their power—and losing the war that threatened not only their lives but their very world.

"What shall we do about the Fellowship, then?" Burgos Harsha asked. "And the Iviomils: we can't simply expect them to be awed by our dreams and go away."

"No," Hanuman said, "that's true. Which is why we must awe them otherwise."

"How, then?"

"We shall hunt them down as thallows do sleekits. Sivan wi Mawi Sarkissian may be the equal of Salmalin, but he can't evade the Order's finest pilots forever."

"But he doesn't have to evade them forever. Only long enough to destroy the Star of Neverness."

"I've considered this danger," Hanuman said. He placed his fingertips against his temple, and the neurologics inside the diamond clearface covering his head glowed like a million purple snakes. "The chances of Sivan successfully falling out around our star while our lightships guard her approach zero. Therefore the Iviomils must have a secret strategy—and what is that?"

"I'm an historian, not a warrior," Burgos Harsha said. "How should I know their strategy?"

"I'm no warrior either," Hanuman said. This, as Danlo knew, was not really true. Hanuman had studied the killing arts since childhood, and he came to war as easily as a snow leopard comes into his claws. "But I *am* a cetic," Hanuman continued. "That is, the cetics once graced me with training in their art. It's as a cetic that I look at Bertram Jaspari now. And what do I see?"

At this, Burgos Harsha and a hundred lords turned to look at Bertram Jaspari, who sat beaming hatred at Hanuman. And then Kolenya Mor said, "What *do* you see, Lord Hanuman?"

"He is waiting," Hanuman said. "If the Fellowship's fleet should attack ours here, in the spaces near the Star of Neverness, the manifold will blaze with lights like fireworks at Year's End. In this chaos, the tells of a single deepship falling out into realspace would be almost impossible to detect."

As Hanuman revealed Bertram's secret strategy, Bertram's face fell mottled into shades of red and cyanine blue. Clearly, he had gambled on cowing the Order into submitting to his demands—otherwise he never would have risked himself in coming to Neverness. But now that it seemed his strategy had failed, he glared at Hanuman in deathly silence.

"As I've said, I'm no warrior," Hanuman continued. "But surely this suggests our strategy. We must attack the Fellowship's fleet before they attack us."

"And leave Neverness and our star naked to the Iviomils?" Burgos Harsha asked.

"Oh, no—of course not," Hanuman said. "We'll leave fifty lightships to guard her. And twenty-five more to hunt down the Iviomils. Even thus diminished, our fleet's ships will still outnumber the Fellowship's almost two to one."

"And what if our fleet doesn't find the Fellowship's fleet before they've fallen almost all the way to Neverness?"

Hanuman fell silent for a long time as he looked out into the center of the room where Danlo sat. In the light falling down through the dome, Danlo's deep blue eyes shimmered like the ocean.

"There may be a way to descry the Fellowship's path through the Fallaways," Hanuman said. "We must ask our scryers if they can see such a path. If so, then we might fall upon the Fellow-ship's fleet by surprise and destroy them."

Now Hanuman faced Lord Pall, and their eyes danced over each other's body and face. Although Danlo knew almost nothing of the cetics' secret system of signs, he knew Hanuman well enough to read his fierce will in the sudden coldness of his gaze. And Lord Pall still possessed a will of his own; Danlo could see this as a twitching of his pink, albino's eyes. As Lord Pall and Hanuman stared at each other, and fingers and eyelids fluttered, a great deal of silent communication flowed between them. But mostly, Danlo thought, even as he and Malaclypse Redring and Bertram Jaspari watched—and a hundred lords as well—these two powerful men engaged each other in a fierce contest of wills. In the end, Hanuman won. Lord Pall's old shoulders shook with anger, and his old vocal chords quivered hoarsely as he addressed the Lords' College in his own voice.

"My Lords," he said, "it would be best if we asked our am-bassadors to leave us now so that we may confer among ourselves. Hanuman li Tosh has offered to guard the warrior-poet during the time of negotiations, and I think this would be best. Also, he has asked for a private meeting with Danlo wi Soli Ringess and is willing to provide accommodations for him in his cathedral. Of course this won't interfere with the negotiations; the pilot will be free to journey to the Academy daily to join Lord Bede in trying to stop this war that we all must dread. We've provided an apart-ment for Lord Bede—his old one in Upplyssa, as it happens. Bertram Jaspari is to remain within the Academy's walls as well. He'll be allowed to send word of his safety to his fleet, if he so wishes."

All at once many men and women protested Lord Pall's strange decision. Most of these were lords such as Ludmilla Katarill and Burgos Harsha, but Bertram Jaspari, too, added his voice to the dissenters. "Lord Pall," he said. "Malaclypse Red-ring and I have come to Neverness as a single embassy, and we must not be separated."

Lord Pall almost smiled, glad at last for the chance to exert the full power of his will. "No, it is just the opposite: you must be separated, for you can't imagine what a danger the warrior-poet might be to you. As you've claimed, you are the Holy Ivi of the Cybernetic Universal Church, and as long as you are in Never-ness, we of the Order mustn't allow any harm to befall you."

With that he looked at Hanuman, who nodded his head at Jaroslav Bulba. Jaroslav then motioned for four of the golden-robed godlings standing near him to pick up the chair to which Malaclypse was bound. With much puffing and sighing, they each managed to get a grip on one of the chair's four legs and heave it—and Malaclypse Redring—to the height of their shoulders.

"I'd like to thank the lords for asking me into their College today," Hanuman said as he stood and bowed. Then he walked over to join his godlings at the center of the room where Danlo still sat silently in his chair. "Are you coming, Danlo?" Hanuman asked softly.

Again, Danlo touched his diamond brooch and glanced at Jaroslav Bulba. And then, to Hanuman, he said, "Aren't you going to ask your underling to bind me with acid wire?"

"Will that be necessary?"

"No," Danlo said. "I . . . will come."

As he stood to bow to Demothi Bede and make his farewells, Hanuman addressed the lords one last time.

"This is the moment of our greatest danger," he said. "But it's also the moment of our greatest possibility. We must never forget that Mallory Ringess will return soon and lead us into our infinite possibilities."

With that he turned and beckoned to Danlo and the rest of his entourage. Danlo paused for the count of three heartbeats as he looked down at his reflection in the polished black floorstones; once again he wondered what might happen if his father actually *did* return to Neverness. Then, after picking up his devotionary computer, he followed Hanuman across the ice-cold floor of the College of the Lords.

A LAW FOR GODS

Do what thou wilt shall be the whole of the law.
—Master Therion

At the heart of the Old City, with its many old buildings sweeping skyward with all the strength and grace of organic stone, stood the cathedral owned by the godlings of the Way of Ringess. It was a glorious assemblage of cut-granite blocks, flying buttresses, and colored glass windows depicting the great events from the life of Mallory Ringess. Originally a sect of Kristians had built it in the shape of a cross; its long axis occupied eight hundred feet of a long city block while the cathedral's arms stuck out from the main body to the north and south. Where this world axis joined the longer one representing the way toward heaven—at the cathedral's crossing, that place of all fire and pain—a great tower had been raised up. With its delicate aretes and intricate stonework, it was very beautiful. Beauty alone, however, would never have been sufficient reason for Hanuman li Tosh to have occupied the rooms at the top of this central tower. But it was very tall as well, and it commanded a spectacular view of the Danladi Square, the Cemetery and the Fravashi Green, and other parts of the Old City; some said that Hanuman liked to stand in one of the tower's arched windows looking out at those districts of Neverness where Ringism had gathered its greatest strength.

Certainly, in the triangle of blocks from the Old City Glissade north to the Ring of Fire, and east to the walls of the Academy, Ringists from across the city had swarmed in the hope of finding apartments or other accommodations. At any time of the day, even late into the night, golden-robed Ringists crowded the narrow streets on their way to cafes or to private meetings or to the great joyances held every evening in the cathedral itself. It must have given Hanuman great pleasure to listen to the click-clack of skate blades against ice, to watch the golden streams of his godlings flowing down the red glidderies, and all too often, jamming the broader thoroughfares, the green glissades and great orange slidderies leading to the other quarters of Neverness.

On the evening after the meeting of the Lords' College, Hanuman summoned Danlo to a private audience at the top of the cathedral's tower. Earlier that day, he had been given a room—a cell—in the cathedral's chapterhouse, one of the smaller buildings that adjoined the cathedral on its northern side. For many hours he had waited alone in his cold stone room, playing his shakuhachi and occassionally exchanging a few words with the hologram of Nikolos Daru Ede. When night fell, with the last of the day's sunlight suffusing his cell's thick clary windows with a pale yellow glow, Jaroslav Bulba and another ronin warrior-poet came to escort him to Hanuman's chambers. They used a sound key to open the massive steel door, and they positioned Danlo between them as they walked down a long, gloomy passageway.

In the closeness of the dead air, Danlo smelled the kana oil perfumes that both these former warrior-poets wore; it was a pungent, pepperminty scent that drove up his nose like a spear and almost obliterated the more organic reek of insect husks and spider webs spread across the dusty old wall stones. It had been a long time, Danlo thought, since this lowest level of the chapterhouse had been used. And even now, when godlings from a thousand worlds might welcome such austere dwellings, only two of the twenty cells were occupied: his and Malaclypse Redring's. They passed by this cell—guarded by two more ronin warrior-poets outside the door—on their way to the stairs at the end of the passageway. It occurred to Danlo that Hanuman kept the other cells empty should they ever be needed for other prisoners.

That he was Hanuman's prisoner, Danlo never doubted. He might still be an ambassador from the Fellowship to Neverness, and Hanuman might keep his promise to allow Danlo to journey to the Academy to join Demothi Bede in the daily negotiations. Nevertheless, it was Hanuman who would order his comings and goings. It would be Hanuman, too, who might order terrible things if the times grew desperate and he decided to use Danlo as a tool that he might break and then cast away.

After Jaroslav Bulba and the other warrior-poet had escorted him up a flight of stairs and through a maze of roofed passageways, they entered the cathedral itself. They passed through the great nave, a hundred and eighty feet high, where cut granite blocks and ornaments of stone fairly floated in space as if touched with magic. The long glass windows still glowed with the day's last light. Each window depicted a different scene from the life of

Mallory Ringess. In one of these scenes—where the Agathanian
god-men healed Mallory Ringess of the terrible wound that had
killed him—the color of red showed brightly against the black
hair, a reminder of how close each man and woman was to blood
and pain and death. But in the adjacent window, a resurrected
Mallory Ringess emerged from the aquamarine waters of
Agathange, and his face was as golden as the sun; his eyes were
like brilliant blue windows inviting any onlooker into that inner
world of starlight and dreams—or out into the universe to follow
the way of the gods.

In preparation for the evening's joyance, golden-robed godlings hurried through the cathedral's chancel as if theirs was the
most important work in the world. Some lit candles or carried
bunches of fireflowers up the red-carpeted steps of the altar where
they set them in vases of blue glass. Others polished the heaumes
used to interface what Hanuman li Tosh told them were record-
ings of the Elder Eddas. In neat rows fairly covering the cathedral's entire floor, the godlings positioned these glittering
heaumes at the exact center of the thousand small red rugs. Soon
Ringists from across the city would swarm the cathedral and take
their places on these rugs; they would pull these heaumes over
their heads and disappear into the cybernetic spaces generated
therein. They would see visions of ancient stars and a lovely,
numinous light; they would hear golden voices whispering secrets
inside their brains. Later, after they had faced away from these
"memories" of the gods, they would tell their friends that they
had perceived the deepest truths of the universe.

Danlo looked at the many heaumes which would run such
deceitful simulations. He looked at the godlings all proud and
golden in their belief that they were leading humanity to a new
phase of evolution. And they looked at him. The news that the son
of Mallory Ringess had returned to Neverness had spread among
the Ringists like fire in dry grass. Many said that this event heralded one far greater: the return of Mallory Ringess himself. They
looked at Danlo dressed in his black pilot's robe, and their faces
showed hope for the future as well as hurt that in the past Danlo
had betrayed them. What he might discuss with Hanuman they
could only imagine. But they must have wondered if Hanuman
would try to win Danlo back to the Way of Ringess. If anyone
could lead such a wild and dangerous man as Danlo to the truth, it
was the Lord of the Way, Hanuman li Tosh.

Still pressed between the two ronin warrior-poets, Danlo
walked through a great archway leading to the tower's stairwell.

The four godlings guarding the stairwell's door bowed to Jaroslav Bulba and allowed them to pass. For what seemed a long time, Danlo and the warrior-poets climbed the turning flights of stairs. No one spoke. The thump of leather boots against old stone sounded as rhythmically as heartbeats. Danlo smelled dust, kana oil and the electrical tang of hot plasma. Flame globes, set into the walls at each landing, cast their colors of crimson and blue across Jaroslav's face and lent an even deeper glow to his hideous mechanical eyes. He looked at Danlo, silently, strangely. Perhaps he was trying to read the tells of Danlo's face to determine if he might pose a physical threat to Hanuman; or perhaps he, like others, wondered at the light that seemed to pour out of Danlo's deep blue eyes like starfire.

At the top of the tower the stairs gave out onto a narrow foyer. There two more golden-robed Ringists guarded a black shatterwood door. After they greeted Danlo politely and bowed to him, one of them, a large young man with the pimply face of one who used jook, knocked at this great door. After Danlo's heart had beat five times, it opened. A tiny woman with red eyes and a suspicious face stood in the doorway. There was something unpleasant about her, almost as if, could one have broken through her purple-black skin, the sweet-rotting smell of old fruit would have escaped like a cloud. Despite her size, she had an air of command. Her name, as Danlo well knew, was Surya Surata Lal. Before her famous family had been cast down (she was Bardo's second cousin), she had been a princess on Summerworld. Now, in her devotion to Hanuman li Tosh, it was her vanity to play the princess once again. When she saw that the warrior-poets might have entered Hanuman's sanctum, she imperiously held up her clawlike hand and told them, "Just the pilot, please. Our Lord has said that Danlo wi Soli Ringess is no danger to him. You may wait outside."

So saying, she pushed the door shut and, with great presumption, took Danlo's arm to escort him into the room. Except for the small foyer beyond the door and an adjoining kitchen, the room filled the entire top of the tower. A dome rose up around Danlo, forming both walls and roof of this spacious room. But the dome was not wrought of clary as he might have expected but rather some opaque substance of a purplish hue. Along the dome's entire circumference, from the floor to a height of eight feet, curving windows had been set to let in the city lights. But this evening the windows were shuttered as if Hanuman wished to shut out all distractions. Hanuman, more than any man whom Danlo had ever known, had the will to concentrate his powers as a magnifying glass might focus the rays of the sun. Raimented in his golden robe and all the furious power of his will, he stood by the western windows waiting for Danlo. He faced inward toward the door, and he bowed quite deeply as Danlo and Surya walked closer to him. "Hello, Danlo," he said.

"Hello, Hanuman," Danlo replied. He looked around room, once occupied by Bardo when he had been Lord of the Way. Then he locked eyes with Hanuman and said, "I see . . . that you have made changes."

Indeed, since deposing Bardo and driving him from Neverness, Hanuman had stripped his sanctum of any reminder of Bardo or his things. Gone were the bonsai trees and all the flowering plants so beloved by Bardo. In their place, Hanuman had moved in Fravashi carpets and flame globes and his old chess pieces set out on a black and white board. And, of course, much cybernetica. There were the usual mantelets and hologram stands, but also many sulki grids, once banned as a forbidden technology. And then there were computers. Hanuman collected computers as some men do art or old wines. Electronic computers, optical computers, a gas computer, and computing machines made of brass gears and chromium switches—all these Hanuman had prominently displayed somewhere in the room. Danlo noticed the quantum computers, too, and hanging over one of the windows, a Yarkonan tapestry whose fabric was woven of neurologics and other computer circuitry.

In truth, although the chamber was large, little room remained for much other than all these museum pieces. Danlo noticed a single shatterwood dining table that might have sat eight or ten people; he saw no other furniture, no clothing cabinets or any bed or other obvious place for sleeping. In looking at Hanuman, at the gleaming clearface that covered his shaved head, he thought that he no longer slept as did other men. It was possible for such personal computers to touch one's brain with theta waves and induce periods of micro-sleep lasting no more than five seconds at any time. From time to time, as Danlo saw—almost from moment to moment—Hanuman's pale blue eyes would fall as empty as an ice-field before returning to their hellishly cold intensity.

"We've come a long way since Lavi Square," Hanuman said. He referred to the day of cold and patience years before when he and Danlo had first met in their test to be admitted to the Order. "And I see I've kept you waiting too long—I'm sorry. I thought you might be hungry, so I've ordered us a meal. Will you sit with me a while?"

With a wave of his graceful hand, he motioned toward the window where the shatterwood table had been set with two plates and accompanying napkins and chopsticks. Danlo remembered too well the last meal that he had shared with Hanuman: when he closed his eyes, he could still smell the char of a snowworm roasted alive and feel the pain of his burned hands. Despite the hurt of that long-gone night, however, he nodded his head.

"I'm glad, you know," Hanuman said. And then, turning to Surya Lal, he told her, "But I'm sorry that we must dine alone. If you don't mind, will you tell Sadira that we're ready?"

Surya, who fancied herself as Protector and Advisor of the Lord of the Way of Ringess, fell instantly sullen. Her little wormhole of a mouth tightened as she looked at Danlo mistrustfully. Clearly, she was loathe to leave her Lord alone with him. And even more, she hated being used as a mere messenger. But because she made a virtue of obedience (and because she loved the power that accrued to her in executing Hanuman's orders), she bowed politely and said, "As my Lord wishes." Then she walked quickly across the room, opened the door, and left Danlo alone with Hanuman.

"An ugly woman," Hanuman said, repeating the observation he had once made upon meeting her for the first time. "But her devotion to the Way has touched her soul with a certain beauty, don't you think?"

Danlo stood holding his devotionary computer in his left hand while with his right, he touched the shakuhachi sheathed in the long pocket of his robe's black pants. "I think . . . that she is devoted to you. I think that she would do anything that you asked of her."

"But how not, since I am the Lord of the Way of Ringess? She's very faithful."

"But faithful to what and to whom?" Danlo asked. "Bardo was Lord before you and she betrayed him. Her own cousin."

Hanuman's cold eyes flashed with anger and old hurts. He looked at Danlo for a long time, then said, "You, who abandoned the Way of your own father, speak of betrayal?"

"I . . . would not speak to you at all if I did not have to."

"I'm sorry that you must," Hanuman said. "And I'm sorry to hear so much hatred in your voice."

"I . . . am sorry, too."

"And yet yesterday, before the entire College of Lords, you spoke of still loving me. What is the truth, Danlo?"

Hate is the left hand of love, Danlo remembered as he closed his eyes. Then he looked at Hanuman openly, deeply, and he said, "I think you know."

For a long time they looked into each other's eyes, and an old knowledge passed back and forth between them. Then Hanuman asked Danlo to sit at the table. He well knew how much Danlo hated sitting in chairs; Danlo's obvious discomfort both disturbed and pleased him.

"I see that you've brought one of the Architects' devotionary computers," Hanuman said, gazing at the imago of Nikolos Daru Ede. "Is this a gift for me to add to my collection?"

Danlo looked across the room at Hanuman's chess set, at the white ivory pieces. The god, he saw, was still missing. Once, as a gift at Year's End, Danlo had carved a replacement god from a walrus tusk that he had found, but Hanuman had broken it and had given it back to him.

"No," Danlo said. "I have no more gifts to give you."

"Well, it was silly of me to suppose that you did."

"This," Danlo said, pointing at Ede's hologram, "is all that remains of another god."

Hanuman nodded his head. "I've heard the story. Is this supposed to remind me of the dangers of reaching toward the heavens?"

"Do you need reminding?"

"I see that you still like to answer questions with questions," Hanuman said. And with that, he stepped across the room, picked up a folded silver blanket, and returned to throw it over the devotionary computer that Danlo had set upon the table. Having obliterated and silenced the Ede imago, he looked at Danlo strangely for a long time. And then he said, "You're still the same Danlo, aren't you? Underneath all the accomplishment and brilliance, still the same."

"I . . . am still I," Danlo said. "Truly. And you are still you."

"Fate," Hanuman said. "Yours and mine, so different—and yet once I thought we might share the same fate."

"And yet here we sit, about to take a meal together as we did as novices."

"Fate," Hanuman said, this time almost whispering. "Strange, strange."

"You . . . always loved your fate, yes? No matter how beautiful or terrible."

Hanuman made no reply to this, but only closed his eyes as if in some private vision of the future. Danlo watched the glittering purple lights of the clearface that covered his shaved head; for the thousandth time, he marvelled at the terrible beauty of Hanuman's face.

"I should think you must be hungry," Hanuman said as he opened his eyes. "I remember how you were always so hungry."

As if a signal had been given—and perhaps in Hanuman's momentary interface with the computer that he wore, it had—the door to the kitchen suddenly opened. A courtesan dressed in gold silk pyjamas bore a platter laden with steaming foods. With her golden hair and lovely form she reminded Danlo of Tamara Ten Ashtoreth. Hanuman formally presented her as the diva Sadira of Darkmoon. Sadira told them that it would be her pleasure to serve them that evening, and she came over to their table and began ladeling a hot ming soup into two blue bowls.

"Please eat," Hanuman said to Danlo, who sat staring at the little green ming beans in their swirling broth. "It's not poison, you know."

With that, they both picked up their spoons and began their meal. The soup course was followed by others, kurmash and curried vegetables and other spicy foods that Hanuman remembered Danlo had once loved. For a long time, no one spoke. The sounds of the room were clicking chopsticks and wine glasses tinking against the hard shatterwood tabletop; when Danlo paused between bites, he could hear the faint wheeze of Hanuman's breath. Hanuman, he thought, did not look well. Despite the surface energy with which he invested each of his motions—reaching for a bowl of pepper nuts or refilling Danlo's glass—a terrible stress seemed to run through his entire body like faults deep within the earth. Once, his lungs had been riddled with cancers that he had almost cured in his burning need to be more than a mere man. But now he was coughing again, between sips of wine, subtly coughing with his mouth closed as if Danlo might not notice. But Danlo could almost feel the pain of Hanuman's lungs deep in his own chest, and he winced every time Hanuman's belly tightened and his diseased breath escaped from his gray lips. The skin across the whole of Hanuman's delicate face, he saw, had a gray-white cast to it like dead seal flesh. There was a dark, hollow look about his eyes, and one eye—the left—twitched slightly from time to time. In peeling the shell off a pepper nut, his fingers trembled. As

Danlo gazed at Hanuman's precisely controlled motions, he suddenly knew a thing about Hanuman and fate: Hanuman knew what a fantastic chance he was taking in fabricating his Universal Computer and leading the Ringists to war. And he knew that if he lost, he would probably be killed, and this presentiment of his death haunted him. As all men do, he feared the blackness of nonexistence, yes, but even more he was terrified of something other, something that Danlo was only now beginning to see.

"You should let yourself sleep," Danlo said. "Sleep is the new life of the soul."

"No, it's just the opposite," Hanuman said. He smiled quickly and confidently as if such bold expressions could ward off the worst of his fears. "If you sleep, you die."

Sleep, Danlo remembered, was the first state of consciousness where one's self was absorbed into the ground of being but unaware of that absorption. Thus, in sleep, according to teachings that were ancient twenty thousand years ago, a man might know the bliss of deep peace. But there were other, newer teachings where the timeless wisdoms had been cast into more modern forms. Some of the cybernetic sects believed that in deep sleep, the mind and memory were downloaded into the infinite computational machine that was the universe. Hanuman, who hadn't wholly escaped the theologies of his childhood, feared this downloading as a stealing or devouring of his soul. It was his will to keep himself for himself only. He would not suffer anything to make claims upon his soul: not sleep or the universe or even the love of his deepest friend.

"I had expected that you would be concerned about things other than my sleeping habits," Hanuman said.

"Would my concern matter?"

"I had expected that you'd lecture me on the evils of our creating the Universal Computer."

"What can I tell you that you do not already know?" Danlo asked. "It is a *shaida* thing. Its creation violates the Law of the Civilized Worlds."

"Haven't you heard me say that the new beings that we are becoming will require a new law?"

"Yes, but whose law, Hanu? Your law?"

"No," Hanuman said softly. "A law for gods."

"And what shall this law be, then?"

As if his chair could not contain the violent energies ripping through his body, Hanuman stood up and walked around the room. With his strange light walk it seemed that he was stepping on coals. (Or that he feared putting his feet to the earth.) Here and there he paused to touch one of his computers; he might have been making some subtle adjustment in their programs or merely paying them reverence. He had a quick, artful body, and Danlo marvelled at his precision of motion, as if every one of his actions might be vital to the fate of the universe.

"Do you really want to know the law, Danlo?" Hanuman turned suddenly, and looked straight into Danlo's eyes. "Do what thou wilt shall be the whole of the law."

"Hanu, Hanu."

"Do what *thou* wilt, Danlo."

"Is this what you tell your godlings, then?"

"It's what I tell myself. It's what I tell you."

"I . . . do not understand."

"Then I must explain it to you," Hanuman said. "How many human beings are capable of becoming gods? So few, really, so few."

"But the Way of Ringess, your whole church, all that you have promised—"

"I've promised that anyone can follow the way of your father and become a god. But not *everyone* can. So few, Danlo, so few."

"And what of all the others, then?"

"They'll have the hope of becoming gods. And thus, in their hope, they'll find happiness."

"I see."

"Do you? Do you see how they burn with the pain of existence? Do you see how badly human beings need to be relieved of their suffering?"

Danlo held the gaze of Hanuman's pale blue eyes, and he saw what he had seen years before: the twisted compassion that burned through every cell of Hanuman's body and tormented him.

"You only relieve them of their freedom," Danlo said. "You lead them to sit beneath your heaumes in this cathedral and lose themselves in a counterfeit of the One Memory."

"Must we reargue our old argument?"

"In the end," Danlo said, "you will destroy them. You will lead them to be less than human, not more."

"Do what thou *wilt*," Hanuman said. "If each man and woman could look inside themselves and discover what the universe has designed them to be, they would discover their fate. Their true will. Then, if they have the courage, if they have the genius, they could free the fire from the flesh. Isn't this freedom what we all desire? Of course it is. The freedom to burn as a bright, eternal flame that can never be extinguished. But this is the freedom that only the gods can know. It's the freedom only they have the will to seize."

"But, Hanu, you—"

"Do what thou wilt shall be the whole of the law. And the only law of the gods is that they must be free to be more. *This* is what the universe requires of them."

Danlo, then, stood up from the table and walked over to the window. Although it was shuttered, in his mind he could see the blazing night sky above the city: the stars and the moons and the great black machine that the Ringists were building in near space. He pointed straight above his head and asked, "Is this your freedom, then? Your will to be be a god?"

"The Universal Computer, when it's completed, will run an almost perfect simulation of the Elder Eddas," Hanuman said. His eyes had hooded over, and he spoke almost by rote, almost as if he were reciting Ringist doctrine to would-be godlings. "It will show anyone who desires it badly enough the way toward godhood."

"So few, you said. So few."

"Fate is fate. But the Universal Computer is designed to help all Ringists."

Here Danlo walked over to Hanuman and looked at him deeply. "There are those who would say it was designed to help one man—and one man only—become a god."

"Perhaps there are." Hanuman's eyes fell cold with menace. "But they should be careful to whom they say such lies."

Just then, as Hanuman and Danlo stood before a glowing gas computer and stared at each other, Sadira of Darkmoon returned to clear their plates. She asked if they would like coffee or tea, and Hanuman used this as an excuse to break eyelock with Danlo.

"Coffee, please," Hanuman said. "And if you will, a plate of the snowball cookies."

Hanuman watched Sadira bow and return toward the kitchen. And Danlo watched him watching her. He saw no desire in Hanuman's eyes, no fire in his body for this lovely woman. He wondered if the rumor were true, that Hanuman was smooth between the legs in practice if not actuality. He supposed that Hanuman, in his great gamble into godhood, had lost any interest in the more sublime of the courtesans' arts—and much else.

"I have heard that the entire Society of Courtesans has been converted to the Way," Danlo said.

"Well, it's always been their dream to wake up our evolutionary possibilities—which they believe are encoded in each cell's DNA. You should know, they call this the 'sleeping god.' "

"I . . . know," Danlo said. He held his breath through the count of ten heartbeats, and then he asked, "Have you seen Tamara? Do you know if any of the courtesans have had news of her?"

Hanuman's eyes grew as cold and cruel as spikes of blue ice. He said, "I had thought you would ask me that the moment that you walked in the door."

"Have you, Hanu?" Danlo stepped so close to Hanuman that he could smell the blood on his breath. His hands ached to close into fists, but with all the force of his being, he willed his fingers to remain open. "Have you seen her?"

Hanuman bravely bore the intense light of Danlo's eyes, then, and he said, "No, I haven't seen her. I have other concerns, you should know."

Hanuman bowed politely, almost mockingly, and he returned to the table and sat down. As if he had been clubbed in the belly, Danlo stood trying to get his breath.

"But if you'd like," Hanuman said after sipping a bit of wine, "I'll have the courtesans make inquiries. Although Tamara lost her abilities as a courtesan, perhaps she found her calling on the Street of the Common Whores. Some of the courtesans have friends there."

I must not hate him, Danlo thought as his fingers savagely closed around the flute in his pocket. Then a bright flash, like lightning, tore through his eye and filled his head with the most intense pain he had ever known. *I must not kill him—no, no, no, no.*

"Of course, I don't think Tamara would make a very good whore—she's really much too proud for that, don't you think?"

Danlo almost fell against his chair, then, and he stood clutching the thick shatterwood arms as he gasped for breath. After a while, the fire in his brain quieted to a hot red burning; his breath came hard and hurtful and deep. And then he thought: *He is testing me. Never killing, never harming another. Never hating. But why, Hanu, why?*

Danlo looked around the various cybernetica scattered through the room. There were more than a few robots, he saw, from simple domestics to the tutelary robots that the Timekeeper had once used to keep order within the Order. He wondered if one of these vicious machines might still be alive and programmed to kill him if he should move to harm Hanuman.

"Please sit down, Danlo."

As Danlo fairly fell into his chair, Sadira appeared with their coffee and cookies. She served them quickly and then left them alone.

"You used to love snowballs," Hanuman said after biting through the powdered sugar crust of a round white cookie. "As I did too, once. But now I'm afraid I find them much too sweet."

Slowly, Hanuman chewed on his cookie, and then his eyes softened. He seemed wounded, wistful, almost infinitely sad. And all the while he looked at Danlo in his twisted compassion for the pain that he had so willfully caused him.

He needs to trust me, Danlo thought. *He needs to trust one other human being. To trust and love.*

As if Hanuman could read his mind (or heart), he said, "I've always loved you for your devotion to your ideals."

Danlo picked up a cookie, then, and took a bite. It was crumbly and buttery, very sweet and very good.

"I've always loved your devotion," Hanuman continued, "even when I've hated the harm that it's caused me."

Danlo quickly finished his cookie and then ate another. And all the while he watched Hanuman, watched and waited.

"Of all people, I've needed your help the most," Hanuman said. "And of all people, you've been the wildest, the most willful. It's only fate, you should know, that your will has opposed mine."

Danlo ate a third cookie, then said, "I . . . have never wanted to oppose you. Your will."

"No—you only act according to your ideals, your vision of what should be. But a time comes when individual ideals must be brought into line with a greater vision."

"Is this what you do, then, Hanu? Is this what you've done with Lord Pall, won him to your vision?"

"Well, I really think I have. Which is why he can see the future as it must be."

"I think . . . . that you only control him through fear, yes? He fears the ronin warrior-poets who are loyal to you."

"Well, then, that's silly of him. As everyone knows, my warrior-poets seek only to serve me and the Way of Ringess." Hanuman tapped his finger against the tabletop and then asked, "And what is it that you fear, Danlo the Wild? Surely not death, as does Lord Pall."

To this Danlo made no reply as he bit into a fourth cookie. His eyes fell deep and fathomless as the twilight sky.

"And yet I think that there must be something that you *do* fear, after all," Hanuman said. "Shall I tell you what it is?"

"If you must."

"Pain," Hanuman said. "There's a level of pain before which even you must surrender."

"Pain such as you have known, Hanu?"

Hanuman rubbed his arm then as if he could rub away the ekkana drug that poisoned his veins and tormented him every moment of his life.

"Once," Hanuman said, "here in this cathedral I asked for your help—do you remember?"

"How could I forget?"

"As one friend to another, I asked. And you refused me."

"I . . . am sorry."

"I need your help again," Hanuman said.

"Truly?"

"I need your help, but this time I won't ask. I'll demand."

"What help, then?"

Hanuman rubbed the diamond clearface where it edged his temples, and then he looked up above the table into the dome as if he could see things that Danlo could not.

"You've been sent as an ambassador to try to stop this war," Hanuman said. "A noble goal—and what if you succeed?"

"Then there would be no war," Danlo said simply.

"Yes, but what if the College of Lords agreed to your Fellowship's demands and the Order began disassembling the Universal Computer?"

"Is that possible, Hanu? Truly?"

"Anything is *possible,* but I'm speaking now hypothetically. If the Order this moment agreed to stop the war, how would it be stopped? Even as we speak, the Fellowship's fleet falls toward Neverness."

"Yes, but—"

"How can this fleet be stopped? I need your help in stopping it."

For a moment, Danlo held his breath as he counted heartbeats. Then he said, "If you'd like, I would do anything to stop this war."

"Then you would carry a message to the Sonderval telling him of what has occurred here?"

Danlo immediately saw the trap that Hanuman had set for him.

To stretch time out in order for him to think, he said, "If I knew how to find him among the stars, I would."

"Do you, Danlo?"

He is not ready to yield to the Fellowship's demands, Danlo thought. *He would only use me to betray the Fellowship's fleet.*

Above almost all else, Danlo hated to lie. And so he sought to evade Hanuman's question, saying, "If you truly wish to stop the war, the Order could parlay with the Fellowship's fleet when they fall out near Neverness."

"But parlays might fail," Hanuman said. "War might be joined and a thousand ships destroyed before the Sonderval realized that we wished for peace. Neverness itself might be destroyed."

"No, no—never that."

"I believe that you know which pathway through the stars the Sonderval will choose to lead his fleet. I believe that he would have told you."

At this, Danlo looked straight into Hanuman's eyes, saying nothing.

"And now, you must tell me," Hanuman said.

"No—I cannot."

"Help me stop this war, Danlo."

"No. I . . . am sorry."

"If the Fellowship's fleet falls out near Neverness, there will be chaos. Bertram Jaspari's Iviomils would try to use this chaos to destroy the Star of Neverness. It's upon you to help me stop this tragedy."

"By leading you to surprise the Fellowship's fleet and destroy it?"

"Of course we wouldn't do that. We seek only peace. Help me, Danlo."

"No."

"Please remember, I don't ask for your help. I demand it."

"I cannot help you."

"No, you *will* not help me. Not now, I see. But one's will can be broken. You should know, even a will of diamond."

Danlo thought of the brooch that he wore on his shoulder, the little piece of diamond and gold that the Sonderval had given him. Its sharp needle was tipped with enough of the matrikax poison to kill him instantly should he plunge it into his arm vein.

"I never dreamed," Danlo said, "that I would live to hear you threaten me this way."

For a moment it seemed that Hanuman's eyes might fill with

tears. But then he found that place inside himself that was all will and desire to burn away any weakness inside himself, and his eyes remained as hard as blue ice.

"I've loved you as I've loved no one else," Hanuman said with great sadness. "But love is irrelevant to the purposes of the universe."

"No, Hanu. It is just the opposite."

"There's a level of pain that will break even you. The warrior-poets, as you should know, know everything about pain."

"I . . . will never help you destroy the Fellowship's fleet."

Again, Danlo thought of the brooch pinned to his shoulder. It occurred to him that if he plunged the needle into Hanuman's neck vein rather than his own, he might end Hanuman's endless pain, and much else besides.

"As you might remember, the Warrior-Poets' ekkana drug causes the most terrible pain," Hanuman said.

"I . . . remember," Danlo said. And then he thought, *I must not touch the brooch. If I do, he will know.*

"Then there are the reading computers of the akashics," Hanuman said. "You must remember how powerful they are."

"Even as I remember the arts that you taught me to confuse such readings."

Hanuman smiled at this as he ground a cookie crumb to dust with his finger. He said, "You're perhaps the only pilot so well trained in the cetic's arts. I'm in awe of your mental powers. But consider pain beyond any pain you've ever known. Do you really believe that if the akashics were to place a heaume upon your head while you were experiencing the fire of ekkana, you could keep from thinking what I demand that you tell me?"

"I . . . do not know."

"Do you believe in miracles, then, Danlo?"

Danlo closed his eyes as he remembered the time on Tannahill when he had gone deep into his mind. There had come a moment of utter freedom and intense consciousness when the light of his mind was his to move as he willed.

"Yes," Danlo finally said. "Yes—it is possible."

"Oh, Danlo, please don't make me do this to you."

"I have never been able to make you do anything."

"Danlo, I—"

"Your will is your own," Danlo said. "And my will is mine."

But Danlo wondered what he truly willed. If he didn't use the brooch immediately, he might never have another chance.

"Your will, Danlo. Your damned will."

In truth, Danlo didn't know if he could withstand the kind of torture with which Hanuman threatened him. But he was certain that he could never stab Hanuman with the brooch's needle. Hanuman might still be won to compassion and the light of reason, and even if this were impossible, he could never harm Hanuman. He didn't know if he could harm himself. And yet if he didn't, if he failed to break his vow of ahimsa this one time and push the brooch's needle into himself, then he might be helpless before the pain of the Warrior-Poets' ekkana drug. And then he would betray the Fellowship, and millions of men and women might die.

Ahira, Ahira—what should I do?

His fingers trembled to rip the brooch away from his robe and slash the poisoned needle through a half inch of flesh and put an end to his torment. And then Hanuman's eyes fell as empty as a cup of air. There came a moment when he might have killed either Hanuman or himself. And then the door suddenly opened and Jaroslav Bulba, his eyes pulsing like ruby lasers, came rushing into the room followed by the other warrior-poet. Almost before Danlo could move, they fell upon him. As they had with Malaclypse Redring, they bound him with silvery strands of acid wire. Quickly, skillfully, Jaroslav unpinned the brooch and held it up for Hanuman to see.

"It's as I warned," Jaroslav said. "It's poisoned, with naittare or matrikax."

"I'm glad that you didn't try to use this against me," Hanuman told Danlo. He pointed at the golden needle tipped with a blackish substance that looked like dried ink. "I believed that you wouldn't—how I love your faithfulness to ahimsa, no matter how foolish."

Danlo knew that it would be useless to struggle against his bonds, and yet struggle he did. He tested the tightness of the acid wire, flexing his shoulders and chest until he felt the wire cutting through his silk robe into his upper arms.

"But I'm afraid I don't believe that ahimsa would prevent you from using the needle against yourself," Hanuman said. "But now you're safe, aren't you?"

At this, Danlo clenched his fist convulsively and felt the acid wire slice through the skin on the back of his wrist.

"Because I love you," Hanuman said, "this one last time I'll ask for your help. Please tell me what I need to know."

"No—I will never tell you."

"That we shall soon see." Hanuman glanced at Jaroslav Bulba and said, "Take him back to his cell."

At last, Danlo ceased the futile movements tearing his flesh. He looked at Hanuman and said, "Do what thou wilt shall be the whole of the law. Is this your genius, then? Your true will? Is this what the universe has designed you to do?"

Hanuman's eyes fell as distant and wan as the Ouray Cloud of galaxies. Then he looked at Danlo and said, "Strange but it seems that it is. *This* universe, you should know, was made not just of heaven but what you have always called *shaida*. And what I've called hell."

"No, no."

"Fate is fate, Danlo. We must love our fate."

"My mother once said that in the end we choose our futures."

"And you have chosen yours, then. Goodbye, Danlo."

At a nod from Hanuman, the warrior-poets pulled Danlo to his feet. Because they didn't wish to carry him, they applied a heat pen to the wire below his waist, which caused the silken strands to melt apart like wax strings and leave his legs free for walking.

"Hanu, Hanu—I am so sorry."

As Danlo found the place inside himself where Hanuman's pain touched him with a fierce white light, he saw tears filling up Hanuman's eyes like melted water spread across blue ice. Then the warrior-poets bore him away, out the door and down to the lower parts of the cathedral where his future awaited him.

PAIN

> *The only true wisdom lives far from humankind, out in*
> *the great loneliness, and can only be reached through*
> *suffering. Privation and suffering alone open the mind to*
> *all that is hidden from others.*
>
> —Igjugaruk, the shaman

Danlo's cell was small, ten feet in length, half again as wide, and scarcely high enough for him to stand up straight without scraping his head against the rough stone ceiling. Although heated with the geyser water that flowed through the rocky ground beneath much of the city, it was still cold—cold enough that even Danlo, who was long used to such hardships, had to wear his thickest wool kamelaika lest he shiver in the dank air. Few amenities graced the cell: a multrum for his toilet needs, hot running water for washing his face and hands, a narrow bed and sleeping furs, a small clothing closet, a chess table with ivory and shatterwood pieces, a single chair, a small rug covering a few of the cold floor stones, and nothing else. Except the window. This was a strip of clary set high along the cell's south wall. Although too thick to allow a clear vision of the street outside the cathedral, it let in a clean, natural light that cheered Danlo and reminded him that the Star of Neverness still shined in the heavens millions of miles above. As long as this star of his birth filled the window with its golden light, he promised himself that he would take courage and hope in the possibilities of each new day. For he would need both these virtues in abundance—and much else—if Hanuman should carry through on his threat to torture him. Hope, as the Fravashi say, is the heart's deepest light, and in Danlo it still blazed like the sun.

That Hanuman possessed the will to torture him he never doubted. Hadn't Hanuman, with his own hands, once murdered the novice called Pedar? Hadn't he raped Tamara Ten Ashtoreth of her memories in order to make Danlo share a portion of his soul's deepest pain? Truly, Hanuman had fallen deeply into *shaida,* and so it would only complete the logic of his life for him to extend this anguish in a very physical way and teach Danlo the full meaning of pain. As Danlo waited for two days in his cell—playing with the chess pieces or playing his flute or counting the beats of his heart—he tried not to think about the various forms that his torture might take. Such thoughts could themselves be the first of his tortures; they could weaken his will to the point where he would gladly confess the fixed points along the Sonderval's pathway, if only Hanuman kept his warrior-poets from drilling holes in his fingers with lasers or touching his face with their nerve knives. This, he thought, was why Hanuman kept him waiting alone so long while great events outside his cell shook the universe. To wait this way was to know the first of hell's fiery circles; in waiting for the sound of the warrior-poets' boots against dark and ancient stones, he supposed he had a glimpse of writhing flames of all the other circles, but time would prove him wrong.

"We must escape," the Ede imago said to Danlo for the hundredth time. Earlier that day, Hanuman had returned the devotionary computer to Danlo so that he might have some company while he awaited his fate. "Don't you want to escape?"

Danlo had set the devotionary computer at the edge of the chess table. As he found, Ede the God had programmed the computer to play chess at the same level of skill as the human Nikolos Daru Ede—which was to say, fairly poorly. Danlo, himself only an average-strong player, beat the Ede imago every game. It amused him that Ede never grew angry or frustrated at his defeats, but only offered each time to play another game. If anything frustrated Ede at all (if he could truly know such an emotion), it was that he could not move the chess pieces on his own. Like a ghost, his hologram might flit between the black goddess and an empty square to indicate his move, but he could no more touch these exquisitely carved figurines of ivory and wood than he could force open the cell's great steel door.

"If we don't escape," Ede said, "the warrior-poets might torture you to death. And then I would never recover my body."

"Perhaps Hanuman would help you recover your body," Danlo said. He stood above the chess table and moved a pawn at Ede's bidding. "He would defeat Bertram and his Iviomils if he could."

"But would he help me return myself to my body? Would he help me return to life?"

"I do not know."

"I doubt it," Ede said. "I think Hanuman is more interested in me as the remaining programs of a dead god than a potentially alive human being."

"I am sorry."

"Do you know what Hanuman asked me after the warrior-poets had escorted you from his chambers? He asked me how I might be taken down."

"And did you tell him?"

"I told him that there was a single word that might take me down," Ede said. "Of course, I didn't tell him what this word was."

"Nor have you ever told me."

"Nor shall I ever. Of course, you wouldn't wantonly take me down, as would Hanuman. I think that he wanted to disassemble the devotionary computer and examine my deep programs."

Danlo moved his knight to a white square at the edge of the board and said, "I wonder why he didn't."

"Perhaps he regards me as your property."

"And do you suppose he would respect the inviolateness of my property when he threatens to mutilate my body?"

"How could I know?" Ede responded, answering Danlo's question with a question as he had learned to do. "But I'm afraid that if you died, Hanuman will confiscate me as *his* property and try to take me down."

"I will not die," Danlo said.

"Can you truly know that, Pilot?"

"Hanuman will not want to kill me. I . . . know."

"That may be true," Ede said. "But you, after all, are only flesh—can you foresee how this delicate flesh will react if burned in hot oil? Your skin might cook away or blacken with gangrene. You might take an infection and die."

"I . . . will not die."

"Or what if the warrior-poets crush your limbs between stones? If the flesh and bones are severely compressed, liquid fat is forced out of the fat cells into the body's other tissues. The fat globules can cause embolisms in the blood vessels of the lungs, kidneys and brain. You might suffer a stroke and be paralyzed, if not die outright."

"Thank you for providing me with such enlightening information," Danlo said as he began a pawn storm of Ede's badly protected god. "How is it that you, who have forgotten the Dragon Opening or the God's Defense, know about such things?"

"Well, if I ever do recover my body, I shall need to know *everything* about the human body, don't you think?"

"I do not know what to think," Danlo said. And then, "But I believe I know why Hanuman returned you to me."

"Why, Pilot?"

"To torture me with your knowledge, yes?" Danlo advanced a pawn toward Ede's god, and he smiled in grim amusement. "Now perhaps we could finish our game without discussing the vulnerabilities of *my* body."

Four times during this period of waiting, Lord Bede demanded to be taken from the Academy to the cathedral in order to visit Danlo. He was appalled that his fellow ambassador should be imprisoned in a tiny cell and held incommunicado. Because he still knew many of the Order's lords and could be most persuasive, he quickly rallied support in the halls of the Academy for Danlo's freedom to meet with others, if not his release. But Hanuman deafened himself to such protests. He knew where his power lay; he controlled Lord Pall and the most prominent of the Order's lords as he did the fingers on his hand. Other peoples and problems within the city worried him much more. In truth, even at the height of his ascendency, Hanuman never managed to elevate himself as Lord of Neverness, as some have claimed. Although he might have striven for the total power of an autarch, there were always those who opposed him.

The harijan sect, in their colorful rags and arrogance, were wont to riot and set themselves aflame at every act of Hanuman's that they didn't like. The astriers, too, most of whom were Architects of the Reformed Cybernetic Churches, shunned all Ringists or contact with Ringism; they shut their children inside their big stone houses and refused to allow any of Hanuman's godlings to skate down the streets where they lived. An entire section of the Farsider's Quarter—the Ashtoreth District—fell into open rebellion against Ringism and the Order. It was said that the astriers there had begun manufacturing lasers and other forbidden weapons, but no one really knew.

Similarly, all the alien races regarded Ringism as a plague upon the galaxy. Many aliens had already fled Neverness in protest, but many more set about organizing the entire Zoo from Far North Beach to the City Wild as a separate city closed not only to Ringists, but to all human beings. For the Elidi, with their elfin faces and golden wings, to act in concert with the Scutari seneschals was almost unthinkable, but so it happened. It was a time of strange alliances and clandestine meetings, cabals and assassinations and plots.

Not all the resistance to Hanuman and the Way of Ringess

occurred in these outlying districts of Neverness. Perhaps the most vexing of the problems that Hanuman faced (other than the war itself) was the secret dissent within the apartments near the cathedral, even within the very ranks of Ringism. This harked back to the very beginning of Bardo's church. To accommodate the Lords of the Order and gain new converts, Bardo had banned the drinking of kalla, the remembrancer's sacred drug. Kalla had been a way for some—for a few such as Danlo and himself—to remembrance the Elder Eddas. But it was a difficult and dangerous way, and so Bardo had enlisted Hanuman's help to devise a new remembrancing ceremony. This Hanuman had done. He had copied his own memory of the Elder Eddas into a computer—along with those of such luminaries as Bardo, Thomas Rane, and the diva Nirvelli. Henceforth, Ringists were supposed to satisfy themselves with pulling a silver heaume over their heads and sitting quietly while other people's memories played through their minds like a cartoonist's dramas.

Danlo, from the beginning, had called this watered-down ceremony a counterfeit of the true experience of the Elder Eddas. And so had others. Even as long ago as Hanuman's Fire Sermon, Jonathan and Benjamin Hur and other Ringists had formed a cult within a cult dedicated to the drinking of kalla. They called themselves, simply, the Kalla Fellowship, and they refused to abandon their sacred drug, even when Hanuman li Tosh began excommunicating them from the church for the crime of drinking it. As they of the Kalla Fellowship saw it, *they* were the true Ringists who practiced the true Way of Ringess. And so the brothers Hur had long held secret kalla ceremonies, first in the rooms of Bardo's house and later in Jonathan's apartment or in the rooms of his friends throughout the Old City.

A few members of the Kalla Fellowship, in defiance of Hanuman, had even managed to smuggle slip tubes of kalla into the cathedral itself; while Hanuman had conducted the usual, false remembrancing ceremony with his computers before the altar, they had held a private joyance in one of the meeting rooms off the nave. Jonathan Hur, of course, was not one of these secret celebrants, for Hanuman had long since denounced him as the chief of the Wayless. But each evening many of Jonathan's friends found their way into the cathedral, undiscovered as the kalla drinkers they really were. In truth, Hanuman never quite determined how many of his Ringists secretly drank kalla. To Surya Surata Lal, he confided his fear that there might have been as many as a thousand of them. These thousand, however, he said, posed a threat to Ringism wholly out of proportion to their numbers. They were like worms in his belly, he said; they were like viruses in firestones that could fracture even the finest of such jeweled, living computers. If he'd had the time and the means, he would have driven them from his church and from their apartments nearby; he would have banished them from Neverness as wayless rebels who had betrayed the truths of Ringism.

The Kalla Fellowship might have formed a truly potent opposition to Hanuman if they themselves hadn't been divided in their purpose. Only a year before Danlo's return to Neverness, as Hanuman's control of Lord Pall became ever more obvious and intolerable, the brothers Hur had fallen into argument with each other. Jonathan Hur, with his bright eyes and lovely face, believed that they who drank the kalla should concern themselves only with the exploration of the Elder Eddas and the realization of the One Memory in each human being. They were pilots of mind and soul, he said, and their path lay among shimmering lights inside each man and woman and not in disputing Hanuman's false doctrines on the icy streets surrounding the cathedral.

Benjamin Hur, however, who was as free-spirited and fierce as his brother was soulful, argued that such divine realizations would be meaningless if not brought back into the real world of stone cathedrals and lightships and murderous men. Quite simply, he wanted to fight Hanuman in any way that he could. It was his purpose to restore Ringism to the force for humanity's evolution that he believed it could be. If this struggle meant infiltrating Hanuman's church and trying to win the godlings back to Ringism's original vision, Benjamin Hur was glad to organize the cells and secret networks of kalla drinkers who might undermine Hanuman's authority. And if fate should demand of him more drastic actions, he was willing to lead a secret war of terror and assassination that would make Hanuman tremble.

Unknown to Danlo, it was Benjamin Hur and his kalla drinkers who distracted Hanuman's energies during Danlo's time of waiting. Once, Benjamin and Danlo had been friends and fellow explorers of the Elder Eddas. Although Danlo had renounced drinking kalla for himself, Benjamin Hur (and his brother) still regarded him as one of their own. But where Jonathan felt content merely to lament the imprisonment of a great soul such as Danlo, Benjamin's protest took a more active form. On the day that Hanuman served Danlo a meal of kurmash and cookies, one of Hanuman's closest godlings, a former horologe named Galeno Astarei, was found dead in the deserted aisle off the nave of the cathedral.

And the following morning, two ronin warrior-poets loyal to Hanuman were murdered as they skated down one of the orange slidderies leading from the Old City Glissade.

The murder of one warrior-poet, of course, is an extraordinary event. But for two such killing machines themselves to be surprised and killed in the clear light of day spoke of plots and prowess almost beyond what was considered possible. When these murders were accompanied by Benjamin's demand for Danlo's release, it truly made Hanuman tremble. He spent most of the next few days in reaction to this loss: doubling the guard around the altar and other strategic points within the cathedral; setting his remaining four warrior-poets to hunting the assassins who had hunted their friends; questioning Ringists of doubtful loyalty and threatening to use his akashics to lay bare their minds.

In his frenzy to discover traitors, he might have begun a purge of his entire church if time hadn't been rolling toward him like death clouds across the open sea. But the Order's fleet awaited his command to strike out among the stars, and fate itself awaited the completion of his Universal Computer. And alone in his cell, his deepest friend, Danlo wi Soli Ringess, waited in silent darkness counting the beats of his heart.

They came for him late at night on the 4th of winter. As Danlo lay sleepless in his bed, he heard the sound of three pairs of boots striking the stones of the corridor outside his cell. He listened to the wind outside the cathedral and to the muffled drumbeat inside his chest, but little other sensa touched his nerves. The window above his bed, he saw, remained as black as obsidian. And then, with the creaking open of the great steel door, a faint light leaked into his cell. He smelled the terrible, sharp essence of kana oil and saw two warrior-poets limned in the hellish glow of the doorway. One of them, Jaroslav Bulba, ordered Danlo to sit in the chair by the chess table, while the other one lit the cell's flame globes. The sudden light, in colors of copper, puce and iron-red, hurt Danlo's eyes. For a moment, he marvelled at the dual nature of light, the way that it could either illuminate in joy or fall like fire into the unadjusted openings of his eyes. And then, as he pulled off the warm furs covering him and stood away from his bed, he saw Hanuman enter the room. It was Hanuman who silently pushed the door closed. And it was Hanuman, with his silent cetic's face, who looked at Danlo's naked limbs and said, "Don't bother dressing, Danlo. You won't need your clothes tonight."

With that, as they had done in Hanuman's tower, the warrior-poets bound Danlo to the chair with circles of glittering acid wire. They told him not to move, lest the faintest touch of the wire cut his ivory skin. This time, Danlo did not struggle. He sat naked in his silvery cocoon of acid wire, feeling the icy coldness of the chair pounding like a stone hammer against the backs of his legs and spine. He began shivering, then. As Hanuman looked down at him with his pale, icy eyes, he began sweating and shivering at the sudden shock of cold.

"It's you who make me do this," Hanuman said. "You and your damned willfulness."

In response to this oft-repeated lament of Hanuman's, Danlo only looked at him strangely and smiled.

"I demand that you tell me what the Sonderval's pathway will be."

"I will tell you," Danlo said, "only when all the stars have fallen from the sky."

"I demand that you tell me now."

"I . . . would rather die."

"Oh, no," Hanuman said, "we won't allow that. In a few more moments, you'll only wish that you could. But I've come here tonight to bring you two gifts close to my soul. The first, of course, is pain."

"And the second?" Danlo asked, almost knowing what Hanuman would say.

"Eternity, Danlo. Eternity and pain, pain and eternity—they are the only two things of which this universe is made."

He nodded at Jaroslav Bulba, then, and hardened his face. Quickly, with the speed of a striking cobra, Jaroslav reached out with a glittering needle held between his fingers and stuck it in Danlo's neck. It took only a moment, this injection of the warrior-poets' ekkana drug. The pain of the tiny needle was almost nothing. Danlo sat waiting, sweating and waiting to feel something more than this little fly-bite of his flesh. He counted heartbeats, one, two, three, four of them. And then like a sudden blast of rocket fire in the cold night air, the drug exploded through his nervous system. The fifth beat of his heart felt like a great stone dropped onto his chest. He gasped at the sudden pain of it.

In waves, as his heart's quick spasm pushed the blood through his arteries, he felt the pain pulsing out through his arms, legs and torso, and up through his neck into his brain. Quickly now, as his heart beat faster, shocks of pain filled every part of him with the rhythmic beating of his blood. The head pain was the worst. He wanted to scream at the agony inside his head, which felt like a red-hot iron being pounded with a hammer through his eye. But other pains took him as well: the fiery coldness of stone against his back; acid wire scorching open the skin of his chest; the burning ache of toes once frozen with frostbite. In truth, the whole of his body shrieked with pain, his muscles and skin and nerves and blood and bones all the way down to the deep screaming of his cells.

"You may scream if you wish," Hanuman said. "The only one who might hear you is Malaclypse Redring, who waits in *his* cell. And to a warrior-poet, you should know, the screams of another are the most heavenly music."

I will not scream, Danlo thought. He clamped his jaws shut with such force that his cheek muscles cramped up hard as knots of wood and the pain of his teeth was like thirty-two spears being driven through his gums deep into the bone beneath.

"You're so damned strong, aren't you? But please consider that it takes approximately four hundred seconds for the ekkana to build to its full effect. And it builds quite slowly. What you are exeriencing now is like the burning of a match compared to starfire."

What Hanuman said filled Danlo with yet more pain, but not because of the content of his words. As the vibrations of Hanuman's voice disturbed the cell's dank air, each booming vowel and plosive consonant sent waves of sound pounding against Danlo's eardrums. Once, Danlo thought, Hanuman's voice had been as sweet as honey, as beautiful as polished silver. But now it filled his head like the sudden roar of ten thousand tigers. That was the hell of the ekkana drug, the way that it tortured one's nerves into transforming normally pleasant sensa into the most hideous of experiences. It was like the way that the gentle dragging of a lover's fingernails across the skin of one's back became intolerable after a bad sunburn.

"Are you counting time?" Hanuman asked. He stood in front of Danlo, looking at him strangely, almost with compassion, and the reflected light off his pale, anguished face hurt Danlo's eyes. "We won't really begin until the ekkana has waxed to its fullest effect. And then we'll have at least six hours before it wanes. Six hours—can you imagine that? In the universe as experienced through the fire of ekkana, even six seconds is an eternity."

Danlo drew in a quick breath, hoping to ease the fierce pain tearing him apart. But the coldness of the air only seared his lungs as if he had breathed fire. He smiled, then, at this thought that suddenly came to him:

The nerves are the reason that man does not easily mistake himself for a god.

"I see you still amuse yourself," Hanuman said. "Savor your will to smile—it won't last."

Danlo tried to speak, to open his mouth in order to tell Hanuman that his will would always be as free as a thallow in the sky, if only he had the courage to follow it. But the pain of moving his jaws, his tongue and lips, caused him to lock into silence.

"It's getting worse, isn't it? Can you feel it in your belly yet? Can you feel it in your cells?"

As Danlo struggled not to cry out or lunge against the acid wire, movements that would only bring him further agony, he felt a spear of pain driving through his belly. Although it had been many hours since his last meal, he could feel the peristaltic waves of his belly muscles squeezing the now-liquid food through his intestines. The squirting of his digestive juices burned him inside in sprays of hot acid. Even the absorption of proteins and fats into his cells hurt him; the very streaming of nutrients into his tissues felt as if he would fill up cell by cell and then burst. It came to him then that every part of his body that quickened his life—from his belly to his blood to his brain—was in continual motion. And the more it moved, the more it hurt.

Pain is the awareness of life, he remembered.

Life, he marvelled, in his last moment of clear thought before pain swept him away, was essentially the movement of matter in highly patterned and organized ways. And it was sheer movement, the continual changing from one state to another, that was the ultimate source of all pain. The greater the movement—as in a man's flesh parting at the rip of a knife or a woman giving birth to her child—the greater the pain. Strange, he thought, that he had never quite seen this until now. Strange that movement itself was pain, for the universe was nothing but matter in motion, from the spinning of electrons in a carbon atom of his blood to the fire of photons streaming out of the heart of the farthest star.

Pain is life, and life is pain, is pain—pain, pain, pain, pain . . .

Ironically, the Warrior-Poets had designed their ekkana drug not simply to cause pain but to free their victims to their greatest possibilities. For pain is like a doorway opening from the dark cavern of one's own being out onto the infinite lights of the universe. But it is a door that few can open. Few can reach their moment of the possible and move through pain into that golden land where one's will flows as wild and free as a waterfall. The greater the pain, the Warrior-Poets say, the greater the possibilities of the will in overcoming it and moving toward the truly human. A true human being would be one who could hold all the pain of his body and soul—and still smile upon the infinitely greater pain of the universe.

It hurts, it hurts, it hurts, it hurts. . . .

"It hurts, doesn't it, Danlo?"

Hanuman's voice exploded like a bomb out of the room's blinding light. Danlo couldn't bear the heat of it.

"It all hurts so terribly much, doesn't it?"

Yes, it hurts, Danlo thought. *Yes, yes, yes . . .*

"Danlo?"

Danlo heard his name, and the fire of it burned his brain and made him sweat.

"Is there something that you wish to ask me?"

Yes, Danlo thought. *Yes, yes, yes.*

"Of course, you may ask me anything you wish."

"How . . ." Danlo finally said.

Forcing this single word from his lips hurt more than the time that he'd had to pull free the barbed point of a harpoon accidentally impaled in his leg.

"How much pain can you bear?" Hanuman asked. He stood there in front of Danlo, his blue eyes shining like ice and his robe blazing like golden flames all around him. "Is that what you wish to know, how much pain you can bear before you start screaming and biting your tongue? Sometimes I think it's the only really interesting question: how much pain can we hold before we fall insane like the rest of the universe?"

"No," Danlo gasped, "not how much. How . . . long?"

For a long time now, Danlo had abandoned the counting of his heartbeats. Although whole days had seemed to pass—in truth, whole years—he knew that the night could not yet be over, for the clary window showed no trace of light. Perhaps it had been two or three hours since Jaroslav had injected him with the ekkana poison. Certainly, he thought, he had long since reached the moment when the ekkana would touch him with its greatest fire.

"It's been only two hundred seconds," Hanuman said. He closed his eyes as the clearface computer lit up like purple glowworms swarming about his head. "Two hundred and ten seconds—scarcely more than half the time until we can really begin. And you should know, only a hundredth of the pain. The effects of the ekkana build exponentially. We could hardly call the pain you're experiencing now real pain."

Not real pain . . . two hundred seconds . . . no, impossible, no, no . . .

Danlo hurt so fiercely that he had to exert the whole force of his will solely to keep from crying out. He didn't see how the pain could get any worse. And then, unbelievably, the pain grew worse. Infinitely worse. Seconds passed, and days and whole eons, and it seemed to take forever for his heart to complete one beat and fill with his burning blood in readiness for the next contraction. So intolerable had his pain become that he wanted to be anywhere else in the universe, even if it meant freezing naked in a snowstorm or being cut with a stone knife or repeating the most agonizing experiences of his life over and over again until the end of time.

To his shame, then, he screamed like a child caught in a tiger's claws, screamed and screamed until he thought his lungs would tear away from his ribs and his heart burst. And then he realized that the only sounds of the room came from the breathing of Hanuman and the two warrior-poets—and the rocket-like whoosh of his own tortured breaths. The scream had been only inside of him, inside his mind. His jaws remained locked, and he wouldn't allow his lips to open.

"It's been more than five hundred seconds," Jaroslav Bulba said in a voice that cracked out of the air like a whip. "I don't understand."

The other ronin warrior-poet, a quick, young man named Arrio Kell, said, "Perhaps the ekkana was old and had lost its potency."

"No," Jaroslav said. "I prepared it from the binaries only three days ago."

"Then he should have reached his moment by now."

"Much before now—I don't understand."

Hanuman, then, stepped closer to Danlo and touched the sweat off his forehead. Even the gentleness of Hanuman's hand hurt him. He willed himself to look straight at Hanuman as he felt Hanuman's fingers test the locked muscles along his face and neck. And then Hanuman looked deeply into his eyes and said, "He *has* reached his moment—I'm sure the ekkana has waxed to its full effect."

"But no one," Jaroslav said, "has ever reached his moment without screaming."

"Well, Danlo isn't like other men."

"You speak of him almost as if he's a god."

"Almost," Hanuman said, softly, strangely. "Well, his father *is* Mallory Ringess. Even when he was a man, he wasn't like other men either.''

"Even warrior-poets," Jaroslav said, "cry out when touched with the ekkana. Has he no nerves? Is there something wrong with his brain?"

"No, he has nerves," Hanuman said. "Watch this."

He drew his fingernail across the scar on Danlo's forehead and watched as he jumped forward in his chair; to Danlo, this light touch felt as though this old wound were being reopened with a red-hot knife.

"Do you see the eyes?" Hanuman asked. "How he cries out inside?"

"I would rather hear him cry out *outside* until the walls shake and the air hisses and he burns away his voice."

"Then we should begin," Hanuman said.

"It's past time," Jaroslav Bulba agreed. He drew his long, killing knife from his cloak and held it pointing at Danlo.

"One moment," Hanuman said. Then he turned to Danlo. "Tell me the fixed-points of the stars along the Sonderval's pathway."

Danlo felt his heart beat once, twice, three times with the force of tidal waves crashing against a rocky coast. And then he said, "No."

"No?"

"No."

Although it hurt his chest and throat to utter this single word, it hurt even more *not* to let its iron-cold sounds force open his lips. It took all his will to say it, simply, quietly, without the taint of pain or hatred discoloring his voice.

"Damn you, Danlo!" Hanuman shook with rage, his fine jaw trembling, and his belly, and his hands—and he couldn't stop looking at Danlo with his pale, tear-haunted eyes. "If there were a God in this universe, He would damn someone as cruel as you. But there isn't, so I must. *I* must, do you understand? I really must."

Then he nodded at Jaroslav Bulba, and said, "Begin with the fingers."

Hanuman must have previously orchestrated the course of Danlo's torture and discussed it with the warrior-poets, for Jaroslav and Arrio Kell knew exactly what to do. With Danlo's forearms bound fast to the arms of his chair, his hands and fingers remained free to move. For most of the time since the ekkana had touched him, he had clenched the fingers of either hand into a hard fist. Now Arrior Kell stepped closer to Danlo and used his own hard fingers to pry Danlo's open. He bore down on the knuckles of Danlo's little finger, the one encircled by his black diamond pilot's ring. He pressed this appendage of muscle and bone flat against the chair's hard arm. The ivory tone of Danlo's skin stood out in contrast against the black shatterwood; in the light of the flame globes, his little fingernail sparkled like a jewel.

I will not cry out, Danlo promised himself. *On pain of death, I will not cry out.*

He willed himself to watch as Jaroslav touched the point of his knife against the tip of his finger. And then Jaroslav drove this diamond-steel point beneath his fingernail; he jiggled it to the right and left, working up deeper toward the quick of his nail. It seemed that he was trying to slowly lift away the whole nail as he might shell a nut. Blood spurted, and Danlo's throat clutched— and his belly seized up with agony in his urge to cry out. He tried to jerk his arm away from the killing knife, but could not. Acid wire cut his arm. He tried to move his whole being away from the fire burning up his arm, but he could not escape the knife, the blood, the terrible nearness of pain.

Oh, God; oh, God; oh, God; oh, God. Oh God—I want to die.

As Jaroslav finally cut the nail entirely away from Danlo's bleeding finger and held it up with glee as if he had found a ruby, Danlo ground his teeth together and lunged against the wire imprisoning him. Almost every muscle in his body convulsed at once; he felt his spine pop with the strain of it and an intense urge to vomit. It was then that he began to think about death. There was nothing clear or ordered about these thoughts; so overwhelming had his pain become that he could no longer apprehend the truths of the universe in words, concepts, or reasoned ponderings. All he knew was pain, the fire of pain and the endlessness of pain. And the terrible logic of pain: that pain must end but only when he died. If pain was life, which was only the movement of blood down toward the open veins of his fingertip and nerve signals burning up his arm toward his brain, then it could all stop so easily. Stop the moving of his cells, and he would die. At death, he knew, there would be no lifting of his soul away from the flesh, no encoding of his selfness as a program in a computer or other such fancies. There would be nothing but the cessation of movement, the quieting of consciousness and life. Peace, stillness, silence. To move not would be the end of pain, and he longed for this neverness of existence with every breath that came tearing like a knife down his throat. He wanted to will his heart not to move, to die from the terrible pain of life with all the inevitability with which he had been born.

To die, to die, to die, to die—oh, God; oh, God; oh, God, oh, God!

"Damn you, Danlo!"

This was Hanuman's voice, falling somewhere out of the blinding light inside Danlo. But so great was the confusion of Danlo's pain that he heard this voice as his own.

"Damn you, Danlo—why don't you cry?"

And Danlo heard this as, "Why don't you die?" And he wanted to open his bleeding lips to give Hanuman (or himself) the answer to his question, but he was afraid that if he did, he would scream so hard that the shock waves of sound would tear through his chest and stop his heart from beating.

Oh, God, no. No, no, no—I will not die.

For a long while—almost forever—Jaroslav Bulba worked on the other fingers of Danlo's hand. And with each fingernail, with every time he carved flesh with the point of his knife or used it as a drill to push down through nail and nerves into the bone, he grew more frustrated. And more curious, more devoted to his art. If he had had his way, he might have begun drilling through Danlo's eyes into his brain or carving open his chest to see if Danlo's heart beat all quick and red the same as any other man's. But Hanuman wouldn't allow any wanton mutilations of Danlo's flesh. He truly did not wish him to die. And so, with sharp motions of his hands or piercing looks, he bade the warrior-poets to keep to their plan. They would torture Danlo concentrating on those nerves most easily accessible through thin layers of skin or muscle. And so Jaroslav's knife found its way into the nerve centers of Danlo's elbow, his testicles, and the trigeminal plexus behind the cheekbones of his face.

When these tortures failed to elicit the desired result, Arrio Kell pulled a mars stick from one of his pockets. He held a flaming match to one end of the rolled-up tube of jambool while he puffed at the other. And then, with a thick blue smoke billowing out of his nostrils, he jammed the red-hot tip of the mars stick against the skin of Danlo's belly. There came a sizzling sound of sweat vaporizing and the cells of Danlo's body bursting open and giving up their water to the intense heat burning into him. The smell of cooked flesh hung heavily in the air. There were other smells, too—kana oil, old furs, dust, Hanuman's bloody breath—and all these terrible sensa together made Danlo gag as he whipped his head back and forth and refused to scream.

"This is hopeless," Jaroslav Bulba said. He stood next to Arrio Kell, and the robes of both warrior-poets were spattered with blood. He looked at Hanuman. "You wish your friend alive—but nine of ten men would have already died from the pain. And the tenth would have fallen mad."

"Perhaps he is the Eleventh," Hanuman said. He referred to that rare being out of warrior-poet theology who could transcend all pain in his journey toward the infinite.

"Even the Eleventh finally dies," Jaroslav said. "As all men must."

"All *men*," Hanuman agreed. And then he said, "I'll ask him the question one more time."

Again Hanuman looked at Danlo and asked him about the Sonderval's pathway through the stars. But Danlo remained silent, shaking his head as he gasped for air.

"It's time we brought in the akashic," Hanuman said. He turned to Arrio Kell and told him, "Go up to the cathedral and tell Radomil Morven that I require his services."

With a white towel, Arrio wiped the blood from his hands then pulled on a golden cloak to hide his blood-stained robes. He bowed to Hanuman before leaving the cell.

"I wish you'd let me take the eyes," Jaroslav said, looking at Danlo. "Drilling up the optic nerves causes the most unbelievable pain. Then, too, the fear of eyelessness might make him tell you what you want."

"Perhaps later," Hanuman said, calmly, reasonably, as if they were discussing a future dinner engagement. "But now we'll wait for the akashic."

As it happened, they didn't wait long. Soon, Arrio returned escorting a wizened old man named Radomil Morven. Once, he had been a master akashic of great renown, but in the early days of the Ringist church, he had deserted the Order to serve Hanuman—and to gain the reward of godhood before his heart gave out or some misfortune stole him from life. He came through the cell's doorway carrying the tools of his art as if they were weights made of lead. He shuffled over to where Danlo sat, sighing and wheezing as he set a little hologram stand down on the chess table next to the devotionary computer. With his gnarly fingers, he drummed the shining surface of the heaume that he would place upon Danlo's head.

"I know the need of what you've done," Radomil said to Hanuman as he pointed at Danlo. He looked at Danlo's flayed fingertips and the flap of skin hanging down over his bloody face.

Then he covered his mouth with his hand for a moment as if he might vomit. "But you should have called for me immediately upon injecting him with the ekkana. This torture was unnecessary."

"That's not for you to judge," Hanuman said.

"If you'd had more faith in my art," Radomil grumbled, almost ignoring the coldness falling over Hanuman's eyes, "even the ekkana wouldn't have been necessary."

"So you've told me."

"You open him with knives and acid wire, but my computer can open him much more efficiently."

"We shall see," Hanuman said.

"I could simply have examined the pilot upon one pretext or another," Radomil pressed on. In his willingness to argue with there Lord of Way of Ringess, he seemed utterly confident of his value to Hanuman. "Perhaps we could have told the godlings that Danlo wi Soli Ringess required our help in recovering lost memories."

In truth, Danlo had a nearly perfect memory, and he had never needed another's help in remembering anything. Hanuman, of course, knew this—as did almost anyone who knew Danlo or had been connected to Ringism from the early days. That Radomil seemed to have forgotten this well-known fact spoke much about the power of fear in undoing his ability to reason. Fear ran Radomil as it did most men; he feared decrepitude and disease, exploding stars and blood and the opinions of his fellow Ringists. Ironically, however, as with most men, most of what he feared would never come to pass, even as he blinded himself to dangers that hung over his head like a killing knife suspended by a single hair.

"But why," Hanuman asked quietly, "must we tell the godlings anything at all?" He looked at Jaroslav Bulba, then, quickly and subtly, and there was death in his icy, blue eyes.

No, Hanu, no, Danlo thought. *No, no, no; no . . .*

"Well, look at this poor pilot!" Radomil said, advancing toward Danlo's chair. "Look what you've done to him! He's an ambassador to the Order—what will we tell Demothi Bede when he comes to ask for Danlo's presence in the College of Lords?"

Hanuman suddenly turned the full force of his gaze upon Radomil and asked, "Do you trust me?"

And Radomil swallowed nervously and said, "Of course, Lord Hanuman."

"Then you must please trust me to solve these little problems."

"As you wish."

"And now can we please begin?" Hanuman asked. "Danlo has been waiting almost forever, and I don't wish to prolong his distress."

As Radomil Morven bent over Danlo to place the akashic's heaume upon his head, Danlo finally found his voice. "He . . . will . . . kill," he whispered. "You . . . kill you."

He tried to say more, tried to warn Radomil that he would never be allowed to tell any Ringist of what had happened in Danlo's cell that night. But as he opened his bloody mouth, the air fell against his much-bitten tongue like flames, and his jaw locked in sudden agony. If Radomil understood the meaning of Danlo's blood-frothed words, he must have discounted them, foolishly supposing that Danlo was only trying to forestall further torture.

"There," Radomil grunted as he adjusted the heaume. He turned to the display of Danlo's brain glittering from the hologram stand. All the gross structures from the cerebrum to the almond-shaped amygdala were lit up in various colors. At a word from Radomil, the hologram might shift to a deeper level, displaying the violet streaks of neural pathways through the temporal lobes or even the firing of individual neurons in the language centers. "Oh, he's in pain, very much so," Radomil said. "I've never seen this kind of pain before."

While Radomil pointed out various red, cloudlike bursts of light clumped around the brainstem and parietal lobes—in truth, in every part of Danlo's brain—Hanuman looked on with great interest as if he were still a journeyman cetic receiving a lesson. The warrior-poets, too, were ready to take advantage of the akashic's art. Jaroslav Bulba wanted to rip his knife across Danlo's feet, thighs, belly and eyeballs, just to see which parts of his brain would flare into light. But Hanuman would not allow such experiments. He kept himself concentrated on his purpose.

"Shall I ask him the question now?" Hanuman said to Radomil.

"Yes—before he faints from the pain. I can't believe he's borne this kind of pain without crying out or fainting."

"And where should I tell the warrior-poet to concentrate as I ask the question?"

Radomil cracked his old knuckles and said, "Tell him to

sheathe his knife. The pilot already has enough pain—any more would only drive him away from his ability to speak."

"I've called you here only because he *won't* speak," Hanuman said. "I need you to read his mind."

"But he still must speak, in his mind. In words, in numbers that have a precise representation in the frontal lobes. Too much pain will only cloud this representation."

"But too little pain will enable him to direct his thoughts as he will. He's adept in the cetics' arts, you should know."

Radomil did not ask how Danlo had acquired such prowess, nor did Hanuman tell him that he himself had revealed the secrets of his art to Danlo many years earlier. For a while, as Danlo rolled his wounded tongue through the blood filling his mouth, the two men debated the best way to gain the information that Hanuman sought.

"You're a master akashic," Hanuman said at last. He bowed deeply to Radomil, but his eyes remained cool with the disdain that cetics have for any of the lower practitioners of the mental arts, particularly specialists such as akashics. "One of the finest akashics I've ever known. I bow to your judgement. We'll begin only with words. And if words alone fail, then we'll ask the warrior-poet to accompany them with his knife."

With this compromise, Hanuman took Danlo's untouched hand in his and asked, "What are the fixed-points that the Sonderval must have revealed to you?"

And these words, like red rocket tailings, burned through Danlo's mind: *No, no—I must not think in words. No, no, no . . .*

"Again," Radomil said, studying the lights of the holographic display. "Ask your question again."

"Danlo," Hanuman said, and then he repeated his question.

"He's thinking 'no' and 'words,' " Radomil said. "He's trying not to think in words."

"Of course he is," Hanuman said.

"The more words that you speak, the harder his task will be."

"Of course—that must be true. Which is why I must find the right words."

Again, Hanuman asked his question, but this time he embellished it with queries as to the color of the Sonderval's eyes and the sound of the Sonderval's voice—any sensa that might associate with words spoken at the moment when the Sonderval had divulged the fixed-points of the stars along his pathway.

I must not think the words, Danlo thought. *The numbers, the fixed-points of . . . no, no, I will not. I will not, I will . . .*

"Keep speaking," Radomil told Hanuman. "We're very close."

Hanuman spoke then, and his voice, like a silver knife, cut through Danlo's ears and touched the deepest part of his brain. And Danlo closed his eyes and tried to melt away these words with all the fire of his will.

I will my will my will . . . My will is free like a thallow in the sky; I must have the courage to follow it.

"Remarkable," Radomil said. "Such a remarkable will he has. He's trying to think only in images—and I believe he's succeeding."

Will of heart fire heart beating white wings cold air blue sky . . .

For a while, Hanuman spoke softly to Danlo, asking about the Sonderval's fleet and the pilots who followed him. He began saying the fixed-points of stars that might lie along the Sonderval's pathway; it was his hope that one of these sets of points might trigger a clear memory in Danlo. When this failed, he began asking about the death of the Devaki tribe or why Danlo had allowed Tamara Ten Ashtoreth to leave him. These questions were crueler than the diamond-steel of Jaroslav's killing knife and cut Danlo down to his soul. They almost set loose an avalanche of emotions that might have broken him. But his will, like that of all men and women, was truly free, and this one time in his life he had the courage to follow it.

Sky blue behind blue black space screaming silence wild white starchild shimmering light beyond light light light . . .

"Well?" Hanuman finally asked.

"I can't read anything but these images," Radomil said. "I'm sorry."

Hanuman gently grasped Danlo's other hand, the one whose flayed red fingertips oozed blood. He squeezed these wounded fingers, then. With his hard little hand, he squeezed once, hard, and he must have felt the pain shooting like electricity up Danlo's arm, for he shuddered in violent spasms and suddenly let go. To Radomil he said, "And now what do you read?"

"Scarcely more than pain," Radomil said. "Pain as bright as light."

Light light light firelight fire fire fire . . .

"Please take the nails off his other hand," Hanuman said to Jaroslav.

"I'd rather take out his eyes," Jaroslav said as he began moving his knife beneath Danlo's thumb nail.

Hanuman ignored this and said to Danlo, "The fixed-points—what are they? You'll never be free from this pain until you tell me what they are."

Pain pain pain . . .

For a moment, as Danlo lunged against the acid wire and felt his thumb explode with fire, he thought that all he wanted was to be free from this hideous pain. To flee the burning agony of his existence like a worm burrowing beneath the snow—this tempted him almost more than he could bear. To fight pain or to escape it altogether had become almost the whole of his desire. But he might escape pain straight into words and thus betray the information that Hanuman so desperately sought. And so he turned in another direction. He remembered his deepest desire then, and he willed himself to soar higher (or deeper) into that brilliant star that blazed at the center of his being like a fiery red heart. Into the starfire he fell, gladly, freely, like a thallow soaring into the sun.

Pain.

As feathers become fire, he became his pain; pain was his life's beginning and end, and it went on and on forever in a universe that was nothing but pain.

Pain.

"This is useless," Radomil said. He looked at the display of Danlo's brain, all lit up with a brilliant red fire. Then he looked at Danlo, who sat with his eyes closed, all the while relaxing his chest and shoulders as if opening his heart to all the pain in the world.

Jaroslav Bulba cut loose yet another fingernail, then stood in front of Danlo with his dripping, red knife. To Hanuman, he said, "This *is* useless. If I didn't know that it was impossible, I'd think that he drank an antidote to the ekkana earlier tonight."

But no antidote for the ekkana poison existed, and Hanuman said, "No, he'll feel its fire all his life."

"And how long must that be?" Jaroslav asked, looking back and forth between Danlo and Hanuman.

"I don't know," Hanuman said with a terrible sadness in his voice. "How could I know?"

"Let me take his eyes, now," Jaroslav said.

Hanuman leaned closer to Danlo, then, and he gently pressed his fingers against Danlo's closed eyelids.

"Let me take his life," Jaroslav said with surprising compassion. "He's earned this freedom—no man more."

Hanuman stepped over behind Danlo's chair. He pressed his

fingertips against the great artery along Danlo's throat, and said, "How strongly his heart still beats."

"We could wait a few more days," Radomil said in his wheezy old voice. "After the effects of the ekkana have quieted, there are other drugs we might give him. And then, with most of his brain clear from the pain, I might read—"

"Can anyone read this man?" Hanuman asked softly, almost as if he were speaking to himself. "Have *I* ever been able to read him?"

"Let me take his life," Jaroslav repeated. "If he's reached his moment of the possible and gone on, then there's nothing else to do."

And Arrio Kell added, "If it's his fate to be the Eleventh, he'll have gone beyond all pain and you'll never read him."

Pain beyond pain. Fire beyond fire. Light beyond light inside light light light . . .

While the two warrior-poets stood arguing Danlo's fate with Radomil and Hanuman, something strange began to happen to Danlo. Inside himself, in that space of all fire and pain between his lungs, it seemed that he could feel heartbeats other than his own. He thought perhaps that they might be Hanuman's; he had always felt connected with him soul to soul as if they were twins joined at the chest and floating in their mother's womb. And then the beats seemed to come closer to him, as with a man walking toward him beating a drum. He could *see* this man: a young godling with a jook-pocked face hurrying into the cathedral and making his way through the corridors into the chapter house. His golden cloak flapped behind him like an angel's wings.

Danlo waited a few moments, and then he could hear the man, too, not only with this mysterious sense for which he had no name, but with his ears. And then Hanuman and the warrior-poets heard him as well. There came the distant whoosh of a door being opened, the slap of hard boots against stone. These sounds abruptly stopped outside Danlo's cell. Danlo's heart beat once more, and then someone's knuckles beat against the great steel door. "My Lord Hanuman," a voice called out, "I must speak with you immediately."

Hanuman motioned for Jaroslav to open the door. This he did, and a fervent-looking man wearing a golden robe hurried into the room. Jook pocks scarred his face, which was still red from his journey through the cold streets. His name, as Danlo remembered, was Ivar Zayit, and next to Surya Surata Lal or Jaroslav Bulba, he was the most trusted of Hanuman's godlings.

"Come closer, then," Hanuman said as he stepped over to th
farthest corner of the cell. "Please, catch your breath and calr
yourself."

This Ivar did, and then he cupped his hands over Hanuman'
ear and began whispering. After a few moments, Hanuman pulle
away with a jerk as if he couldn't bear such an intimate touch b
another human being.

"You may free the pilot," Hanuman said to Jaroslav. "There'
nothing of help that he could tell us now."

"What news has Ivar brought, then?"

"*This* news," Hanuman said softly. "This news that will soo
be all over the city. Near Mara's Star, by purest chance, a cadre c
twenty lightships discovered part of the Fellowship's fleet. An
the fleet discovered them. There was a small battle. You shoul
know, two of our pilots survived to return to Neverness. The
will be no surprising the Sonderval now. He'll wait for us ther
around that damned star—or one close by such as Orino Luz."

"He may wait, but would it be wise for Salmalin to lead th
Order's fleet against him?" This question came from Radom
Morven, who considered himself a natural strategist in all matter
concerning war—as many men who know nothing about war ar
wont to do.

"Would this be wise?" Hanuman mused. His eyes paled for
moment like blue ice obscured by clouds. The neurologics twist
ing through the clearface on his head lit up in a million strands c
purple wire. Then he said, "Ivar Zayit has just come from th
Academy, where the entire College of Lords is meeting to deter
mine whether such a course of action would be wise."

"But surely it's upon the Lord of the Order himself to decid
whether or not to send out the fleet," Radomil said. Despite hi
skill at reading men's minds, he still hadn't quite read the subtl
play of power connecting Hanuman to Lord Pall.

"Surely that's true," Hanuman said. "But Lord Pall value
farsighted counsel. Which is why he has sent for my help i
making this decision."

"What will you counsel, then?" Jaroslav asked as he wipe
his knife with a blood-spattered cloth.

"First," Hanuman said, "that you cut the pilot free and hel
him to his bed."

"As you wish," Jaroslav said.

With a blindingly quick motion, he sheathed his killing knif
and drew a blade of another sort from a pocket of his cloak. Thi
little tool was not really a weapon at all, but only a heat knif

which he used to cut Danlo's bonds. In a moment—in a hiss of scorched acid wire and a sickening smell like burning hair—Jaroslav slid the heat knife down the silvery cocoon imprisoning Danlo. It took Arrio Kell scarcely more time to glue shut the wound on Danlo's face and to fit ten krydda-filled skin tubes over Danlo's wounded fingers. Then the two warrior-poets helped him walk to his bed; they gently pulled the furs up covering his naked body almost as if they were tucking in a child for the night.

"Secondly," Hanuman said as he looked at Jaroslav with his deadly cold eyes, "I would like you to escort Radomil back to his apartment."

"That really won't be necessary," Radomil said. He, too, looked at the warrior-poet, perhaps remembering how easily his knife could find its way into a man's flesh.

Hanuman came up close to Radomil and put his hand on his shoulder as if they were old friends. "I'm sorry but I must insist. The streets are dangerous at night, and we of the Way have many enemies."

"But Lord Hanuman—"

"Please allow me to repay your efforts here tonight. You've seen much that would be hard for others to see." With this, Hanuman turned to Jaroslav and said, "Please return him now. You know the way, don't you?"

Jaroslav stared at Hanuman for a moment, and murderous daggers of understanding passed back and forth between their eyes.

"I know the way," Jaroslav finally said. "It will be my pleasure."

He laid his hand on Radomil's arm and steered him toward the door.

"And now," Hanuman said, "Arrio will escort *me* back to my chambers. Where I shall consider what counsel to give Lord Pall."

Ivar Zayit stood next to the cell's chess table, watching Radomil collect his akashic's heaume and holographic display with his trembling hands. Then he looked at Hanuman and asked, "And how may I serve you, Lord Hanuman?"

"You'll come with me," Hanuman said. "I'll need you to wait outside my chambers, and then convey my counsel to Lord Pall."

Ivar Zayit bowed his head in acquiescence to Hanuman's wishes. And then, almost as if he were executing one of the movements of his killing art, Hanuman pushed out his palms to usher out everyone from Danlo's cell. But before leaving himself, he stepped over to Danlo's bed and checked the pulse along Danlo's

throat. And then, moving his lips close to Danlo's ear so that n
one else could hear him, he whispered, "I know you're consciou:
I know you understand me. And I know your pain, but you mad
me share it with you, do you understand? *Do* you? Do you really
I'm sorry, but the pain will lessen in a few more hours. Anothe
eternity, I know, but after that you should try to sleep. Slee|
Danlo, and heal yourself of your wounds, and you still migl
live."

For a moment, Danlo lay shrouded in his furs like a corps
Then he opened his eyes, and a deep blue fire poured out of hin
all the terrible beauty and brilliance of his soul. Hanuman shuc
dered to see this, as if looking at this sunlike thing inside Danl
would cook his face and eat his own eyes down to the bone. A
last, he had to break the connection between them and look awa}

"No, I will not sleep now," Danlo whispered. His lips wei
bleeding, and his tongue—and he could barely form the words i
his mouth. "If I sleep, I die . . . you said, Hanu. If I sleep,
die."

"Goodbye, then," Hanuman said.

"Hanu, Hanu—goodbye."

Hanuman stood away from the bed and whispered, "I'm sorr}
Danlo." Then he backed out of the room and shut the doo
leaving Danlo alone.

Only when I am alone am I not alone, Danlo remembered *I*
pain I am never alone.

As Danlo lay back in his cold bed and stared at his cell's lonj
dark door, he opened himself to all the pain inside him. An
something inside him opened then. Like a door opening onto a
the golden, shimmering pain in the universe, his heart moved an
he felt the movements of other hearts far away. In truth, he felt th
movement of molecules and planets and stars, lightships and mei
and of other things—perhaps everything. All the universe fron
the center of his bed to the uttermost galaxies of the Grus Clou
moved with a beautiful but terrible purpose, and it all hurt. Move
ment itself was the essence of pain, the electrons of hot blue sta»
and of his own blazing eyes spinning and shimmering and cor
necting to that golden moment at the beginning of time when a
matter and memory were one.

Everything remembers everything, he thought. *Everything, ev*
erywhere.

In another moment of time—in the nowness of streamin
blood and knives of pain spinning through every part of hi
body—a clear light shined upon events that had recently occurre

far away. With open eyes and open heart he remembered the battle of which Ivar Zayit had spoken. He could *see* these blindingly quick movements of lightships and blackships and all the other ships of the Fellowship's Tenth Battle Group, commanded by his friend, Bardo.

There were other ships, too. In the deep space around a blazing blue star called Mara's Star (and in the even deeper spaces inside his own mind) he saw a cadre of twenty Ringist lightships surprise the ships of three of Bardo's pilots. That is, the Ringist pilots must have thought they were surprising them, just as they must have supposed that the three ships floated alone and helpless to attack. For they fell against them like wolves surrounding shagshay ewes, but as they did so, the main body of Bardo's battle group fell out of the manifold against *them*.

It was a trap well-baited and quickly closed. There came flashes of diamond and light bursts every time a window to the manifold opened. Bardo himself, in his *Sword of Shiva,* sought out the leader of the Ringist pilots. This was Charl Odissan in the *Phoenix Rising,* a lightship famous for the golden and scarlet hues impregnated in its black diamond hull. After a series of furious feints and fenestrations through the manifold's many windows, Bardo managed to map the *Phoenix Rising* into the heart of Mara's Star. He must have seen it vanish from realspace like a piece of ice vaporized by a heat gun. But he certainly couldn't have seen it reappear at the fixed points that he had chosen deep inside the star. He couldn't have beheld the look of surprise in Charl's brown eyes or heard his final scream.

Danlo, however, lying five hundred light-years away in a cold bed, did. He watched as the star's terrible fire burned away the diamond skin of Charl's lightship, and then quickly blackened the toffee-colored skin of Charl's handsome face. He watched and he waited almost forever, and he felt Charl's final heartbeat as an anguished scarlet burst inside his own chest. He almost screamed, then. In the solitude of his cell and the sudden aloneness of his soul, he opened his mouth and wanted to scream out all the infinite pain inside himself.

No! No, no, no, no . . .

But he couldn't look away from this brilliant, blazing reality. He saw and felt and remembered and knew—and he knew that what came into his mind like a fireflower opening in the sun was true.

Ahira, Ahira, he prayed, *mi alasharia la shantih Charl Odissan, shantih, shantih.*

He might have prayed for all the other pilots and peoples caught up in this terrible war, but he couldn't move his lips or find the voice of his deepest self. Suddenly, the pain grew too great. It exploded inside him like a star falling supernova, and all he knew was fire and infinity and a terribly beautiful light beyond light.

MARA'S STAR

Fear not, and be not dismayed at this great multitude; for the battle is not yours but God's.
                              —from the Chronicles of Israel

Only the dead have seen an end to war.
                              —Plato

The next ten days were the strangest of Danlo's life. He spent all this time alone in his cell, usually lying in his bloodstained bed, eating the soft foods that one of Hanuman's godlings brought him, and healing. Healing and yet not healing. Although his burns quickly scabbed over and nubs of shiny new nails began forming at the base of each finger's quick, the ekkana drug still seared him as if every tissue of his body had been stung with Scutari venom. He could no more escape his pain than he could sublimate himself into vapor and pass out the cracks of his cell's steel door.

It was the paradox of his existence during this period of nightmare sweats and unheard screams that the worse his pain became the more easily he could bear it. During those terrible moments when his blood and bones seemed to dissolve into a molten lava that burned his insides with its fire, he himself could dissolve into fire, the fire into light. In his wildest agony, he could find a place so hideously hot that it felt as cold as ice, a frenzy of motion so violent that it whirled around a center of stillness, clarity and peace. Like a white bird taking refuge at the eye of a firestorm, he could rest at this center beneath a calm blue sky while hellish winds raged all about him.

But, inevitably, there came other moments even more terrible where his pain would subside merely to a fevered torment as if each cell of his body had been burned in the sun. Then he would become all too aware of his suffering; he would feel himself *as* a separate self trapped in the agony of pure existence. He would feel his blood boiling through his veins and arteries, scalding him deep inside. Often, he covered his face with his pillow and screamed like a snow tiger caught in boiling tar. He screamed and wept and raged until his voice gave out; he passed into delirium and hellish visions, and then awoke whispering once more his prayer that God would let him die.

But he held onto life more fiercely than a tiger clasping a young bull in its claws. Four times each day Hanuman's godling brought him his meals, and he always forced himself to eat, even though every mouthful of food burned his throat and stomach as if he had swallowed acid. Two times each day, in the morning and evening, Hanuman sent a cetic to his cell. This man—his name was Daman Nelek—tended Danlo's wounds and taught him various mental arts that he might use to fight the fire of the ekkana poison. Although Danlo tried not to hate Daman Nelek for being a cetic, he drank in his words as if gulping cool water. Night and day he practiced tapas and shama meditation and other arts for living with his pain. It didn't really help much, but was all that he could do.

It was from Daman Nelek that he learned of the events occurring outside his cell. Daman brought the news of the city: in the Great Circle near the Street of Embassies, the harijan had rioted yet again; movements of foodstuffs into the Ashtoreth District had been delayed or blocked altogether, causing the worst hunger in Neverness since the Dark Year; and two of Hanuman's warrior-poets, Kiritan Wu and Jamil Turkmanian, had slipped their killing knives into three of Benjamin Hur's assassins who had killed their friends.

And the news of other worlds: on Heaven's Gate, the Ringists had begun a pogrom against those whom they called the Wayless, murdering almost a million men and women in a single night; a new supernova—possibly the work of Bertram Jaspari's Iviomils or some dread god—had appeared in the spaces beyond Darkmoon; and of most immediate importance, Lord Pall had commanded the Order's fleet to move against the Fellowship where they gathered around Mara's Star.

"Everyone is expecting a battle," Daman Nelek said as he glued a swatch of thinskin over the oozing burn on Danlo's chest. He shook his silver-haired head in amazement at how well Danlo was healing. Danlo, who had always been quick to recover from any wound, was amazed himself at how quickly his burns and lacerations gave way to new flesh. It was almost as if the ekkana had quickened his whole being and fired his cells into a new state of regenerative possibilities. "I expect the war will be over before

Lord Hanuman lets you out of bed. So please try to rest, Danlo wi Soli Ringess. There's no stopping it now."

During the days that followed, Danlo did keep to his bed although he had difficulty resting. Sleep, as he had once known sleep—those long hours of easy breathing and unconscious return to his deepest self—became impossible. Often he meditated for hours to ease his pain. Often he sweated through nightmares and dreams of terrible violence that seemed much more real than any dream. And then, on the evening of 18th of winter, he came awake with a trembling in his belly and blood on his lips. In the chaos of his sleepless sleep, it seemed, in his writhing and working his jaws to scream out "no!" he had bitten his cheek. He tried to climb out of bed but could not bear the pain of movement. He lay back swallowing his own blood and shuddering at the terrible, iron-red taste of it. He faced the long, dark window, looking for the stars. Only the brightest of lights pierced the foot-thick clary pane: perhaps Bellatrix and Agni and, if the hour were as late as he guessed, even the blood-red radiance of Veda Luz.

Or perhaps the faint, almost ghostly lights dancing in the window were only a trick of his vision, no more real than the snowstorms of lights that he could induce by pressing his thumbs against his closed eyelids. He lay back in his soft white furs, and a strangeness fell over him, a coldness and marvelous clarity as if he were laying back in the snow outside and looking up at the bright black sky. For a moment, his pain left him. Or rather, he still hurt terribly, but he didn't mind that he hurt. Pain was the awareness of life, he remembered, and he only thrilled to feel it spreading through him as if he had drunk the purest ice water. And then, suddenly, there in the window—in the deep clary pane or perhaps in the deeper window of his own mind—shined a star. It was red-orange, the color of a bloodfruit and almost as bright as Gloriana Luz. From the constellation of the other stars around it, he knew that it must be Mara's Star.

Pain is the awareness of life. Pain inside pain, awareness inside awareness inside . . .

Inside Danlo's dark and silent cell, as he lay with his eyes open on infinity, something opened inside him. In a moment of terrible beauty, he felt his awareness spreading out like rays of light into the universe. There came a shimmering interconnectedness of all things, a touching of faraway planets and comets and blazing stars. In truth, the vision that fell over him was not really like seeing at all, as a god might look out over the wonders of the galaxy. It was more like seeing from within, as if he were the seeing part of whatever piece of matter or spacetime in which he found his awareness focused. And even more, it was more like *being:* rocks or ice or blood or starlight or the black diamond crystal of a lightship's shimmering hull.

At first, in this vastening outward into infinity, he became no specific thing, but rather the flow of matter and consciousness inside all things, that truly *was* all things. And yet that wasn't quite right, either, for he was within and without, all at once. And everywhere at once. This marvelous new way of apprehending reality allowed him to move through the Holy Ivi's palace on faraway Tannahill no less the depths of a hydrogen atom in his own brain.

The totality of the experience might have crushed him under like a tidal wave if he hadn't chosen a single place to center his awareness. At the center of the 25th Deva Cluster of stars, out near Orino Luz, a single star shined like a great red eye. Mara's Star, it was called, and it illuminated the thirty-two thousand ships of the Fellowship of Free Worlds that waited for the Order's fleet to attack. As if Danlo had himself become this star, his awareness bathed the swarms of ships in an intense, numinous light. And this is what he saw:

The Sonderval, in his prominent ship the *Cardinal Virtue,* had divided his fleet into fifteen battle groups. Against the redness of Mara's Star, they gathered together around the Sonderval's First Group forming a vast, diamond wheel through space. The Sonderval had arrayed five battle groups—the Second, Third, Fourth, Fifth, and Ninth, commanded by Helena Charbo, Sabri dur li Kadir, Aja, Charl Rappaporth and Richardess—in an inner circle surrounded by the remaining nine groups on the outer rim. There, Cristobel and Alesar Estarei were the pilot-captains of the Eleventh and Twelfth Groups while nearby, closer in toward the fire of the star, Bardo led the ships of the soon-to-be-famous Tenth Battle Group.

It was an unprecedented disposition of ships with which to give battle; but then as far as anyone knew, no battle ever fought by human beings in space (or during the Man-Darghinni wars) had been like the one that the Fellowship would fight with the Ringists. The Sonderval had spun some thirty-two thousand ships into a vast, shimmering web of diamond and black nall while Salmalin the Prudent led perhaps forty thousand ships against him. In the spaces of the Civilized Worlds, no such numbers had ever come together in battle, or indeed for any purpose. And most of the ships were deepships or longships, fireships or goldships or blackships whose hulls were wrought of purest nall. Only 756 lightships, divided unequally between the two fleets, showed themselves like bright diamond needles darting among lesser vessels. During the Pilot's War, only lightships had fought lightships; but as the Sonderval and many others immediately understood, *this* war would be very different.

To begin with, its battles would be much more static. In the Pilot's War, Mallory Ringess had led his sixty-six lightships against those of Lord Leopold Soli in a great running battle across the Fallaways from Ninsun to Gehenna Luz. And even then, commanding the finest of pilots such as Helena Charbo, Delora wi Towt, Jonathan Ede and others, Mallory Ringess had found the close coordination of these few lightships difficult. To lead thirty thousand ships from star to star and keep them together in the midst of flashing diamond and death and windows to the manifold opening in bursts of light would be impossible, and the Sonderval knew this. And so he had devised a different strategy. He would choose spaces suitable to his plan and then provoke Lord Salmalin into a battle. The provocation—Bardo's near-annihilation of a cadre of Ringist lightships—had already been accomplished. It only remained for the Sonderval to choose the site of the coming battle and array his forces wisely, and this he did. As he told Bardo and his other pilot-captains, he would try to adapt the strategy that Hannibal Barka had used against the Romans at Kannae thousands of years earlier on Old Earth.

"We'll lay a trap for the Ringists," the Sonderval told his pilot-captains by light radio. This was on the evening of the 11th of winter, as time is measured in Neverness. "We'll spin a great web of ships through space with my ship at its center. And when Salmalin attacks, we'll close on his ships and destroy them."

At Kannae, Hannibal had arrayed his cosmopolitan Karthaginian army against a Roman one much superior in numbers. At his center, in a curious crescent-shaped formation, he had placed himself and his Spanish and Gaulish warriors, who liked to fight naked except for their long shields. They were brave but ill-disciplined, and almost certain to give way before the great crush of Roman armor massed against them. On either side of these wild men, Hannibal had divided the cream of his infantry: his African veterans, dark-faced men with sharp swords and murderous intentions. On his left flank, he drew up his heavy cavalry, and on his right, his incomparable Numidian light horse led by Maharbal the Great.

When the battle began, the Karthaginian heavy cavalry began

to destroy the armored knights on the Roman's right flank while
on the left flank, Maharbal's horse warriors—the finest in the
world—drove off the cavalry of the Roman allies. Meanwhile, in
the center, the Roman legions advanced on Hannibal. They struck
like a great steel hammer, using their spears and short stabbing
swords to drive into the lightly armored Karthaginian line. Inevitably, the crescent of Spaniards and Gauls with Hannibal at its
center began to bend backward and give way. Encouraged, falsely
sensing victory, the Romans pushed even deeper into the
Karthaginian center, so deep that Hannibal's African veterans
formed two jaws of steel on either side of the excited Romans. At
a signal from Hannibal—a blaring trumpet—the Africans began
to close on the Roman legions like a lion's jaws on fresh meat.

So tightly packed were the Romans into a sweating, bloodthirsty mass that they could scarcely wield their swords or raise
their shields. The two arms of Hannibal's cavalry completed the
trap. Having driven off or slain the Roman knights and their allies,
they wheeled about and fell on the Roman army's rear. Thus
having completely enveloped the Roman legions on the front, two
sides and rear, the Karthaginians began to slaughter their sworn
enemies. Sixty thousand Romans died in one afternoon, including
two consuls, eighty senators and twenty-nine tribunes of noble
birth. The golden signet rings of the fallen Roman knights alone
amounted to three bushels in weight. In the history of the human
race, it was the greatest number of men killed in a single battle
until the wars of the Holocaust some two thousand years later.

Certainly the Sonderval, that most vainglorious of men, hoped
to repeat Hannibal Barka's historic victory. But history never re-
peats itself. The Sonderval had spent his life training to be a
mathematician and pilot, not a general. He knew little of leading
great masses of men and women trembling with battle-fear inside
their black nall ships. His genius lay in applying the theorems of
probabilistic topology and piloting his lightship alone through the
galaxy's stars. True, he had fought with Mallory Ringess in the
Pilot's War and had distinguished himself for his command of
the peculiar tactics of warfare in space. And so had some of his
pilots and pilot-captains such as Alark of Urradeth and Bardo.
But he commanded no such corps of hardened veterans as
Maharbal and Hasdrubal and Mago and the other Africans who
had followed Hannibal over the Alp mountains into Italy. Most of
his would-be warriors were as new to battle as baby foxes born on
a bright winter day. And the space of a sun-baked battlefield on
Old Earth is very different from the space of deep space out near

a red giant star. Ultimately, it was space itself that would defeat the Sonderval and rob him of his victory.

And so as the citizens of Neverness enjoyed a night of clear, cold air and great vistas of blazing stars, five hundred light years across the Fallaways the Sonderval drew his fleet into a great shimmering web. His thirty-two thousand ships faced coreward in the direction of Neverness's cool yellow star. As the Sonderval had calculated, it was from this direction that the Ringist fleet must approach. Of course in deep space the words "direction" and "approach" have different meanings than they do on the fields of a faraway planet. The Ringist ships wouldn't charge steadily as horses galloping across a dusty plain; rather they would fenester from stellar window to window in hundreds of discrete jumps. And they wouldn't come at the Fellowship's fleet from the east, south, north or west, but would fall suddenly out of thousands of the billion billion point-exits spread out in the black space near Mara's Star. Not even the Sonderval—not even a god—could exactly predict which point-exits these would be. But the great mass of them were concentrated in three great spinning thickspaces half a billion miles coreward of Mara's Star. In the coming battle, these thickspaces would play a crucial role, similar in strategic importance to the Round Top Hills in the battle of Gettysburg just before the Holocaust. The Sonderval arrayed his fleet facing these thickspaces, and commanded his pilots to watch and wait.

There came a moment when the first of the Ringist ships began to fall out of the opened windows throughout the two thickspaces. The lightships appeared first like a sudden flurry of ice crystals falling out of a winter night. Then came goldships and blackships, thousands of them, and all the other ships of the Ringist fleet. This falling out took more than five hundred seconds, for the Ringist fleet was badly coordinated and most of Salmalin's pilots had little experience in the most noble of all arts. The assembly of their fleet into their respective cadres required another five hundred seconds. If the Sonderval had been quick to attack, he might have destroyed the Ringist ships as they fell out of the manifold in their ones and twos and hundreds. But in truth, his fleet was almost as badly coordinated as Salmalin's. He couldn't trust his pilots—other than his lightship pilots—to execute the kind of complex maneuvers necessary to catch the Ringist ships the moment that they fell out of each window. Then, too, he couldn't have guessed that this gathering operation of Salmalin's ships would take so long. Wisely, he restrained the more impetuous of his pilots and kept to his original plan.

And so it was the Ringists who attacked, not the Fellowship. As the Sonderval had hoped, Salmalin led his fleet toward the gleaming web of ships spread throughout a thousand miles of space. But he did not lead them straight toward the Fellowship's center, in the manner of iron-disciplined Romans marching foot by foot over a plain of hard earth. Space is three-dimensional, not two, and in any case the topology of the underlying manifold makes the idea of a straightforward approach in a single direction meaningless. It was always possible for the Ringist ships to fall out of windows to the flanks of the Fellowship fleet and behind them as well—and even hull to hull in their very midst. That few such point-exits existed in the segment of space where Fellowship's fleet waited was no accident. The Sonderval had chosen his "terrain" with all the care of a general examining a battlefield for boulders and depressions which his enemy might use to hide. He had calculated that Salmalin would not gamble his fleet on an approach through these few point-exits. Not for nothing was the Lord Pilot of the Order known as Salmalin the Prudent.

Salmalin the Prudent was also Salmalin the Stolid. He knew little of war and had the imagination for even less. The whole of his martial wisdom might have been encompassed by such maxims as "never divide one's forces" and "strike at the enemy's weakest point." These he obeyed as dutifully as a novice bowing before one of his masters. And so when he fell out of the manifold in his new ship, the *Alpha Omega* (which had replaced the one that Bardo had stolen), his untutored eye looked out across a few hundred miles of space and picked out the weakest point of the Fellowship's fleet.

There, at the center of a great wheel of ships surrounded by fourteen other such wheels, floated the *Cardinal Virtue*. This distinctive ship with its long, sweeping lines occupied the point closest to the Ringist fleet. The other ships of the First Battle Group were arrayed around the Sonderval in a curious lens-shaped formation bulging out toward the Ringists. To Salmalin, it must have seemed that the arrogant Sonderval was courting glory by exposing himself so. In any case, this central First Battle Group so near to the Ringist fleet—and so nearly isolated from the lightships and blackships of the other battle groups—clearly comprised the Fellowship's weakest point. And so there Salmalin ordered his cadres of ships to concentrate their attack.

At least six thousand Ringist ships leapt forward toward the

First Battle Group. The Ringist fleet had been ordered very differently than that of the Fellowship. Salmalin's 451 lightships had been divided among twenty cadres, it being thought that the pilots of the Order would fight best among their own kind. Similarly, the ships from the Ringist worlds—from Arcite, Heaven's Gate, Thorskalle, Farrago and all the others—fought together with their worldmates in cadres as small as twenty ships and as large as five hundred. For this first strike against the Fellowship's center, Salmalin chose five cadres of lightships and thirty cadres of lesser ships from thirty Ringist worlds. Thus his lightships outnumbered those of the First Battle Group one hundred and ten against twenty, and his other ships fell against the Sonderval's 2,000 goldships and blackships in a force greater by more than three times.

In the opening seconds of the battle, it seemed that the Sonderval's trap might work as he had planned. Even if they had been ordered to do so, the ships of his battle group could not hold against the Ringists. Pilot fell against pilot, trying to force an enemy's ship into an open window and map it into a point-exit within Mara's Star. The pilots of the Ringist lightships slipped in and out of realspace like a hundred and ten diamond needles stitching a terrible pattern in black velvet. Where they encountered lesser ships—especially the cumbersome deepships—they quickly sent them to their deaths in this fiery hell.

But sometimes lightship would fall against lightship. Sometimes, as when the Order's Yoko Jael tried to slay Lara Jesusa in the *White Lotus,* there would occur a wild, intricate dance in and out of the manifold as of light beams twining around each other. Three of the Ringist pilots—Taura Tetsu, Sarojin li Kane, and Riesa Eshte in the *Cube of Space,* perished this way when they made a mathematical misstep and their deadly dance carried them into the fire. But three of the Sonderval's pilot's perished, too, including one of his finest, Zapata Karek who had fought with Mallory Ringess in the Pilot's War and distinguished himself and his ship, the *Sagittarius Bridge.* And the Sonderval might have lost even more of his precious lightships if his pilots hadn't been under strict orders to fall back from the Ringist fleet.

For pilots with as much élan as Arrio Blackstone or Valdamar Tor, such orders were like stone walls imprisoning them, for the essence of piloting a lightship is that one must always move freely where one must. Then too, it was hard for the lightship pilots simply to abandon the less skilled pilots of the lesser ships. But fortunately, the Sonderval had ordered these blackships and goldships to fall back as well, and this they gladly did wherever they could.

And so the great lens of ships comprising the First Battle Group, under the fierce assault of the Ringists, began to buckle and bend backward through space. The Ringists ships poured like a stream of glittering sand in toward the center. And every moment or so, the black glass of space filled with flashes of light. Every time a lightship or goldship opened a window to the manifold, light would flash out and illuminate the swarm of packed ships. Other lights lit up the night as well. Many of the Fellowship and Ringist ships had mounted laser cannon in preparation for this battle. Laser light was useless against the diamond hulls of the lightships or the blackships' extremely dense black nall. But some of the blackships—and especially the goldships and fireships—were built so that the pit projected out of the hull's side like a clear bubble. Inside these pits, which were usually made of clary, the pilots floated and guided their ships by sight as much as interface with their ships' computers. Thus when making planetfall or skimming above the mountains of some alien continent, they could see more easily. But this construction also left them vulnerable: a blackship mounting laser cannon might target a pilot alone in his clary pit and send a beam of killing light streaking through space and easily penetrating the relatively thin clary bubbles. One pilot, Kasimir of Urradeth, claimed that after correcting for the diffraction angles through the curving clary pits, at a distance of a hundred miles, he could send a laser beam burning through the pupil of his enemy's eye.

All the pilots in all the ships, of course, were vulnerable to the hydrogen bombs that some of the criminal Ringists such as Thorskallers used in violation of the Three Laws. However, these weapons of such terrible historic importance played little part in the Battle of Mara's Star. Compared to laser light or the lightning movements of the ships flashing in and out of the opening windows, hydrogen missiles fired at an enemy ship were slow, hideously slow. Then, too, with the ships of both fleets at first packed so densely together, an exploding hydrogen bomb might easily incinerate the ship of friend as well as foe. During the entire course of the battle involving some seventy thousand ships, only fifty-five such missiles were fired. And they accounted for the destruction of only two goldships and one blackship. In the black dome of space, the great blossoms of hydrogen-generated light provided a terribly beautiful fireworks but little more.

With the Sonderval's First Battle Group thus engaged in the

center, and five groups waiting in the inner circle, the pilot-captains of the other groups on the rim of the Fellowship's fleet began the maneuver upon which the battle would hinge. At nearly the same moment, the Sixth, Seventh, Eighth, Tenth, Eleventh, Twelfth, Thirteenth, Fourteenth and Fifteenth Battle Groups fell off through space and struck toward the Ringist's flanks. It was their hope to face the Ringist cadres—most of which were composed of lesser ships from one of the Ringist worlds—and smash them. Aside from Bardo's Tenth Battle Group, however, only the Eleventh and Twelfth groups, led by Alesar Estarei and Cristobel the Bold in the *Diamond Lotus,* came close to executing this plan.

But the battle is to the swift and strong, and all the battle groups faced the problem of coordinating their ships as they fell through the manifold, which inhibited their speed. And all the groups except the lucky Eleventh and Twelfth found that, while most of the cadres they fought were composed of lesser ships, at least one lightship cadre strengthened the swarms of blackships falling against them. Only Bardo, of all the pilot-captains, succeeded in overcoming the two lightship cadres—and the many lesser cadres—arrayed against him. He owed his success to three things: first, except for the Sonderval, of all the seventy thousand pilots in their ships to look out the red flames of Mara's Star, he was probably the finest. Second, he proved to be a great leader of women and men; his innate compassion enabled him to see the problems and fears of even the least of his pilots where the Sonderval would show only contempt. This most undisciplined of men in his personal life understood how to impose discipline on innocent pilots from Simoom and Vesper and other worlds and encourage them. And third, he had an inborn genius for war.

It was Bardo's innovation to divide his group into twenty sets of a hundred ships each, and to appoint one of his lightship pilots as commander of each set. Almost everyone in the Fellowship's fleet considered this to be a waste of the lightships and their pilots. It would only hamper their mobility, his critics said; it would only destroy their ability to streak from star to star as they had in the Pilot's War and concentrate their force on the lightships arrayed against them. But Bardo gambled that any loss of mobility would be more than offset by an increase in strength. Being himself a very powerful man, he believed in strength as the foremost martial virtue. He also believed in the cultivation of knowledge. After all, before founding the religion that he now fought, he had been Master of Novices at the Academy. As he put it to one of his commander pilots, Ivar Rey in the *Flame of God,* "If we don't teach these poor blackship pilots the noblest of arts, who will? And if a pilot takes to the pit of his ship, he should be a *pilot*, by God! Otherwise, he's as useless as a third leg on a whore.''

And so Bardo had spent almost all his waking hours before the battle teaching his commanders how to teach the lesser pilots the noble art of falling through the manifold. And while it was impossible to take a gentle woman from Solsken and transform her overnight into a warrior-pilot the likes of Lara Jesusa, there were many tricks and techniques that she might learn in order to use her blackship to a greater effect. Two thousand such women—and men—as Bardo reasoned, in a great battle group of ships might vex even the finest lightship pilots.

When the battle finally came, Bardo spent almost every electrifying second in helping his twenty commanders to help the lesser pilots in the sets that they led. That day on the 18th of winter in deep space, he accomplished what no other pilot-captain did: While leading his two thousand ships like a kitikeesha drake at the head of his flock, he kept flowing a simultaneous stream of communication with Ivar Rey and Duncan li Gur and his other set commanders. And then later, in the fire of battle with his group spread out over more than a million miles of realspace, he both led and inspired his commanders to fight at the same time. He did this by a demonstration of rare prowess, what the envious Richardess would call the finest flowering of the pilot's art.

Some said that like some mythic subatomic particle he managed to be two places at once, but it wasn't so. So quick and precise were the mappings of his lightship from window to window that it only *seemed* that the *Sword of Shiva* had a double streaking through space. One moment Bardo would appear to advise the rashest of his commanders, Odinan Rodas, not to overextend his set of ships, while the next moment would find him urging Yannis Helaku to take his set straight into a swarm of undisciplined blackships. And *between* these moments he might find help for some poor goldship pilot unable to make a point to point mapping or even fight off a pair of Ringist lightships harassing his hard-pressed 17th set.

Three times during the first movement of the battle he fought one-on-one duels with other lightships. And three pilots of Neverness, including Darrio of Urradeth in the *Infinite Dactyl*, he slew. And the miracle of it was that he never abandoned his set commanders to their own fates or diverged from his purpose. Amidst streaking laser beams and exploding hydrogen bombs and win-lows to the manifold flashing open, that day the *Sword of Shiva* was the brightest light in deep space. In his brilliant diamond lightship, like some ancient god of war come to life, Bardo led his pilots and they followed. They cut into their enemy's ships with a rare fury, either dispersing them or destroying them altogether. In little time, the entire sunward flank of the Ringist fleet collapsed. And then, as the Sonderval had hoped, Bardo led his Tenth Battle Group in a great wheeling movement to take the Ringists in their rear.

But he was the only one of the Sonderval's pilot-captains to fully complete this encircling maneuver. Alesar Estarei and Cristobel the Bold, leading the Eleventh and Twelfth Battle Groups (if 'lead' is the right word), did manage to turn the coreward flank. But they left too many of their enemy's ships undestroyed behind them, and too many of their own. In their wild dash around the Ringist fleet they simply abandoned the slower of their goldships and blackships, which amounted to almost half their groups. They were very lucky not to encounter any Ringist lightships; if they had, they never would have fought free to circle around the Ringist flank. Or at least only the lightships would have done so. As it was, these two battle groups joined Bardo's attack of the Ringist rear much reduced in force. The Sonderval had calculated that of the nine battle groups attacking the Ringist flanks, four or five would win through to complete the encirclement. But with Bardo's mostly intact group and only half each of Alesar's and Cristobel's, only the equivalent of two full battle groups arrived to fall against the astonished Ringists.

It was not enough. Bardo's circling maneuver had taken his group near the three thickspaces from which the Ringists had merged like a swarm of comets. In defense of these spinning thickspaces—and as a sort of rear guard—Lord Salmalin had left three cadres of lightships and fifty lesser cadres. While Bardo's two thousand battle-drunk pilots attacked them like thallows falling out of the sky, Alesar and Cristobel led their fragmented groups against the rest of the Ringist rear.

It was now that the great flaw in the Sonderval's strategy stood out like a wormrunner's diamond illuminated by a laser beam. In battle on foot, with swords and shields, the sudden appearance of the enemy in one's rear can strike terror into a whole army. The fear of cold steel in one's back is as ancient as it is terrible, and it can cause even the bravest of warriors to throw down their arms and surrender. In his planning of the battle, the Sonderval had calculated on such an effect. But he had reasoned from analogy and metaphor, which was always a dangerous thing to do.

In truth, this battle with lightships in space was not much like the slaughter befalling the Roman legions at Kannae millenia earlier. The lightships—and blackships and all the other ships—had no vulnerable "backs" to protect. They could fight backward as easily as forward—or to either side, or up or down. (Or, considering the manifold's complex topology, in or out, or through, or between.) Encirclement *could* render a great swarm of ships nearly useless. If they were compressed into a volume of space containing too few point-sources, only a few dozen ships at any time might open windows to the manifold and make mapping with which to maneuver. Although the six thousand Ringists ships massed against the Fellowship's center felt some effects of such compression, the failure of the Sonderval's Sixth, Seventh, Eighth, Thirteenth, Fourteenth and Fifteenth Battle Groups in completing the encirclement allowed the Ringists far too much freedom to fight. And so the Sonderval's strategy failed on two counts. And so the Fellowship began to lose the battle.

It began and ended with the collapse of the Sonderval's First Battle Group. Within a thousand seconds, their strategic movement of falling backward through space became a rout. With the Ringist fleet molested in the rear by only the Tenth, Eleventh and Twelfth battle groups, their main force of ships turned to pulverize the Sonderval's center. His remaining battle groups—the Second, Third, Fourth, Fifth and Ninth—proved to be no help. At this point in the battle they were supposed to close in like diamond teeth upon the encircled main body of Ringist ships and tear them apart. But the Ringists were too many, and these five central battle groups of the Fellowship found themselves fighting for their very existence. As the battle entered its second movement, it was these ten thousand ships that found themselves in danger of encirclement. In truth, except for the Eleventh and Twelfth Battle Groups and Bardo's incomparable Tenth, the whole of the Fellowship fleet had come close to falling apart.

Bardo was perhaps the first one to appreciate this. The Sonderval, fighting like a furious shagshay bull surrounded by wolves, immersed in the middle of what the ancients had called the fog of war, had neither the time nor perspective to appreciate the extreme peril of the Fellowship's position. He couldn't guess that the entire Second Battle Group commanded by Helen Charbo in the *Infinite Pearl* was about to be caught in a thinspace and nearly annihilated. He couldn't see what Bardo saw: that the battle might yet be won (or at least not completely lost), but only if the Fellowship drove the Ringist cadres from the three great spinning thickspaces, and soon.

In the first seconds of his attack, Bardo saw that the ships of his Tenth Battle Group would be too few to accomplish this objective. And so he ordered his twenty sets to fall back for a moment and regroup near a barren, cratered planet half a million miles from the first thickspace. Leaving Lara Jesusa in temporary command of all twenty sets, he took another few precious moments to abandon his battle group and fall off into the manifold. He made a mapping to a point-exit a few million miles away. His ship, the *Sword of Shiva,* fell out into realspace. And there, in the bright red light of Mara's Star, he found Cristobel's Eleventh Battle Group fiercely pressing into the Ringist's rear. He found Cristobel the Bold and his beautiful ship, the *Diamond Lotus.* By light radio, he sent his imago beaming into the pit of the *Diamond Lotus* from which Cristobel led his attack. He spoke to Cristobel; he invited Cristobel likewise to send an imago of himself into the pit of Bardo's ship. Thus, with lightships flashing through space and the battle raging all around them, with the fate of the Civilized Worlds (and perhaps much else) hanging upon their actions, they paused for a few moments to talk.

"I must ask you to join in the attack of the thickspaces," Bardo said. Although his great, graceful form that appeared in the pit of Cristobel's ship was made only of light, he seemed almost real. With his battle armor of black nall and his flashing black eyes, he was an imposing figure of a man.

"And abandon the Sonderval's plan?" Cristobel asked. He was a large, leonine man with a pointed face and an always-lurking sneer to his voice. He had quick, green eyes that never failed to find the weakness in others. "I would have thought that you, of all his pilots, would remain faithful to his plan."

"And I would have thought that you'd be the first to betray it."

"Oh, no," Cristobel said. "I'll see his plan executed perfectly—as will everyone else."

"Even if it means our defeat?"

Cristobel fell silent as he looked at Bardo. And Bardo instantly understood that Cristobel *wanted* the Sonderval's plan to fail: it would show the entire Fellowship the Sonderval's failings as Lord Pilot. And leave the way open for Cristobel's own ascendancy.

"How quickly you lose hope," Cristobel said. "How faithless you are."

Bardo's face fell purple with anger, but he restrained himself. He said, "My faith is to the Fellowship and to the Sonderval himself, not to his plan."

"How convenient for you."

In space, two hundred miles away, a hydrogen missile suddenly exploded, sending a shock of photons pinging against the hulls of the *Diamond Lotus* and the *Sword of Shiva*. For a moment Cristobel broke interface to speak with two of his battle group's lightship pilots, Vadin Steele and Rohana of Urradeth. And then he reappeared to resume his conclave with Bardo.

"Is it clear to you that we're losing the battle?" Bardo asked

"No—is it clear to you?"

In the pit of his ship (and in the pit of Cristobel's), Bardo closed his eyes as he interfaced a computer simulation of the manifold. In this numinous space beneath space, ten thousand ripples of light flowed outward in circles and interfered with each other in a hideously complex pattern. To read the tells and determine the movements of the tens of thousands of ships of the two fleets was nearly impossible; it was like looking at the boiling black sea after a meteor storm and trying to determine the exact location where every bit of sizzling iron had plunged into the water.

Nevertheless, when Bardo broke interface and looked at Cristobel, his eyes were like black pools filled with thousands of flickering lights. He said, "I can *see* the ships of the two fleets. I can see the battle as it unfolds."

"Oh, you can see it, can you?"

"By God, I can. The lights blossoming outward like a field of fireflowers—there's a pattern there. If you look deeply enough, a terribly beautiful pattern to the way the ships must open the windows to the manifold and move."

"I never knew that you were a mystic," Cristobel said.

"I can see the two fleets as they are, right now. I can see the battle as it must unfold. As it *will.*"

"I never knew that you were a scryer as well."

Bardo's eyes fixed on Cristobel as if he could have drowned him in the anger that he felt boiling inside. But he said only, "Ah, too bad. It's already too late."

"And a doomsaying scryer, at that."

Just then Bardo looked down at his huge, trembling hand. If his imago had been made of matter, not light, he might have slapped Cristobel's sneering face.

"We must take the thickspaces," Bardo said. "There'll come

moment when the Sonderval will see that the battle is lost. He'll ave to call for a retreat. If we hold open the thickspaces, our hips can fall through and regroup around another star."

"And how will the Sonderval know that we hold the thickspaces?"

"I've sent him messages by light radio telling him that we'll ttack. I've also sent Odinan Rodas to find him should those messages never be received."

"Then we should wait for the Sonderval to advise us of a new lan."

"No, too long, too far," Bardo said. He held his hands cuping each other and then suddenly moved them apart as if demonrating the way that a battle among lightships and black ships evitably spread out through space. "We're at least ninety million miles from the First Battle Group. It would take more than a ousand seconds for his signal to return to us. And longer still r him to make his decision. Too, too long."

"But he, not you, is Lord Pilot and—"

"Even now we waste time talking," Bardo growled. "We ust take the thickspaces. And we must do it now."

"*I* must continue to follow the Sonderval's laughable plan. nd so should you."

"You, of all men, I knew I couldn't reason with," Bardo said. And that's why I must command you to fall with me against the nickspaces."

"*Command* me? Does a monkey command its master? By hat right?"

"By the right of what's right, by God!"

"You fall against the thickspaces, then, if that's what you want do."

"By God I will! And after the battle is lost, in remembrance of very pilot who died because of your heartlessness, I'll fall gainst *you.*"

At this, despite himself, Cristobel's quick green eyes showed instant concern. He asked, "What do you mean?"

"If we meet on the street or in a bar, I'll squeeze your throat ntil your eyes pop out of your head. If we meet in deep space, ll hunt you ship to ship and send you into the nearest star to join e poor pilots whom you betrayed."

"*You,* hunt *me?*"

"As I once hunted seals on the ice of the sea."

"Pesheval Lal will hunt Cristobel the Bold?"

Bardo, who had been born Pesheval Sarojin Vishnu-Shiva Lal,

smiled sadly, then said, "As the solar winds of the core stars blow through the galaxy."

"I don't believe you," Cristobel said. "There was a time when you were a coward."

"Was," Bardo admitted, nodding his head.

"Pesheval Lal—we used to call you Piss-All Lal because you were so afraid of the fourth year novices that you used to wet your bed every night."

"But now," Bardo said softly, "Bardo is Bardo. And it's Bardo in the *Sword of Shiva*, not Pesheval Lal, who will fall against you."

"I'm a better pilot than you," Cristobel said. "If you fall against the *Diamond Lotus*, you fall to your death."

At this boast Bardo just stared at Cristobel. He stared and stared, and his black eyes blazed with a desire to find out who the better pilot truly was. All his life he had struggled with the fear that had once led him to be a coward; now he was willing to risk his life to move beyond his fear into something finer and much vaster. And Cristobel saw this. There was a wildness of the soul—a true boldness—shining as a deep light in Bardo's eyes. Cristobel must have feared that, despite his name, he himself lacked this light. And he must have feared that Bardo could see through him as easily as he might a jellyfish.

"We'll not fall against each other," Bardo finally said. "Because you'll do as I've asked."

There was a moment. As Bardo and Cristobel stared at each other, there came a moment when they both knew who was the better pilot and the better man. Leadership is made of such moments; it is a subtle almost ineffable quality, at its best when it doesn't have to threaten, as Bardo had threatened Cristobel. But now, in the truth of what passed between their eyes, as lasers flashed outside their ships and windows to the manifold opened in bursts of light, Bardo threatened no longer. He only touched Cristobel with the fire of his heart and the greatness of his soul. And this was enough.

"As one pilot to another," Bardo said, "I'm asking for your help."

Cristobel looked away from Bardo down at his hands. At last he said, "Very well, then, if you ask my help, I'll lead my ship against the thickspaces."

Bardo did not waste time exulting in his victory. He thanked Cristobel, then said, "I'll go to find Alesar Estarei and ask him help as well. I'll tell him that you and your ships will rendezvous with the Tenth Battle Group near the fifth planet."

"Very well."

"Farewell, Pilot," Bardo said. "And fall well, by God. Fall well."

With that, Bardo's imago faded into nothingness as he took his ship back into the manifold. It took him only a few moments to find Alesar Estarei, in his *Vivasvat*, three million miles away leading the Twelfth Battle Group against a few ragged cadres of Ringist ships. And it took him only a few moments more to persuade Alesar to join him and Cristobel at the fixed-points in space near the fifth planet.

In less than ninety seconds, the ships of the Tenth, Eleventh and Twelfth Battle Groups gathered together under Bardo's command. While the main battle raged some ninety million miles away through the light-torn spaces around Mara's Star, Bardo led his groups in a lesser battle. Even with Cristobel's and Alesar's help, however, he still had only thirty-nine lightships against the sixty-two defending the thickspaces. And his lesser ships numbered only four thousand against five thousand. But the battle *is* to the swift and the strong; the training and coordination of the Tenth Battle Group gave them greater speed, and Bardo's great strength of purpose fired all his pilots with a rare will to fight.

If the Ringists had possessed a similar will—to watch lightship destroy lightship and die down to the last pilot—they might have repelled Bardo's attack. But, in truth, few men and women are willing simply to stand and die. In the face of such fierceness, the Ringist pilots began to lose heart and then to panic. The blackship cadres from Clarity and Maniwold fled the thickspaces first, followed by those from Melthin, Eanna, Kittery and Rollo's Rock. Within a hundred seconds, the whole of the Ringist force holding the thickspaces began to evaporate like ice crystals in a hot sun.

Only the pilots of the Ringist lightships found the courage to face the likes of Lara Jesusa, Yannis Helaku, Duncan li Gur and Ivar Rey in the *Flame of God*. But then an event occurred that gave pause to even the most bloodthirsty Ringist pilot. Bardo took the *Sword of Shiva* into successive duels with three lightships, the last one with Syeira Chu in the *River of Time*. And then, having sent three of the Order's finest into the hell of Mara's Star within ten seconds, he fought a simultaneous duel with both Dag of Thorskalle and Nicabar Blackstone. Using a brilliant mathematics that he had once discovered—Bardo's so-called Boomerang Theorem—Bardo looped back along his serpentine pathway through

the manifold and reappeared in realspace just as Dag of Thorskalle and Nicabar Blackstone were about to make a mapping.

It is probable that they thought they had forced Bardo into a
Japanese Fold or other such trap; they no doubt had calculated
that they would surprise Bardo when he fell out into realspace at
one of two probable fixed-points. But it was Bardo who surprised
them. In a tenth of a second, he made a mapping for the two
doomed pilots—and *Odin's Spear* and the *Ark of the Angels* vanished into the night. Into the star that had already consumed so
many men and women in its terrible fire. But these were two of
the Ringists' heroes, pilots who had braved the Hell's Gate and
fought with Leopold Soli in the Pilot's War. When their friends
such as Ciro Dalibar and Kadar the Wise saw what Bardo had
done, they decided to join the other Ringists in fleeing the thickspaces. As their cadre master Nitara Tal reminded them, they
could always regroup and return later with a greater force.

The way was now open for the Fellowship's fleet to retreat. If
Bardo had now advised the Sonderval of his great victory, it
would have taken at least five hundred seconds for the message to
reach him. Radio waves are slow, creeping at light speed through
space like worms across black sands. Five hundred seconds, in a
battle such as they now fought, were almost forever; in such a
segment of time an entire fleet of ships might be destroyed. And
so Bardo had taken a great gamble. Envisioning the struggle for
the thickspaces as it would unfold, he had picked the latest possible moment when Tenth, Eleventh and Twelfth Battle Groups
would have driven off the Ringists. And then, in his first message
to the Sonderval (the one delivered by Odinan Rodas in the *Diamond Rose),* he had promised that the thickspaces would be open
by this time. That Bardo beat this guess by fifty-four seconds
would always fill him with pride.

And so the Sonderval's call for retreat rang out to the Fellowship's fleet. He ordered every pilot from every battle group to find
a mapping to a point-exit within the three thickspaces that
Bardo's ships held open. He said that they should map through to
Kesava, there to fall out and regroup around that little blue star.
His hard-pressed pilots in the center—those of the First, Second,
Third, Fourth, Fifth and Ninth Battle Groups—needed no further
encouragement to flee the deadly spaces of Mara's Star. Especially for the trapped women and men of the Second Battle Group
under Helena Charbo, they welcomed their Lord Pilot's command
as if God himself had promised them a new life.

Within seconds, the three thickspaces filled with ships falling out of the manifold—and falling almost instantly back in on their quick journey across the stars to Kesava. Goldships and deepships and blackships fell out as the stellar windows opened in thousands of quick flashes. At first this great swarming of ships was like ten thousand fireflies gathering into a shimmering cloud. And then space itself came open in vivid reds and pale running blues, a brilliant fireworks of silver and gold and violet and all the other colors of light. Mostly, the lightships were the last to arrive and fall through. And the last of the last were the lightships of the Sonderval's First Battle Group.

However, the Sonderval himself never arrived. In order that as few as possible of his group's lesser ships would be lost, he had ordered his thirteen remaining lightships to guard the retreat of First Battle Group. Although surrounded by three cadres of Ringist lightships and perhaps sixty cadres of lesser ships, the Sonderval's lightship pilots streaked in and out of the manifold in a dazzling pattern meant to beguile and vex the Ringists. With élan and a rare display of their art, they kept them at bay—but only for a few moments. This was enough time for the last of the blackships to escape into the thickspaces, and for the First Battle Group's lightships to flee as well.

But one of the lightships, the *Rose of Armaggedon* piloted by the young Arrio Ajani, became trapped in a folding thinspace. No point-exits to realspace could he find that weren't guarded by at least one of the Ringist lightships. The moment that he fell out into the black crush of the night, one of the Ringist pilots would quickly send him to his death. The Sonderval might have abandoned him to his fate; some said that it was his duty to do so. Certainly, his arrogance aside, he couldn't have thought that Arrio possessed an equal importance to himself, not as pilot, not as an inspiration to the Fellowship. Perhaps something in Arrio—his youth, his eagerness to prove himself as a pilot, his bright brown eyes—called to the Sonderval.

There are mysteries to the human soul, marvels that unfold endlessly down to its deepest depths. For no reason that the Sonderval ever told anyone, he decided to help Arrio Ajani. And so rather than make a mapping to the thickspaces and the freedom that lay beyond, he took the *Cardinal Virtue* against the ten lightships attacking Arrio. He must have known that he was giving up his life. The battle *is* God's, and although the Sonderval piloted his ship with all the grace and knowledge of a god, *this* battle he could not win.

Like light itself, the *Cardinal Virtue* fell in a glorious shimmering fury against Jin Takenya and Konane Jael in the *Silver Snake*. In a moment of time, he destroyed them. But then in the next moment, Salome wi Maya Hastari, in the *Golden Butterfly*, and Yevatha li Tosh, caught him mapless and helpless as a naked man trapped on the ice of the sea. It was Salome Hastari who claimed to have sent the *Cardinal Virtue* into Mara's Star. In the last moment of his existence as a man, there was a grim smile on the Sonderval's lips and a strange, wild look in his eyes. And then the atoms of his blood and his brilliant, beautiful brain fused into light. Thus died Thomas Sonderval, Lord Pilot of the Fellowship of Free Worlds, master of the Great Theorem, discoverer of the Hell's Gate, rival and friend of Mallory Ringess.

He did not die in vain. Arrio Ajani made use of his sacrifice, taking the *Rose of Armaggedon* into the first thickspace and thence escaping to Kesava. Other than a few hundreds of stragglers from the other groups arriving by the moment, the whole of the Fellowship's fleet other than the Tenth, Eleventh and Twelfth Battle Groups had now fallen through to the imagined safety of this star. Then Bardo commanded Alesar Estarei and Cristobel the Bold to take their groups through as well, and this they did. His set commanders, Lara Jesusa and Duncan li Gur and all the others, began leading their ships through in good style. Of all the fleet, the *Sword of Shiva* was the last ship to abandon the violent spaces of Mara's Star. Bardo himself held this point of honor out of bravura and concern for his other ships, yes, but also because he wanted one last look at the order of the Ringist cadres should they decide to follow the other ships.

But the Ringists had suffered enough of battle for one day. Salmalin the Prudent, having survived two lightship duels and a near miss by an exploding hydrogen bomb, was in no mood to pursue the Fellowship's fleet. Prudently, he ordered his cadres to fall back to the spaces of the more easily defended Morriah Double, there to reassemble and console themselves over the death of friends and battlemates. For their losses had been staggering. Sixty-three Ringist lightship pilots (eight accounted for personally by Bardo) had fallen to their deaths inside Mara's Star. And at least six thousand of the lesser ships would never be seen again. The Fellowship's losses were even more fearsome: seventy lightships and eight thousand lesser ships, more than a fifth of the entire fleet. And, as everyone would soon learn, if not for Bardo's brilliant leadership, the day would have gone much worse.

And all this—and much more besides—Danlo saw as he lay wounded in a little stone cell many trillions of miles away. He saw each of the thousands of ships as they came apart within the fires of Mara's Star. He heard the final screams of many of the pilots, and felt the terrible quick heat of hydrogen plasma burning them alive. He said prayers for the dead pilots of both fleets whom he had known: "Nicabar Blackstone, *mi alasharia la shantih,* Ona Tetsu, *mi alasharia,* Charl Rappaporth, *mi alasharia,* Thomas Sonderval . . ." In truth, he prayed for everyone. The names of all the fifteen thousand pilots who had died in the battle came to him like voices whispering in the wind, and he spent the rest of the night saying their names in remembrance.

And when he had finished, there was blood on his lips and a fierce pain stabbing through his head. His burns tormented him as if he himself had fallen naked into the fires of Mara's Star. "*Shantih, shantih,*" he whispered in formal ending to his prayer. "Peace, peace." But then, as he looked off into the endless shimmering stars of the universe, his eyes deepened with a wild pain, and he knew that there would be no peace. For the greater battle was still to come, and only those few who had died had seen an end to this terrible war.

THE NINE STAGES

*Know, my godlings, the power and the glory of the infinite
Ninth: it is as vast and deep as all the universe; it is as
bright as a new star, as perfect and indestructible as pure,
eternal light.*
— from the *Devotionaries* of Lord Hanuman li Tosh

The first official news of the battle came to Neverness on the 21st
of winter in the year 2959. On that bright, sunny day a pilot of the
Order, Nitara Tal in the *Olber's Paradox,* fell out of space to tell
of the Ringist's great victory. Of course, since the Ringists hadn't
managed to destroy the Fellowship's fleet and their losses had
been terrible, their victory wasn't quite as crushing as Nitara
made it seem. And this wasn't really the *first* news that the people
of Neverness had of the killing frenzy near Mara's Star. Two days
earlier, on the 19th of winter when Danlo arose to eat his morning
meal of toast and coffee, he told the godling who served him of
what he had seen in the star fields of his mind. The young godling—Kiyoshi Telek—then told a friend of Danlo's marvelous
vision, and this friend in turn told at least five other godlings. By
midday, every Ringist coming in and out of the cathedral wanted
to discuss this miracle.

Danlo was already famous for his great remembrance years
ago, his experience of the One Memory. Some said that the scryers, in their visions of times yet to be, were really remembering
the future; they believed that Danlo's vision, if true, must be
nothing more than an act of scrying. But others pointed out that
no scryer had ever described future events in such terribly beautiful detail. (Perhaps the cynics said, out of the scryers' fear of
being exposed as false prophets.) By day's end, the rumor of
Danlo's feat had spread throughout the city. It seemed that even
the lowliest harijan or wormrunner wanted to debate whether it
was possible for a man to apprehend the lightning flashes of
events occurring far away in space.

And then, two days later, Nitara Tal stood before Hanuman li

Tosh and Lord Pall and Lord Mor—and all the others in the College of the Lords. And her description of the battle almost exactly matched Danlo's vision. This unexplained phenomenon delighted some of the assembled lords and amazed them all. And it frightened Hanuman li Tosh. Hanuman had always known that Danlo could look into his heart, and now he feared that Danlo could look into his secret doings as well. Out of fear, then, he laid secret plans to destroy the source of his fear.

But others had other plans. While Danlo met each day of pain and solitude with courage—playing his shakuhachi and willing himself to heal—Demothi Bede campaigned for his freedom. As did Jonathan Hur, who sent various members of the Kalla Fellowship into Hanuman's cathedral on missions to undermine Hanuman's authority. Through the icy streets of the Old City the winter wind whistled—along with whispers of Hanuman's iniquity. By the 24th of winter, even some of Hanuman's closest godlings began to wonder why the Lord of the Way had decided to keep Danlo as a prisoner.

Of course, Hanuman had devised a fiction to justify this crime. He maintained that Danlo was only a "guest" seeking sanctuary in the cathedral's chapterhouse; he had come there to pray for an end to the war. As for Danlo's burns and wounded fingers, he explained these in the simplest of ways: Out of despair and compassion for all those who had burned to death inside Mara's Star, Danlo had mutilated himself. This was the Alaloi way, the way that Danlo had been taught as a child; once, as a young novice, Danlo had slashed his own forehead with a sharp rock in atonement for the death of all eighty-eight members of the Devaki tribe. And now the faces of fifteen thousand men and women screaming like wraiths in the starfire haunted Danlo.

In truth, Hanuman said, this terrible vision had broken Danlo's mind. It had made Danlo imagine that the very cetics sent to heal him—and Lord Hanuman himself—had tortured him. Hanuman admitted that he feared not only for Danlo's sanity but his very life. It was possible, Hanuman said, that having failed in his mission to stop the war, Danlo would find a way to join the fallen pilots in death.

No one called Hanuman a liar, to his face. Ivar Zayit, the godling who had witnessed part of Danlo's torture, would not talk to anyone about what he had seen, nor would the two warrior-poets, Jaroslav Bulba and Arrio Kell. And as for Radomil Morven, he seemed to have disappeared from the city. His friends who came to the cathedral to make inquiries were given to under-

stand that if they didn't wish to disappear as well, they should
concern themselves with professing their faith in the Three Pillars
of Ringism and following the Nine Stages toward godhood.

As Danlo gained strength and his fame spread to even the
darkest districts of the Farsider's Quarter, one man schemed to
force Danlo's release. This was Benjamin Hur, he of the fierce
spirit and fiery face. It was Benjamin who first suggested that
Danlo should be the leader of the Kalla Fellowship; if they could
secure Danlo's freedom, he said, even the most devoted Ringists
might leave Hanuman like glittlings drawn by the sun. Surely
Danlo must see that he had no hope of stopping the war otherwise. If only they could convince Danlo to take his rightful place
as his father's chief disciple, then they might begin the long work
of restoring Ringism to its purity and purpose.

And so Benjamin Hur set loose a time of terror not seen in
Neverness since the Dark Year when the Great Plague had come
to the city. He gave his fanatical followers rings filled with matrikax poison should they ever be captured and called them his
ringkeepers to honor them. It was a ringkeeper who slew Deror
Chu in revenge for Danlo's torture, and three more who died
beneath Jaroslav Bulba's flashing knife in a partially failed attempt to assassinate these two warrior-poets.

One woman—her name was Pualani Keth—smuggled a body
bomb into the cathedral and was only stopped from blowing up
herself and Hanuman at the last moment. A keen-eyed godling,
trained by Hanuman himself, read the tells of terror on Pualani's
face and ordered her taken away to an empty cell for a scanning.
(He also ordered the poison ring ripped from her finger before she
could break it open and drink its deadly contents.) There, in the
screaming darkness below the chapter house, Jaroslav used his
knife yet again to cut the bomb from Pualani's swollen belly.
When he was finished, he held up a sphere of bloody white plastic
explosive the size of a newborn child. He declared that the bomb
would have been quite sufficient to vaporize Hanuman as he had
stood on the red-carpeted altar conducting the evening remembrancing ceremony; it might even have destroyed the cathedral
itself. Before dying of what the warrior-poet did to her then,
Pualani confessed her mission to bring down the cathedral—and
all those false Ringists who had betrayed Mallory Ringess besides.

After this, Hanuman ordered scanners placed at entranceways
of the cathedral's eastern and western portals. He posted godlings
around the entire block on which the cathedral stood, and woe

betide the curious passerby who wandered onto the cathedral grounds hoping for a better look at the great flying buttresses and graceful stonework sweeping out into space. But he could not secure the entire city. At the college of Lara Sig on the Academy, a ringkeeper managed to fire a heat bomb into the apartment of Lord Alesar Druze, and thus, in a gout of flames, died one of the most rabid of Ringists. That Benjamin Hur had dared to take his terror into the once-inviolable buildings of the Academy shocked the staid academicians. They called for patrols along the Academy's Wounded Wall, as well as nightly curfews and random searches of anyone coming or going on the surrounding streets.

And then, on the 34th of winter, a much greater shock struck the city. Unknown to Benjamin Hur, a ringkeeper named Igasho Hod contrived to build a bomb in the secrecy of his house in the Pilot's Quarter. Although Igasho displayed the golden armband proclaiming his devotion to Ringism, he also wore a mechanic's green robes. In truth, he was a much-trusted master mechanic who had access to the various laboratories of Upplyssa at the heart of the Academy. Over a period of many days he smuggled the pieces of a laser out of the Academy and brought them to his house. He smuggled out jars of heavy water as well. After separating out from this water a sufficient quantity of deuterium, he fashioned a small, crude but very effective hydrogen bomb. And then, by sled, he crossed the city and went out to the drugworks and food factories on the plain southeast of the Hollow Fields.

Beneath the hundreds of glittering clary domes were the hydroponics, gardens and vats growing the plant foods and cultured meats on which the citizens of Neverness liked to dine. Igasho Hod piloted his sled down a narrow glittery running through the center of these domes. And then he simply abandoned it. He snapped on his skates and fled to a vantage point on the lower slopes of nearby Urkel. And then, using a simple radio signal, he activated the laser that triggered the bomb. In the hold of the sled, a beam of ruby light flashed out for a moment and heated the heavy hydrogen to its fusion temperature. And then, in the next moment, a much more brilliant flash of light split the sky.

The fireball generated in the explosion almost instantly boiled outward in all directions. And as it burned, it rose into the atmosphere, condensing water and sucking up dust from the cratered earth to form a great mushroom cloud. Many miles away, some thousands of people in Neverness were blinded by the initial light flash; and many more were horrified to behold the death cloud rising into the air. And from his vantage point on a rock promontory on the slopes of Urkel, Igasho Hod donned a pair of dark goggles and watched as the bomb's blast wave shattered every dome and food factory not already vaporized by the hellish heat. Although he knew that at least two hundred men and women working in the factories and drugworks had just been burnt to blackened husks, he smiled grimly at his success. In war, he reasoned, people die. It was his hope that he had given Benjamin Hur the leverage to humble Hanuman and force his hand, and he had to be glad of that.

But of course he had done no such thing. When Benjamin Hur learned that it had been one of his ringkeepers who had destroyed the food factories, he was horrified. Now Hanuman would condemn Benjamin Hur and his ringkeepers as criminals, and rightly so. Benjamin feared that Igasho's insane act would only help strengthen Hanuman's authority. For now, in the face of deep crisis, the panicked people of Neverness would want an autarch to restore order. The Lord of the Way of Ringess might become the Lord of the City, in name as well as fact, if only he found a way to assure the people of their daily bread.

This, it seemed, would be difficult to do. Igasho's bomb had completely destroyed the food-producing capabilities of all the factories. The tinkers promised that new factories might be built within forty days, and the agronomists hoped for small crops of algae and bacteria a few tendays after that, but no one knew what truly might be possible. The Lord Ecologist estimated that the city's entire store of food—the warehoused grain, the larders of the private kitchens and dormitories, the iced desserts of the free restaurants and the frozen meats waiting to be grilled—would last no more than a single tenday. And so the hungry millions of Neverness would have to place their hope in the great deepships filled with kurmash and wheat, and plying the Fallaways on emergency missions from Yarkona, Urradeth, Askling and others of the Civilized Worlds. Although it quickly became tiresome to admit it, everyone feared that the maneuvers between the Ringist and Fellowship fleets would cut off the stream of golden grain on which their lives depended.

It was on the morning of the 35th of winter that Danlo first learned of this disaster. On a day of spotty sun and brief snow showers dusting the streets outside his cell, he arose to the sound of the great steel door creaking open. Kiyoshi Telek, a young man with a golden face smiling above his golden, godling's robes, entered carrying a tray of food. According to his habit, he set it down atop the chess table and asked if Danlo was healing well.

"Truly, I . . . am well," Danlo said, gasping out his habitual response. Although the flesh of his body had healed as well as it ever would, the ekkana still touched his lungs with fire with every breath that he took. "And how do *you* fare, Kiyoshi?"

"Oh, very well, Master Danlo."

Kiyoshi, who had once been a journeyman historian, respected Danlo's accomplishments as a master pilot, and he addressed him as if they were still both faithful Ordermen. Because he liked Danlo—and because something about Danlo held him as if he had come into the presence of a brilliant new star—he always lingered to talk to him.

"What news do you have of the war, then?" Danlo asked.

Although Kiyoshi kept his usual smile frozen on his face, his soft brown eyes filled with sadness and fear. Danlo followed Kiyoshi's gaze, then, and he noticed that his usual breakfast of bloodfruit, roasted bread and coffee had been reduced to bananas, boiled rice and a thin, green tea.

"I'm sorry, Master Danlo, but something terrible has happened."

Quickly, he explained that a hydrogen bomb had destroyed the food factories. It was a most inexplicable tragedy, he said, for no enemy ships had been found near Neverness and none of planetary defense satellites had detected any missile fired from deep space.

"Lord Hanuman has said that it must be the work of one of Benjamin Hur's wayless murderers. Have his ringkeepers fallen mad, then? Who but a madman would destroy the very food he must eat in order to live?"

"I . . . do not know," Danlo said.

Once, he remembered, as a curious young novice he had visited the food factories to see with his own eyes how the strange and civilized people of Neverness got their food. And now he closed his eyes, trying to envision a blackened crater and fused sands where once the gleaming clary domes stood. He, who had seen so much so far away, hadn't even dreamed this great event occurring only miles from where he sat on his bed playing his flute. He couldn't see the dark, damned face of Igasho Hod, for his mysterious inner vision failed him and it would be two more days before this doomed man claimed credit for his crime.

"And now there's no more bread," Kiyoshi said as he pointed at the food tray. "And everyone seems to be hoarding coffee."

Danlo stepped over to the chess table and used his fingers to pop a slice of banana in his mouth. He had always had a fondness for this strange, sweet, sticky fruit, which some believed had evolved in the rainforests of Old Earth.

"And Lord Hanuman has said that we must preserve all the bloodfruits that we can," Kiyoshi went on. "He's afraid that a time will come when we'll need the ascorbic acid as a preventive against scurvy."

As Danlo fingered another slice of banana, it occurred to him that Hanuman might have ordered him treated with special consideration and given him an undue portion of food. And so he picked up his dish of sliced bananas and held it out to Kiyoshi. "Have you eaten?" he asked. "Are you hungry?"

"Thank you, Master Danlo, but the cathedral's kitchens haven't quite run out of food yet. I dined this morning much as you."

"I see."

"But everyone is saying that if the shipments don't soon arrive from Summerworld, Lord Hanuman will have to begin rationing. *Then* there'll be hunger, I suppose."

Danlo's eyes filled with something bright and painful as he saw the anxiety clouding Kiyoshi's face. He said, "Yes, that is possible. But most of what we fear never comes to pass."

"Have *you* ever been hungry, Master Danlo? I haven't. I've lived all my life in Neverness within five blocks of a dining hall or restaurant."

"I . . . have been hungry before," Danlo admitted. He stared at the sliced bananas, all the while remembering his first journey to Neverness when he had driven a dogsled across the frozen sea.

"Were you very hungry, then?"

"I . . . almost starved to death. I had to eat Jiro, who was my friend."

At this fantastic statement, Kiyoshi's eyes widened, with horror as much as fear. Although many wild stories about Danlo wi Soli Ringess circulated through the city, Kiyoshi had never heard this one before. "You ate a *human being?*"

"No," Danlo said, smiling with amusement despite the sadness he felt deep in his throat. "Jiro was a dog. When I set out from Kweitkel for Neverness, seven dogs pulled my sled. But I had bad luck hunting seals, and our food ran out. The dogs died one by one. I . . . had to eat them all."

He closed his eyes and said a silent prayer for the spirit of his lead dog: *Jiro, mi alasharia la shantih*. And then for the other dogs as well: *Bodi, mi alasharia la shantih, alasu laya Kono eth Atal eth Luyu eth Noe eth Siegfried, shantih, shantih.*

After a moment, Kiyoshi shook his head as if he couldn't quite believe what he was hearing. He said, "You ate the flesh of a *living* being, then?"

"No—it is as I have said. All the dogs had died."

"But they *had* been alive, hadn't they? You said that one of them was your friend."

"Yes, truly, he was. Jiro gave up his life so that I might live."

"And you were able to eat him?"

"Life . . . lives off of other life," Danlo said simply. His eyes were deep blue pools of light, at once full of mystery and sadness. "That is the way the world is."

"But I've heard that you've taken a vow of ahimsa."

"That is true," Danlo said. "But at the time, I had not."

Kiyoshi thought about this as Danlo began to eat. He watched Danlo shovelling clumps of rice into his mouth with a pair of chopsticks. And then he asked, "But what would you do now, if a hunger came to the city?"

"Then I would be hungry, like everyone else," Danlo said, smiling.

"But would you eat a dog or a sleekit, to save your life?"

"I would not kill an animal," Danlo said. "Nor, by the demand of my hunger, would I cause another to kill an animal for me. But if I chanced upon a sleekit killed beneath the runners of a sled, I would eat it."

Kiyoshi's lips pulled back in disgust, and he said, "Well, I wouldn't. I could never eat anything that had a face. I'd rather die."

"I am sorry."

"It's a horrible world, really," Kiyoshi went on. "Horrible that everything has to eat everything else just to live."

"But this is the only world there is, yes? The only world . . . that could be."

"But we can change the world, can't we?"

Danlo, who always wolfed his food when he was hungry, finished chewing a huge mouthful of rice. And then he said, "We cannot change its essential nature."

"But why else are we here, if not to evolve and make things better?"

Danlo smiled and said, "Every time a woman gives birth to a new child and teaches him a new song that she has composed, the world evolves and becomes better."

"I'm not so sure. Our lives can be so futile."

"No, our lives are the songs that sing the universe into existence."

Now it was Kiyoshi's turn to smile, and he said, "What I meant was, our *human* lives can be so full of hate, pain, murder, meaninglessness. We were meant to be so much more."

"Truly," Danlo said, and he took a sip of tea.

"When we've become gods, we'll move beyond such things."

"Do you think so?" Danlo asked. Although the tea wasn't very hot, he drew a quick breath against the lava he felt burning down his throat.

"Only a god could become free of suffering."

"No, it is just the opposite," Danlo said. He took another sip of tea, and he fell into a moment of shama meditation as he tried to cool his tortured nerves. And he then remembered: *Pain is the awareness of life. Infinite life, infinite pain.*

"Only a god could know what it's like to shine with a light beyond suffering and death," Kiyoshi went on. "Lord Hanuman has said that each man and woman is a star."

"Truly, we *are* stars," Danlo said, closing his eyes. As he moved into remembrance, his voice fell soft and deep: "We shimmer and whirl and cry out at the miracle of hydrogen exploding inside our hearts. We are angels dancing in the fire, spinning sparks of wild joy into the night."

And then, after long moment of silence, he whispered, "We are the light inside light."

Kiyoshi waited a while for Danlo to return to himself. He watched Danlo open his eyes, and he gazed at the light that seemed to pour out of him like a deep, blue, liquid fire. Like many Ringists, he was slightly in awe of Danlo. "Lord Hanuman has said that only by becoming fire will we ever become free of its burning."

Danlo began scooping the banana slices out of his little blue bowl and eating them. Their slight acid burned his stomach. Once or twice, he had to hold his breath at the pain of it. "Lord Hanuman . . . would know about burning," Danlo gasped.

"Yes, and therefore," Kiyoshi continued, "he has said that we all must become lords of fire and light. This is the way of the gods."

"I remember that he said this," Danlo said after taking a sip of tea.

"A god, at least, wouldn't have to fear hunger."

"What do you mean?"

"A god would never be hungry."

"Even if he had no food?"

"But a god wouldn't have to eat food," Kiyoshi said. And then he smiled at himself. Although he was as devout as any Ringist, he liked to step back even in the middle of his most serious debates and regard his beliefs with a bit of humor. "What's the point of being a god if you have to eat?"

"I see," Danlo said. "And how would a god acquire the energy with which to move, then?"

"Well, the universe is full of energy, isn't it? A god would be able to draw energy directly from the universal source."

"I . . . see," Danlo said, looking deep into Kiyoshi's eyes.

But, in truth, Danlo didn't really understand the newer doctrines of Ringism because he had been gone from Neverness too long. And so Kiyoshi explained how each man and woman could become a god. As they sat in Danlo's cold cell sipping tea (Danlo was glad to share his cup), Kiyoshi began with the fundaments of the Three Pillars, stressing the importance of a clear remembrance of the Elder Eddas. For most people, he said, these remembrances would be perfected only when the Univeral Computer was complete and each godling could interface a nearly perfect simulation of the Elder Eddas. Only then would this vast knowledge of the gods work its miracle upon those who could apprehend it. Touched with this godfire, as Hanuman called it, women and men would begin to feel a burning deep inside their bodies' cells. And then the "Sleeping God" would awaken, and they would begin their great transformation toward the divine.

"I know of the Sleeping God," Danlo said. "This is just the potential of our DNA, yes? I know that the courtesans have a theory about this. They dream of waking up the cells, the whole bodymind. This is the whole purpose of their art, to wake human beings up."

He didn't add that Bardo had incorporated this doctrine into the Ringist canon largely as a sop to the Society of Courtesans, which he had hoped to convert. Kiyoshi, who had come to the Way of Ringess long after Danlo had left it, seemed unaware of the history of the very religion that he embraced. As Danlo gazed at Kiyoshi's golden, trusting face, he saw no point in relating how well Bardo's manipulations had worked.

"If you know about the Sleeping God," Kiyoshi said, "then you know almost everything. What else is the Way but a way of awakening our potential to become gods?"

He went on to tell of the Nine Stages, which Hanuman had set as a formal doctine only within the last year. All human beings, he said, on their great journey from child to god had to pass through each of these stages; none could be skipped. The first three stages—the basic biological, emotional-sexual and intellectual competencies—most people managed well enough if nurtured with compassion and care. But many there were who grew to adulthood in the most barbarous of conditions; often they fell victim to disease, neglect, hunger, rape, slel neckers, mind masters or even war. They were like flowers given too little water and sun, like bonsai trees growing to a stunted maturity in tiny pots. And so they would have difficulty evolving into the fourth stage, which was that of the devotional. Almost all godlings, Kiyoshi said, had reached the devotional stage of psychic sensitivity, compassion, love, selfless service and a mystical sense that their lives were interwoven with the greater life of the universe. Such devotion was necessary before they could move on to the next stage of full mysticism.

"The fifth stage is critical to all the higher ones," Kiyoshi said. "This is the complete development of the mystical sense. The ability to fall into samadhi, to experience the oneness and interconnectedness of everything and integrate it—this is very difficult."

Danlo reached out to the teapot to refill their cups. "Are you speaking now of the samadhi of the yogin or of cybernetic samadhi?"

"Well, samadhi is just samadhi, isn't it? It varies only according to its intensity, to the degree that one can surrender and become vastened in the greater One."

Here Kiyoshi paused to see if Danlo agreed with what he had said.

"Please go on," Danlo said, and he burned his lips sipping his too-hot tea.

"Well, nothing could be vaster than the cybernetic spaces," Kiyoshi said. "Potentially, with a computer vast enough, with a perfectly realized simulation, our entire universe would be only as a grain of sand on a beach falling off to infinity."

"I see," Danlo said, burning his mouth again.

"And so the cybernetic samadhis are the most intense, the most total. The way information fields open out into infinity in all directions, the electric connections, the flowing out of the self into the vastness—I'm sorry, but I'm really not describing this well.

"No, it is just the opposite," Danlo said smiling. "Please go on."

"The flowing *into* the self of pure Self, all possible universes concentrated in a single moment like lightning that grows ever more brilliant—the integration of this mystical experience can take years to master."

"Truly," Danlo said.

"But such mastery," Kiyoshi said, "prepares the way for the sixth stage, that of remembrancing. It's only in the sixth stage that one can fully apprehend the Elder Eddas and attain a clear vision of the One Memory."

Danlo closed his eyes as he returned to a moment of deep, clear light. He was aware of the way that this light inside light eternally differentiated itself, falling into form, willing and whirling and becoming and evolving. All memory was locked up inside this light. In a way, matter and memory and pure consciousness were all one and the same thing, and he was aware of himself as a billion billion burning drops of light that flowed together into a single, shimmering ocean.

"Everyone knows that you had a clear vision of the One Memory," Kiyoshi said when Danlo opened his eyes and looked at him. "A great remembrance—as so few have had."

Danlo took a sip of tea and continued looking at Kiyoshi, but he said nothing.

"You and Lord Hanuman, Nirvelli, Thomas Rane—we're fortunate that all of you have copied your memories of the Elder Eddas for the rest of us to interface. It helps to open us to the possibilities of the sixth stage."

"But my remembrance was never copied," Danlo said.

"No? But why?"

"Because I would not allow it to be."

"You wouldn't? But why not?"

"Because such an experience is *experience,*" Danlo said. "It can be lived but not copied."

At this, Kiyoshi's face fell into disappointment and doubt. He said, "Well, perhaps it can't be copied *perfectly,* but I can't see the real difference between Thomas Rane's remembrances of the Elder Eddas and my experience of them when I interface a remembrancing computer."

"There is all the difference in the world," Danlo said. "It is the difference between lightning and . . . a lightning bug. Between what is real and that which is only a pale imitation."

Kiyoshi frowned again, even as Danlo smiled and passed the cup of tea into his hand. Unlike most people in Neverness, Kiyoshi had little fear of contagion or disease, and so he gladly pressed the cup to his lips and took a sip. "Since I've never had a great remembrance of my own," he said, "I wouldn't know about this difference that you speak of. But still, I must be grateful for what I've seen of the Elder Eddas. It gives me hope that someday I might move into the sixth stage or even beyond."

"I did not mean to dampen your hope," Danlo said. He reached out and squeezed Kiyoshi's ungloved hand. "Please tell me about these other stages that lie . . . beyond."

And so Kiyoshi went on to describe how remembrancing prepared the way for enlightenment. In this, the seventh stage, a man or woman who followed the Way of Ringess would experience the possibilities of the god within. There would be a living of the Elder Eddas, a heightened and permanent new awareness of the numinous fire that animated all things. One who attained this exalted seventh stage would himself blaze with a transcendental radiance in and through the body. The eyes would overflow with light like jeweled cups trying to contain an ocean. Wherever the seventh stage master walked, he would leave luminous streamers of love and joy in his wake.

And then, if he could endure the burning pain of it, would come the penultimate stage, which Hanuman called transfiguration. As the aspiring godling came finally and fully awake, the Sleeping God inside would cry out in a great, golden voice that rang from depths of each atom of his being to the farthest reaches of the universe. Each cell of the body would sing at a higher pitch and resonate with every other. The DNA would awaken to its infinite possibilities and begin to work permanent biochemical changes in the body and brain. As the eighth stage master adapted to this higher energy state, his whole being would literally radiate light like a star. This was the end of two million years of human evolution—but only the beginning of endless billions of years of movement into godhood, the ninth and final stage.

At some point in this infinite ninth stage, some said, a god would leave his body behind, vanishing in a blaze of light. Others held that a god would choose to remain human in form while helping all other godlings to their final transfiguration. But almost everyone agreed that a god would be able to transform and transcend his being at will; as Kiyoshi told Danlo, what was the point of becoming a god if not to be a master of matter and energy, a lord of fire and light?

"After enduring the refining fire of transfiguration comes the release into light," Kiyoshi said. "A god shines like a star, but a god can also drink in the light of the sun."

Having finished the last of the tea, Danlo sat on his bed holding the empty blue cup in his hands. "Drink in . . . how?" he asked.

"Through the cells—every cell of his body."

"Would a god's DNA code for chloryphyll, then?" Danlo smiled playfully and provocatively, but also with a rare feeling for Kiyoshi's ability to examine his beliefs with a good humor. "Would the cells of his skin begin turning green like a kesava leaf as he stood naked in the sun?"

At this, Kiyoshi smiled as well and said, "How could I know? Only one human being has attained true godhood, and he left Neverness years ago."

He went on to tell of the attainments of history's sages, past and present. According to Lord Hanuman, he said, Jesus the Kristoman, Lao Tzu, the Narmada and numerous godlings had risen to the fifth stage. Fewer had mastered the sixth stage of remembrancing: of the ancients, only Jin Zenimura, and of the Ringists, only Thomas Rane and Surya Surata Lal. (Once, Hanuman had counted Jonathan Hur as a sixth stage adept, but as time passed and the Kalla Fellowship became ever more estranged from the main body of the church, Hanuman had demoted Jonathan to the fifth stage. And Bardo had been demoted even further; if one believed Lord Hanuman, Bardo had barely the soul and wit to have completed the intellectual development of a rather precocious child.)

The seventh stage occupied the heights of a lofty mountain, and there only Gautama the Buddha and Nirvelli sat. And at the mountain's very peak, listening to the divine wind of the world roaring like a billion rockets, Lord Hanuman himself shined like a star all alone. He looked down at all the other godlings struggling to fly up to the eighth stage, and he drew them on like a beacon in the night. And, because he was after all still a man, he looked up towards the heavens, too. He searched the bright constellations of stars for sign of Mallory Ringess, who was the only one ever to have become a real god.

As Kiyoshi fell silent with a look of intense longing in his eyes, Danlo smiled sadly. He stepped over to the chess table and took up the empty rice bowl in his hands. And then, one by one, he began picking off the rice grains still stuck to the bowl and eating them.

"And what of Nikolos Daru Ede?" Danlo asked. He glanced at the imago of Ede beaming out of the devotionary computer atop the chess table. A program of curiosity seemed to freeze

Ede's soft, round face. "There are countless people in the galaxy who believe that Ede became the greatest and only real God."

Here Kiyoshi frowned and squeezed his hands together anxiously. "Lord Hanuman has said that Ede was the greatest charlatan in history. And that the Architects who believe in his godhood are the worst of the Wayless."

He didn't add that many Ringists, led by Surya Surata Lal, were calling for the war to be extended and waged upon the Architects of all the Cybernetic Churches, who bitterly opposed the rise of Ringism. Surya Lal claimed that the Architects were degraded human beings willfully and hopelessly stuck in the lowest of the stages. They should be rounded up and quarantined on prison planets, she said; they should be injected with slel viruses that would eat away the blockages in their brains and open them to the truth of the Way. But even then it would be doubtful if they could ever ascend through the nine stages. One of the godlings had overheard Surya telling Hanuman that perhaps it would be best simply to euthanize them and spare them the torment of their low and hopelessly human lives.

Because Danlo didn't like what he saw in Kiyoshi's eyes, he frowned, too. But then, upon noticing that the Ede imago was looking at him with insult written upon his glowing face, he almost smiled. It occurred to him that here was one god, at least, who would never have to eat again—unless he somehow managed to revive his frozen body and cark himself back into his old and hopelessly human form.

"Do you believe, then," Danlo asked, "that my father became the first god in the history of the universe?"

"Well, certainly the first to have arisen out of the human race."

"And that he would have transcended the need for food and drink?"

"I think I believe that he transcended much more than this. Have you heard the testament of Masalina Raizel?"

"No," Danlo admitted, shaking his head.

"Well, everyone knows that Mallory Ringess left Neverness on Year's End in 2941. Masalina was meditating among the rocks of the Elf Garden that day. She said that as she was looking up at the stars, she saw a tremendous flash of light—so bright that it dazzled her. But she was certain that the light came from the peak of Atakel, and not the sky. Others saw this light on the mountain that night, too."

"Truly?"

Kiyoshi's face was now all sunshine and gold, and he said, "Everyone knows how Mallory Ringess liked to climb Atakel to be alone. Well, this was his final aloneness and illumination before his reunion with the greater illumination of the stars."

"Then you believe that my father became . . . this light?"

"What else could I believe?"

"You believe that his human body transfigured itself into pure light?"

"Well, the flash that Masalina saw was very bright."

Danlo smiled as he closed his eyes, making a quick calculation. Then he looked at Kiyoshi and told him, "If all the atoms of all the cells of my father's body were transfigured this way, the energy released would be almost a hundred trillion trillion ergs."

Kiyoshi, the would-be historian, asked, "Is this a lot?"

"It is the equivalent of a thousand hydrogen bombs," Danlo said. "It would have vaporized the entire city and reduced the slopes of Atakel to lava. If Masalina had seen what she thought she did, she would have been much more than just dazzled."

"Perhaps your father found a way to transfigure without releasing so much energy."

At this, Danlo shook his head. "There are laws giving the equivalency of matter and energy, yes? The Einstein set them forth on Old Earth before the Holocaust."

Danlo thought that he had made a rather keen point, but such reasoning seemed not to persuade Kiyoshi, who said, "Well, who is greater, a low-stage, wayless ancient out of history or a god? Surely a god would be able to remake any of the laws which constrain a mere human being."

As Danlo had no answer to this, he stood picking the rice grains from his bowl and staring at Kiyoshi.

"I think I have to believe that your father transfigured into light," Kiyoshi said. "Such a light would be totally free; it could fall anywhere in the universe."

Danlo almost reminded him that this light, even if free, would fall very slowly across the long, black deeps of the universe. And then it occurred to him that if his father could remake the fundamental laws, perhaps he could remake spacetime itself so that light moved as quickly as a tachyon.

"But what of my father's lightship, the *Immanent Carnation?* It vanished on that day as did my father."

A lightship, Danlo thought, *could* fall almost infinitely faster than light; that was their glory and their purpose.

"I suppose that if Mallory Ringess could transfigure himself into light," Kiyoshi said, "he could cause the atoms of his ship simply to disassociate and evaporate into the air."

Danlo smiled grimly as he envisioned the terrible energies that it would take to evaporate the beautiful diamond hull of a lightship. Then he said, "If my father has gone out into the universe as pure light, how could he ever return to Neverness?"

"I'm sure that he could regather the rays of his being into his old form, if he wished," Kiyoshi replied. "He did promise that he'd return."

Danlo held his hand open toward the wan light filtering in through the window. "Perhaps he is returning now, even as we speak."

"Perhaps," Kiyoshi said, smiling. And then, more seriously, "He *will* return, you know. And he'll lead us to right the world's injustices so that everyone can move through the nine stages to become a god."

"And then?"

"And then we'll remake the world—the whole universe."

The whole universe.

Danlo closed his eyes, then, and a lightning flash of apprehension sliced through the dark veils of his mind. For a moment (or a year) he fell through black, empty space. And then there, hundreds of miles above the city of Neverness, Hanuman's Universal Computer appeared. It was a vast, almost-complete black sphere glowing dully in the light of the sun. With every breath that Danlo took, the microscopic assemblers that swarmed its surface added neurologics to the computer's mass, and it grew.

The whole universe.

For a long time, Danlo had wondered why Hanuman called this ugly machine his *Universal* Computer. Was it because he believed that it would run any possible program or simulations of reality almost universal in their scope? Truly, Danlo thought, and yet he sensed that Hanuman's great design was something much more. Somehow Hanuman hoped to use it to remake the universe: to rid the world of injustice and suffering, of hate and war and disease and death. But exactly how Hanuman thought a computer the size of a moon could accomplish this impossible feat, Danlo didn't know. He almost saw it. A dark and vast shape struggled to take form before his inner eyes. But it was as if he stood on a frozen street with his back to the sun, looking at his shadow. No matter how hard he stared or how quickly he moved, this image always receded before him like a black, faceless wraith twisting across the ice.

"You could help, you know."

Kiyoshi's voice fell like the crack of an iceberg into the room. Danlo immediately opened his eyes and looked at him.

"You could help us all become gods," Kiyoshi said.

This statement truly astonished Danlo, who said, "*I*? I . . . am only a wayless pilot of the Fellowship, yes?"

"I think I have to believe that you're something much more than this," Kiyoshi said.

"What, then?"

"Did you know that many of the godlings are saying that you, as well as Lord Hanuman, have attained the eighth stage? They say that you're a lightbringer, that you've returned to Neverness to help guide the church to its destiny."

On Tannahill, Danlo remembered, the men and women of another church had called him Lightbringer. But that had been an accident of history: because he had dared to look upon the infinite, inner lights of his own mind, the Architects of the Cybernetic Universal Church believed that he had fulfilled an ancient prophecy. But he had told no one on Neverness of this fiery ordeal. That Kiyoshi had named him as a lightbringer astonished him. He might have smiled at the strangeness of it all, but Kiyoshi sat looking at him with such hope and longing that he felt like crying instead.

"Do *you* believe that I have attained the eighth stage, Kiyoshi?"

"Well, it's possible, isn't it? Possible for any man, but for the son of Mallory Ringess himself . . ." Kiyoshi's voice faded off into the quiet of the little cell.

"And what if I have, then?"

"Then you should take your place as a lord of the church."

"But the church already has a lord, yes?"

"But you and Lord Hanuman were once the closest of friends. Many are saying that he'd welcome you to stand by his side—like a double star."

"I have sworn that I would never take part in this religion again. In any religion. I am sorry."

"I'm sorry, too, Master Danlo."

For a moment, Danlo wondered if Hanuman might have sent Kiyoshi as either a messenger with a subtle summons or as a spy. That this only now occurred to him amused him deeply, for it seemed an obvious strategem. However, Kiyoshi sat looking at him with such a trusting face that he knew he was no spy. He felt

Kiyoshi's heart opening to his, and he knew that Kiyoshi had spoken from a truth deep inside.

"I am glad that you came this morning," Danlo said as he returned the rice bowl to the tray. "It is always good to see you."

At this, Kiyoshi stood up and bowed deeply. "I'll come again with the midday meal. But I can't promise you kurmash or coffee."

"But you can promise me your company," Danlo said, smiling. "I would gladly trade three good meals for that."

"You might not say that in another ten days," Kiyoshi said. He picked up the tray and returned Danlo's smile. "Not if our food runs out and the shipments don't arrive."

"No, I might not," Danlo admitted. "But now is only now, yes?"

"Thank you for reminding me of that, Master Danlo. I'll look forward to talking with you again at your next meal."

"I look forward to that too, Kiyoshi."

Kiyoshi bowed once more before opening the door and walking back into the cathedral. One of Danlo's guards—a ronin warrior-poet named Dorjan Noy—quickly slammed it shut with a great ringing of steel. When Danlo was finally alone, he knelt down by the chess table and picked up three grains of rice that had fallen to the floor. Two of these he ate immediately, and then he sat staring at the third grain that shined in the palm of his hand like a little white worm.

The whole universe, he thought.

He closed his eyes again, and an image came to him: He saw trillions upon trillions of tiny worms eating their way into an round, red apple the size of the sun. When they had devoured it completely from the inside, its bright red skin burst open in a blaze of light. As the light died, there in the emptiness of space, he saw that the worms had gathered into a single, writhing mass. And they were no longer white but black as charred corpses—as black and vast as Hanuman's Universal Computer. And then this vast, black ball of death moved through the star fields of the galaxy at tremendous speed, sucking out the light of each star as it passed. And growing, always growing into the darkness that it created until it swelled to the size of the Vild.

The whole universe.

When Danlo at last opened his eyes, he saw that the grain of rice was still only a grain of rice. He licked it off his hand and savored the taste of it in his mouth a long time before chewing it carefully and swallowing.

THE PARADOX
OF AHIMSA

*All life lives off life: the grass feeds the shagshay, and
the shagshay feed the Devaki. And when we die, our
bodies feed the grass.*

—from the Devaki *Song of Life*

*The life of each living being resonates with the life of
every other; all life must be respected as the equivalent
of one's own. Therefore, do no harm to any living thing;
it is better to die oneself than to kill.*

—Fravashi teaching

As it happened, Kiyoshi Telek did not arrive with Danlo's next
meal, nor would he serve him again for a long time. Around
midmorning, having spent an hour playing his flute, Danlo decided to search in his wooden chest for the book of poems that his
father had once given him. Although he had long since memorized every poem on every page, it comforted him to hold the old,
leather-bound book open on his lap as he recited the rhythms and
rhymes of the ancients.

It had been a long time since he had practiced this rare art of
reading, however, and so he found the book buried at the bottom
of the chest beneath his spare furs, kamelaikas and other possessions. To get at it, he began removing each revered object and
laying it on the bed. There was the clear, diamond scryers' sphere
that had once belonged to his mother, and his carving tools neatly
wrapped inside an old seal-leather bag. With these chisels and
gravers, he had once carved an ivory chess piece from a walrus
tusk that he had found. This chess piece—a white god that Hanuman had once broken into two pieces in an act of calculated
cruelty—he set next to his skate blades. And next to that went the

little, cubical, necklace-devotionary given to him by Hannah Ivi en li Ede, the High Holy Ivi of the Cybernetic Universal Church.

The cool touch of each of these things stirred deep memories in him; when he unwrapped the point of his old bear spear from its oilskin, he instantly recalled the bite of blue cold air and the crunch of *soreesh* snow beneath his sliding skis. He remembered how Haidar, his found-father, had carved this beautiful leaf of flint and given it to him as a birthday present. And now, in the quiet of his cell, he marvelled at its fearful symmetry. It was as long as his hand from wrist to fingertip and as sharp as the diamond-steel of a warrior-poet's killing knife. In the light streaming through the window, it glowed almost bloodred.

He was just about to set this deadly stone sliver next to his other things when he heard a great boom as of a bomb exploding on the streets outside the chapterhouse. So powerful were the shock-waves of this blast that he felt the reverberations through the stone floor and resonating with the flint point still gripped in his hand. And then, even as he stood there watching, the outer wall of his cell began to crumble apart like a paintstone beneath a pounding pestle, and he suddenly knew that no one would serve him meals in this little room again.

What Danlo didn't know—then—was that during the night one of Benjamin Hur's ringkeepers had managed to slip past the godlings that guarded the cathedral. After other ringkeepers had sabotaged the flame globes on the nearby streets, this ringkeeper used the confusion of the swirling snow and the sudden darkness to spray an invisible paint on the outside wall of what he thought was Danlo's cell. The street lights had soon been restored and the cathedral grounds checked for trespassers—but of course none were found. And meanwhile, even as the godlings returned to their cold and lonely duty, the paint did its work.

For it was a very special paint: one of Benjamin Hur's tinkers had mixed it from a quickly drying adhesive and a solution of programmed bacteria dissolved in water. These microscopic stone-eaters clung to the white granite of the chapterhouse like ticks on a snow tiger. Within seconds, the bacteria began to release acids that tore the hard granite into tiny molecules. Some of these molecules they ate and digested; others passed from their membranes as a sludge-like waste or remained untouched. Within minutes, the bacteria began to reproduce swarms of new bacteria which continued their silent and nocturnal feast.

And all this had occurred while Danlo slept or sat talking with Kiyoshi about the nine stages toward godhood. Hanuman's tinker had made precise calculations: after a fixed number of generations, according to their program, the bacteria had all suddenly died. If not for such a precaution, they might have continued to eat their way through the entire chapterhouse and the rest of the cathedral—and perhaps through the lovely stone houses on the surrounding streets and the very bedrock of Neverness Island itself. Such bacteria swarms had been know to reduce entire planets to balls of dust, which is why the penalty for using this technology throughout the Civilized Worlds has usually been death. That Benjamin Hur dared to violate the oldest of laws bespoke his fear that in this war to end all wars, much more than mere planets was at stake.

But his tinker's mindless little robots did their work well; they touched nothing except this outer wall of the chapterhouse. And even this expanse of foot-thick stone blocks they did not tear down altogether, but left standing in the semblance of a wall. Any godling who chanced to look towards Danlo's cell would have been unaware that the stonework there was as porous as a sponge and as soft as chalk. Danlo himself was unaware of this—until he felt the bomb explode outside and the air ring with the sound of it. Men in facemasks and furs came for him then. They used steel shovels to tear apart the wall of his cell as if bashing their way into a snowhut. One moment Danlo stood before his bed, holding the flint spearpoint in his hand and staring at the wall; and the next moment the wall caved inward in a shower of rotten stone, dust and wind-driven snow. A blast of bitterly cold air stung Danlo's face and rattled the white feather that he wore in his hair. Through the hole where the wall had been came the sudden brilliance of white snow and the shimmering, blue sky. One of the men with shovels quickly regarded Danlo through a pair of dark snow goggles; he might have been looking at a child who didn't realize that his old world had just shattered forever and a new life lay before him.

"Danlo wi Soli Ringess, you know me, don't you?" With a crunch of crumbling stone beneath his boots, the man stepped into the cell. He ripped the mask from his face then, and Danlo saw that it was Tobias Urit, with his red beard and his red, robust demeanor. Once, they had drunk the sacred kalla together in dreams of the future and in innocent fellowship. Once, Tobias had been a gentle man. But now he was the first and fiercest of Benjamin's ringkeepers. "Benjamin Hur has sent us, so you must please hurry."

Four other men dressed much as Tobias crowded around the

opening in the wall. They had all dropped their shovels, brandishing instead other weapons in their place. Two held bullet guns in their gloved hands, and two more aimed lasers toward the street. The two with the bullet guns rushed through the cell and positioned themselves by the door should Danlo's guard be foolish enough to open it.

"Please hurry—we won't have long before they come," Tobias repeated. He held up Danlo's black sable fur so that Danlo could more quickly thrust his arms into it.

Although Danlo had need of great speed, he paused a moment to gather up a few of his things. He stowed his bamboo flute in one of the leg pockets of his kamelaika; the diamond sphere, carving tools, spear point and broken chess piece, he dropped into his other pocket. He moved to sweep up the devotionary computer, but Tobias quickly told him to leave it behind, that the boxlike machine would impede his escape. And so reluctantly, Danlo left it where it sat, on the chess table.

"I will return for you," Danlo told the Ede imago. "As soon as I can, I will return and help you recover your body."

"It's all right," Ede said. "I can wait a hundred years—or a thousand. Goodbye for now, Danlo wi Soli Ringess."

Danlo quickly bowed his head to him, and then paused another moment to tell Tobias something.

"You know me, Tobias," he said. He looked at the two masked ringkeepers waiting by the door for the warrior-poet to enter. "You mustn't harm or kill anyone for my sake. I . . . will not allow it. I will die instead."

Tobias' eyes hooded over with a dark anger, then, but he reluctantly made a grunting noise that sounded as if he had given his assent. And then he led Danlo outside into the brilliant sun. Too many days spent in the semi-darkness of his cell had weakened Danlo's eyes; the fierce white light almost blinded him. The fiery pain of it would have been bad enough all of its own, but with the ekkana still tormenting his nerves, he wanted to scream like a sleekit suddenly flayed and dropped onto a hot grill. Fortunately, Tobias had thought to bring a spare pair of goggles (and a facemask), and these Danlo pulled over his head as quickly as he could. After a few moments of their rush through the newly fallen snow, halfway across the cathedral's grounds, Danlo found that he could see again—but he almost wished that he couldn't.

Toward the end of the block where the cathedral rose up like a lovely granite mountain, the street and part of the grounds had been blown open in the bomb's blast. Neither sleds nor godlings could easily pass by this steaming crater. A few who had tried lay dead in the snow, the victim of four more of Tobias Urit's ringkeepers. Obviously they had used their bullet guns to kill them: Danlo had never before seen the effects of these terrible weapons, and he marvelled at the great gouts of flesh that the lead bullets had torn from their bodies. The beautiful snow with its billions of sparkling crystals was spattered with blood and in many places had been reduced to a red slush. Danlo almost abandoned his escape, then; he almost walked back towards the cathedral to await the certain attack of Jaroslav Bulba and the cadres of godlings with lasers and bullet guns of their own. But Tobias Urit and his ringkeepers would surely try to defend him, and many more men and women might die.

"Quickly now," Tobias said, pulling the sleeve of Danlo's furs and leading him toward the street. He glanced at the bodies sprawled about the bomb crater, and he said, "I'm sorry about them, but if we're to avoid killing anyone else, we must hurry."

For a moment, Danlo hesitated. He dug his feet into the snow like an embattled shagshay bull and looked at Tobias. And then he looked up at the houses and apartments opposite the cathedral. Although the street itself was nearly deserted, foolish men stood by open windows to see how Danlo's escape might unfold. A random bullet or beam of laser fire might easily find their too-curious faces. A few children looked out of these windows as well; as Danlo's gaze fell upon the bright, black eyes of a young boy standing on a balcony, he finally decided to flee this street of death as quickly as he could.

"No one else," Danlo told Tobias. "You must promise me this, yes?"

At that moment, down the block, golden-robed men armed with bullet guns began to pour from the cathedral's western portal.

"I promise this, then," Tobias spat out. "Now please hurry."

And so Danlo followed Tobias to a big, red sled waiting on the street. Another of Tobias' ringkeepers piloted the sled; he sat in the cockpit frantically waving his hand, beckoning Tobias and Danlo to jump into the back of the sled. This they soon did, along with a third ringkeeper who sat by Danlo's left side. With Tobias pressing him from his right, with the smells of sweat and blood and fear thick in the air, the pilot ignited the sled's rockets and it thundered into motion down the icy red street.

They almost broke free from the district around the cathedral without incident. The sled roared down the wide glidderies almost heedless of the skaters who were quick to jump out of their way. The bitter wind ripped at Danlo's face mask and sent particles of spindrift shattering against his goggles. Within seconds they neared the great green glissade that divided the Old City in two. Only a few of the district's glidderies gave out onto this thorough-fare. Tobias had obviously arranged which one they must take, for near the Cemetery, the sled's pilot made a sharp, slicing turn across the red ice and steered his way onto a little street lined with three-storey apartments. Danlo remembered this street well from his nightly forays as a journeyman: It crossed the Old City Glissade and led into a maze of lesser streets surrounding the Fravashi Green. In one place, half a block before the intersection, the street narrowed to scarcely more than an icy ramp ten feet wide.

"Get out of the way!" the sled's pilot yelled at the skaters in front of him. He waved his hand in front of his face as if shooing away a cloud of furflies. "Get out of the way!"

But he had to let the sled slow almost to a crawl lest he smash into an astrier woman dressed in rich brown furs and a pair of young godlings perhaps on their way to the afternoon remem-brance at the cathedral. These three women—and others—reluc-tantly edged to the side of the street to allow the sled to pass. But there were those who weren't so quick to move. Three other god-lings, sporting their eye-catching golden furs, stood on the ice down the street blocking their way. They sported bullet guns, as well. They pointed these guns straight ahead as they waited for the sled to approach.

"Run them down!" the ringkeeper sitting on Danlo's left shouted to the pilot. "Run the murderers down!"

One of the godlings fired his gun, then, and a bullet exploded through the air and smashed into the sled's windshield. A spiderweb fracture spread across the curving clary pane, but the plastic was too tough to shatter altogether.

"No!" Danlo shouted back. "We can just leave the sled and skate away."

But at this naive suggestion, Tobias sat shaking his head. "They'd shoot us in the back. Or we'd be trapped on another street—Hanuman must have already emptied the cathedral of his guards. No, we'll have to keep to our plan."

"No, I will not allow it."

"Run them down," Tobias called out to the pilot.

"No, no . . ."

"Run them down *now!*" he yelled as he pulled out a gleaming laser from inside his furs.

"No!" Danlo screamed as the sled suddenly rocketed forward.

Many things happened almost all at once. One of the godlings fired his gun again, and a bullet blew out a piece of the windshield. This plastic shard flew back through the sled and cut through the facemask of the ringkeeper sitting on Danlo's left. He cried out like child, immediately clasping his hand to the ragged, bloody wound. And Tobias leaned his heavy body over the side of the sled to get a better angle of fire. As he did this, Danlo lunged against him. In truth, he fairly flew out of the sled in his rage to get at the laser. He almost caught this murderous shining thing with his hand even as Tobias fired upon the three godlings. The laser beam instantly burned through Danlo's glove across the back of his hand. The smells of charred leather and cauterized skin flew out into the air. Danlo cried out in agony then, even as the ringkeeper on his left recovered his will, grabbed Danlo by his furs and yanked him back to his seat in the sled. He—his name was Kantu Mamod—wrestled with Danlo, trying to pinion his arms and restrain him. And all the while the sled shot forward, a great red bullet of plastic streaking down the red ice of the street.

Other, smaller bullets flew in the opposite direction. They finally blew out the windshield of the sled. One of the bullets nipped off a piece of Tobias Urit's left ear, but he seemed not to notice this slight wound. After somehow managing to get his laser targeted again, he almost instantly killed two of the godlings blocking their way. The third one, a young woman dressed only in a sleek, gold kamelaika, stood dumbly holding her wounded breast as if she couldn't quite believe that the effects of a laser on human flesh were as terrible and as real as she had been told.

"Get out of the way!" the sled's driver shouted yet again. But it seemed that she couldn't move, and so the rocketing sled slammed into her belly, throwing her into the air like a child's doll. Danlo, still struggling with Kantu Mamod (and still reaching for Tobias Urit's laser), would always remember the sickening thud and crunch of breaking bones. Just as her face froze with shock and terror, he touched eyes with this woman, touched the last light of her soul. And then her body hit the hard ice with a slap and a crack, and the sled broke free of the cathedral district. In moments, they crossed the Old City Glissade and lost themselves in the snake's nest of streets that lay beyond.

To any skater who passed by them, they must have posed a frightful sight: two large men with their bloody white facemasks and the frantic pilot trying to steer his windowless sled. And Danlo, held as prisoner in the rear seat, his mask hanging from his

neck as a result of his fierce struggle with Kantu Mamod. Danlo's
face had fallen dark and full of wrath; one of the godlings who
witnessed this part of his escape would later remark how terrible
he had been to look upon just then. If Danlo hadn't vowed never
to harm another human being, he might have ripped the laser from
Tobias Urit's hand and used it to club his head. He sensed that he
had the strength to do this. As his heart beat like a pulsing star
and his blood swelled his limbs with liquid fire, he felt that he
could break free from Kantu's grasping hands and rise up to
destroy both these men. He could wait for the pilot to slow the
sled around a corner of some narrow street before jumping out
onto the ice and skating away. So badly did he want to do this
murderous thing that his eyes blazed with a bright and terrible
will. His vow of ahimsa *required* him to escape from these men
who had killed on his behalf. And yet it also required him not to
harm them, even in escaping. As he tasted blood in his mouth
from where Kantu's elbow had split open his lip, he remembered
that it would be better for him to die than ever to harm another.

"Damn you, Danlo wi Soli Ringess!" As the sled turned
along the purple gliddery at the northern edge of the Fravashi
Green, Tobias Urit pressed his palm to his bleeding ear and
cursed. "Damn you—you almost made me dead!"

Tobias glanced out at the many people skating down the paths
of the Fravashi Green, so-called because many livaya bushes na-
tive to Fravashing grow there. But few seemed now to be looking
their way; the sled's pilot had slowed them to a more stately
speed, and both Kantu and Tobias had removed their hideous face
masks.

"You . . . promised," Danlo whispered into the wind. But
he ennunciated these words with so great a fire that Tobias heard
him clearly.

"Well, I had to break my promise—otherwise we'd all be
dead."

Never killing, never harming another, Danlo remembered. *It is
better to die oneself than to kill.*

He closed his eyes against the glare of the icy street, and he
recalled the face of the young woman run down by their sled. He
recalled other faces, too, lovely women and men and children who
had died during this short life of his that seemed suddenly much
too long. He wanted to die then, too. Ahimsa required him to
die—or else others might be run down or burnt by laser fire just
so he might live. And yet he couldn't simply kill himself, couldn't
wrest the laser from Tobias Urit's hand and burn out his own

anguished, beautiful brain. The essence of ahimsa was that all beings must honor the life of every other being, even their own.

How can I die without dishonoring my life? How can I live without causing more death?

"Turn left at the next street," Tobias said to the sled's pilot. "And then an immediate right."

For a few moments, they slid down an almost-deserted street, and the pretty, old stone buildings flew by on either side of them. Tobias had pulled on a knitted wool cap which covered his mutilated ear while Kantu Mamod used his face mask to stanch the blood flowing from his wounded jaw. Danlo saw that Kantu's nose was bleeding, too. He remembered then knocking his head into Kantu's face by bad chance during their struggle.

"Damn you, Danlo wi Soli Ringess," Kantu Mamod said as he daubed the blood from his swollen nose. "I think you broke it."

Instantly, Danlo felt the hot burn of guilt and compassion burning up his throat. It pained him that he had caused Kantu pain; and it pained him even more that he should feel any sort of compassion for the slight wounds of this murderous man.

"I . . . am sorry," he said. "Here, let me see, perhaps I can—"

"We'll tend our wounds when we get to the apartment," Tobias snapped. And then, as the pilot slowed the sled in front of a large white-stone apartment building faced with lacy iron balconies, he told Danlo, "You'll come inside with us; Benjamin Hur has asked me to bring you to him, and I've promised that I shall."

"But you have already broken one promise today," Danlo said, and his eyes flashed with dark blue lights. "Why not another?"

"I won't argue with you about what I've had to do," Tobias said. His red face reddened even more deeply. "You'll stay close to us, or else we'll knock you off your feet and drag you through the city."

Danlo said nothing but only stared at Tobias through the clear winter air.

"Can't you see how important you are to us?" Tobias asked. "Now come with us, please."

With that, he motioned toward the apartment building, and three more ringkeepers rushed out the door. They came up to the sled and stood by as Tobias, Kantu and Danlo climbed out onto the street. "Keep close," Tobias ordered them. "Keep close to Danlo wi Soli Ringess, and don't allow him to skate away."

And then he slapped the sled's red plastic shell, and to the driver, he said, "Thank you, Yurik. I hope I'll see you later tonight."

With that, Yurik fired the rockets yet again, and the sled jumped forward and disappeared down the street.

"Now let's all please hurry," Tobias said. He waited a moment while the three new ringkeepers and Kantu Mamod surrounded Danlo to the front, rear, and either side. And then he led them up the white granite steps into the building.

After passing through the entrance hall where yet two more ringkeepers were stationed, they entered a large apartment at the building's rear. Tobias mentioned that the Kalla Fellowship had taken over the entire building; the apartments on all four floors were full of ringkeepers sleeping in makeshift beds and sitting down to their common meals as they plotted the downfall of Hanuman li Tosh. The apartments were full of other things as well. Immediately upon walking through the door, Danlo noticed that the front fireroom had been stripped of all furniture and stocked with bags of kurmash, sleeping furs and spare skate blades—and, of course, with bullet guns and lasers and eye tlolts and knives and other weapons of assassination and war. Along one wall of the room stood a great workbench, and there the circuitry and parts of some sort of explosive device were laid out as casually as with a table set for dinner. The jewels of a laser, too, lay ready to be assembled.

Danlo almost expected Benjamin Hur to step out from one of the sleeping chambers to greet him and glory in these deadly treasures, but it was not to be so. As soon as one of the ringkeepers had shut the door, a team of two efficient-looking women tended Tobias Urit's and Kantu Mamod's wounds, quickly gluing shut their lacerated flesh and applying a salve of thinskin for protection. Meanwhile, other ringkeepers made ready a change of clothing: plain brown furs to replace their outerwear and black facemasks instead of their bloodstained white ones. One of them asked Danlo to remove his white feather, and this he did. But when she wanted to cut off his long, black hair altogether, Danlo refused. With his face mask and the hood of his furs pulled up over his head, he said, no one would be able to tell who he was. Tobias agreed that such hair-cutting would be unnecessary. Furthermore, it would take time to cut it properly, and Tobias didn't want to waste another moment. When he saw that their preparations had been completed according to his plan, he led Danlo, Kantu and four other ringkeepers toward the door.

"We'll skate across the city," he told Danlo. "It will be much harder for Hanuman's godlings to track us on skates than to pursue the sled."

"Where . . . are we going?" Danlo asked.

"Benjamin Hur keeps another apartment down on the Street of Smugglers," Tobias said. Before pulling on his new face mask, he wiped the sweat from his red beard and then told Danlo exactly how to find this apartment. "If we become separated, I would ask you to go there by yourself."

"It might be better if we became separated, yes? Then no one else would be killed because of me."

"But then *you* might be killed, Danlo wi Soli Ringess, and I can't allow that."

"I . . . am sorry that you cannot."

"Will you promise me that you won't try to escape? We'll skate much more quickly if we skate freely."

For a moment, Danlo considered this. "Why should you think that I would honor my promise, then, when you would not honor your own?"

"Don't make me beg you," Tobias said though clenched teeth.

"Very well, then," Danlo said, "I promise not to escape."

Danlo stood still for a moment, and his eyes shimmered with the light of events as they might unfold. If he *did* try to escape, Tobias' ringkeepers would only continue to hunt him through the streets, and many more innocents might be harmed or even killed. He decided that it would be best for him to confront Benjamin Hur as soon as possible. In the end, it was not Tobias but Benjamin who was responsible for all that had happened that day. Danlo's best hope of ending the violence that swirled around him like the winds of a storm—and perhaps the greater violence throughout the city—lay in cooling the fires of Benjamin's heart and reminding him of the dream they had once shared.

"I promise not to escape," Danlo said again. "But I promise as well to try to stop you if you try to harm anyone else on my behalf."

At this, Kantu Mamod touched his broken nose and looked at Tobias, who said, "We understand each other, then. Now let's please go."

And so they went out onto the streets. The building's rear door let out onto a little alley, almost as dark as a tunnel beneath a mountain. But after a short hike through the newly fallen snow, they reached a bright purple gliddery where they snapped in their skate blades and joined the throngs out to find their midday meals.

Tobias took the lead, positioning Danlo in the center of the
ringkeepers who followed him. Although none of them laid their
hands upon Danlo or crowded his personal space, he understood
from their extreme sensitivity to his motions that they would not
allow him to strike off down the ice on his own. Apparently,
Tobias had little faith in his promise. But then that is the way with
human beings, that those who cannot see their own essential nobility cannot see it in another.

Despite the heavy flow of skaters, they made swift progress,
turning on to a green glissade that almost immediately intersected
the East-West Sliddery. Tobias might have led them onto this
wide orange street, but he feared that Hanuman's godlings might
search it as an obvious route into those parts of the city where
Ringism held little sway. Therefore, he pointed their way onto a
gliddery leading toward a rather dangerous district known as the
Bell.

Danlo well-remembered the twisting glidderies there, for he
had explored them almost street by street during his wild days as a
journeyman. After they had crossed the Way—the broadest street
in the city and the only one officially made of white ice—they
passed into crowded streets little used by the godlings and academicians who clung to the safety of the Old City. It was a beautiful
day, with a patina of new powder melting beneath the strong noon
sun. In this bright, open light, with the colors of purple ice and
white snow and the red and brown furs of the manswarms a glory
to behold, the Bell seemed no more threatening than Resa Commons. With Tobias leading his ringkeepers in such a tight formation, no wormrunners would accost them with offers to sell stolen
firestones or demands that they pay money for their protection. At
worst, they might have to fend off a few whores hoping to earn a
handful of City disks. If they encountered none of Hanuman's
godlings, they might expect to exit onto Strawberry Street in
peace and thence make their way to the Street of Smugglers.

And then, just after they had passed across the purple and
green checkered intersection with the Long Glissade, their peace
was broken. Outside a well-known restaurant, a long queue of
people stood waiting on the street to take their meals. Danlo remembered eating at this very restaurant himself on the day after
he had begun designing his lightship; it was a free restaurant,
specializing in the plain but hearty foods of Urradeth. The men,
women and children who stood kicking their skate blades into the
purple ice were mostly of the poorer sects: hibakusha and harijan,
autists and aphasics and common whores. But today, quite a few

astriers stood in line as well, along with various merchants, wormrunners and even an exemplar from Bodhi Luz. And they all seemed impatient and angry that they should have to wait beneath the open sky. Such lines, one astrier woman loudly complained, hadn't been seen in a thousand years. And a harijan man dressed in bright but ragged yellow silks wondered if the shortages would soon close the free restaurants altogether.

He, as with most of the civilized men and women standing along the street, had never known hunger or even imagined having to go a day without eating; for him, the right to eat was as natural as breathing air, and food had always been as forthcoming as the light of the sun that shined steadily day after day. All he had ever had to do was to walk into a restaurant, grab a bowl and be served. In truth, the free restaurants still had plenty of food to serve. But the private restaurants had almost run out of the cultured meats, the spices and oils and rare fruits from which they concocted their famous dishes. Thus they had recently raised their prices beyond the means of all but the rich or the most extravagant. This inflation had driven even the astriers to the free restaurants—as well as many others. And so it had become almost impossible to sit down to a simple meal of kurmash without waiting in line for an hour.

It was as Danlo and his escort were passing along this line of would-be diners that a fight broke out. A nervous harijan boy was dancing about trying to dig designs in the ice with his skate blades. But he had the misfortune to collide with a wormrunner standing next to him, and one of his steel blades skived the wormrunner's fine boots. When this cruel man saw the scratches that the boy had made, he fell into a fury. "Look what you've done!" he shouted. Without warning, he cuffed the boy's ear, knocking him to the ice. The boy's father, a small but rather violent-looking young man, turned in line to see what had happened. Without bothering to help his son, he immediately pulled a knife from beneath his quilted silks and tried to stab the wormrunner in the face. But the wormrunner already had his laser out; he simply burned the poor harijan man through his eye and spat on him as he fell and joined his sobbing son on the ice. Then he spat again and called out, "Why should anyone have to wait for greasy kurmash and a few rotten nuts?" With that, he glanced at the man that he had so casually murdered and skated off into the street.

But his line of flight took him directly towards the ringkeepers surrounding Danlo. The wormrunner rudely pushed through a group of barefooted autists, but when he came to Kantu Mamod, he found that this man was not so easily moved. "Get out of the way!" he shouted as he lifted his arm to sweep Kantu aside. On any other day Kantu might have allowed the wormrunner to pass. But Kantu, eyeing the wormrunner's laser and the evil work that it had just done, would not let him close to Danlo. He whipped out a knife of his own and closed with the wormrunner. He was much quicker than the harijan man had been; he slashed the steel knife across the wormrunner's wrist, cutting the tendons and causing him to drop the laser. And then, to the cheers (and cries of horror) of the multitudes on the street, he plunged the knife into the wormrunner's heart, killing him instantly.

Danlo, of course, true to his word, tried to stop this killing. But it all happened very quickly. By the time he had turned to face the advancing wormrunner and descried his intent, Kantu Mamod already had his knife out. "No!" Danlo shouted as he lunged for the knife. But even as he began to move, Tobias Urit and two other ringkeepers came up behind him and locked their arms around him. All at once, Danlo's whole body convulsed like that of an enraged tiger. But it was already too late; by the time he had broken free and had reached Kantu's side, the wormrunner had dropped to the street spouting fountains of blood across the purple ice.

"No!"

Danlo called out this single syllable with all the force of the winter wind; he screamed so hard that his throat burned and his voice suddenly died in a gasp of hot breath and pain. He had almost no time to reflect on this further murder, however, because at that moment a man in a golden cape and face mask skated right up to Kantu Mamod. While many onlookers foolishly crowded around them, this man looked at Kantu Mamod's bloody knife. Then he looked at Danlo and the ringkeepers who had moved to surround him with their bodies.

"Please remove your masks," the man said to them. He spoke smoothly, but his voice was edged with steel. "Remove your hoods and masks."

"Leave us alone," Kantu said hotly, pointing his knife at the man. Drops of steaming blood rolled off the steel point and fell burning holes in the ice. "I don't know who you are, but you've no right to ask us this."

"I didn't *ask*," the man said. "Remove your masks now, or I shall remove them for you."

Tobias Urit pushed close to Kantu then, and said, "We were

out to take our meal when this wormrunner went mad. And now we intend to continue our journey."

"First remove your masks."

"That we can't do," Tobias said. "Not for a nameless man who wears a mask himself."

At this, the man suddenly nodded his head as if bowing. And then, with a single, swift motion, he swept the mask from his face and said, "I'm Nigel of Qallar. And that man whom you're protecting is Danlo wi Soli Ringess. I recognized his voice when he cried out."

"It's a warrior-poet!" one of the ringkeepers standing in front of Danlo cried out. Nigel's curly black hair and copper skin gleamed in the sun. "It's one of Hanuman's warrior-poets!"

This news finally encouraged the onlookers to want to flee the street. But such a great mass of people could not move out of the way very quickly. In a moment of time, Nigel's killing knife magically appeared in his right hand while he held a black tipped needle-dart in his left. And in the next moment, Tobias Urit pulled his laser free from his furs, and the four ringkeepers near him drew their knives from their pocket sheaths as quickly as they could.

"No!" Danlo cried out again.

Tobias Urit might have killed the warrior-poet, then. Unlike most men, the sight of a warrior-poet gripping his killing knife did not shock his nerves; there was no slight hesitation of terror that the warrior-poets often relied on to strike their victims dead in a flash of steel or quickly injected poison. In truth, it had been Tobias Urit, along with Benjamin Hur himself, who had executed two other of Hanuman's ronin warrior-poets. But Tobias could not bring himself to raise his laser and fire upon the waiting warrior-poet. In the end, he found his honor as all men must try to do. When he looked upon the swarms of women and children (and men) screaming just behind Nigel of Qallar, he couldn't fire his laser lest he miss and perhaps burn an innocent boy through the eye. And so he pocketed this terrible weapon, and moved to draw out his knife instead.

"Go!" he shouted, digging his elbow into Danlo's ribs. "Skate away as quickly as you can! I'll meet you later."

"No," Danlo said. "No, I have promised to—"

"Skate now, I said! You can't stop this, so please go!"

Just then, Makan Krishnan, the ringkeeper in front of Danlo, began to draw a bullet gun from beneath his furs. Out of fear of the warrior-poet's poisons, perhaps, he seemed not to care if he

sprayed lead bullets about like a mustilox defending himself
against a wolf. But Danlo would not allow him to fire this mindless weapon. He locked his hand on the cold, steel barrel, thereby
immobilizing the frustrated ringkeeper for a moment. And in that
moment, the warrior-poet moved. "No!" Danlo shouted, even as
the warrior-poet flung his dart at the ringkeeper's face. The little
needle tore through the ringkeeper's leather mask and penetrated
his cheek. He jumped, then, as if he had been struck by lightning;
he convulsed and shuddered and froze, and then he fell against
Danlo like a toppling statue. His soft, brown eyes fairly oozed his
fear at being paralyzed and unable ever to draw another breath.

No, no, no, no!

Danlo gently lowered the dying ringkeeper to the street. And
then, in yet another moment of time, he hesitated—but not out of
terror. He had vowed to try to stop Tobias and the other
ringkeepers from killing anyone, but how could he do this? If he
grabbed Tobias' knife arm, he would only help the warrior-poet to
kill Tobias, as with the stricken ringkeeper that he held in his
arms. But if he moved to fend off the warrior-poet's deadly
knife—if by some miracle he actually caught the knife in his body
or hand—he would only make it easier for the ringkeepers to do
their bloody work. As the sunlight poured down like gold across
the ringkeeper's lifeless eyes, Danlo saw that all that he had done
that day had only hastened the dead toward their fate. And nothing that he could do now would prevent more killing; the coming
blood storm was as inevitable as the rising sun.

"Skate, Danlo, skate!" Tobias cried as he slashed his knife
toward the warrior-poet.

And so Danlo skated. He whipped off his encumbering furs
and fairly exploded off the ice. He did not want to see this battle
between the ringkeepers and the warrior-poet. And yet, in the
moment before he turned to concentrate on the icy street before
him he beheld an astonishing thing: the lone warrior-poet with his
killing knife charging five similarly armed men. It was terribly
unequal odds. But fate favored the warrior-poet, for he had
trained his whole life with this weapon for such a moment, and he
exulted in the exercise of his dread art.

Almost instantly he fell into that electric state of being where
external time slowed down even as the firing of his brain and the
nerve impulses singing through his limbs accelerated. He was no
longer a man, but rather a fury of pure movement. He whirled and
slashed and ducked and parried; his knife was a striking serpent's
fang, a blur, a flash of lightning. His golden furs swirled about

him like flames, and his golden, armored kamelaika turned Tobias Urit's and Kantu Mamod's blades. The three other ringkeeper's, in their terror and confusion, seemed only to get in each other's way. Danlo saw one of them cry out and fall clasping the bright white coils of intestines that spilled from his opened belly. And then he saw no more—no more than the purple ice powdered with white snow, the spaces between the screaming people in their brown and ochre furs, and the deep blue sky beyond. He skated as fast as he could; in only moments, he left the violence of the street behind him.

No, no, no, no . . .

For a while, the only sounds that Danlo could hear were the click-clack of his steel skate blades beating against the ice and the screams of the hurrying people all about him. And then came other sounds: the whooshing wind, birds singing and the distant roar of rockets. He heard his heart beating in quick, explosive pulses like a bomb detonating over and over inside his chest. He had always been the fastest of skaters, and with the warrior-poet making a butchery of the ringkeepers, he had need of great speed. He skated and skated, and the hardness of the ice beneath his blades sent shockwaves of pain shooting up through the bones of his legs. He skated with a rare wildness and grace of motion, and as he skated, he prayed that he would leave the warrior-poet far behind him.

Boom, boom, boom, boom.

Although he hated leaving the ringkeepers behind this way, he decided that he could best honor their lives—and their deaths—by fleeing. That they would die beneath the warrior-poet's flashing knife, he felt certain. There came a moment when he could almost feel the booming of their separate hearts; he sensed their lifefire as cries in the wind, as vibrations in the ice, as a pain deep within his own wild heart. And then another moment four of their hearts suddenly stopped.

Doom, doom, doom, doom.

Once, near the intersection with the Street of Friends, he turned to look for the warrior-poet. All he could see behind him, with his eyes, was a great stream of people flowing down the gliddery, their colorful furs shimmering in the sun. But with a deeper sense of vision, he became aware of the warrior-poet pursuing him. This knowledge came to him in different ways. As if scanning the manifold for a lightship, he read the tells of the street, the ripples of fear running from man to woman to man. He felt this fear himself as an acid burning in his belly. From far away, like the ringing of a distant star, he picked out the individual clack-click-clack of the warrior-poet's skates. He saw him, then. In the deeps of his mind, lightning flashed, and this afterimage blazed like fire: the warrior-poet skating in a hellish fury of accelerated motion. His golden cape billowed behind him; his glittering knife dripped blood as he flung aside the screaming people who blocked his way down the purple ice.

To die, to die, to die, to die.

Danlo wondered then, if the time had come to stop and wait for the warrior-poet—simply to stand and die. But if he opened himself to the killing knife, the sacrifice of Tobias Urit and the others would be in vain. And, in truth, he did not want to die but to live. And so he skated. He didn't fear that the warrior-poet would shoot at him with a laser or bullet gun; his kind disdained the use of such weapons. He skated very quickly, and moment by moment, his only concern was that he didn't collide with any of the other skaters who got in this way. He darted and bobbed and shifted and weaved; he flashed down the gliddery like a streak of light. The wind tore at his black kamelaika, and the strong sun stung his eyes. As time closed in like the clouds of a winter storm, his whole universe narrowed to the shimmering purple corridor of ice that lay before him. The ringing of a thousand pairs of skates vibrated up through street and touched the rhythms in his blood. Steel glinted and silk swished, and he seemed to sense with perfect accuracy when the skaters in front of him would suddenly move and an opening appear. He fairly flew through these gaps in the manswarm like a lightship falling through an endless series of windows into the manifold. He skated and skated with an almost perfect freedom of motion; so intense was the wild joy surging within him that he felt like a great white owl soaring through the sky.

To fly, to fly, to fly—it hurts, it hurts, it hurts.

In his mind, he saw the warrior-poet skating like a whirlwind, closing the gap between them. And yet, he knew that if he kept his courage, he could outdistance him, for the warrior-poet could not maintain his frenzy of accelerated motion very long before completely burning out. The problem was with pain. Danlo felt it building like a firestorm within him. With every stroke and glide, with every heartbeat and breath, tendrils of pure flame twisted along his tortured nerves, nearly paralyzing him. Only his will kept him from collapsing into a weeping, shuddering wreck of a man. But even the most adamantine will can be broken, and he knew that soon his will to move would dissolve beneath the ek-kana poison like diamonds dropped into mirax acid.

It hurts, it hurts, it hurts, it hurts.

As he gasped at the burning sword of pain stuck beneath his ribs, the streets quickly flew by: The Street of Aphasics, the Street of Heaven, the Street of Neurosingers. And still the warrior-poet pushed closer through the living stream of furs and silks that separated them. He sensed that this Nigel of Qallar tracked him by the tells of the men and women crowding the streets; the warrior-poets were almost as adept at the art of reading faces as the cetics. If he could find a deserted street before the warrior-poet sighted him, he thought, then he might duck into a building and hide. But in this district of tenements, free restaurants and shops, there were no deserted streets. No deserted *legal* streets, that is. As with all of Neverness' segregated districts, the dwellers of the Bell had built various illegal streets connecting its webwork of glidderies to those of surrounding districts. Some were no more than narrow alleys giving out into tunnels beneath the district barriers. Few knew all of these streets, and still fewer used them for fear of being caught and fined or trapped alone in some dark underpass by a slel necker. Over time, as the city officials discovered them, they were destroyed street by street, but new ones were always springing up like worms from a corpse.

Oh God, it hurts, oh God, oh God!

Once, on a dark night of burning flesh and betrayal, Danlo had followed Hanuman li Tosh down one of these twisting streets. He remembered it well; he wondered if it was still there, connecting with a little gliddery just off the Street of Cartoonists. As he gasped for breath and darted around a fat astrier wearing an illegal snow tiger fur, he *saw* this street in his mind: every dip, every turn, every rill and divot in the old white ice. Only, he was seeing it not from memory, but as he had seen the stellar windows and the flashing lightships around Mara's Star. It existed in the now-moment just beyond the purple glidderies ahead of him. He felt as certain of its reality as the arteries and veins that connected the burning tissues of his body. He could escape down this little tube of ice, he knew. If he were willing to trust that the vision he saw in his mind was true, he could escape the murderous warrior-poet into freedom of the district beyond.

Oh God, oh God, oh God, oh God!

But trust is one thing, and gambling one's life on a mysterious inner sense quite another. For if he turned down this illegal street only to find it closed, it would almost certainly become a death trap. He would have to retrace his path down the long, walled street—by which time the warrior-poet would have discovered his loophole and moved to backtrack him. If he chose instead to skate straight ahead into the manswarms, he *might* still escape the district via the Long Glissade and thence to the Serpentine which twisted through the heart of the Farsider's Quarter. It was still unknown, he thought, who would give out first, the warrior-poet or himself.

Yes or no, yes or no, yes no yes no . . .

In the end there is always a choice. But if one listens to the truth of one's heart, only one way to choose. And so Danlo made a sharp turn down a little gliddery of no name, and he found his street. He skated down it with all the speed and certainty of a falcon diving through the air. At the end of a block lined with apartments and shops, the street itself suddenly ended—or so it seemed. For there, between two crumbling old imprinting shops, was the narrow walkway of ice that he had seen. He followed the walkway where it broadened into a tunnel. This dark tube of ice cut through the embankment of snow separating the Bell from the Diamond District. And all was exactly as he had seen, and suddenly there was light for the tunnel was blessedly open. And then, after a few more moments of striking steel and gasps of cold air, he was through. He made his way onto a piss-stained alley between two brothels. And then he exited onto Strawberry Street where the air smelled of rare perfumes and burning jambool, and the connecting streets were as red as frozen blood.

The light, the light, the light, the light.

The streets about him were more open than those of the Bell and the buildings newer and more brilliant. He remembered, then, that the Diamond District had been named not just for the trade in firestones and Yarkonan bluestars that occurred there, but for its buildings, many of which were faced with white quartz cut from Atakel. All this lovely crystal caught the sun so that the whole district sparkled like diamonds, from Strawberry Street to the Street of Imprimaturs. As he paused a moment to get his breath, he marvelled at the beauty of it. And then he remembered something else. The Street of Imprimaturs, if he followed it far enough toward the Merripen Green, eventually gave out onto the Street of Smugglers. And on that infamous street, Tobias Urit had said, he would find the apartment of Benjamin Hur.

The dead, the dead, the dead, the dead—mi alasharia la shantih.

After he felt sure that he had lost the warrior-poet, he struck off down Strawberry Street, past all the procurers and wormrunners and silk-clad whores. The intense light of the district dazzled him and hurt his eyes—and this pain was as nothing next to the blazing fire of his heart. Even so, he still skated as quickly as he could. For he had promises to keep, and the faces of all those who had died that day tormented him far worse than any physical pain or poison.

THE FIRST PILLAR
OF RINGISM

Know, my godlings, the three great truths that we all must
live by: that Mallory Ringess became a real god and will
one day return to Neverness; that all men and women can
become gods; that the path toward godhood is in
remembrancing the Elder Eddas and following the Way of
Ringess. These are the three pillars that hold up the
heavens toward which we all must strive.
     —from the *Devotionaries* of Lord Hanuman li Tosh

Danlo found Benjamin Hur's apartment in a neighborhood of
obsidian cloisters, hospices and many fine, three-storey blackstones. There, near the Merripen Green, the Street of Smugglers
suddenly straightened and became much less seedy and dangerous
than it was only half a mile to the east. If one followed it far
enough to the west, it emptied into the Serpentine where it curved
around the Winter Ring and passed through the safest (and most
boring) part of the city: the well-ordered and tree-lined blocks of
the Ashtoreth District. But the streets around Benjamin's apartment were safe enough—or had been until war came to the city.
Now that Benjamin's ringkeepers had fairly taken over all the
nearby buildings, no one wearing the godlings' gold dared to
enter this part of the Farsider's Quarter for fear of being killed as
an assassin or spy. Even the wormrunners and whores avoided it.
As Danlo skated up to the door of a lovely blackstone built between two cafes, he felt the eyes of the street and the surrounding
buildings watching him, watching and waiting.

Boom, boom, boom, boom.

With the edge of his fist, Danlo knocked on the door. It was an
unseemly way to announce himself, drumming on the hard wood
as if hammering on a piece of bone. But his knuckles hurt from
the cold, and he couldn't bear the pain of knocking in a more

civilized manner. Everything about him hurt: his hands, his heart and especially his throbbing, burning head.

The door suddenly opened, and a man standing in the foyer called out, "Who are you? Remove your mask so that we can see who you are."

Danlo saw then, that this pock-faced man was pointing a laser at him. Three other men stood about him with lasers in hand guarding the doorway.

"I am Danlo wi Soli Ringess," Danlo said as he removed his mask. "And who are you?"

At the saying of Danlo's name, the man's manner almost immediatly gentled. "I'm Lais Martel," he said. "But what happened to Tobias Urit and the others?"

Quickly, as the wind whooshed through the opened doorway, Danlo recounted what had happened outside the restaurant in the Bell. And then he said, "The warrior-poet pursued me for a while. But I think I lost him."

"You *think?*"

"I . . . am almost certain that I did."

"Well, come in, then, Danlo wi Soli Ringess. It won't do to stand in open doorways with a warrior-poet on the loose."

With that, Lais Martel pulled Danlo inside the building and slammed the door. Then he led him down the hallway to the apartment of Benjamin Hur.

"This is it," Lais said as he paused before a black, shatterwood door. "Benjamin has been waiting for you—we've all wondered why you were late."

After another round of knocking, another man—a nervous and rather gentle ringkeeper whom Danlo remembered as Karim of Clarity—opened the door. He invited Danlo into the apartment's main fire room. Danlo immediately bowed to Lisa Mei Hua, Poppy Panshin, the Masalina, and Zenobia Alimeda, all of whom sat around the room on chairs or couches as if they had been anxiously awaiting Danlo's arrival. At the very center of the room, pacing tracks into an expensive Fravashi carpet, was Benjamin Hur, one of the founders and the would-be warlord of the Kalla Fellowship.

"Danlo!" he cried out as he rushed forward to embrace him. "I'm glad you're well—but where are the others?"

Again, Danlo told his story. Benjamin, with his great hooked nose and green tiger's eyes, listened with a ferocity of purpose quite terrible to behold. Moment by moment, his anger built until it exploded out of him like pus.

"Do you see?" he raged. He turned away from Danlo toward a little man sitting on a plush, velvet couch. "The only way to restrain Hanuman and all his godlings and warrior-poets is to kill them before they kill us!"

"Hello, Danlo," the little man said, standing and bowing politely. Then he too came forward to embrace him. "As usual, my brother shows no restraint himself."

"Hello, Jonathan," Danlo said, returning his bow. He looked at his old friend, Jonathan Hur, and a flush of memories warmed him inside. "I am glad to see you. I am glad . . . that you were invited today, too."

At this Jonathan exchanged glances with his brother, then said, "But I wasn't invited, I'm sorry to say. I came here straightaway only after I'd learned that Benjamin had engineered your escape."

"Well, I would have invited you," Benjamin said, staring at him. "After Danlo had arrived safely and I had a chance to speak with him."

So saying, he invited Danlo to sit in one of the hideous velvet chairs opposite the couch. But Danlo preferred the floor instead, and so he dropped down onto the carpet facing the couch. Jonathan, quick to follow his lead, sat crosslegged near him, and Benjamin grudgingly did the same. Poppy Panshin, a big woman bred on Yachne as a waiting womb for the aristocracy's genetic experiments, eased herself off the couch and sat as near to Danlo as she could—as did Lisa Mei Hua, the Masalina and Zenobia Alimeda. Such easy gathering together on a Fravashi carpet recalled happier times when they had passed a bowl full of kalla from hand to hand around a circle. Even Benjamin, in all his fierceness, must have felt the pull of deep memories, for he smiled as he lost himself in the deep blueness of Danlo's eyes.

"Would you like some tea?" Benjamin finally asked. "You must be cold."

"Yes, that would be good," Danlo said.

At this, Karim of Clarity abandoned his door duty for a moment, and stepped over to the tea service sitting on top of one of Benjamin's fine, inlaid tables. All around the apartment, as Danlo saw, were many fine things: Yarkonan tapestries, kevalin sets from Clarity, Mirrian vases and flame globes, Golden Age paintings and much else. Benjamin explained that he had recently taken over the apartment—and the whole building—from a dead wormrunner who had owed the Kalla Fellowship a debt. He hadn't had the time, he said, to sell off all this pelf and to use the money to buy laser jewels, diamond steel, nall armor, matrikax poison and other weapons of war.

"Here we are," Benjamin said as Karim laid the tea service at the center of the carpet.

While Karim returned to his post by the door, Benjamin poured a golden tea into little blue cups and passed them around the circle. The symbolism of this ceremony was not lost on Danlo—or any of the others. They each remembered the cool and slightly bitter essence of kalla, as well as the rising stream of racial memories known as the Elder Eddas. But the tea was only tea: hot, tannic and much too sweet.

"We must count Tobias and Kantu, all the others, as dead," Benjamin said as he took a sip of tea. "I'm sorry, Danlo—but at least you're here."

"I . . . am sorry, too."

"We're all sorry," Jonathan said. And then he looked at Benjamin. "And we'll continue with our sorrow until you put a stop to this madness."

Benjamin scowled, then, and Danlo thought that the differences between the two brothers couldn't have been more striking. There sat Benjamin with his flashing green eyes and all his rage at the injustices of life. And only four feet away, Jonathan Hur, he of the gentle soul and bright brown eyes as soft and sweet as melting chocolate. He was an urbane young man with a mischievous turn to his face suggesting that he liked to play at the important activities of life rather than taking things too seriously. But his demeanor was deceiving; he was really the most purposeful of men. Before the war, he had been a master holist of no little reputation—one of the youngest masters at the Academy—and he still wore the brilliant cobalt robe of his profession. From their first meeting in Bardo's house years ago, Danlo had instantly liked him, as he had Benjamin. Both brothers, he thought, despite their surface dissimilarities shared a great love of life. They both had hearts of fire, and they both burned to bring forth the beauty and truth inside everyone willing to drink kalla with them.

"This isn't the time," Benjamin told Jonathan, "to begin our old argument."

"But what better time time could there be?" Jonathan asked quietly. "Since here sits Danlo as a result of our desire that he lead us against Hanuman."

Benjamin's face fell heavy with anger, and he said, "Danlo is here as a result of careful planning and the sacrifice of too many good men. If we had relied on your desire and your methods only, he'd still be rotting in his cell."

"But your methods have only brought Hanuman's wrath down upon us. And now the whole city faces starvation because of what your man did."

"Igasho acted without my knowledge. Do you really think I would have allowed him to build a hydrogen *bomb,* much less use one?"

"I don't know what to think anymore."

"Jonathan!"

Jonathan's eyes grew even softer, and for a moment it seemed that he might weep for his brother, for all that had become and all that he would never be. And then he said, "Even if you didn't command Igasho, he still acted to please you. He must have thought the bombing was consistent with this madness you've already brought to the city. And who can blame him?"

"It's Igasho who was mad, not I," Benjamin said. "He made a choice—as we all must do."

"You've made your choices, too."

"I've only chosen to make the truths of the Elder Eddas known to all people everywhere—is this so wrong?"

"And you would do this by murdering them?"

"I'd execute Hanuman li Tosh and all his kind," Benjamin said, "if they keep *our* kind from the One Memory."

"But no one can keep anyone from this," Jonathan said softly. He looked down at the blue cup in his hands, and then smiled at Zenobia Alimeda and Lisa Mei Hua who had followed him to Benjamin's apartment. Finally he looked across the circle at Benjamin. "Has Hanuman kept *you* from our ceremonies?"

"No, but he—"

"No," Jonathan interrupted, "only your desire to oppose him in violence has kept you from drinking kalla with us."

Now Benjamin touched eyes with Poppy Panshin and the Masalina, a rather fleshy-faced man who had once been a famous neurosinger on Silvaplana. Benjamin then glanced at Karim of Clarity standing patiently by the door. Once, they had met almost every night in Jonathan's apartment in the Old City to drink kalla with Jonathan, Zenobia and Lisa Mei—and others. But as Hanuman had grown ever more powerful, they had followed Benjamin down cold and corpse-strewn streets into this lonely part of the Farsider's Quarter.

"We've all vowed," Benjamin said, "to abstain from drinking kalla until Neverness is safe for everyone to do so."

Jonathan smiled sadly, then, and said, "But until it *is* safe, shouldn't we be as lights for those who have never drunk the kalla? Shouldn't we be as diamond windows transparent to the Eddas so that all people can see their own possibilities?"

"Lights can be snuffed out," Benjamin said. "Windows can be broken."

"But one light can ignite ten others. And each of those ten, ten more."

"Oh, Jonathan, you're such a dreamer! And dreamers so easily die."

"I'm not afraid to die."

Just then all the fierceness melted out of Benjamin's hard green eyes, and it seemed that he might weep. Then he said, "I've never doubted your courage—only the wisdom of your way."

"And I've never doubted your compassion—only your ability to find it."

For a while, as the afternoon wore on and they drank tea, the two brothers argued their old argument. Danlo learned how the two factions of the Kalla Fellowship had split apart, and how each hoped to reconcile the other to its way. He learned other things as well. According to Benjamin, that very morning Igasho Hod had been found dead in an alley off the East-West Sliddery. His ring had been broken open, and his lips were blue from the effects of the matrikax poison: apparently he had killed himself in remorse for destroying the food factories and incinerating so màny helpless people. Benjamin made it seem that Igasho's death somehow atoned for his terrible act, but Jonathan found this argument absurd. Jonathan brought news of his own, then. He told of five deepships full of Yarkonan grain that had been lost as the Fellowship and Ringist fleets manuevered through the Fallaways. Everyone was expecting another battle soon, he said. And now that there would be no shipments of grain for at least another ten days, everyone was expecting the first pangs of hunger.

"What will you say about the wisdom of your way when you hear children crying because they have nothing to eat?" Jonathan asked his brother.

But Benjamin chose not to answer this unanswerable question; instead he stirred his tepid tea with his finger and looked at Danlo. "You see, we've been fighting this way since we both could speak. But Jonathan is older and cleverer than I, so he always wins."

All this time, Danlo had kept his silence as he listened. And now he smiled gravely and said, "I do not think that either of you has won anything."

At this, Benjamin's eyes flashed angrily, and he squeezed his cup so hard that his hand trembled, causing tea to spill over the dead wormrunner's carpet. "Damn you Jonathan!" he said. "I should never have let you in the door. With all your damn compassion, you've softened Danlo so that he has no will to resist what Hanuman has done."

Now it was Danlo's turn for anger. Only, where Benjamin showed the fierce emerald eyes of a tiger, Danlo's eyes were wild, blue, blazing stars.

"What do you know of will?" he asked, rubbing the old scar on his forehead. And then, as the shooting pain behind his eyes quieted for a moment, his voice dropped almost to a whisper, "What do you know of compassion?"

Benjamin glanced down at the tea stain on the carpet, then, and said, "I didn't mean to insult you, but I see now that there's little hope you'll lead us against Hanuman."

"I *would* lead you," Danlo said.

At this Benjamin suddenly looked up hopefully.

"I would lead you, but only if we could find a way to oppose Hanuman's works with *satyagraha.*"

"I'm unfamiliar with this word," Benjamin said.

"It means 'soul force,' " Danlo said. He explained that the Fravashi, in their making of the language of Moksha, had borrowed it from the ancient Sanskrit. "There must be a way . . . to oppose Hanuman in nonviolence with all the force of our souls."

"But that's no opposition at all—only a deepening of Jonathan's dream!"

Danlo closed his eyes a moment as he remembered a beautiful and terrible light inside light. "It is much more than that," he said.

"Did this soul force of yours keep the warrior-poet from slaughtering my men?"

"No," Danlo admitted. "But you cannot even dream how great the force of our souls truly could be."

"I didn't bring you here today to listen to this."

"Did you think that I would simply abandon my vow of ahimsa, then?"

Benjamin motioned toward Karim of Clarity with his laser, and he said, "Did you think that you could just walk in here and persuade us to lay down our arms?"

"I had hoped that I might," Danlo said, smiling sadly.

"Your vow of ahimsa caused at least one of my men to die. You say you grabbed Makan's arm, allowing the warrior-poet to strike with his dart?"

"That . . . was not my intention," Danlo said. "I only wanted to prevent him from harming the warrior-poet. And more, from firing his bullets into the crowd."

"Well, you succeeded, didn't you? And now Makan is dead."

Danlo looked down at his hand that had grabbed the barrel of Makan's gun. He could still feel the cold metal burning his fingers, burning like a bolt of lightning up the nerves of his arm and neck into his head. "I am sorry that he is," he finally said.

"And what if Makan *had* killed the warrior-poet?" Benjamin demanded. "Then Tobias and the others might still be alive."

"I am sorry," Danlo said, still staring at his hand.

"You might have traded one life for five, don't you see?"

At this Danlo suddenly looked up and locked eyes with Benjamin. "Am I only a merchant, then, to trade this way?"

"No, you're a man," Benjamin said. "And men sometimes must make difficult choices."

"I have already made my choice. Never killing, never—"

"You're a man who might lead other men," Benjamin interrupted. Here, Zenobia, Poppy and Lisa Mei all looked at Benjamin, who quickly said, "Men *and* women. Can you even dream how many might follow you if only you'd lead them?"

"Follow . . . only to kill, then?"

"But wouldn't you kill a few so that the many might live?"

"No."

"If fate gave you the chance, wouldn't you kill Hanuman to save a hundred children from starving?"

"Hanuman . . . was my deepest friend."

"Only one man, Danlo! Wouldn't you kill one man to save ten thousand men and women from dying in this stupid war?"

For a moment, Danlo closed his eyes as he counted the beats of his heart.

Boom, boom, boom, boom.

"One man against ten thousand, Danlo. Only one mad, evil man."

Doom, doom, doom, doom.

At last, after Danlo had opened his eyes and drawn a deep breath, he looked at Benjamin and told him, "No, I am sorry—I will not perform this kind of calculus of killing. It is either wrong to kill or it is not. I . . . believe that it is wrong."

"*Always* wrong?"

"Yes, always," Danlo said.

But just then his eyes clouded with doubt, for suddenly, in his mind, he saw something that terrified him: a young boy lying in his arms, his beautiful face ravaged with pain and hunger. The boy had great courage and pride, but not enough fire inside to keep him alive, and so Danlo watched the light fade from his eyes—eyes that were as clear and deep as liquid diamonds.

"No, no," Danlo murmured, "no, no, no . . ."

Benjamin seized upon Danlo's moment of weakness, then; he came over to Danlo and laid his hand upon his arm. "Will you lead us?" he asked.

"No," Danlo said, still staring at the deep, blue eyes that stared at him out of memory and time. "No—the soul force, the fire, there must always be a way."

Misunderstanding him, Benjamin now jumped up and crossed over to one of his tables inlaid with blue lapis stones and gold. He opened the drawer and closed his hand on a shining laser. "This," he said, presenting the laser to Danlo, "is how the soul must manifest its force in a world of men such as Hanuman."

"No," Danlo murmured again.

Benjamin stepped across the circle closer to Danlo. He knelt, holding the laser out to him. "Please take it, Danlo."

Danlo saw that Poppy Panshin, Karim of Clarity and the Masalina were all watching him, their hopeful faces urging him to take up the laser. Jonathan Hur, he saw, held his breath as he stared at him, as did Zenobia Alimeda. And Lisa Mei Hua, who should have followed Jonathan in all his gentleness, seemed secretly to wish that he would take the laser and somehow lead the two halves of the Kalla Fellowship to defeat Hanuman.

"Please, Danlo." This came from Benjamin, who held the glittering laser before him. And then three other voices—those of the Masalina, Poppy and Karim of Clarity—joined him. "Please, Danlo."

Please, Father.

Danlo listened to voices outside and inside, from eons past and moments yet to be. He saw ten thousand pairs of eyes looking at him, Jonathan's soft brown eyes and Benjamin's and many, many others. And always the one pair of eyes that haunted him, the secret light, blue inside blue—it was such an agony to behold this terrible and beautiful blueness that he wanted to pull his own aching eyes from his head.

Please, Father.

It seemed forever that Danlo gazed at the laser gleaming in the light of the late afternoon. And then he said, "I cannot."

"Your father would take the laser," Benjamin said. "If he ever returned as everyone believes he will, he'd do what needed to be done."

"I . . . am not my father."

"No, you're certainly not," Benjamin said. Then he sighed and stood up to return to his place in the circle.

Please, Father, Danlo silently prayed. *Please do return and bring an end to this madness that you began.*

"It's ironic that Hanuman preaches that your father will one day return," Benjamin said, almost reading Danlo's mind. "If your father ever *did* return, Hanuman would wish he hadn't."

"I think you're wrong to assume that Mallory Ringess would do violence to Hanuman," Jonathan said.

"Well, Mallory Ringess knew about the proper use of force, didn't he? He had a violent soul, and he knew about killing."

"He knew about compassion, too," Jonathan said. "If Mallory Ringess returned, he'd find a way to deal with Hanuman without more murder."

"By being a diamond window through which Hanuman could see his deeper possibilities?"

"Why not?"

"By being a light?" Benjamin continued. "Do you really suppose that Hanuman would just look upon Mallory Ringess' shining face and be dazzled into dismantling this false religion that he's made?"

Jonathan looked to Zenobia and Lisa Mei as if for confirmation, and then said, "It wouldn't really matter what Hanuman did or didn't do. If Mallory Ringess returned, he'd tell the people the truth about what he was. And then there would be no more religion called Ringism."

"Do you really believe that?"

"At least, there would be no religion as it is now. Mallory Ringess would only have to walk into the cathedral and show the godlings the way to remembrance the Elder Eddas. He could lead the whole city in a mass kalla ceremony—can you imagine a million people passing bowls of kalla from hand to hand up and down every gliddery and glissade?"

"Now *that* is a lovely thought," Benjamin said. For the first time that afternoon, Danlo saw him smile. "A very lovely thought."

Jonathan smiled then, too, and said to his brother, "I wish he *would* return. I never met him—I suppose I'd really like to know if he really became a god.''

''I would too,'' Benjamin said. ''But he won't return—if he were able to, he would have done so by now.''

''At least we're agreed that we mustn't hope for this,'' Jonathan said.

Benjamin sighed as he looked across the circle at Danlo. ''This *satyagraha,* this soul force of yours, is really a lovely concept. I wish I could see how we could use it to bring Hanuman down. But I can't.''

Just then Danlo removed his flute from its pocket, and he played a single, soft note. And as he breathed into long bamboo shaft and stared at Benjamin, an idea came to him like a fireflower opening in the sun.

Again, Benjamin sighed, ''You're a lovely man, Danlo. But you're not your father. I'm afraid you'll have to choose between Jonathan's way or mine.''

I am not my father.

Now it was Jonathan's turn to try to persuade Danlo of the wisdom of his way. He said that in the Old City, near the Ring of Fire, an apartment was being prepared for Danlo. His plan was to bring Danlo to this apartment in secret, where he would live and gather others to him in secret remembrance of the Elder Eddas. At night, he might steal out into the dark streets and journey among the kalla worshippers throughout the city. He would be a light to them, a diamond window, a living embodiment of the principle of *satyagraha.*

''You're not your father,'' Jonathan said. ''But you *are* Danlo wi Soli Ringess—everyone knows you've had a clear vision of the One Memory. In time, if you could help bring others to their own remembrance, much might be changed.''

I am not my father.

Benjamin watched Danlo carefully, clearly dreading that Danlo would approve this plan and join his fate with Jonathan's. But then Danlo surprised him, saying, ''I am sorry, Jonathan. Truly I am.''

''You won't lead us, then?''

Jonathan's face, in all its dreaminess and dissapointed hopes, was hard to look at just then. Danlo could hardly bear to tell him that his plan was much too passive, not at all the deepest expression of the soul's beautiful and truly terrible force.

''I will not lead you the way that you want me to,'' Danlo said.

"We do not have the time to lead the people toward the One Memory, now."

"Why not?"

"Because Hanuman will not allow us to." Danlo closed his eyes as he remembered the terrors of the war that the Iviomils had fought with their fellow Architects on Tannahill. Dreams were more precious than diamonds or firestones, but when people were murdered by a warlord's death cadres, they might have no time to realize them. "Now that Benjamin has so spectacularly arranged my escape, I am afraid of what Hanuman will do."

"But what will you do, then?"

I am not my father.

"I will oppose Hanuman with all the force of my soul."

"But how? Since you've rejected both Benjamin's way and mine?"

"I have my own way."

"And what is that?"

"I will be a brilliant mirror showing Hanuman just as he is."

"I don't understand."

"I will be a blazing light showing the godlings the *shaida* of the religion that they have made."

"But how, Danlo?"

"I will give them more diamonds than they can hold in their hands. I will give them firestones too dazzling to behold."

Now Benjamin began laughing softly even as his fierce green eyes shone like emeralds. He said, "I know you, Danlo. You have a plan."

"Yes—I have a plan."

"What is it, then?"

"I cannot tell you."

"But you must."

Danlo looked around the circle at Poppy Panshin, Lisa Mei Hua and the Masalina, with his fleshy and fearful face. And then he looked back at Benjamin and said, "Any of you might be captured and questioned beneath a warrior-poet's knife."

"We know the risk we take," Benjamin said.

Just then a bolt of pain shot through Danlo's head, and he told them, "I will not allow Hanuman to have reason to torture you with the ekkana."

"But this is why we wear our rings," Benjamin said. He made a fist and showed Danlo his glittering ring filled with matrikax poison. Then he nodded at Karim of Clarity, Poppy Panshin and the Masalina, who held up their rings as well. "We would each of us die to protect you or your plan."

"I know that you would," Danlo said, smiling sadly. "But rings can be taken before they might be used."

"Well, there are other ways to die."

"I will not allow anyone to die for me," Danlo said. "I am sorry."

A sudden silence fell over the room like a descending *morateth* cloud; Jonathan and Benjamin traded glances with the others sitting around the circle, but no one seemed to know what to say.

And then Benjamin finally looked at Danlo and told him, "Well, at least you'll stay here with us—it would be much too dangerous for you to take Jonathan's apartment in the Old City."

"I will stay neither there nor here."

"But you've no place else to go."

"I have the whole city. The . . . whole world."

"I meant that there is no place safe," Benjamin said. Then he looked down at the laser still in his hand and sighed. "There is something I should tell you, Danlo. Our efforts to help you escape did not unfold exactly according to our plan."

Danlo saw the anxiety fall over Benjamin's face, then, and he said, "It is not only that Tobias Urit and the others died, is it?"

"No, there's more than that." Benjamin placed his tea cup to his lips as if to drink, but it was empty. "It seems that the disassemblers we used to dissolve the walls of your cell were not programmed with great enough precision. I'm afraid they dissolved the walls of other cells as well."

Now Jonathan was staring at his brother in horror as if he had just learned that a bacteria swarm was about to eat the face of the entire planet. But Benjamin's news was not quite so catastrophic as that. He swallowed once, sighed, cleared his throat, and then said, "I'm afraid that Malaclypse Redring has escaped as well. No one knows where he has gone. But he'll be hunting you, Danlo."

For a long time Danlo sat on the soft Fravashi carpet, silently blowing into the ivory mouthpiece of his flute. And then he said, "Yes, he will."

"Don't you see? It's too dangerous for you to leave here."

"Nevertheless, I must leave."

Benjamin looked at Karim of Clarity, who still stood with his laser by the door. "I'm not sure that I can let you," Benjamin said.

There was a moment, then. Danlo blew a long note on his flute; the music was high and haunting like the call of the snowy owl. Then he looked at Benjamin, who almost gasped at the light streaming from Danlo's eyes. In truth, Danlo was really much wilder and fiercer than Benjamin, and for a single moment he let blaze the full force of his soul. And then he put down his flute and asked, "Are you really willing to be my jailer, Benjamin?"

But Benjamin, transfixed by what he saw in Danlo's face just then, couldn't answer.

"Many died to aid my escape," Danlo said. "Do not let their sacrifice be for nothing."

At last Benjamin found his voice; he looked down at the carpet and said, "All right—I won't hold you then."

Danlo bowed his head, then suddenly stood up as he placed his shakuhachi back in its pocket.

"You're not leaving *now*, are you?" Jonathan asked.

"Yes," Danlo said.

"But where will you go?"

"That I cannot tell you."

"But you've no apartment, no money, no friends—at least no friends whom Hanuman's spies won't watch."

Danlo crossed to the room's drying rack where he found his face mask and goggles. At a nod from Karim of Clarity, he found a spare fur there, as well, and put it on. Then he turned to face Jonathan, Benjamin and the others. "I would like to thank you all for your concern for me."

"But how will we find you if we need you?" Benjamin asked. "And what if you need us?"

Danlo considered this for a moment. Then he said, "From time to time I shall skate down this street—wearing a different face mask and furs. If you need to talk with me, set a blue bowl in the window of the front apartment, and I shall come in."

"Very well," Benjamin said, nodding his head. Then he and all the others stood to embrace Danlo and wish him farewell. "Stay to the Farsider's Quarter," Benjamin advised. "It's dangerous, but I'm afraid that if you go near the Old City, you'll be taken."

Danlo bowed and said, "Farewell Benjamin." Then he bowed his farewells to each of the others and walked out into the hallway. The ringkeepers there opened the outside door to let him out onto the street.

I am not my father, he thought.

As he skated down the sliddery into the heart of the Farsider's Quarter, he smiled beneath his dark, leather mask. Soon he turned onto lesser streets where none of the men and women passing by would see his his face or know who he truly was.

HOPE

*Our first and last hope must always be to follow the way
of Mallory Ringess and to behold his miraculous
transformation even as we hold his image forever inside
ourselves.*

—Hanuman li Tosh, Lord of the Way of Ringess

Nearly thirteen years before, Danlo had come to Neverness across
six hundred miles of the frozen sea. Starving, frostbitten and
alone, he had found his way onto the icy sands of North Beach
where a Fravashi alien called Old Father had befriended him and
offered him shelter in his house. And now, as he skated alone
away from Benjamin Hur's apartment, he realized that he was
very near the Fravashi District, where he presumed that the white-
furred Old Father still guided his students in the daily Moksha
competitions and the mystical art of plexure.

His path took him along the Merripen Green and crossed the
East-West Sliddery. And then it cut across the corner of the
Fravashi District, where many old houses remain as a testament of
the importance of the Fravashi in Neverness over the last three
thousand years. Danlo very badly wanted to make a detour down
the streets of these squat, one-storey dwellings and pay his re-
spects to Old Father. But he feared that Hanuman's spies might
keep a watch for his arrival. And so instead he turned onto a
gliddery leading west through a neighborhood of old tenements
and whitestone hospices.

Here, in this nothing neighborhood of autists, harijan,
hibakusha and other castaway peoples of the city, he might have
found refuge. He might have taken residence in one of the free
dormitories, and taken his meals every day in a great commons
room, sitting at table before a gas fire and eating with strangers.
But because he did not wish to be known for who he was, he
would have had to keep his mask covering his face, and this
peculiarity might have drawn unwanted attention. And so he

crossed onto a little red street leading directly into that part of the city where no one lived.

This was the City Wild, a great expanse of yu trees, gentle hills and streams running through ravines untouched by the hand of man. The founders of Neverness, wishing to include in their great city a swath of raw nature, had ordered these acres of forest to be left in their wild state. For three thousand years the city had grown across the tip of Neverness Island, and the various districts—the Ashtoreth District, the Darghinni and Elidi Districts and all the others—had been added one by one. As the pressure of too many people caused the building of huge tenements and towers, many had argued for the cutting of the City Wild's trees. But the Timekeeper had never allowed such a desecration; indeed, he had permitted the building of only a few paths through this cold and wild forest. Those wishing to experience the splendors of nature, he said, could brave the snowdrifts and steep ravines on skis. The more timid souls could always take solace in the Merripen or Gallivare Greens, those soft fields of flowering plants and carefully tended trees nearer to the city's hotels and restaurants. And so especially in the deeper parts of winter, the City Wild has always been a place of songbirds and solitude, where a man might lose himself for whole days and encounter no other human being.

Such distance from the inquisitive eyes of the city was exactly what Danlo desired. At one of the free shops just off the East-West Sliddery, he acquired a pair of skis, a stove, lamp, sleeping furs, saw, knife and other tools he would need to begin his time alone in the forest. But he found no food. It was strange, he thought, that the free shops had been almost totally emptied of food while they fairly bulged with furs, kamelaikas, skates, goggles, heated boots, lip balm and other necessities for living within a frozen city such as Neverness. He realized that the weakest part of his plan was that he would have to emerge from the City Wild at least twice each day to take meals in the free restaurants of the surrounding districts—that is, if the grain shipments ever arrived from Summerworld or Yarkona and the lords of the city kept the restaurants open.

He entered the City Wild along a green glissade that ran straight across the entire city, from South Beach to the Hofgarten. Here the ice was well kept and the skating easy. Here, too, were great yu trees rising up straight and grayish-green, and the even greater shatterwood trees that reminded him of his first home on the island of Kweitkel. In truth, much about this forest was similar to the wild forests on the islands far to the west of Neverness: the

feather moss and fairy finger growing on the tree trunks, the snow
apples and iceblooms and anda bushes blazing red and orange
with fireflowers. Near where the glissade intersected a sliddery
that cut through the forest from east to west, he found stands of
snow pine and bonewood thickets uncommon to his home island
but still familiar nonetheless.

He well-remembered the names of these plants, as well as
those of the few animals who lived among them. There was *Liliji,*
the fritillary, and two species of loons that he knew as *Aditi* and
Liolya. There was *Churo,* the sleekit, and *Aulii,* the snowworm
who made their homes beneath the snow. Sometimes flocks of
pilits or kitikeesha would find their way onto one of the City
Wild's frozen lakes; but just as often, some clumsy farsider on
skis would come crashing through the trees and drive these pretty
birds away. Over three thousand years, almost all the larger animals had adandoned this little woods. Gone were the wolves and
bears and mammoths who had once lived there. Gone too, it
seemed, were the snowy owls. As always when Danlo entered the
wild part of the world, he listened for the cry of this rare white
bird who held half his soul. But the only sounds of the forest were
the wind swirling through the trees, the tinkle of spindrift snow,
and the far-off tapping of a tititit bird.

About half a mile into the Wild, he left the sliddery. He ejected
his skate blades and put on his skis. He struck off north toward a
little ridge he remembered that cut through the heart of the forest.
In truth, he remembered almost every rock and tree of this al-
most-wild woods, for during his time as a student in Old Father's
house, he had come here almost every day. He remembered the
smells of the red yu berries and the pungent fragrance of the
fireflowers; he remembered how good it was simply to slide his
skis through the newly fallen *soreesh* snow. In little time, he
found the place that he was seeking. This was a ridge of granite
rocks running from southwest to northeast. He hoped that it might
provide a shield against the west wind, that murderous wind of
deep winter that he knew as the Serpent's Breath. Close to the
ridge, on the south side, grew a protection of another sort: a copse
of snow pine interspersed with bonewood thickets. It was Danlo's
hope that this wall of vegetation would act as a shield against the
searching eyes of anyone who might ski close by.

And so, on the narrow snowfield between the ridge and the
bonewood thickets, he set to work building his house. From the
pack that he had acquired in the shop, he removed a long, steel
knife. So keen were his memories of what Jaroslav Bulba had

done to him with his killing knife that he was almost reluctant to touch it. For a while he held the blade gleaming in the sun of the late afternoon. How strange, he thought, that this brilliant thing could be used to cut out a man's heart as well as in the cutting of snow. But after all, the knife was only a knife, and today he would use it only for this latter purpose.

About a hundred yards from his house site, blown up against the ridge, he found a drift of snow. It was *kureesha* snow, as he had once called it: all wind-packed and hard and easy to work. Immediately, he began cutting snowblocks the size of a man's chest. The dark blue sky wouldn't hold the sun much longer, and soon it would grow dark and very cold. As quickly as he could, he bundled these blocks into his furs and dragged them along the ridge to his house site. Many times he made this short journey, cutting blocks and then dumping them on the circle of snow that he had packed down with his skis. When he saw that he had enough, he began shaping the blocks with his knife, shaving off the sparkling ice crystals and planting the foundation blocks around the circle down into the snow. Working inward and upward, he set the next circle of blocks and then the next. It fairly astonished him that he could work so quickly, for it had been almost half his life since he had built similiar snow houses out on the frozen sea. But his hands, much more than his eyes or mind, seemed to know just how to cut the curving blocks and to fit them together into a growing dome. Soon, it seemed, he was setting the last circle and then whittling away at the crunchy snow of the last block, the key block that he set into the highest part of the curving roof.

Having completed the main body of the house just at sunset—the white dome was higher than his head—he spared not a moment to admire his handiwork. For he still had to build the tunnel, that long tube of snow that would serve as an entranceway and keep out the howling wind. He finished it beneath the light of the flame globe that he had set on a rock. The forest had fallen so dark that he could barely see the trees rising toward the starry sky. And it was very cold, almost blue cold—the kind of cold that could freeze the life inside a man's limbs and steal his breath away. He badly wanted to take shelter inside his new house, then. But the wind was up, blowing particles of spindrift against his face mask and driving through the chinks between the blocks of snow.

And so, with his numb fingers and shivering arms, in the deepening cold of the night, he went around the outside of his house packing snow into every chink that he could find. And when he had finally finished this brutal labor, he stood back on the cold, squeeking snow and lifted his face to the stars. *"Wi leldra pelasu mi shamli se halla, se kareeska,"* he prayed, calling for his ancestors to bless his new home. Despite the pain of his cold face muscles, he smiled at how easily he had fallen into his old ways. And then without further cermony, he dragged his skis, furs, pack and all his possessions through the tunnel into his living space beneath the dome.

At first, the interior of his snow house was very cold. But he set the plasma stove onto a little rug at the center of his single room, and the air warmed quickly. Indeed, soon it was so warm that he stripped off his furs and began building the shelf of snow that would serve as his bed. He worked to the light of the flame globe, set also at the room's center. Lovely lights of amethyst, turquoise and topaz suffused the curving walls of snow, causing each individual ice crystal to sparkle like a jewel. With his bed complete, he had only to spread out his thick sleeping furs to be ready for the night. In the morning, he thought, he could cut wood poles with which to make drying racks for his clothing and boots and otherwise make his house habitable.

He might have slept, then. He might have dived beneath his warm, silken shagshay furs and reflected upon the events of this remarkable day. Instead, he went outside to make his piss-before-sleeping. He put on his fur coat, walked out into the woods, and stood with his back to a pine tree facing south. A man, he remembered, must always piss to the south, sleep to the north and pray to the east. And die to the west. Soon, he thought, it would come time for him to make this journey: either to die the real death or to die to the man that he had always known.

He stood there in the cold and almost silent night listening to the faint movement of the wind through the trees. He smelled snow and yu berries and death: The long, dark vapors of it were heavy in the air and almost as real as his steaming breath. Far above, out in the blackness of deep space, the stars shined like a billion bits of newly fallen snow. The stellar winds blew through the universe in single, fiery breath, and he listened to this faint sound, too. He looked toward the Vild at the supernovas, the *blinkans* as he had once called these fierce blazing lights. He remembered that the radiance of one of these supernovas—Merripen's Star—would soon fall over Neverness in all its terrible glory and whispers of death.

He feared the coming of this starlight; he feared the death of his world, and so he turned to the east for a while to pray. And there, as he looked towards the horizon just over the dark outline of the mountains, Atakel and Urkel, there in the east he beheld the glow of the Golden Ring. This great swath of living gold colored the stars amber and ruby red; it swirled and rippled and flowed with beautiful patterns and purpose—and for a long time he prayed that its purpose would be to shield his world from the Vild's killing light.

But just as he took an icy breath and hope leaped in his heart, he looked straight up above the city. In near space, across only a few tens of thousands of miles, Hanuman's Universal Computer loomed all black and huge as a moon. It blocked out the familiar stars, Shesakeen and Kefira Luz and others that Danlo had known since childhood. In truth it seemed to eat the stars like some vast black hole made by the hand of man. Seeing that the Golden Ring would not grow near the spaces of this monstrous machine, he nearly despaired. And when he thought of Bertram Jaspari's Iviomils waiting somewhere in spacetime—waiting to use their hideous *morrashar* to destroy the Star of Neverness—he felt something black and heavy and utterly cold gnawing at the soft tissues of his belly. He remembered his own purpose, then. He let the starlight fall across his cold, naked face, and he prayed for the courage to embrace the strange fate that he had chosen for himself.

Despite the sweet song of a panditi bird filling up the forest, he slept badly that night. Sometime toward morning he began dreaming his old dream, the one that had first come to him during his sojourn on the beach of the false earth inside the Solid State Entity. In this dream, in the exotic and fevered land of nightmare, a tall gray man used steel scalpels, lasers and drills to cut at his flesh. The man sculpted his body and face, transforming him into a beautiful tiger.

He always awoke from this dream sweating and trembling to scream and move; always the taste of blood filled his mouth. And on *this* morning of cold blue air and sunlight filtering through the domed snow blocks above him, he tasted a terrible hunger as well. He realized that he hadn't eaten since the morning before when Kiyoshi Telek had served him breakfast in his cell of the chapterhouse. And so he quickly put on his kamelaika, boots, furs and face mask, and went outside. He skied back through the forest toward the orange sliddery that ran through the trees.

The air was clear and sweet, and the drifts of snow sparkled in the early light. After leaving his skis buried in the snow behind a great shatterwood tree, he clipped in his skate blades and pushed off toward the nothing district north of the Merripen Green. He saw only one other skater, a man dressed in hooded furs much as himself. In little time, he exited the City Wild via the green glissade that had no name. The cafes and restaurants of the Farsider's Quarter and the entire city of Neverness lay before him. He had only to choose one of the free restaurants to take his morning meal, and then he could begin fulfilling his plan to bring down Hanuman li Tosh.

Eating took much longer than he had hoped. Three of the restaurants that he found had run out of food, and at the fourth, he had to stand outside on the street for two hours waiting in line with scores of other hungry people. The cold was bad enough, but the smells of garlic, cilka and coffee wafting from a nearby private restaurant tormented him—and everyone else impatiently clicking their skate blades against the ice and grumbling at the unfairness of life. The icy air vibrated with tension and the sounds of wormrunners and autists hawking up gouts of morning phlegm. Quite a few of them passed their time smoking jook and jambool and other potent drugs. The muddy brown smoke spilling out of their pipes seemed only to aggravate the emptiness in the pit of Danlo's belly. And when he finally took his place at a long plastic table inside the restaurant and sat down to his breakfast— one bowl of boiled kurmash as thin and pale as soapy water—his belly writhed and howled for more food. But he was not allowed a second helping; the restaurant's ushers quickly collected his empty bowl and fairly pushed him back out onto the street. There, he saw, the line of hungry people waiting down the red ice had grown even longer.

He spent the rest of the morning making inquiries in the district's various cutting shops. He would skate up and down the busy streets, knocking at doors and asking the whereabouts of a once-famous cutter named Mehtar Hajime. Although many of the cutters whom he questioned offered to sculpt his body at the most reasonable of prices—changing his blue eyes to green, enlarging his sexual organs, or carving his vocal cords so that he could sing like a Fravashi alien—no one seemed to know where Mehtar might be found.

And so he extended his quest into other districts, working down through the Farsider's Quarter from the Merripen Green along the Street of Cutters and Splicers to the Diamond District. He entered the Bell and searched the shabby shops on the glidderies near the Street of Neurosingers; he skated back along the

Serpentine and explored the dangerous neighborhoods just south of Rollo's Ring. There, in a little shop protected with iron doors, he spoke with a cutter who had once known Mehtar. This cutter, a plump and proud-seeming man wearing the white cottons of his profession, eyed Danlo suspiciously and wouldn't let him through his doorway. "What do you want of Mehtar Hajime?" he asked.

"I seek his services," Danlo said.

"Who are you?" the cutter asked. "Why don't you remove your mask so that I can see whom I'm talking to?"

"I am sorry," Danlo said, standing in the open doorway like a beggar. "I cannot do that."

"Why not? Do you suffer from the tabes? Perhaps one of the fleshrotting funguses? Or are you one of the unfortunates burned in the blast of the food factories?"

"I suffer only from the cold," Danlo said. "It has fallen cold early this year, yes?"

"Well, I can't just invite inside some faceless man wearing a mask."

"But can you tell me where I might find Mehtar Hajime, then?"

"It's been almost twenty years since he practiced his art," the cutter said evasively. "He used to have the finest shop on the Street of the Cutters."

"Yes, I stopped there," Danlo said. "The shopfront is blue obsidian carved with figures of exemplars and the double-sexed. A cutter named Alvarez had taken over the shop."

"That's the place—did you happen to see the carving above the door?"

"The carving of an Alaloi man killing a mammoth with his spear?"

"You've a good eye," the cutter said. "Mehtar was most famous for sculpting men into the shape of the Alaloi. It seemed that almost everyone wanted to be as hardy and strong as these primitives. Such transformations were quite popular a generation ago."

"But no longer, yes?"

"Are you interested in such a sculpting for yourself?" the cutter asked.

Danlo kept silent for a moment, and then answered his question with one of his own. "Do you know if Mehtar might have trained any apprentices in his art?"

"Perhaps he did, perhaps he didn't," the cutter grumbled, suddenly beginning to lose interest in Danlo. "How should I remember? It's been almost twenty-five years."

"But do you know of any other cutters who might have his skill in this kind of sculpting?"

"Have you tried Paulivik's shop? I've heard that Paulivik the Younger is almost as good a cutter as his father."

"I *have* tried that shop," Danlo said, gently knocking his boots against the doorframe to keep his feet warm.

"Well, I can't help you further. I can regraft a burned face or make an exemplar, but to make a man into a beast-man, no, no—I won't do such barbaric sculptings."

"The Alaloi are not beast-men," Danlo said quietly.

"I won't argue with a faceless man," the cutter said. "If you seek Mehtar Hajime, seek in the stars. I heard that he left Neverness years ago."

So saying, he bowed his head quickly as if forced to acknowledge an autist or some other lesser human being. And then he slammed shut the door.

The Alaloi are not beasts, Danlo thought as he stood in there in the cold. *They are human beings—true human beings.*

Because he was cold, tired and very hungry, he decided to abandon his quest for the day. On a gliddery just off the Serpentine, he was very lucky to discover a restaurant fairly overflowing with food. Although he had to wait in line for most of three hours, when he sat down with other hungry strangers in their furs and half-frozen faces, he found that he could eat as much as he liked. This was a great deal. When Danlo was truly hungry, he could eat like a ravenous tiger. And so he gorged on kurmash and blacknuts—and ming beans in curry sauce, and fried snow apples, and most miraculously, coffee and glazed crescent bread for dessert. He ate so much that his belly bulged like that of a woman gravid with child. When he had finished this feast, he could barely stand up. Skating through the windy, nighttime streets was a torment. Twice he had to sit down on the snow-covered benches and breathe deeply lest he lose his meal. It was late when he finally entered the City Wild and found his skis in the snow where he had left them. And by the time he found his house in the clearing beneath the ridge, it was very late: although he had memorized his path along the crusts of snow—every rock, root and tree—the forest was dark and deep, and he had to ski with great care. At last, however, he crawled into his house and lit the flame globe and stove. He threw off his clothes; he settled down naked into the warmth of his sleeping furs. And when he awoke the next morning to the warbling of the loons, he found himself as hungry as any bird and ready to begin eating once again.

In the days that followed, Danlo searched almost the entire city for this lost cutter named Mehtar Hajime. The alien districts of the Zoo, of course, he avoided, as he did the streets surrounding the Academy. And he left the Ashtoreth District alone; the astriers and Architects of the various cybernetic churches who made their homes there would never have allowed anything so sordid as a cutting shop to blight their stately neighborhoods. As the weather grew colder—and it was very cold, almost the coldest winter in memory—he considered contracting for the services of Alvarez or Paulivik the Younger or some other cutter who might be able to sculpt a rugged Alaloi hunter out of the softer clay of a more modern man. But Danlo did not like to give up so easily.

And so as the season's storms blew clouds of snow down the icy colored streets, he dared the neighborhoods of the Old City and the Pilot's Quarter, but to no avail. Each day he would set forth into the city with the highest of hopes, and each night he would return to his house a little more tired and discouraged. And a little hungrier. Almost daily, it seemed, another score of restaurants closed their doors, and the lines outside the remaining open ones grew even longer—in truth, so long that on some days he had to choose between eating or continuing his quest. That he often chose the latter bespoke the calling of his fate; deep inside he sensed that, like sands through an hourglass, time was quickly running out.

He made one other quest as well. He took advantage of his days on the streets to ask after a former courtesan named Tamara Ten Ashtoreth. To every cutter he spoke with—and every harijan, wormrunner or whore—he asked if they knew of this beautiful woman who had once promised to marry him. But no one did. He searched for her in every shop or cafe that he entered, on every glissade or gliddery. He would look deeply (and much too boldly) at every passing woman, hoping to catch sight of her lovely face. Once, on the East-West Sliddery, in the bold stare of an astrier woman adorned in her brilliant blond hair, he thought that he had found her. But when he looked more closely, he saw that this woman's lips were not so full as Tamara's nor did she carry herself with Tamara's natural grace; her eyes were cold and blue, not warm and brown as Tamara's, not alive with all Tamara's fierce inner fire and pride.

By the 45th of winter, he was almost ready to abandon both these quests when he had what seemed a stroke of luck. Because

Tamara had once possessed a great skill in the arts of pleasure—before Hanuman had raped her mind and ruined her as a courtesan—Danlo feared that she might have left this sublime profession for the much less exalted practice of a common whore. And so he searched for her on the Street of the Common Whores; he searched as well the nearby Street of Musicians and the Street of the Ten Thousand Bars. He even knocked at the doors of the body shops down on Strawberry Street, and was almost glad that none of the whores there knew of her. But one of these tired-looking women knew something else that interested him greatly. Her name was Sumi Gurit, an older woman with many living tattoos that writhed beneath her fair skin in the most lurid of ways. She overheard him talking with a cutter whose shop specialized in bringing women (and men) back to their youth. And when this cutter, too, sent him away unenlightened as to the whereabouts of Mehtar Hajime, she approached him on the street and said, "Perhaps I can help you."

"Yes?" Danlo said, moving toward the side of the street away from the other skaters. Many wormrunners and wealthy people promenaded past the brothels, stopping here and there to bargain with evil-looking procurers who stood outside windowless doors. "Do you know where I might find Mehtar Hajime?"

"Perhaps I do," Sumi Gurit said. "Why don't you take off your mask so that we can speak more intimately?"

"I am sorry, but I cannot do that."

"You've a handsome voice and handsome way of moving," she said. "Why won't you let me see if you've a handsome face to accompany all this handsomeness?"

"I am sorry," Danlo said again. He looked at Sumi's naked arms, belly and legs, and for a moment he marvelled at her ability to withstand the cold. But then he remembered that many whores carked their blood with juf and other glycol drugs, the better to be able to display their wares. "I am seeking only this cutter—not company."

"I'm sorry, too," Sumi said as she brushed up against Danlo and ran her fingers through the furry hood covering his head. "And I'd like to help you—perhaps we can help each other."

"How . . . can I help you, then?"

"Would you like to have dinner with me? I know of a restaurant not far from here that serves the finest of cultured meats."

"This is a private restaurant, yes?"

"Of course—did you really think I'd want to stand outside a free one all night just to be served a bowl of watery kurmash?"

"I am sorry, but I haven't any money."

Sumi eyed Danlo's dark, rich furs and his fine kamelaika, and she said, "Of course you must have money."

"No, truly, I do not."

"Then how did you hope to gain the services of a cutter such as Mehtar Hajime?"

Danlo dropped his hand down into his fur's great pocket, and he felt for the silken pouch that he had secreted there earlier. But he said nothing.

"It's been hard to make contracts with everyone hoarding money just to buy a little food," Sumi told him.

Danlo squeezed the silken pouch and felt the curving hardness of what lay inside, but still he didn't speak.

"I'm hungry," Sumi said.

For a long time, Danlo just stood there on the street gazing at her in silence.

"I'm cold," Sumi said, looking at him with her sad, old eyes.

At last, Danlo drew his hand from his pocket. He held the silken pouch tightly, like an owl gripping an egg in its talons. And then, with his other hand, he unfastened his furs and shrugged them off in one fluid motion. He came up to Sumi; he touched her ice-cold arm. "Here," he said, gently draping his furs over her shoulders. "It is very cold tonight, yes?"

In the dim light of the cold stone row houses, he stood there with nothing more to cover him than his thin wool kamelaika and his face mask. The wind whipped down the street, pulling at his hair with its long, icy fingers. Many days earlier, he had removed the white owl's feather that he liked to wear in his hair. And now, with every whore who skated by seeming to appraise him as she might a diamond ring, he hoped that no one would take note of his hair. He remembered Bardo once telling him that he had unique hair inherited from his father; it was long and glossy and black—and shot with rare strands of red.

"Thank you," Sumi said as she looked at him, searching beneath his mask for his deep blue eyes. She seemed almost ready to cry. "I think you're very kind. You didn't just give me your furs because you want to find an old cutter, did you?"

"No," Danlo said softly. He watched his steamy breath hang in the air.

"This is a beautiful fur," Sumi said as she ran her fingers over it. Although she looked down at the silk pouch that Danlo still gripped in his hand, she made no comment about it. "And I think you must be a beautiful man."

"And I think that you are a beautiful woman."

"Oh, no, I'm too old to be beautiful like I was," she said. "But I can still try to repay a little kindness."

Danlo smiled at her, then, all the while thinking that she truly shined with *shibui,* a kind of deeper beauty that only time can reveal, much as the wind and water sculpt the rocks above a stormy sea.

"Mehtar Hajime once sculpted a friend of mine," Sumi said. "She had already been brought back to youth at least five times, and all the other cutters had told her that they couldn't help her. But Mehtar Hajime made her young again—young and beautiful."

"I have heard that he was the best cutter in the city," Danlo said.

"There's no sculpting he couldn't make," Sumi said. "I was very sad when he closed his shop."

"I am sorry."

"I kept hoping that he might open another one; but instead he bought a house on the Tycho's Street."

"The Tycho's Street . . . that lies in the Pilots' Quarter?"

Sumi smiled as she nodded her head. "It's a strange place to find a cutter, I know, but I'd heard that he no longer practices his art."

"But you kept track of him all the same, yes?"

"I'm afraid I did—I suppose I always hoped that he might be able to help me someday, when I needed a last return."

"I see," Danlo said touching eyes with her.

"But this is just the foolishness of an old woman. Even if he would agree to do a sculpting, I could never afford his services, now."

For a long time, Danlo simply looked at her, and something passed from him to her, something warm and fluid as water and yet bright and blue as starfire. "You do not need his services," he said.

"Thank you for saying that," Sumi said. "Thank you for your furs."

"Thank *you,*" he said, bowing.

She returned his bow with surprising formality, and then smiled at him. "Would you like to return to my rooms with me? It's very cold."

"I am sorry, but I cannot."

Her eyes clouded with sadness as she sighed, "I'm sorry, too. But I wish you well, whoever you are."

"I wish you well," he said. And then he whispered, *"Halla los li devani ki-varara li ardu nis ni manse."*

"What does that mean?"

" 'Beautiful is the woman who touches the heart of a man.' "

With that he smiled beneath his mask and bowed one last time. And then he skated off down the street, past all the wormrunners and procurers and other women who whistled at this strange man in the black kamelaika and long, flowing black hair. The wind pierced this single garment like ten thousand icy needles, and he should have been very cold. But strangely, for the first time in many days, he felt the sweet liquor of hope warming him deep inside. Hope touched his heart; it was as beautiful as a woman's smile and as terrible as the fires of the sun. All the way back to his house in the woods he kept dreaming of the future as it still might be, and he never minded for a moment that he had given his furs to a cold and lonely woman.

The next morning he awoke to a new covering of snow over the woods and blue cold air, the *kaleth ri-eesha* as he had once called this biting coldness after snow. Without his furs, the making of his piss-upon-arising was an agony of chattering teeth and shivering belly. He was hungry, too. He well knew how the body, devoid of the fires of food, could quickly fall into hypothermia and frostbite. And so his first task of the day would be the procurement of new furs. He made his usual journey through the trees into the city; only this time the cold chilled his limbs so that he could barely move his skis. In truth, the cold nearly killed him. Three times, he felt the terrible temptation to just lie down in the snow and let the dreamy confusion of cold carry him over to the other side of day. But then he remembered his purpose, and he clenched his teeth to halt the painful crack of enamel against enamel. He skied as quickly as he could to burn what little glucose remained in his muscles. And then, when he had snapped in his skate blades and reached the glidderies just to the east of the City Wild, he ducked into a private restaurant just to drink in a few drafts of warm air.

Because he had no money, he soon had to leave this heaven of roasted breads and cinnamon coffee that he longed to taste. But he found other restaurants and shops, and even a warming pavilion just off the Long Glissade. In this way, he worked his way east along the streets near the Gallivare Green. There, in a neighborhood of fine obsidian blackstones four storeys high, he finally found a shop stocked with much good—and free—clothing. He might have picked out a new parka of spun plastic, but instead he chose a great, hooded shagshay fur, as brilliantly white as the snow. This had been worn by other men; it was stained with wine and smelled of old sweat and smoke, but he liked the deeper warmth of fur, the silky and natural feel of it. In such a marvelous fur, he thought, he could survive even the worst of deep winter's cold.

He ate no breakfast that morning. He crossed the Old City Glissade and hurried north through the evenly spaced purple streets of the Pilot's Quarter. Soon enough, he found the Tycho's Street and followed it towards the Sound where it intersected the North Sliddery. There, on the corner of these two streets, in a neighborhood of lovely white granite chalets, he found the house that Sumi Gurit had told him belonged to Mehtar Hajime. But when he knocked at the door, he found it instead occupied by a rich wormrunner named Kaloosh Makovik. This suspicious old man rather rudely informed him that yes, a Mehtar Hajime had once owned the house, but that he had sold it to Kaloosh himself several years before. He told Danlo that he didn't know where Mehtar might be found; and then he ventured to offer Danlo a bit of advice: "You should keep to your house, whoever you are. I've heard the harijan are robbing anyone they find alone. This is no time to be wandering about the city looking for the services of a retired cutter."

And with that, he fairly slammed the door and left Danlo standing alone in the cold. Danlo might have abandoned his quest, then. He might simply have given up and enlisted the services of a lesser cutter, for he was very close to despair. But then, by a rare stroke of chance (or so it seemed), as he was skating back down the Tycho's Street, he suddenly came upon an old friend. He saw him coming out of a flower shop, and recognized him immediately: it was Old Father, with his great height, white fur, and large, golden eyes.

"Excuse me," Danlo said, skating up to him, "but aren't you the Fravashi Old Father who—"

"Ho, ho, indeed I am!" Old Father called out in a musical voice that spilled from between his marvelously mobile black lips. For a moment, he eyed Danlo's black face mask as he smiled in his mysterious, alien way. Then his voice dropped lower than the longest vibrating string of a gosharp, and he said, "Ah, ah—it is good to see you again, Danlo wi Soli Ringess."

Danlo froze as he looked about the crowded street. But none of the astriers and academicians coming and going from the street's many shops seemed to be paying them any attention. Even so, he motioned for Old Father to move off the main part of the street toward an alley that cut between two old buildings.

"How," he asked, his voice rough and thick with the cold, "how did you know who I am?"

"But who else would you be?" Old Father asked. "Oho—who else could I think you are?"

Danlo wanted to rush up and throw his arms around this friend from his past, but one doesn't simply embrace a Fravashi Old Father, especially not on a public street in the middle of the Pilot's Quarter.

"I missed you, sir," Danlo said softly.

"Ha, ha—and I missed you. I kept hoping that you might knock at the door to my house."

He went on to say that he had heard the news of Danlo's escape from the cathedral. Indeed, he believed that for many days, Hanuman's spies had watched his house in case Danlo decided to seek shelter there.

"I was afraid that it would be so," Danlo said. "Otherwise I would have wanted to see you again as soon as I could. It has been more than five years."

"So, it's so," Old Father said. "And much has happened to you since then—I've heard the most incredible stories about you these past days."

Danlo, standing with his back to the alley facing Old Father, looked about the street again to see if anyone might be watching him. He said, "I should go soon, yes? I am afraid my being with you places you at risk."

"Ha, ha—yes it does, yes it does!" Old Father sang out. "But I never minded the risk of talking with you."

Old Father smiled in his Fravashi way, his lips pulling back to reveal his strong, flat teeth and his great golden eyes lighting up like twin suns. Danlo suddenly remembered how much he loved this old alien who had truly been like a father to him since his first days in Neverness.

"But *I* mind," Danlo said softly. "I would not want anything to happen to you. I am sorry."

"Ah, oh—then go if you must. Go, go, go! But, where will you go? I've worried that you've been wandering the streets since your escape."

"I . . . have a place to live," Danlo said. "It is as safe as any place in the city."

"Good, good—then I can cease *my* wandering the streets knowing that you have a peaceful place to sleep."

Danlo looked at Old Father's long, white-furred limbs, and he remembered how he always moved quite slowly and painfully due to the arthritis that inflamed his old joints. "You have been searching for me? Thank you, sir, but you should not have troubled yourself."

"Oh ho, but the universe is made of little else than troubles," Old Father said. "But never too many that I wouldn't want to help my favorite student."

"I wish that you *could* help me," Danlo said, remembering his utter failure to find the cutter named Mehtar Hajime. For a moment, his voice fell heavy with despair. "But no one can help me, now."

"No?"

"No—I am sorry."

Fravashi Old Fathers, he thought, helped their students to learn the language of Moksha or the art of plexure in which two differing realities are held together at once in the mind. They helped them learn to play the flute or that it is wrong to harm another living thing, but they couldn't possibly help find a lost cutter who obviously didn't wish to be found.

"Ah, oh, aha—so many troubles," Old Father said. "Why don't you tell me what is presently troubling you?"

Danlo saw no point in burdening Old Father with unnecessary information, but something about this golden-eyed alien made him want to trust him with his life. And so he took a deep breath and said, "I am looking for a cutter."

"Oh, ah—and not just any cutter, I think."

"No—his name is Mehtar Hajime."

At this, Old Father's eyes suddenly began glowing softly with a dreamy and faraway look as if he were remembering something. And then he said, "Ah, yes, of course, Mehtar Hajime."

"You have heard of him?"

"I have. And what is more, I know where he might be found."

This astonishing claim caused Danlo to back up slightly and regard Old Father with something like wonder. "Where, then?" he asked.

"Look to the Street of Mansions in the Ashtoreth District," Old Father said. "I'd heard that, having grown very rich, he bought a house there."

"But how?" Danlo stared for a moment at Old Father's fathomless eyes, and for the thousandth time, he thought that there was something very mysterious about this Fravashi alien whom he called Old Father. "How could you have possibly known?"

"Oho, you will be wondering if this is just a fantastic chance or happy fate. But what if it's neither? So, it's so: I've been in the city for a long time, and I hear many things."

Perhaps, Danlo thought, Old Father *did* hear many things. But certainly it was a far chance that they had met here on this little street today just when Danlo had almost given up hope of finding the cutter.

"Thank you, sir," he said. "It was good to see you again, but I should say goodbye now before it falls too late."

"But why are you looking for this cutter? Oho—why are you looking for a cutter at all?"

"I cannot tell you that, sir."

"I see, I see. Well, I suppose it has something to do with your quarrel with Hanuman li Tosh. Ho, ho—I'd heard that he tortured you."

"Yes, he did," Danlo said softly. He closed his eyes for a moment as he felt the heat of the glowing iron nail that seemed forever lodged in his brain.

"And yet you seek a cutter and not revenge?"

"Never harming another even if he has harmed you. You taught me, sir."

"Ah, well, well—I hope I didn't teach you *too* well. It wouldn't do to let torturers such as Hanuman go on harming others."

"No, truly it would not."

"Then you have a plan, ha, ha? You would use the *satyagraha* to oppose him, and this cutter Mehtar Hajime is part of your plan?"

"Yes."

"Ah, oh—so, it's so, then." Old Father fell silent as he looked for Danlo's bright, blue eyes beneath his face mask. "But you must be very careful, I think. You've changed since I last saw you. In you the soul has grown very great, and you can't even dream what forces might come into your hand."

So saying, he bowed stiffly and awkwardly, all the while moaning at the pain of his grinding joints. And then he laid his hand upon Danlo's arm and smiled his sunny smile. "Your soul may be great, truly, truly, but dark times can dim the light of even the brightest star. Please promise me that whatever happens, you'll never give up hope."

"All right, then," Danlo said smiling. "I promise, sir."

"Please promise that you'll never give up."

Although Danlo made no reply to this, in words, he bowed to Old Father, and his dark, wild eyes blazed with his promise.

"Oho, goodbye, then, Danlo wi Soli Ringess! I promise *you* that I shall see you again in better times when our souls can fly free."

And with that, Old Father moved off down the street leaving Danlo to wonder how this mysterious, old alien always seemed to appear in his life just when he needed him the most.

CHAPTER 14

THE FACE OF
A MAN

*Nikolos Daru Ede was the man born to be God. His
human face was soft, round and full of light; His divine
face is more brilliant than the sun. His human smile was
like a light being turned on in a dark room; His divine
smile is like the radiance of a billion billion stars. When
his human lips, so full of life, laughed, a breath of sweet
air blew through the hearts of those who loved him; when
His divine lips let loose with laughter, the heavens
themselves shake with joy. His human eyes were as bright
and black as onyx stones; His divine eyes are as black and
deep as all the infinities of space and time.*
   —from *The Birth of Ede the God*, 142nd Algorithm

It was later that day that Danlo found his way onto the Serpentine
and followed it around the Winter Ring where it dipped south for
half a mile before twisting yet again through the quiet neighborhoods just above the Ashtoreth District. In fact, the Serpentine
formed both the northern and western boundaries of the Ashtoreth
District, which spread out between this snakelike street and the
cliffs of South Beach. Thus, of all the districts in the city, it was
the largest, the most well-defined and contained.

It also proved to be the most difficult to enter. While it wasn't
true that the whole district had been closed to outsiders such as
Danlo, many streets, even whole neighborhoods, were. The peoples of a hundred cybernetic churches—the Architects of the Infinite Life, the Universal Church of Ede, the Fostora Separtist
Union, and of course, the Cybernetic Reformed Church, among
others—made their homes on these broad, straight, tree-lined
streets. And almost all of them opposed the rise of Hanuman li
Tosh and the new religion of Ringism. If they had acted together,
they might have posed the most powerful counterforce against
Hanuman in the city; but of course the cybernetic churches could

no more cooperate than different nest-groups of Scutari. The most they could do was to agree that no Ringist should enter their peaceful district. But even this was more a shared sentiment than a realized plan. Architects such as those of the Fathers of Ede patrolled some neighborhoods as ferociously as snow tigers walking the bounds of their frozen territories; while elsewhere, in the neighborhoods just off the Long Glissade, the gentler Cybernetic Pilgrims of the Manifold couldn't see the point of defending their isolated streets.

It was Danlo's bad luck to encounter a group of the more militant Architects just as he tried to turn off the Serpentine onto a gliddery leading through the heart of the district. Five men of the Universal Architects had blocked the street with sleds, which they stood behind, sliding their skates back and forth on the red ice and grumbling at the cold. They wore white shagshay furs much as Danlo—only theirs were newer and finer, and unstained with wine. As Danlo skated up to the barricade, they looked askance at his worn furs and his black face mask. One of them, a rather well-fed man whose face was red from the cold, motioned for Danlo to stop. He then skated a few feet closer and said, "I don't think I've seen you before—what is your name?"

Danlo looked up and down the street, at the great stone houses and yu trees rising up from the snow-covered lawns. He decided that if these men lived in any of these houses, they must be rich, as the Architects of the Ashtoreth District often were.

"I have not been on this street for many years," Danlo said, trying to evade the man's question. "I am just passing through."

"Well, you won't pass through unless you give us your name and remove your mask."

Danlo saw that the man held a homemade laser down by his side. His friends were all armed too, but quite irregularly: one of them sported a needle gun, another fingered what seemed to be some kind of jeweled, ceremonial sword, while the fourth and fifth men brandished shatterwood clubs.

"Neverness is a free city, yes?" Danlo looked at the man who had stopped him. "Her streets have always been free."

"Well, that was before the war," the man said. "If you wish the freedom of the streets, why don't you return to the Street of Smugglers or wherever it is that you've come from?"

"I only wish to find a man—he lives on the Street of Mansions."

"The Street of Mansions!" The red-faced man with the laser eyed Danlo suspiciously. "What is you purpose there?"

"I . . . cannot tell you."

"Why? Why not?"

Now all five men moved a little closer to Danlo. Their faces were grim with mistrust and fear.

"I cannot tell you . . . why I cannot tell you," Danlo said. "But surely my purpose is my own."

"Keep your purpose to yourself, then," the man said. "But keep out of our streets."

"Does the Street of Mansions belong to you, then?"

"We don't care about the Street of Mansions—but we've sworn to keep strangers such as you from our streets."

"Which . . . streets?"

The man with the laser waved his arm wildly. "*This* street, of course. And the next three streets over toward the Serpentine where it curves toward South Beach. We can't guard every street in the district."

"But others guard other streets, yes?"

"Some do, some don't. I don't really know."

"I see."

"Now go away. We don't want to have to force you."

Again, Danlo looked at the faces of these five soft men, and he thought that they were as unused to violence or force as baby kittens kept inside a rich woman's apartment. But they had weapons, and they *were* men—and therefore they could always fall into violence as easily as struck matches.

"Farewell," Danlo said, with a bow. "I wish you well."

He retreated back up the street, then, and made his way back onto the Serpentine. He followed this great pulsing street southwest through even richer neighborhoods. Four times, he tried to enter the district along other streets, but he was stopped and turned away much as he had been the first time. Undeterred, he skated the Serpentine to its very end, where it emptied into the Long Glissade just above South Beach. And then he looped back around this great green street eastward and tried to enter the district through its soft underbelly.

There, in one of the loveliest and most out-of-the-way neighborhoods in the city, he finally found his way in. Although a few richly dressed astriers and Architects shook their heads at his shabby appearance, no one challenged him. He found the Street of Mansions only a few blocks from South Beach. Great yu trees covered with red berries rose up above the street, while the great stone houses stood far back past the snowy lawns, protected by stone walls or glittering steel fences. The whole street—and it was

only five blocks long—seemed strangely deserted. The only
movements were the wisps of wind-driven snow and the loons
rattling about in the branches of the trees. Danlo was struck with
the beauty of the neighborhood, the perfection of colors: the ruby
red street, the white snow and white granite houses, the green fir
needles—and beyond, the blue on blue sky. That no one skated
the street in order to drink in all this beauty fairly astonished him.
But then, it was always that way in rich neighborhoods. The rich,
he had found, shut themselves away from the cold teeth of the
world, much as spirali took refuge inside their shells.

In truth, gaining access to the dwellers of the Street of Mansions was almost as hard as opening the hardest of spirali shells.
Although the street itself was unguarded, all the houses were.
Each of the steel gates in every wall along the street was closed.
And in the warming pavilions behind these gates, men armed with
clubs stood ready to turn away any poor harijan who might be
foolish enough to come begging for food or shelter. These men—
many were huge, blond-haired Thorskallers recruited for their ferocity—were quick to turn Danlo away. He worked his way down
the north side of the street, rapping his knuckles against each steel
gate and asking after the cutter called Mehtar Hajime. But no one
seemed to have heard of him. And then, after he had come to the
end of the street and was ready to begin with the houses on the
south side, he suddenly remembered a thing. Almost twelve years
before, on a night of beer and shared confindences, Bardo had
once mentioned Mehtar's full name: Mehtar Constancio Hajime.
And now, standing in the cold by yet another ice-hung gate, for no
reason that Danlo could put to words, he had a strange sense that
he should begin asking for the cutter by his full name.

This he did. He knocked at four more gates, and four times he
was turned away no richer in information. But at the fifth gate,
one of the guards told him, "I've never heard of a Mehtar Constancio Hajime. But there's a man, Constancio of Alesar, who
lives across the street three blocks over—the third house from the
corner. Maybe he can help you."

Danlo smiled his thanks and bowed to the guard. Then he
quickly retraced his path down the street. When he came to the
third house from the corner—a grand affair of white granite and
pillars holding up the sculpted blocks of the portico—he skated
up to the steel gate fronting it once again. Again he knocked, all
the while keeping his eyes on the inner light fence of flashing
lasers that ringed the lawn. The lone guard stepped out of the

warming pavilion and stared at Danlo through gleaming steel bars.

"You again," he said. He was a tall man, taller even than Danlo, and he chewed at his blond mustache as he looked for Danlo's eyes behind his mask. "I thought I told you that I didn't know a Mehtar Hajime."

"I have learned that his full name is Mehtar Constancio Hajime. And that a Constancio of Alesar lives in this house. This is a coincidence, yes?"

"I don't really know—nor do I care."

"Could it be that Constancio of Alesar once had a different name?"

The guard's face was grim and red from the cold. He said, "Constancio never speaks of his past. And I've been his guard only a couple of years, so there's little that I can tell you."

"But you could tell *him* that a man seeks to speak with him, yes?"

"What is your name, then?"

Danlo stood there on the ice for a moment and then said, "I . . . am Danlo of Kweitkel."

"I've never heard of Kweitkel—is it far from Neverness?"

Danlo thought of the icy island of Kweitkel where he had been born. It lay only six hundred miles across the frozen sea. But to a man making such a journey by dogsled, it was farther than the stars of the Gilada Inferiore.

"It is very far," Danlo said. "Few have heard of it."

"Well, Danlo of Kweitkel, I can't think of why I should disturb Constancio on the chance that he'd want to speak with you."

Danlo, having anticipated this moment, drew his hand from the pocket of his furs. He held a little figurine of carved ivory that he had made during the long nights he had spent out in the woods: a broad-shouldered Alaloi man poised with his seal spear. "This is a present for Constancio," he said.

"It's fine work," the guard said as he fingered the carving. He looked at Danlo expectantly. "Very fine work."

Again, Danlo dropped his hand down into his furs and removed a carving of a great white bear. "And this is for you."

"Very, very fine," the guard said as he took the bear and began turning it over in the sunlight. "Living in Constancio's house, one develops an eye for fine things—which I'm sure you'll discover if Constancio wishes to speak with you."

So saying, he pocketed both figurines and told Danlo, "Wait here while I announce you."

Without a bow, the guard turned and skated up the path to the house. Danlo remained outside on the street, all the while wondering why Constancio had not installed a fone with which to communicate between house and gate. It seemed strange that he would openly sport the illegal lasers of a light fence while eschewing a much lesser technology.

After a while—a very long while, considering the coldness of the day—the guard returned. With much shrieking of steel, he opened the gate and said, "Constancio has agreed to see you. Please follow me."

He led Danlo up the walkway to the steps of the house's portico, where they both ejected their skate blades. However, there was no need for him to knock at the great white door, for it hung open to the cold. And there, waiting in the doorway, stood a tall man with steel-gray hair and a face as gray as the ice-mists of the sea. His gray eyes studied Danlo's eyes, and it almost seemed that he could see through his black mask and lay bare the bones of Danlo's face that lay beneath.

"I am Constancio of Alesar," he said. "And you are Danlo of Kweitkel—a planet that no one has ever heard of and exists on none of the maps."

So saying, he nodded for the guard to return to his post and then invited Danlo inside his house. They walked together through the entrance hall, which was hung with many fine tapestries and lit with flame globes. After passing through a sun room filled with expensive furniture—and with gosharps, Darghinni sculpture, Fravashi carpets, cases of alien jewelry, and hundreds of other things—they entered Constancio's tea room. There Constancio invited Danlo to sit at a little table inlaid with triangles of lapis and marble. An insulated coffee urn sat at the table's exact center, and next to it, two cups. As Danlo eased himself down onto a chair of purest, carved shatterwood, he looked up at the tondo paintings hanging on the wall. Colors of absinthe, sapphire and tangerine swirled and flowed in lovely patterns according to each painting's program. The effect of this outlawed technology on Danlo was both soothing and hypnotic; he had to force himself to look away and concentrate on Constancio sitting across the table.

"You'll soon be hot in such fine furs," Constancio said, examining Danlo's clothing. He himself wore only a quilted silk robe of purest gray. "Why don't you take them off?"

Danlo shrugged off his furs then, and he sat at the table in his kamelaika and black face mask. The rich, intoxicating smell of the coffee was a pain almost greater than he could bear.

"You've unusual hair," Constancio remarked as he poured the coffee. "It's not often one sees such a rich black mixed with strands of red."

Danlo was so thirsty (and hungry) that he gulped his coffee, burning his mouth. He gasped in a breath of cool air, and then asked, "Are you by chance the same Mehtar Hajime who once owned the finest cutting shop on the Street of Cutters?"

Constancio's gray face seemed to grow even grayer and grimmer, if that were possible. He said, "Who am I, then, you wish to know? Who is anybody? Who is that we were born to be?"

"I . . . do not understand."

"Who are *you*, Danlo of Kweitkel? Who were you born as, and who do you wish to be?"

This time, when Danlo drank his coffee, he sipped it slowly and more carefully. "I have told you my name," he said. "And if you'd like, I will tell you my purpose, too."

"Please, do tell me," Constancio said. He looked down at the figurine of the Alaloi hunter that he held in his hands. And then he looked back at Danlo.

"There is a kind of sculpting that Mehtar Hajime once made better than any other cutter in the city," Danlo said. "It is said that he could transform any man into an Alaloi."

Danlo looked at this tall, elegant man sitting across from him, and he wondered if he could truly be Mehtar Hajime. Mehtar, according to Bardo, had worn the rugged, hairy body of an Alaloi man, shaped by himself.

"I think I remember that style," Constancio said, dragging his fingernail along the figurine's nose. "It was many years ago, around the time of the Quest, when Mallory Ringess transformed himself into an Alaloi."

"I have heard that it was Mehtar Hajime who transformed Mallory Ringess."

"Well, during these frightful times, one hears many things about Mallory Ringess." Constancio's eyes seemed to bore into Danlo's like steel drills, and he said, "It's quite unusual to sit drinking coffee while wearing a mask. Why don't you remove it?"

"I am comfortable as I am," Danlo said. "Does my wearing a mask discomfort you?"

"No, no, not at all. All men wear masks of one sort or another, don't they?"

"Truly, they do," Danlo said. And then suddenly, as surely as he knew the lines of his own nose, he knew that Constancio of Alesar had been born as Mehtar Hajime. If Mehtar could change his first form into that of an Alaloi, surely he could have changed himself yet again into the gray-faced Constancio. "Why is it then that you wear the mask of a changed name?"

"My name is Constancio of Alesar," Constancio said.

"And mine is Danlo of Kweitkel."

For a while the two men sat across from each other at the little table, sipping their coffee and staring at each other. And then at last Constancio broke the silence. "This is a fine piece of work," he said, holding up the figurine. "How did you acquire it?"

"I carved it from a piece of ivory," Danlo said.

"You really made this yourself?"

"Yes . . . truly."

"Then you are as good at carving ivory as you say Mehtar Hajime once was at carving flesh."

"Was . . . once?"

"It would have been twenty years since Mehtar sculpted an Alaloi."

"I had hoped that even if Mehtar had changed his name and retired," Danlo said, "he would still be a master of his art."

Constancio looked down at his hands, which were long and lithe and very well made. "It's said that the flesh always remembers what the mind forgets. A man could return to Neverness after a hundred years and still know how to skate her streets."

"Then you believe that Mehtar could still sculpt a man into an Alaloi?"

"As well as you've made this figurine."

"And the price for such a sculpting—it would be high, yes?"

"Very high. Mehtar would have to come out of his retirement, of course. And then there would be the cost of new lasers, drills and drugs—and setting up another cutting shop."

"I see," Danlo said, looking about at all the expensive objects in the room. He noticed the silvery strands of a Darghinni hang-nest displayed in a clary case, and he wondered that Constancio could have acquired such a priceless thing. "How high, then?"

"Ten thousand city disks."

"Ten *thousand?*"

"That's what I said."

"But only a rich man would possess so much money."

"And are you not rich, Danlo of Kweitkel?"

"No, truly I am not."

"Then how can you hope to know what it is like to be as strong and full of life as an Alaloi man?"

Danlo sat in his chair remembering his childhood among his adoptive Alaloi brothers and sisters. He remembered that although his spear casts had been farther and truer than Choclo's (and almost any other of his near-brothers), Choclo had always defeated him in wrestling, manhandling him to the ground with a shocking strength.

"Ten thousand city disks *is* a heavy sum," Constancio continued. "But even that is not enough."

"What do you mean?"

Constancio waved his hand at a Fravashi carpet hanging from the wall. He said, "Look about my house and you will behold many fine things. But not as many as even ten days ago. I've had to trade three tondos and a carpet for an insultingly small supply of food. And soon, I'm afraid, very soon the price of even kurmash will shoot off toward infinity. In such times, it's never possible to have too much money, never, never."

"I have no money," Danlo said as he touched the precious blue stones of the table. "I never have."

Constancio looked at him in disbelief, and then continued, "I should have left the city when I had the chance. I was afraid this Ringism madness would lead to war."

"Why did you stay, then?"

"Because I thought that Neverness would be safer than any place else."

"But the universe is everywhere just the same, yes?"

"Just so. And that's why the only real safety is in things."

Danlo examined his fine coffee mug, blown from the rare ruby glass of Fostora. He said, "You have many things—do you feel safe?"

"I've prepared for this day all my life. I'm as safe as any man in the city."

"Have you many friends, then?"

"Once God betrayed me, and then my people betrayed me— now I put my faith elsewhere.

"I am sorry," Danlo said as a strange light came into his eyes.

But his compassion seemed only to anger Constancio, who said, "How could you hope to accomplish what you wish if you haven't any money?"

"I have brought something else."

"What, then?"

"This," Danlo said, and he reached into the pocket of his furs.

He drew out the silken pouch and untied the drawstring. Then, with a quick motion, he emptied into his hand a shimmering diamond sphere.

"My God!" Constancio said, almost gasping for breath. "That can't be real—may I hold it?"

Danlo gave him the sphere and watched as Constancio turned the flawless diamond between his sweating hands. Brilliant lights flickered beneath the sphere's curving surface with a many-colored fire.

"A scryer's sphere," Constancio said. "How did you acquire it?"

"I . . . cannot tell you."

Constancio looked long and deeply at him, then. After a while, he said, "You have unusual eyes. Such a rare, deep blue. Did you know that Mehtar once sculpted a pair of eyes such as yours?"

"Truly?" Danlo said, although he knew very well the story of how Mehtar Hajime had once sculpted his mother into an Alaloi.

"In fact, she was a scryer herself," Constancio said. "Her name was Katharine the Scryer—she was the sister of Mallory Ringess."

He went on to describe the sculpting of the members of the quest that Mallory Ringess had led to the Alaloi people. Katharine, he said, had once blinded herself as all scryers do during their terrible initiation ritual. And Mehtar Hajime had grown for her new eyes, which he had implanted into her newly sculpted face.

"Strange that you should have her eyes," Constancio said. "So dark, so blue—like liquid jewels."

Danlo suddenly looked down at the tabletop; he felt a spear of light stab through his left eye and burn through his head and face. He wondered if Constancio knew the story of how Mallory Ringess had fallen into love with Katharine—all the while unaware that the woman whom he would lay with was his sister.

"I had heard that Katharine died upon the quest to the Alaloi," Constancio said.

Yes, Danlo remembered, *she died giving birth to me.*

"I have also heard that a scryer's sphere is supposed to be returned to her sister scyrers upon her death."

"Yes, that is their way," Danlo said.

"Well, *this* sphere, if it's not a counterfeit, was obviously never returned."

"It is not a counterfeit," Danlo said, still gazing at the blue tiles of the table.

"Danlo of Kweitkel," Constancio said. "Such a strange man with such strange and beautiful eyes. Why don't you remove your mask so that I can see your eyes more clearly?"

"No—I cannot."

"If Mehtar is to sculpt your face, much more than just your mask will have to be removed."

Danlo suddenly looked up; beneath his mask, his eyes flashed like blue fire. He said, "This sphere is worth ten thousand city disks, then?"

"That is hard to determine," Constancio said craftily. "But if it's a true scryer's diamond, I should think that it would buy a sculpting."

"I . . . do not seek just any sculpting."

"But you've said that you wish to wear the flesh of an Alaloi man."

"Yes, truly—but not just any Alaloi man."

"I'm afraid I don't understand."

"There was a man whom Mehtar once shaped into an Alaloi. I wish to be shaped the same as he."

"And who was this man?"

Danlo paused a moment to take a deep breath, and then he said, "Mallory Ringess."

"Mallory Ringess!"

For a long time the two men only stared at each other across the tea table, and neither of them said a word. And then Danlo finally spoke in voice that was almost a whisper, "I had hoped that Mehtar might have kept the holograms that he must have made of Mallory Ringess' face. I had hoped that he might still be able to work a new sculpting from these holograms."

"That's a rather long hope, isn't it?"

"Is it truly?" Danlo asked. From the way that Constancio's gray eyes suddenly hardened with concentration then, Danlo knew that he had guessed right: that a collector of valuable things such as Constancio would never have thrown away something so dear as a hologram of Mallory Ringess's face.

"Even if Mehtar *had* kept the holograms," Constancio said, "I don't understand why would you wish to look like Mallory Ringess."

"Is that so strange, then? Isn't this a time when almost everyone in the city dreams of becoming a god in emulation of Mallory Ringess?"

"But you're asking to be sculpted into the shape of a primitive man, not a god."

"But Mallory Ringess wore this shape just before he became a god, yes?"

"Well, everyone knows that he left Neverness wearing the body that Mehtar made for him," Constancio said, rather proudly. "But only the Ringists believe that he became a god."

Danlo was silent a while, and he felt Constancio's eyes burning into his like lasers.

"Are *you* a Ringist?" Constancio asked.

"No—it is just the opposite."

"You oppose Ringism, then? Well, that's good. Many in this district do as well. It will make your visits here easier."

"Then you believe that Mehtar will be able to make such a sculpting?"

Constancio carefully replaced the scryer's sphere back in its silken pouch. The pouch itself he dropped into a pocket of his robe. "If this sphere proves real, then I'm sure that Mehtar would be able to make the sculpting that you desire."

At the sudden disappearance of this diamond sphere, Danlo felt a burning hollowness in the pit of his belly. It was the only thing of his mother's that he owned, and he couldn't quite believe that he would never again hold it in his hands.

"There is one thing that I must ask," Danlo finally said. "No one must ever know of this sculpting."

"Of course, of course—you wish your privacy, as anyone would. As I wish for myself."

At that moment, Mehtar's eyes fell as gray as old snow, and Danlo could't tell whether or not he should trust him.

"I must ask that no one be told my name."

"There isn't a man in the city better at keeping secrets than Constancio of Alesar," Constancio said.

"If these requests are not honored," Danlo said, "then I must ask you to agree that the price of the sculpting is forfeit and will be returned."

Constancio patted his bulging pocket then and said, "Your secrets are as safe with me as I will keep this beautiful sphere."

Danlo stared at this almost unreadable man for a moment and then extended his hand. Although Constancio must have regarded the touching of flesh against naked flesh as the most barbaric of customs, he clasped Danlo's hand in his to seal their agreement.

"When can we begin, then?" Danlo asked.

"Well, there are many preparations to make, drugs and tools that might be difficult to acquire. I should say at least twenty days."

"I had hoped that it might be sooner than that."

"The sculpting itself will take at least three times as long."

"I . . . may not have so much time."

"Would you hurry the making of a great work of art?"

"No," Danlo said. "But sometimes the greatest art springs forth like a fireflower in midwinter spring."

"It *is* possible for a great cutter such as Mehtar Hajime to cut more quickly. But despite all pain blocks and drugs, such cutting would be much more painful."

"I see."

"There would be the shock to many of the body's tissues, all at once, the accelerated healings. The drills and drugs and lasers—it all burns so terribly, you know, and the nerves can stand only so much trauma."

"I . . . see."

"Have I then persuaded you that a quick cutting would be both foolish and full of chance?"

Danlo closed his eyes at the sharp pain that always lurked just beneath his forehead. He felt his heart beating too hard and his blood pulsing through his brain. The ekkana drug still licked every tissue of his body with tongues of fire, and all his nerves from his toes to his head still writhed and burned.

"I . . . would ask that Mehtar make his cutting as quickly as he could," he finally said.

"You have courage," Constancio said, taking a sip of coffee. He looked across the table and lost himself in the depths of Danlo's eyes. "Great courage, I think. And you'll need all of it to become what you desire to be."

"When can we begin, then?"

"Return here in eighteen days. If chance falls well upon us, it should be possible to convert one of the rooms of his house into a cutting chamber by that time."

"Thank you," Danlo said, bowing from his chair. Then both he and Constancio stood up and bowed more formally.

"And when you do return," Constancio said, "if you have trouble entering the district, you should say that you are a guest in my house. If anyone seeks confirmation of this, I'll instruct my guards to say that it's so."

"Thank you," Danlo said again. "Until then, I wish you well."

"And I wish *you* well, Danlo of Kweitkel. If the war doesn't annihilate us all, in a very short time you'll know the joy of becoming the man you wish to be."

I am not my father, Danlo thought for the ten thousandth time.

As Constancio accompanied him to the door, he kept thinking of his father. He felt his father's design in his own long nose, his bold face bones, his long black and red hair. He looked inside himself, then, and saw the face of Mallory Ringess staring back at him. It was a face transfigured by the pain of countless sculptings: strong, wise and noble, and yet cut with an underlying savagery. In his proud countenance was written the story of man's primitive origins and the transcendent fate that awaited anyone who had the courage to become his true self. Although Danlo was not his father, and never could be, if he kept his courage then very soon this wild and beautiful face of his father's would be his own.

TAMARA

*What is a child? A child is an instantiation of an ideal of
our minds and the completion of our personal programs.
We conceive a child, and the mother nourishes herself with
elements of carbon, hydrogen, oxygen and nitrogen—and a
child is born. We can say that it is the program of these
elements to come together as a child, just as it is the
child's program to grow into a woman or man. A woman
and a man may make many children together—fifty is not
too many—each child programmed to utilize ever more
elements of the universe until every atom of every speck of
dust around every star from the Milky Way to the Sagara
Spiral finds itself subject to our programs. We can say that
this whole, cosmic, creative process is the program of the
universe. And so we come to the deeper answer to the
question: What is a child? A child is the means by which
our individual programs become one with the Universal
Program; a child is the architect who will reshape all
matter and remake the universe itself into a paradise
designed for our children's children.*
                    —from *The Principles of Cybernetic Architecture,*
                                        by Nikolos Daru Ede

The days that followed were the grimmest of Danlo's life. As
deep winter approached, the weather grew even colder. The occa-
sional light, powdery snows of the season gradually gave way to
relentless blue-black skies devoid of any cloud or particle of
moisture. The air felt so dry and cold that breathing could be a
torment of iced nostrils, coughing and frosted lungs. Twice, despite his mask, Danlo almost suffered the pain of freezing his
face. Eating rich foods would have fed his body's fires, but he had
much trouble finding restaurants that still served even watery
bowls of kurmash. He might have kept to the relative warmth of
his snow house in the woods, but he felt that he should search the
streets and try to take at least one meal each day.

And then, suddenly, on the 50th of winter, it seemed that the whole city suddenly ran out of food. As the Fellowship and Ringist fleets manuevered for what everyone prayed would be their final battle, the grain shipments from Yarkona and Summerworld were completely cut off. One by one, hour by hour, the restaurants began to close, the free ones first followed by most every private restaurant from the Hollow Fields to the Hofgarten. The next day, thirty thousand men and women of the harijan sects swarmed the Merripen Green to demand that the Order open their food reserves and feed the hungry city.

But, in truth, the Order had no reserves. There was hunger in the halls of the Academy no less than on the Street of Smugglers. Lord Audric Pall sent a messenger to the Merripen Green to inform the harijan of the masters' and novices' pain and privation. However, the myth of the Order's buildings bulging with barrels of kurmash and bags of rice had infected the people's minds. No one believed this messenger—Lord Alesar Druze himself—and the harijan had rioted, pelting Lord Druze with snowballs studded with ice.

The violence spilled over into the surrounding streets. The enraged harijan broke windows of hundreds of shops and forced their way into the closed restaurants only to find them as empty of food as clam shells washed up onto a beach. They broke into the apartments of rich wormrunners looking for a little bread with which to feed their children; a small army of harijan even stormed Hanuman's cathedral to appropriate the supply of foodstuffs rumored to be stored in the vast, underground crypts. Only with difficulty did Hanuman's godlings and guards drive them off. When the battle was over, two hundred harijan lay dead on the street outside the cathedral's western portal, while many more nursed bullet wounds or flesh seared black in the fierce heat of the flashing lasers. Fifty-four Ringists died that day, too, and thereafter Hanuman li Tosh resolved to arm each of his would-be gods with lasers and close the entire Old City to anyone refusing to follow the Way of Ringess.

As Danlo awaited the surgeries that would shape him into the form of his father, he might have done best to avoid the city's dangerous streets. But even if it had become impossible to find the smallest kernel of kurmash or rotten bloodfruit, he still burned with the desire to fulfill a more private quest. And so every day he made the journey through the City Wild and skated the icy glidderies looking for Tamara. And the harder that he looked, the greater and more poignant grew the feeling that she was looking for him, as well.

Once, near the green and orange checkered intersection of the Street of Embassies and Hotel Row, he thought that he saw her. He was skating among a throng of richly dressed diplomats, pilgrims and other farsiders trapped in Neverness when he felt a strange tingling sensation at the back of his neck. It was as if someone were tickling the flesh there with an electrical current or the tip of a knife—or with her eyes. He suddenly ground his skates into the ice and turned. And there, past the many panicked people hoping to find a meal in one of the nearby hotels, he saw a flash of blond hair and lovely dark eyes out of his deepest dreams. He saw this vision of a woman melt into the manswarms so quickly and completely that even though he darted between other skaters in pursuit of her as fast and gracefully as he could, he lost her yet again.

And there was something else, too. Later, when he would relive the moment in his mind in all the vivid colors and textures of a phantast's painting, he would remember seeing a pair of long, naked hands and flashing red rings. His sense of propriety told him that his memory must be faulty, that no one except an autist would go about ungloved in such deadly cold weather. And no one except a warrior-poet (and only one warrior-poet at that) would dare to wear red rings for all to see. He wondered if his brain, weak with hunger, had only hallucinated these brilliant images. Or perhaps he had only drunk in various fragmented sensa of the street and reassembled the pieces into a pattern with special meaning to him. And yet, his memory *was* his memory. He had come to trust this window to deep reality as he did the truth of his own eyes. And so thereafter, in skating the streets from the Bell to the Fravashi District, whenever he felt the cold, burning touch of another's eyes upon him, he made it his habit to turn and look for Tamara, to watch and wait and listen.

And then one day, by purest chance it seemed, he found her. It was the day before his scheduled return to Constancio's house for his first cutting. The sky rippled with a deep, liquid blueness, and it was cold, in truth too cold to be wandering the streets on any business less important than immediate survival. Nevertheless, late in the afternoon, with the sun slanting pale yellow over the mountains to the west, he took his time skating down the Street of Musicians. A few times he paused before the warming pavilions to listen to the sweet notes of the kytherals and ocarinas spilling out into the air. Near the Street of the Common Whores he even found a flutist from Solsken who played a shakuhachi similar in sound to his own.

There he lingered for a long while, his skate blades fairly frozen to the red ice as he drank in this beautiful music of the breath and soul. Few others, however, stood there with him. And fewer still had money to spare for even the finest of virtuosos or improvisatori. He himself had only a handful of baldo nuts, which he had found in the forest beneath crusts of snow. It was as he was placing these nuts in the flutist's thanksgiving bowl that he heard a sound that filled his throat with old pain and intense longing. From far off down the street it came, like the peals of a golden bell and a viola's vibrating strings, all at once. He well remembered this lovely music made upon a gosharp, for Tamara had played this barbaric instrument with all the passion and grace of a master courtesan.

In only moments he found himself a block farther along the Street of Musicians. And there, in front of a private restaurant with its closed, steel doors, he saw her sitting on a white shagshay fur playing for group of aficionados. There were two wormrunners in black sable furs and an astrier man weighed down by a heavy chain of platinum about his neck. An exemplar eight feet tall from one of the Pipal worlds stood with his eyes tightly closed as he almost leaned against a stout woman who wore a look of ecstasy on her face. And the attention of all these people—and others—fell upon the lone woman sitting with a golden gosharp in her lap.

Danlo's eyes fell upon her, too. She had the hood of her dark furs thrown back, the better to hear the music that she made, and her long, blond hair cascaded over her shoulders like sunlight. Her eyes were as dark and brown as coffee; ten thousand times during the past years he had seen these lovely eyes looking at him in hope and longing when he closed his own. Her face showed signs of bitter seasons and want, but was still beautiful for all the suffering that she had borne. It was an older and leaner face, truly, but one that radiated all of Tamara's wild joy of life that he had once called *animajii*. Tamara, he remembered, had always lived as joyfully as a tiger playing in the sun. And like a tiger, she'd always had her claws sunk deeply into life—it was one of the things that he loved most in her.

"Tamara, Tamara," he whispered. But with the air itself moving with the gosharp's music, no one heard him. "Tamara, Tamara."

He stood there on the street watching Tamara's long fingers

play over the gosharp's strings with all the fluidity and grace of running water; he marveled that she could move her fingers at all, for her hands were naked to the icy air. He attributed her hardiness to *animajii*, this pure fire of life flowing through her limbs and driving her to make such soulful music despite the terrible cold. He remembered well the fire that filled her inside; he remembered himself filling her with his own wild fire, and he fairly trembled to take her beneath the furs of her bed as he had on the night that they first met so many years ago.

Tamara, Tamara.

After a while, she finished playing and put down her harp. The exemplar dug in his pockets for some money to give her, nothing so precious as a city disk, but he was nonetheless pleased to drop a few gold davins into her bowl. The astrier man astonished everyone by taking off his platinum chain and coiling it like a long silver snake next to the exemplar's coins. He bowed to her and said, ''I've never heard a harpist play so well; perhaps you can use this to buy a little food.'' Others gave other things: a twist of toalache, a bag of dried snow apples, a fireflower picked earlier from the Hyacinth Gardens. They bowed, too, and hurried off to complete their errands.

Danlo was the last to give thanks for Tamara's music. He stood there staring at his empty hands, ashamed that he had nothing to put into her bowl. And then he remembered the stone that he had found five days before as he wandered the sands near Tamara's old house on North Beach. He took it out of his pocket and held it gleaming in the light. It was smooth and round and not much larger than a baldo nut; swirls of crystal white cut though a cool, blue-gray in a lovely pattern like that of a spider's web. Tamara, he remembered, had once kept seven oiled sea stones on the windowsill of her tea room. He thought that she might like this stone, so he placed it in her thanksgiving bowl.

''Oh, that's beautiful!'' she said as she sorted through her bowl. She held Danlo's gift in her naked hand, and she seemed more pleased with this simple stone than with either the gold coins or the platinum chain. ''I've always loved beautiful stones.''

''I . . . had hoped that you might,'' Danlo said. He stood there in his white furs and black mask, all the while gazing at Tamara's face. For the moment, only the two of them remained on this part of the street. ''I wish I had more to give you; you will not be able to buy any food with a stone.''

''No,'' Tamara agreed, weighing the coins and the platinum chain in her other hand. ''But there's almost no food to buy anyway. I rarely receive such gifts as these, you know, but even so, who's willing to trade a bag of rice for mere gold?''

Danlo looked at her for a while, and then said, "You must be hungry. I am sorry."

Then Tamara smiled at him sadly and said, "You must be hungry, too. Almost everyone is."

"Truly, I *am* hungry," he said. "But in listening to you play, the beauty of the music, like silver waves, like the sea singing to the stars . . . there were moments when I forgot my hunger."

Tamara, who had always loved compliments almost as much as chocolate candies, laughed softly for a while. It was her old laugh: a little sadder, perhaps, but still rich and warm and full of life. "You speak so beautifully," she said. She looked at him strangely. "Such a beautiful voice, too—have we met before?"

Danlo smiled then because he thought his voice sounded hoarse with the cold. He stared at her a long time before saying, "I have heard you play before."

"Oh, really? I've only recently begun playing on the streets. But I was a courtesan once years ago—perhaps we made a contract together?"

A sudden pain blossomed behind his left eye as he remembered how Tamara had once given her promise to marry him. Because he couldn't speak just then, he looked down at their shadows wavering upon the ice.

"My name is Tamara Ten Ashtoreth," she said. "But I'm afraid you have me at a disadvantage. Why don't you take off your mask so that I might see whom I'm talking to?"

Danlo stood with his head bowed down, almost completely unable to move. He looked for his reflection in the ice, but the dull, red gliddery showed little sign of how Tamara must have seen him: the white ruff of his furs, his black face mask, his deep blue eyes overflowing with warm salt water and light.

"Why don't you take your mask off?" she said softly.

At last, with his heart beating against his ribs like a fist, with a single swift motion, he ripped the mask from his face. And then he looked up and locked eyes with her.

"Oh, no!" she gasped. She had begun wiping her harp with a silk cloth, but when she saw Danlo for who he really was, she put it aside and stood up as if to flee. "Oh, Danlo—I thought I'd never see you again."

"I . . . always prayed that I would see you."

She stared at the lightning bolt scar cut into his forehead and the other more subtle scars of suffering and experience that time had cut into his face. She said, "I'd heard that you had left the city. That you were one of the pilots chosen for the Vild Mission. There was to have been a second Academy established somewhere in the Vild, wasn't there? I thought you'd never return."

"I . . . had to return."

He took a step closer to her, then, but she suddenly remembered her need to keep a distance between them, and she held out her hand. "No, Pilot—please."

"Tamara, Tamara . . ."

"No, Pilot, no, no."

Danlo stood there clenching his fingers into fists, not knowing what to do. And then he said, "It is very cold. Would you like to sit a while in a cafe? I have not been able to find one that serves coffee, but there is still hot tea if you do not mind drinking it without honey."

"That *would* be nice," Tamara said. "But I'm waiting for someone."

A shard of steel sharper and colder than a warrior-poet's killing knife drove through Danlo's left eye just then. He winced and said, "I see."

Something in his voice must have touched her, for she suddenly decided to step closer to touch *him,* and she let her cold fingers slowly burn down his face from his eye to his chin. "Oh, Pilot, I'm sorry, but I'm afraid that nothing has changed."

"You still don't remember me, then?"

"I remember only our last meeting in the Mother's house."

"But in all this time there has been nothing else?"

"I'm sorry."

"No images, no dreams of the moments that we spent together?"

"Well, I do remember saying farewell in the Mother's house," Tamara said gently. "Perhaps it would have been best if that really *had* been our farewell."

"No, no," Danlo said. "Seeing you here, now, your eyes, your blessed breath . . . it is like finding the sun after years of falling through black space."

She laughed for a moment and said, "You're a beautiful man—it's not hard to see why I must have loved you."

"Do you remember the word *imaklana?* This love magic between a man and a woman that is instantaneous and yet eternal, too?"

"I remember that you've spoken of this before."

"And you do not believe that it is true?"

She looked at him sadly and said, "I suppose a part of me must still love you. But I can't *feel* it. And I think I really don't want to. I'm sorry."

"I . . . am sorry, too."

He closed his eyes against the hot tears that he felt welling there. He remembered how Hanuman's rape of Tamara's memories had destroyed much else in her that was beautiful and good. He raged, then. His tears dried up like pools of water beneath a blazing sun, and when he looked again upon Tamara and the harsh winter light pouring down upon the street, his eyes were full of nothing but wrath.

"Oh, Pilot, you're still so angry." Tamara took a step backward, almost to the edge of the fur spread over the icy street. "You've still so much hate. So much despair."

"Yes," Danlo said, and the sound of this single word escaped his lips with all the force of a death wind blowing in across the sea.

"And I'm still afraid of this hate, you know. I'm still afraid of you."

At that moment, Danlo's eyes were like blue-black holes into his soul. Because he didn't want Tamara to see the bottomlessness of his emotions, he looked down at the skate tracks in the street and said, "I have always wanted to find a way to stop hating."

"But why hate at all?" Tamara asked. "Why hate the world just because I happened to contract a virus that destroyed my memory?"

"It is not the world that I hate," Danlo almost whispered. "It is a man."

"But why? Who is it, then?"

"It does not matter."

"Please tell me."

"I cannot."

"Is it Hanuman?"

Danlo smiled at the lively intelligence that he saw in her eyes, the way that her mind loved to move. He looked at her for a long time but said nothing.

"Well, I suppose a lot of people hate him," she said. "Because of the war, because of what he's done."

He bowed his head in acknowledgement of Hanuman's perverting of the Way of Ringess, but still he remained silent.

"But that's not why *you* hate him, is it?"

"No," he said.

"But why, Pilot? Please tell me."

"No."

"Is it because Hanuman fell into love with me that first night, too?"

"Then you remember things about you and Hanuman, yes?"

"I remember that I never loved him. That I never *could* have loved him."

"I see."

"So you needn't hate him because of me."

Danlo watched the sunlight playing on her golden hair, and he smiled sadly.

"But you *do* still hate him so fiercely," she said. "There's something I'm not understanding about you and him, isn't there? Why won't you tell me?"

"I do not wish to hurt you."

"But how could your quarrel with Hanuman possibly hurt me?"

He took a breath of cold air, coughed, and closed his eyes for a moment. And then he looked at her and said, "Because it was not a virus that destroyed your memory. It was Hanuman."

"What? What are you saying?"

He told her then what Hanuman had done to her: under the guise of recording her memories of the Elder Eddas for his remembrancing computers, one night in deep winter he had lured her into the chapterhouse of the cathedral. There he had slipped a cleansing heaume over her head and carefully destroyed her memories of Danlo one by one. And in her confusion and despair afterwards, he had pricked her neck with a tiny needle, injecting her with the viruses that caused the Catava Fever. But these had been killed viruses, not live; Hanuman had used them only to fool any virologist who might examine Tamara afterward into believing that she had been afflicted with this terrible disease. He had hoped that no one would ever suspect him of this crime, and almost no one ever had.

"But surely Hanuman wouldn't have told you what he did," Tamara said. Just then a big, black zamboni rolled down the street, melting and smoothing the ice for the afternoon's skaters. She waited for this huge, humming machine to pass, and then asked, "How can you know this?"

"I *know,*" Danlo said. "I know Hanuman. At Year's End, in the cathedral, I gave him a gift and he told me with his eyes."

At this, Tamara's eyes flashed with anger for a moment, but then she breathed deeply and asked, "Why didn't you tell me?"

"When I saw you in the Mother's house, you had already suffered so much."

"Oh, Danlo," she said. Her face softened and she looked at him strangely, as if she were more concerned with his sufferings than her own. "Then you believe that Hanuman did all this to take me away from you?"

"Yes, truly," Danlo said. "But it was more than that."

"What do you mean?"

Danlo pressed his hand to his throbbing head; he took a breath of icy air, held it a moment and sighed. And then he told her, "Hanuman wanted to give *me* a gift. All his life, he had felt the pain of life so keenly, so deeply. I have never known a man who felt so alone. Alone and yet not really alone. He was always so close to the one thing that he would love above all others, the one thing that he *needed* to love, but never quite could. This is just the beautiful, blessed world, yes? The . . . terrible world. There is a life inside all life, a light inside light, and it all shines so terribly brightly. Look deeply enough inside a rock and you will see how it comes alive with the most marvelous light from within. But he could never quite bear to behold it; he never really wanted to see himself just as he is. The light—in him, it is truly as bright as any star, and it connects him to the light inside everything else, and he always hated that. He was always so afraid of losing himself, one light among an infinite number of others. He hated himself for this fear. But he could no more stop being afraid than he could escape the pain of being alive and alone. And so he despaired. He always suffered such a rare and terrible estrangement. And after his remembrance of the Elder Eddas, in being forced to look upon the light of his own memory, the One Memory, it grew almost total.

"I have looked for a way to see how it must be for him. To say this to myself, in words. I think that the only color he truly knows is black. But this is a black inside black, yes? It is as far from the blackness of my face mask as that color is from white. It is a black with an inside and an infinite depth, a bottomless cavern, a black so totally and truly black that one can never quite behold it because it reflects no light. This utter blackness, this neverness of light—this is all that he sees now when he looks inside himself. His soul is broken. And he knows this. But rather than seek healing, he calls all this blackness and despair his fate, and he wills himself to love it. He . . . has always wished for me to love it, too. For me to understand not just with concepts or words, but to know it from within. He wanted to burn this blackness into me so that he wouldn't be so alone. This was his gift to me. And this was why he destroyed your memories."

After Danlo had finished speaking, they both stood there looking at each other as if trying to enter each other's soul through their eyes. From far down the street came the click-clack of skate blades against ice, and the wind was up, driving crystals of old snow against the shop windows and closed doors. And then Tamara smiled at him sadly, with all the pain in the world. "Oh, Danlo," she said, touching his face again, "I didn't know."

"I did not want you to know," he said. "You had already lost so much of yourself. I did not want you to grieve over what I had lost, too."

Tamara rested her hand on his, and said, "But I lost only my memories; it would seem that you lost much more than this."

"No, no—there was a moment in the Mother's house when you had almost forgotten who you truly are."

"That was a bad time," she admitted.

"But I have not forgotten. You have always been just yourself, yes? Your splendid self. Even now, you worry more about me than you. So much love, Tamara, so much compassion. I have always loved this in you. I . . . always will."

Tamara had never been one to deny her best attributes or to diminish herself in any way. But the rape of her mind had softened her pride. She squeezed Danlo's hand, and told him, "I only wish I could love as you do. There's something about you, something I don't remember seeing before."

"A few moments ago, you were afraid of me because of my hate."

She looked at him strangely again, and nodded her head. "And that's what I don't understand. A few moments ago, there *was* hate. This burning blackness of yours beyond black. But now there's so much light in you—it's as if a star had suddenly burst. I wish you could see yourself. Your face, your eyes. Oh, dear Danlo, you've such beautiful eyes, so wild, so full of light. I've never seen anyone's eyes come so alive. When I said farewell to you in the Mother's house, your eyes were almost dead, and I wanted to die, too. I *was* so terribly afraid of you; I think I was aware of only this fear. But now you return from the stars like this. I think you've gifts other than the one that Hanuman gave you. So much love—what you think you see in me is only the barest flicker of what pours out of you like the sun."

Danlo watched the breath escape Tamara's lips in wispy, silvery puffs. And then he said, "It has always been easy for me to love you. Impossible . . . not to love."

"Oh, I think it's more than that, much more than you and I."

"You always believed that love was the secret of the universe," he said, smiling. "That through love, men and women, stars and galaxies—everything—would awaken."

"Through *love,* Danlo."

"Do you still believe in love, then?"

"Of course I do. In a way, whether you look into the heart of an atom or the heart of the world, it's all there is."

"I wish I could believe that."

"Look into your own beautiful heart," she said, "and you'll find a love far beyond the love of a man for a woman."

"I . . . know that there is," he said. "I only wish I could hold it. But sometimes it is harder than holding the reflection of the sun's rays upon the sea."

"But you're so close to it, aren't you?"

"Sometimes I swim with the dolphins and seabirds in the light; but too often something black and infinitely vast pulls me down like a rock."

"I think you understand Hanuman too well."

"Truly, I do."

"But at least you still fight. There's such a war going on inside you."

"I *do* fight," he said. For a moment, his eyes grew even brighter, like twin blue diamonds. "There is always this eternal war, yes?"

"I suppose that's true," she said. "I can certainly see how it is that you and Hanuman have come to make war against each other."

"I wish that it did not have to be. But Hanuman would say that it was our fate."

"Hanuman didn't have to give you the gift that he did, did he?"

"No," he said, covering her hands with his gloves to protect them from the wind. "But I did not have to try so hard to show Hanuman the glory of the world, as I have always seen it."

"What do you mean?"

He smiled strangely, sadly, and then said, "All that I am, all that I have ever hoped to be . . . this has touched Hanuman deeply, yes? Touched like fire against his naked heart. I am afraid that I killed something in him. I am afraid that much of who he is, I made him to be."

"But he has made his own choices, hasn't he?"

"Yes, and I have made mine. We both made a war of our souls against each other and brought it into this religion about my father."

"But you can't blame yourself for what Hanuman has done with the Way of Ringess."

"Can I not? We made war, willfully, and now this war has been brought to the stars."

"But that's all so tragic. So sad."

"Yes," he said.

"And it's so wrong for you to blame yourself this way. You didn't start this stupid war any more than you can stop it."

For a moment, his eyes burned with a strange, wild light. And then he told her of his journey from the Vild to Sheydveg and the gathering of the Fellowship of Free Worlds. He told her how he had come to Neverness as an emmissary of peace, only to be thrown into a dark cell by Hanuman. About his torture, however, he said nothing.

"But how did you come to be here, wandering the street in a mask?"

"Benjamin Hur and his people arranged my escape. They almost tore down the walls of the cathedral."

"Were you hurt?"

"No," he said. "But many were. Many . . . were killed."

"Oh, that's terrible," she said. "There's been so much killing since the war started."

"Then you didn't know?"

Tamara shook her head. "I'm afraid I haven't paid enough attention to politics these past years."

"I see."

"And really, before the war, it was easy to ignore what Hanuman was doing. All his plans and secret murders didn't touch very much of the city."

"Not this part of the city, perhaps."

"But this is where I've lived. I haven't gone near the Old City in almost five years."

"Not even to visit the Mother?"

"I'm sorry, Danlo, but the Mother died soon after you went to the Vild. There's a new Mother, now."

She went on to tell about the affairs of the Society of Courtesans, how Helena Turkmanian had been replaced by Zofia Omusan, a harridan completely enchanted by Hanuman li Tosh.

And then she said, "And that's all I know. Since I left the Society, I haven't talked with any of my sisters."

"Then you have no connection with your old life?"

"Almost none," she said, smiling mysteriously. And then she pulled her hands from between his and looked down the street at the other skaters. "It's falling late, you know."

She returned to her fur where she finished wiping down her gosharp and placed it in a hard, silver case. Then, kneeling, she quickly rolled up the fur with the skinside facing out; she tied it securely and set it on the ice by the gosharp. In watching her precise and yet graceful movements, Danlo remembered the great care that she had always invested in the simple living of life. She seemed to love the feel of the soft, silken fur, the sound of the wind, even the harsh red light off the ice of the street. In truth, she seemed to love almost everything that she could touch or see, and he had always loved this about her.

"I am glad that I found you again," he said, digging at the ice with the tip of his skate. "It was good to see you."

"It was good to see *you.*"

He started to bow his farewell, then, but just as his eyes dipped past hers, she looked over his shoulder behind him and broke into a smile. A sudden, fierce love lit her face like the light of a flame globe. Danlo dreaded beholding the focus of her affection, but even so, he broke off his bow and forced himself to turn around. And there, down the street past the closed restaurants and shops, he saw a woman and two children dressed in shagshay furs skating quickly toward them. He had only to count ten beats of his heart, and the two children—both boys about five years old—had sprinted close enough that Danlo could see their windburned faces.

Ahira, Ahira, he whispered to himself. *Ahira, Ahira.*

The boy on the right resembled the woman straining and puffing to catch up with him; he had flaming red hair and a softness about his fat, fair cheeks as if he had rarely missed a meal. But the boy on the left was lean and built for speed like a falcon. His long, sharp nose cut the wind, which had blown back his hood and whipped his hair wildly about his head. His hair was almost totally black; Danlo saw that immediately. And his eyes were like twin blue jewels: dark, lively and overflowing with delight.

Oh, Ahira—I did not know.

In a few more moments—in a flurry of laughter and grinding skates—the dark-haired boy won the race and fairly flew into Tamara's arms. Their love for each other spilled out of them with all the sweetness and intensity of blossoming fireflowers. While Tamara used her fingers to comb the boy's hair back from his forehead, he wrapped his arms about her waist and buried his face in her furs.

"Mama," he said, suddenly pulling back and reaching into the pocket of his furs. "Look what I've brought you!"

In his little hand, wrapped neatly in a clear thinskin, he held a sandwich much torn and compressed into a mass of crumbly bread. Tamara took it from him as if being presented the rarest of firestones, and she said, "Thank you, Jonathan—but wherever did you get this?"

Before he could answer, however, the other woman and boy skated up to them and called out a greeting. In the confusion of quick words and easy laughter, Jonathan finally noticed Danlo standing by his mother's side. He looked at him, then. He boldly met Danlo's gaze and held it much longer than a five-year-old boy should have been able to do. And in this touching of their eyes, in the light of this wild young soul that was so similar to his own, Danlo instantly saw that Jonathan was his son.

This knowledge came to him differently than had his vision of the battle of Mara's Star. It was more immediate and much more physical: he felt it burning like a fire in his belly and in the synchronized movements of their breath. Something inside every cell of his body, perhaps as deep as the DNA, seemed to resonate with the lifefire of this beautiful child and sing along the lines of his blood. This marvelous song—in truth, it was really much more like the cry of a great white bird far out over the sea—called to him from a secret place inside his heart. Its sound came poignant and clear, and went on and on and on.

Tamara, Tamara, he asked himself, *how is it possible?*

He turned to look at Tamara, then, with her soft, dark eyes so full of love. And Tamara looked at him. He didn't have to tell her that he knew Jonathan was his son. Somehow, she knew that he knew—he could see it in her fierce pride and the way that she looked at Danlo as if to say, "Do you see this beautiful child that we have made?" And he *did* see this miracle of creation, this child of his dreams sidling up to the warmth of Tamara's furs even as he continued to stare at Danlo. As Danlo looked at Jonathan, there came a moment of terrible beauty as if love and suffering, joy and sadness, past and future were all one. And for the second time in his life, he fell into love.

How is it possible?

Tamara, still holding the sandwich in her hand, noticed that the other woman and boy were eyeing Danlo suspiciously. Always one to respect decorum, she rather belatedly made the presentations.

"This is Pilar Kiden and her son, Andreas wi Novat Kiden," she said, nodding at the red-haired woman and the other boy. Then she turned and used her free hand to pull the hood of Jonathan's furs over his head. "And this is *my* son, Jonathan Ashtoreth."

As she spoke, Danlo bowed to each of them in turn. And then Tamara smiled at him and said, "And this is Danlo wi—"

"Danlo of Kweitkel," Danlo hurriedly interrupted, not wishing for Tamara to speak his full name. "I am called Danlo of Kweitkel."

"Danlo is an aficionado of the gosharp," Tamara explained to Pilar, all the while looking at Danlo in puzzlement. "And he's a wonderful musician himself."

For a while, they all stood about discussing the difficulty—and danger—of playing music on the street in such a climate of cold and uncertain times. And then Tamara returned to the miracle of the sandwich that Jonathan had given her.

"I'm so hungry," she told her son as she began to unwrap the sandwich. "But have all of you eaten?"

"We found a restaurant, Mama. We had sandwiches, too."

"The truth is, it wasn't really a restaurant," Pilar said. Except for the color of her skin, which was almost pink and marred with the rare malady of pigmentation called freckling, she was a good-looking woman. She was a few years older than Tamara, big-boned with an open and kindly face. Her body was almost as stout as Bardo's, and like Bardo's, it suggested all the solidity and strength of the earth. "We found a house just on the west side of the Merripen Green. A couple of wormrunners had converted the lower floor into a dining room. They were serving sandwiches today. The bread is a little old—I think the wormrunners must have been hoarding it quite a while. And I can't imagine where they found any cultured meat."

"*Is* it cultured meat?" Tamara asked as she used her finger to gently tease the two slices of bread apart. Careful not to let a single crumb fall to the street, she inspected the thin slices of reddish-brown meat sitting in their bed of wilted kava leaves and curry paste. "I've heard that some of the wormrunners have been poaching shagshay and other animals from the northern part of the island."

"I *think* it's cultured meat," Pilar said. "I hope it is."

"I do, too," Tamara said. She sniffed the meat and then broke off a crumb of it and placed it on her tongue. "I really wouldn't want to eat an animal unless I were starving."

"But we *are* starving," Pilar said. "Before our sandwiches, Andreas and I hadn't eaten since yesterday."

Danlo, remembering his first journey to Neverness across the sea when he had lost count of the days in which he had had no food, smiled grimly but said nothing.

"Well, it *does* taste like cultured meat," Tamara said. "I think it tastes all right."

"I thought it tasted all right, too," Pilar said.

All this talk seemed to confuse Jonathan, who had never seen the cultured meats grown in the vats of the food factories, much less the flayed flesh of a dead animal. In truth, he just wanted his mother to eat. "Aren't you hungry?" he asked her.

"Of course I am," she said, taking a nibble of the sandwich. "But are you still hungry, too?"

"No, Mama—why don't you eat?"

Tamara gently broke the sandwich into two pieces then, and offered one to Danlo. She said, "I know *you're* hungry."

"Thank you, but no," Danlo said, shaking his head. "I do not eat meat."

"But it's cultured meat, I'm sure."

Since Tamara had forgotten so much about him, he explained a little about his vow of ahimsa and how he thought that the growing of animal tissues in cold, plastic vats did violence to the spirit of all animals. And then he said, "Please, go ahead and finish your sandwich."

"But you could have the bread," Tamara said, breaking off a piece of the crumbly brown bread. "Couldn't you?"

"I will eat tomorrow," Danlo said, thinking of the long next day that he had planned to spend in Constancio's cutting chamber. Although they hadn't formally agreed to such arrangements, he felt certain that Constancio would feed him in order to sustain his strength through the coming surgeries. "So please."

Tamara, needing no further encouragement, lifted her sandwich to her lips with great enthusiasm and bit off a piece. Although she was very hungry, she ate with elegance and was careful not to let any particle of bread or meat fall to the ice. Then, too, she considered it cruel to eat in front of hungry people, and so with every skater who passed by her—wormrunners, harijan or autists—she would hold the sandwich inside her furs

for a moment and stop chewing. Thus it took her quite a while to
finish her meal.

While Jonathan and Andreas began a game of bump-and-skate
across the street's darkening ice, Danlo chatted with Pilar about
the unusual coldness of the season. And all the while he stole
glances at Tamara as she ate her sandwich. He loved watching the
bunch and flow of her strong jaw muscles and the deft motions of
her hands. She took joy in all the simple motions of eating and
seemed intensely grateful for the gift of life. In the way that she
looked at Jonathan, as he laughed and struck steel against ice and
fairly tore up and down the street, there was a bright and natural
goodness, like sunlight on a false winter day. There was hope and
pride and fierce protectiveness, but there was another thing, too.
Tamara loved life, and she loved love, but deep inside she was
always so terribly afraid of losing it. This was the secret of her
soul. Danlo saw that if anything ever happened to Jonathan, she
would want to die. The brilliance and totality of her love awed
him. It caused his eyes to burn and his throat to ache and his heart
to beat in a waves of red, throbbing pain.

Tamara, Tamara, he thought. *We have a son.*

After Tamara had finished her sandwich, Pilar bowed to Danlo
and said, "It's falling cold; we should be going. But I'm glad to
have met you, Danlo of Kweitkel. I wish you well."

"I wish you well, too," Danlo said, returning her bow. "You
and your son."

With that, Andreas broke off his game and came over to make
his goodbyes. While the two boys leaned against each other shoulder to shoulder, trying to push each other off balance, Tamara
looked at Pilar and said, "Thank you for taking Jonathan today.
What can I give you for the sandwiches?"

"But you took Andreas three days ago—don't you remember?" Pilar asked. "And fed him *two* meals."

"But that was just kurmash. I'm sure the wormrunners would
have charged much more for cultured meat."

"Haven't I told you that these things always come out evenly
in the end?"

"Here," Tamara said, reaching inside her pocket for the platinum chain that the astrier man had given her. "I've had a very
good day—please take this."

Pilar's eyes lit up at the beauty of this glittering thing, but she
said, "Oh, no, I couldn't—this is worth much more than a couple
of sandwiches."

"But it might not be in a few more days. And as you've said, these things always come out evenly."

"Oh, Tamara, no, I really couldn't."

"Yes, you really *can,* and you must."

Tamara gently took Pilar's hand then, and opened her fingers so that they might hold the chain. So great was the force of her will that Pilar made no more protests.

"Thank you," Pilar said. Then she bowed yet again, swept her arm around Andreas, and the two of them skated off down the street.

"I love Pilar," Tamara said. "After I had lost my memories, during that horrible time when I hardly knew who I was, she took care of me."

"I am glad," Danlo said. "She seems an easy woman to love."

Tamara nodded her head as she put her arm around Jonathan and drew him closer to the warmth of her body. To Danlo, she said, "Would you like to accompany us to our apartment? There are things we should talk about, but it's growing cold and I should take Jonathan inside."

"Yes, I would like that," Danlo said. "Do you live far?"

"No—it's only a few blocks from here."

She bent to collect her rolled-up fur and gosharp, and Danlo moved to help with these things. Tamara gave him the fur, but the much heavier gosharp in its silver case she kept for herself. She was a strong woman who had no trouble carrying it in one hand even as she held Jonathan's hand with the other. Together they led the way up the street with Danlo following a few skate strokes behind. They passed the Street of Ten Thousand Bars and turned onto a little gliddery lined with blackstone tenements. Faint smells of garlic and roasted bread wafted out into the air; it seemed that although the restaurants were all closed, more than a few people still kept private stores of food and were cooking their evening meals behind closed doors. Danlo smelled other things, too: the lovely fragrance of Tamara's hair, the rank molecules spraying out of the speech organ of an alien Friends of Man and, almost everywhere, the smell of fear.

This last was much more than the acridness of sweat beneath old furs. It was the hurrying of the people as they skated with purpose and passed shadowed alleys; it was wormrunners avoiding coughing autists, and harijan with tight, shrunken bellies, and the inability of men and women to meet each other eye to eye. Danlo was very glad when Tamara left the street and opened the

door of an old tenement. Arm in arm with Jonathan, she led
Danlo up a flight of worn stone stairs and down a hallway lit with
flame globes. Danlo liked the play of warm colors across the walls
of the hallway. He liked it that the building seemed clean and well
kept. And then Tamara opened the door to her apartment, and he
liked it even more that they would have a space to be alone out of
the shivering cold.

"You have to take off your boots," Jonathan informed Danlo
as they all stood on a large cotton carpet inside the door. "It's one
of our rules."

As Danlo knelt to unlace his boots, he looked about and saw
that the space in which Tamara and Jonathan lived was almost as
small as the interior of his snow house. In truth, there were only
two rooms: the fire room in which they stood and an adjoining,
fur-lined area too tiny to be dignified by calling it a sleeping
chamber. Even the fire room was misnamed, for it was graced
with neither fireplace nor plasma hearth. Danlo remembered how
Tamara had liked to dance naked in front of a blazing wood fire,
and he wondered if she felt the lack of hot flame tongues licking
at her body. Still, the room was warm enough, for along one wall
ran a radiator fairly gurgling with water piped up from the hot
springs beneath the city. And it was warm in other ways, too.
Tamara had filled it with carpets and flowering plants and paintings that she and Jonathan had made. In a corner of the room
opposite the door, she had set up a little electric stove. Sometimes, she said, on their lucky days, she would boil kurmash there
or heat up a pot of tea.

"Would you like a cup of tea?" she asked as she took Danlo's
furs and hung them on a wooden drying rack. "I've been saving a
Summerworld green for just such an occasion."

While Danlo sat crosslegged on the floor and Tamara made the
tea, Jonathan stole off into the sleeping chamber as silently as a
snow leopard. He returned a few moments later holding in either
hand his two most prized possessions: a small, simple five-holed
flute made of black shatterwood and a black clary model of a
lightship nearly two feet long. He set the flute on the carpet near a
cushion; he came over to show Danlo the lightship, pointing out
the areas behind the fuselage that housed the rockets and spacetime engines.

"I'm going to be a pilot someday," he told Danlo. And then,
after telling the story of the battle of Mara's Star that he had
heard from Andreas, he said, "If there's another war when I'm

bigger, I'll have my own ship and fight battles around the stars. Do you think there'll be another war?''

At this Danlo smiled sadly and said that he didn't know. And then he looked at Jonathan and told him, ''When I was a boy, I wanted to be a pilot, too.''

Jonathan clearly approved of Danlo's ambition; he smiled at him knowingly as if they both shared a secret, then said, ''I want to take my lightship to the stars of another galaxy. My mother once told me that not even Mallory Ringess has journeyed so far.''

For a while, Danlo sat with Jonathan recounting the journeys of great pilots such as Rollo Gallivare, the Tycho, Leopold Soli and Mallory Ringess. And then Tamara came over with their tea, which they sipped from delicate little blue cups. Twice, Tamara refilled these cups before asking Jonathan to pick up his flute so that they could begin his evening lesson. Danlo watched carefully as he listened to him play a song that Tamara had taught him. And Jonathan kept looking at him, occasionally missing his fingering and trilling out a sharp, skirling note in his desire to please Danlo. When he had finished, he put down his flute and said, ''I just learned that yesterday, so I'm not very good at it yet. But I can play the first two Songs of the Sun—would you like to hear them?''

''No, Jonathan, it's late and you should be asleep soon,'' Tamara said.

''But I haven't had my story.''

''I'll tell you two stories tomorrow night,'' Tamara said.

Although Jonathan could be a willful boy—in truth, more willful even than his mother—it was not his way to whine or argue. But neither did he like to defy Tamara outright. And so, as he often did, he simply pretended not to hear her. ''Will *you* tell me a story?'' he asked, turning to Danlo.

Danlo noticed Tamara smiling her approval, and so he looked at Jonathan and said, ''This was one of my favorite stories when I was a boy.''

While Jonathan scooted over and sat in his lap, Danlo told him of the Two Friends. On the third morning of the world, he said, wise Ahira had befriended the youth named Manwe, teaching him to hunt, to mate and to take joy in the beauty of the newly created world. And to fly. Manwe was the first human being to fly, and he took to sky with all the rare grace of the snowy owl. Together he and Ahira soared over green-shrouded islands and the cold blue sea. They flew around the world, wing nearly touching hand, feasting on fish and occasionally tricking Totunye, the great white bear, out of his dinner of seal meat or salmon. And then, on the third evening of the world, they flew up beyond the sky. They looked down upon the forests and mountains and the sea's white ice. Their bright eyes shimmered in the nighttime sky like silver lights, and this was how the first stars came to be.

"But stars are really fusion fires of hydrogen and helium, aren't they?" Jonathan asked as Danlo finished his story.

"But how do you really know that? Have you ever touched a star?"

At this, Jonathan laughed and said, "No—they're too far away."

"Stars *are* fusion fires," Danlo said. "But they are also something more."

"But stars can't really *see,* can they?"

"Haven't you ever looked at a star and seen it looking back at you?"

Again, Jonathan laughed, and he looked at Danlo for a long time. He said, "You're a strange man."

"Truly, I am."

"And you have a really big face."

"Thank you," Danlo said, smiling, not knowing how else to respond.

"Will you tell me another story?"

Here, Tamara finally interrupted and said, "No, Jonathan, it's time to sleep now." She stood up and came over to lift him off Danlo's lap.

"I *will* ask you a riddle," Danlo said. "It is the first of the Twelve Riddles—my grandfather asked me this when it was time for me to stop being a boy."

Jonathan didn't wait to see if this might be all right with his mother. He simply looked at Danlo and said, "I love riddles."

"Very well, then—how do you capture a beautiful bird without killing its spirit?"

"Do you mean capture by putting it in a cage?"

"Perhaps. But there are different ways of capturing things. A star captures a comet with gravity; a flower captures a butterfly with bright colors and the smell of nectar."

"That's a really hard riddle."

"Yes—I know."

"It *would* kill a bird's spirit to put it in a cage, wouldn't it?"

"Truly, it would."

"That's a really hard riddle," Jonathan said again as he looked up at the ceiling and tapped his chin with his finger. "What's the answer?"

"I do not know."

"But you *have* to know—you asked the riddle."

"Still, I do not know."

"But your grandfather asked you."

"My grandfather died before he could finish the riddle. I have been searching for the answer to it almost all my life."

"What if it has no answer?"

"I know that it does."

"What if it has no answer—and that's a kind of answer. Like one of the Fravashi koans, you know, what was the shape of your face before you were born?"

Danlo looked hard at his son, then, and his face was shaped with wonder and pride. "How does a five year old boy know about Fravashi koans?"

"My mother teaches me all the time. I'll have to know a lot to enter the Academy—that's the only way to become a pilot."

"I think that you would be a fine pilot."

Even though the talk had turned onto one of Jonathan's favorite topics, he was not easily sidetracked. "I still want to know the answer to the riddle," he said.

"Perhaps someday we can solve it together."

"I'd like that."

"I would, too," Danlo said.

For a long time Jonathan just sat on Danlo's lap looking at him. And then Danlo took out his flute and played a short goodnight song. While he breathed down the long bamboo tube, he wondered how it was possible that everything in the souls of two people could come streaming out through the eyes. At last he finished playing and sat smiling down at Jonathan. Then Tamara, who still stood above them watching and waiting, reached down and grasped her son's hand. With his other hand, Jonathan touched the lightning bolt scar on Danlo's forehead and told him, "I love you."

After this, Tamara took Jonathan into the sleeping chamber. Danlo heard sounds of teeth being cleaned, swishing water, spitting and rippling furs. He heard Jonathan say that he was still hungry. Then came the music of Tamara's soft, lovely voice reassuring him that there would be more food tomorrow. She sang him a sweet little song and perhaps kissed him goodnight. Soon she reappeared in the fire room, shutting the door behind her. She came over to Danlo and sat facing him.

"I've never seen him take to anyone the way he has with you," she said.

"He is a lovely child."

Tamara looked down at the floor for a moment and then said, "I've often wondered if I should have told you."

"You knew, then? Truly, in the Mother's house—you knew."

"Actually, before that. The night that I went to the cathedral, I knew I was pregnant."

"I see."

"I've calculated that we must have conceived him a few days before that."

"I see."

"You haven't asked me how I know he's ours."

Danlo smiled mysteriously and extended his fingers toward her. "Do I have to ask if this hand is mine?"

"Still I should tell you that although I can't remember us being together, I always took precautions with my clients."

"But not with me?"

"It would seem not. I like to believe that I loved you so much that I wanted your child."

"I . . . believe that."

"Thank you," Tamara said, almost whispering. "Thank you."

"But why *didn't* you tell me, then, in the Mother's house?"

"Because I had to say goodbye to you," she said. "I *had* to, don't you see?"

"I do see," he said. He touched her hand, then held it gently. "But he is my son, and you should have told me."

"But what would you have done? Would you have stopped being a pilot? Would you have abandoned your quest to the Vild?"

"The choice should have been mine to make."

"I'm sorry, Danlo." Her fingers trembled against his as she squeezed him hard and looked at him. The strength of her hand was astonishing.

"I am sorry, too," he said.

"I always wanted him to have a father, you know."

"Then you never told him about me?"

She shook her head and smiled. "Not exactly. He knows only that his father was a pilot who was lost in the manifold."

Danlo looked down at the model of the lightship that Jonathan had left on the carpet. "I see," he said. "So you gave him your name."

"Should I have given him yours? This isn't the easiest of times to be a Ringess, is it?"

"No," he said, thinking of how he had presented himself to Pilar as Danlo of Kweitkel, "it is not."

As he said this, a sudden concern clouded Tamara's face. "You said that you escaped from Hanuman. Is he hunting you? Is that why you were wearing a mask?"

"Yes."

"Do you need a place of refuge, then? Would you like to stay here?"

"Thank you, but I have a place."

"But you'll visit Jonathan, won't you? To solve your silly riddles?"

"I am afraid that my coming here might put you at risk."

"We haven't anything to eat—how much more risk could you bring?"

He squeezed her hand gently as he looked at her face, the lines of pain and the leanness of it. "You are right, there is always risk, yes? So if you'd like, from time to time, I will bring you what food I can."

"But you haven't had enough to eat yourself!"

"But Jonathan is my son. And you were almost my wife."

At this, she let go his hand and sat silently weeping for a while. And then, through layers of tears she looked at him and said, "You're a beautiful man."

He moved closer to her and touched her wet cheek. He touched her forehead, her eyes, her glistening hair. "I still love you," he said.

"But I still *can't* love you," she said, taking his hand away from her. "I'm sorry, but I can't love any man."

"Then there has been no one else since we were together?"

"No one that I've loved. No one that I've let into this room."

"I see."

"There have been times when I had to do things for money," she said. "And lately, for food."

"I . . . am sorry."

"Please don't be. I trained as a courtesan, remember? I was once with exemplars with fortunes and whole days to spend in the pursuit of ecstasy. How much easier it is to please a man who cares for nothing except a little quick pleasure."

"But today you were playing your gosharp, yes?"

"Well, I do what I can. The wormrunners will still trade for food, but some will settle for nothing less than firestones or gold. And some want only flesh.''

"I will bring you all the food that I can find," Danlo said again. "Only there is something that I . . .''

He paused a moment considering whether he should tell Tamara of his coming surgery and his plan to bring down Hanuman li Tosh.

"What is it, Danlo?''

"I . . . must change myself. My appearance, in body and face. I've contracted with a cutter. There will come a time, and soon, when I will want to wear my mask even when I am with you.''

"And all this is because you don't want Hanuman to find you?''

Danlo nodded his head. And then, because he liked always to speak the truth, he said, "Because I do not want him to find me . . . as I am.''

"What do you mean?''

He closed his eyes as he held his breath and counted his heartbeats. Then he looked at her and said, "At this moment, Bardo and Richardess and Lara Jesusa and other pilots whom I have known are manuevering in their lightships among the stars to fight Hanuman. Benjamin Hur is fighting him with lasers; Jonathan Hur tries to fight him with light and love. I . . . must fight him in my own way.''

"But how, then?''

"I cannot tell you more than this.''

"What you're doing—it's very dangerous, isn't it?''

"Yes.''

Tamara looked down at her hands, which were trembling slightly. She suddenly locked her fingers together and said, "Now that Jonathan has found his father, I couldn't bear it if he lost him.''

For a while Danlo watched the room's soft lights play in her eyes as he sat silently looking at her.

"Oh, Danlo, what are we going to do?'' She undid the collar of her silk robe and drew forth the necklace that she wore next to her skin. She held its single pearl in her hand so that he could see it clearly. "You made this for me, didn't you? I don't remember your giving it to me, but I don't know how else I could have acquired it.''

He looked at the large, black pearl shaped like a teardrop. He remembered finding it and cleaning it and fastening it to the necklace's black and red string, which he had braided from strands of his own hair. "I did make it for you," he said. "It was a symbol of our promise to marry each other."

She turned the pearl so that its smooth surface shined with flecks of silver and pink. "I've traded or sold all my other jewelry, but I couldn't bear to lose this."

"It is only a pearl," he said. "Only a little piece of an oyster."

As she looked at him looking at this lovely, little thing, she began to weep again. And she said, "I wish I could keep my promise to you. But I can't."

"I know," he said softly. "I know."

"But I would still like to wear it as a promise of our friendship with each other."

"Please wear it, then. I would like you to."

With that they rose up to embrace each other. For a long time, they just stood there touching foreheads. Then Danlo put on his face mask and furs and stepped over to the door.

"When will we see you again?" she asked.

"Perhaps the day after tomorrow. I . . . will bring something for you and Jonathan."

With that, he stepped across the room and opened the door to the sleeping chamber. He stood silently looking down at Jonathan asleep beneath his furs. And then he whispered a prayer for him, "Jonathan, *mi alasharia la, shantih, shantih,* sleep in peace." He went out onto the street then, and as the bitterly cold air found the eyeholes of his mask, he wondered how he would be able to keep this promise to his son and the woman whom he loved.

THE STARVING

The belly is the reason that man does not easily mistake himself for a god.

—Friedrich the Hammer

All life can be seen as the evolution of matter into forms that compete for the universe's free energy. The acquision of energy and its entrapment in the chemicals such as glucose and glycogen is life's fundamental work; it is a terrible urge felt by fireflowers and fritillaries, no less the alien Scutari or Elidi birdmen or the newly created organisms of the Golden Ring. And the source of almost all this energy is light.

A star shines, sending its trillions of trillions of photons singing through black space. Somewhere, in the icy seas off the island of Kweitkel or in the red chlorophyll of a little maker, a single photon strikes a particle of matter. This brief interaction—lasting not much more than a hundred millionth of a second—lifts one electron from an electron pair to a higher level. And then the electron falls back to its ground state, giving off excess energy like a mad wormrunner scattering on the street a pocketful of golden coins. Life has learned to catch the electron in its excited state and to use its energies for the purposes of life. Thus life, over untold eons and ages of forgotten stars, has spread through the universe and learned to hold ever greater concentrations of energy. Bacteria have learned this; sleekits have learned this; and next to the gods, human beings have learned this terrible necessity of life most ruthlessly of all.

From the time the first women and men stood upright on the veldts of Old Earth beneath the blazing sun, human beings have always been good at the getting of food. Food is nothing more than energy trapped in kurmash or honey—or in blood cells or muscle or the sweet fat girdling the ribs of a shagshay ewe. For a god such as the Silicon God, all matter everywhere might be food for his black, sucking maw, but a man's meats are fewer in source. It is only when these sources begin to vanish like snow eaten by the sun that the hunger of humanity is revealed in all its awesome ferocity. Then, in the worst of times, women will betray their children and men slay other men over a few handfuls of rice. They will make war against each other, all against all, and even the best of them might fall desperate and be forced to abandon lesser virtues for the sake of something to eat.

In the days following the closing of the city's restaurants, as Danlo submitted to the first surgeries that would transform him into the shape of an Alaloi man, the competition for food in all quarters of Neverness grew fierce. There were more riots, among the harijan, of course, but also in quiet neighborhoods such as the Nori district peopled by refugees from the Japanese Worlds. Hibakusha, astriers, wormrunners, Ordermen—who among the living of Neverness did not feel the sickening bite of hunger during those long, cold days? Even the aliens suffered the pain of empty bellies. From the Zoo came reports of Elidi nestlings dying for want of nectar and cultured sweetmeats. And the Scutari. The Scutari seneschals, according to their way, were slaying their newly hatched nymphs whom they could not feed. Since their religion held it as a cardinal sin to waste meat, they ate their young with reverence and abandon. And then, when their hunger grew fervent enough, they attacked the Elidi aerodome and carried off dozens of Elidi children before they were driven away.

A few of the more devout (and desperate) Scutari even braved the streets outside their quarter; they stalked the darkened glidderies outside the Hofgarten, hunting human beings. But this proved to be a grave mistake. When Hanuman li Tosh learned that three of his godlings had been taken and sucked clean of their flesh down to their bones, he organized cadres of Ringists to cordon off the entire Zoo from the rest of the city. At least three of these cadres actually entered the Scutari district on a mission of revenge. It was said that the cadres had broken into a huge cluster-cell and slayed some thirty Scutari. And it was whispered, in the cafes and streets, that the wormlike bodies of the dead Scutari had mysteriously disappeared, perhaps sold to the wormrunners who operated the many burgeoning secret (and illegal) restaurants.

It was the wormrunners, certainly, who organized and operated the hunts on the northern part of Neverness Island. From sleek red jammers skimming above the forests scarcely higher than the treetops they aimed their lasers at shagshay, silk belly and mammoth—and snow tigers and wolves and any other animal that they could find. The bolder among them even led forays out onto the ice hundreds of miles from the city. There, using infrared sensors, they took bears and seals and even plotted how they might hunt the great whales who swam in the waters of the southern oceans. In public Hanuman denounced this slaughter. But secretly he realized that the city's need for food was growing more desperate by the day; the flesh of the murdered animals, however little when divided among millions of people, might buy him the time he needed to conclude the war and bring the construction of his Universal Computer to completion.

As deep winter approached, even the tychists were praying for an end to the war. On the 82nd came news that cheered almost everyone: It seemed that Ringists had managed to engage the whole Fellowship fleet out near the Alohir Double. Everyone expected that this would be the war's final battle. But then the following day, Salmalin the Prudent sent a pilot in a lightship to tell the College of Lords that they had fought only a skirmish and had destroyed only a handful of their enemy while losing ten lightships and forty-two blackships of their own. And on the same day, Benjamin Hur delivered another blow. Deciding on a test of strength, he led a team of his ringkeepers against an Old City apartment block housing two full cadres of godlings.

The raid was a complete surprise and a complete success: His ringkeepers captured hundreds of lasers and heat tlolts and killed at least fifty of Hanuman's most devoted followers. And they captured something else as well. In one of the apartments, fairly carpeted with dead bodies and blood, Poppy Panshin discovered machinery for making viruses and other bio-weapons. Although none of the various blue vials or needle darts was found to contain a single live virus, two of Poppy's ringkeepers had panicked and had spread the news to their friends. Soon, like a fire in a field of dried kurmash touched off by a lightning stroke, the whole city burned with the rumor that Hanuman li Tosh had developed a slel virus that would eat holes in the volition centers of his enemy's brains, thereby rendering them helpless to resist conversion to the Way of Ringess.

This rumor lent an even greater urgency to Danlo's plan to unseat Hanuman as Lord of the Way of Ringess. During the dark days of that darkest of seasons, no one seemed to know what to believe, not even Danlo. And so he resolved to complete his change as quickly as possible. In one of Constancio's large sleeping chambers filled with robots, strange-looking machinery, stinking chemicals, drugs and gleaming tools, he lay on a hard steel table and gritted his teeth as the cutter opened almost every part

of him. The deep bone work came first. Almost every bone in his
body from his toes to his skull had to be steeled with layers of
new bone, the tendon attachments built up and strengthened.

The pain of such procedures almost killed him. Once, as Constancio was drilling through his elbow, one of the pain blocks
suddenly failed. (Constancio later explained that he had bought
the glittering nerve machine from an undependable wormrunner).
Despite the shama meditation which Danlo practiced continually
throughout his surgeries, he had cried out and jerked his arm, as
chance would have it, straight *into* Constancio's drill. The diamond bit had torn down the length of Danlo's forearm, chewing
up muscles and ripping through nerves, arteries and veins. The
blood from this accident sprayed over both of them so they resembled two wormrunners trying to butcher a still-living mammoth.
Constancio had to spend the rest of the morning repairing the
damage. "It's fortunate that I've had the foresight to clone spare
nerves," Constancio explained as he teased apart two of Danlo's
tendons with his scalpel. "Otherwise it would be quite a few days
before you could use your arm."

"I . . . am sorry that I moved," Danlo gasped.

"But it wasn't your fault," Constancio said. "I should have
acquired the blocking machine from one of the shops along the
Old City Glissade. And I *would* have, but all the best shops have
been emptied of the best machines. How many poor people have
been burnt by lasers or heat tlolts in this war that Benjamin Hur
fights against the Ringists? Too many, and I'm afraid that the pain
of burns is almost too terrible to bear. *Much* worse than bone
pain, which is hot and deep but doesn't last long."

Just then Danlo lay flexing his fingers and grimacing at the
astonishing pain shooting down the length of his radius bone.
Again he gasped, "It lasts . . . long enough."

As Constancio adjusted the level of a new blocking machine
and injected Danlo's arm with a numbing drug, he whistled a
bright little tune as if he were very happy once again to be sculpting human flesh. "I've observed that you feel pain more acutely
than my other clients," he said. "But you seem also to have a
remarkable ability to control it."

Danlo explained, then, how an encounter with a warrior-poet
had left him permanently poisoned with the ekkana drug.

"Remarkable—truly remarkable that you are even able to
skate outside in the cold, much less lay beneath my lasers without
screaming. Pain blocks or not, you must still feel the touch of
them like fire."

"Truly, I do," Danlo said.

"Then perhaps it would better if I took you into unconsciousness."

"But if you did this, you would have to work more slowly, yes?"

"It helps me avoid nerve damage if you consciously move the various muscle groups and limbs at my request," Constancio admitted. "And the nerves take the longest to repair."

"Then I should remain conscious, yes?"

"Only if you can bear it."

"I think I must."

"There *will* of course be times when you'll have to be unconscious. As when we begin working on your spine."

"I . . . see."

"You don't fully trust me, do you?"

"Do I trust you?" Danlo asked. "I think I must trust you. In the end, between men, trust is all there is, yes?"

In truth, however, he had once heard a story about Mehtar Hajime that caused him to doubt. It seemed that Bardo, years ago in a chance encounter on the street, had pushed Mehtar sprawling to the ice for being rude to a harijan man. In revenge—this is how Bardo always told the story—when it came time for Bardo to be sculpted and accompany Mallory Ringess on his journey to the Alaloi, Mehtar had played a cruel trick on him. Unknown to Bardo, he had implanted in his flesh timed hormones that later caused Bardo's membrum to harden into a permanent state of tumescence. Much later, when Bardo had returned from the quest, he had found another cutter to undo the work that Mehtar had done. But for a long while thereafter Bardo had suffered the opposite and quite unbelievable problem (for him) of softness in his mightiest of parts. In hope of exacting a little revenge of his own, he had searched for Mehtar in the cutting shops up and down the streets of the Farsiders' Quarter but had been unable to find him.

But for all Danlo's misgivings as to Constancio's essential purity of intention, the work went smoothly enough. Only in one respect did Constancio disappoint him—and this had nothing to do with his profession of sculpting human beings into strange and sometimes powerful new shapes. As Danlo had hoped, on those days when he had to spend both morning and night in Constancio's converted sleeping chamber, Constancio fed him rich meals of kurmash, pulses, nuts and fruit so that he might keep his strength and heal quickly and well. But when Danlo had asked for a little extra kurmash to take home to Jonathan and Tamara, Constancio had refused to help. "That wasn't part of our contract," Constancio reminded him coldly. "You traded a scryer's sphere for your sculpting. Well, I'm sculpting you, and much more as well. It's not every cutter who would fete you with the finest of foods as if you were an exemplar."

Danlo hated to argue or to bargain like a merchant. But then he thought of Jonathan chewing on mint sticks to ease the pain of his empty belly, and he told Constancio, "Surely the sphere is worth much more than my sculpting."

"What is anything's true worth?" Constancio said. "If this war doesn't end soon, I might not be able to trade your sphere for a single baldo nut."

"But surely you would not need to. You have hoarded much food, yes? *Years'* worth, I think."

Constancio, who must have feared anyone spreading a rumor that he kept large stores of food, lied to Danlo, saying, "No, no—I've barely enough to feed my servants and myself for a few more days. And you. I've given you the best of what I have, and still you ask for more."

"Only a little kurmash for my wife and son."

"And I've told you, that's impossible."

"Have you ever been truly hungry?" Danlo asked. "Have you held a child in your arms and felt the emptiness of his belly in your own?"

"No, of course I haven't. It's been precisely to avoid such barbarisms that I chose the career that I did."

"I see."

"But if it's any satisfaction to you, soon enough I'll be starving along with everyone else. And so will you when your sculpting is completed."

It was later that day that Danlo began his brief career as a thief. Although he had always been the most honest and trustworthy of men, he took to hiding a little of each meal in the folds of his napkin. This food—rice, almonds, ming beans or dried blood-fruit—he surreptiously emptied into the great pockets of his furs at the first chance. And then, after the day's cuttings, he would smuggle it out of Constancio's house, past his guard at the front gate and out into the streets. As often as he could, far after dusk, he would knock at the door to Tamara's apartment and then hurry inside to provide a little midnight feast. When Constancio remarked Danlo's rare appetite, the way that food almost magically disappeared from his plate, Danlo admitted that he had always been able to eat enough for two men. It was a matter of a quickened metabolism, he said, the way that his body's fires burned hot and deep.

"Strange," Constancio said. "But it must be true. I've never seen anyone heal as quickly as you have—even with the benefit of drugs or the form-field machines. I cut you and glue you shut, and three days later, there isn't even a scar."

As Constancio said this to him, Danlo smiled and closed his eyes. He remembered well that once he had healed much as any other man. But something had changed inside him, something that his torture had begun and his sculpting had only accelerated. It was as if the shock of hunger, drugs and pain had quickened his whole being. Now, deep inside himself, inside the cells of his heart and brain, he felt something beginning to move. Perhaps it was his DNA itself, uncoiling like trillions of tiny snakes; but it felt more like fire, like a countless number of infinitessimal flames swirling and spinning and burning into him new possibilities of life. In truth, he felt more alive than he had ever been before. He felt stronger and hungrier, like a great, beautiful tiger, so burning and insatiably hungry that he could have eaten enough for three large men.

"I suppose we should finish your sculpting quickly," Constancio said. "Otherwise you *will* eat the last of what little food I've stored."

In the next few days, Constancio watched Danlo more carefully, making sure to keep him company at each of his meals. Part of this was only fascination with Danlo's remarkable metabolism and powers of healing. But partly, too, he must have suspected Danlo's thievery, for under the guise of scientific curiosity, he began to measure ever ounce of kurmash and count every almond that went onto Danlo's plate.

Danlo wished that he might do as a mother wolf or father thallow and bring home in his stomach food that might be regurgitated many hours later and eaten. But he was still human, after all, and he didn't have that power. And so he took his stealing to its next level. Rather than surprise Tamara and Jonathan every evening with his purloined tidbits, he began returning straightaway to his house in the City Wild. There, early in the morning beneath the towering shatterwood trees, he hunted out sleekit mounds buried beneath layers of snow. With a hand axe made from a piece of good flint, he chopped into the mounds, robbing them of the baldo nuts that the sleekits had stored against the coldest days of winter.

Although he was careful to take only a few dozen nuts from

any mound, he realized that he was bending his vow of ahimsa if not breaking it altogether. True, the furry little sleekits might have gathered nuts in abundance that winter and might not miss a mere handful. But just as easily, his violation of their food stores and home might cause their young to starve or even die. He consoled himself with the fact that he didn't really *know* that he was causing the sleekits any harm. And it warmed him inside whenever he opened the door to Jonathan's apartment and saw his eyes light up at the round, brown baldo nuts, which he gobbled down roasted or raw or simmered in one of Tamara's makeshift (but delicious) soups.

Even so, it was not enough food. Never again, it seemed, would the people of Neverness know the comfort of one meal following the next, as day follows night. On the 5th of deep winter, a shipment of wheat berries from Darkmoon arrived at the Hollow Fields. For a few days the free restaurants opened and doled out the grain in carefully measured rations. Although Tamara gave her son as much of her ration as she could, he always seemed to want more—even if he always pretended to fullness before he had finished half his bowl and seemed more concerned with Tamara's hunger than his own. By the 12th, the flesh began melting from his small body like a candle slowly burning itself down. Sometimes he would sit on Danlo's lap for a long time listening to stories or trying to solve their riddle of how they might capture a beautiful bird; but just as often he would lie listlessly on one of the carpets as he held his empty belly and stared at the paintings on the wall.

One night, soon after Constancio had begun the first work on Danlo's face, Tamara took Danlo aside and told him, "I'm worried about Jonathan."

They were sitting together by the stove in Tamara's fireroom, all the while listening to Jonathan tossing and turning beneath the furs in the sleeping chamber. Danlo had his mask off, and he ran his fingers across his sore, reddened jaw. He looked at Tamara, at her gaunt but still beautiful face. "I am worried about him, too," he said. "And I am worried about you."

"I'm so hungry, Danlo. I never thought it could be so bad."

"I am sorry."

"I never really thought about it, food, you know—I always took it for granted, like water or air."

"Perhaps we should be thankful, then. It is said that thirst is even more terrible than hunger."

"How could anything be more terrible? Have you really looked at Jonathan these past few days? I'm afraid he's *dying.*"

Danlo, who was only too familiar with starvation, took Tamara's hand and said, "No, he is far from that. He is a strong child still with much life in him."

Somewhat irritably, for she was very hungry, Tamara pulled her hand away from him and waved it toward the other room. "What you really mean is that there's still a little something of him left to starve. But it's so little, really—sometimes it seems he's nothing but bright eyes and bones. *He's* so little, so terribly little, and I can't bear to see him suffer this way."

Danlo touched his tongue to the inside of his throbbing jaw, which Constancio had been working on in preparation for implanting huge new teeth. He tried to beam a smile toward Tamara, and he said, "It will not be much longer."

"What do you mean?" she asked, clearly alarmed.

"Only that soon the war will be over and there will be food again."

"But the war could go on for *years!*"

No, I will not let that happen, he thought. *I must end it all, and soon.*

"I think that things are coming to an end," he said. "But this will be only a kind of beginning, yes? Where all things are possible."

He closed his eyes then, and the trillions of separate flames inside each of his cells seemed to flare in a single direction, straight towards his heart. The light of this marvelous fire grew ever deeper and more brilliant until it shined like the sun.

"I can feel it beginning," he said. "I . . . can almost see it."

"Oh, Danlo—what are you talking about? The war? Do you really think that anything good could come out of this stupid war?"

"I know that it will."

"I'll never understand you. Your son is *dying.*" Tamara's jaw was trembling, and she swallowed again and again, perhaps trying to fight back her tears.

"He is not dying. I will not let him die."

"But he's so hungry!"

"We are all hungry, yes?"

"But most of us grow thinner, not thicker."

As Danlo sat looking at her, he was very aware of how his arms and legs beneath his kamelaika fairly rippled with thick, new muscles. Although he was still very lean, his chest and shoulders had been deepened so that he exuded all the power and vitality of a great white bear. His hands, too, were no longer the hands of a modern human being. So long and thick were his fingers, so massive his palm bones, that it seemed he could easily crush a man's skull merely by squeezing it to splinters.

"Truly, I have not starved as others have," he said. "But to eat while others go hungry, to *need* to eat—sometimes this is even harder, yes?"

He told her then of the terrible necessities of life among the Alaloi. Sometimes, once every hundred winters, when some disaster befell the shagshay herds and seals could not be found, meat would become so scarce that a whole tribe might face starvation. During these "hunger days," it became the duty of each hunter to eat in order to keep up his strength—otherwise he would soon grow too wasted to bring back food for the rest of the tribe. This need of the men to eat robbed food from the mouths of the women and children. Sometimes the weakest of them starved and died. Watching a young child's limbs turn to sticks while one's belly churned with fresh meat was said to be almost the worst agony that a man could ever know. But it was better, much better, than letting the whole tribe go over to the other side of day.

"I know you've brought all the food that you could," Tamara said. "And I know that you're doing what you're doing because you have to. I just wish I understood why."

"Would understanding make the hunger go away?"

"No, of course not. But if we're to starve to death, I'd at least like to know how you plan to bring Hanuman down."

"I will not let you die, Tamara."

"I *can't* die, you know, as long as Jonathan still lives."

"I . . . would do anything that I can so that you do not starve."

"Would you really?" So saying, she bent over and pulled a leather purse from beneath the rug. She opened it and shook out a handful of diamond disks. "Would you take these, then?"

"If you'd like," he said, as she poured the city disks into his hand. "But why?"

"I've heard that the wormrunners are selling fresh meat. If you should chance to find one of these wormrunners on the street, you'll need money."

"I see."

"It's just money, you know."

Danlo stared at the glittering disks in his hand and said, "I have never had any money of my own."

"From what I've heard, it should be enough to buy at least ten pounds."

"Ten pounds . . . of shagshay meat? Or snow tigers murdered from the air without a prayer for their spirits?"

"It's just meat, you know. It's already dead—stored in some wormrunner's cellar. You'll have done nothing to cause the animal's dying."

"Do you truly believe this?" he asked. "Isn't it the diamond coins of men such as I that cause the wormrunners to murder the animals?"

"But they're *my* coins, not yours," she said. "And the meat would be for me and Jonathan."

Suddenly, with a click of diamond against diamond, Danlo closed his fist. He said, "I will take your money, then. But I must think about this—I cannot promise that when the time comes, I will buy this meat."

Tamara looked off into the other room where Jonathan lay breathing heavily and occasionally moaning in his sleep. Then she looked back at Danlo and said, "I'd do anything to keep him from starving."

"And I have said that I will do what I can do. What I *can*, Tamara."

"I understand," she said. "How could I ever ask any more of you?"

"Do you know where these wormrunners with meat to sell might be found?"

"Pilar told me that her friend, Averil, bought some on the Serpentine just above the Winter Ring."

"That is a dangerous neighborhood."

She nodded her head. "I know. I've been afraid to go there after dark, but I think that's when the wormrunners make most of their trades."

"You, afraid? You used to skate anywhere in the City wearing your spikhaxo."

He was referring to the finger gun that she once wore built into a leather glove. The spikhaxo fired little darts tipped with naittare, a poison so deadly that it could reduce a strong man to a quivering wreck of a human being within seconds.

"Well," she said, "that was before the war—before I had Jonathan."

"I see."

"I was hoping that *you* might be willing to return home by way of the Serpentine some night.

"I . . . think that I would be willing."

"Thank you, Danlo. And if you *do* find one of these wormrunners, please be watchful. I'd want to die if anything were to happen to you."

It was two nights later, as Danlo was skating home along the Serpentine, that he found his wormrunner. Or rather, his wormrunner found him. Because it was very cold, he had stopped inside a warming pavilion to take advantage of the hot air jets blowing up from beneath the street in measured pulses. The restaurants along the great sliddery were all closed, as were most of the cafes and shops. Only a few hard men and women braved journeys this time of night, and few skaters passed him by. Although the Serpentine was usually well-lit, the cluster of flame globes above the warming pavilion had been broken, causing the orange ice and the nearby shops to be almost swallowed up in darkness. It was a place of shadows and shattered glass and warm sussing air. Despite the warmth, Danlo would not have remained long if a large man dressed in rich sable furs hadn't called out a greeting and skated straight up to him.

"It's a cold night, isn't it?" the man said. He had a thick blond beard and bloodshot blue eyes—Danlo caught sight of the wormrunner's rather handsome face as he stepped into the pavilion and used a flame light to ignite a pipe packed with brownish twists of seaweed. "Do you mind if I join you? Would you like to smoke a little toalache with me?"

"Thank you, no," Danlo said. "I do not smoke."

"That's too bad, then. It's a great pleasure in such hard times. And it eases the pain of an empty stomach."

Just then a cloud of grayish smoke billowed out from the wormrunner's pipe and mouth. Danlo stepped back a few feet, trying to find a space of fresh air. Although the pungence of the burning toalache was almost overpowering, Danlo smelled something that disturbed him even more. It was a fainter smell—but thick and deep and slightly sickening. It seemed to steam off the wormrunner's furs and beard and to stain his bloody breath. Danlo drew in a breath of his own, letting the terrible scent play through his nostrils. There came a moment, then, when he knew that the wormrunner had recently handled a quantity of meat; quite possibly, he thought, the wormrunner had secreted a part of some dead animal beneath his flowing furs.

"I remember when that place used to serve the best cultured carnig in the city," the wormrunner said as he pointed across the street at a restaurant with blue awnings and broken windows.

"And now it's closed—now it's almost impossible to find any kind of meat, even in the underground restaurants."

"Truly it is," Danlo said.

"Would *you* be interested in acquiring some meat?" the wormrunner asked, stepping closer to Danlo. He opened his furs, then, and drew out a lumpy thinskin the size of a large bloodfruit. "I've a good piece of fresh shagshay that I could sell to you."

Danlo looked down at the clear plastic wrapping and the dark red mass of meat that lay inside. He sniffed the air again. Although the meat didn't seem overly decayed, he didn't like the smell of it. There was something strange about its scent, something dark and deep that disquieted him and made his belly churn even as hot juices began spurting in his mouth.

"May I . . . see this meat?" Danlo asked.

"Of course," the wormrunner said, unwrapping the thinskin. "I wish I had more to show you, but it's been a busy night."

In the faint light of the one flame globe that still burned, Danlo looked at the meat that the wormrunner held in his hands. He had hoped that he might identify a thigh or perhaps shoulder joint—or anything that might tell him which part of the shagshay this meat had been cut from. But it was too dark to see much more than a bulging, shapeless wad of flesh.

"It's minced shagshay," the wormrunner said, almost apologetically. He looked at Danlo looking at the meat. And then, as a cold wind whooshed down the street, he began to look at Danlo strangely, and more closely, taking note of his tallness, appraising his huge shoulders and the massive muscles of his chest and arms. He looked for Danlo's eyes beneath his face mask, apparently trying to decide if he could trust Danlo with what he had to say next. "If you'd like more meat than this, or a finer cut, I keep an apartment near here."

For a long time Danlo stared at the meat and let its terrible quick essence pierce his nostrils and eat into his brain.

Never killing, he thought, *never harming another.*

"I . . . would like more meat," he suddenly said. He remembered Jonathan sitting on his lap and looking at him so trustfully with his bright, hungry eyes, and he said, "I would like to buy at least twenty pounds worth."

"So much, then? Do you have that much money?"

"How much will I need, then?"

For a while, they stood there in the warming pavilion discussing the cost of meat. Although Danlo had little experience in negotiating the price of anything, he knew enough not to tell this handsome-looking wormrunner how many city disks he kept in his pocket.

"Why don't you return with me to my apartment?" the wormrunner finally said. "That way you can choose your cut, and we can complete our negotiations there."

Danlo gazed at the wormrunner's eyes, all the while wondering if he meant to cheat him, or worse. The wormrunner smiled nicely, openly, warmly. Danlo sensed, then, that the wormrunner's main purpose was not robbery. Truly, the wormrunner sought profit, an exorbitant one, and perhaps this was all that Danlo had to fear.

Even so, he hesitated a moment, thinking, *There is something here that I do not see.*

"Why don't I wait while you bring it here?" he said.

"Twenty pounds of meat?" the wormrunner said. "No, no—I won't carry so much through the streets."

"This is a dangerous neighborhood, yes?"

Again, the wormrunner smiled and said, "I understand your reluctance—what we do is illegal and you don't know me. But there are many about here who do. I never have any trouble selling meat."

So saying, he folded up his lump of meat and put it back inside his furs. Then he glanced down the street toward the closed restaurant; he smiled, again quite nicely. Danlo turned that way, too, and he saw a man standing beneath the light of a flame globe. He had the look of an astrier: the sharp, arrogant face, the calculating eyes, the well-tended body covered in a splendid fur of rare white ermine, with matching hat and gloves. He seemed quite nervous, as any astrier would be in such a place at that time of night.

"Ah, one of my patrons," the wormrunner said. "Would you please excuse me while you decide what you want to do?"

He struck off down the street, then, leaving Danlo standing alone in the warming pavilion. Danlo watched him skate straight up to the astrier. He saw him bow and then lay his hand on the astrier's shoulder as if they were old friends. But the astrier seemed to loathe being touched by one of such low estate; he backed away from the wormrunner as from a rotting corpse, and looked down at the ice.

These are terrible times, even for the rich and proud, Danlo thought.

And then, from a distance of thirty yards, he watched the wormrunner open his cache of murdered meat and show it to the astrier. He saw the astrier wince as if he had been shown a still-throbbing heart ripped from a child's chest; he saw the wormrunner holding up four fingers as the astrier man shook his head and pointed toward the meat with only his fore and middle fingers. And now it was the wormrunner's turn to decline the astrier's offer. He sighed and then he held up three fingers; after a while, the astrier reluctantly inclined his head. With a smile splitting his broad, bearded face, the wormrunner wrapped up the meat and handed it to the astrier. Then he bowed and skated back toward the warming pavilion.

"It seems that everyone wants more meat tonight than I can carry," he told Danlo. "My patron has agreed to follow me back to my apartment. You're welcome to come too, if you wish."

"To bid against each other?"

"No, of course not," the wormrunner said, clearly offended. "I've more than enough meat for both of you. In any case, my patron and I have already agreed on our price."

"I see," Danlo said. And then, "But I saw no money exchange hands."

"Well, I wouldn't ask anyone to pay until he had received the meat."

"But I saw you give him the meat."

"Oh, I don't mean *that* meat," the wormrunner said, smiling. "That was just a little lagniappe to seal our agreement."

"I see."

"Perhaps you'll become my patron, too, and it will be my pleasure to bestow such gifts upon you."

"Perhaps," Danlo said.

"And now, why don't you accompany us back to my apartment? It's only a few blocks away."

Again, Danlo hesitated as he looked deeply into the wormrunner's glittering eyes. And then he said, "All right."

The wormrunner led Danlo back to the closed restaurant where the astrier man joined them. As they skated east toward the Merripen Green, the astrier hung back slightly, eyeing Danlo and his stained shagshay furs with open contempt. Near the North-South Glissade, they turned onto a little red street lined with closed shops and blocks of apartment buildings. Most of these blocks were deserted, but in the middle of one of them, a single open cafe attracted swarms of harijan, wormrunners, hibakusha and other dwellers of this dark neighborhood. Despite the absence of flame globes on the narrow streets (and despite the starved, sunken faces), the presence of all these people hurrying in and out of revolving doors and drinking their weak mint tea behind steamy windows recalled better times of small comforts and the reassuring habits of everyday life.

And then the wormrunner motioned for Danlo and the astrier man to follow him down a gliddery almost as dark as a path through the nighttime forest, and nothing about this lonely, wind-swept street reassured Danlo. The sounds of other skaters striking steel against ice quickly faded to faintness. Danlo heard the click-clack of his own skates, of course, and the astrier's and wormrun-ner's quicker rhythms, but little else. The moaning wind that blew down the street carried the far-off screaming of a hungry baby— or perhaps it was only the howling of one of the Merripen Green's snow cats getting ready to fight. The wind carried other things, too: biting particles of windblown snow and the smell of roasting meat. The smell of meat seemed everywhere to permeate the air, from the wormrunner's blood-stained blond beard to the astrier's furs. When the wormrunner stopped and opened the door to one of the buildings, the scent of raw flesh spilled out into the night.

"Here we are," the wormrunner said as he pushed into the hallway.

Reluctantly, the astrier man followed him inside, and so did Danlo. In this ill-lit hallway, lined with greasy old tiles, dust, dead leaves and other filth, they passed two other people, hibakusha with radiation-eaten faces and smiles of greeting calculated to please the wormrunner. Probably, Danlo thought, the wormrunner paid them to keep silent as to the illegal activities occurring in the building. That the wormrunner truly operated a butcher shop out of his apartment Danlo saw the moment the wormrunner opened the black, shatterwood door. After letting the astrier man go first, Danlo stepped across the threshold and fairly gasped at the sight that awaited him.

"As you can see," the wormrunner said, "we've plenty of meat."

In truth, the little apartment had been completely emptied of furniture and rugs and all other signs of domestic life. In place of these things were clary cases displaying various cuts of meat. Stacked neatly on a bed of snow inside one of the cases, great bloody slabs of what appeared to be shagshay steaks immediately caught Danlo's eye. He saw hunks of muscle and bone resembling loin roasts, and briskets, and other body parts. Pieces of what the wormrunner claimed to be seal meat filled half of one case, while in the case next to it, the hams of a musk-ox shone like brilliant ruby jewels. Something about all this meat disturbed him. It had a strange look to it, as if it had been molded into unusual shapes and injected with preservatives and dyes to brighten its color. It was really much too red, not at all like the meat of these blessed animals as Danlo remembered from his childhood. Perhaps, he thought, the wormrunner didn't know the proper way to dress meat or prepare it for cooking. Certainly the wormrunner would not have prayed for the animals' spirits on their journey across the frozen sea to the other side of day.

Nunkiyanima, Danlo silently whispered to himself, *mi alasharia la shantih. Pela Yaganima, Shakayanima, mi alasharia la, shantih, shantih.*

Next to the shuttered window, the astrier man stood looking down at a case containing long tubes of sausages and bloody bowls full of liver, lungs, sweetbreads, brains and other organ meats. Danlo wondered if he was really interested in all this offal or whether he would ask the wormrunner to wrap up several slabs of shagshay steaks. He wondered for himself how much the wormrunner might ask for twenty pounds of seal meat, which he remembered in all its fat and richness as the sweetest meat of all.

"Would you like a cup of tea?" the wormrunner asked the astrier. He motioned toward the kitchen. "I've a store of Summerworld gold that I can brew while you're deciding."

"Thank you, no," the astrier man said in a thin but cultivated voice. "I'm afraid I must hurry."

"And how about you?" the wormrunner asked, turning to Danlo. His bloodshot blue eyes drilled into Danlo's as if he were searching for something. "Why don't you remove your mask and furs and take some tea with me?"

"I . . . think that I will keep them on," Danlo said.

"Is it too cool for you in here? Would you like more heat?" the wormrunner asked, stepping over to Danlo. "Well, it *is* cool, of course, because we have to keep the meat cool. But I should think that someone as healthy-seeming as yourself wouldn't mind a little coolness."

As if to test his assessment of Danlo's physical state, he smiled and squeezed Danlo's arm in a too-friendly way. Then he patted Danlo's back and shoulder, pressing deeply with his fingers, and he said, "Some of us have escaped the starvation by doing what we have to do. You've done better than most, it seems. Such muscles you have—it must take a lot of meat to feed such a fine body as yours."

Danlo closed his eyes a moment as he remembered the terrible lightness of Jonathan's body, which he could almost feel pressing him close, his little heart beating next to his heart, fast and urgent like a bird's. In his helplessness, in his shame, he felt his eyes burning, and he said, "I would like to buy twenty pounds of meat, or more if that is possible."

"Of course—that amount of shagshay steaks will cost a thousand city disks."

"A . . . thousand disks?"

"It's the finest shagshay, the finest cut."

"And what could I buy for three hundred disks, then?"

"Is that all you have?"

"Could I take twenty pounds of seal meat for three hundred disks?"

"No—but I could sell you twelve pounds for that price."

"I . . . would like more meat than that."

"Of course, of course—I could give you twenty-five pounds of organ meats for four hundred disks."

"Liver, then? Heart meats and brains?"

"Well, that, of course, mixed with intestines and lungs—I make a special mixture for those seeking bargains."

"No," Danlo said. "I do not want offal."

The wormrunner smiled then as if he had suddenly remembered something. "We keep the uncut meat in my cold room. If you're willing to be your own butcher, I might find a twenty pound leg of shagshay that I could sell to you at a lower price."

"Truly? And do you have any larger cuts of seal meat, as well?"

"I'm not sure what we have left—why don't we see?" the wormrunner said. Then he noticed that the astrier man also seemed very interested in acquiring this cheaper meat. He bade the astrier to remove his furs, and he apologized, saying, "My cold room is a bit messy, and I wouldn't want you to stain such fine furs."

He led both of them toward the rear of the apartment where he opened the door to the cold room. He twisted the light key on the wall and motioned for the astrier man to go inside, followed by Danlo. A shock of cold air from the opened window enveloped Danlo as if he had been plunged into icy water. The fetor of old, rotting flesh made his belly clutch and almost heave. His leather boots slipped on the wooden floor, which was greasy with clots of hardened white fat and stained red with blood drippings. In one corner of the room stood a work table similarly spattered with gore, and in the other corner, two wooden tubs perhaps once used for bathing in hot water. But now they fairly overflowed with a slop of blood, bones, and pinkish flayed skin. He might have stared at these vessals of horror for a long time if another sight hadn't struck him with all the force of a lightning bolt. For there, along the far wall, pierced by great steel hooks bolted to the ceiling, hung the flayed, headless bodies of seven dead animals. They were all bright, red bands of meat and white fat and sawed bone. And they were neither shagshay bulls nor silk belly sows nor seals but a much more common animal apparently much easier to trap and kill.

No, it cannot be, Danlo thought. *Man must never be a hunter of other men.*

But they *were* men, or perhaps women, and Danlo saw this instantly, and he knew these hanging corpses for human beings with all the certainty that he knew his right arm was his own. He knew, too, all in a moment, that the wormrunner had lured them into this room much as he had Danlo, and had murdered them there. In truth, the slaughtering of a man could be more safely and efficiently accomplished in this cold room, for any sprays of blood along the wall would not warn off the wormrunner's patrons nor was there a danger that Danlo, in his death struggles, might fall against one of the meat cases and crack it beyond repair. Then, too, it would be hard work moving a man as large as Danlo without using the cold room's hoists and hooks. So Danlo understood the necessity of the wormrunner's ruse and the logic of his being murdered there. But he was not quite prepared to become a headless corpse himself.

He might have instantly turned and fled from the room if the wormrunner hadn't anticipated his actions. In truth, the wormrunner had anticipated almost everything about the slaying of his fellow man for meat. Just as Danlo looked up at the hanging corpses, in his moment of supreme horror and shock, the wormrunner leaped upon Danlo and grabbed him from behind. He was a very strong man, and he pinioned Danlo's arms between their thrashing bodies. This gave the astrier man his golden moment. The astrier—it suddenly became clear to Danlo that he wasn't really an astrier at all but only another wormrunner dressed to deceive prospective victims such as Danlo—had picked up a blood-encrusted axe from the work table. He came at Danlo with this axe. He swung it at his head. He might easily have murdered him, then, as he had many others.

It is not a difficult thing, to murder a man. Immobilize him for only a moment, and sharp steel can bite through even the thickest of skulls. And the wormrunner *should* have been able to keep Danlo from moving during this single moment; half a year earlier, he would have matched Danlo's strength limb against limb and held him still for the killing stroke. But he hadn't counted on the cuttings of Constancio of Alesar; he couldn't have known the terrible, quick strength of Danlo's newly sculpted body. Danlo scarcely knew himself. But even as the astrier swung his axe, Danlo felt a surge of blood swelling his muscles as if starfire itself were pouring through him. He suddenly remembered the skills that he had learned as a child wrestling with his brothers in the snow.

Almost without thought, then, he bent low and snapped his whole body forward like a catapult, heaving the astonished wormrunner over his back into the air. In a shock of breaking bones and curses, the wormrunner collided with the false astrier, knocking him to the greasy floor. It was something of a miracle that neither of them cut themselves against the axe, which flew out of the false astrier's hand and struck the wall. If Danlo had been a different kind of man, he would have picked up this axe and brained these two murderous cannibals. Instead, for what seemed forever, he froze like a snow hare and stared at them.

Never killing, he thought. *Even to save one's own life, never harming another.*

And then his moment of paralysis passed, and he turned to flee from this charnel house. He ran out into the street, pausing only to snap in his skate blades. He flew across the dark ice of unnamed glidderies for a long time, and he didn't care where he went. Although the wind blew keen and cold and he kept gasping for a clean breath of air, he couldn't get the taste of blood and death out of his mouth. His belly was a ball of acid pain and emptiness. He felt the coins that Tamara had given him pulling down like stone weights. He knew then that he would never be able to buy any meat, either to save his own blessed life or even Jonathan's. He knew that he would never be able to *look* at meat again. And never again would he look at men and women without seeing them as meat that might ease the agony of another's endless, burning hunger.

A PIECE OF BREAD

*"Truly, truly, I say to you, it was not Moses who gave
you the bread from heaven; my Father gives you the true
bread from heaven. For the bread of God is that which
comes down from heaven, and gives life to the world."*
—Jesus the Kristoman

For most of a day after his near-butchery at the wormrunners'
hands, Danlo brooded over the continued existence of these two
men. He knew that he should tell someone about the wormrunners' meat shop; the problem was who to tell and how he might
approach them. With the Order controlling only those parts of the
city bounded by the East-West Sliddery and the Long Glissade
(and of course the Hollow Fields), there was almost no rule of law
in the wild streets elsewhere. Danlo might have gone to Benjamin
Hur to ask for redress. But, most likely, Benjamin would have
sent a cadre of ringkeepers to exterminate the wormrunners, and
Danlo wasn't quite prepared to be the initiator of such violence.
But neither could he simply allow other unsuspecting clients to
walk into the wormrunners' apartment looking to buy a little
meat.

As it would happen, fate (and his own wild actions) solved this
agonizing dilemma. Unknown to him at the time, when he had left
the wormrunners writhing on the floor of the slaughter room, he
set off a chain of events that would shake the entire city. And it all
had begun like this: When he had thrown the murderous wormrunner into his friend, the crash of them hitting the floor and their
screams had shaken the entire building. One of the wormrunners'
neighbors, venturing out into the hall to investigate the noise, had
found the door to the apartment hanging open—and much more
besides.

The man probably had known that the wormrunners were selling meat from their apartment illegally. Perhaps he himself had
even bought a few tidbits from one of the meat cases in the outer
room. But he must have been stunned by what he found beyond

the doorway to the wormrunners' slaughter room, for he ran out into the hall crying out an alarm that roused others in other apartments. The wormrunners, dragging their broken bodies across the meat-slimed floor of their apartment, had managed to barricade their door. But a gang of their outraged neighbors had broken it down. They had swarmed the wormrunners and killed them with their bare hands. And then they had gone to other buildings throughout the neighborhood, crying out the word of the wormrunners' abomination. Gaining in numbers building by building, they had forced their way into three other similar meat shops and had slain the wormrunners whom they found cowering inside.

By the next morning, the whole district around the Merripen Green had errupted in a pogrom against the meatsellers; by nightfall, the riots had spread all the way to the Old City. Over the next few days, gangs of armed harijan and others killed hundreds of wormrunners, even those selling nothing worse than diamonds or stolen firestones. They shut down hundreds of meat shops, even those selling real muskox hams and shagshay steaks. Much of this meat they blindly cast into great bonfires ignited from faggots of shatterwood. They cast the bodies of the dead wormrunners and their poor butchered victims into these infernos as well. All through the earliest part of deep winter, a dark, greasy smoke filled the air, and the streets of the city from the Hofgarten to the Ashtoreth District reeked with the smell of burning flesh. Only later, as the starvation worsened, would the people of Neverness realize how much good food had gone up in flames.

It was during this time of fire and midnight executions that Danlo began the final sculpting of his face. Constancio implanted huge, new teeth into Danlo's jawbone, and he thickened the bone all around Danlo's eyes. He flattened out his proud nose, paying special attention to the muscles of the nostrils so that Danlo might be able to close his airways against the cold at will. By the fifteenth of deep winter, Danlo no longer recognized himself. And then Constancio did the delicate work on his vocal cords and eyes. Mallory Ringess had spoken in a bright, bold baritone not easy to duplicate. Three times Constancio had to cut and recut all through Danlo's larynx to get the timbre of his voice just right.

The eyes proved even more difficult to sculpt. Constancio had considered three options for transforming these windows to Danlo's soul: first, he might have implanted bacterial colonies into Danlo's irises to change their color; second, he might have cloned and grown for Danlo whole new organs of sight; and third, he might simply have shaped artificial corneas to cover Danlo's eyes and brighten them from a deep and liquid blue to the piercing blue eyes of Mallory Ringess. It was this last option that Constancio chose, but he kept having trouble with the color. No matter how carefully he matched the blue to the hologram of Mallory Ringess, every time he lifted the artificial corneas onto Danlo's eyes he looked at Danlo in frustration and cursed.

"There's something strange about your eyes," he told Danlo after he had tried on the fourteenth pair of corneas. "The light— too bright, always too bright. Mallory Ringess had eyes that pierced like a laser, but no matter what I do, yours blaze like a star."

Constancio, who was not usually given to mysticisms, attributed this brightness to some inner quality of Danlo's soul that shined through his eyes. He looked down at the gleaming artificial corneas that he held in the palm of his hand, and he shook his head.

"You're a strange man," he said. "And I—I am who I am because I've always achieved perfection in my sculptings. Perhaps we should grow you new eyes and see what you look like after they're implanted."

"But that would take many days, yes?"

"Of course—but I've promised that you shall look exactly like Mallory Ringess."

"Perhaps Mallory Ringess, if he were to return to the city today, would not look exactly as he did when you made your holograms of him."

Danlo, of course, was by now very familiar with the holograms of his father, for he had been studying them the last thirty days in order to be able to mime the patterns of his speech, as well as his facial expressions and mannerisms.

"It's your choice, you know," Constancio said, shrugging his shoulders.

Danlo reached out to touch the artificial corneas, which looked like tiny blue cups and were almost as soft as the tissues of his own tongue. He said, "I have decided, then."

"Very well," Constancio said. "I'll seal them today."

And so Constancio performed the last of the surgeries for which Danlo had contracted. The artificial corneas covering Danlo's eyes could easily be removed by another cutter—or just as easily be left in place for the rest of Danlo's life. When Constancio had finished sealing the artificial tissues to the real corneas curving over Danlo's pupils and irises, he invited Danlo to remove his clothes and to stand naked before a mirror that he brought into his cutting chamber.

"Ecce homo," he said. "Behold the man that I have made."

And Danlo, gazing out through eyes that were the same deep blue eyes he had always known and yet appeared quite differently, beheld an astonishing sight. There stood a great bear of a man, an Alaloi hunter covered in thick black hair almost as dense as fur. His arms were as thick as clubs; his legs were like tree trunks drawing strength from the earth. And his face. His massive jaw and great jutting browridges suggested granite cut from mountains; his eyes were twin chunks of blue ice reflecting the light of the sun. In truth, it was a savage, primitive face out of memory and time, and frightening to look upon, but it bore also a great sensitivity and intelligence. Once, Mallory Ringess had worn such a face. And now Danlo, staring into the mirror, marvelled that the face of his father had become his own.

"I am he," Danlo said in a voice that sounded strange to him. "Truly, I look almost exactly like him, don't I?"

"There's not another cutter in the city that could have done what I've done," Constancio said. And then he pointed between Danlo's legs at his membrum, at the blue and red scars running along the shaft. "Of course, the cutter who made these sculpted clumsily—if you'd like, I could redo them so that the pattern is more evenly spaced."

"Thank you, no," Danlo said. He didn't tell him that it was his own grandfather, Leopold Soli himself, who had cut these scars during his passage to manhood. Nor did he recount how the great Soli had died before Danlo had completed his passage.

"Then we are finished, aren't we?" Constancio said. "I believe the contract has been completed."

"Yes," Danlo said, putting on his clothes. Although the white shagshay fur still fit him, he had had to acquire a new kamelaika and boots to accommodate his thick new limbs.

"Very well," Constancio said, and he led him downstairs through his richly decorated house to the door. "Then we should say farewell. I don't expect I'll see you again—unless you wish to be changed back into your old self or some other form."

"I . . . am happy with this one," Danlo said, making a fist and feeling the great strength of his forearm flow down into his hand.

"I understand. Though I confess it's still a mystery why you should choose to look precisely like Mallory Ringess."

"But you will keep the wondering about this mystery to your-self, yes?"

"Of course, of course. You're entitled to your secrets—you've paid me almost enough to glue my own lips closed."

"And do you remember that this payment is forfeit if you should tell anyone about the sculpting?"

"Of course I remember." Constancio pointed into his sun room, which opened off the hallway. There, set on a black shat-terwood stand, gleamed the diamond scryer's sphere that had once belonged to Danlo's mother. "It's a beautiful thing, isn't it? Beautiful, beautiful."

"Yes, truly it is."

"Farewell, then, Danlo of Kweitkel."

"Farewell, Constancio of Alesar."

The two men bowed to each other, and then Danlo made his way down Constancio's walk, through his gate and out into the street. As always he kept his mask securely fastened. In truth, he skated the streets with every nerve fiber of every sense burning for signs of danger. He prayed that he might finish the last of his preparations before some inevitable encounter exposed him as a mime of Mallory wi Soli Ringess.

And then later that night something happened that threatened to undo his entire plan—and all that was most precious to him in life. As he sat with Tamara and Jonathan in their fireroom, drink-ing a weak green tea and telling stories, he tried to think how he might say goodbye to them. According to his habit, Jonathan had nestled comfortably on his lap; Tamara knelt by the stove roasting a single skewer of baldo nuts, which was all they had to eat. With his dark, sad eyes, Jonathan stared at these nine nuts as if nothing else in all the world could possibly interest him. But when Danlo finished telling of the hunter who talked with the thallow, Jona-than looked up towards his face mask and said, "I like that story, Father."

Danlo smiled because it pleased him to be addressed this way. Ten days ago, all of his own, Jonathan had begun calling him Father, and neither Danlo nor Tamara had the heart to continue the fiction that his father was a pilot lost among the stars. "I like that story, too," Danlo said.

"And I like the way you tell it—the way you make the sound of a thallow. How do you do that?"

"By listening to the thallows speaking to each other," Danlo said. "And by trying to speak to them."

"Your voice sounds different," Jonathan observed. "Is that from calling out like a thallow?"

"My voice, my blessed voice," Danlo said, trading looks with Tamara.

And then, as Tamara's haggard eyes captured all of Danlo's attention, Jonathan did an astonishing thing. Although he was terribly weak with hunger, he reached out with all the speed of a striking serpent and pulled the mask up over Danlo's head. But where Tamara gasped to see the changes cut into Danlo's flesh and almost dropped her skewer of nuts, Jonathan only stared at him and asked, "Why are you wearing a new face, Father?"

"You . . . know that it is I, then?"

"But who else could you be?"

"But you said that my voice sounds different."

"Well, *all* of you is really different, but you're still you, aren't you?"

"Truly I am."

"All of you looks different except your eyes."

"My . . . eyes?"

"Well, they look different, too—they're too blue, like thallow eggs. But they *look* the same. I mean, the way you look at me, the way you look at Momma, at everything—it's all the same."

"I see."

"You once told me that the stars were the eyes of the Old Ones who died. Your eyes are like that, like stars."

"Truly?"

"You know, the way it doesn't matter if it's a hazy night or the Golden Ring colors the sky gold, the stars shine through always just the same."

Again Danlo smiled because Jonathan always said the most astonishing things.

"You have beautiful eyes, Father."

"Thank you. So do you."

"But the rest of your face—why do you want to look like an Alaloi?"

"You know about the Alaloi, then?"

"Of course I do—haven't you been telling me stories about them?"

"Yes, but I have not *told* you that they were Alaloi stories."

"What's it like to be an Alaloi?" Jonathan wondered. "Pilar said that they live in caves and hunt real animals for meat. They must be like animals, to kill animals."

While Tamara brought over the roasted nuts on a plate, Danlo explained to Jonathan about the Alaloi. He told him that the Alaloi were truly human beings—in some ways more human than the men and women who dwelt safely in their heated apartments in cities such as Neverness and never even thought about the great chain of being upon which their very lives depended. All life, Danlo said, lived off of other life. The krill of the oceans ate the plankton, and the whales ate the krill, but over time all life evolved and grew stronger.

"If you look at it deeply enough, life is always savage and cruel," Danlo said. "What makes the Alaloi different from us is only that they have chosen to live closer to the cruelty and not look away."

"Then they aren't really like animals, are they?"

"Truly, they *are* animals, as are we. But they are also something more. What makes human beings truly human is this moreness."

"You told me that you would never kill or harm an animal just to eat," Jonathan said. "Is this what it means to be more?"

"Yes, partly—I believe that it is," Danlo said.

"Then are you more human than the Alaloi?"

"No, not more human. Only more . . . civilized."

Despite his great hunger, Jonathan slowly chewed a baldo nut as he had been taught, then observed, "But you eat baldo nuts."

In truth, that evening Danlo had given all his nuts to Jonathan, as had Tamara.

"Well, I still have to eat something, don't I?"

"But you're *not* eating, Father." Jonathan looked at Tamara kneeling beside him and said, "Aren't you hungry, Momma?"

"I had something earlier while you were with Pilar," Tamara lied. "Now please do eat before your food grows cold."

For a while, Jonathan ate his nuts even as he remained sitting on Danlo's lap. To Danlo, brushing the hair away from Jonathan's face, it seemed that his head was too large for his body, even with his belly ballooning out below the sunken chest in starvation. His skin felt too hot, too, as if he had another fever. But for all Jonathan's privation, Danlo told himself that his son was still strong. And then Jonathan said something that changed his mind and almost caused him to abandon his plan to impersonate Mallory Ringess.

"I'm still hungry," Jonathan admitted after finishing the last nut. He looked at Danlo as if in contemplation of all that he had told him that night. "I can feel my body eating itself. And it hurts, Father—why does it have to hurt so much?"

There came a moment, then, in looking into Jonathan's dark, trusting eyes, that protecting his life became infinitely more important than his plan to bring down Hanuman, more important even than saving the lives of everyone in the world or on the many worlds of the universe itself.

He might truly die, Danlo thought. *He still might die.*

Even if Danlo were to unmask himself that very night, perhaps announcing himself like God at the door to Hanuman's cathedral, Jonathan might continue to grow weaker and weaker as he starved. Danlo, as Mallory Ringess, might indeed cast down Hanuman as Lord of the Way of Ringess and bring an end to the war—only to find that it might take several tendays to restore the food shipments to the city. And in that time, Jonathan very well might sicken beyond hope and go over to the other side of day.

But I cannot let him die.

And so Danlo did not complete his final preparations to mime a god that night, nor the next day, nor even the next. Instead, he spent these precious hours hunting through the City Wild for any kind of food that he could find. Even as the Fellowship's fleet stole among the Fallaways from Karanatha to Veda Luz, maneuvering to fight one last battle, and even as the gods themselves hammered the heavens with their cosmic weapons of war, Danlo gathered frozen yu berries and hacked off pieces of teartree bark which might be brewed into tea or pounded into a paste and eaten. He searched for new sleekit mounds as well. But the recent storms had covered the woods with a thick fur of new snow, making his quest almost impossible. Even though he searched the drifts from the Fravashi District to the Zoo, (and even though he raided one mound with all the cunning and rapaciousness of a wolverine), his labors yielded no more than a few handfuls of nuts. And still it was not enough food. And still, hour by hour it seemed, Jonathan grew weaker.

And so twice, on two bitterly cold nights with the first hint of the Serpent's Breath blowing in from the north, Danlo used his sharp flint spearpoint to open his veins and let a little blood flow into Tamara's teapot. Although not as rich as seal blood, this red elixir of life had been brightened by his lungs and moved by his heart through every part of his body. There was strength in it, as there was sweetness and vitamins in the yu berries that he crushed into the pot as well. A few spoonfuls of teartree paste completed the recipe for blood tea, which Danlo brewed and poured for Jonathan into a little blue cup. Jonathan might have sustained himself on such a power food almost forever, but Danlo could not continue to let his own blood without enfeebling himself to the point of coma and death.

Once, in a near-delirium of weakness and love, he considered sawing off his own arm for food with which to feed Jonathan. He considered killing himself outright, too, and he might have opened his throat artery but for his doubt as to Tamara's will to cut him up and cook him into one of her stews. He realized then that his entire hope for the future had come to shine upon Jonathan like the light of a single star. It was the greatest agony of his life that as he watched Jonathan grow thinner and thinner and fade, the future faded as well and grew ever more tenuous and dim.

One night, after Jonathan had gone to bed, Danlo sat talking with Tamara over cups of hot water. The last of their tea had run out, along with all their food. It suddenly seemed that there wasn't a crust of bread left in the entire city. Tamara hadn't eaten anything for a day, nor had Danlo for two. Both of them were so weak with hunger that they could hardly hold up their heads, let alone hold a meaningful conversation. Danlo's belly hurt, and his wrists where he had cut them. In truth, his whole body still burned with the torment of Constancio's surgeries and the fire of the ekkana drug. And perhaps worst of all was the old pain in his head that flared into a flame whenever he thought about his starving son.

"I do not know what to do," Danlo said, rubbing his chest.

"Perhaps you should go ahead with your plan." Tamara, upon the first sight of Danlo's face after Jonathan had pulled off his mask, had guessed the whole of his plan to mime Mallory Ringess. Almost every night since then, they had discussed what Danlo might do once he announced himself as a man who had become a god. "What else *can* you do?"

"I do not want to leave you alone."

"We'll be all right. We have Pilar and Andreas."

"But you have no food."

"Oh, but no one does—there's not even any meat left to buy from the wormrunners."

"I . . . did not know that any wormrunners had survived the riots."

"Few enough, it seems," Tamara said. "I think they'd be afraid to sell meat—or anything else—even if they had it."

"The poor wormrunners—I am sorry for what happened to them."

At this, Tamara shrugged her shoulders and said, "I've heard that the factories will soon begin harvesting food again."

"But this could be a rumor, yes? Only a rumor that Hanuman has begun."

"Well, I'm sure he doesn't want everyone to lose hope."

"I am sure of this, too," he said. "And I am sure that because of the desperation here, he will press for battle too soon, possibly to the disadvantage of the Ringist fleet."

"Then perhaps it would be best if you waited to announce yourself until after this dreadful battle."

"I cannot do that."

"But why?"

"Because we might lose the battle," he said. "And because if there is anything that I can do, I must not let this battle happen."

"But you—"

"Then, too, Jonathan is starving, and that is another reason that I cannot wait. And you, too, Tamara—almost everyone."

"But I still don't see what you can do about that other than carrying through with your plan."

For a long time, Danlo just sat there on Tamara's carpet, staring at the paintings on the wall. He had his spearpoint at hand, the one that he had used to cut his veins. With this long, symmetrical feather of flint, he tapped the back of his huge new knuckles. If he had been a careless man, the slightest touch of the spearpoint's murderously sharp edge would have left a line of blood marking his skin. But he was not careless. He tapped and tapped, stone against bone, in time with the quick, urgent beats of his heart. And then, after what seemed an eternity of contemplation and remembrance, he said, "There might be one thing that I could do."

"What, then?"

"I . . . could hunt."

Tamara looked at him as if he had just told her that he could fly through space to Simoom without his lightship and return bearing a basket of bread.

"Oh, Danlo, what are you saying?"

"I could make a harpoon and go out onto the sea to hunt seals."

"I don't believe what you're saying. Your vow—"

"This one time, I could break my vow."

"But you told me that it's better to die yourself than ever to kill."

"Yes, but I am not sure that it is better to watch my son die than to kill. Truly, nothing could be worse than watching him die. Or you.''

"But could you really *kill* a seal?"

"I . . . do not know. I could try, couldn't I?"

"But when would you go?"

"The day after tomorrow," he said. "I could make the harpoon tomorrow and leave the next day."

But Danlo didn't leave two days later, nor the day after that. Although he quickly fashioned a harpoon from a piece of walrus ivory and a shatterwood sapling that he cut, he couldn't quite bring himself to venture forth when the time came. He persuaded himself that he should search the city one last time before willfully killing a beautiful animal. And so he skated from the Ashtoreth District to the Bell, looking for an open restaurant, even an underground one selling dubious dishes. He approached the autists in the Merripen Green to see if they might have anything to share. But it seemed that Tamara was right, that Neverness was as barren of food as an ice desert. He thought to explore the private houses of the Fravashi District, perhaps even daring to knock at the door to Old Father's house itself. But when he returned to Tamara's apartment that evening, a new disaster caused him to abandon that plan.

"Jonathan, Jonathan," he said immediately upon opening the door. For there, in the fireroom, Tamara sat with Jonathan on her lap, soaking his feet in a bowl of warm water. He looked at Danlo and weakly smiled a greeting. Although obviously in great pain, he stared and stared as if he no longer cared how much it all might hurt. But Tamara had more than enough concern for both of them. Her lips were tight and almost bloodless with fear; her eyes sought out Danlo's as if to ask why God would want to visit such cruelties on an innocent child.

Without bothering to remove his mask or furs, Danlo crossed the room and plunged his hand into the water. He felt Jonathan's feet down near the toes; the skin was cold as ice and the muscles underneath as hard as frozen meat.

"What happened?" he asked.

And so Tamara told him about the unfortunate events of the day. That morning she had gone to the Courtesan's Conservatory just south of the Street of Embassies to beg for a little food. She had left Jonathan with Pilar and Andreas; with the air over the city having fallen almost dead cold, they had planned to stay inside doing nothing more strenuous than telling stories. But around midmorning a neighbor had knocked on Pilar's door to tell of a food shipment to be distributed later at the Winter Ring. And so Pilar had wrapped the children in their furs and joined the swarms of starving people who crowded this expansive circle of ice. They had waited almost motionless in the cold for hours along with thousands of others.

But no food had ever arrived to be distributed; the rumor proved false. And so the manswarms—many of them harijan— had rioted. In this great crush of humanity going mad, Pilar had barely been able to keep a hold on Andreas. As Pilar later told Tamara, with much weeping and blame of herself, Jonathan had become separated. Although she and Andreas had searched the surrounding district until night came, they had not been able to find him. She hadn't thought that Jonathan had been one of the hundreds trampled and skived to death with sharp skate blades for she had searched the mounds of corpses around the Winter Ring to no avail. Finally, with the cold of night threatening to freeze their faces and feet, they had returned to tell Tamara the terrible news that her son was lost, perhaps wandering the streets alone.

Tamara's first impulse, of course, had been to throw on her fur and go out looking for Jonathan. But even as Tamara was lacing her skates, Jonathan had miraculously showed up at the door. Somehow he had managed to find his way home. But he was shivering with the first touch of hypothermia, and the tips of his nose and ears had fallen white with frostbite. And far worse, his feet had frozen almost all the way up to his ankles.

"It must have been hard for you to skate with your feet so cold," Danlo told Jonathan as he touched his forehead. The boy's ears and nose were red, and his skin quite warm with the flush of restored circulation. Danlo, who had once frozen his feet, too, knew that as the blood began flowing again through Jonathan's veins, he would feel an agony of burning as if his toes had been plunged into boiling water. "You are very brave."

Jonathan looked at him as if to say, "Thank you, Father." But his eyes had fallen glassy with his suffering, and for the moment he seemed to have lost the power of speech.

"It would be better," Danlo said to Tamara, "if a cryologist or cutter thawed his toes."

"Of course it would," Tamara said. "But there's a five day wait to see the cryologists, and neither they nor the cutters have any drugs left anyway. What else could I do?"

"Nothing, then," Danlo said gently. "You are doing all you can."

Tamara looked at him for a long time, and it seemed that she very badly wanted to break down and weep.

"I don't want to go to a cutter," Jonathan suddenly said. "I want to stay here with Momma."

"It's all right, I won't take you anywhere," Tamara said, running her fingers through his thick black hair.

"And I want you to stay, too," Jonathan said to Danlo. "Won't you please stay, Father?"

Much later, after they had finished thawing Jonathan's toes and put him to bed (he had passed into unconsciousness listening to Danlo play his shakuhachi), Danlo took Tamara aside and said, "There is something that I must tell you about frostbite."

"What is it, then?"

"Jonathan's toes were frozen very deep. Without drugs, it might be impossible for even the best cryologist to repair the damaged tissues."

"What are you saying?"

Danlo stood with Tamara in the corner of the fireroom, and he gently gripped her shoulder with his huge new hand. "It might be impossible to save his toes, you know. They were so—"

"No, I don't want to hear this," Tamara almost shouted as she broke away from him. She shook her head and stared down at the blazing stove. "I shouldn't have left him with Pilar today. Really, I shouldn't."

"But what else could you have done?" he asked.

"I don't know," she said. "I don't know what to do now— Oh, Danlo, what are we going to *do?*"

At last, as she touched eyes with Danlo and he touched her face, she began to sob. And then they held each other forehead pressing forehead, and after a while, he couldn't tell which tears were hers and which were his own.

"You did what you had to do," Danlo whispered. "And now I must, too."

"Please don't tell me that you're thinking of leaving now."

"I am sorry."

"But this really isn't the time. It's much too cold outside, and Jonathan will need you now more than ever."

"But he will need his strength most of all. It will be almost impossible for him to face what is to come without food."

"But I *have* food," Tamara suddenly said. She moved over to a cupboard, which she opened. She drew out a steel basket covered with a white cloth and showed it to Danlo. "Look."

Danlo gently peeled back the cloth to reveal three golden

loaves of bread. Nearly half of one loaf had been sliced off, obviously eaten by Tamara and Jonathan earlier. But the other loaves were thick and crusty and smelled as if they had been freshly baked.

"One of my former sisters at the Conservatory gave them to me," Tamara said. "They still have food there, though I think this might be the last of it."

"She must have loved you very much to give you this," Danlo said. "But it will not last very long."

"I know," Tamara finally admitted. "I know."

"Jonathan will need something more sustaining than a little bread if he is to regain his strength. Which is why I have decided to hunt tomorrow."

"So soon, then?"

"I am afraid that I have waited too long. If only I had not waited these past days, Pilar might not have needed to take Jonathan out looking for food."

"But you mustn't blame yourself. How could you have known what would happen?"

How could I have known?

In truth, he *had* known that he shouldn't have waited. Perhaps he had sensed the future. Certainly he had sensed Jonathan's deteriorating condition, that his need for food was becoming immediate and critical. A deep voice, deeper than his belly or brain, perhaps as deep as the atoms spinning in his blood, had whispered that he must go out to hunt. Why hadn't he paid attention to this voice? Why hadn't he immediately followed this urgent whispering? Once, it had been his dream to become an asarya, a truly human being who might have the courage and compassion to say yes to all things. But he had always known that he must look at deep reality as it truly was before he could affirm it. And to behold the world through shimmering new eyes, he must first wake up and learn how to see. Why, he wondered, had he looked away from the truth of Jonathan's suffering? Why hadn't he simply picked up his harpoon at the first chance and hurried off into the wild to hunt his seal?

Because it is wrong to kill, he thought. And then, as he stared at Tamara's soft, waiting eyes, came the deeper voice like the call of the snowy owl or the whispering of the wind: *Because I am afraid.*

"Find some drugs for Jonathan," he told her. "Sell your pearl, if you must."

"All right, then," she said, nodding her head.

"I must say goodbye now. Please tell Jonathan that I will return soon."

"But how soon?"

"Two or three days, perhaps five—I do not know."

Tamara bent over and removed one of the whole loaves of bread from the basket. She held it toward him and said, "Please take this."

"No," he said softly, "I cannot."

"But you'll need all your strength if you're to hunt seals. You can't go without eating for five more days."

"Neither can Jonathan. Or you."

"But there might be a harvest from the food factories. Or a shipment might get through. Or—"

"Or you might have nothing more than this bread until I return."

"But without this bread, you might not return with any meat. If you're so hungry that you stumble into a crevasse or can't wait out a storm, you might not return at all."

"I will be all right."

"But if you're *not* all right, we won't be either. Didn't you once say that a hunter sometimes must eat the best food for the good of the tribe?"

"Yes—sometimes the few must die so that the tribe will live. But you and Jonathan are my tribe now, my whole tribe. If you should die, there would be no point to my hunting a seal."

"I understand," Tamara said. Then she broke off the end of one of the loaves and handed it to him. "But please take this—you should have *something* in you before you leave."

"If you'd like," Danlo said, putting the bread into the pocket of his kamelaika. "Thank you."

He embraced her, and put on his face mask and furs. He went out onto the streets where he was so cold that he could barely stand it. All the way back to his snow house beneath fir trees in the City Wild, his mouth watered and his belly groaned as he thought about this bread. Tomorrow early in the morning, he would make a quick breakfast of it. And then, with a little food energy brightening his veins—no less Tamara's love—he would ski out onto the ice of the sea to harpoon a beautiful animal.

THE HUNT

In the very earliest time,
When both people and animals lived on earth,
A person could become an animal if he wanted to
And an animal could become a human being.
Sometimes they were people
And sometimes animals
And there was no difference.
All spoke the same language.
That was the time when words were like magic.
The human mind had mysterious powers.
A word spoken by chance
Might have strange consequences.
It would suddenly come alive
And what people wanted to happen could happen—
All you had to do was say it.
Nobody can explain this;
That's the way it was.

—after Nalungiaq

At the edge of the city, where the sea meets the rocky shore, lies a collection of stone huts, wooden docks and great clary hangars known as the Quay. In good times—indeed, in all the days since the founding of Neverness except the Dark Year—the Quay had always been a place of bustle and excitement, where men and women came to borrow windjammers, catamarans, ice schooners and other craft with which to venture out onto the sea. During the time of Goshevan of Summerworld a few generations earlier, the sport of dog-sledding had become popular, and so the kennels and sled runs had been added to the north of the main docks. Even in deep winter, there were always those wild spirits who relished swift motion over ice and snow and the bite of cold wind in their faces. Some loved being pulled along at great speed by a color-fully rigged schooner while others preferred the yapping and whines of a team of sled dogs. And so almost every morning for centuries, when the sea froze hard and fast, the people of the city had crowded the mooring slips and sled runs hoping to take a bit of pleasure for the day.

The war, however, had changed everything. As Danlo saw in the early light when he skated nearer the Quay, many of the hangars had been melted and blackened by bombs, perhaps in some raid of Benjamin Hur and his ringkeepers. All the jammers and many of the schooners had long since been misappropriated by the wormrunners using them to bring back their poached animals from the northern part of Neverness Island. The remaining ice boats sat frozen in their mooring ships, shagged with layers of snow. As for the dog sleds, Danlo found many of them intact inside one of the larger stone huts. They were neatly set out in rows, dozens of wooden frames with attached leather harnesses. And the wood was all polished, the runners waxed, the leather traces in good repair. But there were no dogs. Although Danlo searched each of the kennels one by one, it seemed that other raids by hungry people must have carried away the dogs to the cooking pots of the city's apartments and underground restaurants.

This did not surprise him. In truth, he was only too happy to find usable sleds, for he had feared that he might have to make one of his own from pieces of wood scavenged from the forest and various materials that he might find in the shops near the Serpentine. That he would need *some* sort of vehicle for his private quest he had known from the moment that he had announced his intention to hunt. It would be hard enough for him to carry much farther the carving flints, knives, sleeping furs, ice saw, stove, spare clothing, and all the other things that he had stowed that morning into a large nylon pack. And it would be almost impossible for him to bring back a seal without a sled with which to pull it. A fully grown seal, as he remembered, weighed hundreds of pounds, and even he in his powerful new body would not have the strength to carry one more than a few yards.

And so he chose one of the smaller sleds and dragged it outside into the cold salt air. He tied his pack and harpoon securely to the center of the sled; his bear spear, the one that he had recently made from his old flint spearpoint and a new shatterwood sapling, he rigged more loosely in a kind of a sheath. He wanted to be able to grab it quickly at need should some wandering ice bear chance upon him. He still didn't know if he could kill *any* animal, much less a great bear with its soulful eyes and great cunning brain. But with a single spear he might transform himself from a nearly helpless prey animal into a predator that even the Old White Great Ones (or the *Uryu Kweitil Onsu* as he had used to call the mightiest of bears) might fear.

It did not take him long to cut the harness and rig it so that it fit neatly over his shoulders and chest. His parka, made of silky white shagshay fur many inches thick, would act as a pad so that the leather traces didn't cut into his flesh. Although it would constrain him to be thus attached to the sled as if he were a dog, he did not think that it would be truly hard work pulling it unless he managed to kill one or more seals. Then the wooden frame would groan under the weight of dead muscle and bone. Then the steel runners might slice deeply into the snow and freeze fast if he should pause too long to catch his breath. But until that time the sledding shouldn't be too difficult. With a ski pole working in either hand, all he had to do was to lean forward against the harness and slide one ski ahead of the other, over and over, always pulling his light load over the smooth and hard-packed snow.

If he were lucky—if the weather held clear and the snow remained fast and good—he might cover more than thirty miles in a single day. He hoped that he might find the seals of the deep ocean close-in to Neverness Island, for he feared that he would not have the strength for much more than a couple of days of such work, not unless he chanced upon a little food with which to fire his starving body. And if he journeyed *too* far to the west with nothing to eat and found no seals (or found that he lacked the will to take up his harpoon and kill one), his situation would become critical. He might easily collapse in exhaustion, too weak to return to Neverness. Then, spear or no spear, the ice bears would sniff him out and slay him. Or the murderous west wind would fall over him like a great, cold hand crushing him to the ice. Then at last he would return to the world that had given him birth, and his plans and dreams for a golden future would come to an end out on the bitter, frozen sea.

It was very cold when he made his first ski stroke and pulled the sled smoothly over the packed snow. *All journeys begin with the first step,* he thought. And then he remembered the coda to this saying supplied by Justine the Wise: *Unless you can fly.* In the loneliness of the deserted docks, with the dead sails of the ice schooners flapping in the wind, he wished for wings so that he might simply fly over the ice with all the freedom of a thallow. He wished, too, that he might descry a dead seal lying upon the ice and magically transport it back to Neverness. But he knew that *this* journey would not be so easy. In truth, he sensed that nothing about this hunting of seals would be simple or easy. And so as he faced the dark, blue western sky and slid one ski ahead of the other, he prayed for all the courage and strength of life, which was the only true magic there was.

He travelled due west, straight into the wild. With every stroke over the cold squeaking snow, the great circle of the world opened before him and drew him closer to its center. He stood upon the frozen ocean, and everywhere he looked, he saw this ocean. In the sky above him, in the immense cobalt dome of the heavens, wispy clouds called *sirateth* lay like a white fur over the still-dark horizon. What were clouds, he wondered, if not the ocean evaporated and condensed out into the air? Behind him, in the light of the rising sun, the mountains of Neverness Island blurred into a white and indigo massif edged in flame red. The white, of course, was snow, and what was snow if not the ocean's water crystallized into lovely, six-pointed flakes and blown to the four points of the world? As the early morning wind blew soft and steady and the spindrift snow swirled over the ice in beautiful patterns, he had much time to reflect upon the great circle of water and the world, which was nothing less than the circle of life itself.

Terrible beauty.

All his life, it seemed, ever since he could remember, he had marveled at these two aspects of life, the terrible and the beautiful. The beautiful, the *halla* half of the world, lay ever before him waiting for him to reach out with his eyes and simply behold. There was a deep beauty in the way that the sun touched the sea and caused the ice to glow red like heated copper, even though the air was almost dead cold. Beautiful, too, were the iceblooms, the colonies of algae coloring the snow plum and purple and brightening to amethyst as the sun rose higher and the world began to sparkle as if made of billions of tiny jewels. By mid-morning, the sky began to show the yellowish reflection of light off the ice; these iceblinks, or *shonashin* as he had known them in his childhood, had been named because they shimmered so beautifully. It seemed to him, in looking from heaven to earth, that the world was always trying to arrange itself so that he might marvel at its beauty. But the world had other purposes, too, and with every mile that he skied away from Neverness over the endless sea, he became more aware of the terrible nature of life, the *shaida,* the way that the wind and snow and ice seemed always ready to grab him up with their cold, killing claws.

Terrible beauty.

Some miles out beneath the naked sky, he came upon huge,

crystalline pyramids flung up and frozen in the sea. *Ilka-rada* he had once called these striking, turquoise ice-forms, and he marveled at the way the world also arranged itself to kill him with such beautiful things. For if he tried to take his sled through this maze of fissures, spires, blocks and bergs, the slightest misstep might send him plunging into a crevasse or impale him on a jagged spear of ice. Here, too, in all its deadliness and *shaida* splendor, was the ocean. He felt it calling to him even as the world itself called; in the pull of gravity against his blood, he sensed that the world was always trying to reclaim itself even as the ocean sought to reabsorb its water.

Water, water, everywhere, he thought, recalling the lines of an ancient poem. *The world is mostly water.*

He himself, in his straining muscles and steamy breath, was also mostly water. In a way, he was nothing more (and nothing less) than a wave of water moving upon the surface of the ocean. After he had turned south to avoid the band of icebergs, he came across a patch of *sastrugi,* frozen waves making a rippling pattern across the ocean's ice. What, if anything, he wondered, was the essential difference between himself and these pale blue waves? Well, most obviously, he moved—but then so would the waves once midwinter spring came and the oceans ice melted. Then even a child might apprehend the truth that a wave is the ocean and the ocean a wave.

For a while, as he bumped his way across the *sastrugi* field, he consoled himself with the thought that the ocean moved according to the wind and the pull of the moons, whereas he moved himself. He had will; he might conceive of a great purpose such as the hunting of a seal, and thus will his tired limbs to push and glide, to keep moving one ski ahead of the other. As the day wore on and he began to feel faint with hunger, however, it occurred to him that he would need all his will simply to keep from lying down and freezing like one of the *sastrugi* waves. That was the great demand of life in the frigid wild. His awareness must always spread out like wind across the ocean's icescapes and yet also turn toward himself. His icy mustache, his watering eyes, his steamy breath, his blood, even his piss that yellowed the snow— everything about himself reminded him that he must always focus on keeping the water of his body liquid. Always and forever, he must keep the atoms of his being moving in precise patterns inside himself, whipping them with his will, for in the moment that he fell into unconsciousness of life, he would begin his journey to the other side of day.

Pain is the awareness of life, he remembered.

It was a rule of life that the greater the awareness, the greater the pain. Certainly he had pain enough, in his body and soul, to last the rest of his life. Almost everything about him hurt. His toes and fingers stung with the cold, as did his face, even beneath a layer of grease and his black leather mask. His teeth ached fiercely, as did his left eye, with a special, stabbing pain that sometimes took his breath away.

Toward midafternoon, after perhaps twenty miles of sledding over mostly hard-packed *safel* snow, the wind grew stronger and blew particles of spindrift pinging against his goggles. It was this icy, deep cold wind, he thought, that chilled him and caused his limbs such torment. Or perhaps it was Constancio's sculptings of his deep tissues, or the ekkana drug, or simply hunger that sent streamers of fire shooting along his bones and burning through his joints. It was hunger, pure and terrible, that shrunk his stomach into an empty, groaning bag and pounded at his brain like a block of ice being dropped over and over upon his head.

Only by dwelling on greater pains could he mute these screaming agonies of his flesh. And so he thought about Jonathan looking at him with his dark, hungry eyes and the dead eyes of all the Devaki tribe who had gone on to the other side of day. He called up burning images of all the men, women and children of all the other tribes of Alaloi who might be dying of a *shaida* virus at that very moment. And then he let into his heart and lungs and soul the greatest pain of all. This was just the pain of the world, the pain of all life. It lay outside him in cold white ice crystals and seabirds crying in the wind; it howled inside his blood with every cell and each carbon atom spinning in consciousness of its fate to return home.

To return to the center of the circle.

To move mile after mile across the brilliant snow was painful; perhaps the essence of pain was just movement itself, of atoms and consciousness, the way that ice crystals evaporated under a strong sun and even the hardest rocks cracked and eroded in time and washed as silt into the sea. Nothing could hold its form forever. Although Danlo had always known this with his mind, only now was he just beginning to sense the circulation of matter throughout the universe in a new kind of way. At that moment, as he paused to adjust his goggles against the ice's glare, a star exploded somewhere in the Harmony Group of galaxies some forty million light-years away. He saw the flash of this supernova as a deep light behind his eyes and felt the fiery blast of photons, X rays and plasma gas in the exhalation of his own breath.

Nearer to him, on the planet Askling, a group of Ringists ignited a hydrogen bomb and vaporized a million people, while nearer still, three miles across the ocean's ice, a diving thallow drove its talons into a plump snow goose and carried it off to tear it apart. Even from this distance, he was sure that he could hear the goose's screams and frantically flapping wings and see the bright sprays of blood freezing red against the white snow. Beneath this same blessed snow he smelled the fermy droppings of the snowworms and sensed the iceblooms giving off oxygen in almost silent respiration. If he stared hard enough with his burning eyes, he could almost *see* the individual molecules of oxygen streaming out from between the shimmering snow crystals and whirling off into the sky to join with the wind.

And all this was just the circle of life, and who was he to try to break it? It came to him, then, that no matter how great his awareness, no matter what pains he took with life, all his terrible (and beautiful) will wouldn't keep the atoms of his self from eventually flying apart and returning to the world. Even now, as he stood scanning the ice and sky, his breath escaped his lips in puffs of carbon dioxide and water vapor and vanished into the wind. Soon, he knew, in a day or a hundred more years, he would vanish, too, like a drop of rain returning to the ocean.

But nothing is lost, he thought. *Nothing is ever lost.*

That was the miracle of life, that although he and all living things must eventually die, they would remain always within the great circle. The atoms of his body would come together with those of a wolf, a worm and a snowy owl (and a rock, an ice crystal and a breath of the wind), and a new bit of life would be born. It was the purpose of atoms to continually organize themselves in consciousness of the world, to live, to take joy in the sunlight, ultimately to transcend into ever new forms and evolve. For Danlo, as for anyone, it was *shaida* to die at the wrong time, but ultimately dying itself was *halla* because out of this terrible necessity, life grew only vaster, the circle stronger, the world ever more magnificent and beautiful.

Nothing is lost.

There came a moment, then, in gazing at the marvelous blueness behind the deep blue sky, when he melted. His skin and muscles liquified to water, and his eyes, and his blood flowed out of him to rejoin the salt water of the sea. He felt his breath and his mind and all the tissues of his being spreading out infinitely in all directions over the shimmering white ice. Then the whiteness broke apart into violet, yellow, aquamarine and chrome red, and quicksilver and gold, and the ice itself suddenly caught fire, trillions of tiny separate crystals blazing with a single, numinous flame. And for a moment, this fire was in him and he was this blessed fire, and there was no difference. He was the wild, whirling wind and the burning salt running through all the waters of the world and the clear, cold light pouring out of the depths of the ocean.

That night he built a house far out on the ice. As the sky fell dark and the first stars appeared like bright diamonds on black silk, he used his saw to cut blocks of wind-packed, snowhut snow. He was very glad when he had set these blocks into a little dome and he could crawl inside. He was so tired from his exertions in the cold that he almost collapsed onto his sleeping furs. For a long while he lay before his stove watching the flickering plasma lights and letting a little heat soak into his face and hands.

Outside it was as cold as death, but inside his house the air began to warm almost to the melting point of ice. He managed to eat a few mouthfuls of bread, the last of what Tamara had given him. It wasn't nearly enough to fill him, but the goodness of it in his belly was enough to revive him so that he could go about his nightly chores. These were few enough. He had no dogs to care for, only himself. And so he hung his shagshay furs on a drying rack near the stove, and the felt liners of his boots as well. Then he set a large steel pot on the stove and began filling it with snow.

It would take him a long time to melt out enough water for him to drink, that night and the next day, and he wanted to fill his slip tubes before he fell into sleep. In truth, at that moment, with his lips cracked and his tongue almost parched in dehydration, he felt the pain of thirst much more keenly than hunger. As it happened, the snow that he dumped into the pot would take away the first of these pains and part of the second, for it was a special, almost magical snow. Earlier that day, he had paused atop an icebloom to dig out great heaps of purplish snow and pack it into dozens of clear plastic bags. The blooms of algae running through the snow—in bands of blue-green as well as purple—were not dense enough to sustain him altogether. But the algae was a rich food full of life and healing virtue, and if he boiled down enough snow, he might make a kind of soup that was very good to eat. This he did. Then he made another pot of soup, and then another. He might have spent all night melting snow this way, and eating and drinking, but soon enough he emptied his last bag and went outside to make his piss-before-sleeping.

The next morning he awoke to terrible pangs of hunger tearing at his belly. A man, working outside all day in the cold, might burn off as much as six thousand kilocalories of food energy. And a very large man wearing the body of an Alaloi and pulling a sled through the terrible cold of the Starnbergersee might require ten thousand kilocalories worth of seal meat or baldo nuts or berries or whatever else he might be able to find. According to Danlo's calculations, he would have been lucky if he had consumed a tenth that amount of bread and algae. He might have searched out another icebloom to feed his famished body, but such labors would only progressively weaken him.

In truth, he was already very weak. Although he had not starved as long as others in Neverness, he had starved enough. The magnificent body that Constancio had sculpted and fed from his own kitchens was already beginning to waste away. As with Jonathan, he could feel tissues of his chest, back and belly eating themselves, inexorably burning away like the seal fat in an oilstone lamp. His arms and legs were lighter, too, in the sense that muscle was beginning to fall off them. But ironically, they felt much heavier, almost as if Constancio had welded iron limbs to his hip and shoulder joints. Any kind of movement, even tying the laces of his boots, hurt. This terrible weakness frightened him, for he knew that if he didn't find food soon, the starvation would progress to the stage when he could no longer trust his own body.

And so he decided to hunt. He looked out across the ice to the north, west, east and south, wondering where he might find a seal. Beneath the crusts of snow, he knew, should be many seal holes; all during winter when the sea froze, each seal kept open in the ice perhaps a dozen holes in order to breathe and to come up and rest from his journeys hunting fish in the dark, icy waters. In Danlo's youth, with his found-father Haidar, he had always used trained dogs to sniff out these hidden holes. But now he would have to find them another way. For a while, he stood taking in the wind through his nose.

Although his sense of smell was nothing like a sled dog's, it had lately grown very keen. Perhaps hunger had driven him to drink in all the sights, sounds and scents of the world. Or perhaps it was only the ekkana drug stripping his nerves bare and rendering them exquisitely sensitive to the touch of floating molecules and sound waves and light. Whatever the causes of the deep changes rippling through the cells of his body, he could almost hear the worms eating their way through the iceblooms beneath the snow and the jewfish that swam beneath many feet of ice. And he could almost smell the seals. Theirs was a rich, musky scent that nearly permeated the snow and wafted up into the air. But it emanated from no particular direction; try as he might, with his nostrils opening and closing at will as might a dog, he could not detect the source of this beguiling scent. Perhaps, he thought, he wasn't really experiencing the spoor of seals in the now-moment but only remembrancing or hallucinating—in the dreaminess of his hunger, almost anything seemed possible. He might have stood there beside his snowhut half the morning simply sniffing the air if he hadn't recalled a different method of searching for seals.

A shaida way, he thought. *The way of the wormrunners.*

From his sled, he removed a scanner, which he fit over his eyes in place of his goggles. With this ugly machine he could see heat as infrared frequencies of light. It was the simplest thing to look out through the scanner over the miles of the sea and read the ice as patterns and shadings of the color red. Where the ice was thickest, and therefore coldest, the scanner showed crimson darkening to a deep maroon. And in other places, patches of cinnabar predominated, and the brighter reds, the clarets and scarlets and carmines. The seal holes appeared as points of a vivid, almost flame red, for there the ice gave way to the relative warmth of the ocean.

He could even differentiate the active holes from the inactive ones that had been abandoned and allowed to freeze up somewhat. The active holes, down through the ice beneath the surface snow-crusts, were almost like windows to the ocean; the ice glazing the dark, hidden pools of water would be only a few inches thick. Within easy skiing distance of his snowhut, he saw at least five of these holes. They were like drops of bright, burning blood against the other infrared colors of the ice. All he had to do was take up his harpoon, stand over one of these holes and wait for a seal to come up from the ocean to breathe.

To wait to kill that which I must not kill.

After taking a deep breath of air, he put on his skis and went over to his sled. He pulled the harpoon out of its sheath. It was a long, murderous thing both terrible and beautiful to behold. Days before, when he had carved its wickedly barbed head, he had fashioned a ring at its base. Now, in the freezing cold of the morning, he removed a coil of rope from his pack and knotted the end of it through this ring. The head of the harpoon was detachable; the harpoon's shaft fit snugly but unglued into the head's ivory socket. The basic idea behind hunting seals, as he had once hunted these splendid animals, was simple: when a seal came up into his hole, the hunter standing above would thrust his harpoon straight down through the snow crust and impale it. In the seal's writhing agony, the ivory head would work its way into flesh and bone and break away from the shaft. And then the hunter would pull on the rope with all his might and haul the seal out of the hole bellowing and bleeding up onto the ice.

With luck, the harpoon would have penetrated the heart or lungs, almost instantly killing the seal. But more often, the hunter had to dispatch his prey with a blow of a stone axe to the head or by cutting his throat. As Danlo gripped the hard shatterwood shaft of the harpoon in his hand, he thought that he might be able to thrust it down through the hole at the unseen seal. But he didn't know how he could possibly crush the life out of the seal, especially if he chanced to look into the seal's bright, black eyes.

Never harming another, never killing; it is better to die oneself than to kill.

He made a silent prayer to the spirits of all seals everywhere: that they should understand his need and come swimming to leap upon his harpoon. Then, with his harpoon in one hand and bear spear in the other, he marched out across the ice to the nearest hole. He thrust the bear spear down into the snow with the point towards the sky. Although he didn't expect to be molested (most bears hibernated in snow caves through most of the winter), the hungriest bears might have awakened to prowl the ice and seek out active seal holes of their own. It was from the ice bears, he thought, that the Old Ones of the Alaloi tribes must have learned the art of seal hunting thousands of years before. And most of this art consisted simply of the patience to wait.

Sometimes a man had to wait for most of a day for a seal to come to a particular hole; as a boy, Danlo had heard of the great Wilanu, who had once waited four days before killing his seal. Although Danlo did not have the stamina to wait so long, crouching above the snow-covered hole with his harpoon held ready, he would certainly have to wait a period of time. And so he cut blocks of snow and built a shield wall against the howling west wind; he stood with his back to this wall, looking down at the unmarked snow that hid the seal hole. This snow, warmed by the ocean beneath, appeared through his scanner as a bright, almost ruby red. All he had to do was wait with his harpoon in hand for the seal to rise and the snow to flare into a flaming crimson with the heat of the seal's body.

It will look like the snow itself has caught fire, he thought. *Or like a star exploding from beneath the ice.*

He waited all day to see this terrible light. He listened to the wind burning across the ice and tried to count the individual particles of spindrift swirling atop the seal's hole. After a long time, he gave up and counted the beats of his heart instead. Approximately three thousand beats marked the time of one hour; he waited almost motionless in the driving wind for some nine thousand beats before his raging thirst drove him to drink from one of his slip tubes. After another ten thousand beats, he realized that he hadn't brought enough water to last the day. Nor had he eaten enough food the night before to stand so long in the killing cold; he was so weak with hunger that his arm shook and all the muscles of his body trembled. He was afraid that he might collapse at any moment and fall crashing down through the seal's hole into the ocean below.

But he had to stand, to stand and wait, and that was the hell of hunting seals. It was a cold, white hell of chattering teeth and ice crystals stabbing into his nostrils. Twice his fingertips froze, and in the pain of thawing them in his mouth, he remembered how Jaroslav Bulba had driven the tip of his killing knife beneath his bloody nails. After yet another ten thousand heartbeats, his legs had grown so stiff that they seemed almost frozen. It hurt him to move, even slightly, but it hurt him even more to stand silent and still, as he must continue to stand if he didn't want to frighten his seal away. And all these agonies of his body, as terrible as they seemed, were not the worst of what he had to endure. As he counted out another ten thousand beats, one by one, he heard Jonathan's voice crying along the wind and calling him to hurry up and kill his seal. And he heard his own voice crying inside with each passing breath that he could never kill any animal.

Not even a sleekit, not even a worm crawling through the snow.

Finally, far into the night, he abandoned his vigil. In truth, he had really waited much too long, for his body was much too weak to stand for any time beneath the cold stars. He found that his fingers had frozen again, slightly, and his toes. He barely summoned the strength to return to his hut and crawl inside. On this night, he had nothing to drink but melted water and not even much of that. And he had no food at all. And so he lay inside his sleeping furs, sipping from a thermos cup and trying to thaw his icy digits. His body had grown so cold that he shivered, even inside layers of thick shagshay fur. But he could little afford this expenditure of his body's precious energy; he knew that if he didn't find a seal the next day, he would have to return to Neverness with an empty sled.

But I am not a hunter of seals.

All his life, he had had bad luck hunting seals. He had never quite known why. Perhaps (this is how he had thought as a child) one of his ancestors had once killed a rare white seal, an *imakla* animal, and the stain of this *shaida* act had touched all his descendents. Was it truly possible that the bad luck of his childhood and his adoptive ancestors' misfortunes could touch him now? He didn't know. But he sensed that something had frightened the seals away from this part of the ice where he had chosen to hunt. Perhaps it was only the machines and the murderous expeditions of the wormrunners that had driven off the seals. If this were so, then it would be best for him to break camp at first light, to move his sled farther to the west where the wormrunners were unlikely to have gone.

But if it is my fate not to find a seal, I will never return.

Already, he thought, it would be hard enough for him to ski the thirty miles back to Neverness, even if he abandoned his sled and all his other things. It would be a desperate chance to journey in the opposite direction towards the setting sun. Of course, everything about this hunting of seals had been desperate from the very beginning, so how was he to weigh one thin chance against another? He would have to listen to the wind blowing in deadly gusts from the west and Jonathan calling him across miles of ice to the east; he would listen to his breath and his shivering body and the calculations of his brain. In the end, he knew, he must listen to his heart and make his choice.

I must trust my fate, whatever that might be, he thought. *I must choose my fate and make it be.*

In the end, it was his fate that saved him. He awoke the next morning resolved to find a seal farther to the west. He promised himself that he would somehow stand and wait by the next seal hole until he killed his seal—either that or stand and die. But when he crawled from the tunnel of his house, he saw something that changed his mind. For there in the snow, all around his house, were the paw prints of an ice bear. There was no mistaking this spoor, for each of the prints was more than a foot wide and half again as long, and no other animal (except the mammoths of the far islands) made such a huge impression in the snow. He had slept so deeply that he hadn't sensed the bear sniffing at his house.

Of course bears could move across the ice almost as silently as starlight, so he might not have heard the bear even if he had remained awake. More than one hunter had been killed as he sat in his house drinking blood tea at night. A snow house was an easy thing to demolish, especially for a bear who could break into much stronger structures. He remembered how the snowcrusts covering a seal's lair sometimes grew very thick; once, he had watched a bear batter at this covering with his mighty paw until it finally caved in and the bear charged headfirst down through the crumbled snow, only to re-emerge moments later with a seal pup dangling from its jaws. As he stood examining one of the bear's prints and measured the size of the five curving claws, he wondered why this bear hadn't simply crashed his way through his house and grabbed him in his sleep.

Perhaps, he thought, the bear had once killed a wormrunner and hated the taste of man. Or perhaps something in Danlo's scent had put the bear off; just as he would never hunt a white seal no matter how hungry he was, perhaps the ice bears could sniff out something strange and rare about certain men and would regard them as *imakla* animals that they may not kill.

The Old Ones are very wise, he thought. *Very strong and very wise.*

He wondered if the wisest bears might have developed an aesthetics of scent so exquisitely attuned to the world that it would serve them as a kind of worship or faith. For a while he knelt there on the snow laughing because this notion was so incredible that it might be true. And then he realized that he was very hungry and not thinking clearly; the most likely explanation for why the bear had left him alone was also the simplest: that he just wasn't worth killing. Bears preferred to eat seals, and when they caught one, after tearing it open, they most often devoured only the skin and fat, leaving the meat behind. Although Danlo still had some meat left to him, there was almost no fat; his whole body was like leather rope wrapped around bone. A starving body burned its own muscle for energy, an inefficient metabolic process that created ketones as a waste product. With each contraction of his lungs, he exhaled millions of these stinking molecules, and if he could smell his own breath, then so could the bear, even through the snow blocks of his house. Could a bear be wise enough to connect this scent with starvation and thus sense the leanness of his body? Truly, he thought, the Old Ones of the

Starnbergersee must have such powers of mind, for why else would the bear have let him live?

Thara soma anima, Totunye, he thought. *Thank you for my life.*

That this bear was one of the Old Ones he knew from the size of its prints. And he was certain that it was a male; it would probably stand ten feet tall on its hind legs and weigh as much as a thousand pounds. And this, he suddenly realized, was a lot of meat. Although it shamed him to think of this great animal only as potential food moving on paws silently across the ice, he could not help himself, for he was very hungry. He stood up, then, and looked off towards the west where the prints disappeared into the dark ice of the horizon. As the sun rose, he would be able to see these peculiar curving-inward prints more clearly. Following them across the gleaming *safel* snow would not be difficult. And here was more shame, that he would contemplate hunting a noble old bear who had let him live. But what else could he do? He might hunt seals for a year and not find one, whereas this bear was probably prowling the ice only a few miles away.

It is one thing to hunt a bear, he thought. *But it is another to kill it.*

He went back into his house, then, and came back out a few moments later gripping his long bear spear. He thrust it down into the snow for a moment while he rummaged in his sled for the scanner. He began to lift it towards his eyes when it occurred to him that searching for a bear in this way would bring him even more shame. And so he tucked the scanner back into his pack. And then, after a moment of thought, he realized that his shame was nothing against the pain of Jonathan's frozen feet and starving body. This realization touched off a different and deeper shame: that he had almost let the aesthetics of his childhood interfere with what he had to do. Was it really so wrong to use this machine in the service of life? Perhaps he should even wish for a laser or bullet gun to aim against the bear. Perhaps he should find the bear as quickly and easily as possible, and then kill it in any way that he could.

It will not matter to the bear how I find him if in the end he dies.

Again he lifted the scanner from his pack and brought it towards his face. And then, as he gazed at its hellish, glittering lenses, he knew that he could never again put this *shaida* thing over his eyes. He would hunt the bear as his found-father and grandfathers of the Devaki tribe had hunted bears for five thousand years. In truth, it was the only way that he knew to hunt.

If I use the scanner, I might detect the bear more easily through his heat. But there might be other things that I would not see.

There was an art to hunting, an attunement to the shapes and sounds of the world and all the animals who lived in it. A wormrunner, firing his laser at a pack of wolves from the safety of a hovering windjammer, had no such attunement. His way was all science and slaughter, the mechanical production of vast quantities of fur and meat. A wormrunner would scorn the tracking of a bear over the ice by his spoor just as he would laugh at the Alaloi hunter's superstitious prayers to the spirit of the hunted animal. But Danlo knew that the spirits of all animals called to each other, sometimes even to human beings. In truth, each spirit was interconnected with every other in complex ways, even as the *halla* nature of the world shimmered everywhere like the interwoven strands of a spider's web, if only one knew how to see it.

As Danlo put away the scanner for the second time, he realized that he had been trained since his early childhood in this rare art of seeing. This was the great genius of the Alaloi totem system. He, as with all Alaloi men, had learned a hundred words for what civilized people would think of as simply ice. There was *malku* and *silka* and *morilka,* the death ice which looked thick enough to support a man's weight but would crack open treacherously beneath his feet. Having these words close to his lips, he perceived the subtle turquoise shadings of *ilka-rada* and the whorls and variations of the frozen sea where a wormrunner might only have seen a uniform expanse of white ice. The Alaloi worldview was not only a lens allowing him to behold the world more truly than he could by looking through a wormrunner's scanner, but a way of living among the ice-locked islands of the western ocean.

A wormrunner could never live this way, so close to the ice and sky. A wormrunner would die where an Alaloi child would thrive, and that was why the wormrunners and other civilized human beings set out into the wild with their lasers and heated parkas and windjammers. And that was why Danlo would not use the scanner. Not because it was morally wrong to do so, but because this machine would be like a dark, necromantic crystal pulling him from one worldview into another. He would hunt the bear with a flint-tipped spear and all the strength of his muscles; he would slide his skis over the *bureesaha* snow much as any Alaloi man, and anything that broke this close connection with the world might cause him to fail or even kill him.

Lo luratha lani, Totunye, he prayed. *Siliji ni moranath.*

Then he bent over his pack and pulled out a pair of goggles different from the polarized ones that he had worn on his journey from Neverness. These were nothing more than a leather headband and a single curving piece of wood that fit over his eyes. A narrow slit running across the center of the wood let in a little of the world's light, not enough to make him snowblind, but enough so that he could see. He had carved the goggles one night as he had sat telling stories to Jonathan; he hadn't been sure why, nor why he had brought them on his journey out onto the ice. But now, as he fastened them around his head, he was very glad to have them. Now, he thought, he would be able to look at the marvelous, frozen world and see it just as it was. He realized that something deep and mysterious had driven him to make the goggles and hunt as an Alaloi man; even now as he picked up his bear spear and faced the rushing wind, he could almost hear his fate calling him.

He tracked the bear for most of the morning straight towards the west. It seemed that the bear himself was on a mission, either hunting out a favorite collection of seal holes or perhaps returning to his den. The tracks ran over the hard pack snow almost as straight as the East-West Sliddery, curving in places only to avoid an open crevasse or a patch of *ilka-rada*. As the sun rose higher, the iceblinks appeared in the sky, wispy saffron brush strokes against deep cobalt blue, and the air warmed, slightly. Danlo felt this warmth in gentle gusts of wind that poured through the slits in his goggles and touched his naked eyes; in truth, his whole body felt warm, strangely warm as if the thrill of hunting the bear had fired his heart and blood where food alone could not. He felt himself suddenly more awake, more alert, more alive. He could almost smell the bear's thick, smoky scent on the wind; he could almost hear the bear's black claws slicing through the snow somewhere ahead of him. Although beneath this newfound vitality he was still very weak, he used his skis to skate the fast snow, pushing and gliding over the silky whiteness at a speed that the bear couldn't match. With every mile that he moved over the frozen tissues of the ocean, he seemed only to grow stronger, as if the reflected light off the purple iceblooms sustained him and the wind breathed new life into his mouth and nose. He felt the veneer of civilization falling away from him, peeling back in layers to reveal a wilder and deeper self. The world before him became like a mirror, a vast shimmering circle of white ice that showed him to himself: a truly splendid and powerful animal hunting another animal with all the wild joy that was his by right of birth.

I am Danlo, son of Haidar, the Tiger Slayer, he remembered. *I am Danlo the Wild, son of Mallory Ringess.*

He realized that it was the last of his energy. It came only as a result of *lotsara,* the burning of the blood, that rare art of metabolizing the body's remaining fat reserves in order to lend it a final burst of life. All Alaloi men are taught this art upon coming into manhood, and they use it to keep from freezing to death when caught in the fierce winds of a *sarsara* or in other extreme situations when they must fight for their lives.

Danlo had starved too long, and so the marvelous heat he felt burning up from his belly and rushing out to his arms and fingers would fade, and soon. But he almost didn't care, for the pursuit of the bear absorbed him utterly. Before him lay the whole world and all the things in it: the ice frozen in wind-ripple patterns; the wispy *shetha* clouds high in the sky; the swirling *anasha* snow. There was bear sign, too, things that the bear left behind him other than his huge tracks: a piece of paw fur ripped off by a patch of razor ice; a bit of blood frozen into ruby crystals; an eyelash; the tip of one of his black claws, broken off where the bear had scratched at a feather trapped in a block of clear *kleensu* ice. Danlo tasted a drop of this frozen blood; it burst into fire in his mouth with the tang of burning iron, and the power of it spread through his body like a magical elixir.

He also tasted the bear's piss, frozen into yellow slush like a patch of *malku* snow. From its rank-salt flavor, he knew that the bear must have been eating the iceblooms, a food he would only consume if he could find no seals. He confirmed this when he broke open a piece of the bear's dung and saw the blue spiricules of a snowworm twisting through the darker matter. Perhaps, he thought, this bear had become a connoisseur of snowworms and knew the richest iceblooms where he would most likely find them.

Oh, bear, where are you going? Please tell me where you are going.

A couple of miles into his quest, he came across a huge impression in the snow where the bear had lain down, perhaps to take a nap. He thought that the bear, like himself, might be very tired and weak with hunger. Or perhaps the bear had only been basking in the sun. He remembered that bear fur, although it looked white, was really quite colorless. Each of the millions of hairs from the nose to tail was nothing more than a very thin, clear tube allowing sunlight to pass through it to the black skin beneath. Some of the sunlight, of course, would refract off the hairs and scatter in all directions—hence the bear's seeming white hue. But much of it would be absorbed as heat by the skin's blackness, and in this way the great white bears had evolved a very efficient way to keep warm.

As Danlo paused a moment himself to rest and to scan the ice ahead of him, he began remembering everything that he had ever learned about bears. Especially their powers: he remembered that a bear could walk over the icepack continuously for days or swim in the ocean for a hundred miles without stopping to eat or sleep. A bear, sniffing at the blue cold air, could smell a live seal three miles away, and a dead, decaying one at a distance of more than twenty miles.

I must be very careful in stalking this bear, he thought. *For if the wind shifts and he smells me, he may stalk* me.

So far, his stalking had been easy and relatively safe, for he had skied almost straight west, into the wind. But the wind might suddenly die, or the bear might veer off towards the north or south—or perhaps circle back along his path to seek out an icebloom or favorite seal hole. The night before, he thought, this bear had let him live for some unknown reason. But today, he might suddenly decide to hunt him, perhaps just for the sport of it. Sometimes bears were like that. With bears, one never quite knew what they would do. And so, as the sun climbed higher in the sky, Danlo became ever more aware of the nuances of snow and ice and the movements of the wind. Almost as if he were a bear himself, he paused more often to sniff the air and look about him at the four points of the world.

A whole art of hunting an animal, he remembered Haidar once telling him, *is to become that animal.*

This becoming, he thought, was more than just recalling the bear's habits and trying to guess what the bear would do next and where he might go. It was feeling the power of the world through his feet, and feeling his own terrible power course through him every time his legs moved and he connected once again with the ice or snow. It was a sense of playfulness undergirded by an unshakable confidence in his ability to survive even the worst winter storm. Above all, it was *animajii,* the wild joy of simply being alive and tasting the marvelous tang of salt water or basking in the golden rays of the sun.

I am not I. I am Totunye, of the Old Ones, the Uryu Kweitil Onsu.

At least twice, his close identification with the bear helped him continue the hunt when he might have been stymied. Around midday, he came to a great dish of *rashuwel* many miles wide

where shallow dunes of windblown snow had obliterated the
bear's tracks. He might have plowed straight ahead and then spent
hours circling the *rashuwel* on the other side in hope of discovering where the tracks reemerged onto the hardpack snow. Instead,
he immediately turned to the south and after a hundred yards,
picked up the bear's tracks again. It seemed that the bear had
avoided the *rashuwel* altogether. Blowing snow, while not really
dangerous or difficult to cross, can tickle a bear's nose and make
him sneeze. And *this* bear was an Old One, after all, who obviously possessed a keenly developed sense of propriety. He would
consider such sneezing beneath his dignity. And so he had chosen
to make a slight detour on his way toward his destination—that is,
if he truly had a destination and wasn't just wandering the ice in
search of seals.

Another time, later in the day, Danlo came upon a *varulia*.
This was a mile-wide patch of dark, churning water where the
ocean current had kept the ice from closing. The bear's tracks led
right up to the edge of the *varulia* and simply gave way to the
ocean. Since Danlo could not directly follow the bear, this time he
had to choose between circling the *varulia* to the north or south.
But the *varulia* might be ten or twenty miles long; as he examined
the ice right and left, he could see no end to it, for the black
ribbon of water vanished into the horizon in both directions. He
stood there for a while wondering which direction he should
choose. And then, at last, he thought to pile up many pieces of
pack ice into a mound. When he climbed this mound, he could
see farther.

To the north, the *varulia* closed into a sheet of hard ice at
perhaps four and a half miles distance, where to the south it froze
up not more than three miles away. Circling to the south, it
seemed, would save him some miles of his journey. But the ocean
current flowed swiftly through the *varulia* from south to north;
common sense told him that the bear would let the current carry
him northwards for a few miles, perhaps all the way to its end,
before he climbed out onto the ice on the other side and shook
himself dry. According to this logic, then, Danlo should circle to
the north. But there are always senses beyond mere logic. Somehow Danlo knew that the bear wouldn't let the current sweep him
down the length of the *varulia*. He could almost *see* the bear
swimming hard against the current, trying to keep a straight
course to the west. Perhaps the bear simply wished to resume his
journey across the ice in as direct a line as possible. Or perhaps
another reason led him to take this harder way.

The bear was of the *Uryu Kweitil Onsu,* almost certainly past his prime. But not far past, Danlo thought. With a strange tingling running through his spine into his own arms and legs, he sensed that the bear still fairly quivered with a tremendous vitality and wanted to test his strength against the icy ocean waters. It was really a matter of pride. Therefore the bear would swim straight ahead. And therefore, the southern route around the *varulia* should prove the quickest after all, as Danlo found when he circled it in this direction and found the bear's tracks reemerging from the ocean almost exactly where he had envisioned they would. He might have rejoiced in this small triumph, but he had skied eight miles to the single mile that the bear had swum, and he had fallen even farther behind. With the sun itself falling toward the purplish horizon, he knew that he had to find the bear, and soon, or else risk losing him in the growing darkness.

I must follow the bear, even into the night, he thought. *I must follow my fate, lo-mirala mi halla.*

As he pushed ahead toward the sun, he thought about another Alaloi saying concerning fate: *ti-anasa daivam.* This could be translated as an imperative to love his fate—or that he should suffer his fate in silence and acceptance. *Anasa* meant both to love and to suffer; to an Alaloi man opening his heart to the terrible beauty of the world, there was no almost difference. If it was truly his fate to die alone out on the windswept sea, then he should sink down to the ice and face west one last time. He should pick the ice out of his eyes in order to behold the infinite glory of the world. Even in the agony of his freezing limbs and his final breaths, he should give thanks for being alive. He should thank his father and his mother and all life for bringing him into life; he should marvel that of all the beings that had been born since the beginning of the world, it was his fate to have lived at this time, and to die.

Ti-anasa daivam.

But it was his fate to find the bear. He came upon him just before sunset. As he crested a shallow dune, he almost immediately descryed a small yellowish-white dot against the faintly blue ice a mile ahead of him. He drew in a breath of cold air, and froze into motionlessness. With the sun so close to the edge of the world, the ice and sky fairly blazed with colors, and it was hard to see. Nevertheless, he stood for a long time facing west, drinking in the dazzling light of the world. For the count of ten beats of his heart, the dot did not move. After another fifty beats, the dot still appeared as no more than a hump on the ice or a snowblock. But then Danlo looked harder, reaching out with his eyes and opening them to the varying wavelengths of light despite the pain of such seeing.

After a while, he could make out the form of the bear. He sat with his back toward Danlo as he stared straight ahead and down at the ice. Danlo stared, too, stared past the bear at the dark circle of an open seal hole. Here, where the warm Kalikak current flowed swiftly up from the south, the ice was less thick than in other places, and the seal holes would be open to the air, as this one was. The bear sat waiting for a seal to come up and breathe, waiting as patiently as any Alaloi hunter. He might wait yet for hours, frozen to the ice, watching and waiting. And when the seal at last came up, he would explode into motion; with lightning speed, he would use his paw like a war hammer to strike the seal's head and kill it. And then he would drag the seal up onto the ice and begin his feast.

Ti-anasa daivam.

For a long time, Danlo stood there on the sparkling snow, watching and waiting himself. He almost couldn't believe his good luck. The bear's whole attention was focused on the seal hole; it might be possible for him simply to walk up to the bear and take him from behind. With the wind still blowing steadily from the west, the bear would not smell him. In truth, when he opened his nostrils and let in the wind, *he* could smell the bear. It was a dark, musky scent almost intoxicating in its aliveness. It excited Danlo to sense the bear in this way, and he suddenly found himself moving over the snow closer to its source. But he moved slowly, gracefully, silently. Almost silently: as he slid one ski ahead of the other over the soft, *kushku* snow, the faint suss of wood through shifting white ice crystals fell over him like the sound of thunder. He prayed that the bear would not hear him. He prayed that the wind whooshing along the ice would drown out such lesser sounds, and so it happened, for the bear didn't once move his head or even twitch his ears.

Ti-anasa daivam, follow your fate.

For what seemed like forever, Danlo stalked the bear. As he drew closer, he could see the bear more clearly. The bear sat with his rump low to the ice, his great shoulders hunched up and his long neck and snout pointed straight towards the seal hole. All his fierce concentration pointed in this direction, too. Danlo thought it somewhat arrogant of the bear to sit this way, facing the wind. True, he could sniff about more effectively in this attitude, but it left him more vulnerable to being stalked from behind. Obviously, then, the bear feared nothing that moved across the ice, neither the wind nor other bears nor even man. It was possible, Danlo thought, that this bear had never seen a man. None of the Alaloi tribes hunted this far to the west, and most of the city's wormrunners had been killed in the recent riots. That was the great mystery and power of the bears (at least of the *Uryu Kweitil Onsu*), that they should fear nothing in all the world.

Ti-anasa daivam.

At a distance of a hundred yards, Danlo stepped out of his skis and sank down low, his belly to the snow. Still gripping his bear spear, he inched his way forward, taking care to avoid any of the projecting spurs of *ilkeesh* that might have torn at his parka and sent the slightest of sounds ripping out into the air. He crept across five yards of cold snow and then ten. Beneath him, beneath layers of snow and ice, the ocean rushed all salty and warm like the blood of the world. He listened to its deep murmur for a while, just as he listened to the rushing of his own blood and the bear's. After another five yards of such painstaking stalking, he sensed the connection between the bear and himself growing ever stronger. At any moment, he feared, the bear might turn to look at him. And so he lay motionless in the snow for a while and covered his black face mask with his white mittens.

Once, many years before, he had seen a bear employ just such a strategem while stalking a group of seals playing upon rock. In order not to be seen against the white ice downwind of this rock, the bear had crept silently forward, always holding one white paw over his black nose. After Danlo had counted out a hundred heartbeats, he began moving forward again in a similar manner. He kept one hand close to his face, the other clamped around his spear. At thirty yards, the scent of the bear grew almost overpowering. Danlo felt the growling emptiness of his belly and the terrible screaming hunger of every cell of his body. He remembered a word, then, *waashkelay,* which meant simply "meat hunger." He realized that on some deep level, the grains and pulses and other vegetable foods that he had eaten for so many years had never truly satisfied him. Always, buried in the tissues of his heart and belly, there had burned a deep desire to consume the meat of another animal and to taste the marvelous red tang of blood once more.

Ti-anasa daivam.

After he had crept very close to the bear—no more than twenty yards away—the wind softened and the world fell almost silent. He could almost hear the bear's deep, patient breaths. He himself tried to breathe more softly and slowly, and to quiet the booming thunder of his heart. His entire concentration fell on the bear like the light of the sun. They were the only two beings on all the surface of the sea; here, beneath the deep blue sky, in the loneliness of the blue-white ice, it was almost impossible to imagine that human beings lived in a great stellar city not more than sixty miles away. The great war that his kind fought among the cold stars seemed impossibly distant, almost as if it had happened in a different age of the universe long ago.

The Alaloi tribes a thousand miles to the west wouldn't know of this war, although they might look up at the nighttime sky and wonder at the growing mass of the Universal Computer that devoured the familiar stars like some dark, *shaida* moon. They couldn't dream that the strange, glistering lights that they called *blinkans* were really supernovas, or that men in blackships from far away might soon turn their star-killing machines upon the sun. And Danlo couldn't dream this either, for just beyond the bear, caught for the moment between heaven and earth, the sun blazed all golden-red like some mysterious fire burning away both past and future. For him (and for the bear) there was only this eternal now-moment between the beats of his heart when the sky stood still and the wind did not move.

Ti-anasa daivam.

At last, however, the bear himself moved. But he didn't surge forward to the rising of the seal from its dark hole; rather he turned in curiosity to look behind him. Danlo knew that it wasn't his smell that caused the bear to move, nor any sound, for he had frozen once again, this time becoming just another white mound against all the other mounds of wind-blown snow. No, it was something other, some mysterious connection between them almost pulsing along the ice. Danlo knew that the bear would see him. Bears eyes aren't very good, and any other bear might have perfunctorily looked his way, blinked a few times, and then turned back to the seal hole. But *this* bear would look straight at him and see the white fur of Danlo's parka as the fur of another animal and not as snow. Therefore, Danlo smiled to himself and ripped off his face mask and goggles, the better to see. Then, in an explosion of muscles coming alive and powdered snow flung out into the air, he leapt to his feet and charged the bear.

It was the only thing that he could do. He had to get inside the bear's circle, and quickly, or he might lose his chance of killing him. Most animals, he knew, had such a circle of fight-or-flight. To remain outside this circle allowed an animal simply to turn and flee; but if one stepped in close, within striking distance, then the threatened animal would have no choice but to fight for his life. Danlo did not want to give the bear any choice. Although he sensed that the bear would fight no matter what he did, just for the sheer singing joy of fighting, he still might run away. After all, the bear might see him as a truly strange and fierce animal, with his flashing blue eyes and his long spear pointed straight towards the bear's heart.

Ti-anasa daivam, he prayed. And then, *Never killing or harming another being, not even in one's thoughts.*

There was a moment, then. The bear, stunned and outraged at Danlo's unbelievable aggression, charged *him*. He bellowed and snorted and burst across the snow at a frightening speed, seeming barely to touch its sparkling surface. Then as the two of them came together, he rose up to his full twelve feet of height like a great white god. He was a huge bear, truly one of the Old Ones, fifteen hundred pounds of fur and bone and great bunching muscles as hard as shatterwood. He stood snarling down at Danlo with his black lips pulled back from his teeth. And Danlo stood below on the soft snow with his spear held ready, all the while staring at the bear's black nose, his black tongue, his fathomless black eyes. Although his huge teeth were white and sharp as daggers, Danlo knew that bears rarely struck with their teeth. They preferred to kill by paw and claw, and these terrible weapons the bear held out wide to his right and left above Danlo's head. He was so close to the bear that he could smell his steaming breath and feel its heat. At any moment the bear might swing his paw downward with all the force of a falling tree; at any moment Danlo might push his spear upward toward the bear's exposed chest. Danlo's heart beat once and then twice, very quickly, very hard. And then the moment finally came, the moment between life and death. The moment *of* life and death. He stared at the bear, and the bear stared at him, watching and waiting. For what seemed like an eternity, Danlo felt himself become a strange being rising up out of the icescapes of a strange and silent world.

I cannot kill him—never killing or harming another, not even . . .

But the bear could kill him. Without warning, the bear suddenly swung his paw down towards Danlo's head. He moved with astonishing speed. Danlo only just managed to jump back far enough to escape the hard black pads of the bear's mighty paw. But the sharp claws raked the air an inch from Danlo's eyes and caught his furs, ripping through to the skin and muscle beneath. A pain like five knives of fire burned through his chest, but all his awareness focused on jerking free from the bear's claws and avoiding his gnashing teeth. This he finally did. Snow sprayed all about them, and the bear snorted at the smell of blood suddenly staining Danlo's white furs. Again the bear reared up and flailed out with his other paw. And again Danlo moved back, avoiding the blow. And then he himself moved with lightning speed, in towards the bear.

He astonished himself at the ferocity of his attack; perhaps he even astonished the bear. For the bear had almost certainly never seen a human being before, and he seemed not to know the power or purpose of a spear. There came a blinding moment when Danlo struck upward, aiming the flint spearpoint at the soft spot just beneath the bear's ribs. All the strength of his body and being went into this single thrust. At first, however, he couldn't tell if he had pierced the heart spot, for the setting sun behind the bear filled his eyes with a brilliant white light and exploded inside his brain. All around him the ice shimmered like diamonds beneath the deep blue sky. And then the bear let loose a long, low, dreadful bellow, and he knew. He stood on the blood-spattered snow, fighting for breath, fighting for life, and he drove the spear home. A terrible strength welled up from inside him. His blood burned through his veins, and his breath steamed from his mouth, as wild as the wind. He kept pushing forward with the spear, forward and upward, all the while letting the weight of the bear's death struggle drive the shaft deeper. The bear tried to bite him and catch him with his paws, but he was in too close, so close that he could almost lick the long white fur of the bear's belly.

Again and again the bear bellowed and shook and raged. Danlo felt the bear's great power and life shuddering down the spear's shaft, pouring out in sprays of bright red blood. Some of this magical substance got into his eyes, and its intense saltiness burned worse than tears. Even in his killing drive, he wanted to weep for the bear, and even more, for himself. For he felt himself caught up by fate, even as a single ice crystal is swept away by the wind. But then, as the bear murmured and weakened and the light went out in his eyes, Danlo knew that he had moved to a deeper purpose. In truth, he was not a helpless ice crystal at all; when he looked inside his fiery heart, he saw that all the force and fury of the wind was just his own furious will toward life. In the end, he had chosen. He had killed the bear out of all the wild joy of life, in utter freedom, and this was a terrible and beautiful thing.

Ti-anasa daivam.

At last, as the bear stopped struggling, the fire went out of Danlo. The bear became a dead weight at the end of his spear which he couldn't possibly hold up. In truth, he couldn't even hold up himself. And so both he and the bear collapsed at the same moment, crashing to the ice with such force that it almost cracked. For a long time, Danlo just lay there next to the bear on the cold snow, panting for breath. He couldn't move, not even to turn his face away from the bear's belly or to let go of the spear that stuck out of the great, bloody wound there. And he didn't want to move, because he had no strength left, not even enough to open his mouth and cry out at the immense pain of it all. He almost couldn't feel his arms or legs. The weakness sucking the life out of his body was so terrible and total that he wanted to die. It would be so easy to die, he thought. He only had to watch the sun sink slowly behind the dark, blue horizon and let the terrible coldness of the sea carry him over to the other side of day.

Follow your fate.

As the sun disappeared beyond the rim of the blazing ice, however, he remembered why he had come to this place of life and death. Slowly, he let go the spear and moved his hand towards the snow; it was like moving underwater and so painful that he wanted to scream. All around the bear's belly and chest, the blood from his wound had turned the snow red. Danlo managed to grab up a heap of bloody slush and lift it towards his face. He ate it slowly, letting the ice crystals melt in his mouth and the blood run down his throat. After a long time, he felt something move inside him as if the bear's blood had lit his life's fire once more.

Again he ate some of this magical snow. And again, many times, scooping up handful after handful of snow and sucking the sweet red blood out of it. Because he was famished, he thought that he could have eaten all the blood of the sea itself. But his stomach had shrunken into a hard, empty bag, and the raw blood caused it to writhe and heave. Suddenly, he had to turn to cough, and he vomited up great clots of blood. But he was so hungry that he couldn't help eating even more snow. And again he vomited, and again he ate, many times until it seemed that each time in this dreadful cycle, he vomited a little less and ate a little more. Certainly, there was no lack of blood to consume, for it still poured out of the bear as if he himself had drunk the wine-dark ocean.

After a while, he felt a little strength returning to his exhausted body. He got up on his hands and knees and scooped some snow into his mouth, this time clean white snow without the slightest stain of blood. And then he crawled over to the bear and opened his huge black mouth. He let a trickle of water pass from his mouth to the bear's, giving him a last drink of water. And then he closed the bear's dark eyes and said a prayer for his spirit. *"Pela Uryanima, mi alasharia la shantih,"* he whispered. "Go to sleep, Great One, go to sleep."

He himself wished for sleep almost more than food—perhaps even more than fulfilling his promise to bring home food to Tamara and Jonathan. But to sleep was to die, for his body was freezing fast with the terrible cold of the night. Already his blood-soaked mittens were turning to icy gauntlets around his hands. He had to move now or he would not survive until morning. And so he drew out his knife and set to work. He cut open the bear from his throat all the way down the belly. He cut through skin and fat and muscle, and he marveled that the design of the bear's body was very much like his own.

Quickly, for the wind had risen and the stars were coming out, he cut off great hunks of blubber and gobbled them down like candy. He cut out the liver and drew it forth steaming into the air. He bit off the very tip of it, chewing in delight and letting its rich, iron taste revive him. The rest of the liver he cast into the snow as offal, for it fairly oozed poisonous concentrations of vitamin A. And then, with his diamond-steel knife, he broke open the ribs and sternum and cut out the heart.

The *ardu* he had once called this great, central organ. He ate most of it standing on the freezing slush looking up at the stars. Haidar had once told him that the heart of a bear held a great power. It held the bear's very lifeforce, his *anima,* and as Danlo gazed at the familiar constellations of his childhood and partook of the bear's flesh, he felt some of this life pass into him. He marveled at the fire he felt warming his belly; he looked down at the bear, all white fur and dark ruby jewels of meat shimmering in the starlight, and he marveled at how his death had given him new life.

There is no life that is not something's death; no death that is not something's life.

He knew that he would have to butcher the bear, and soon, or else the body would freeze into a great solid mass of flesh impossible to move. Because he didn't think that he could complete this work in the cold of the wind, he tramped over to a nearby patch of *kureesha* snow and began cutting blocks for a snow house. He cut many blocks, for on this night he would need to build a very large house. It didn't take very long to fetch these blocks back to where the bear lay and begin setting them into the snow. He built the house around and over the bear. He stood on the blood-frozen snow, stepping around the bear and shaping block after snowblock so that it fit the rapidly rising, curved walls. When he was almost finished, he removed the plasma stove from his pack and set it near the center of the dome. It would provide a little heat and enough light to work by while he fell upon on the bear again with his knife.

Nothing is lost.

And so, moving carefully but swiftly inside his house of snow, he cut the bear into pieces. In order not to waste the bear's great gift of life, he took out many plastic bags from his pack and filled them with the blood that still leaked from the bear's body. He filled them with chunks of sweetbreads, as well, and brains and blubber and meat, so many pounds dark red meat that he didn't know if he would be able to transport all of it back to the city. At first, this hard, bloody work exhausted him. More than once he had to lay down to rest upon the huge, white fur-skin that he had flayed from the bear. But as he rested, he ate, great masses of raw bear flesh, particularly the fat, which his body almost instantly burned to give him new energy. Strangely, as the night deepened, he seemed only to gain strength. He could feel his belly working hard around the bear meat, and his heart and his blood. He could almost feel the cells of his arms and legs swelling and replicating themselves, moment by moment, building new layers of muscle as the flesh of the bear became his own.

Nothing is lost.

Sometime toward morning, he tended his wounds and finally lay down to sleep. All around the cold, icy walls, he had stacked the many plastic bags full of meat. The bear, occupying most of the center of the house, had been reduced to little more than a blood-encrusted skeleton. But the bear still lived. In him, of course, and outside over the sea's starlit icescapes wandering the great circle of the world. When he closed his eyes, he could hear the bear's spirit calling him. His great, low voice sang along the wind and built into a roar. He told Danlo that he had given his life to him for a great purpose. A time would come, and soon, when Danlo would have to be strong even as the bear had been strong. In the end, his flesh and blood belonged to the world, as did his breath, his dreams, his very life.

Nothing is ever lost.

And so he fell asleep marveling at the great mystery of all that had happened that day. He listened to the wind as it moved over the ice and built; he listened to his breath and counted the beats of his heart, and he marveled at the mysterious strength building inside him with all the inevitability of a winter storm.

THE BREATH OF
THE WORLD

> *Do not fear to die, for death is merely the liberation of our
> immortal pallatons from our mortal bodies. The question
> arises as to what happens to our pallatons when encoded
> as pure information into a universal computer? Do we
> simply exist in stasis like letters on the page of a book or
> do we flow with all the power and beauty of a lightning
> storm? What degree of reality can the running of this
> immortal program produce? I propose that the
> instantiation of our selfness as a pallaton is more real
> than a breath of fresh air; it is more immediate and
> powerful than the rushing of the wind.*
> —from *Principles of Cybernetic Architecture*
> by Nikolos Daru Ede

It took Danlo four days to return to Neverness. The first day he
spent in skiing back to the first of his snow houses to fetch his
sled, and the next in pulling the empty sled back over the ice
westward to his second house where he had cached the bear meat.
He feared that another bear might sniff out this marvelous treasure in his absence, and so he hurried back across the *sastrugi* and
glittering *anasha* fields with all the speed that he could manage.
He was glad to find his kill untouched, just as he had left it.
Working quickly in the cold morning light, he loaded the many
meat bags onto his sled, which he covered with a plain white
cloth. Although it seemed like a lot of meat—he estimated that he
had bagged at least eight hundred pounds of muscle, organs, blubber and blood—he wanted all of it to provide for the needs of
Tamara and Jonathan and their friends. And so he fit the sled's
leather harness over his chest and began to pull. But the sled
didn't move. He might have jerked to the right and to the left to
break the sled's runners free from the ice, but the wounds that the
bear had left in his chest still burned like fire. Very reluctantly, he

unloaded a couple of hundred pounds of meat and stored it under a covering of snow near the house; this extra meat would do Jonathan no good if he died of starvation before he had the chance to eat it. Danlo told himself that he could always return for the meat if he had the chance. And if not, then another bear would find it, or the scavenger birds when the strong midwinter spring sun began to melt the sea's snow.

At first, his journey homeward proved difficult, for he was still too weak to pull such a load over sixty miles of rough ice. But it seemed that with every mile he moved beneath the dark blue sky, he grew only stronger. He kept a bag of blubber and meat chunks just inside his blood-stained furs where it was warm and wouldn't freeze. As he skied, he ate, dipping his hand inside his parka again and again and removing a bloody gobbet which he devoured with his strong white teeth. Although he had no means of weighing out these tidbits, he later guessed that over the four days since killing the bear, he ate some thirty or forty pounds of meat. Some of it his cells burned for energy, but most of it was converted to hard new muscle layered down all along his lean body.

It fairly astonished him how quickly he gained weight; sometimes it felt that if he could keep eating this way, the whole mass of the world would flow into him and swell him with its strength. He healed quickly, too. The wounded skin and muscles over his chest gave way to healthy new flesh as if the cells there were metabolizing and dividing at a wildly accelerated rate. In truth, ever since he had eaten the bear's heart, his whole being rippled with new life. He felt some marvelous and fearful thing remaking him deep inside. He felt it driving him, even as the wind screamed and pushed at his back like the breath of God. Although he himself felt almost as powerful and indestructible as a god, he knew that it was still possible for a winter storm to catch him in its icy talons and delay him for as long as a tenday. And so he drove his skis hard against the snow, and he hurried back to Neverness where his son and the woman whom he loved would be waiting for him.

He arrived at West Beach in the middle of the night. He pulled his sled across the snow-covered sands as silently as he could, for he didn't wish to meet anyone or to endure some roving pack of harijan questioning him and ripping back the cover of his sled. But it was very late, and with the wind whipping clouds of spindrift through the darkness, no one was about. The streets near the beach were also deserted, and so he made his way into the City Wild unmolested. There, among the groaning shatterwood trees, beneath the light of the cold stars, he unloaded his sled and cached the bear meat in his snow house. The best of this meat—perhaps twenty pounds of rib steaks—he secreted in the inner pockets of his furs. He placed a few bags of blood and blubber there as well. And then he skied through the forest toward the heart of the city to pay Tamara and Jonathan a visit.

Between the forest and the edge of the Merripen Green he encountered only a few people who took one look at him stalking down the dark icy streets and shied away from him as from an angel of death. And when Tamara opened the door of her apartment, she let loose a cry of dismay at the sight of his bloody furs and red-encrusted mittens. She stood there in a quilted sleeping robe blinking her tired eyes and staring at him. After quickly looking up and down the hallway, she ushered him inside and said, "Oh, Danlo, I was beginning to think that you wouldn't come back. Seven days you've been gone—so long!"

"It is good to see you," he said as he took off his face mask and unzipped his furs. He quickly embraced her. "I thought about you every day."

She stood near him to take his furs and hang them on the drying rack near the door. "You can't go about the city like this. You look like you've been to war and murdered someone."

"I *did* murder someone," he said, as he began pulling the meat packets from his furs. "It was Totunye, a bear, a great-grandfather of a bear. I always had such bad luck hunting seals."

"Oh, no—I really didn't think you could kill *anything*. I'm so sorry that you had to do this for us."

"I . . . am sorry, too."

He looked about at the small, sparsely furnished apartment with the plasma stove in the corner and the pretty paintings on the wall. He looked toward the sleeping chamber, and he listened for Jonathan's deep breath of sleep beyond the closed door. Something about these two rooms immediately disturbed him. A faint fetor as of rotting flesh hung in the air. He worried that one of the meat packets or blood bags had somehow gone bad, and so he turned to examine them before Tamara put them away. But the contents of each one remained fresh and frozen; during his short journey from the City Wild, his body's heat hadn't had time to work at the meat. He wondered if Tamara had secured some meat in his absence. Perhaps Jonathan, like a sleekit, had hidden a tender tidbit beneath the shagshay fur or in some nook somewhere in the apartment and had then forgotten about it. But then, when Danlo turned to look at Tamara's gaunt face and soft, haunted eyes, his belly tightened, and he suddenly knew the source of this terrible smell.

"Jonathan," he said, softly. "It is Jonathan, yes?"

"What do you mean?"

He stood facing the door of the sleeping chamber, his nostrils opening and closing. He almost whispered, "I have smelled this before."

In truth, since the moment he had first stepped inside the apartment, he had known that Jonathan was very sick. The smell center of his brain, touched into life by a few powerful molecules floating in the air, had triggered a cascade of memories which he had tried to forget.

"I really can't smell anything," Tamara said, looking at him. "You must have keener senses than I."

"It is the frostbite, yes? His toes. Then the drugs did not help?"

"I wasn't able to buy any, Danlo. It seems that with all the cold this winter, everyone has frozen ears or toes and has needed drugs. Pilar and I tried all the cutting shops from the Merripen Green to the Long Glissade, and even the wormrunners, those who are still doing business. No one has any drugs."

"I see."

"I gave him an herbal tea—it was noria root and a few other things that one of Pilar's friends had put together." Tamara's eyes were glazed and dull with pain, and she suddenly seemed much older than her years. "I've tried to feed him what I could and keep him warm. I even prayed for him—I've done everything I could think of."

"I know that you must have," Danlo said.

"He's been asking for you, you know. Every day—really, every hour."

"I would like to see him."

"Now?"

"Yes. Even if he is sleeping, we should wake him and feed him some blood tea as soon as it is ready."

Tamara bent her head in agreement, and she moved off to open a bag of frozen blood and prepare a pot of tea. When she had finished melting this dark, crystalline mass and mixing it with teartree paste, she poured out the steaming red liquid into a mug and then stepped toward the sleeping chamber.

"Wait," Danlo said, putting his hand on her shoulder. "You should drink this yourself. And then bring Jonathan his tea."

"No, Jonathan first—I'm not really hungry."

Danlo looked at the stark lines of her face, the sunken eyes and cheekbones standing out beneath the pale skin. Truly, he thought, she was very hungry. He said, "There is plenty of food now. You should not be afraid to eat. Please."

"All right," Tamara finally said. She drank the mug of tea, quickly, almost compulsively, blowing on it between gulps to keep from burning her mouth. And when she had finished, she poured herself another mug and would have drunk that, too, if Danlo hadn't stopped her.

"You should give your stomach some time before drinking more," he said. "Or else you will lose what you have drunk."

She nodded her head and led him into the sleeping chamber. And instantly, the smells in the room fell over Danlo like a dark, heavy cloud and choked him so that *he* almost vomited. He smelled sweat and fear and the moistness of diarrhea that sometimes leaked from Jonathan's starving body. And he smelled something else, something much worse, the dark and terrible thing that was eating away Jonathan's flesh and poisoning his blood.

He lay beneath two thick shagshay furs sleeping fitfully and all curled up like a babe inside a womb. Danlo well knew the chills of starvation that no amount of clothing or coverings could drive away. And so he was very reluctant to expose Jonathan's naked body to the room's cold air. But he had to face the source of this terrible smell, and he gritted his teeth as he reached for the light key on the wall. And then he held his breath and peeled back the furs to look at his son's frostbitten toes.

Ti-anasa daivam.

As he had feared, the toes on both feet had fallen black with gangrene. And worse, the blackness had spread almost to the ankles, where bands of dark blue and streaks of red gave way to the paler, still-healthy tissues. His son's feet were rotting off his body, and they stank of decay and death.

Ti-anasa daivam.

Just then Jonathan moved his legs and moaned in his sleep, and Danlo dropped back the covers. "Jonathan, Jonathan," he whispered.

"I'm sorry," Tamara said, standing by Danlo's side. "I think I've waited too long."

"Yes," Danlo said. But there was no anger or blame in his voice, only compassion for Jonathan—and Tamara.

"I kept hoping that I'd find a cryologist or cutter who had the drugs to heal this," she said. "And then, when it began to spread past the toes, I hoped that you'd return, with meat, of course, or any kind of food that we could give him to build up his strength before. . . . Oh, Danlo, I just couldn't *bear* to take him to the cutters like this. I wanted to save his toes, and now I'm afraid that he'll lose both feet. But he's so weak, he's not ready for that. I don't even want to take him outside on the streets, and I'm so afraid, Danlo, so stupidly, stupidly afraid.''

She wept, then, and she and Danlo stood above the bed holding each other and watching Jonathan sleep. After a while, she began to whisper her deepest fears. She told him of a cutter down on Nirvanna Street who had dealt with the results of the season's cold weather in the cruelest and crudest of ways. Even before his drugs had run out, where other treatment might have been possible, this cutter had fallen into an amputation frenzy, hacking off fingers, ears, noses and toes at the first sign of frostbite. He claimed thus to have saved many lives. But many there were who wandered about the city crippled in their limbs and missing parts of their faces. And many more, it was said, had died of infections after submitting to such horrible surgeries. As Tamara told Danlo, she feared taking Jonathan to such a cutter almost more than she feared for his life.

''There is one cutter who might be able to help him,'' Danlo said. ''He would still have the cryonic drugs. And antibiotics and immunosols as well.''

''The cutter who changed you?'' Tamara quietly asked.

''Yes. And if he cannot save the feet, he can at least keep Jonathan from pain and infection.''

''I can't bear for him to lose his feet.''

''I know,'' he said, touching her face. ''But after the war is over, he can always have his feet regrown.''

''By your cutter?''

''No—he would ask too much money. But the Order will have to persuade the city's other cutters to restore everyone who has lost fingers or toes to frostbite.''

''Won't *your* cutter ask for money to heal Jonathan's feet?''

''He might. Do you have any money?''

Tamara nodded her head and stepped into the other room for a moment. She returned carrying a bag of gold coins. ''It's all I have left.''

Danlo hefted the jingling coins in his hand and then tucked them into the pocket of his kamelaika. He said, ''It is almost dawn. After Jonathan has had his tea, I will take him to the cutter.''

"I'll come with you, then," she said.

"All right—if you'd like."

"He's my son," she said. "He's all I have."

After that, she gently shook Jonathan awake. At first, he seemed dazed and confused, the lethargy of sleep combining with the apathy of starvation. But when he saw Danlo kneeling on his bed, he smiled weakly and tried to sit up. This proved quite difficult for him to do. His arms and legs had begun to form contractures, almost freezing them in a curled-up, fetal position. The act of straightening his tortured limbs caused him to wince and cry out in pain. For a moment, the furs fell back to reveal his starved body. Danlo was shocked at the changes that only seven days had wrought in his son, for he seemed little more than a skeleton covered with skin. He stared at Danlo with his sad brown eyes, the lenses of which had clouded over and the whites discolored with an unusual bluish hue.

"Father," he said, "you're home."

"Yes, I am home."

Danlo moved over to pull the furs around Jonathan and hold him while Tamara pressed the mug of tea to his lips. Although he was so weak and light in his body that Danlo wanted to weep, he drank the blood tea as greedily as a wolf pup sucking down his mother's milk.

"Did you kill a seal, then?" he asked after he had finished his tea. "Mama said that you went out on the sea to hunt seals."

For a while they sat there on the bed as Danlo recounted the story of his killing the bear. Twice, Tamara got up to pour another mug of tea for Jonathan—and for Danlo and herself. Jonathan would have drunk even more of this bloody elixir, and perhaps have gobbled down a fat steak as well, but he seemed suddenly sick in his belly, and Danlo told him that he must wait before eating anything more. And so they waited.

Danlo drew forth his flute and played a song for Jonathan. And when he had finished, Jonathan asked for another, and he lay all curled up listening to the music that filled the room like lovely, floating pearls. With the rising of the sun, the white curtains over the window began to glow with a deep light. Tamara stared at this reddish glow as if she dreaded the breaking of the new day. And then, while Danlo breathed into his flute and counted his heartbeats, she sighed and closed her eyes, staring inside herself. She seemed to be looking for a different kind of light that might give her strength to face the coming ordeal.

When morning finally arrived, they dressed Jonathan in his

kamelaika, a torturous task since they had to work the tight fabric up and over his swollen feet. Once, he jerked uncontrollably at the cold, and this sudden motion caused the leg zipper to scrape across his foot. He screamed, then, a soft, high, strangled sound terrible to hear. He pleaded with Tamara to let him stay in bed. So great was his fear of cutters that he grabbed at the bed's furs, refusing to leave. But Tamara told him that Danlo had found a cutter who would be gentle with him. This man, she said, had drugs that would heal his feet. At last, Jonathan let go of the covers and clutched at Tamara instead. He buried his face in her breasts and murmured, "No, no, he'll hurt me—I don't want to die, Mama."

Tamara looked at Danlo in silent despair, then, as she tried to blink away her tears.

"I will not let you die," Danlo said, laying his hand on Jonathan's head. "I promise."

For a long time Danlo and Jonathan looked at each other. Something bright and fiery in Danlo's eyes must have given Jonathan hope, for after that he made no further complaint. He allowed Tamara to slip on a pair of silk-lined slippers and his outer furs. Then Danlo bundled him with the two bed furs, wrapping him up as snugly as a frittilary in a cocoon. After putting on his own face mask and nothing more (Danlo didn't dare to wear his blood-stained furs in the daylight), he lifted Jonathan in his arms. The boy seemed as light as a bag of feathers. Although he would have to carry him a long way through the city, he wished that he was much heavier.

It was a bitter morning and really much too early to be skating about on the uncertain streets. The air smothered them like ice water, a temperature that Danlo knew as *hurdu,* a wet blue cold falling quickly to dead cold. The frozen glidderies seemed as darkly purple as a bruise. The sky itself was darkening with gray-white bands of *ilketha.* Later that day, he feared, would come the *moratetha,* the death clouds of a full winter storm. Already the wind had begun gusting from the south, driving tiny ice crystals against the windows of the shops. Danlo, dressed only in his thin kamelaika, should have been very cold. But the heat of Jonathan close against him and his own intense inner fire kept him from shivering. Even so, Tamara insisted on stopping at a clothing shop down on Silver Street, one of the few free ones that were still open. Tamara, who was always wiser in the ways of money than Danlo, paid the shopkeeper a small bribe to dig out a fine shagshay fur that he had hidden at the back of the store. The thick white fur would keep Danlo warm, and almost as important, keep any passerby from wondering who would be skating about the city almost naked in a black kamelaika.

They made the journey down the Serpentine to the Ashtoreth District without incident. They passed by autists dressed in rags and starving harijan and hibakusha dying of various diseases. And others. Despite the many layers of fur wrapped around Jonathan, somewhere near the Winter Ring he began shivering from the cold. But he was always cold these days, he said, and he told Danlo not to worry. He lay quietly in Danlo's arms trying not to cry out when Danlo hit a sudden bump in the ice or shifted to adjust his weight. He looked up at Danlo with an almost infinite trust brightening his clouded eyes. And Danlo looked down at him, more often than was wise given the ill-kept surface of the streets. But he could not help himself. He thought that even through the furs separating him from Jonathan, he could feel his heart, his little *ardu,* beating quickly like a bird's. He could certainly smell his feet; it was the smell of death: the dead, blackened tissues of his feet sending out gases that mixed with the other death smells hanging heavy in the air.

On almost every street, it seemed, smoke issued from the plasma ovens burning the bodies of those who had died during the night. Although Danlo covered Jonathan's face against the taint of charred flesh and burnt blood, the boy couldn't help trembling with fear, especially when they turned down Loyang Street with its many hospices giving shelter to the city's most desperately sick. Danlo felt close to trembling himself, with fear for Jonathan, and with love. He felt his own feet all warm and quick with life; if he could have pulled them from his boots and sawed them off to save Jonathan's feet, he would have. But in the end, each of us must bear the pain of life alone, no matter that there are those who would suffer with us. In the end, all Danlo could do was to skate, to hold Jonathan close to him and pray that he would choose some other morning to make the journey to the other side of day.

When they turned onto the Street of Mansions, Tamara gave a start of recognition, for she had once lived in a fine house just off the nearby Long Glissade. In truth, her mother and many of her brothers and sisters still lived there—and hundreds of her cousins and her greater family lived in the surrounding neighborhoods. They were all astriers and good Architects of one of the Cybernetic Reformed Churches. And they had all turned away from Tamara; when she had left her family to become a courtesan, they had disseised her, formally denying her bread, salt, wine, and communion with any of the Church's holy computers. To them, it was as if she had never been born. She was less than dead—as was her son and any other children she might ever bear.

"I went to my mother," Tamara said as they glided down the tree-lined street. "When the hunger began, I begged her for food—you might not know it, but the Church asks all astriers to keep a seven-year store of food. Most keep less than a year's worth, but my mother is the *Worthy* Victoria One Ashtoreth, and she always followed the eight duties so terribly strictly. There's *plenty* of food in her house. I know. But my mother wouldn't even open the door for me. Or for her own grandson. She pretended not to see us. Oh, Danlo, how can anyone be so cruel?"

But Danlo had no answer for her. She seemed lost in her memories, and her usually soft, brown eyes had fallen almost bright black with anger. In the face of her deep pride, it was astonishing that she had gone to her mother for help. Only her love (and fear) for Jonathan could have driven her to such a desperate act. Hers was truly a deep, deep love, pure and elemental; gazing into her darkly savage eyes just then was like looking through cracks in the ice down through layers of rock into the fiery heart of the world. As he watched her skating in step by his side, all the while stealing fiercely adoring glances at Jonathan, he thought that she would do almost anything to keep him from harm. Where he had killed a bear for Jonathan, she might possibly slay another human being in defense of his life. Certainly, she would die for him; as Danlo felt the weight of her son pressed up against his own heart, he marveled once again at the terrible and beautiful power of love.

Ti-anasa daivam.

At last they came to Constancio of Alesar's house, with its surrounding wall and shiny steel gate. Danlo banged his fist against the steel bars, and a harsh grating sound rang out onto the street. He waited a few moments and then knocked again. After a while the tall blond guard whom Danlo had befriended during his previous visits came out of the nearby warming pavilion. The guard—his name was Siegfried Olafson—seemed irritable and tired. He skated up to the gate with his hands held out as if to shoo them away. But when he saw Danlo's familiar face mask and the eyes that stared out at him from beneath it, he frowned a moment, and then smiled.

"Danlo of Kweitkel," he said, bowing politely. "I didn't expect to see you again."

"I have come because I need Constancio's help." Danlo held up Jonathan so that Siegfried could see his face. "This is my son, Jonathan. And this is his mother, Tamara."

"I wish you well," Siegfried said, "but I'm afraid Constancio won't be able to help you."

"My son is very sick," Danlo said. He told Siegfried about the frostbite, then, and how Jonathan's feet had fallen rotten with gangrene. "I . . . have hoped that Constancio would have the cryonics to save his feet."

"Maybe he would; maybe he wouldn't. But he doesn't want anyone else coming to him for any more cuttings—he told me this himself."

"I like to believe that he would still want to help me," Danlo said. "As he helped me before, yes?"

"I'm sorry, but you've wasted your time."

Holding Jonathan with one arm, Danlo dug in the pocket of his furs for the bag of coins that Tamara had given him. He gave it to Siegfried through the steel bars.

"Will you please take this to Constancio? It is all that we have."

Siegfried pulled at his icy mustache for a moment, and then closed his fist around the coins. "All right—if you ask. Please wait here."

And with that he turned to skate up the walkway to the house. Danlo, whose arms ached from carrying Jonathan across half the city, sat down on the purple ice while Tamara stood there gazing through the gate at the line of flashing laser lights that made a fence around Constancio's property. Beneath the ruff of her furs, her face was wind-burnt and calm, although Danlo knew that inside she must be fairly trembling with impatience. It was hard to wait on that cold, lonely street. The bitter wind blew off the sea from the south, and the sun was little more than a dark, red smear behind the deepening clouds. Jonathan continued shivering and suffering in silence as he looked up at Danlo for reassurance. Danlo could do little more than touch eyes with him. He thought of the Alaloi word for waiting, *vania,* and he marveled at the courage that Tamara and Jonathan showed in waiting for their fate to unfold.

After a while, Siegfried returned still clutching the bag of coins in his hand. "I'm sorry," he said. "But it's as I told you—Constancio won't see you."

After Danlo had stood up again, Siegfried passed the coins back to him through the steel bars. Danlo moved to put them back in his pocket, but just then Tamara sidled over to him and took the coins instead. She weighed them in her hand, which caused the coins to chink against each other inside the leather bag. And then she looked at Siegfried and said, "You've taken a coin for yourself, haven't you?"

Siegfried's face fell red with blood as he spat at the walkway. Almost instantly, the frothy white liquid froze into ice. "And what if I have? Shouldn't I be paid for my labors?"

She flashed him a dark, dreadful look and then turned to Jonathan. With a fierce resolve, but gently and with almost infinite grace, she peeled back the furs cocooning him. It took her only a moment to remove his slippers, and then she quickly covered him up again—all of him except his feet.

"Look," she said as Siegfried recoiled in horror at what had happened to Jonathan. The wind blew the stench of rotting flesh straight into Siegfried's face. "My son is fighting for his life."

"I'm sorry," Siegfried muttered. "These are bad times."

Tamara put Jonathan's slippers back on him and wrapped the bed furs about him again. She said, "Why don't you return to ask Constancio for his help once more?"

"I'm sorry, but he wouldn't give it."

"Not even for a child who has nowhere else to go?"

"I'm afraid not—Constancio hates children."

"Has he no heart, then?"

"Well, not a *human* heart. I'd heard that he replaced his real heart with an artificial one years ago. I think he was afraid that the nerves there would misfire, and it would just stop beating."

Tamara stared at Siegfried for a long time before saying, "Why don't you open the gate so that I can talk with him?"

"No, I'm afraid that's impossible. Now please go—it's too cold to stand out here arguing." Siegfried looked at Danlo and said, "Please take your woman and your son away from here before they freeze to death."

"We'll go, then," Tamara said to him. "But first give us back the coin."

"What?"

"Your master can choose to help us or not—I suppose that's his right. But we shouldn't be charged just for asking his help."

"Well, these are bad times," Siegfried said again.

"Give us back the coin. Please."

Siegfried thrust his hand into his pocket as if to honor her request. But then he said, "It's just a coin—now go before it's too late."

Again, Tamara fixed him with her dark eyes. "Have *you* no heart?" she asked.

"I have a son of my own," Siegfried said. "On Thorskalle—it's a poor place, as you may know. My son is very bright, but we've had no money for an education. After the war is over, I'll return there, and every coin I've earned serving Constancio will go toward buying him a place in one of the elite schools."

"I'm sorry about your son. But at least he isn't dying."

"And neither is yours—he's already dead. There isn't a cutter in the city who will be able to help him. You should save your coins for those who really need them."

At this, Tamara leaned closer to Jonathan and put her hands over his ears to keep him from hearing Siegfried's cruel words. But it was too late, for he looked at Tamara with panic in his eyes as if Siegfried had just stuck an icy dagger of fear into him.

"Give us back the coin," Tamara demanded again. "It may be that this single coin will make the difference in our affording the services of a cutter who could help him."

There was a moment, then. Tamara locked eyes with Siegfried, and they struggled with each other, his will against hers. Finally, he reached into his pocket and cast the golden coin through the bars of the gate. It rang against the street's ice and lay there glittering.

"Take it, then, if it means so much to you. Now go before I send the robots against you."

As Tamara bent to retrieve the coin, Danlo swallowed against the rage he felt burning up his throat. All this time he had remained nearly motionless, listening to his racing heart and staring at Siegfried. During the days of his transformation, he had come to think of the man as his friend, but his petty thievery made a mockery of such sentiments. In trying to steal the coin, he had tried to steal the life of his son. Truly. And this betrayal touched off in Danlo a terrible, black wrath. He instantly hated Siegfried. He wanted to use his powerful new body to break down the gate and strangle him. But it is one thing to kill a bear for his meat, and another to harm a fellow human being for simply being human. In the end, Danlo forced himself to breathe deeply the cold air smothering him and to look away from Siegfried. Then he shifted Jonathan in his arms and turned to skate away.

Never harming another, not even in one's thoughts.

For a long time he and Tamara skated up the Street of Mansions toward the Serpentine. The wind howled and their skate blades struck the street in a rhythmic cutting of steel against ice.

Finally, near the Winter Ring, they paused to take shelter inside a
warming pavilion. They sat on a scarred, old wooden bench. As
Danlo held Jonathan near one of the hot air vents to warm him,
Tamara rested her naked hand on Jonathan's head. He was all
curled up inside his furs, staring off into the air; he seemed listless
and not to care anymore what happened to him. For Danlo (and
Tamara as well) this apathy was more terrible than if he had cried
and bitterly protested his fate. It made Danlo want to cry out in
rage and rail against his own bitter fate.

"What are we going to do?" Tamara asked as she leaned her
head next to Danlo's and whispered to him.

And he whispered back, "You know what we have to do."

"No, I can't."

"We have no choice."

"I'm afraid it will kill him. If he's to die anyway, I'd rather it
be at home, in bed, without all the pain."

"But a cutter might still be able to save him."

"But the pain, Danlo—I just can't bear for him to feel all the
pain."

Danlo sat looking into Tamara's eyes, which were shiny with
tears like two dark mirrors. *Pain is the awareness of life,* he remembered. And then, *Pain is the price of life.*

"We have no choice," he said again.

"I know," she said. "But it's just so horribly unfair."

"Truly, it is."

"For everyone, really, it's *all* so horrible, isn't it?"

"Yes."

"But why, Danlo? Why does it have to be this way?"

"I . . . do not know."

She sighed and took a breath of air. And then another, and
another, and she closed her eyes for a while to gather her strength.
At last, she looked down at Jonathan and said, "All right—I'm
ready."

Danlo smiled at her courage. Because she could not see his
face beneath his mask, he tried to let all his own courage and love
of life pour out through his eyes. The High Holy-Ivi of the Cybernetic Universal Church had once named him the Lightbringer,
after all, and he should have been able to find a few golden rays of
hope for the mother of his child and the only woman whom he
had ever loved. But the star that had once burned so brightly
inside him had nearly gone out. He felt dead inside, as dark and
cold as ashes. And so he could do little more than to lay his hand
on her shoulder and say, "I know that it will be all right."

They found a shop on the Street of Cutters and Splicers not far from Tamara's apartment. It belonged to a man named Rodas Alabi whom Danlo had met during the days when he had searched the city for a cutter who could sculpt him. Danlo had instantly liked Rodas, with his big, easy smile and knowing eyes; he had sensed that Rodas was a fine cutter (and he had heard this from others), and so it seemed only natural that he should come to him with his son.

Rodas' shop was small and simple, fronted with nothing more than plain white granite. The plain wooden door opened onto an outer room where Rodas' clients waited to be served. That day only two others—a pregnant astrier woman and a rich exemplar—were there ahead of them. Danlo sat with Tamara and Jonathan on soft, blue cushions opposite them. He set Jonathan on Tamara's lap, and then looked across the cold room. The harijan and exemplar were discussing their respective afflictions without shame or care for who might be listening. The exemplar complained of a pair of too-tight boots that had caused a corn to grow on the side of his toe; he had come to the cutter to have the painful callous removed. The astrier woman, it seemed, had come to have her baby removed. She told the man that she wouldn't give birth to a child whom she couldn't feed. "I can't even feed myself," she said in a high voice that whined like a cloud of furflies. "It's a terrible world where a mother has to make this kind of choice."

After a while, the door to the inner rooms opened, and an autist staggered out. He was perhaps a young man, but his long, stringy hair had gone white and he seemed nothing more than rags and bones. Obviously, the cutter had removed his nose and both his ears, for bandages of clear thinskin covered these raw, red, newly-made openings to his head. Most others would have worn a face mask to hide such disfigurements, but the man was an autist, after all, much used to playing upon people's pity in order to beg a few coins from them. Although autists are supposed to have little sense of reality (as opposed to that transcendent ground of being that they call the realreal), he immediately singled out Tamara as someone who might help him. Without a glance at the astrier woman and the rich exemplar, he stepped straight over to Tamara. He held his hands cupped before her like a bowl. "Please, good woman," he said. Because his gaping nasal cavities were covered with the clear thinskin, he was forced to breathe through his mouth. This caused him to speak in a high, twangy voice hard to listen to. "May the good God smile upon your kindness."

Out of compassion, if not pity, Tamara reached into the pocket of her furs to find a coin for this wretched creature. But before she could give him one, he looked at Jonathan who was staring at him boldly without loathing or fear. He suddenly broke the bowl of his hands and shook his head at Tamara. And then he reached into his own mildewed furs and pulled out a smooth, gray dreamstone. He gave it to Tamara and said, "For the boy, to dream the good dream and walk through the real with his dream body. That he might walk again through the lesser real with his lesser body."

Danlo smiled at the autists' belief that human beings, in communion with the realreal, can dream the world into existence. He smiled at the autist. He wished the world could be so simple that a simple dream might save Jonathan's feet; nevertheless, he was grateful to the autist for his blessing.

"May the good God dream you well," Danlo said to the autist. Once, as a young man, he had eaten rice balls with the autists in the Merripen Green and learned from the autist dream guides how to dream their communal, lucid dreams. "And may you dream the good God and dwell in the realreal."

For a long time, the autist stared at Danlo's brilliant blue eyes and looked at him strangely. And then, quite mysteriously, he whispered, "Never forget your dream."

He turned to leave the shop, but before he could reach the door, the exemplar spat out, "Filthy autist."

And then the autist, smiling, reached into his greasy hair to pluck out a few of the lice that made their home there. He threw the little insects straight at the exemplar's head. When the exemplar fairly dived off his cushions to avoid being infested, the autist smiled again and said, "Filthy rich man. Your life is only a bad dream."

With that he bowed low, opened the door of the shop, and was gone.

Shortly after this, Rodas Alabi emerged from his inner rooms. He had a round, kindly face and a once-round body much reduced by hunger. He wore a fresh white cotton kimono; obviously the garment must have been new since it was impossible to find soap with which to do laundry. He came straight over to greet Tamara, Danlo and Jonathan. He took one look at Jonathan's glassy eyes and shivering body, and announced, "I'll take you next."

Of course the exemplar, who had been waiting longer than Jonathan, protested this decision. But the cutter quieted him with a single look. Then he turned to nod at Danlo and Tamara. "Why don't you bring the boy back?" he said.

They followed Rodas through the open door and then down a short hallway into a room of cushions and bright red rugs spread from wall to wall. Two fireplaces full of blazing wood logs kept the room warm; various green plants in brightly painted pots filled the room with fresh oxygen. Windowless as the room was, it might have been dark except for two fires and the electric lamps that gave forth a clean, white light. It was almost too bright to be comfortable, but Rodas had brought them here to examine Jonathan, and he needed a strong light with which to see.

"It's his feet, isn't it?" he said. He pointed at Jonathan, whom Danlo had propped up against a few cushions. "Let's get his furs off, then."

While Tamara unwrapped the furs to expose Jonathan's feet, Rodas held his breath as if he expected a blow to his belly. And then, at the sight of the blackened limbs, he exhaled suddenly and sighed, "Well, then, I've seen too much of this lately."

"Can you help him?" Tamara immediately asked.

Rodas stared off at the wall for a moment and then looked at Jonathan straight in the eyes. He said, "I can't save your feet, Jonathan, because there aren't any of the medicines left. But I think I can save your life. Do you understand?"

Jonathan, all curled up and shaking with fear as much as cold, slowly nodded his head. "You have to cut off my feet—will it hurt very badly?"

"I don't have any of the pain medicines left," Rodas said. "But I can use a nerve block; we'll do what we can."

"I'm afraid," Jonathan said.

"I know you are," Rodas said. He patted Jonathan's head and then traded long, grave looks with both Danlo and Tamara. "If all goes well, I can have both feet off in less than five minutes."

"So . . . quickly?" Danlo asked.

"I'll have the assistance of Fostora-made surgical robots. There is only one thing. . . ."

"Yes?"

Rodas led Danlo over near the crackling fire where they could have a space of privacy. He said, "The surgery *will* be quick, but you'll have to help. You and the boy's mother."

"Help . . . how?"

"You'll have to hold him down."

"I see."

"Can you do this?"

Danlo took a long, deep breath, and then said, "I think so. Yes."

"I'm having restraints made to fit my chair," Rodas said. "But they're not ready yet. Who would ever have thought I'd have to resort to such barbarisms?"

But Danlo had no answer for him. All he could do was to look at Jonathan as he lay trembling on his furs and staring up at Tamara.

"Very well," Rodas said. "And the boy's mother—will she be able to help, too?"

Danlo waited while his heart beat five times, and then he said, "Yes—she is very strong."

"Very well," Rodas said again, and he walked back near Tamara. "We should begin soon."

"And what will the cost be?" Tamara asked.

"There will be no cost to you," Rodas said. "Not for this."

"But your time, your tools, your—"

"Others pay what they can," Rodas broke in. He looked off toward the door that led to his outer rooms where the astrier woman and exemplar waited. "There are still many rich people in Neverness."

"Thank you," Tamara said.

Rodas nodded to Danlo, who squatted to lift Jonathan into his arms. Despite the room's heat, Jonathan was shaking and shivering more violently now. He looked up at Danlo with his sad, knowing eyes and said, "Please, Father—I'm afraid."

"It will be all right," Danlo said. He brushed the hair back from Jonathan's forehead and looked at him. "Truly, it will be all right."

He followed Rodas and Tamara out the door into the hallway, then. Rodas showed them into a brilliantly lit room of white tiles and other hard surfaces. The air stank of burnt flesh and ozone and some disinfectant that smelled like stomach acid. Rodas bade Danlo to lay Jonathan on a large chair occupying the room's center. This gleaming black machine—there was no other word for it—adjusted itself to fit the angles of Jonathan's small, contracted body. Although it looked quite forbidding, with its covering of scleen plastic, a soft, thermal inner gel provided Jonathan with heat as well as a relative degree of comfort. The scleen was very hard and very smooth; it could easily be wiped clean of blood and the bacteria that might infect Rodas' clients.

"Mama, Mama," Jonathan said, looking up at Tamara.

Rodas covered Jonathan's naked body with a plain white sheet. He apologized for having no clean coverings that Tamara and Danlo might wear, nor any way of providing them means to wash.

All his disinfectant, he said, had to be saved for the chair and various objects of the room, and of course, his cutting tools.

"These are barbaric times," he said. "But we'll do what we can."

He bade Danlo to hold down Jonathan's upper body and positioned Tamara over the boy's legs. After swabbing the ankle area with a little of the strong-smelling disinfectant, he strapped a nerve block to Jonathan's right leg just above the knee. This long, black curving computer looked something like a piece of body armor that one might wear for a particularly vicious game of hokkee. But, in theory, it would generate a powerful field that would block all signals running up the nerves of Jonathan's leg. If all went well, Jonathan should feel almost no sensation below his knee and certainly no pain.

"We're almost ready," Rodas said.

He rolled one of his Fostora-made surgical robots up to the right side of the table. This was a great, glittering thing of lasers and needles and many kinds of diamond-steel drills and saws. Its fifty tentacle-like arms could be fitted with retractors and suctors and clamps—or fiber opticals or tlolts or any of the other ten thousand tools that might be used upon a person's flesh. Most importantly, these arms might be programmed for various surgical tasks. As Danlo leaned gently on Jonathan's shoulders and pressed him down against the table, Rodas snapped various tools onto the hands of each arm and made the proper programming. Then he traded long, grave looks with Danlo and Tamara, and said, "Please don't let the boy move."

Now Danlo leaned harder against Jonathan, while Tamara fairly lay across Jonathan's thighs as she held his lower legs. And Jonathan looked up at Danlo and said, "Please, Father—don't let him hurt me."

At first, all went well. Rodas began with the right foot. His plan was to take it off just below the joint, thereby leaving the bone intact and making a regrowth easier. He activated the robot, and it suddenly went to work in a fury of flashing steel and pulsing lasers. The many robot arms performed an intricate dance, circling Jonathan's leg like so many writhing snakes. Their coordination was unbelievable. Tiny scalpels cut through skin, nerves, tendons and ligaments while the lasers worked to cauterize the severed blood vessels. During the two minutes of this surgery, Jonathan experience little pain. The worst of it, for him, was the weight of Danlo and Tamara holding his curled-up body straight. And, of course, the sounds: steel whirring against the bony ten-

dons; the suck of cartilage being pulled apart; and the hissing of
the lasers as their heat vaporized Jonathan's blood. A stench of
ozone and cooked flesh mixed with the rot of gangrene and enveloped the table. Danlo could no more escape this terrible smell
than he could avoid looking down into Jonathan's eyes or quiet
the hammering of his own heart. His heart beat quickly a hundred
and eighty-four times before Rodas said, "Very good," and
turned off the robot. He could feel his own blood pulsing up
through his throbbing head, and down along his spine, through his
legs and into his feet.

"Please, Father—is he finished yet?"

As it happened, Rodas was finished with the right foot. With a
loud thump, he cast the blackened member unceremoniously into
a waste container. Then he moved toward the nerve block and told
Tamara and Danlo, "I'm sorry I only have one of these—hold
him tightly, now."

As he unfastened the nerve block and moved to strap it to
Jonathan's other leg, Jonathan's whole body suddenly contracted
as if jolted with electricity. "Oh, oh!" he cried out, "it hurts, it
hurts!"

Rodas rolled the robot over to the other side of the table while
Danlo caught Jonathan's eyes and told him that the pain wouldn't
last long. And Tamara began singing him a song to take his mind
off the fire eating away at the stump at the end of his leg:

> Little child, little child,
> Dancing down the starry Wild.

"Barbaric," Rodas muttered as he made a slight adjustment in
the robot's programming. "It's barbaric that I should have no
drugs to give him."

But it seemed that Jonathan's pain might be just bearable and
the worst of his torment over. He lay against the table listening to
Tamara's singing, all the while gripping Danlo's arms with his
little hands, moaning and gasping for air and trying to be brave.
Danlo wanted to weep at the courage and pain that he saw in his
son's eyes, and he was awed by his terrible will to live.

Ti-anasa daivam.

And then Rodas began to cut off the other foot. Once again,
cold steel began to bite through skin and bone, and lasers flashed
out to touch Jonathan's arteries with their ruby fire. This time,
Jonathan jumped at the crunching and sucking sounds of his flesh
coming apart, for although he didn't yet feel the pain of it, he

knew that he soon would. "Please, Father," he gasped, and the hurt of his right leg became the agony of his left, and there was no difference. Danlo hoped that this time, when the surgery was finished, Rodas might leave the nerve block in place a while longer to ease Jonathan's pain. Or perhaps they might even give him a few coins in exchange for the use of the nerve block, for a few days while Jonathan's stumps were healing. Danlo looked down at Jonathan lying so helplessly beneath his weight, and he thought that he would do anything to ease his pain.

Boom, boom, boom. Danlo counted the beats of his heart and prayed that Rodas might amputate the left foot as quickly as he had the right. *One hundred twenty-one, one hundred twenty-two, one hundred twenty-three* . . .

And then, quite suddenly, as Rodas was cutting through the Achilles tendon, the nerve block failed. Rodas would later discover that its power cells had gone dead. But in the moment, all he could do was to grit his teeth at the terrible scream that ripped through the room. For the count of three heartbeats, Rodas continued guiding the robot through the great tendon, and Jonathan continued screaming in agony.

"Ahhhh!" he shrieked out in a high, terrible cry. "Ahhhhhh!"

Tamara, furiously gripping Jonathan's thrashing legs, looked at the robot's dozens of arms snaking around Jonathan's foot. "Stop it!" she said to Rodas. "Can't you stop it—you're killing him!"

"No—we're almost done," Rodas said. "Another minute, please."

"Ahhh, ahhh, ahhhhh . . ."

Boom, boom, boom . . .

"Please, please," Tamara begged as the tears flooded her eyes. "Please stop."

Please, Father.

As Danlo pushed down on Jonathan's shoulders, Jonathan shook his head back and forth, and he never stopped screaming. His eyes had fallen wild and almost mindless, as if they might jump out of his head. But once, between breaths, in gathering strength for a further round of screaming, Jonathan looked up at Danlo in full lucidity. And there was nothing in his eyes except terrible pain and a terrible awareness that he could never escape it. Laser light burned through his flesh, and he begged with his eyes for Danlo to make the agony go away, but there was nothing that Danlo could do. It was the worst moment of his life. He counted the beats of his racing heart, all the while praying that Jonathan's little heart wouldn't suddenly fail from the fire tearing through him.

Please, Father—let me die.

"No, no," Danlo whispered. "No, no, no, no."

After another thirty seconds (thirty years for Danlo, and for Jonathan, thirty thousand), Rodas shut down the robot and stood back from the table. He rubbed a sponge soaked with disinfectant over Jonathan's raw stumps and then sprayed them with bandages of thinskin.

"Mama, Mama, please," Jonathan cried out, "it hurts, it hurts."

"I'm sorry," Rodas said as he unfastened the nerve block and examined it with disgust. "But new power cells are impossible to come by these days."

"Please—I want to go home."

Tamara dressed Jonathan, then, and picked him up to hold him. She sat on the far end of the table (that part not spattered with tiny bone fragments and blood), all the while rocking back and forth and holding her head against his as she resumed her song:

> *Come and play, come and play,*
> *Dancing down the Milky Way.*

This quieted Jonathan, a little. He sat in Tamara's lap, shaking and murmuring in pain. He seemed not to care what had happened to his feet. It took all his strength simply to look up at Tamara and say, "Please, Mama—take me home."

At a nod from the cutter, Danlo wrapped him in his white bed furs. He stood by the bloody, black chair looking at Jonathan and trying to get his breathing right.

"Do you live far from here?" Rodas asked.

"No, only a few blocks."

"Good. Keep the boy as warm as you can, and make him drink, even if he doesn't want to. I don't think that he'll fall into shock but . . ."

"Yes?"

"There's a great danger of infection—do you understand?"

Danlo inclined his head once and traded long, knowing looks with Rodas. And he asked, "Is there nothing you can give him, then?"

"No, I'm afraid not. The whole city is empty of drugs."

"I see."

"I'm sorry," Rodas said. He laid his hand on Danlo's shoulder. "But the boy is strong, so don't lose hope."

After that, Danlo and Tamara put on their furs. Tamara gave Jonathan into Danlo's arms and led them back to the outer room where the harijan woman still waited for Rodas to rid her of her baby. (The exemplar, it seemed, had decided to seek the services of a less busy cutter.) When they went out into the street, they found that it had finally begun to snow: tiny, broken flakes of *raishay* as cold as death. The sky was all closed-in gray and clouds of swirling white. They skated in silence back through the snowswept streets to Tamara's apartment. None of the other people hurrying through the storm greeted them or even looked their way. It didn't take them very long to trudge up the tenement's stone steps, to walk down the hallway, close themselves behind a hard, shatterwood door and put Jonathan to bed.

They spent the next day in simply caring for Jonathan. Tamara made him many pots of blood tea and sang him songs. Once, she ventured to cook up a bear steak dripping with juice and fat, but Jonathan couldn't stomach such a rich food. It was left to Danlo to eat the meat, and this he did. He did all that he could to keep up his strength so that he might devote himself to his son. Mostly, when Jonathan wasn't sleeping, he told him stories about the animals' adventures during the first days of the world and played his flute for him. Although Jonathan cried out often at the pain of his throbbing stumps—a soft, murmuring music of his own— sometimes he fell into a silence as vast and deep as the sea. His eyes glazed like ice over water, and he seemed to be looking inside himself at a dark, desolate place towards which no one could journey except himself. Then Danlo would breathe deeply and count the beats of his heart; then he would look upon Jonathan with all the light of his love and pray for him.

Early the following morning, Danlo and Tamara learned of something that only further darkened their spirits. It had nothing to do with Jonathan, at least not directly. A lightship arrived at the Hollow Fields, and its pilot, Faxon Bey, like a leper carrying a plague, brought war news that almost no one wanted to hear. He told of another skirmish fought between the Fellowship Fleet and that of the Ringists: it seemed that the pilot-captain named Bardo, in command of two battle groups, had nearly destroyed a full cadre of Ringist ships out near the Orenda Double. And worse, on the planet Cilehe, the Ringists and their enemies had used laser satellites against each other and exploded hydrogen bombs; they had released both info and biological viruses to infect human

beings and the computers upon which their lives depended. Faxon
Bey said that at least seventy million people had died. And this
wasn't the worst of his news.

As he reported to the Lord of the Order, Audric Pall, the planet
Helaku High was no more. Its star had fallen supernova, instantly
vaporizing five billion people and everything else that lived there.
And it was almost certain that Bertram Jaspari's Iviomils, with
their *morrashar,* had caused the supernova. The rumor spreading
through Neverness like some wild plague held that the Iviomils
were waging a war of vengeance. Or perhaps they were campaign-
ing for Bertram Jaspari's release. Since they hadn't been able to
approach the Star of Neverness, they had taken their terror elsewhere. They had fallen quite mad, of course, and everyone feared
that they would destroy the Civilized Worlds one by one if they
weren't themselves destroyed first.

"It must all end soon," Danlo told Tamara over cups of blood
tea while Jonathan was sleeping. No matter how slow or fast
Danlo breathed, he couldn't rid himself of the fierce pain that tore
through his head. His chest hurt, too, as if his heart were pushing
out against his ribs. Although he hadn't known a soul on Helaku
High, its destruction was too much like that of Alumit Bridge,
whose Narain people he had known very well. "My time is coming soon—I must do what I can to end this *shaida* war."

"Are you thinking of leaving us, then? You're ready to go
ahead with your plan, aren't you?"

"Yes, I am. But I will not leave Jonathan like this. First, he
must get well."

But Jonathan did not get well. In truth, all during the second
day since the amputation of his feet, he grew only weaker. He fell
into fever, and the tissues around his stump reddened like heated
iron and began to drain with the pus of infection. At first Danlo
and Tamara tried not to worry, for Jonathan's fever seemed slight.
But then Danlo remembered that those who have starved usually
do not develop high fevers or show typical symptoms of illness,
even during the most acute of infections. As the storm howled
through the streets outside and buried the city in many layers of
freezing snow, Jonathan lay almost motionless staring off at the
window. Each hour, it seemed, his pain grew worse. There came a
time when he turned away from the cups of blood tea that might
have strengthened him, and then, a little later, he refused even
water.

"There must be something we can do," Tamara whispered to
Danlo as they stood over Jonathan watching him try to sleep.

"There must be something *you* can do. Didn't your people use herbs for curing infections and fevers?"

"*Lalashu,* my blessed people," Danlo said, remembering. The pain behind his left eye throbbed with all the dark energy of a pulsar. He began calling to mind memories of the sisters and brothers of his tribe, terrible images of blackened eyes and bleeding ears and white, frothing lips. Once, he had tried to save his people from the slow evil that had infected them. He had melted snow for drinking water and had kept the oilstones burning warm and bright; he had made blood tea and rubbed hot seal oil on the foreheads of the dying. He had even prayed for their spirits as his found-father, Haidar, had taught him to pray. But in the end he had saved no one. "Truly, my people did use herbs and other power plants. But it was the women's knowledge—I never learned what might help against this kind of fever."

"Perhaps we still might find a cutter with antibiotics or immunosols," Tamara said.

"But you have already been to almost every cutter in the city."

"Well, perhaps a wormrunner, then."

"Tamara, Tamara," he said softly, "only one such as Constancio of Alesar would have these miracle drugs. And they would not be for sale for a hundred bags of gold coins."

"But we can't just stand here and watch him die!"

"No," he said, smiling gravely, "we cannot."

With that, Danlo knelt on the bed beside Jonathan and gently shook him awake. "Jonathan," he said, "there is something that I must teach you about dreams."

It was a last, desperate attempt to cure Jonathan of his infection. Danlo knew that there was little hope. Even so, he taught Jonathan the autists' techniques for entering into a communal dreamspace. There was a way, he explained, of retaining an awareness of dreaming even while one was dreaming. And more, a way of consciously willing the shape and substance of the dream. The cetics would say that such conscious dreams were only vivid simulations of reality. But the autists spoke of awakening into the dream; they sought that marvelous feeling of coming alive into one's own interior landscapes where the sense of reality becomes almost overwhelming. This, they said, was the realm of the real. They believed that here one's dreams had immense power. And so did Danlo. At least he sensed the possibilities of pure consciousness.

Once, on Tannahill thirty thousand light years away, he had

almost looked into that hidden place where matter's consciousness of itself burns like a deep, blue fire. Where matter *moves* itself and continually creates itself out of a light inside light that shines everywhere the same. If life had a secret, he thought, it was in this conscious creation. Life could quicken and evolve; it could will itself to change into new and marvelous forms. Ultimately, it could cure itself of any disease.

Infinite possibilities.

"*Mi alasharia la shantih,*" Danlo said to Jonathan. "Close your eyes and go to sleep."

And now this cure became the whole of Danlo's dream. He tried to share it with Jonathan. But Jonathan was too young, too sick, and there was too little time for new teachings. And, in truth, although Danlo was supposed to be the Lightbringer and had made promises to Old Father, he had almost lost hope. And so he could not quite open that golden door to deep consciousness where all the energies of eternity blaze like ten thousand suns.

He tried to explain his defeat to Tamara: "The universe has one soul only. And it is always dreaming—it dreams itself into existence. Dreams form and flow like liquid jewels from this single soul. In a way, there is only one dream that takes many shapes in many minds. The autists believe that when we participate in this dream, we help create the universe. Truly. The more perfectly we enter the dream, the greater our power to create. If we dream as God would dream, our will towards creation becomes very great—then there are infinite possibilities, yes? But I . . . was not able to dream the One dream. At least, I did not dream it well. And so like a tidal wave it broke my dream for Jonathan into diamond dust and swept it away."

As Danlo's dreams failed him, so did Jonathan begin to fail. He was never able to enter into the lucid dreaming state along with Danlo and visualize his body's white blood cells devouring the alien bacteria like so many sharks snapping up plague-ridden blackfish. He had his own dreams to which he surrendered utterly. He had his own consciousness, deeper than the ocean, and it was only of death. He dreamed of dying, he told Danlo, and it was not like falling into a dark, icy crevasse but rather like flying straight up through the brilliant blue sky into the sun.

"Please, Father—it hurts so bad," he said.

"The infection creates pressure on the nerves," Danlo said as if he were reciting from a medical lesson. He had always believed in telling the truth to Jonathan as far as it was possible. "When the bacteria multiply, the tissues swell and press upon the nerves in your legs.''

"It hurts everywhere," Jonathan said. "I can feel the bacteria eating me inside—they're in my blood."

"In your blood," Danlo said softly. *Uma lot, your blood, my blood—my son.* "I . . . am sorry."

"Please, Father—it hurts, it hurts."

Once Jonathan had decided on death, it was astonishing how quickly he faded. He was like a cup of tea that has sat on an icy windowsill too long, like a lamp that has burned almost its last drop of oil. When Danlo pressed his lips to his forehead, his skin felt almost cool as if his body had given up trying to fight the infection. Gradually he lost the power to move. With his head on Tamara's lap, he lay on his side all curled-up and frozen with contractures. He couldn't even lift his arm to grip the cup of water that Tamara encouraged him to drink. His face had fallen pale as bone. Danlo remembered that a body in starvation loses its muscle and fat more quickly than its blood. This creates a relatively larger volume of blood and causes the weakened heart to work even harder to move it. Danlo sensed that if Jonathan were to die, it would be because his heart suddenly seized up and stopped. Gazing at him as Tamara stroked his dark hair and sang him another song, he sensed that this failure of his heart might come very soon.

"Jonathan, Jonathan," he said. And then, looking at Tamara, he whispered, "Tamara, Tamara."

Tamara sat there for a while staring at nothing. Her beautiful face had fallen gray with anguish, doubt and fear. Danlo thought that he had never seen anyone so tired. She seemed haunted by her love for her son. She had a dream of her own, and now this dream was dying even as Jonathan moaned softly and struggled to breathe. And then she looked at Danlo. In her dark eyes there was an utter hopelessness and yet an utter denial of what must soon come.

Ti-anasa daivam.

Strangely, it was Jonathan who gave Tamara the courage to face his death. He knew that he would soon make the journey to the other side of day, and he was no longer afraid. Although he was only a very sick boy lying in his mother's lap, his whole being fairly shimmered with a willingness to leave life behind. Later in the day after the storm had broken and the sky had begun to clear, he looked up at Tamara and said, "I want to go outside."

"What?" she said. "What are you saying?"

Jonathan could barely move, but he turned his head just
enough so that he could see Danlo. "Please, Father—please."

"What is he talking about?" Tamara said to Danlo.

After gazing at Jonathan a while, Danlo nodded his head and
told Tamara, "The old men and women of my tribe, the children,
too—when they were close to their moment, we would take them
outside to sit beneath the sky."

"You've told him too many stories, you know."

"I am sorry."

Jonathan looked up at Tamara and said, "I want to go down by
the sea. Where you used to take me to the beach. Please, Mama."

"No, that's really impossible." And then to Danlo, almost
without thinking, she said, "It's horribly cold outside—I'm afraid
it would kill him."

Danlo almost smiled at the absurdity of what Tamara had just
said, but then he watched as Jonathan called out to her with his
eyes like an osprey caught in the closing ice of the sea. Something
deep and beautiful passed from him to her and from her to him. It
was terrible to see, for Tamara's eyes instantly filled with anguish
and tears, and yet marvelous, too, in the way that Jonathan's eyes
came alive one last time with a soft and gentle light.

"All right, then," Tamara finally said to him. "If it's what you
want."

With that they dressed Jonathan and wrapped him again in the
bed furs. Danlo and Tamara both put on their outer furs and boots;
Danlo made sure that his face mask was in place before lifting
Jonathan and carrying him out the door.

Ti-anasa daivam.

It was hard skating through the city. The storm had left much
snow, which the plows had pushed to the side of the major streets
in great, gleaming white mounds. But on the lesser glidderies near
Tamara's apartment, the red ice was pink with a patina of untouched snow, and even the East-West Sliddery was fouled with
patches of frozen slush. The wind blew away the last clouds of the
storm, revealing a sky so darkly blue that it seemed almost black.
Even as the last heat of Jonathan's body escaped through his furs
into the air, the heat of the world, as little as it was, radiated
upward through the sky and vanished into space.

They crossed the West Beach Glissade and made their way
along a gliddery through stands of shatterwood trees. And then
they ejected their skate blades and walked along a footpath
through yu trees and bonewood thickets down to Diamond Beach.
This was one of the city's wild beaches, with its pristine forest

quickly giving way to vast expanses of windswept dunes and hardpacked sand covered with snow. At the edge of the beach, where the frozen *sastrugi* waves caught the light of the late afternoon sun, the Great Northern Ocean opened for miles before them. Once, years before, Danlo had crossed this ocean towards the east and miraculously found the city of Neverness waiting for him. And now he sat with Tamara and Jonathan on a driftwood log looking out towards the endless ice of the west, the direction that one must always face in dying.

Ti-anasa daivam.

"It's cold," Jonathan said. He sat in Tamara's lap gazing at the sun as it lit the horizon in colors of chrome red and shimmering gold. "I'm so cold."

In truth, it was very cold: a harsh, biting blue cold falling quickly to deep cold. Even the numerous birds that usually flocked the beach had fled, leaving only a few gulls and scrawcaws to hunt snowworms along the ocean's edge. Soon, when night came, it would turn dead cold, and then it would be very dangerous to sit unprotected in the wind. Since Danlo did not want to hasten Jonathan's journey—it being the oldest of teachings that one should always die at the right time—he gathered up a heap of deadwood from the thickets above the beach and set it ablaze. Soon the heat from the fire began to melt the ice glazing their log; it warmed their hands and faces and gave off a crackling orange glow against the fall of night.

Ti-anasa daivam.

Because Jonathan requested it, Danlo brought out his flute and played a bittersweet music that he had composed for Jonathan some days earlier. It was a simple song, really, but a powerful one that seemed to enchant Jonathan and hold him with its soft, murmuring melody. Jonathan lay totally still on Tamara's lap. He gazed off at the intense blueness of twilight as he listened to the beautiful music that flowed over the beach and soared off into the sky. Now the first stars appeared like bright diamonds: Ninsun and Araglo Luz and the brilliant Moriah Double that formed the eye of the mighty Bear constellation. There were the *blinkans*, too, the great glisters of light that were the remnant radiance of old supernovas. And now Tamara began to sing for him, words of love and light that welled up from deep inside her heart. She would later tell Danlo that she couldn't remember these words, for they formed up in the moment like delicate ice crystals from the moisture in her breath and were immediately lost to the wind.

Ti-anasa daivam.

For a long time Danlo played his flute as he watched the gulls gliding along the frozen surf and looking for signs of snowworms. It seemed that Jonathan was watching these beautiful white birds, too, for his eyes remained open and unblinking in their direction. Danlo couldn't tell, however, if he were truly seeing them or something else. Perhaps, in the way of the birds, he perceived a sky *behind* the sky, a blue so deep inside blue that it flowed like water. Colors—black or cobalt or the silver-white of the stars— would not appear as finished events only, but rather as tones moving in time. For his son, he prayed, the changing colors of early evening would be like music to his eyes. But he feared that he was seeing otherwise.

Perhaps phantasms or spirits haunted his dying sight. Perhaps he looked up into the heavens only to see the dark birds of night descending upon him, the death birds with their shining black talons and terrible screaming cries. God, as Danlo's found-father had once taught him, was a great silver thallow whose wings touched at the far end of the universe. Or perhaps God was the rare white thallow, *Ahira*, whom some called the snowy owl—no one really knew. But it was certain that God eventually devoured all things: oceans and planets and stars, and even innocent children who liked to watch the birds soaring above a frozen beach.

Jonathan, Jonathan.

"Father . . . Father."

Danlo, upon hearing Jonathan call to him, put down his flute and knelt beside him in the cold snow. He had taken his mask off so that he could play more easily; now he drew in close to Jonathan to hear what he had to say.

"Father," he murmured. His breathing was labored, ragged and weak. "How do you . . . ?"

Jonathan's voice faded off, and Danlo knelt by his side waiting for him to finish his question. What had he wanted to ask? Was it the riddle that they had both puzzled over?

> *How do you capture a beautiful bird*
> *without killing its spirit?*

Had Jonathan, dwelling in that twilight land between day and night, somehow solved the riddle?

As Danlo listened to Jonathan struggling to breathe, he thought that he would never know: neither what Jonathan had wanted to ask him nor the answer to the riddle itself. For Jonathan never spoke to him again. He lay with his head pressed against

Tamara's chest, all the while staring at Danlo. After a few hundred heartbeats, he began staring *through* Danlo as if gazing at the brilliant stars of some faraway galaxy. His last words were for Tamara, she who had borne him and brought him into life. "Mama, Mama," he said. "Mama, Mama." And then he fell as silent as the frozen sea.

"Jonathan," Danlo said. He removed his mitten and laid his hand on Jonathan's cold forehead. *"Mi alasharia la shantih,* go to sleep, now, go to sleep."

And Jonathan closed his eyes as he breathed softly the icy air smothering the beach. Danlo watched the furs covering Jonathan's belly gently rise and fall. After a long time—two thousand and fifteen of his own heartbeats—he could no longer see the furs moving. He held his face near Jonathan's face, and he felt very faintly his son's breath touching his lips and burning over his eyes. And then, after another three hundred heartbeats, he felt nothing. Jonathan lay as still and quiet as a stone. Danlo pressed his lips to Jonathan's cold lips, waiting for him to breathe again. He waited a long time, uncountable moments of time. His heart drummed steadily and quickly inside him as it always had, and yet he could no longer feel the individual beats. There was only a single great pressure there, a swelling, a terrible red fire, like that of a star about to explode. He kissed Jonathan on the forehead, softly but fiercely. Then he stood on the snow and stared at the western sky where the stars of the Owl constellation pointed the way out into the universe.

"Mi alasharia la shantih, sleep in peace, my son."

He turned to lift Jonathan away from Tamara. She sat on the log by the glowing fire stunned and almost unable to move. Frozen tears glistened like pearls stuck to her cheeks. But she was not weeping now; all she could do was to stare at Danlo as he held Jonathan in his arms and looked up into the bright black sky.

"No," Danlo whispered. He held Jonathan so that the starlight fell over his body and face. He himself let this cold, white light fill his eyes like millions of icy needles stabbing at his brain. "No, no—please, no."

Ti-anasa daivam, he thought. *Live your life and love your fate.*

But how could he live now that Jonathan had lost his life? In truth, his son had lost everything: life, love, joy, and all that he might ever have become. And he himself had lost almost everything. Now the great chain of life and being that had begun on Old Earth five billion years ago was finally broken. Danlo stood there in the near-darkness, and he thought of his father and his grandfather, and all his ancestors back to the man-apes who had walked the burning veldts of Afarique in all their splendor and pride. And he wondered at his mother and his grandmother—all his mother's mothers who had grown into young women in the womb of their Mother Earth. And none of these millions of men and women who were of his body and blood had died in childhood.

What were the chances that on a planet of fierce predators, cold, hunger, disease and never-ending war, where half the children born did not see their fifth birthday, not a single one of them would have died as a boy or wailing babe? *Almost infinitely small.* It was truly a miracle that they had all lived to beget children of their own. And yet, here he stood on a windswept beach on a faraway world as a result of this miracle. Everything that moved or breathed or spread its leaves in the morning sun had been called into being despite the almost infinite odds against it, and that was the miracle of all life. It was one reason that it was so infinitely precious.

The whole world, Danlo thought, should want to weep at each little piece of itself lost to life in all its marvelous possibilities. As he himself wanted to weep, but could not. All he could do was to look toward the cold sky remembering how Jonathan liked to laugh and ask him riddles. He had lost this beautiful boy forever; he had lost a son who would have grown into a beautiful man. And thus he had lost the man who would someday have been his friend. It was all gone, now: his grandsons, his granddaughters and great-granddaughters, too—all his children's children. And more than anything else, the one child that he had ever loved as his own. For a long time he stood there beneath the blazing stars holding Jonathan in his arms, and the rage at what he had lost built inside him like all the fires of creation.

"No," he whispered again. And then something inside him broke. It came from within him, this terrible and deep wrath that shook him down to his bones. He drew in a deep breath and pulled back his head—and then he called out to the heavens like a wounded animal: "NO!"

His voice built louder and louder. It startled Tamara and shook the air; it thundered across the beach, pounding in wave upon wave against the ice crusts and shimmering snow dunes. In truth it wasn't the cry of an animal at all, but of a very powerful man, and perhaps even more. His was a deeper and finer voice, the voice of his father cut by Constancio of Alesar, and cut now with all the pain and passion in the world. The voice of a god: he wanted all

the world to hear him; he wanted his protest against the insane
cruelty of life to carry up into the sky and ring out across the
stars. He wanted the gods of the Cataract galaxies to know that
Jonathan had suffered torment and death to no purpose; he
wanted the whole universe to know. And God. Especially God,
who had betrayed him and his son and all that he had ever
dreamed. He cried out a single word, long and terrible and deep,
that God at last might wake up and behold the horror of creation
and the futility of all life.

"NOOOOOOO!"

At last, he thought that he understood Hanuman li Tosh. The
great tree of life, spreading its many-flowered branches towards
the heavens, reaching with its roots back to the beginning of time,
was rotten at its very heart. The universe itself was flawed. And
worse, misbegotten, blighted, diseased, utterly *shaida* in its essential nature. And Hanuman had always known this. And thus he
pitted himself against existence itself, and desired with all his soul
that the universe should be made differently. What courage this
required of him, to shake his fist at the heavens and demand
redress for all the pointless sufferings of life! What genius, what
will, what strength! As Danlo stood on the frozen snow holding
Jonathan and calling out to the stars, he doubted whether he himself would ever possess such a terrible strength. In truth, he
wanted only to die. And more, he wanted never to have been born,
so that he would have been spared the pain of life, and thus
sparing Jonathan, too.

NO!

Even as he was pushing this cry outward to the sky with his
mind and belly and every beat of his heart, Tamara came over to
him. She waited until he ran out of breath, then laid her head on
Jonathan's chest and began sobbing. He saw that as terrible as
was his own pain, Tamara's was infinitely worse. That was the
truly unbearable thing about pain, that it had no limit or end. In
realizing this, in feeling Tamara's wracking sobs as they shook
Jonathan's little body, he laid his head gently atop Tamara's head
and sobbed, too. After a while he looked up again at the stars.
And Tamara stood away from Jonathan as she sought out Danlo's
eyes in the light of the dying fire.

"It is all right," he croaked out, trying desperately to find
something to say. "Nothing is lost."

"What? Oh, Danlo, what do you mean?"

"Nothing is truly lost," he said again, although he did not
believe anything of what he told her.

And yet. And yet. As he stood there in the wind letting his breath out in puffs of silver-black steam, he remembered something that he had once learned. Each breath of his body contained some one thousand billion trillion atoms, mostly of nitrogen and oxygen and carbon dioxide. And the entire atmosphere of the world held about the same number of breaths. Thus every time he drew in a lungful of icy air, he inhaled an average of one atom from each of the breaths swirling about the world. And with each exhalation, he returned an atom to each breath, over and over as his belly rose and fell. And Tamara did, too, and Benjamin Hur, and Hanuman li Tosh, and all the other millions of people who lived in Neverness. And not just they, but the mothers of the Patwin tribe, and the fathers of the faraway Wuyi tribe in the west of the Ten Thousand Islands—all the people on all the oceans' islands. And the bears and birds and snowworms and whales, and all the other animals of the world who lived and breathed, also contributed their own breaths to the breath of the world.

Between the rising of the bloody sun and its setting over the sea, a man might take ten thousand breaths, and each one would vibrate with thousands of atoms breathed at some time by each living being. And not just the living. In the movements of the clouds and wind, the world's air continually circled Icefall day after day, year after year, millenium after millenium. The atoms of life evaporated and condensed and diffused and swirled everywhere in an everlasting global metabolism, and none of them was ever lost.

And so Danlo stood on the starlit snow, and he breathed in air that had once filled the lungs of Rollo Gallivare, the great Lord Pilot who had founded Neverness three thousand years before. And before *that* historic event, thousands of years before, the ancestors of the Alaloi had come to Icefall in their long silver ships. And before they had destroyed those ships and carked their human forms into the shape of primitive men (even as Mallory Ringess and Danlo had done), they had looked out upon Icefall's fir-covered islands and deep blue sky, and they had sighed at the immense beauty of the world. And with each sigh they had sent into the cold, clear air atoms carried in their ships and in their bodies.

Once, they or their ancestors had breathed these bits of oxygen on Silvaplana, Darkmoon, Arcite, Sheydveg and Sahasrara—and every other world going back to Old Earth. Thus they had carried with them the cries of ecstasy of Danlo's far-great-grandparents mating beneath an acacia tree in Afarique, as well as the Newton's cry of triumph when he discovered that everything in the universe pulled at everything else no matter how infinitessimal its mass or how great the separation in space.

As Danlo let a little air flow past his lips, he let in ten thousand atoms from breath of the Buddha delivering the Fire Sermon in Uruvela and ten thousand more from the last despairing words of Jesus dying on a wooden cross and surrendering up his spirit to the heavens. It was all inside him now, the breaths of the ancients and the breaths of the dead members of his tribe, too. And the dying breath of Jonathan: it burned inside Danlo's throat and chest with each draught of cold air as if he had breathed in starfire. As long as he lived, he would feel the heat of it touching his eyes and searing the soft tissues around his heart.

Nothing is lost.

He stood on the beach facing the wind, which was nothing more (and nothing less) than the wild white breath of the world. Even as he continued holding Jonathan against his chest, he watched the wind blow shimmering crystals of spindrift snow across the frozen sea. And then he looked up at the sky. There, the vacant spaces between the stars drew his gaze as if sucking him down a black and infinitely deep crack in the universe.

Most of the universe was as empty as a cup drained of blood tea. Everywhere he looked, whether toward the Detheshaloon or the Morbio Inferiore, it seemed that there was only darkness and nothingness, the utter neverness of light, love and life. And yet he knew that even the most barren patch of space contained a few atoms of hydrogen or helium spinning in the dark. These tiny bits of matter were just the exhalations of the stars; as with all matter everwhere, they might pass from star to star and eventually fuse together into light. But they could never be destroyed. Nothing in the universe or of the universe could ever truly be destroyed, and that was the miracle of creation. The universe preserved all things, atoms and X rays and photons, dying plaints and hopeless cries— and even the silent prayer of a silent, heartbroken man.

Nothing is lost.

With the setting of the Wolf moon in the west, Danlo remembered how Jonathan liked to watch the world's six moons rise at night and make their way across the sky. He remembered many things about Jonathan: his intelligence, his curiosity, his courage, his great love for his mother that had always lit up his deep, blue eyes like sunshine. He promised himself, then, that he would do everything possible to remember Jonathan, in his dreams and in his heart, with all his will and every atom of his being.

Nothing is lost.

Somehow, he thought, the universe itself must have a way of remembering Jonathan and all those who had ever lived and died. He stood staring at the shimmering stars, and he wondered at this strange idea that had taken root in his mind. Did he truly believe it? He *had* to believe it, or at least act as if he did. After all, he had made promises to Old Father, and to himself. Someday he might look God in the face and learn the truth of how the universe (or anything at all) remembered anything. But for now it would have to be enough that he and Tamara looked inside themselves to behold the bright, lovely child that they had made.

Nothing is lost.

"Tamara," he said, stepping nearer to her. "We must say goodbye to him now."

"No, I can't."

"We must bury him before it grows too cold."

Tamara wept again at the reality of Jonathan's body lying dead in Danlo's arms. She stood swaying in the snow, shaking her head back and forth against the wind. And then she composed herself and said, "Couldn't we just uncover him and let him freeze? After the war, there will be drugs again, and the cryologists might be able to revive him and cure his infection."

"No, it is too late," Danlo said. "When one has died from being sick so long the way Jonathan was sick, such revivals are impossible. The cryologists refuse even to try. It is against their ethics. The brain—"

"Please, Danlo."

"Tamara, Tamara," he said softly, "not even the Agathanians could bring him back to life."

"But didn't you once tell me that the Solid State Entity had such powers? Couldn't you carry Jonathan frozen in the hold of your ship and hope that the Entity might restore him?"

The Solid State Entity, he thought, possibly *could* make him live again. At least She—the goddess whom he had known as Kalinda—might be able to create an almost perfect copy of the son they had loved. But he knew that if She did, he would never truly be the same.

"He would be different, in his soul," he explained to Tamara. He stared off at the stars as he remembered his sojourn on the earthlike world that the Entity had created. "Someday, in looking at his eyes, in touching his breath with your own, you would discover this difference. And it would tear out your heart."

"But shouldn't we *try?*"

"No, it is too late," he said again. "He died at the right time."

"How can there ever be a right time for a child to die?"

"I . . . do not know. But for everything, there is a time. Even for the gods."

"I just can't stop hoping."

"I . . . am sorry."

"I can't just walk away and leave him as if he no longer exists."

"In a way, he will always exist," he said. "Nothing is lost."

"Oh, Danlo, I wish I could believe that."

Danlo took a deep breath of air, and then he explained to her how all the breaths of Jonathan's life still circled the world in the swirling wind. He told her of his theory that the universe remembers everything, but it gave her little solace. She just wept, and shook her head, and touched her fingers to Jonathan's closed eyes as she said, "No, he's gone."

"No, Tamara, he is—"

"Gone, gone—I suppose I know that nothing can bring him back. But if he *is* gone, I don't want to bury him beneath the snow. That's such a ghastly, barbaric thing. He'd only remain frozen forever like the body of Ede."

"But what do you want to do, then?"

"Return him to the world, like his breath."

"By taking him to one of the crematoriums?"

"I suppose there's no other choice."

"There might be another way," he said. He looked down at Jonathan lying so quiet and still in his aching arms. Although his son was almost as light as air, he had gradually grown very heavy. "We could make a pyre and creamate him ourselves."

"Now? Here?"

"Yes, why not?"

"It would have to be a very big fire," she said.

Danlo looked off at the bonewood thickets and yu trees above the beach. He said, "There is much wood in the forest."

"All right," she said. "Let's make a pyre, then."

Actually, it was Danlo who made the pyre, not Tamara. Because she couldn't bear to leave Jonathan's body alone in the snow, she sat on the log again holding him near the little fire that Danlo rekindled from a few pieces of wood that he had piled up earlier. And then he turned to the greater fire that he would build farther down by the sea. To make this second fire hot enough to consume Jonathan's entire body, he calculated that he would need a great deal of wood. And so he walked up into the forest and returned carrying bunches of dry bonewood in his arms. He trudged across the dunes weighed down by this load until he came to the frozen waves at the edge of the beach. There, on the moon-lit ice, he set down the wood, sighed and drew in a breath of cold air. Then he went back up to the forest to find more wood.

Many times he made this tiresome journey between the forest and the sea. In truth, he worked long into the night, gathering bundles of sticks and hauling logs over the crunching snow. He built the pyre wide and high: by midnight, it had almost reached the level of his eyes. And all this time Tamara sat watching the pyre grow. She sat holding Jonathan's cold body against hers, holding him tightly as she rocked back and forth in front of the fire. She let her head fall against his as she sang him songs and sobbed terribly when her words failed her; it was her way of saying goodbye.

After Danlo had heaped the last log on the pyre, he returned to where Tamara was sitting and took Jonathan's fur-wrapped body from her. Together, in the moonlight, they walked back down the beach. Because it would be unseemly to treat Jonathan's body as if it were only a bundle of wood, Danlo cradled it with one hand while using the other to climb to the top of the pyre. There he lay it between two logs facing towards the west. One last time, he kissed his son on his cold lips. Then he climbed down and stood on the ice as he looked at Tamara.

"Are you ready?" he asked.

Weeping softly now, Tamara could only nod her head in assent.

"All right, then," he said. He pulled a box of matches from his pocket and struck one into flame. He held it to the tinder which he had stuffed into a pocket of twigs near the base of the pyre; almost instantly, the tinder and the surrounding wood caught fire and began crackling with a bright orange light. With a whoosh, the combustion sucked oxygen from the blowing wind. In moments, it seemed, the flames leapt from stick to stick and from log to log, and soon the whole pyre roared with bright, blazing fire.

"Mi alasharia la shantih," Danlo said. "Sleep in peace, my son."

And Tamara, standing by his side, murmured, "Goodbye, goodbye."

For a long time they watched the pyre burn. The leaping flames lit up the beach and shot off into the sky. The wood, dry as

bone, popped and snapped and sent showers of sparks spinning
into the night. So intense did the fire's red heat become that Danlo
and Tamara had to step back a good many paces to keep from
singeing their furs. In little time, it began consuming Jonathan's
furs and then the body of Jonathan himself. Danlo tried not to
notice the pungent smell of roasting flesh. In truth, he tried not to
breathe, but the wind blew the fire's smoke straight towards his
face. It fell over him (and Tamara) in dense, dark, bittersweet
clouds. After a while, Danlo gave up and simply endured the
burning in his lungs and his eyes.

Nothing is lost, he thought. *Nothing is ever lost.*

He drew out his flute, then, and played a requiem for Jonathan.
As the flames built brighter and brighter and the pyre's smoke
vanished in the wind, he played a sad, clear song that soared
above the beach with all the beauty of a flock of thallows. Tamara
joined him. She sang softly to the music, words of love and light
that might guide Jonathan on his journey to the other side of day.
For many moments, there was nothing in all the world except this
playing and singing. The fire reached its peak in ferocity and heat,
and then slowly fell off as it consumed its fuel. After thousands of
beats of Danlo's heart, it grew dimmer and cooler and began to
die. And all this time, Danlo played and played in remembrance
of Jonathan as he gave his breath to the world.

Nothing is lost.

Long past midnight, when the pyre had burned down to nothing more than a few glowing coals and cold black ashes, Danlo
finally put away his flute. He stepped down to the edge of the
beach where the fire's intense heat had melted the ice of the sea
itself. He used his naked hand to sift ashes, but he could find
nothing left of Jonathan's body, not even a fragment of a bone. In
places, the ashes had mixed with the melted sea water, forming a
kind of mud. He scooped up some of this dark matter, then, and
smeared a slashing mark across his forehead. Almost instantly,
the bitter wind froze the wet ashes to his skin.

Ashes—there is nothing left but ashes, he thought. And then,
Everything is lost.

He stood up and walked across the snow, swaying in the wind
like a drunken man. He came over to Tamara and fell against her;
he pressed his head next to hers and wept bitterly with her for a
long, long time.

THE RINGESS

*I must speak to you of the god within each of us. This god
is lord of fire and light. This god is fire and light, and is
nothing but fire and light. Each of us is this god. Each
man and woman is a star that burns on and on with
infinite possibilities. I must speak tonight of becoming this
star, this eternal and infinite flame. Only by becoming fire
will you ever be free from burning. Only by becoming fire
will you become free of pain, free of fear, free of hatred,
sorrow, lamentation, suffering and despair. This is the way
of the gods. This is the way of the Ringess, to burn with
the fire of a new being, to shine with a new consciousness
as bright as all the stars, as vast and perfect and
indestructible as all the universe. This is the way of
Mallory Ringess, who watches over all the people in the
City where he was once as human as you and I.*

           —from the Fire Sermon of Hanuman li Tosh

The coming of morning brought no joy to either Danlo or Tamara.
At first light, having completed their vigil by the sea, they returned in silence to Tamara's apartment. As soon as they had shut
the door behind them, Tamara stumbled into her sleeping chamber
and fell sobbing against her bed. Nothing that Danlo could do or
say eased her suffering even slightly. After she had wrung her
body dry of tears, she lay silently staring at the cold, empty neverness of her life as if she were willing herself to die. It was a
terrible thing to see. In truth, Danlo feared for her life. He feared
that she would use her cooking knife to open the veins of her
wrist or simply walk out the door without her furs and find some
dark, abandoned alley where she could lay down upon the ice and
let the cold carry her over to the other side of day.

    And so Danlo kept a watch over her. And as he watched, he
waited for his own pain to cool from the red heat of glowing iron
to a more bearable degree of suffering. But it did not. For as he sat
by Tamara drinking cup after cup of blood tea, all the while star-

ing at Tamara's untouched cup, he tried to remember all the moments that he had ever spent with Jonathan. Because he had a phenomenal memory—an almost perfect memory of pictures—he could quite easily see Jonathan playing with his toy lightship or the wonder in his eyes when Danlo told him about the shimmering colors (and terrors) of the manifold. And all this memory haunted him.

Memory, as he discovered, could be a truly terrible thing. Over and over he replayed in his mind each of his decisions and actions leading up to Jonathan's death. He saw with perfect clarity the night that he and Tamara had created Jonathan out of lust and love, and he looked once again upon his denial of the possibility that Tamara might have been with child when he had abandoned Neverness for the mission to the Vild. If only he had found Tamara and stayed to protect her and Jonathan as he grew from babe into a bright-eyed boy, then perhaps he might have seen the war coming and would have left the city for some safer place. Or, having returned years later, if only he had found them sooner or hadn't delayed so long in hunting for food, then Jonathan might not have frozen his toes and sickened and died.

If only, if only . . . If only he could keep himself from remembering, then the images burning through the back of his eye into his brain might go away, and the terrible pain in his head might stop. He realized then that all this terrible memory was his way of journeying into the past in order to change it, as if he could thereby restore Jonathan to him and create a different present. Once, years before, he had wanted to become an asarya, a great-souled human being who might say yes to all things. But now he dwelled in the dark cavern of remembrance grasping at glowing phantasms as they streaked through the blackness inside him, and this was just the opposite of affirmation. In truth, it was the essence of hell, and as he sat pressing his thumb against his aching eye, he thought he would go on and on falling through the void forever.

Later that night, as if shaking herself out of a nightmare, Tamara finally roused herself. She sat up rubbing her swollen eyes and gripping her belly, which gobe had cramped into a hard knot of pain. And then she looked straight at Danlo.

"Thank you for sitting with me," she said, "but there's really no point in your staying here any longer."

He smiled sadly and shook his head. "There is all the point in the world. You—"

"I shall be all right," she broke in. "I've decided that I have to be."

"Truly?"

"I'm not the only mother who has lost a child in this terrible war. In this city alone there must be hundreds."

"I am afraid that there must be thousands."

"And there are children who have lost their mothers—their fathers, too. I've decided to remain to help them."

"To remain here in Neverness?"

"To remain among the living, Danlo."

"I . . . see."

"The war won't last much longer, you know," she said. She picked up her cold cup of tea and took a sip. "It *can't* last much longer. And when we've won, or lost, and there's food in the city again, I shall be free."

"No, no," he murmured. He touched her tangled, tear-stained hair. "I do not want to lose you, too."

"I know this must be hard for you," she said. "But really, you lost me years ago when Hanuman took away my memories."

"I do not want to lose you again—not this way."

"I'm sorry, Danlo."

"Hanuman," he whispered as if uttering some forbidden word. "The more deeply I look into the past, the more clearly I see him staring back at me with his *shaida* eyes."

"You must hate him now more than ever."

"No, it is just the opposite. I must find a way *not* to hate him. I must find a way to forgive him, with all the force of my will."

"*I* can't forgive him," Tamara said. "I wish that it was he whom we burned last night and not Jonathan."

Danlo shook his head sadly and said, "No, no—never killing, never hating or harming anyone no matter what he has done to you."

"After all that has happened, you're still devoted to ahimsa, aren't you?"

"I . . . must be. More than ever."

"But isn't it time you completed your plan to bring Hanuman down?"

"Yes," he said, "it is time."

"Then you'll leave me tomorrow, won't you?"

"If I can," he said. "If I can, then I must."

"Will you show me where you've stored the bear meat before you leave? I'd like to give some to Pilar and Andreas—and others, too."

"Yes, of course," he said. "It is *shaida* to waste good meat."

After that they drank their cups of tea and collapsed into the sleep of exhaustion. They awoke the next morning long before first light. They waxed Tamara's skis, put on their furs, and made their way through the deserted streets to the City Wild. It was cold in the forest, so bitterly cold that Danlo had to light a fire outside of his snow house to keep Tamara from shivering and freezing her limbs. Although the sun still had not risen, the starry sky glowed in the east above Urkel with the first blue of dawn.

"The meat will keep all winter," Danlo said as he stood next to Tamara by the crackling fire. He pointed at the little dome of snow half-buried in a fresh, gleaming, white drift. "Unless you know of a safe place near your apartment, it would be best to keep it here. There are many men who would murder for this meat."

"I won't hoard it, you know," she said. "I'd like to give it away to those who need it most."

"Of course," he said. "But please keep a little for yourself."

Tamara said nothing as she stared at the fire's flickering flames; her beautiful face, glowing red-orange in the firelight, betrayed neither hope nor fear nor even the slightest care for herself or her life.

"I must prepare myself now," he said softly. "Please excuse me."

With that, he went inside his snow house, with its many stacks of plastic-wrapped bear meat. From a pile of clothing and furs near the foot of his bed, he drew out a fresh, formal pilot's robe. It was a black and cut all of a piece to be close-fitting in the body and loose around the legs. He stripped naked and then slipped this silken garment over his skin. After quickly putting back on his white shagshay furs, he gathered up a few of his possessions, and went back outside to Tamara.

"It will be cold today," he said, sniffing the air. The sky had now lightened to a pure, cloudless blue, and only a few of the brightest stars still remained of the night. "Cold but very clear."

He came over to Tamara and spread a newl skin over the fresh snow near the fire. And then he laid out his bag of carving tools and the necklace-computer that Harrah Ivi en li Ede had once given him. There too he set the two halves of the ivory chess piece that he had once carved for Hanuman, the white god that Hanuman had broken in anger and flung back in his face. The last thing that Danlo gave up was his shakuhachi. The bamboo flute, in its black leather case smelling of woodsmoke and wind, he held lovingly in his hands a few moments before laying it next to the chess piece.

"Would you please take care of these while I am gone?" he asked.

"Of course I will," she said, nodding her head slowly. Then she bent down to pick up the flute. She did not ask him when he might want his things back, for either his plan would succeed and he would return soon, or it would fail and most likely he would never play his flute again. "Are you ready to leave, then?"

"No, there is one last thing that I must do."

So saying, he pulled at his pilot's ring which he wore around his little finger. Because the ring had recently grown too tight, he had to lubricate it with a little bear grease and twist hard before he got it off. After staring at this shimmering thing for a few moments, he pressed it into the center of Tamara's naked hand. Then he drew over his head the silver chain that Bardo had given him years before. Hanging from this chain was a ring wrought entirely of black diamond, another pilot's ring: the very one that had once belonged to his father. He took the ring off its chain and slipped it over his finger. It fit perfectly—as it should have, since Constancio had carved Danlo's knuckles according to the ring's dimensions.

"Please keep my ring for me," he said to Tamara.

Tamara held the ring up to see it better. It sparkled all bright and black in the light of the rising sun. "Why don't you just wear your own ring?" she said, now looking at Danlo's little finger. "It seems the same as your father's."

"Truly, it does," he said. "But each pilot's ring is unique. The carbon atoms of the diamond are stived with iridium and iron. This makes for an atomic signature that the scanners in the Pilot's College can read, yes?"

"I didn't know that."

"Few do," he said. "It is one of the secrets that pilots are not supposed to tell."

"Then why are you telling me?"

Danlo held his fist up to the sun. "Because, with this ring, I am no longer a pilot of the Order. I am Mallory Ringess, who was once Lord Pilot and Lord of the Order—but who is now a god."

"I think I understand."

He pointed to his pilot's ring that she held between the thumb and forefinger of her hand. "Someday I hope to return for my ring, so that I can be a pilot again."

He embraced her, then, and kissed her forehead. She gathered up his things and tucked them down into her pocket. And then she retrieved a haunch of bear meat from inside the house and hid it beneath her furs, which caused them to bulge out over her belly as if she were pregnant.

"Goodbye, Danlo," she said. "I wish you well."

"I will go with you to the edge of the forest," he said.

"No, there's no need. I'd rather find my way back alone."

"If you'd like," he said. And then, "Perhaps it would be best if you returned to your apartment and stayed inside. This might be a dangerous day to be out on the streets."

"I suppose it might be," she said, looking at him.

"Goodbye, Tamara. I wish you well."

Again he embraced her, then watched as she snapped on her skis and struck off across the sparkling snow. After a few moments—in truth, after a few hundred beats of his heart—she disappeared among the great shatterwood trees, one proud, lone woman lost in the wild white forest.

And now it begins, he thought. *Ahira, Ahira—give me the strength to do what I must do.*

Because he was hungry, he brought out a packet of steaks and unwrapped it. He roasted the dark, rich meat over the fire. He took a long time in cooking it, and longer still to eat it. He sat on a snow-covered rock, chewing the bloody meat as he watched the sun climb higher in the sky. His plan called for him to reveal himself as Mallory Ringess, but he did not want to do so in the early morning when few people would be about. And so he waited and watched the sky; he ate and ate and filled his belly with the bear meat. And when he could eat no more and wait no longer, he wiped the grease from his lips. He pulled his mask over his face, against the cold, of course, but also because he did not want to be recognized until the right moment. And then he put on his skis and made his way through the snow to the paths that cut through the northern part of the City Wild.

I am not I. I am Mallory wi Soli Ringess, son of Leopold Soli, son of the Sun—and brother to Kalinda, Ede, Maralah, Pure Mind and all the galaxy's other gods.

He found a little gliddery that debouched onto the Run, a broad thoroughfare running west to east from the Quay all the way through the Pilots' Quarter to the Elf Gardens at the foot of Atakel. It was the second greatest street in the city and the only one whose ice was colored blue. He followed it through the City Wild where it emerged just north of the Fravashi District. Almost immediately—in the half mile between the edge of the forest and the Run's intersection with the Long Glissade—he noticed a great many people crowding the streets.

Once, nearby attractions such as the Hofgarten and the Promenade of the Thousand Monuments (and many fine restaurants) had drawn the manswarms to this part of the city. But for many days the war and deep winter's cold had driven the more prudent of them inside their hotels and houses, and so it surprised Danlo to see even exemplars and farsiders skating about in the noonday sun. One of them, a little diamond-seller from Yarkona, informed Danlo of the news spreading through all the quarters of the city like flame globe's light. It seemed that a huge shipment of rice had arrived at the Hollow Fields and would be distributed at various free restaurants from the Elidi District to the Academy. Everyone appeared quite excited. As Danlo glided down the bright blue street, he heard whispers of hope and even a few prayers that the war itself might be near its end. He hadn't seen such optimism lighting the people's faces since the beginning of the starvation many days before.

In truth, not everyone in Neverness had starved equally. It is always this way in highly civilized places where people share neither plenitude nor privation. Although few except the wormrunners had actually prospered (and these only for a while), many of the richest citizens seemed little marked by hunger or want. Danlo saw many such men and women as he skated toward the richest part of the city. Exemplars and astriers and quite a few professionals of the Order crowded the streets leading to the Hyacinth Gardens, the Gallivare Green and Hotel Row.

There was almost the usual bustle among the Run's fine shops, if none of the gaiety of better times. Soon, perhaps, if the rumor of a food shipment proved false, the people's mood would turn ugly and fearful again. But right now, in the golden sun, they awaited their rations of free rice as if looking for manna to fall from the heavens.

According to his plan, Danlo made straight for the Great Circle, where the Run and the Way come together. Although not the exact geographic center of the city, many consider the Great Circle its heart, for the intersection of these two greatest of streets divides Neverness into her four unequal quarters. The Great Circle itself is nothing more than an open ring of blue-white ice little more than a quarter-mile in diameter. Around it flow the lanes of traffic coming off the Run and the Way—and the great orange glidderies leading to the Farsiders' Quarter and the Academy. For three thousand years, the people of Neverness have converged upon the Great Circle everyday at noon to skate figures in the ice and meet with friends for coffee and conversation. Before the war, the kiosks around the rim of the Circle had done a brisk business, selling everything fr om puffed kurmash to steaming Summerworld teas laden with spices and honey. Now, of course, they were mostly closed except for a few vendors with stores of toalache and other drugs to offer. At various strategic points, musicians had set out their gosharps or drums on colorful carpets, and they played while men and women in rich furs skated about trading rumors and smoking their pipes.

None of the musicians, however, occupied the stage at the center of the Circle. This was a platform of yellow-painted wood usually reserved for orchestras or the troupes of wandering courtesans who liked to entertain the manswarms with their exotic dances. By tradition, though, anyone could mount this stage to address his fellow citizens. In centuries past, the Timekeeper had stood upon it to declare war upon the Order of Warrior-Poets and the Narmada had recited his Sonnets to the Sun. And here, as well, autists had gathered to share their lucid dreams with the elite of the city, and hibakusha had bared their radiation-eaten faces and pleaded for an end to all war everywhere. Many would-be visionaries had used this stage merely to rant and to shout out their prescriptions for how the universe might be arranged more justly; many madmen had stamped their boots against the resonate wood and babbled out their claims to be God. Danlo himself had listened to these wild women and men as they vexed the manswarms all about them. And so as he skated toward the stage and then climbed its five wooden steps, it didn't surprise him that almost no one looked his way.

I am Mallory Ringess. I am Mallory Ringess. I am . . .

Slowly, he removed his goggles and pulled the mask back over his head. The cold wind cut through his dense black beard and stung his face, that rugged visage of an Alaloi hunter that Constancio had sculpted twice, once for himself and once years before for his father. Now, with his bright blue eyes, he looked at the people milling about below the stage. A few of them had turned toward him; as if struggling to retrieve an old memory, they seemed to be wondering who this familiar yet strange-looking man might be. Then Danlo threw back the hood of his furs, and the sunlight played over his long black hair and his strong, splendid face. One of the onlookers—a rather stout astrier matron—pursed her lips into an "O" and let out a gasp of astonishment. A couple of men turned to see what had caught her

attention; when they beheld Danlo standing all radiant and proud
above them, they jumped back and used their hands to shield their
eyes as if they couldn't quite believe what they were seeing.

"Look!" one of them cried out. "Look at that man!"

"No, no," his friend said, "it can't be."

"It is he," the first man said. "It must be he."

Now an exemplar skated over to them, and a blue-furred eschatolgist, and four godlings in their golden robes. And all this
time Danlo had remained silent as he stood above them, watching
and waiting. The wind murmured in his ears, the wild west wind
that was the breath of his dead son and his lost father. He opened
his mouth to speak, then. He drew in a deep breath of air, and
then let it pass back out through his throat and lips to rejoin the
greater breath of the world.

"I am Mallory Ringess," he whispered. He stared out at the
many faces turning toward him. Could he ever act as if this were
really true? Would any of the dozens of people now gathering
around the stage ever believe that here stood a man who had
become a god? "I am Mallory wi Soli Ringess."

"What? What did he say?"

"I don't know," the tall exemplar sighed. "Did you hear what
he said?"

Up on the stage, Danlo swallowed against the dryness in his
mouth. He clamped his jaws shut as his cheek muscles worked
and he counted the beats of his heart. And then he pulled open his
lips and cried out, "I am Mallory wi Soli Ringess, and I have
returned to Neverness!"

For a moment, no one moved. His voice—the deeply rich and
resonant voice of his father—rang out across the ice of the Great
Circle. Half a hundred men and women held their breaths and
froze rigid with amazement; and then half a hundred more abandoned their conversations and toalache smoking and made their
way nearer to the stage.

"I am Mallory wi Soli Ringess, and I have returned!"

A young merchant from Tria fairly dripping in diamonds and
other jewels laughed loudly and pointed his finger toward Danlo.
"Look, it's another madman who thinks he's Mallory Ringess."

"It *is* Mallory Ringess," an old woman standing next to him
said. She wore the golden robe of a devout Ringist and an expression of awe on her withered old face. "Can't you see that it's the
Ringess?"

"No, it can't be—you're mad, too," the merchant said. But
then, a few moments later, he admitted to another merchant that

he had seen a hologram of the famous Mallory Ringess only once years before. "It *can't* be he, can it? Are we all mad?"

During the next few hundred beats of Danlo's heart, most of the people skating about the ice ring converged upon the stage. Word of the miracle occurring in the Great Circle seemed to be almost instantly communicated to the manswarms on the nearby streets such as the Run and the Way, for hundreds of curious men and women began streaming into the Great Circle and crowding the ice. In very little time they stood shoulder to shoulder packed as densely as a flock of *kitikeesha* birds. Astriers and wormrunners and ambassadors, neurosingers and hibakusha and professionals of the Order wearing their new golden robes—they all pressed nearer to the stage to get a better look at this man who claimed to be Mallory Ringess.

Far out, at the edge of the ring, he descryed three of the alien Friends of Man and two white-furred Fravashi. The taller of the two Fravashi, he thought, might even be Old Father, his teacher from his youth who had given him his bamboo flute and much else besides. It seemed that this splendid, golden-eyed being was watching him as if wondering what he would say next; it seemed that all the different peoples of the city stood before him in their thousands and were waiting for him to continue speaking.

"I am Mallory Ringess," Danlo said in a voice that was at once strange to him and hauntingly familiar. "I am Mallory Ringess, and I have returned to the people of the city that I love."

Near the stage, a small woman looked up at him with awe illuminating her face. She fairly swooned in her long blue furs as if she had recently drunk many goblets of wine. But then she recovered her strength (and her wits), and called out, "Mallory Ringess—it is good to see you again after all these years."

Danlo turned to smile upon her as if the sun itself were pouring out of his eyes. Her knew this woman from his days at the Academy; her name was Maria Paloma Sakti, a master eschatologist who was an authority on the origins of the Silicon God. What her relationship had been to his father, Danlo couldn't guess. But he remembered that many of her fellow masters at the Academy had called her Maria of the Gods, and he supposed that his father might have addressed her thusly as well.

"Maria Paloma Sakti," he said, bowing his head slightly. "Maria of the Gods—it is good to see you again, too."

A murmur of approval arose from the two academicians nearest to Maria and spread out among the other Ordermen around them like waves upon the sea.

"And Alesar Kwamsu," he said, bowing to an historian dressed in a godling's golden robes, "it is good to see you so well."

Now Danlo looked farther out at the people circling him like hundreds of many-colored rings. He saw Eva li Sagar and Ravi Armadan and Vishnu Suso, the Lord Horologe, who still wore a horologe's bloodred robes. And one by one, he called out to each of these men and women whom he knew: "Lord Suso, it is good to see you again. Master Kim, Viviana Chu, Willow of Urradeth, Rihana dur li Kadir—it is good to stand among you once more."

Twenty names he called out, and then twenty more, choosing only the oldest of masters who would certainly have been at the Academy at the time of Mallory Ringess. To each of them he bowed, and then he looked out over the thousands of other faces turned toward him.

"It is good to return to you, even in such terrible times. It is good to return, so that the city and all the Civilized Worlds might return to order."

Near the stage, a young man dressed in the ocher robes of a neologician stood tapping his skate blade against the ice. He was still a journeyman, perhaps only eighteen years old, and, as it happened, he had come to Neverness from Gehenna while Danlo was out exploring the Vild; Danlo knew that he had never seen him before. This intelligent journeyman, in all his skepticism and pride, had shunned wearing a godling's golden garments as he might a poisoned robe. The other journeymen at the college of Lara Sig (and his masters, too) knew him as a fierce critic of Ringism and the twisted words of Hanuman li Tosh. And so it surprised none of his friends standing near him when he cleared his throat, looked straight up towards the stage and called out, "Are you really a god? What does it *mean* to be a god?"

Now fifty thousand other faces looked toward Danlo, waiting to hear how he would respond.

Nadero devam acayer, Danlo thought. *By none but a god shall a god be worshipped.*

And then, to the journeyman neologician and thousands of others, he said, "It means seeing more than the eyes can see; it means knowing more than the mind can know."

The journeyman stuck out his chin and sniffed in a bit of cold air. And then he called out again, "And what is it *you* know that we do not?"

At this, a cadre of golden-robed Ringists moved closer to him, perhaps to pick a fight with him or chastise him for his unbelievable effrontery. But then Danlo held up his hand and smiled as he shook his head to stay them from any possible violence. He gazed at the journeyman's intelligent face wondering what he might say. And then suddenly, even as he had remembered the words to an unknown poem years before and had seen the battle of Mara's Star as it unfolded across many light years of space, the journeyman's name burst into brilliance in his mind.

"Thaddeus Dudan," he said to the journeyman. "That is your name, isn't it?"

In truth, it *was* his name, and Thaddeus Dudan, the young journeyman neologician from Lara Sig, suddenly pulled back his head as if Danlo had slapped his face. While the ordermen crowding close around him began to talk of the miracle that Danlo had just worked, Thaddeus looked up at Danlo in awe as if Danlo could read his mind.

"How?" he asked hesitantly. "How did you know?"

"I know many things," Danlo said. His voice swelled out like a great liquid wave across the Great Circle and was taken in and passed mouth to mouth by the thousands of people now swarming the nearby streets. "I know the mappings between any two stars, and I know that the number of stars in the universe is infinite and that they shine everywhere the same. I know the neverness and the darkness of light of the Detheshaloon; I know the hearts of men and the minds of gods. I know the white thallow alone in the sky; I know the snowworm dreaming in his icy burrow. I know the scream of a mother giving birth to her child; I know the great loneliness of the sea. And I know that all these things—men and gods, stars and thallows and snowworms and mothers and children—must continue even as life itself continues.

"I know that we are not robots blindly run by our passions; I know that we have the freedom to create ourselves and to choose which future we shall create. I know the Elder Eddas, for I have remembranced them as deeply as a whale diving down into the depths of the Great Northern Ocean. Everything is there, in the Elder Eddas: stillness and motion, darkness and light, and the memory of all that has been and possibilities of all that might ever be.

"How shall I speak to you of what I know? I know that there is a light inside light that shines through everything. It is like a dance of starlight, an endless photon stream, always moving, always beautiful, impossible to really see. And the colors, shimmering, dissolving into each other, the infinite points of silver and violet and living gold—all the colors, and no colors that man has ever seen before or imagined seeing. I know that the deep consciousness of all things is a single, shimmering substance more brilliant than any color and quicker than any light. And all creation comes from this consciousness.

"This is the secret of life. I know that life must continue in consciousness of itself even as it creates itself, on and on into a golden future without limit or end. *We* must continue. We who hold all the many-colored rays of starlight in our hands must finally grasp our infinite possibilities. But we will see nothing and create nothing if we blind ourselves with hydrogen bombs and explode the very stars. If we continue making war against ourselves, we will *not* continue to be. I know that billions of people have already died in this war. I know that gods have died and whole nebulae of stars have died, too. And I know the way to stop the killing and to end the war. This is why I have returned. I am Mallory wi Soli Ringess, Lord Pilot and Lord of the Order, and I have returned to Neverness to bring peace."

At this, a tremendous cheer rang out across the Great Circle. All at once, fifty thousand people gasped out their desire for peace, and in the cold air their many separate breaths gathered into a single, silvery cloud. Seeing that his moment had finally come, Danlo motioned toward Thaddeus Dudan and told him: "Go to the Academy and find Lord Pall. And find as well Lord Kutikoff, Lord Mor, Lord Parsons, Lord Harsha and Lord Chu— all the Lords of the Order. Send for as many masters as are in residence at Borja, Resa, Upplysa and Lara Sig. Tell them that I have returned. Tell them to go to the Cathedral of the Way of Ringess and wait for me. Tell them to escort Bertram Jaspari and Demothi Bede there as well. There I shall speak to them all—and to Hanuman li Tosh who calls himself Lord of the Way of Ringess."

For the count of three heartbeats, Thaddeus Dudan hesitated. Then he bowed deeply and said, "Yes, Lord Mallory." He turned toward the eastern part of the ice ring and began pushing his way through the many men and women craning their necks to get a better look at the man (or god) who stood on the stage before them. It took a long time for Thaddeus to reach the edge of the ring, where the Academy Sliddery gave into the broad band of streets girdling the Great Circle. And then he was gone, just another dot of reddish color lost into all the brilliant colors of the manswarm.

One door, and one door only, opens onto this brilliant future that I have seen. But which door do I choose? And where do I find the key to unlock it?

Danlo stood on the stage, gathering in his breath and looking out over the people of the city. In the vast swarms around him he saw Gamaliel of Darkmoon and Mahamira, the great diva, and hundreds of others whom he knew. In the south quadrant of the ring nearest the Farsiders' Quarter, he caught a glimpse of a face that might have been Tamara's. But when he looked more closely, looked for the sad brown eyes of this fiercest and loveliest of women, she seemed to have vanished into the awestruck throngs. Likewise, at the outermost part of the Circle, a glint of color as of red rings flashing in the sun drew his gaze. His heart beat once, and then twice, and he thought that he saw Malaclypse Redring skulking behind one of the abandoned food kiosks. The warrior-poet—if it were really he—wore a plain brown fur over his deadly form, and he slipped from kiosk to kiosk, working his way around Danlo's back. No one seemed to notice him. And on this brilliant day when ten thousand doors opened onto the future, few of the manswarm would have cared that a warrior-poet walked among them, for all their cares had been given over to a man whom they worshipped as a god.

"Who will come with me?" Danlo cried out. "Who will stand by my side and come with me to the cathedral?"

As he had expected, fifty godlings in their golden furs surged toward him to be closer to him. And fifty thousand others slid their skates against the ice and shouted as one, "We will come! We will come!"

Slowly, Danlo made his way down from the stage. Many godlings awaited his descent onto the ice of the ring; they swarmed around him, vying with each other to lay their hands upon his white furs or even daring to touch his face. For a few moments Danlo allowed himself to suffer such intensely personal adorations. Then he held up his hand to ward off further familiarities. His black diamond pilot's ring shimmered in the sunlight, and he told them: "Come with me, then!"

He instructed twelve of the godlings nearest him (one of them happened to be Madhava li Shing with whom he had roomed at Perilous Hall) to let no one else close to him. And then, with these godlings acting as a golden-clad vanguard, he made his way toward the eastern quadrant of the Great Circle. Slowly, almost magically, the sea of people around him parted and allowed him to pass. And almost immediately, they fell in behind him and his escort, following as closely as they could.

After a long time, Danlo reached the Academy Sliddery and skated past the Hyacinth Gardens. Here, with the scent of fireflowers burning through the air, the crowds of people grew even thicker. Word of the return of Mallory Ringess had electrified the citizens of Neverness and had spread from street to street before Danlo. Along the stretch of ice fronting the Museum, a great many people blocked his way. But they too made a path for him and then joined him, reinforcing the army of his followers. They streamed off the Gallivare Green and the Street of Embassies in their thousands.

By the time that Danlo approached the Courtesan's Conservatory, where Tamara had once trained in the arts of ecstasy, he led a host of men and women at least half a million strong. At the intersection of the Serpentine, he turned south for five long blocks as he led his godling vanguard through the heart of the Old City. And the cheering thousands behind him buoyed him onward like a great, swelling wave of humanity. So loud was the roar of the voices through the streets that the very stones of the towers all around Danlo seemed to shake. Soon, in only a few more blocks, his host of godlings and others would break upon the cathedral. And then Danlo would pound on the great doors with the diamond ring that had once belonged to his father, and Hanuman li Tosh would be forced to open them and let him inside.

They will be waiting for me there. Hanuman and Surya Lal and Bertram Jaspari. And Lord Pall and Lord Harsha, who knew my father well. And Malaclypse of Qallar, of the two red rings— he, too, will try to find his way inside.

Somewhere, he thought, inside the cathedral or on some darkened street, the warrior-poet would try to trap him and determine whether or not he was truly a god. Perhaps he would ask him to complete a poem that only a man who has refused to become a god could answer. Or perhaps he would assume that Danlo as Mallory Ringess had already transcended his humanity and would try to slay him for the sin of moving godward.

By none but a god shall a god be slain.

Just south of Danladi Square, the Cathedral of the Way of Ringess rose up in all its glory. Its beauty overshadowed the nearby buildings, many of which, in their glittering sweeps of organic stone, were beautiful indeed. As Danlo skated closer, his gaze fell upon the long stained-glass windows depicting the famous scenes of his father's life. In the intense sunlight, the reds, golds and blues of the windows sprayed out into the air and seemed to drench the entire cathedral in color. Above the crossing, where the arms of the cathedral joined the building's main body, the central tower looked down upon the granite flying buttresses and all the graceful stonework below. And it looked up as well, for Bardo had ordered the tower surmounted with a great golden dome. Here, Danlo knew, inside the tower's rooms, Hanuman li Tosh spent his nights looking up into the sky at the Universal Computer and at the Golden Ring. Here, too, beneath this glittering golden dome, he would have been waiting when some godling knocked upon his door and brought word of the coming of Mallory Ringess.

I am Mallory Ringess; I am Mallory Ringess; I am Mallory wi Soli Ringess. . . .

The streets nearest the cathedral were lined with golden-robed godlings chanting: ''Mallory Ringess! Mallory Ringess! Mallory wi Soli Ringess!'' Their desire to leap forward to greet their god was great, but their discipline was great, too, and they had been instructed to clear a way for Danlo and his vanguard. And so they kept to the sides of the wide glidderies as Danlo passed by them, and all the while they cheered and chanted his father's name.

When Danlo drew close to the cathedral's western portal, he saw that the three great wooden doors had been thrown open. Other godlings—Hanuman's cathedral police—stood beneath the huge stone archway of the central door waiting for him. Despite the fervor of the moment, he noticed that the original carvings of the Kristian saints and prophets in the archway had been replaced with organic stone sculptures of Katharine the Scryer, Shanidar, Balusilustalu, and Kalinda of the Flowers, all of whom had helped Mallory Ringess become a god.

After ejecting his skate blades, Danlo climbed the shallow steps leading up to the portal. The shouts of half a million people drowned out the sound of his boots pounding against stone; the ringing in his ears almost silenced the pounding of his heart. And then he passed through the doorway, and the godlings there fairly fell on their faces in their eagerness to bow to him. They allowed the godlings of Danlo's vanguard to pass inside as well, but then they closed ranks to bar anyone not dressed in a godling's golden robes. But their numbers were too few, and the fervor of the manswarm following Danlo had grown too great. In only a few frantic moments, men and women dressed in the Order's many colors—and harijan, hibakusha, and astriers, too—swept the cathedral police out of their way and surged inside.

''Mallory Ringess! Mallory Ringess! Mallory wi Soli Ringess!''

Thousands of godlings packed the great nave of the cathedral;
they stood along the walls and between the pillars of the aisles
calling out his father's name. The sound of their voices reverber-
ated from the stonework and the windows, and rose up to fill the
cathedral's magnificent vault high above. To mark the return of
Mallory Ringess, thousands of candles in their golden stands had
been set afire. But there was little need for their flickering, yellow
flames, for the noonday sun rained down upon the cathedral and
light streamed through the windows in lovely parallel lines of
crimson and emerald and a deep, cobalt blue. As Danlo walked
deeper into the nave, he felt this light like starfire upon his face.
He felt many, many pairs of eyes burning into him, too. He made
his way past the rows of adoring godlings straight toward the
chancel. There, to the right of the red-carpeted altar, stood Surya
Surata Lal, Thomas Rane, Nirvelli and Mariam Erendira Vasquez,
who had once been the Order's Lord Eschatologist. They waited
in silence along with Delores Lightstone and Lais Motega Mo-
hammed and the other elite followers of the Way of Ringess.

To the left of the altar, the Lords of the Order had been gathered as Danlo had instructed. There were a hundred and twelve of
them that day: Jonath Parsons, Rodrigo Diaz, Mahavira Netis and
Nicobar Yutu, who wore a new golden robe, and others. Since
Danlo's visit to the College of Lords, many lords had traded in
their colored robes for those woven of a godling's gold. Kolenya
Mor, the present Lord Eschatolgist, had been the first of them to
convert so openly to Ringism, and Alesar Druze, Sasha Chu and
Oklani wi Nuri Chu had followed her example along with some
seventy-five others. Now Eva Zarifa, the Lord Fabulist, sported a
gold robe with purple armbands to denote her profession rather
than the reverse. Burgos Harsha, however, the Lord Historian, still
wore his old brown robe and declared that he always would. And
Lord Pall still wore his cetic's orange robe.

As Lord of the Order, he wished to distance himself from
Hanuman li Tosh and the Way of Ringess. He pretended to an
autonomy of his position in which few now believed; almost everyone at the Academy suspected that Hanuman subtly controlled
Lord Pall, even as a master programmer's virus might invade and
run a robot's operating systems. Lord Pall, of course, still acted as
if all the power of the Order was his alone. This terrible old man,
with his bone white skin and blackened teeth, had positioned the
lords and masters of the Order near the altar according to their
rank.

Farthest away, almost to the aisle where many godlings shifted about to get a better look at Danlo's entrance as Mallory Ringess, he had commanded the master academicians to gather as a group some three hundred strong. Closer in stood such minor lords as Lillith Jesusa and John Raizel. Although Demothi Bede was no longer of the Order, Lord Pall had invited him to wait by his side a few feet from the altar, along with Kolenya Mor, Morasha the Bright and Burgos Harsha. Demothi Bede, who had floated for many days with Danlo in the pit of his ship on their journey to Neverness, seemed not to recognize Danlo for who he truly was. Lord Pall, too, obviously accepted Danlo as Mallory Ringess, for he stood staring at Danlo with his pink, albino's eyes as if bitterly regretting that here walked one who had a better claim than he to the Lordship of the Order.

"Mallory Ringess! Mallory Ringess! Lord Mallory wi Soli Ringess!"

One other man awaited Danlo's approach through the nave with loathing and dread. This was Bertram Jaspari. As the false Holy Ivi of the Cybernetic Universal Church and commander of fleet of ships that would destroy the Star of Neverness, he stood with chains binding his arms against his bloodred kimono. He might have bowed his head in shame at all the atrocities he had committed and plotted to commit, but instead he defiantly pressed his thin, blue lips together and glared hatred at this man whom he believed to be Mallory Ringess. "Hakra!" he spat out as he watched Danlo make his way among the thousands of godlings. According to his interpretation of his Church's teachings, it was the worst of crimes for a man to become a god. In all his sanctimoniousness, he acted as if Mallory Ringess's crime of hubris had somehow cancelled out his own. "Hakra! Abomination!"

All these people (and many more such as Thaddeus Dudan and Master Jonath who had once been Danlo's tutor at Borja) Danlo took note of as he walked past the cheering manswarms. But then, as he came closer to the altar, almost the whole of his attention fixed upon Hanuman li Tosh, who stood alone on this elevated platform waiting for him. He had positioned himself across from the table holding the golden urn and the blue bowl used in countless kalla ceremonies. He himself was resplendent in his long, golden robe. The diamond clearface molded to his shaved head glittered with a billion bits of violet light, a sign that he was in almost continual interface with some cetic computer, possibly even the Universal Computer itself.

Had any of the godlings chanced to look toward the altar, they would have seen Hanuman beaming out a dazzling smile as if he had been awaiting the return of Mallory Ringess with gladness and love. But this was a sham. Not for nothing had Hanuman trained as a cetic to master every nuance of expression and emotion. His eyes—his infinitely cold, pale, *shaida* eyes—had not fallen inward with visions of other-worldly beauties or prophecies finally fulfilled. Instead, they fell upon Danlo with a cold fury terrible to behold. Almost no one in the cathedral was aware of Hanuman's true passions except Danlo. And even Danlo was able to pierce the icy glaze of Hanuman's face only because he had known him as well as anyone ever could.

He is afraid, Danlo thought. *He is afraid, for I bring the one thing that he truly fears.*

As Danlo's heart boomed in his chest like the Vild stars exploding into fire, his eyes drank in Hanuman's eyes. And Hanuman's unwavering gaze drew him onward, deeper into the nave of the cathedral. Hanuman seemed to have aged terribly since their last meeting; his eyes were bloodshot and sunken in their hollow sockets as if he hadn't slept in many days and had hardly deigned to eat. At last Danlo approached the steps to the altar. There, Jaroslav Bulba and three other ronin warrior-poets stood blocking Madhava li Shing and the eleven other godlings of Danlo's vanguard from getting too near to Hanuman. But they allowed Danlo to pass. And so as he had done once six years before on the evening of Year's End, he climbed the shallow steps one by one to stand on the altar with his deadliest enemy and his deepest friend.

I am afraid, too, he thought. He looked up above the altar at the cathedral's eighty-two windows, focusing on the one showing Mallory Ringess' blessing of Bardo before his ascent to the heavens. The sunlight streamed through golden glass and lit up Mallory Ringess' strong, noble face. The last time that Danlo had stood here, the fierce deep winter wind had blown in this great window, showering the altar with bits of colored glass and nearly killing Hanuman. On that night of broken gods and broken dreams, he had almost killed Hanuman himself. Out of hatred and fear, he had almost used the heavy urn to break open Hanuman's brains, but at the last moment he had saved him instead. And now, on this glorious day of his return as Mallory Ringess, he was afraid once again. More than anything else, he feared that he would let his hatred of Hanuman and all that Hanuman had done well up and overcome him. And thus betray him. *But I must not hate—I am Mallory Ringess, who is beyond hate or fear. I am Mallory Ringess; I am Mallory Ringess; I am Mallory wi Soli Ringess.*

"Mallory Ringess! Mallory Ringess! Lord Mallory wi Soli Ringess!"

As the thousands of people in the cathedral swayed and chanted and shouted out the name of Mallory Ringess, Hanuman bowed low to welcome Danlo. And Danlo, who was much taller than Hanuman, bowed, too—not quite as low as Hanuman, but low enough not to break the electric connection of their eyes.

"Lord Mallory! Lord of the Order! Lord of Lords!—Lord of the Way of Ringess!"

If he were truly to act as his father, Danlo thought, then he must embody only the godly emotions. Fear and hatred were as far beneath him as the world's dirt was beneath the sun. But wrath—the pure and blindingly bright *ira dei* before which the very heavens must tremble—that was something must vaster. In wrath black and bright a god might return to Neverness to avenge wrongs and restore justice to a war-ravaged people. He might chastise the wicked and perhaps even slay those who had visited horrors upon the innocent, whether they be man, woman or child.

I cannot slay him, but I can remove him as Lord of the Way of Ringess, here and now. I am Mallory wi Soli Ringess, Lord of the Way of Ringess, and I—

"Lord Mallory wi Soli Ringess!" Hanuman suddenly called out. He held up his hand to quiet the godlings swaying ecstatically throughout the cathedral. If he suspected anyone of impersonating Mallory Ringess, he gave no sign. He stood between golden candelabra blazing with light and vases filled with freshly cut fireflowers—and all the while he stared at Danlo with a terrible intensity as if each cell of his body was burning from deep inside. Only a few feet of the altar's red carpet separated him from Danlo. But the distance between their desires and dreams (and perhaps their souls) had grown as great as the light-years between the stars. "Lord Mallory, I have told the people that you would return, and on this glorious day, you have come before us to fulfill the truth of the first pillar of Ringism."

As Danlo took a step nearer to Hanuman, the people around him finally began to grow quiet. Immediately upon ascending the altar, he had shrugged off his furs, and he now stood in his formal pilot's robe, the only one in the cathedral dressed entirely in black. The elite of the Way of Ringess gathered impatiently below the altar, as did the lords and masters of the Order. Thousands of godlings spread out through the nave like a sea of rippling gold. Here and there, harijan dressed in colorful but ragged silks joined them, along with neurosingers, arhats, astriers and all the other

peoples of Neverness. So great were their numbers that they
spilled out the cathedral's open doors and swarmed the surrounding streets. In truth, the whole of the Old City for many blocks in
any direction had filled with men and women waiting for Danlo to
speak so that they might know the glorious and terrible justice of
a god.

This is the moment, Danlo thought. *And my voice is the key
that will unlock the door.*

But he was afraid to speak. He was afraid that Hanuman, in all
his cetic training and deep familiarity with Danlo, might detect
some slight tell or pattern to his speech and expose him for who
he truly was. He might openly challenge Danlo to prove that he
was Mallory Ringess; thus Danlo had put on his father's pilot's
ring in the event that he should be tried or tested.

*One door, and one door only, opens onto the future. But will
Hanuman let me open it?*

Danlo looked down at the black diamond ring all sparkling and
brilliant around the little finger of his right hand. He took a step
closer to Hanuman, and he filled his lungs with a deep breath of
air. He was afraid that Hanuman would try to keep him from
speaking. Hanuman must have known that Mallory Ringess—the
true Mallory Ringess in all his pride and wrath—would punish
him for the terrors that he had unleashed in the Ringess name.
Would Hanuman try to have him assassinated, here atop the altar
with its scarred, old carpet stained as red as blood? Would he
allow Malaclypse of Qallar into the cathedral and stand by in
feigned horror as Malaclypse broke through the cordon of cathedral police and fell upon Danlo with his killing knife? Or would
he simply slay him himself, with a poisoned needle or a hidden
laser, and announce that a stronger god had slain a lesser one, and
that the Way of Ringess had now become the Way of Hanuman li
Tosh?

*He cannot allow me to speak, for I am Mallory Ringess. I am
Mallory Ringess; I am Mallory Ringess; I am Mallory wi Soli
Ringess.*

But he did not see how Hanuman could silence him. Even if
Malaclypse had found his way into the cathedral, Hanuman
couldn't count on the wild chance that he might try to slay Danlo.
And it would be a desperate thing for Hanuman to have him
assassinated or to execute this act himself. Assassins could always
be caught, tortured and made to reveal their masters. And the
slaying of Mallory Ringess, at this time and in this place, would
touch off riots and would cause suspicion to fall upon Hanuman

with all the certainty of the rising sun. Even so, as Danlo breathed in deeply, his eyes swept out to the central loggia above the nave, looking behind the fine stonework of the balconies for assassins or robot lasers. And he took yet one more small step closer to Hanuman; he wanted to make it as difficult as possible for anyone to fire upon him without also incurring the risk of slaying Hanuman.

"Lords and masters of the Order," he finally called out. His voice flowed out of him steady and clear, and it rippled with power. The thousands of godlings in the cathedral immediately fell silent at the terrible beauty of this godly voice; even Hanuman li Tosh looked at him strangely as if in awe at hearing the voice of Mallory Ringess for the first time. "Lord Hanuman li Tosh, Princess Surya Surata Lal, all those of you who have donned the golden robes of a godling and followed the Way of Ringess; ambassadors and citizens of Neverness and all those of you who have ever sought the secret of life in the remembrance of the Elder Eddas, I have returned so that we all might fulfill the truth of this eternal quest. I have come before you from the stars across the universe to bring justice to the Civilized Worlds and an end to war."

Here, Danlo paused a moment to allow the godlings to let loose a tremendous cheer that pounded through the nave from wall to wall and shook the long, glass windows in their casings. And then he drew in another breath of air and opened his mouth to continue speaking. "I have returned to bring justice, but there can be no justice as long as—"

"Death to autarchs! Death to false gods!"

Just then, from the crowd of godlings nearest the altar, a large and cruel-looking man who might have once been a wormrunner interrupted Danlo. All in one moment, Danlo felt his belly tense up at the sound of this voice, even as he saw Hanuman li Tosh subtly move his eyes in a cetic sign directed toward this golden-robed man. And then a terrible thing happened. The man drew forth a bullet gun of gleaming chrome and aimed it straight toward the altar.

"Death to false gods! Death to Hanuman li Tosh!"

Many things happened almost all at once. A hundred men and women crowding near the altar cried out in terror, while a hundred more covered their faces or tried to duck low toward the smooth stone floor. The man with the gun screamed out in hatred, while three of the nearby cathedral police immediately closed upon him. One of them, a young godling with flaming red hair and fire in his eyes, managed to knock the assassin's arm off its mark. He held it locked straight upward while the gun exploded into life. Three times gouts of flaming hot gas burst from the muzzle of the gun, sending metal bullets smashing against the hard granite of the vault high above them. At least one of the bullets blew out a section of glass from one of the windows directly above the altar—as it happened, the very window of Mallory Ringess saying farewell to Bardo that had shattered inward once before. This time, only part of the window shattered, and only a few bits of violet and gold glass rained down upon the altar.

Almost without thinking, Danlo moved closer to Hanuman to shield him from this shower of sharp, glittering glass. He almost couldn't help himself. It was as if the gun's explosion had hurled him back in time to a moment when his essential love for Hanuman had overcome his hate. And now he found himself suddenly embracing Hanuman, bowing his head down over Hanuman's head, letting the flying pieces of glass cut through his thick black hair or spray against the black silk robe covering his back and neck. Some of the cathedral police near the altar also shielded themselves from this glass, but others swarmed the assassin and disarmed him. And still others—along with Jaroslav Bulba and three of his warrior-poets—rushed up upon the altar to throw their bodies around Hanuman and Danlo.

"Protect him!" Hanuman cried out as he pushed away from Danlo. For one shattering moment of time, he met eyes with Danlo and stared at him strangely. Then he caught Jaroslav Bulba by the sleeve of his robe and motioned toward Danlo. "Protect Lord Mallory Ringess!"

While the cathedral police below the altar wrestled the would-be assassin to the floor and bound him with acid wire, Jaroslav Bulba and twenty other godlings swarmed around Danlo. They covered Danlo with their bodies, shielding him from the bullets or the laser light of other assassins—and shielding him as well from the eyes of the thousands of godlings spread throughout the nave. Thus concealed by this wall of golden silk, Jaroslav Bulba came up behind Danlo and stuck a black-tipped needle in his neck. At the same time, other godlings took hold of Danlo's arms and waist, even as Danlo suddenly surged forward wildly and shouted out, "No!"

But it was too late for him to break free. The paralytic drug that Jaroslav Bulba had injected into him almost instantly froze his muscles into motionlessness much as a strong cold wind might steal a man's breath away. "No!" he cried out again. "I am Mallory wi Soli Ringess and I—" But then his voice choked off as if some invisible hand were squeezing his throat. His legs gave way and he fell against Jaroslav Bulba and the godlings surrounding him. Five of the godlings proceeded down the steps of the altar to clear the way while Jaroslav Bulba and five others followed buoying up Danlo in their arms.

"Out of the way!" Hanuman called out. He pushed away from the godlings remaining on the altar, foolishly—or so it seemed—exposing himself. He stood facing the godlings and all the peoples of the city standing below the altar. His smooth, silvery voice cut like a sword through the pandemonium spreading through the cathedral. "Make way for Lord Mallory Ringess! He must be taken to safety!"

Danlo, who was caught between the bodies of Jaroslav Bulba and three other ronin warrior-poets, struggled to speak and to move. But he could do little more than to watch Jaroslav's deadly violet eyes and wait for his captors to take him to safety. This they soon did. They bore him through the nave of the cathedral, through throngs of women and men nearly frantic to know whether or not their god had been struck by one of the assassin's bullets. Danlo felt Jaroslav's hot breath in his face and felt blood trickling down his neck where a sliver of flying glass had cut him. High above him, sunlight and wind streamed through the hole that the bullet had torn open in the beautiful window; all around him, the breath of hundreds of godlings broke into the air as they gasped out their fear for Mallory Ringess' life.

And then the warrior-poets swept him through a great archway mounted with stone pinnacles and a sculpture of Mallory Ringess that looked out upon the nave. They half-carried him down a short passageway to the main stairwell that led up through the central tower. Someone opened the doorway to the stairwell and pushed him through. For a moment the stones of the stairwell echoed with the chant of ten thousand godlings calling out his name: "Mallory Ringess! Mallory Ringess! Lord Mallory wi Soli Ringess!"

I am Mallory Ringess, Danlo thought. *I am Mallory Ringess, and I have returned across thirty thousand light-years to end the war.*

And then suddenly the doors banged shut behind him, cutting off the voices of the godlings, and there was a silence as deep as space.

THE BATTLE OF
TEN THOUSAND SUNS

*In death thy glory in heaven, in victory thy glory on
earth. Arise therefore, Arjuna, with thy soul ready to
fight.*

—Bhagavad Gita 2:37

The ronin warrior-poets brought Danlo to Hanuman's sanctuary
at the top of the tower. As before, it was crowded with sulki grids,
hologram stands, computers and other cybernetica. The flame
globes had all been lit in anticipation of Danlo's arrival. They cast
a rainbow light upon Hanuman's chess set on its black and white
board: his old set of carved ivory and shatterwood pieces that was
missing the white god. Danlo's devotional computer—the one
that he had carried with him across the thousands of light-years of
the Vild—had been brought from his cell in the chapterhouse and
positioned on a table near the chess set. But as with so many days
before, Hanuman had covered it with a white null cloth impervi-
ous to sound or light. Hanuman motioned toward the cubical
bulge beneath this cloth and explained that he could not bear
Ede's constant chatter.

Because Hanuman kept no bed or couch for sleeping, the warrior-poets laid Danlo down on one of the Fravashi carpets near the
eastern quadrant of the room. Danlo, still under the grip of the
warrior-poet's paralytic drug, could make no movement of his
body other than blinking his eyes. As Jaroslav Bulba knelt to
check his pulse and his breathing, he lay back on the carpet staring up at the long curving windows of the dome above him. He
gazed upon the deep blue sky and the sections of the purple-
colored dome that blocked out the sky; from time to time, Jaroslav's face would hover straight above his like a spider suspended
in space, and then he would gaze at Jaroslav's hideous, red, jewelled eyes.

"I've never seen a god before," Jaroslav said, looking down at him. "Mallory Ringess—there was a time when I would have had to slay you for being a god. That is, if you really *are* a god, as everyone says you are."

Danlo's heart beat three times, and he blinked twice as he stared up at this ronin warrior-poet who had once tortured him. But he could not turn his head away from him, nor could he speak.

"You will be wondering about the drug that I injected into you. Unless you are given the antidote, its effects are permanent."

I cannot move, Danlo thought. *But I must move; I must will myself to move.*

"Permanent paralysis," Jaroslav said in a voice without pity or heart. "But we can keep you alive with feeding tubes almost forever, if Lord Hanuman wishes you alive."

I must will myself to move. I must turn and lie here facing west if it is my time to die.

After a long while—Danlo counted some three thousand heartbeats—he heard the sanctuary's doors open. From the sound of footsteps against stone he thought that two or more men had walked into the room. When one of these men began speaking, his voice echoed off the optical and quantum computers and the Yarknonan tapestries hanging between the windows. He instantly recognized this smooth, silvery voice for it belonged to Hanuman li Tosh.

"Well, he doesn't look so godly now, does he?" Hanuman said. He came over to the carpet and stood above Danlo; his cold blue eyes looked down upon Danlo like two pale moons. To Jaroslav Bulba, standing by his side, he said, "Please give him the partial antidote now."

"Are you certain of this, Lord Hanuman? If he is really a god, then—"

"Oh, I think that he's as human in his body as you or I. Give him the antidote so that I might speak with him."

"As you wish, Lord Hanuman."

While Jaroslav stepped into view with a needle held between his fingers, another man shifted about in back of Hanuman. Danlo could hear the crinkling silk of his garments but could not see who it was. And then he felt the cold sharp bite of the needle entering his flesh. His face, neck, jaws and throat began to tingle and burn. After his heart had beat twenty times, he found himself able to open his mouth, slightly. And then Hanuman spoke to Jaroslav again, saying, "Please leave us now. Wait outside the door until I call for you."

Danlo's heart beat four more times, pumping the new drug through his arteries, muscles and nerves. He managed to turn his head just enough to see Jaroslav Bulba gather up the other warrior-poets and move off toward the door.

"The antidote," Hanuman said to Danlo, "will cancel the paralysis of your face and head. The warrior-poets make the subtlest of drugs—you should know, we've other antidotes that will allow other parts of you to move. Or your whole body, just as it was before you were poisoned."

With great effort Danlo pulled his head straight backward, trying to get a better look at Hanuman and the man who stood hiding behind him. "Hanuman," he finally gasped out. He licked his lips and swallowed against the fuzzy dryness in his throat. "Hanuman li Tosh . . . I am—"

"Mallory Ringess," Hanuman said as he moved over and knelt by Danlo's side. "Mallory wi Soli Ringess is the god—or man—whom you have mimed. But I know who you really are."

With that, he motioned to the man behind him, and Constancio of Alesar stepped into view.

"Danlo," Hanuman said, looking down and locking eyes in the way he had done with Danlo since their meeting in Lavi Square many years before. "Danlo wi Soli Ringess—you are he, aren't you? I know that you are. I know that this man has recently sculpted you so that you might mime your father."

Danlo turned to stare at the tall, gray man named Constancio of Alesar. The paralysis of his tongue and lips had almost completely left him, and he found that he could give voice to all the wrath that he felt burning up inside him.

"Go away," he said in a deep and dark voice. "Go away and never return."

"I'm sorry about your son," Constancio said. At these words, Hanuman's eyes locked upon him like searchlights, and he stood looking back and forth between Constancio and Danlo. "I'm sorry, but there was nothing I could do."

"You might have *helped* him," Danlo said. "You had the drugs, the cryologist's art—it was within your power to save his life, and you let him die."

"I'm sorry, but it was too late. And we had already concluded our agreement, don't you see?"

"I . . . see," Danlo choked out. He stared at Constancio, and his eyes burned with his anger. And then he said, "You promised. You were to keep the sculpting a secret—we touched hands to seal our agreement, yes?"

"Well, it was wrong of you to impersonate a god," Constancio said. He fairly cringed under Danlo's intense gaze, and he looked off down at the bare floorstones beneath the carpet. "And it was wrong of me to try to keep your secret."

"You agreed that if you told anyone, the price of the sculpting would be forfeit. The sphere belonged to my mother. Please return it to me, now."

At this, Constancio looked at Hanuman as if the drug had paralyzed not only Danlo's body but his mind. "He's mad," Constancio told him. "I should never have agreed to sculpt a madman."

Hanuman looked at Constancio strangely, as if he were more of a mechanical puzzle to be solved than a living human being. And then he asked, "But you did sculpt him, didn't you? And you can prove this, as you have said?"

Again, Constancio nodded. And then he said to Hanuman, "Will you please hold his head still?"

With a sad, grim smile, Hanuman clamped his hands around Danlo's forehead and jaw. It took all his strength to immobilize Danlo, for just then Danlo raged at his betrayal and helplessness, trying to shake his head from side to side with all the power that he could summon. At last, when Hanuman had won this battle of wills, Constancio reached into the large black bag of tools that he carried and removed a laser scope. While holding open Danlo's left eyelid with one hand, he shined the intense light around in a little circle where the bright blue iris gave way to the white. "Do you see the seam?" he asked Hanuman. "I've sealed artificial corneas to the eyes. They can easily be removed, if you wish."

"Please," Hanuman said, holding Danlo's head even more tightly.

After numbing each of Danlo's eyes with a topical anesthetic, Constancio sprayed first the right and then the left with a solvent. In only moments, he had taken out the corneas to reveal the same deep, liquid blue eyes with which Danlo had looked out at the world ever since he had been a child.

"It's well that you've provided evidence of his miming," Hanuman told him. "Thank you for coming forward."

"Thank *you*, Lord Hanuman," Constancio said, bowing.

"Please don't tell anyone about this miming."

"Of course I won't," Constancio said. "You have my promise. And now I should like nothing more than a passage from Neverness, as *you* promised."

"Of course," Hanuman said. He gazed out one of the western

windows at the blazing sun. For many days now, the rumor of the Iviomil's threat to destroy the Star of Neverness had struck terror into the peoples of the city. Some of them, desperate to flee the starvation and the coming apocalypse, had offered to sell heirloom firestones or parts of their bodies (or even their very children) for a passage in one of the blackships that occasionally departed from the Hollow Fields. No day went by that Hanuman, as the true Lord of the City, wasn't besieged by a hundred such requests. "I *have* promised you a passage, haven't I?"

So saying, Hanuman strode over to the door and opened it. He motioned for Jaroslav Bulba and one of the other warrior-poets to enter the room. According to some secret signal from Hanuman, they positioned themselves on either side of Constancio. "I've promised this man a passage away from Neverness. Please see that he leaves the city today."

With a quick bow of his head, he bade farewell to Constancio and then walked with him and the warrior-poets to the door. He shut it himself. Then he spun about and returned to the carpet where Danlo lay staring at him.

"He's truly a great cutter," Hanuman said. As he studied Danlo's face and savage form, his eyes fell as cold as a thin blue milk that has frozen into ice. "But I hate traitors who break their promises."

Danlo, who still struggled in vain to move his arms and hands, looked at Hanuman and said, "Then you plan to murder him, yes?"

For five beats of Danlo's heart, Hanuman continued looking at him in silence.

"He will never leave Neverness, will he?"

And then Hanuman smiled sadly and said, "Of course he will. I have *my* promise to keep. After he's dead, he'll be burned in a plasma oven, and the smoke from his body will leave the city before the day is over. He'll have his passage from Neverness."

"I see."

"I should think you'd want him dead."

"I . . . do not. You must know that I do not."

"Never killing, then? Never harming another despite what he had done to you?"

"In all that Constancio has done, in all that he has failed to do, he has only harmed himself. His . . . soul. I wish him no further harm."

"You're too damn noble—I've always said that."

"I am sorry."

"I didn't know that you had a son. *I* am sorry that he's gone. With all my heart, Danlo."

For a while Danlo looked at Hanuman as his eyes burned and filled with tears. He could still feel the touch of Jonathan's dying breath upon his face and smell the smoke of his burning body.

"Was he Tamara's child, then? Tamara's and yours?"

Danlo closed his eyes as the bright flames of memory burned through his mind, but he remained silent.

"Then Tamara still lives in Neverness, doesn't she?" Hanuman the cetic, aimed his silvery voice at Danlo like a knife. "I think that she's lived here all this time; I think that she bore your child years ago, and you abandoned him in your silly quest to the Vild."

Now Danlo opened his eyes and stared straight at Hanuman. He said, "I do not wish to speak of Tamara. Nor of my son."

"As you wish, then."

Danlo looked up at the curving, purple sections of the dome above him. He ground his teeth against all the despair and hate he felt poisoning him. And then he said, "I should never have gone to Constancio to be sculpted."

"Perhaps not," Hanuman said. "But you mustn't blame him for your betrayal. You should know, it was you who betrayed yourself."

"Truly?"

"Do you suppose that your father would have tried to save me from an assassin's bullet? Do you think that Mallory Ringess would have shielded me with his own *body?*"

"I . . . do not know what my father would do."

"The way that you *looked* at me, Danlo. On the altar, just after the window broke and the glass came down, there was a moment—it was all in your eyes, you should know. All in your dear, damned, wild eyes."

"My eyes," Danlo said. *"My* eyes, now."

"Yes, well, the artificial corneas can be replaced, can't they? If we should wish to continue this ruse. But as for now, I'm almost certain that no one but myself could have seen you for who you truly are."

"Then the godlings still believe that I am Mallory Ringess?"

"They *do* believe this, Danlo. You must know how deep and terrible is their need to believe."

Again Hanuman knelt on the rich, colorful carpet with his knees almost flush against Danlo's chest. He reached down to touch Danlo's forehead for the heat of fever; he touched his eyes, throat, arms and belly, testing the muscles for the tells of paralysis. Although Hanuman's hands and fingers had always been as hard as iron from years of his practicing the killing arts, they fairly trembled with a new weakness as if the strain of touching Danlo tormented him. In truth, the strain of the starvation and the war (and his secret dreams) had weakened his entire body. It was shocking to see the ghastly changes that only a few tendays of time had wrought upon Hanuman since his torture of Danlo. His face had fallen white as shatterwood ashes and seemed to have aged ten thousand years. From time to time, his eyes showed flashes of the hellish fire that raged inside him and still kept him moving. But just as often they glazed over with an icy film of despair and seemed devoid of life. His movements, once as fluid as quicksilver, were pained and uncertain like those of an old man.

It was as if he had made a secret and *shaida* pact with death where he would be allowed to remain alive forever—but only at the cost of becoming a talking, breathing, calculating corpse terrible to behold. Long ago he had murdered the most beautiful parts of himself to become as strong and immortal as a god; long ago he had taken the blazing mantle of the prophet upon himself. But at last the fire of what he most desired (and feared) had grown too hot and bright to bear. Even as Danlo watched, this wild and infinite flame was consuming Hanuman from the inside out. Like a chain reaction of supernovas blowing apart the core of a galaxy, there was nothing to stop it. Soon, he thought, it would burn away the last of Hanuman's humanity, leaving little more of the man that Danlo had once loved than bone and pain and his terrible will toward his own fate.

"I know that the godlings have always believed what you wanted them to believe," Danlo finally said. "What have you told them about me, then?"

"I've told them that you're unharmed. And that you've been taken to safety until there's no further threat of assassination."

"I see."

"Of course, in such times as these, there are always those nihilities who would assassinate vaster souls, even potential gods."

"But it was you whom the assassin aimed his gun at, not I."

"So it seemed."

Danlo watched the clearface computer as it glittered all around Hanuman's head and bathed his face in a hellish purple light.

"I think that I understand," Danlo said. "The assassin was one of your warrior-poets, yes?"

"Actually, he was a godling whom Jaroslav Bulba has trained. He's been taken to a cell in the chapterhouse—as it happens, across from your old cell. For *his* protection, of course. You should know, he's admitted to being a ringkeeper; we've told the godlings that Benjamin Hur ordered him to try to assassinate me."

"I see," Danlo said again. And again, he tried to move his arms and legs, but could not. "But wouldn't it have been simplest if you had ordered him to assassinate me?"

"Simplest, perhaps, but not safest. To assassinate the great Mallory Ringess—that would have been a wildly dangerous thing to do. Even to have *feigned* an assassination attempt against the Ringess might have turned the entire church against me. I couldn't blame such an attempt on the ringkeepers; I'm afraid the people's suspicion would have fallen upon me. Then, too . . ."

"Yes?"

"It would be hard to find any godling willing to assassinate his god."

"Even one of your warrior-poets?"

At this Hanuman smiled and said, "Even Jaroslav Bulba believes you to be Mallory Ringess. Even he was reluctant to touch you with his needle."

"And what does your false assassin believe, then?"

"Only that he has helped me to discredit Benjamin Hur and his silly ringkeepers. The whole city has seen how his man, in all his carelessness, almost assassinated *you.*"

Danlo's left eye felt as if one of the splinters of glass from the window had driven straight into the black opening at the center of the iris. Although he desperately needed to rub away the stabbing agony of it, he couldn't move his arm. "I had thought that you would want to silence me," Danlo said. "But I could not see how you would."

"You really couldn't? You, who have always seen so much?"

"You were always cleverer than I in such things, Hanu. Always more subtle."

"Perhaps," Hanuman said. "But even so, your plan was subtle enough. Really, it was quite brilliant. Despite the dangers and the chances against it, it came within a breath of succeeding."

One door, and one door only, opens upon the golden future that I have seen, Danlo thought. *Ahira, Ahira—why did I choose the wrong door?*

"Of course your father would have executed this plan differently," Hanuman said. "He was always a great strategist and tactician—a true warlord. Despite your father's famous boldness, he would never have simply walked into my cathedral and placed himself at my mercy."

"I did not count on your mercy, Hanu."

"No—you tried to seize the moment and depose me. But your father would have eschewed such a strategy as lacking elegance, much less common sense. Somewhere in the city he would have established a base from which to operate. Perhaps even in the Pilot's Quarter or near the Ring of Fire. And then upon announcing himself, he would have gathered his friends and followers around him. Benjamin Hur's noisome ringkeepers, of course, and most of the Order. The aliens, too, would have flocked to his bloody banner. The harijan, the neurosingers, the tychists—they would have swarmed forth street by street until they overwhelmed the whole city. I wouldn't have stood a chance of stopping him."

Danlo, lying helpless on the Fravashi carpet, breathed deeply against the pain in his head, and then said, "Truly, I considered such a plan. But there were two reasons that I could not follow it."

"Please tell me."

"I did not want to touch off open war within the city. There has already been enough death in Neverness."

"And your second reason, then?"

"My second reason was similar: If you saw that your defeat was certain, you would have fled the city and tried to continue the war from the stars. I did not want you to escape."

"But, Danlo—you can't win a war without fighting a war."

"I . . . had to try."

"Your devotion to ahimsa amazes me. You might have won everything."

"And in winning this way, I would have lost all that truly mattered. There was a chance that I could have ended the war without further killing."

"Well, chance has fallen against you, and you've lost. Your fate has betrayed you, Danlo."

One door, and one door only, opens—

"Which is why you lie here before me paralyzed and waiting for me to decide your fate."

Danlo took another breath as his heart beat hard up through his throat and head. "It would be simplest for you to kill me, yes?"

"Simple, yes, but silly," Hanuman said. "You must know that

I can't simply paralyze your heart and lungs and provide you with a passage away from Neverness as I have with that treacherous cutter.''

Danlo closed his eyes as he listened to the sounds all about him and inside him where his heart beat like a booming, red drum. He could almost feel the rhythmic chants of ten thousand men and women vibrating up through the stone beneath him; he could almost hear the long, dark roar of half a million people standing outside the cathedral and shouting out his name: "Mallory Ringess! Mallory Ringess! Mallory wi Soli Ringess!"

"They're still waiting for you," Hanuman said. "Or, I should say, for your father. They've waited all their lives for him to return."

"And you cannot simply send them away, can you?"

"No, I'm afraid it would be dangerous to try to disperse them, now."

Again, Danlo closed his eyes, and he almost saw the soundwaves of half a million voices pounding against the sanctuary's sealed windows and threatening to shatter them inward. He said, "Yes—truly it would."

"You should know," Hanuman said, "the cutter wasn't the only one to come forth since I had you brought here. Others have asked to speak with you—that is, with your father."

"Who, then?"

"Lord Harsha and Lord Mor—they knew your father well. Bertram Jaspari, too."

"Bertram Jaspari? What does he want of Mallory Ringess?"

"Who knows? To plea for his own freedom, perhaps. Perhaps just to rage, to threaten and to try to control a god."

"I do not wish to see him."

"No—and I do not wish to see *you* like this. But there's one whom you would wish to see."

"Truly?"

Hanuman nodded and said, "A Fravashi alien named Old Father has knocked on the doors of the eastern portal. I believe that this is the very Old Father who tutored you before you entered the Academy."

"Strange," Danlo said. "Strange that he should have come here."

"Then he doesn't know that you're miming your father?"

"I am not sure. He knew that I was looking for Constancio, but not why."

"I wish I could believe you, Danlo."

"I . . . almost do not care anymore what you believe."

"But you care about this Fravashi alien, don't you?"

"What do you mean?"

Around Hanuman's head, the clearface lit up for a moment, and he said, "I invited him inside the cathedral. But he told me the silliest thing: that he couldn't enter buildings of more than one storey or more than fifty feet in height."

"But this is true! It is said that being in such buildings drives the Fravashi mad."

"Surely this is just superstition. Which is why I invited this Old Father to wait in one of the cells of the chapterhouse."

"You . . . have imprisoned a Fravashi Old Father?"

"Only until Jaroslav Bulba determines his part in this plot against me."

At this Danlo suddenly gasped as if Hanuman had kicked him in the belly. "Hanu, Hanu—you cannot torture a Fravashi Old Father!"

"Can I not? I'd torture the entire universe to reveal its secrets, if I had to. As it has tortured me."

Danlo could find no words for the horror he felt eating at his insides like a twisted worm. So he simply lay there on the carpet staring at Hanuman.

"You should know," Hanuman said, "I've sent my warrior-poets for Tamara. They'll find her and bring her here, too."

"But why, Hanu? She took no part in my plan."

"Perhaps not," Hanuman said. "But she is the key that will unlock the door."

"What . . . door?"

"The door to your heart. The door to your damned will. You're the one being that I can't torture, Danlo. But if the ekkana drug and the warrior-poet's killing knife won't open the nerves of your soul, then I must find other means."

"No!" Danlo shouted. In all his sudden and terrible hatred, the veins jumped along his neck, and his head jerked upward against his paralyzed body. "No—you have already tortured her once! You raped her of her memories, and that is enough!"

"It's never really enough," Hanuman said. He placed his hand upon Danlo's forehead and gently pushed his head back down to the carpet. "There's no end to pain—you should know that. But I don't want to torture Tamara. And I don't really need to, do I?"

Because Danlo couldn't resist the force of Hanuman's entire body, he finally stopped raging and let his neck muscles relax.

But there was fire in his eyes and hate in his heart, and he couldn't look at Hanuman just then.

Never killing; never harming another, not even in one's thoughts.

"It must have been terrible for Tamara to have lost her son," Hanuman said. "She's suffered so much already—why make her suffer more?"

"No!" Danlo cried out again. And then, in his wrath, he lapsed into his milk tongue, *"Elo los shaida! Shaida eth Shaida! Shaida, shaida, shaida!"*

He fell silent, then, and after his heart had beaten nine times, Hanuman looked at him and said softly, "It's *shaida* to inflict such suffering—I know. Do you think I didn't feel the pain of it when I ordered Jaroslav to run the point of his knife beneath your fingernails? Do you think I didn't die a little when Tamara lost her memories and wanted to die? *Shaida,* as you say. But you should know, out of all the manswarm's billions, a few chosen people will reach the point where certain seeming evils are not only permitted but required of them. Evolution demands this, fate itself demands this. Who are these people, then? Only those men and women who burn to be more than women and men. Only the rare ones who would gladly gouge out their own eyes with red-hot pincers if only they might be replaced with new, jeweled eyes that see farther and deeper into the higher frequencies of light. Once I called them true human beings: they who can endure the burning that never stops, the sheer hell of this universe, all the frenzy and the lightning. And not just endure the flames but rejoice in it. *I* burn, Danlo—only you really know how I've always burned. And so I've been chosen to embrace what others think of as evil. This is my fate, and I accept it. The truth is, I love it. Just as it was your fate to love and embrace ahimsa and let your son die."

"No, you are wrong," Danlo said as he shook his head back and forth. "You are truly wrong."

At this, Hanuman shook *his* head and smiled painfully so that the dead white skin of his face broke into many cracks and his lips pulled back from his teeth. "I've already sent a pilot—Krishnan Kadir—out to our fleet. He'll tell Lord Salmalin, and everyone else, that Mallory Ringess has returned and promised to end the war. To end the war—how else to accomplish this but by fighting a final and decisive battle? I've ordered Lord Salmalin to lead our ships against the Fellowship Fleet immediately. The battle is beginning even as we speak. How can we not win? We've the superior numbers. And every pilot of every lightship and blackship will know that Mallory has returned to lead them into battle, in spirit if not in the actuality of his lightship. They'll fight for their god; they'll fight like the godlings they are and destroy Helena Charbo and Cristobel the Bold and your fat friend Bardo—and every pilot who falls with them. The stars themselves will light up with the ships that they incinerate. The whole of the Fallaways from Ultima to Farfara will be ours. All the Civilized Worlds— three thousand worlds, three trillion human beings. And then we'll be free to fulfill the dream of all those who follow the Way of Ringess. Such a dream, Danlo, such a beautiful and perfect dream. *This* is the fate that I've chosen to embrace.''

For a while, Danlo lay beneath the sanctuary's dome simply breathing and counting his heartbeats. And then he looked at Hanuman and said, ''You have already used my return as my father to inspirit your fleet's pilots, yes? Then there is no need to threaten Tamara.''

''I only wish that this were so,'' Hanuman said. ''After all, the battle *might* be lost—this treacherousness of chance is the nature of war, isn't it? Other battles might have to be fought. If so, I might have to ask more of Mallory Ringess than that he simply return to Neverness only to vanish into my cathedral. You might have to appear before the godlings again as your father, Danlo. In fact, I'm certain that I'll ask this of you. Eventually, we'll win the war, and we'll have to consolidate our victory.

''Three thousand worlds, you should know, three trillion people. And more, perhaps a thousand times as many, on all the worlds of the stars out near the Vild, and inward, closer to the core. You shall speak to them all. And I'll help you find the words to speak. In person or by hologram—it doesn't really matter. Lord Mallory wi Soli Ringess! He has returned at the hour of humanity's greatest need to lead all the race towards its glorious fate! The First Pillar of Ringism has been fulfilled! And now the whole human race will long to realize the promise of the Third Pillar.

''Seeing you, in all your glorious, new, sculpted form, who will doubt that the path toward godhood lies in the remembrance of the Elder Eddas and following the Way of Mallory Ringess? And when my Universal Computer is completed, I'll provide them with a remembrance of the Elder Eddas vaster than their vastest dreams. I'll provide them with a Mallory Ringess whom they'd die to follow—and you shall assist in this sublime creation. This is *your* fate, Danlo. This is the glorious and golden future that I've chosen for you.''

Now the pain in Danlo's eye grew worse, and he ground his

teeth together to keep from crying out. And then he gasped in a quick breath and said, "You wish me to become a robot programmed by my fear for Tamara, yes?"

"Not *become*, Danlo. We're all of us already robots who haven't yet embraced the freedom of the refining fire."

"No, you are wrong," Danlo said. "I am not a robot. My will is always my own. And I will never follow your *shaida* dreams."

"Do you really believe that Tamara could endure the touch of the ekkana running like red-hot steel along her nerves? Do you really believe that *you* could endure her agony?"

"No, no," Danlo murmured, and he closed his eyes. "No, no, no."

"I should like to give you the antidote so that you can move again. There are better ways of controlling the body than with paralytic drugs."

"No," Danlo said again. He looked straight at Hanuman. "I will never speak your words as my own."

"Words," Hanuman said. He stood up and stepped over to a shatterwood stand holding up one of his cybernetic museum pieces. This was a glittering thing of chrome and buglike computer eyes, and was about as large as a man's head. Hanuman picked it up and held it toward Danlo so that the light of the flame globes reflected off one of the seven curving glass eyes.

"Your words have been recorded—every word that you've spoken in this room. Other computer eyes recorded your image when you stood to address the godlings in the cathedral. You should know, there are simple cetic programs that can break your words down to their constituent phonemes and reassemble them into any words in the Language of the Civilized Worlds. Similarly, your image can be fracted and morphed—Mallory Ringess can be made to stand before the manswarms and speak my words as only an impassioned god could speak. On the holograms that I shall create, if not in actuality."

Danlo felt an acid burning in his stomach as if he had just eaten a piece of bad seal meat. He said, "This is just the technology of the outlaw cartoonists, yes? They who slel images of beautiful men and women and create fantasies to sell down on the Street of Dreams."

At this Hanuman smiled and said, "But I shall give your image freely to aspirant godlings on every world from Solsken to New Earth."

"Then you already have what you need, yes? You have captured me in your computer—like one of your dolls."

Danlo turned his head to look at a low and squarish table topped with dead, gray glass. When brought to life, the liquid crystals beneath the glass would form the most complex and beguiling shapes, in colors that ranged from flaming red to tangerine, absinthe to violet. The patterns of pure information would glitter and vibrate and organize themselves into ever more intricate patterns. Once, Hanuman had used this table to display these dense informational structures that most cetics knew as artificial life but that he called dolls.

"I'd rather have your participation as a man, in the flesh," Hanuman said. "Or rather, as a man who has become a god. I would ask you to walk among the people and speak with them. I don't want to keep you locked away in this room forever."

Near the table, Danlo saw, resting on top of a marble stand, was a black cetic's sphere glittering darkly in the light of the flame globes. Wrought of crystalline neurologics that would generate an almost infinitely dense information field, it had once supported entire ecologies of artificial life. Once, years before, Hanuman had called it his universal computer; he had used it to create the dolls displayed within the table. It had been the first of the computers that he programmed to evolve a life of pure information.

"I do not see," Danlo said, "how you could ever trust me to speak to anyone."

"I trust you to follow your heart, what you believe to be true. I always have."

"My . . . heart," Danlo said, straining to look up at Hanuman.

Upon seeing Danlo's discomfort, Hanuman walked over and picked up a golden pillow from near the edge of the carpet. With great gentleness he tucked it under Danlo's head.

"I have my dream as you have yours," Hanuman said.

"Your *shaida* dream."

"So you've always called it. At least, since the day in the Shih Grove when you first began to understand. But, Danlo, please consider that you've only *begun* to understand. How can you judge what I've done as *shaida*—or *halla*—until you've glimpsed the end towards which all my acts have been directed?"

Are snow apples gathered from thorns? Danlo wondered, remembering words that his grandfather had once taught him. *Does the Tree of Life bear* shaida *fruit?*

"I . . . have *seen* what you've done," Danlo said. "I have

watched your warrior-poet cut away my fingernails with his knife; I have watched my son starve before my eyes."

Again, Hanuman knelt by Danlo's side. He brushed the hair out of Danlo's eyes and laid his hand upon his head. Although he spoke no words just then, Danlo could see the pain softening his ice-blue eyes. Despite what Hanuman had said about loving his fate, Danlo knew that he really hated each of the many acts that had driven him toward it. Hanuman had always had a rare sensitivity to suffering—to his own and that of others. With every captured ringkeeper whom he had tortured since the beginning of the war, his face had been cut with deep new lines as if one of his warrior-poets had gone to work upon him with his killing knife. With every child who had died screaming in his mother's arms, he had truly died a little inside, too. The sound of his heart was now one long, dark, terrible scream. Danlo could feel it in the pulse of Hanuman's trembling fingers; he could hear it in the thunderous beating of his own.

"Hanu, Hanu—there is no end to the universe," he said. "There is no end to life. And therefore there is no end toward which we might direct our acts. Truly, there are only acts and living beings. The acts *of* living beings. Each blessed act should be *halla*, not *shaida*. As each blessed being is *halla*, too. You cannot simply murder a man to save ten men—or ten thousand. Such a calculus is itself *shaida*."

Hanuman removed his hand from Danlo's forehead and stared at the lines cut into his palm. And then he said, "Then you wouldn't sacrifice an innocent child if you knew that he would grow up to be an Igasho Hod who would explode a hydrogen bomb and cause ten thousand other innocent children to starve?"

"No," Danlo said. And then he closed his eyes for a moment, and he saw Jonathan's bright blue eyes staring at him out of the darkness of memory. "I would take Igasho Hod as child and teach him to know *halla*."

"But what if you knew that the only way to stop the Iviomils from destroying the Star of Neverness was to execute Bertram Jaspari? What if you *knew* this, Danlo? Wouldn't you want to cut his throat yourself?"

"But how could such things ever be known?"

"What if you were a scryer, Danlo? What if you could see the future?"

Danlo, who was himself the son of a scryer and had more than once fallen into prescient visions, lay there shaking his head. "But there is no future frozen like ice in time. There are only futures, yes? For each human being alone, ten thousand futures—or ten thousand trillion. Each moment of time flowing into each moment, onstreaming into strange and terrible beauties as the future is born. The simplest act . . . might have consequences impossible to see. It is like a stone dropped into the center of the ocean. The ripples keep moving outward upon the starlit waters in all directions, touching everything forever. There are infinite possibilities, Hanu. Truly infinite. And that is why no one can see the future.''

"No, you're wrong," Hanuman said. "I can."

For a moment, Danlo lay completely still as he stared at Hanuman and fell into the icy blueness of his eyes.

"It's not that I can see which of your wild and bloody futures will be," Hanuman said. "Rather, I can see which future *must* be."

Suddenly he rose to his feet and moved over to the shatterwood dining table where he had set Danlo's devotionary computer, covered with its null cloth. With a quick motion of his arm, he swept back the cloth to reveal the glowing hologram of Nikolos Daru Ede. For many days, the Ede imago had waited beneath the cloth with the infinite patience of a machine, even as he beamed his eternal and godly smile at no one.

"Hanuman li Tosh, my master and jailkeeper, the answer to your question, of course, is computational origami.'' The Ede imago spoke as if no time had passed since their last conversation. But he must have been very aware of every moment that he had spent cut off from receiving information from his environment, for he aimed a wide grin at Hanuman and said, "In the five hundred thousand seconds since we last talked, I've remembered how I folded together the different lobes of my brain. All the gods that I have known have depended upon this art.''

Obviously, during the days in which Danlo had sculpted himself into the form of his father, Ede and Hanuman had occasionally spoken with each other. Ede was about to continue their last conversation when he (or rather the computer eyes studding the devotionary computer) noticed Danlo lying helpless on the floor.

"The infolding increases the complexity according to the square of the number of . . . Mallory Ringess!" The Ede imago suddenly turned his full attention upon Danlo, who was looking up at him from the carpet. "You're Mallory Ringess, aren't you? Then you've returned while I've been shut away in a dark and lightless place.''

Just then Hanuman came between them and shook his head.

"We'll speak of origami some other time. Now I want to speak of other things."

He held his hand out toward the Ede's bald head and bright black eyes. Then he looked at Danlo and said, "Nikolos Daru Ede pursued his own fate as a god, and the greatest of all man's religions arose around this miracle of evolution. You should know, I've regarded his ontogenesis *as* a miracle since I was three years old. I was trained in this belief, of course. All good Architects are. But where my father—and every other Architect in the Cybernetic Universal Church—condemned anyone who tried to emulate Ede as a wicked *hakra,* I always regarded such hubris as heroic. *Each man and woman is a star*—such a heretical and heroic dream, isn't it? I always wanted to be a hero, Danlo, and I wondered why no one else in my church wanted this, too. Well, of course a few of them did, secretly like me. But they couldn't even discuss their dreams with anyone else—they were afraid of the punishments. Do you remember how I used to talk about the deep cleansings that my father was always threatening in order to eliminate hubris and the other negative programs? The way the cleansing computers would erase one's memories like a censor blotting out a painting with black ink? How I feared these cleansings, how I hated the dark cleansing cells and the readers with their hateful computers. Their *shaida* computers, as you would say. The truth is, I hated everything about Edeism and the Cybernetic Universal Church. It's a sick and hurtful religion designed for nihilities such as my father was. I think that much of what I've done since my father died has been in reaction to the suffocating orthodoxies of the church. But deep down, mine was the rebelliousness of a child because I didn't really understand."

Hanuman turned to the Ede imago and bowed before him with seeming great compassion. He said, "Ede, as a man, was a great man. But of course he was a failure as a god. Do you remember Kostos Olorun? As the first High Architect of the Cybernetic Church, he wisely decided not to follow Ede's path into godhood. Who was he to survive the vicious evolutionary struggles among the gods? Who was anyone? And so instead he chose power over men on many worlds. He created a doctrine of limitation and promulgated it in the *Facings*. Do you remember his words? *I* can never forget them: 'And they turned their eyes godward in jealousy and lust for the infinite lights, but in their countenances God read hubris, and he struck them blind. For here is the oldest of teachings, here is wisdom: no god is there but God; God is one, and there can be only one God.'

"Only one god—or only one man who incarnates the Godhead or moves toward it. The elite of all the universal religions have always known this. There was only one Kristoman born of a virgin mother. The Buddhists called for men and women to walk the eightfold path toward enlightenment, but how few of all the billions ever crossed over the sacred river to become buddhas? And what of Jin Zenimura? He actually created a billion Wise Lords—in name only. So it's always been. So it must always be."

Now both Danlo and the Ede imago were watching Hanuman closely, waiting to see the end towards which his words were directed. And then Hanuman looked straight at Danlo and said, "It's *dangerous* to unleash man's spiritual energies. And foolish, and futile, too. Most people are nihilities. Most people are too stupid and lazy to practice even most basic mental disciplines. But they're still *people*, after all, if not true human beings. We must always have compassion for their suffering. It's upon us, the elite, to make their lives bearable, even meaningful. But how to do this? They can't really become buddhas; they can't really become gods. But they can *believe* in these impossible dreams.

"Therefore the elite of the universal religions have always substituted belief in the Infinite for the experience of it. We all need God—but only in small and measured doses. Who can look upon the burning bush and not be destroyed in its flames? Who can bear the heaven and hell of each moment blazing in time? Who can shine like a star? And so, for all but a few of the manswarm, the rare ones who are truly human, it is better to glimpse such a miracle through a dark glass or to grasp it through words only. This is why I had to stop the drinking of kalla in our church. This is why I've provided a remembrance of the Elder Eddas through interfacing the Universal Computer. Because I love people, Danlo. I always have, and I always will."

At this, Danlo managed to smile grimly, and he said, "You love people . . . as a tiger loves lambs."

"No," Hanuman said, walking over to him. "As a shepherd loves sheep."

"But you've already slaughtered billions of your sheep in this *shaida* war."

"It's a terrible sacrifice, I know. But soon, I'll bring an end to the war, even as you promised the people in the Great Circle. I'll bring an end to war itself."

"Truly?"

"I'll bring the first true order to all the worlds of man. Order, peace, happiness—it's what the people truly crave."

"But Hanu, blessed Hanu, you—"

"I'll build a church for all time and all people. I'll create an eternal institution for the betterment of our race."

"But, Hanu, the blessed people, on this world and every other, the *shaida,* the true suffering—"

"I'd relieve them of their suffering."

Danlo blinked his burning eyes a moment, and then said, "No—you would only relieve them of their freedom."

"I'd give them long and golden lives."

"No—you would only relieve them of their lives. Their . . . true life. You would kill them, in their spirits, in order to save them."

"I only want to make a better world."

"But the world is just the world, yes? The blessed world."

"You don't really understand," Hanuman said.

"No—I understand too well."

"Your grief over your son has blinded you. You still don't see it, do you?"

"See . . . what?"

"The flaw, the damning flaw. There's a fundamental flaw in all human beings that goes far deeper than the capacity of any religion to heal. The truth is, the flaw cuts through all things of this world down to the heart of the universe itself."

"I still believe," Danlo said, "that the universe is *halla,* not *shaida.*"

"But, Danlo, look at yourself! Look at your life! For just one moment, look at life in this universe, just as it is!"

For a while Danlo lay watching Hanuman, and like a wave swelling vaster and vaster, an immense sadness filled his eyes. And then he said, "I think that you have always hated life."

"Perhaps I have," Hanuman said. He stood looking at Danlo, and looking inside himself, too. Although he remained as still and silent as a cetic, Danlo thought that he might be grieving for the beautiful child that he had lost in becoming a man. "You must know that I've hated what I've had to do in life. But even more, I hate a universe that would allow me to do it."

"Oh, Hanu, Hanu, you—"

"And you do, too," Hanuman quickly broke in. "Look inside your heart and you'll see it."

No, no, Danlo thought. *Never hating, even in one's heart, never—*

"*I* see it," Hanuman said. "When I look inside you, there's only fire and ashes."

Jonathan, Jonathan, mi alasharia la shantih. Danlo lay silently praying as he drew in a deep breath. He felt a fire hot against his face and burning inside his chest. *Are you truly inside me, now?*

"Your son," Hanuman whispered. "What did the cutter say his name was? Jonathan. Jonathan—he was a beautiful child, wasn't he?"

"Yes—truly he was."

"He shouldn't have died, you know. He should never have suffered and died."

"But he *did* die," Danlo said. "I burned his body on a pyre of bonewood down by the sea."

"If the universe had been made differently, he wouldn't have had to die."

"What . . . do you mean?"

Hanuman, now quite excited, swept his hand toward the dome above them. There, in the evening sky, thousands of miles above them, the Universal Computer hung all silent and still like a vast, dark moon. He said, "I'd like to encourage you to follow your heart. I'd like to show you the end toward which I've suffered and striven. To share my dream with you."

"I do not wish to share your dream."

"Not even if you could see how Jonathan could live again?"

"No," Danlo said. He closed his eyes tightly as he listened to the wild thunder of his heart. "He is only ashes, now. He is only a breath upon the wind."

"He *could* live again, you know. And Tamara's memories of you could be restored, and she could return to you."

"No, no—not this way. It is not possible."

"The Alaloi people could be healed of the virus that afflicts them. All people everywhere could be healed—the universe itself could be made whole and *halla.*"

"No, I do not see—"

"It's what you've always dreamed, Danlo."

What I have always dreamed.

Danlo closed his eyes, then, and lay quite still facing the sanctuary's gold and purple dome. His eyes fluttered like butterflies beneath his eyelids as if he were truly dreaming. However, he was not dreaming at all, but only seeing intense flashes of light inside the dark universe of his mind. He saw the *Sword of Shiva* and other lightships streaking near a hot white star, and he immediately knew that the pilot-captains had chosen Bardo as Lord Pilot of the Fellowship Fleet. He saw ten thousand blackships falling through space and opening windows to the manifold. And with each of these man-made flaws in the cold, clear crystal of space-time, a flower of light blossomed in the blackness like a newly created star. And then Danlo opened his eyes, and he saw that this light was not only within him but without. In the sky above him, in the spaces near the Universal Computer, many of these light-ships falling in and out of the manifold had lit up the night. Elements of the Fellowship Fleet—perhaps entire battle groups— were at that moment vying with the Ringist pilots for the fate of Icefall and the Star of Neverness.

It has begun, he thought. *The last battle of the war has begun.*

Danlo saw that the Ede imago was watching him from across the room, and he said, "You know who I truly am, yes?"

"Danlo wi Soli Ringess," the Ede imago said, beaming out a smile. "It isn't hard to deduce that you've tried to usurp Lord Hanuman by masquerading as Mallory Ringess."

"Once," Danlo said, smiling ironically, "you hoped that I *would* bring him down. So that you might recover your body and be human again."

"Well, I've other hopes, now."

"I see."

"Please forgive me," Ede said, "but I told you long ago that my only power was that of words. And now Lord Hanuman has need of my words."

"I see."

"I have my dream, too," Ede explained.

Danlo nodded his head in acceptance of Ede's new alliance, and then he said, "Once, you would have advised me not to trust Hanuman. Not to follow him into any web of lies in which he might try to ensnare me. What do you advise, now?"

"Only that you follow your heart, as Lord Hanuman has said."

"All right, then," Danlo suddenly said. He turned to look at Hanuman still standing silently by his side. "Show me what you have dreamed."

In the sky far above the sanctuary, more lights flashed out into darkness. And Hanuman li Tosh, Lord of the Way of Ringess, smiled down upon Danlo as the clearface computer suddenly blazed in a hellish violet radiance about his head. Danlo heard him draw in a deep breath, just as he heard the breaths of thousands of godlings thundering through the streets outside the cathedral. The whole of Neverness, it seemed, was calling for him and waiting for him to walk among them once again. And then Hanuman bowed his head slightly, and the interior of the dome surrounding him came alive with a dark and otherworldly violet glow. There came a moment when the cold floor beneath Danlo gave way and he felt himself falling. And then there was neither coldness nor light nor sound but only the terrifying black void of a new universe that went on and on without end.

THE UNIVERSAL COMPUTER

What I'm really interested in is whether God could have made the world in a different way; that is, whether the necessity of logical simplicity leaves any freedom at all.

—The Einstein

If this is the best of all possible worlds, what must the others be like?

—Source Unknown

Danlo knew then what he had suspected ever since his first meeting with Hanuman in the sanctuary: that the dome surrounding them was wrought in part of powerful neurologic circuitry. In truth, the whole of the dome was like a huge purple and gold heaume encompassing not only their heads but their entire bodies. Once before, on Alumit Bridge, Danlo had entered a similar chamber. But where the neurologics woven into the walls of that faraway room had allowed him to interface a planetary computer network called the Field, he now turned his awareness toward a much vaster and infinitely more profound computer.

For the entire sanctuary encoded the workings of Danlo's brain as radio waves and beamed them up through space to the Universal Computer. The sanctuary was like a window to the lightning-quick information fields of this ungodly machine. And the Universal Computer ran the programs that Hanuman had written for it, and beamed rivers of pure information back to the neurologics of the sanctuary. Thus Danlo finally faced the universe that Hanuman had made. He fell for a long time into a dazzling darkness; he fell on and on into the dazzling dream of a man who would be as God.

Never before—not even in the room of the Narain Transcendentals on Alumit Bridge—had he experienced such a total interface with a computer. The sanctuary's logic field that pulled at his brain was very powerful. Perhaps, he thought, the cybernetic arts of the Order's cetics were much advanced over that of the Narain. Or perhaps it was the paralysis of the warrior-poet's drug that caused him almost completely to lose the sense of his body. He could not feel his arms, legs, buttocks or back against the carpet of the sanctuary; he couldn't feel his belly or the breath as it filled his chest. It seemed as if the very tissues of his being had melted and flowed away like water. Only a faint burning behind his eyes reminded him that he was still a human being in a human body.

And then, as the Universal Computer sent streams of photons flashing through its millions of miles of optical circuitry and the field surrounding him intensified, even this old and familiar pain almost vanished. He became aware of himself as a different kind of body. Now, in this space of the alam al-mithral, which is what the cetics called their computer-generated reality, he looked upon his cybernetic self as a being woven of billions of bits of pure, glittering information. He floated naked and alone in a black void, at once fully human and completely other. His fingernails sparkled like white diamonds; the skin encompassing his godlike form glistened with flecks of aquamarine, emerald, topaz, violet and ten thousand other colors. And his eyes—his eyes had returned to the deep and secret blue of the midnight sky. In truth, his eyes shined brilliantly like liquid jewels with a blue inside blue fire that astonished him. He had never dreamed that Hanuman, with a simple computer program, could capture the essence of his eyes so perfectly. He had never dreamed that Hanuman (or any cetic) could capture him so completely in any cybernetic space, and this dread of losing his true self was almost too terrible to bear.

I am not I. I am flaming crimson and glowing copper and streaks of blue-white light. I am light beyond light. I am light light light. . . .

It was very strange, he thought, that he could see his own eyes. Usually, upon instantiating into a surreality, various aspects of one's selfness would be represented symbolically or pictorially as images that were more or less human. In the fifth degree of instantiation, subtle programs would generate an icon almost exactly like that of the realtime person interfacing the computer. The icon would cark out into a cybernetic space and experience a simulated world in almost the same way as a man walking among a field of fireflowers. As with a man in the real world, one's perception and point of view would be directed outward away from the icon's eyes towards various objects that the computer conjured up and made almost real.

As Danlo fell through this strange cybernetic space called the alam al-mithral, it should have been impossible for him to look upon his own face. He was aware of himself as an icon of many flowing colors, for he could gaze at his hand as easily as a child watching himself reach toward the sun. But he could also see himself floating in the void from many angles all at once: he could look up at the naked soles of his feet or down upon the sable and flame red hair falling down his back. It seemed that his awareness, and perhaps even his consciousness itself, had cathected many points of space all around him. He wondered, then, if it was Hanuman's purpose to share his vision of this surreality, which might well be of everything within it. If Hanuman were truly playing God to his own private universe, then perhaps he would wish to dwell within it and perceive it with all the power of the divine.

> *This is my world, Danlo. Thank you for joining me here.*

Hanuman's voice spilled out into the blackness all around Danlo, coming from everywhere and nowhere. It echoed in the void a million miles outward in all directions and pounded in unseen waves against his icon's chatoyant skin. Like the wind, it whispered in his mind—his very real and human mind which must still exist inside the cathedral's sanctuary in the real world almost infinitely far away.

"I . . . cannot see you," Danlo said. He was aware of himself as a gleaming icon speaking into the endless darkness. Because he had no idea of which direction he should aim his words, he simply opened his golden lips and said, "Why don't you instantiate as an icon so that I might see you?

> *I prefer this degree of instantiation.*

"This is seventh degree, yes?"

In the sixth degree of instantiation, that of transcendence, the computer generates a transcendental self that can appear at different places almost simultaneously. Often this self is represented as an icon of pure light or tachyon beams that can flash from one point in space to any other almost infinitely quickly. In the seventh degree of instantiation, there is no self separate from the surreality being created. And therefore there is no need for an icon to move about within the computer's creation. In cybernetic vastening (or cathexis, as the cetics call this final degree) one *becomes* the entire field generated by the computer's program. In a way, one becomes the program itself, and this, the cyber-shamans say, is the ultimate vastening of human consciousness.

"But Hanu, no one can instantiate in the vastening degree for very long—it is too dangerous, yes?"

In truth, the seventh degree of instantiation was terribly dangerous. And therefore it was forbidden to all of the Order, even the cetics—and especially those cetic masters and computer adepts who called themselves cyber-shamans.

Of course it's dangerous. And of course it's forbidden—as it should be for almost everyone.

Danlo, still lying on the carpet of the sanctuary, shook his head in sadness at Hanuman's hubris. And he saw (and felt) his icon floating in the alam al-mithral shake his head, too. Many were the cetics, he thought, who had lost themselves into their computers.

"I can see myself," he said. "My face, my eyes. You have programmed it so that I am experiencing aspects of the seventh degree, yes?"

Of course I have. It's a most subtle program, you should know.

"I do not wish to become vastened as a computer program— even one that is infinitely subtle."

What do you wish, then?

"Only to see what you have created and to return to my true self."

Very well, Danlo. This is what I've created.

Suddenly, in almost no time at all, a terrible, quick light filled the darkness surrounding him. In a vast, incandescent sphere centered at his eyes, it exploded outward with a speed much greater than that of true light. For a moment, he had to hold his hand shielding his eyes against the brightness of it. And then, a moment later, the space around him coalesced to a brilliant clarity, and he found that he could see outward to the ends of the universe almost infinitely far in all directions.

"My . . . God!"

For there, spinning in space that was now the essence of light itself, he saw many earthlike worlds. There may have been ten million of them—or many more. They filled the void around him like perfect, spherical jewels floating in a sunlit sea. There was something strange about his perception of these computer-generated worlds, for he could see the most distant of them with the same degree of resolution as the nearest. In truth, wherever he looked, at whichever world, he could make out the lines of the continents all around the circumference of the globe—all at once and from many different angles. The power of such seeing almost blinded him; it sent waves of nausea vibrating up through his belly and made him dizzy. After a while, however, he adjusted to this near-omnivision and began to study these worlds that Hanuman had made. Each of them, he saw, was exactly the same: a blue and white glory of deep oceans and soft blankets of clouds, an almost perfect replica of Old Earth. Not even the Solid State Entity, he thought, possessed such a drive to create. Not even Ede the God, in all the fullness of his power, in all his mysterious and terrible urge to design new worlds and new races of human beings, had ever dreamed of making so many earths.

"How . . . many are there?" he asked. His voice resonated in his throat like a golden gong. And almost immediately, Hanuman answered him.

Now there are exactly 25,490,056,343 worlds. And in each second of computer time, more are generated.

"But why so many?" Danlo wondered. "And why *earths*, Hanu? Why are all these worlds the same?"

Because it's my will to create life as it could fully be. In a world—a whole universe—as it could fully be.

"But, Hanu—what kind of life could this *truly* be?"

Shall I show you, then?

"Yes, if you'd like."

As quick as light, Danlo found himself streaking down toward one of the earths. He fell through this space that wasn't really space, and then entered the earth's atmosphere that was composed of pure information rather than real air. But at first it *felt* like real air. It felt almost as biting and cold against his naked flesh as the *sarsaras* that blow through Neverness when deep winter gives way to midwinter spring. *Almost,* Danlo thought. The glittering skin over his cheeks and nose tingled with a chill almost as if he were facing a real wind. But he felt no belly-cold, none of the terrible iciness of true cold that would pierce to the bone like ten thousand steel needles stuck into every part of his body.

This, he thought, was one of the limitations of computer simulation. True cold was aching teeth and freezing blood and ice crystals bursting open the cells of one's fingers and face; it was more than the firing of clusters of neurons registering the pain of such an event inside one's brain. The consciousness of cold—and consciousness itself—was spread among the body's four trillion cells, and deeper, down to the chains of proteins and lipids that formed the matter of living flesh. In a way, each spinning hydrogen atom in a water molecule felt the loss of its energy in vibrating more slowly and falling into coldness. And therefore it was impossible to simulate this sensation completely from the touch of the dome's neurologics upon his brain alone.

I am not truly cold, Danlo thought. *I am not . . .*

And then he felt and heard his teeth chattering, and he was not so sure. He could not tell whether this sensation of enamel cracking against enamel originated in his real body lying in the sanctuary or was only part of the program that drove his icon closer to Hanuman's earth. And then, as he glided down to the lower and warmer layers of the atmosphere, his shivering suddenly ceased. He felt the soft breezes of a tropical ocean blowing over his nearly weightless body. Strangely, however, he couldn't feel the heat of the sun. Nor could he find any such orb blazing above him, even though he searched the blue sky from horizon to horizon.

> **There is no sun to see, Danlo. Because there is no sun.**

"But how . . . . ." Danlo's words died into the wind as he flew over the ocean toward a broad, glittering, white beach. "How can there be no sun?"

In this entire universe, there are no stars because light shines everywhere upon all things.

"No . . . stars?" Danlo said, gazing up into the heavens.

Truly, he thought, there *were* no stars, but neither was there darkness, for Hanuman could not abide the absence of light. And then, as quickly as a diving sparrowhawk, he fell down to the beach which glittered everywhere with a light that came from nowhere—at least nowhere that he could see.

"It . . . is very beautiful," he said, and his words floated like pearls out into the warm, wet air. He looked out at the ocean's clear turquoise waters and lapping waves; he watched the seagulls soaring along the beach and crying out in the sheer joy of flight. In truth, it *was* quite beautiful, but more as a painting is beautiful than a real beach. For much was lacking in this scene that the computer conjured from its programs. The surf reeked only slightly from smells of seaweed and salt, and there was none of that fermy essence of life living and dying that had excited him since his first taste of the sea as a child long ago. And the beach, although as pristine and perfect as he might wish, was not quite truly perfect after all. The sand gleamed in its sweeps and dunes for miles up and down the beach, as real sand should, but when he looked more closely down at his feet, he could not descry the millions of fine grains of which real sand was made.

You are thinking that this sand is not quite real. As with the very matter of this world itself. But it is real. It's as real as you wish it to be.

For a moment, Danlo became aware of just how much he hated interfacing the same computer as did Hanuman and sharing the same thoughtspace. And then, as he stared at the sand all around him, he saw the smear of whiteness give way to billions of separate grains of sand. He stared and stared, and it was as if his eyes had suddenly gained the power of microscopes, for he could see each grain in all its glittering perfection. They were like tiny white diamonds cut all the same, like a vast treasure of jewels that Hanuman's computer had heaped into dunes for him to behold.

But it is still not real, he thought. *No matter how powerful the program, the computer cannot make this sand real.*

He bent down to scoop up a handful of sand and to hold it before his eyes. And then suddenly the uniform whiteness of its tiny crystals gave way to bits of color that looked like feldspar and other minerals, and minute flecks of shell and basalt rocks as black as night stood out among the grains of ground-up quartz.

> *The simulation is not perfect, Danlo. I know. But it can be made as perfect as one might wish. As it will be when the Universal Computer is completed.*

Danlo let this warm, powdery sand that wasn't real sand sift between his open fingers and fall down to the dunes at his feet. He looked out at the whitecapped waves breaking in the ocean's shallows and the dark green jungle above the beach. This world that Hanuman had made lacked much detail, particularly in the articulation of the trees and landforms far away. And although the computer's program might be able to correct for this hazy amorphousness, increasing detail and resolution according to the focus of Danlo's attention, it could never perfectly simulate the entire world. To accomplish such a miracle would require a computer the size of the world. And so it was with the universe of other earths all about this spinning earth; Danlo remembered an eschatologist once saying that the simplest complete model of the universe was the universe itself.

The universe itself—the whole universe. There can only ever be one universe.

Just then he gazed off at the jungle to the east where a great hill rose up above the emerald foliage. And there, upon the flat top of the hill, white-washed houses and marble buildings gleamed in the ever-present light of the world. Obviously, he thought, Hanuman—or someone—had built a whole city to look out over the sparkling ocean waters.

> *Why don't you walk through the jungle to the city—you'll find a path leading there above the beach.*

At this, Danlo searched the wall of jungle that rose up above the beach sands. A few hundred yards away he saw a break in the greenness where a path snaked off through the great trees. He made straight toward this path, then. He trudged up across the dunes and entered the jungle. In being enveloped by the thick canopy above him he might have expected a darkening, as of a million leaves blocking out the sun. But there was no darkening;

the bark of the trees and the jasmine vines encircling them stood out as brightly as any of the rocks and shells along the beach.

It was a strange jungle, he thought. The rising path was set with slabs of white marble, making the walking very easy. No lianas hung down from the tree limbs to ensnare him as he passed by; no undergrowth blocked his way. In little time, he had walked many miles farther through vegetation of every conceivable variety. Towering above him were ebony trees and sycamores and ironwood. And cedars and mahogony and tamarinds—it seemed that Hanuman had caused every type of tree from every clime of Old Earth to grow in this enchanted forest. There were many shrubs as well, holly and huckleberry and indigo, and magnolia and mountain lilac and others that he could not quite identify.

In truth, he saw much strange flora that might have been of alien origin—or perhaps only a creation of Hanuman's computer. And almost all of this lush vegetation bore nuts or flowers or fruit. The branches of every tree and bush were heavy with pecans, almonds, papaya, guavas, mango, lemons and a hundred kinds and colors of berries. Danlo had never seen so much hanging food; it was as if the entire jungle were a larder packed with delicious things to eat.

There is enough food here to feed a city of people—or ten thousand cities.

There were enough flowers in the forest, as well, to fill ten million vases. Bright sprays of African violets and orchids fairly exploded from the green curtain of the leaves. There were trilliums and roses, too, and pansies, honeysuckle and snapdragons. Great swarms of bees and butterflies flitted from flower to flower lapping up nectar; the whole of the jungle fairly vibrated with their buzzing and fluttering wings. As Danlo walked farther into the jungle, a riot of other sounds fell out among the flowers. Monkeys chattered high in the canopy to the music of cockatoos and macaws and other brightly plumed birds. Every tree, it seemed had its family of squirrels, all of which seemed curiously unafraid of the many snakes twining their sinuous bodies around the lianas and the boles of the teak trees. Danlo wondered if he himself should fear these snakes, for he saw adders and asps and others which he knew to be poisonous. But this jungle did not seem to be a place for fear. Even if he should dread the death of his icon's glittering body, he did not sense that any of the animals—even the cobras and the fire ants—wished him any harm. And then, when he rounded a bend in the path and climbed higher up the green-shrouded hill, he came upon a sight that astonished him. For there, pressed up against a lilac bush, a great orange and blackstriped tiger crouched as if waiting for him to come closer. And closer he came, and he saw that the tiger wasn't really waiting for him at all, but rather working at the food that lay pinned beneath her paws.

"Ahira, Ahira," he whispered, "it is not possible!"

Danlo had expected to look down upon the corpse of a waterbuck or an antelope; instead he saw the tiger clawing apart a very large bunch of bananas. In truth, the tiger had piled up pomegranates and apples, as well, and she was busily tearing apart and eating this fruit with all the contentment of a monkey.

> *I've taught all the cats and carnivores of this world to eat fruit, Danlo. I've taught the ants to eat banana peels and seeds and the mosquitoes to drink nectar instead of blood.*

The path took Danlo very close to the tiger, who appeared not to notice him as he stepped by. He saw (and heard) the tiger licking at a piece of sticky banana caught between her claws. She purred as harmlessly as a housecat in Neverness, and seemed as gentle and tame as a dog.

She is as alive as any of the life of this world, he thought. *But all of her animajii has left her. She is a creature of the wild whose wildness has been taken away.*

Truly, this fruit-eating tiger had lost the essence of tigerness itself. Could Hanuman see this? Had he ever watched a snow tiger stalking a shagshay bull through a dark forest and seen the mysterious fire lighting up her wild, golden eyes?

He does not know. Because he has always looked away from the one thing that he truly wishes to see.

After Danlo had climbed for perhaps an hour, he emerged from the jungle and came upon a broad field of grass sloping upward toward the city. Now he could plainly see the city's walls running around the circumference of the hilltop and the main western gate. He wondered why there should be walls at all. He wondered why the people of the city should even live in houses when they might easily dwell in the jungle without fear of darkness, mosquitoes or hunting tigers.

> *The wall is to remind my people that they are separate from the world that I have created for*

them. And people must always live in houses, or
they are not really people.

Just as Danlo approached the gate, whose great wooden doors
stood open, he turned for a moment to survey the glittering green
jungle and beach below him. He saw puffy white clouds forming
over the ocean in almost geometric patterns and a flock of parratock birds bursting from the trees in a glory of bright red, yellow and blue feathers. He wondered, then, if this marvelous
performance might have been designed solely to please his eyes.
Once, he thought, as a young cetic, Hanuman had been content to
design bits of information and the rules by which they inter-
acted—and then to step back and watch these artificial atoms
evolve into artificial life. Hanuman had called this life dolls, and
once upon a time it had been his pride that his dolls should evolve
and live their lives solely according to the initial rules that he
programmed for his universe. To interfere in any way once his
universe had been created and set running he would have considered inelegant. Clearly, however, in the many days since that time,
he had abandoned the necessity of logical simplicity for other
purposes.

But what is his deepest purpose? This I still cannot see.

He turned once more, then, and passed through the gate. No
one stopped him. Indeed, no one stood guard by the gate, because
the people of the city had no one or nothing to guard against.
Immediately he found himself on a broad, tree-lined boulevard
leading through the city's heart. Buildings faced with white marble rose up on either side of the street, and many people filled the
adjacent walkways and lawns. It surprised Danlo that none of
them seemed able to see him or otherwise apprehend his still-
naked form. They streamed out of the buildings as if they had
been called to a feast or some special event. And all these women
and men (he saw no children) were of a single racial type, almost
as if they had been cut from the same chromosomes. Their skin
shined a deep golden brown, the color of wildflower honey, and
their hair was as straight and black as Danlo's; their eyes were at
once soft and bright like black jade. With their flaring noses and
wide, sensuous lips they were a handsome people—in truth, a
people whose lithe and symmetric forms embodied the ideal of
human perfection. They might have done well to go about the
streets naked and unashamed. But both men and women wore
white silk pantaloons and a large flowing shirt gathered in and
tied at the waist with a purple silk cloth. Most sported jewelry of

some kind: golden rings and silver torques and snakelike armlets of hammered copper. They seemed at once a barbaric and ultra-civilized people: primitive in their culture and yet almost godly in their comportment and awareness of their purpose in life.

There are no wormrunners or autists in this city, Danlo thought. *No murderers or madmen.*

Many people were emerging from long rectangular buildings that might have been bathhouses; many more were pouring down the steps of glittering granite structures that seemed to be churches or cathedrals. The manswarms filled the central boule-vard and swept Danlo along toward what seemed to be the center of the city. He wondered if it might be time for these people to take their midday meals. But he saw no restaurants on either side of the street. Indeed, he saw no food pass hands among the men and women seated on benches beneath the trees, nor did he detect any sign of hunger on their handsome faces. It occurred to him, then, that with the jungle outside the city's walls so full of food, they might simply pass outside the gate and pick whatever fruit they needed whenever they wished.

> *No, you are wrong, of course. The fruit in the jungle is for the animals only. My people have transcended the need to take their nourishment from the flesh of nuts or fruit. They have better things to do with their lives than to spend their time eating.*

Danlo remembered then that Hanuman had always regarded the getting and eating of food as one of life's unpleasant necessi-ties. He had never taken much joy in the steaming bowls of kurmash or the other delicacies that Neverness had to offer. And now, as he told Danlo, he had created a race of people who did not have to soil their golden lips with grease nor stoop to relieve themselves of their bodies' dark, steaming wastes.

> *The air itself nourishes them, you should know. The various shells and fruit rinds in the jungle decompose into nutrients that are taken up by the wind. All they need do is breathe and their lungs are filled with all they need to sustain them.*

Because Danlo wanted to know more about the ecology of this artificial life, Hanuman explained that the droppings of the animals over the whole of the world decomposed into the nutrients from which the forests grew. The trees, he said, continually sucked up nutrients from the soil and made the fruit for the animals to eat.

"And when the animals die," Danlo asked, "do their bodies decompose into these nutrients, too?"

But the animals don't die, Danlo. Nor do the trees or the flowers or the grasses. On all my earths, nothing ever dies.

Danlo, standing by himself for a moment beneath a great tree by the side of the street, drew in a quick breath of air. Then he said, "If nothing ever dies, then how is there room for new life to be born?"

Nothing is born, either. Almost nothing. There's little need for the complications of birth since all life in this universe has almost evolved to its highest and most perfect state.

Danlo looked around him at the river of women and men streaming toward what seemed to be an open square. Now he understood why he saw no children among these people. He remembered that Hanuman had always avoided children as if they reminded him of some tragic event that had occurred in his own life long ago.

"You have said that *almost* nothing is born. That life has *almost* evolved to its highest state. I do not understand, Hanu."

Well, I don't wish to mystify you. Why don't you walk toward the square with the rest of the people?

Thus bidden, Danlo rejoined the throngs crowding the street. He noticed again that he was invisible to these people. And more: one man, hurrying along, brushed up by him—and Danlo watched as the man's hand passed through his glittering right shoulder as easily as Danlo might have moved his own hand through a light beam. Hanuman gave him to understand that as a specially created being, he was wrought of a different substance than the other people of the world.

I am like an angel of God sent to watch over these people.

In little time he passed into the great square, which was now packed from one end to the other with people in their gleaming white pantaloons and shirts. One of them, a beautiful young woman (in this impossible city, all the women and men remained forever young) stepped out of the crowd and mounted a set of marble steps leading up to a plain white marble altar at the square's exact center. And with every step she took upward, a great cheer issued from ten thousand throats all at once. Finally, she took her place at the top of the altar above all her friends and city-mates; she knelt on the hard stone and bowed her head as if in prayer. And everyone in the square joined her, kneeling and praying to the God who had created them.

They are praying to Hanuman, Danlo thought. *Even though they do not know his name, they still pray to him.*

And then Danlo felt wave upon wave of love pour through him like sun-warmed honey. So intense was this love that he could hardly stand; as the sweetness of it filled all the tissues of his being, he wanted to kneel down and pray, too. He understood that in sharing the same thoughtspace as did Hanuman, he shared something of Hanuman's sensations and passions. And at that moment, as the Universal Computer wove Hanuman's cybernetic dream from bits of information and pulses of light, it touched the pleasure centers of Hanuman's brain with a golden fire. At that moment, as the people of the city worshipped Hanuman (along with trillions of other men and women on all the billions of other cities of this universe's other earths), Hanuman felt a vast and incredible shock of love tear through him as if he had been struck by a lightning bolt.

Danlo shared only a fraction of this cybernetic samadhi—even so it was almost enough to knock him from his feet and render him empty-eyed and speechless. He understood, then, something of Hanuman's terrible addiction to his computer. As each moment in the outer world of Neverness' cold and icy spires passed slowly by, Hanuman would turn inside to the light of his private, inner universe. And moment by moment throughout all the rest of his life, his need for computer-generated bliss would grow greater until it became almost infinite in its longing.

You are wrong, Danlo—my people know the name of their God. Listen to them pray.

And Danlo listened, and he heard the thousands of the people in the square chanting: "Hanuman, Lord Hanuman, Lord of Fire,

Lord of Light—you are the Light of the World, and we are the Children of the Light."

After a long time of this chanting in which these words were repeated many times, one of the men kneeling nearest the altar stood up and adjusted the orange silk cloth encircling his waist. Danlo immediately understood this orange color to be a badge of priesthood; he noticed that many other men and women kneeling around the altar wore similar belts. Then the standing priest swept his arms toward the heavens and called out according to ritual, "Lord Hanuman, one of your children is ready to return to you. Her name is Ituha the Pure, and we have found her worthy of the Light."

There followed a long round of testimonials where various people in the square would stand and tell of Ituha's goodness, her generosity, wisdom and other virtues. Then one of the priests verified that Ituha had completed every step along the ninefold path toward enlightenment. All that remained was for Ituha herself to proclaim her desire to be reunited with Hanuman and beg to be released from her human form. And this she soon did.

"Hanuman, Lord Hanuman, Lord of Fire, Lord of Light—take me in your blazing arms and lick the flesh from my body with your fiery tongue!" Ituha now knelt with her hands covering her heart as she looked up into the cloudy blue sky. "Let me feel you burning inside; let me burn and burn away; let me return to you in light."

Thus having completed the ritual, Ituha bowed her head and waited. All the people in the square waited, too, and a silence fell over them as if the air itself had sucked away all sound. Danlo, who still knelt at the edge of the square, tried to count the beats of his heart as he waited and watched the sky. But at the center of his glittering and godlike body, where his heart should have been, he felt nothing move. And then suddenly the ground shook and an irresistible force pounded at his chest as a great, golden voice fell over the square:

> *Ituha, my child—I find you worthy of the Light and invite you to come to me.*

It was Hanuman's voice, amplified and deepened a thousand-fold. And now it seemed that not only Danlo could hear it, but all the men and women waiting in the square. For they shielded their eyes as the sky opened and a great flash of light streaked down through the atmosphere straight toward the altar. This golden light fell over Ituha the Pure and wrapped itself in snakelike flames around her body. It almost instantly burned away her silken garments. And then it burned its way into her flesh, and she writhed at the touch of its fire, not in agony but in ecstasy. She opened her mouth to scream out in joy: a long, deep and beautiful sound that excited the manswarms in the square to scream out as well.

And the firelight burned even deeper into her, and her whole body began to glow like heated copper. Brighter and brighter grew this light that was consuming her until her tissues began unravelling from her bones like thousands of blazing threads of yarn. And each thread dissolved into a billion bits of color that glittered and swirled about the altar. And then each bit, like a tiny star, burst into a glory of pure white light. It seemed that every atom of her being contained an almost infinite quantity of light. The radiance of this miraculous event filled all the square; it expanded outward to illuminate all the streets of the city and the entire world itself. After a few moments, the godly light coalesced into a great glittering stream shooting up from the altar into the sky and out into the universe beyond. It blazed for a long time, and then it was gone—and so was the body of Ituha the Pure. The top of the altar was as bare as a white stone found along the beach; not even the golden rings that Ituha had worn nor even her ashes remained.

> *My child has returned to me in Light; let this Light fill all your days until you return to me as well.*

As Danlo stood watching this transcendent event, he let this light fill all his mind. And then a strange thing happened. For a moment, he returned to the real universe of blazing stars and lightships falling against each other in fury and hate. He saw Bardo's *Sword of Shiva* flashing in and out of the manifold as he pursued other glittering diamond ships of the Ringist fleet. The battle between the Ringists and Fellowship fleet boiled all around him. And then, as if the Universal Computer's program sensed that its simulation of Hanuman's artificial worlds was not quite strong enough, Danlo felt an incredibly powerful logic field pulling at his mind, pulling him back to the city on the hill on this impossible and surreal earth.

> *There is no reality but this reality, Danlo. Please remain here with me.*

And so Danlo stood once more in the square by the altar as the women and men lifted their faces toward the heavens and cried out, "Hanuman, Lord Hanuman, Lord of Fire, Lord of Light— you are the Light of the World, and we are the Children of the Light!"

Their ritual having been completed—Danlo couldn't tell how often they gave one of their own into Hanuman's fiery maw—they stood as a single body of people. That a real battle occurred in the spaces about the Universal Computer and might at any moment destroy their entire universe, they seemed not to have the slightest inkling. They only laughed softly and spoke words of hope to one another concerning the miracle that they had just witnessed. And then they visited with one another for quite some time, all the while recalling Ituha's purity and desire to transcend her human form; they spoke of their own desire to join Ituha in Light some-day and other matters that were dearest to their hearts.

As Danlo eavesdropped these many conversations, it occurred to him that each man and woman expressed their aspirations in a very similar manner. In truth, each conversation, taken as a whole piece or word for word, was almost identical to every other. They sounded much like parratock birds squawking out little dialogues and homilies that had been programmed for them. At last, as it grew closer to the hour for bathing and singing, they congratu-lated each other at having witnessed yet another vastening. Then they melted away in their ones and tens until the square grew almost empty.

Now you understand whence the light of this universe arises.

Danlo, who was still kneeling, stood up at last and turned to look at the faces of the people who remained in the square. None of them seemed able to hear Hanuman's now-diminished voice. None of them seemed able to see Danlo, who smiled and said, "This is just the same light that shines everywhere and falls upon the trees and flowers, yes?"

Light is always light, Danlo.

"It is an interesting ecology that you have created," Danlo said. "But if nothing is ever born in this world, I do not under-stand how the people retain their numbers."

> *I have said that almost nothing is born. Just as
> the vastening of one of my children is a rare
> event, so is the birth.*

"I see."

> *If you would witness the birth of a new child, go
> out of the city to the east meadow just above the
> jungle.*

Because Danlo *did* wish to behold the miracle of new life
coming forth into the world—even if both the world and that life
were more artificial than a Gilada pearl—he did as Hanuman bade
him. He passed out of the square onto the great boulevard leading
to the eastern gate; he passed by prayer pavilions and many music
houses where the people of the city were singing devotionals and
other holy songs. As upon Danlo's entrance to the city, no one
stood guard at the gate. He found the meadow unoccupied as well.
He made his way through the long, swishing grasses down the
slope until he came to the mango-laden trees of the jungle.

"Is this where you mean?" he asked. He spent a while walking along the line of the jungle as he searched for some sign of
another human being. He cast his eyes to the left and to the right,
looking for perhaps a brightly colored blanket upon which a
young woman might lay in order to give birth to her child. But he
saw nothing and no one; only the macaws and the monkeys talking in the trees provided him with any company. "There is no one
here."

> *You're wrong, Danlo. You are here.*

For a moment Danlo stared at the glittering flesh of his hand.
Then he stared at the city's gates above him; he scanned the entire
meadow about the city, thinking that he might see walking toward
him some young woman that Hanuman had sent to him. He wondered if Hanuman might expect him to mate with such a woman,
here and now on these soft green grasses rippling in the wind; he
wondered if it were possible, in the tremendous time accelerations
of the computer's program, for this woman to grow gravid with
his child and then to push him forth into the world laughing in joy
even as he watched.

"I do not understand," he finally said.

*Of course you're the child's father. And in a way,
you're the mother as well.*

"I . . . do not think that I *want* to understand."

*The child is inside you, Danlo. His name is
Jonathan. He's inside your memory and your
mind, and it's you who shall give him birth.*

Once before, on a pristine and beautiful earth inside the Vild,
the Solid State Entity had looked inside his mind and recreated
Tamara from his memories. This Tamara had been very real. She
had been wrought of real elements of carbon, hydrogen, nitrogen
and oxygen even as he was wrought; she was a beautiful woman
of soft, brown eyes and loving hands and breath that whispered
deep dreams in his ears with all the urgency of the wind. He
might have remained almost forever with this Tamara on this lost
earth, but in the end he had had to leave her because she was not
quite the *true* Tamara, his beloved who wandered the streets of
Neverness pregnant with his child.

If the Solid State Entity, in all Her godly power, could create
only an imperfect mime of Tamara, then how could Hanuman
hope to use his Universal Computer to simulate Jonathan with any
degree of exactness? And yet he clearly had confidence in his
ability to create a doll that would be identical to Jonathan. From
the first, Danlo had feared that this might be Hanuman's plan. He
had supposed that he might easily turn away from this *shaida*
simulation of his son whenever he chose. But now that the moment had come, he was not so sure. He seemed to have as little
will as one of Hanuman's dolls. In truth, he was exhausted,
drugged, defeated and still grieving terribly over Jonathan's death.
He almost didn't care if he himself lived or died. And so because
he wanted to know the true power of Hanuman's computer (and
because he longed to hold Jonathan again and look into his dark,
wild eyes), he agreed to what Hanuman proposed.

"Jonathan, Jonathan, *mi alasharia la shantih,*" he whispered.
"Sleep in peace—but forgive me for dreaming you to life again."

According to Hanuman's instructions, Danlo began to visualize Jonathan as completely as he could. Because Danlo had a truly
remarkable memory—an almost perfect eidetic memory in which
he could see each individual hair follicle of the down on Jonathan's cheek—he found this an easy feat to accomplish. In a
moment's time, an image of Jonathan as bright and clear as a

bluestar diamond sparkled inside his mind. (His very real brain-mind inside his skull, which must still lay motionless along with the rest of his body on the carpet of Hanuman's sanctuary beneath the blazing battle that raged across Neverness' sky.) Danlo apprehended this brilliant image with his eyes no less than his mind. And the dome of Hanuman's sanctuary read the lightning storm of serotonin and other neurotransmitters firing Danlo's neurons and encoded these electro-chemical events as pure information. It communicated this information to the Universal Computer. And like a paint machine adding a daub of bright color to a nearly complete canvas, the Universal Computer very slightly augmented the program that it was running. In this way, on the earth of the universe that Hanuman had created out of nothing but information, on a grassy meadow beneath an artificially blue sky, Jonathan wi Ashtoreth wi Soli Ringess came to be born again.

"Jonathan, Jonathan," Danlo whispered. "Jonathan, Jonathan."

He came into being in the space three feet in front of Danlo. In a way, his instantiation was the opposite of Ituha the Pure's vastening. Even as Danlo might use his lightship to open a window to the manifold, the air before his eyes ripped apart to reveal a brilliant white light. Almost instantly this light spilled out over the meadow and began to break apart into swirling bits of color. Each bit organized itself according to the program that built Jonathan's body. And so the Universal Computer wove Jonathan's hair of glittering bits of information and similarly fashioned his face. It sculpted his slender arms, his chest, belly, legs and feet. Because Danlo chose to remember Jonathan as he had been before freezing his feet, his toes were healthy and whole and took on the warm ivory flesh tones of the rest of his skin. In truth, his whole body and being were as healthy as Danlo could have wished—and as nearly perfect as he had ever dreamed.

"Jonathan, Jonathan," he said.

And Jonathan opened his bright, blue eyes and said, "Father—you're still wearing your new face. But its all glittery like silver and gold."

"You . . . can see me, then?"

"Of course I can see you," Jonathan said. He ran his small hand over his silken shirt and pantaloons, which were cut the same as those worn by the people of Hanuman's city. "Why shouldn't I be able to see you?"

"Well, the other people could not see me."

"Why not?"

"It . . . is hard to explain." In truth, Danlo did not understand himself why Jonathan should be able to see him where the other dolls couldn't. "Perhaps it is because I am not fully instantiated in this world."

"But what does that mean?"

"It means that . . . I am not quite I."

"But who else could you be?"

Danlo smiled at the innocence of Jonathan's question, then said, "Don't I seem different from you, Jonathan?"

For a while Jonathan stared at the glittering ruby and sapphire lights of Danlo's body. And he said, "Well, *all* of you is really different, but you're still you, aren't you?"

"Truly I am. In my deepest self—in my true self—I am always only I. It is the same for you, too, and for everyone."

"All of you looks different except your eyes."

"My eyes," Danlo whispered, remembering. He realized then that this recreated Jonathan was mimicking words that the real Jonathan had spoken in Tamara's apartment not so long ago. "My blessed eyes."

"They're blue inside blue just like your first eyes, Father. So they *look* the same. I mean, the way you look at me, the way you look at everything—it's all the same."

"I see."

"You have beautiful eyes, Father."

"Thank you. So do you."

Just then Danlo took a step forward to touch Jonathan's face and hold him in his arms. But his hand fell upon Jonathan's cheek like a shower of light; he couldn't feel Jonathan's warm, downy skin nor could Jonathan feel his hand touching him.

Jonathan, Jonathan—I cannot touch you, he silently lamented. *I can never touch you again.*

For a while he stood there letting the glittering lights of his hand illuminate various features of Jonathan's face. And then a familiar voice spoke out of the jungle:

> *Of course you can touch him. If you desire a greater degree of instantiation, then I shall make it so.*

Slowly Danlo nodded his head and whispered, "Yes, please do."

In almost no time the colors of Danlo's skin across his hands, arms and the rest of his body began to flow together and blend into a single, pure ivory tone. His long hair spilling down over his shoulders shined a brilliant black shot with strands of red. He suddenly found himself wearing the black kamelaika of a pilot; its warm and supple smoothness was as comforting as a second skin. He hesitated to test the sensibility of his first skin. Although he could feel the gentle wind brushing against his lips and his long eyelashes, even as he had while falling down to this earth, he still didn't know if the Universal Computer's program would allow him to touch a tiger or a monkey or one of Hanuman's other dolls. Or a child.

Jonathan stood there on the grass looking at him with his dark, sparkling eyes as he waited for Danlo to touch him. At last Danlo did. He reached out his hand and ran his fingers through Jonathan's silky brown hair. He felt the slight hollow at the back of Jonathan's neck, the softness of the skin. Then he dropped to one knee and hugged Jonathan to him, fiercely yet gently because it would be so easy to hurt him. There was something infinitely tender and good about holding a small child. Jonathan's hair smelled fresh and sweet, and his little body molded itself to Danlo's as if it had been made to fit there. And his eyes: The infinite trust that Danlo saw shining there touched his own eyes with something that was at once beautiful and terribly sad. He felt tears burning in his eyes then, and he watched as one of these tiny drops of saltwater fell down and touched Jonathan's cheek. In the unselfconscious way of a child, Jonathan wiped the moisture away with his finger and stood there looking at him in puzzlement as to why his father should be weeping.

After they had broken their embrace, Jonathan stooped to pluck a bright yellow dandelion from the rippling grass. Then he pointed up in the sky where a flock of white geese were flying along the line of the ocean. "I love birds," he said. "Do you remember the riddle that you asked me about birds?"

"Yes, I do."

"I love riddles—will you ask me the riddle, Father?"

Danlo smiled as he wiped the tears from his eyes and said, "All right, then, if you'd like—how do you capture a beautiful bird without killing its spirit?"

"That's a really hard riddle," Jonathan said.

"Yes—I know."

"It *would* kill a bird's spirit to put it in a cage, wouldn't it?"

"Truly, it would."

"That's a really hard riddle," Jonathan said again as he looked up at the sky and tapped his chin with his finger. "What's the answer?"

Again Danlo smiled because although this Jonathan looked and felt almost exactly like his dead son, he was still reciting words like a robot programmed to please him. "I do not know the answer to the riddle," he said.

According to his memory (and the program of the Universal Computer), he expected Jonathan to reply: "But you *have* to know—you asked the riddle." But then Jonathan surprised him, saying, "I wonder if a bird even *has* a spirit."

"Everything has a spirit," Danlo told him. "In a way, everything *is* just spirit and nothing else."

"I mean, I wonder if a bird has spirit as you and I."

Jonathan's essential philosophical inquisitiveness (no less his brilliance) had always delighted Danlo, and now he stood across from his bright-eyed son smiling at this unexpected question. He thought that the Ai program of Hanuman's Universal Computer might be much more subtle than he had imagined, for it seemed that it had almost captured something of Jonathan's essential nature.

"I know that a bird's spirit is just the same," Danlo said.

"But how could you know that?"

"But how could I *not* know? How could you not know? Haven't you ever watched an osprey skip along the ocean's waves just for the sheer singing joy of it?"

"But perhaps it's really only hunting fish."

"Only?"

"How could you *really* know what it's like to be a bird unless you become one yourself?"

"In all my life," Danlo said, "that has been one of my greatest joys."

"What has?"

"Becoming a bird." He looked off toward the north where the rocky cliffs gave way to the deep blue ocean. He wondered at Hanuman's program for this world; he wondered if he might see a snowy owl, the beautiful white bird with whom he shared his soul. *Ahira, Ahira—you are I, and I am you.*

"But, Father—you can't *really* become a bird, can you?"

"Truly, I can. Just as a bird can become a man."

"A bird can become a *man?*"

"Of course—haven't I ever told you the story of the Woman Who Loved Seagulls?"

"No, I don't think you have."

"Well, then," Danlo said as he knelt down and patted the grass, "sit with me here awhile and I shall."

And so for a long time Jonathan sat on Danlo's lap listening to his story even as he had once done in Tamara's apartment before he had died. Danlo loved the weight of Jonathan against him, just as he loved the look of wonder that lit up Jonathan's eyes when he told him how Mithuna of Asadel Island had flown with the gulls every evening at sunset before turning back into a woman at dawn's first light.

After he had finished, Jonathan kissed him and jumped up to play on the grass. Then he moved over to the edge of the jungle, where he began climbing an apple tree fairly bursting with bright red fruits. Very quickly he climbed quite high—high enough to worry Danlo. But it occurred to him that he had nothing to fear, that there could be no true accidents on this world because there was no true chance, and surely Hanuman wouldn't have programmed his computer to cause Jonathan to lose his grip or grab onto a rotten branch? Surely not, and yet even so, he hovered beneath his son with his arms held ready in case he should somehow slip and fall out of the tree.

This simulation is not perfect, Danlo thought as he watched Jonathan sit on a limb high above him and bite open a crunchy apple. *But it is very good.*

Just then, speaking out of nowhere, Hanuman's voice startled Danlo out of his reverie:

> *The simulation can be made as good as you wish,*
> *Danlo. Every moment that you spend*
> *remembering your son and visualizing him, every*
> *moment that your icon interacts with his, my*
> *computer adds to the program encoding his*
> *selfness. In a way, it's you—with the aid of my*
> *computer—who is bringing him to life and*
> *sculpting him to perfection.*

Danlo watched as Jonathan plucked an apple off its stem and tossed it down to him. He caught the apple in his hand and took a bite. It tasted tart and sweet, almost like a real apple.

And then, speaking to the sky, he said, "The simulation of my son *is* remarkable. It is almost perfect. But, Hanu, it can only ever be *almost* perfect."

Is it perfection that you require, then? Or the love of your son?

"I . . . do not know."

And the love of Tamara Ten Ashtoreth. You could bring her here, too, and restore her memories of you. You could heal her, you know. You and she could live with Jonathan in this paradise together as you were meant to be.

For the first time, Danlo began to doubt his opposition to the building of the Universal Computer. Truly, in recreating Jonathan out of sparkling bits of information, it had done a miraculous thing. Who knew what other wonders it might work? Danlo saw in his mind a burning image of a healed Tamara looking at him as she had at their first meeting in Bardo's house years ago. He saw himself holding her, and she him, in burning passion and blessed love. His longing for her fired every cell in his body; it caused his throat to choke with emotion and his head to ache with a sharp and terrible pain.

"Tamara, Tamara," he whispered to the sky. "Why shouldn't I bring you here? Why shouldn't we dwell here forever with our son? All that awaits us in the other world is separation, pain and death."

Here, you should know, there is no more death forever. There is no disease, either. If you wished, you could bring all the tribes of your Alaloi people here. And thus heal them of the Plague virus.

"To heal my people," Danlo said. "This is what I have always dreamed."

It is what I've always dreamed of too, Danlo. To heal the universe of its essential flaw.

"To heal the universe," Danlo said. He looked out at the ever-bright sky as he remembered the deeper and bluer sky of the world of Icefall. Once, upon the death of his entire tribe, a boy who hadn't quite completed his passage into manhood, he had set out beneath this blue inside blue sky on a great quest to find a cure for the world's pain and the *shaida* nature of the universe. And now, it seemed, he had almost completed his journey.

> *To heal the universe—the whole universe.*

"Father, why are you so silent?" Jonathan called down as he took another bite of apple. Although he didn't really need to eat the fruit for nourishment, he had no problem enjoying its texture and taste. "What are you thinking, then?"

The whole universe—I can heal the whole universe.

For what seemed a long time, Danlo looked up through the green leaves of the tree to watch Jonathan so happily eating his apples.

> *You can create the universe, you know. You could remain here with me, and create a whole universe all your own.*

The whole universe.

Danlo looked to the east at the great jungle that covered the rolling hills all around him. The trees fairly groaned beneath their weight of red, yellow and orange fruits while tigers called to each other to come mate and play. Were these tigers any less beautiful than those of Icefall? Were the trees? Wasn't a single tree wrought of pure information, in its glorious lacework of leaves, almost as magnificent a creation as a real tree? Didn't it fill his eyes with its loveliness and touch his lungs with sweet-smelling fragrance?

"It's beautiful, here," Jonathan said from his branch high above. "Can't we stay here forever, Father?"

"It . . . is possible that we could," Danlo said.

"Couldn't we bring Mama here, too? I miss her so badly."

"I miss her, too."

"We could live anywhere in the world where we wanted, couldn't we? Anywhere in the whole universe."

The whole universe.

Danlo looked southward over the tops of the trees. There, a set of mountains rose up to form the beginning of the great coastal range. A few of the higher peaks showed white with ice and snow. From many miles away, Danlo could see this newly fallen snow; even as he concentrated his focus of vision, he could descry individual snow crystals glittering in all their intricate and lovely six-pointed symmetry. Were any of these beautiful crystals any less

real than the snow that had stung his face and chilled his fingers
as a child?

"If we *did* choose to remain here," he called up to Jonathan,
"where would you want to live?"

"On our own world, Father. Couldn't we have a world all of
our own?"

"I suppose that we could."

"Couldn't we *create* a world of our own? You and I, Mama,
too? Couldn't we make it as we wished it to be?"

Just then Jonathan, biting hard on a fat red apple to leave his
hands free for climbing, came down from the tree. After he had
jumped onto the grass in front of Danlo, he handed him the apple.
And then he pointed to the mountains north of them and said,
"I'd always want mountains like these, only with more snow like
Atakel and Urkel. I'd miss the great white bears if our world was
too warm. I'd miss the shagshay herds and the ice hawks."

Yes, Danlo thought, looking northward, he too would want
great, towering mountains whose slopes were shagged with many
layers of ice and snow. He would want white foxes and shatterwood trees, wolves and wolverines and thallows who nested
high up in the rocky crags. In a universe of his own creation,
anything would be possible.

The whole universe.

Far out over the sea, many miles to the west, he at last caught
sight of a brilliant white bird soaring into the sky. It was Ahira, he
saw, the snowy owl—the wisest and wildest of all animals. When
he looked very hard, he could see Ahira's mysterious orange and
black eyes looking back at him. A shock of recognition burned
through his brain and leapt along his spine like a lightning bolt; it
touched every part of him with its electric fire. This splendid bird
seemed almost as real as anything he had ever beheld. Just as
Jonathan, pressing up against his side, felt almost as real as a real
child.

He wondered, then, at the true nature of reality. There was
something utterly strange about it that he could approach but
never quite apprehend. It was as if in looking at reality too
closely—like examining the grains of light and darkness in a foto
of a familiar face—it became ever less real. Wasn't reality, like
the perception of a foto, merely a construct of his mind? Didn't
he, after all, in the firing of his brain's neurons in precise ways,
create his own universe? And if this were so, if the reality of this
electronic universe were truly as real as the one that he had left

behind, raging in war and exploding its stars, then why not remain here forever?

The whole universe.

For an endless moment, Danlo stared west at the glittering waters of the sea. It came to him then that he had reached the last of his courage and will. His great journey to reach the center of the universe that had taken up most of his life was finally over, for he had no more strength to go on. As a boy he had buried all eighty-eight members of his tribe and then buried his grandfather, as well. Soon after that, he himself had nearly died trying to find the fabled city of Neverness. Starving, frostbitten and alone on the ice of the sea, he had had to eat his best sled dog in order to stay alive. And then, after the regeneration of his flesh, and all his hopes and dreams, as a young man he had lost Tamara to the rape of her memories and had lost Hanuman as a friend. How much loss could one man bear? How much suffering could the universe inflict upon a man before he shook his head in utter denial and turned away from it?

Suffering had no end, he thought, and infinite were the streets of the City of Pain. Still as a young man, he alone had survived a chaos space inside the manifold where ten other fellow pilots had become lost; he had lived to journey on into the heart of the Vild and become witness (and catalyst) of the death of the Narain people and their entire world. And then he had returned to Neverness, only to be imprisoned and tortured with knives and the hideous ekkana drug. And as terrible as this torture of his flesh, it had been nothing next to the anguish of watching Jonathan starve and scream as the cutter had taken off his feet. O blessed God!, he wondered, how much suffering could one universe hold?

Jonathan, Jonathan, mi alasharia la shantih, you are dead—I felt your dying breath upon my lips and burned your body down by the sea.

But now Jonathan lived again and pressed his head up against Danlo's hand. All the dead and the dying could be redeemed, healed, made almost real. Even those friends and fellow pilots who were dying in this moment in the battle for the Star of Neverness. He himself, as creator of his own universe, could accomplish this miracle. All that he needed to do was to surrender, to give in to his desire to escape the senseless suffering of life. Truly, he thought, there was always a time to admit defeat and simply give up.

No, I must not, Danlo thought. *I have promised Old Father that I would never give up.*

Not defeat, Danlo, but victory. The victory of a
man who has the courage to become a god.

"No, no," Danlo said, "I never wanted to become a god."

No, you always wanted even more. Well, then,
look up away from this world and you shall know
the full power of interfacing the Universal
Computer.

Thus bidden, Danlo circled Jonathan's body with his arms as he pulled his head back and looked up through the sky to the universe beyond. The glaring blueness suddenly gave way to a pure black, and there in the yawning void a million other earths appeared. He stared at these spinning blue and white jewels for a while and then his vision exploded outward in an expanding sphere as it had before. A million more worlds burst into view, and then ten million. Soon he found himself able to look upon all twenty-five billion worlds of the universe, all at once. And not just to study them, as an astronomer through a telescope, but to dive down hawklike with his mind's eyes through layers of atmosphere and instantiate at will in whatever city or forest that he chose.

On one earth he watched as a race of blond-haired giants danced around a crackling woodfire in a clearing and howled out their praises to a god named Hanuman. And on another earth, he saw a pygmy-like people building a tower of white marble straight up into the sky. He saw earths whose people had evolved so far toward perfection that the air above their cities fairly flickered with the lights of many men and women returning to their god. Other newly created earths were spectacular with virgin forests and clear, tropical waters teeming with thousands of species of fish; they but awaited the coming of human beings to fulfill their purpose.

And all this—and million times a million times more—he saw all at once, all in the same moment. And the miracle of it was that he understood all that he saw, and that he could truly *see* each person on each separate earth, not collectively as a colorful smear of humanity, but one by one like pearls upon an infinitely unravelling strand. He could see rocks and trees and shells along countless white sand beaches—anything that he wished to see anywhere.

And the power and pleasure of such vision made him want to melt away into the lightning information storms of the Universal

Computer. This great machine, floating in the space of another universe almost infinitely far away, seemed as near as the vivid field of vision just behind his eyes. In truth, it was as if a new lobe had been miraculously grafted onto his brain—a lobe as vast as a moon. He felt no separation from it. He *was* the Universal Computer, and it was he. He sensed its programs and information flows in almost the same way that he did any other part of his mind.

Crystal-like complexes of ideas and patterns of thought formed up and flashed through him at tremendous speed. He found himself able to apprehend these patterns at a glance; it was like understanding, in a nanosecond, all the words that human beings had ever uttered, or written down, or thought. He could *feel* his intelligence expanding out toward infinity in a great, electric rush that thrilled him with a sense of his vast power. He watched a hundred people on a hundred worlds going about the business of their artificial lives, and he perceived the programs that animated each of them. And then he looked upon the faces of a million people, and then all ten billion trillion people on all the twenty-five billion earths.

He saw the men and women (and children) dissolve into glittering bits of information, each one into its own unique pattern. And he saw how each of the individual programs encoding their selfnesses sprang from a single master program that ran the Universal Computer itself. That ran him, that *was* him, at least in this moment when he shared total interface with Hanuman. He himself was nothing but information rushing at the speed of light and forming itself into patterns. Off and on, off *or* on, a trillion trillion light pulses flashed through the computer's optical circuitry every ten trillionth of a nanosecond. This godlike radiance filled all the interior of the dark, moon-sized Universal Computer; it filled all the interior of Danlo's mind like ten thousand supernovas exploding into light. In a moment of time, he became this light that filled an entire universe; he became the light that *created* the universe itself.

White bright light glittering blazing becoming all that is I am God my God I am one alone so always totally alone like a seed buried beneath black rotting earth I am the one who creates roses burst forth out of dreams inside dreams like perfect diamond crystals without pain fear suffering no disease no death no flaw no life as life as it has been has been so terrible while the acorn dies in becoming the oak spreading out infinitely beneath the sun whose son kills the father kills the sun all suns within that universe

*because life is the disease that has no cure except in creation of
this universe out of dreams of infinities of worlds and stars all
matter energy spacetime information collapsing coalescing folding into the one perfect universal computing God out of nothing
but pure information like white bright light* . . .

For what seemed an eternity, Danlo dwelled at the center of
this brilliant white sphere of cybernetic samadhi. All reality
seemed to dissolve into swirling, glittering bits of information
that might be tessellated like tiny diamond tiles into an infinite
number of possibilities. If his mind had had lips and a voice, it
would have gasped in pure pleasure at the temptation to remain
here forever and create his own universe. But at last he returned to
the meadow below the city. He found himself holding tightly onto
Jonathan and marveling at the soft, woody smell of his hair.

The whole universe, Danlo. The whole universe.

"It . . . is almost perfect," Danlo said as he stroked Jonathan's hair and looked off at the seagulls gliding over the ocean.
The interface with the Universal Computer had almost unnerved
him, causing him to stand unsteadily and gasp for air.

*Remain here with me and we shall make it
perfect.*

Danlo's whole bodymind still crackled with the lightning-like
ecstasy with which Hanuman's computer had touched him. He
knew then that in sharing interface so deeply, Hanuman had
shared his great dream and perhaps even something of his soul.
And it all lay before Danlo like an endless ocean streaming outward in all directions. He wanted to drink in the totality of this
dream all in one huge swallow, but because he had now returned
to the limitations of his human self, he had to be content with
apprehending it sip by sip. He saw that Hanuman *needed* to share
his great vision with one other person; only then might the pain of
his terrible aloneness go away. And so Hanuman was trying to
capture him as a flower does a bee with the sweetness of its
nectar.

. . . *falling down upon fields of flowers melting golden into
honeysuckle sweetness goodness truth beauty love love love* . . .

There was a moment. Danlo stood breathing in the heavenly
fragrance of the fruits and flowers bursting out of the world all
around him, and he wanted to remain there forever. He wanted to

say, "All right, then, Hanu—if you'd like." These words were as close to his lips as the taste of honey on his teeth. But then he looked off into the deep blue sky behind his eyes, and he began to remember.

"If I *did* remain here," he said, "I would be betraying those I left behind."

Upon hearing the pain and indecision in Danlo's voice, Jonathan broke free from his embrace and turned to look at him. "Who, then, Father?" he asked.

And Danlo replied, "Your mother—the *real* Tamara. She . . . who would give her last piece of bread to the children who are still starving in the streets of the city. And the Ayame and Tausha tribes out on the islands west of Kweitkel—all the Alaloi tribes. All the people who have suffered in this *shaida* war. All people everywhere."

"But why can't we just bring them all here?"

"Because it would be—"

"Why can't we bring *everything* here?"

Danlo smiled at his son's naivete and said, "The whole universe? Every suffering bit of creation? Would you bring every rock and tree and tiger and snowworm and star of the other universe into this one, then?"

"Why not?"

"It . . . is not possible."

"But why, Father?"

"Because in order for the Universal Computer to completely simulate the real universe, it itself would have to be infinitely large."

At this Jonathan only smiled, mysteriously and knowingly, and yet hopefully, too. It occurred to Danlo that Hanuman would have smiled thusly as a child before he had lost his innocence. And then he remembered something that he had seen during his total interface with the Universal Computer, a terrible and tragic thing that Hanuman had done when he had been little more than a child. And he remembered something else as well. Suddenly, like a light being turned to full power inside a dimly lit room, his inner sight illuminated the totality of Hanuman's dream. The utter horror and hubris of it caused him to gasp as if struck between the ribs with a hokkee stick and to drop to one knee. "My God," he cried out, "it is not possible!"

But it *was* truly possible; at least it was possible that Hanuman would attempt to accomplish what even gods such as the Solid State Entity or the April Colonial Intelligence must have regarded as insane. For he truly dreamed of making his Universal Computer infinitely large. All his plans were designed toward this great purpose. After he had led the Ringists to destroy the Fellowship of Free Worlds in the battle that Danlo could almost feel flashing and pulsing all about him, he would begin consolidating his victory.

The Ringists, they who served him in bringing forth a golden future, would finally complete the construction of the Universal Computer. That is, the first phase of its creation would be completed. Then Hanuman would use its vast computing power to discover the secret of manufacturing and manipulating tachyons, those glittering and almost imaginary particles that could travel through spacetime infinitely faster than light. He would exult in possessing this technology that the gods themselves used to communicate information across thousands of light-years in a moment; then in triumph he would initiate the Universal Computer's second phase.

All across the three thousand Civilized Worlds—and in ten thousand times as many star systems containing dead, unpeopled worlds—his Ringists would carry in the holds of their deep ships the disassemblers and other robots used to tear apart matter into its constituent elements. Asteroids, comets, interstellar dust, even whole planets—all would be food for the maw of his galaxy-wrecking machines. And then, from the holds of the deepships as well, his faithful godlings would release other self-replicating robots. Assemblers tinier than a blood cell would use the clouds of elements to remake themselves explosively a trillion times over; it would be like dropping a bacteria colony into an ocean of sugar. And they would fabricate millions of miles of neurologics and optical circuitry as they built other black, moon-sized lobes identical to the Universal Computer. Hanuman calculated that the stars of the Fallaways alone contained enough matter to make a billion of them. And just as Ede the God, master of computational origami, had folded together the many millions of component parts of his nebula-sized brain, Hanuman would begin connecting the lobes into a single computer that spanned twenty thousand light-years of realspace from Ultima to New Earth.

The third phase of constructing the Universal Computer would be the utter triumph of the Way of Ringess. As Lord of the Civilized Worlds, Hanuman would bring his new religion out to the other peoples of the galaxy. He would win them to his vision, either with words or electronic samadhi or war. He would excite them to build yet more billions of lobes of the Universal Computer's brain. Somewhere along the way of this crusade, perhaps in toward the light-drunk spaces of the core, his Ringists would come across the Iviomils who had destroyed the star of the Narain people. In a lightning duel of ships falling through the manifold and flashing laser lights, they would capture or kill these deadly Architects once led by Bertram Jaspari. They would capture the deep ship containing their *morrashar* and study this star-killing machinery. And then the same robot factories that had built the components of the Universal Computer would begin building new *morrashars*, millions upon millions of them. The factories would build robot blackships as well. With the Universal Computer programming and setting the mappings of the ships from star to star, Hanuman would send this death fleet out to the farthest reaches of the galaxy.

And then would come the terrible fourth phase of the Universal Computer's making. After many hundreds or thousands of years (after Hanuman had tortured the Agathanian engineers and had wrested the secret of immortality from them), he would turn upon the trillions of Ringists whom he had promised to lead toward godhood. In truth, he would lead them down into the dark and endless cavern of death. It would be the greatest betrayal in the history of the human race, perhaps the greatest in the history of the universe. For Hanuman planned nothing less than the extermination of all human beings everywhere. All *beings* everywhere: every man, alien and animal around every star of the Milky Way galaxy. He would do this because he no longer needed them to help elevate him toward the divine, and because in his great compassion, he wished to spare all life the horror of what was next to come.

This was the killing of the stars, the exploding of the stars into light that would eventually put out the light of the entire galaxy. The stars, in falling into supernovas and dying, in the incredible heat of their blazing plasma furnaces, would use up their hydrogen and helium atoms to manufacture lithium and oxygen and silicon and cold black iron—all the elements of material reality. Hanuman would need these elements to construct ever more lobes of the Universal Computer, for much of the matter of the universe was bound up into the stars.

Using his robot fleets of *morrashar* blackships like swarms of locusts, he would destroy the stars of the Sagittarius and Orion Arms one by one and ten thousand by ten thousand. He himself would long since have removed his physical person to safety, perhaps on one of the earths that Ede the God had once created in the Vild or on a new earth that he would make at the edge of the galaxy out near the stars of the Magellanic Clouds. For Hanuman would now be the greatest of the galaxy's gods in actuality as well as dreams, and all the stars from the core out to the Ivory Double would be his to use as he pleased.

In truth, all the other gods of the galaxy—The Solid State Entity, Chimene, Iamme, Pure Mind, the Silicon God, the Degula Trinity and perhaps even Mallory Ringess—would have been slain in the explosions of the supernovas, if not during the first rush of destruction, then certainly in the chain reaction when the densely packed core stars blew out the entire center of the galaxy in a vast wave of light and death. This terrible killing light would seek out all the huddled human beings on all their natural and made-worlds floating in space; it would put an end to *Homo sapiens'* great galactic adventure begun on Old Earth so many thousands of years before. It would also destroy millions of lobes of the Universal Computer, melting off many miles and layers of optical circuitry and sometimes even vaporizing an entire moon-sized lobe in a flash.

But always Hanuman's fleets of robot black ships would follow in the wake of this destruction and release its swarms of assemblers upon the glowing dust and other debris. New lobes of the Universal Computer would be continually refabricated and interfaced with the older lobes in brilliant streams of tachyons crisscrossing the galaxy; every part of this godlike machine would be connected to every other in an almost infinitely complex network of interflowing information. And thus someday, farwhen, after perhaps ten million years or more, the entire galaxy would be remade as a cloud of trillions of diamond-skinned lobes that would be a single, vast, black, glittering computer.

And then, in the fifth and final phase of the making of this *shaida* thing, Hanuman would turn his ice-blue eyes outward and gaze across the dark and endless void at other galaxies. Having accomplished what few other gods would have dared to attempt (and having created perhaps the greatest and most concentrated intelligence in the universe), his hubris would have grown as vast as the Universal Computer itself. No god and nothing would remain to come between him and the fulfillment of his dream. Ages earlier, a would-be god named Mallory Ringess had proved that there existed a one-to-one mapping between any two stars of the universe—and thus that a lightship or blackship might fall almost anywhere in spacetime in a single fall. But such mappings could be hideously difficult to find; between two stars of different galaxies, they could be almost impossible. Indeed, no pilot of the Order had ever succeeded in journeying out from the Milky Way, not even to one of the nearer galaxies such as Draco or Fornax.

But now Hanuman would use the Universal Computer to overcome the limitations of man's mathematics. With its almost infinite computing power, it would discover mappings between the stars of the Magellanic Clouds (those few million stars that Hanuman allowed to remain untouched by his galaxy-killing machines) and those of Leo, Sculptor and Andromeda and all the other galaxies of the Local Group. Hanuman would then send millions of *morrashar* death ships and deepships containing both disassemblers and assembling robots out to these blazing, far-flung stars.

In each of the twenty galaxies of the Local Group, Hanuman would set loose a wave of destruction similar to the catastrophe that had overcome the Milky Way. But he would create as well. Like some black, malignant crystal almost infinite in size, the Universal Computer would grow explosively ever outward, absorbing dark matter and cosmic rays, as well as the remains of quasars and nebulas and blue supergiant stars. How long it might take for it to encompass the three million light-years of space from the Anur dwarf galaxy to Triangulum, Hanuman couldn't know. But by that time, however far in the future that it be, Hanuman's patience would have grown almost infinite along with his power.

Inevitably, the Universal Computer would begin absorbing whole clusters of groups of galaxies. From the Canes Ventici Cloud out to the Pavo-Indus and Cetus clouds of galaxies, the Universal Computer would continually convert all matter into circuitry or other computer parts before incorporating it into itself. It would swallow up thousands of galaxies: the ring galaxies and the ellipticals and the lovely, sparkling swirls of stars in spiral galaxies like the Milky Way. Even the rare Seyfert galaxies, whose bright cores radiate strongly in blue and ultraviolet light, it would deconstruct, digest and remake in its own form. The Grus Cluster of galaxies would die to its program to grow toward infinity, as well as the Virgo Cluster seventy million light-years distant and all the other clusters in the Local Supercluster.

The superclusters are like brilliant knots in the long, glittering strands of galaxies that weave the glorious tapestry of the universe. And now this beautiful piece of work would all unravel and come undone as the Universal Computer tore apart the Coma, Perseus and Hercules superclusters, all of which lay within a billion light-years of what would be left of the once-marvelous

Milky Way. The Universal Computer would grow ever outward devouring the stars, on and on, until it had consumed and folded up the whole universe. And someday, farwhen, after many millions of years, there would be almost nothing left of the universe except this single, crystal-like machine and a god named Hanuman li Tosh.

He would dwell on his earth at the center of what he had created. Perhaps he would keep tigers or monkeys or other tamed living things as pets; perhaps he would even keep a few million human beings this way as well. Sometimes he might sit in a forest clearing and let the blowing leaves brush against his hair; sometimes at night he might walk along a darkened beach crunching shells into the sand and letting the light of the stars fall across his face. But there would be only a few dim stars left to behold.

In any case, Hanuman had never cared for the world's marvels or the glories of creation. He would have his own creation now, and he would face it not with his eyes or living senses, but only with his mind. Whenever he chose—and this would be almost every moment of his endless life—he might stare off and interface the Universal Computer, which would now be truly universal in its scope and power. He would be finally and totally alone, even as God is alone, without the sound of a real ocean to make his heart beat faster or the touch of a woman's breath upon his eyelids. Outside, the stars would have died and all would be as dark and hard as the black diamond shells that encased the moon-lobes of his computer. But inside there would gleam a brilliant if artificial light, for Hanuman would have all eternity with which to play with his dolls and to shape pure information into a whole universe without pain, suffering or flaw.

The whole universe.

Danlo, still crouching down on one knee and gasping in horror of what he remembered, finally managed to stand back up. He looked around at the rippling grass and the blue sky beyond the meadow. And again he noticed that the clouds floating above him like puffy white dreams seemed almost too-perfectly shaped.

"No." He uttered this single, simple word with a sureness that came from deep inside his belly. "No."

Upon hearing this, Jonathan came over to him and said, "That's really the only way to save everyone, you know. To bring them here from the other universe."

"To kill all the people, then? All the stars? All things . . . everywhere?"

"But, Father—isn't every living thing doomed anyway? In the end, doesn't everything that lives just suffer and die?"

"Yes, truly everything does, but—"

"Life is a disease that has no cure. No cure except extinction."

"No—that cannot be true."

"The flaw, Father—the fundamental flaw runs down to the fabric of the universe itself."

Danlo looked at his son sadly and said, "Is the only way to save the universe, then, to destroy it?"

"It's hard," Jonathan said, "but didn't you teach me that true compassion is the hardest thing in the world?"

"Do you think that it is compassionate to *murder* people?"

"But they don't really die, do they? If they can be brought here to this universe, if they can be made to live forever without suffering—isn't this really the only way they can live without the dread of death?"

"No," Danlo said again. "No."

"The whole universe can be healed of its flaw and perfectly recreated here. Is it wrong to want to save the universe, Father?"

At that moment it was hard for Danlo to look at Jonathan, so he closed his eyes and took a breath of air. And then he remembered something important, something that he should never have forgotten.

"Jonathan," he said softly as he looked off toward the beach and the world all around them, "even if the Universal Computer grew infinitely large and the simulation of the universe became perfect, it would still be only a simulation."

Jonathan stepped closer to him and threw his arms around his waist. And then he looked up with his deep blue eyes and asked, "Aren't I real, Father?"

Gently, Danlo reached behind him and pried Jonathan's fingers apart; gently he placed his hands on his son's chest over his heart and pushed him away.

"No," he said, struggling to breathe, "you are not real."

"Won't you help bring Mama here and everything else?"

"No, I will not."

"Please, Father."

"No."

"But why not? I don't understand."

With a sudden but graceful motion, Danlo swept his hand out toward the city where many of the people would be gathering for an hour of prayer. Then he looked into the jungle at the lovely parratock birds with their brilliantly colored plumes and bright little eyes. In a way, he thought, all these dolls were perfect— perfect like diamond crystals frozen in ice. Because each of the almost infinitely many parts of the world did not die and were not reabsorbed into an ever increasingly complex web of creation, there could be not true evolution here. And so the universe as a whole was freezing up into a vast, single crystal without flow or true consciousness.

"Please tell me why you won't help me, Father."

At last, as tears built in Danlo's eyes, he turned toward Jonathan and said, "Because all this life that you have made . . . is so unalive."

And Jonathan just stared at him silently for a long time as the innocence melted from his face like honey beneath a glaring red sun. And then he said, "Damn you, Father."

Because Danlo couldn't speak just then, he looked at the soft locks of hair falling across his son's forehead.

"You might have saved me, you know. You might have saved everyone."

Danlo continued to gaze at his son who wasn't really of his flesh or spirit or heart but only an instantiation of images out of his and Hanuman's mind. "No, no, I—"

Damn you, Danlo!

These words came not from Jonathan's lips but fell down from the sky like thunder and shook the ground upon which Danlo stood. He clasped his hands to his ears, but he couldn't seem to shut out the deafening sound that rolled out all around him.

Damn you, damn you, damn you! I've offered you the whole universe. I've created a heaven for you, and you choose only hell. You should know, it's your choice, Danlo.

And then the sky opened and a bolt of lightning tore down through the air and struck Jonathan full upon the forehead. He staggered backward as blue bands of electricity crackled and sizzled all about his body like glowing snakes. "No!" he cried out as his eyes opened wide with the sudden and terrible pain. "Please, Father—help me!"

Despite himself, Danlo leaped forward to save his son. But he was too late, for Jonathan's silken garments suddenly burst into bright orange flames as if they had been soaked in sihu oil. Danlo fell over him and bore him down to the ground, all the while trying to beat out the flames with his hands. But the fire burned only hotter and hotter; it burned Danlo's hands and face and then it began burning deep into Jonathan's flesh. He lay beneath Danlo shuddering and writhing and screaming as he pleaded, "Father, Father—please help me!" The terrible heat began to char Jonathan's skin; soon a black crust formed over his chest and across his face and began spreading over his whole body. As the fire worked deeper and deeper, his skin cracked open and red liquids leaked out before bubbling and steaming off into the air. The stench of roasting meat caused Danlo's belly to heave. "I don't want to die! Please, Father—don't let me burn to . . . ahhhh! Oh, Father, it hurts, it hurts, it hurts!"

For what seemed forever, Danlo held the burning body of his son in his arms as he felt himself burning too. And then he looked down at the twisted piece of charcoal lying motionless on his lap; he watched as what was left of Jonathan's body fell apart into ashes in his hands. "Jonathan, Jonathan, *mi alasharia la shantih,*" he whispered. Slowly he stood and lifted his blackened and bleeding hands toward the sky. "No!" he cried out. "No, no, no, no!"

And the sky answered him:

Your choice, Danlo. It's always been your choice.

Upon these words, the ground beneath him suddenly softened as if soaked by water and turned to mud. He felt himself being sucked downward for a long time into warm, rotting loam. And then the sense of oozing materiality all about him dissolved into a stark, cold nothingness as he began falling into a dark cavern without light or sound, without bottom or end. He fell almost forever; through whole universes as vacant as a dead man's eyes, through the neverness of all his dreams and hopes for life, he fell and fell, on and on. He was utterly alone like a stone spinning through space, and he fell down through the black and breathless night, and then down at last through the golden dome of Hanuman's sanctuary and back into the hell of his drugged, burning, paralyzed body.

THE FACE OF GOD

There is a war that opens the doors of heaven. Glad are the warriors whose fate is to fight such a war.
—Bhagavad Gita

When things look like a nightmare, wake up.
—Source unknown

Danlo opened his eyes to look up upon the clear, curving windows of the sanctuary's dome. He found himself still paralyzed and lying on the Fravashi carpet that covered the cold stone floor. He felt the golden pillow that Hanuman had placed beneath his head; he felt cold currents of air falling across his face and a burning behind his eyes, but he still couldn't feel most of his body. For a moment he let the light of the familiar deep winter stars play across his eyes, and then he turned his head to see Hanuman standing above him.

"You should know, it's your choice," Hanuman said, looking at Danlo in all his helplessness. "It's always been your choice."

Danlo saw that the clearface molded to Hanuman's skull had quieted to a glossy purple, as if he had temporarily turned away from the Universal Computer.

"My choice," Danlo forced out. "Yes, truly it is."

Painfully, he turned his head away from Hanuman to gaze at the objects of the room. The sulki grids and the many computers glittered in the light of the flame globes; the chess set with its missing white god still stood ready for someone to play with its ivory and black shatterwood pieces. And nearby, on top of the dining table where Hanuman had left it, the devotionary computer still beamed forth the hologram of Nikolos Daru Ede.

"You have made your choices, too," Danlo said. For a while he looked closely at the chess set, and he could see a tiny crack running through one of the black squares of the board. And then he remembered the terrible thing that he had seen during his total interface with the Universal Computer. He turned back toward

Hanuman and said, "I know that you murdered your father, Hanu."

With a sad, bitter smile, Hanuman bowed his head to Danlo. And then he said, "I had to kill him, you should know. It was the only way that I could keep him from violating my mind. My *self*. It was the only way I could leave Catava and come to Neverness to pursue my fate."

"I . . . am sorry."

"Please don't be. For me, really, it was the beginning of everything. It opened a door that made all things possible."

One door and one door only opens upon the golden future that I have seen, Danlo thought. But now, as he looked at Hanuman's icy blue eyes shot with blood and the pain of his terrible fate, he saw that this single iron door remained bolted and closed forevermore. *One door only . . .*

Through the cold dark windows of the sanctuary, Danlo stared out upon the nighttime stars. In places, to the south and east, the yellowish haze of the Golden Ring obscured their brilliance while directly above him in near space, the looming vastness of the Universal Computer devoured the stars altogether. It was as if the hand of God had smeared a great circle of black paint against the shimmering heavens. And yet even in the darkness near this growing machine, many lights flashed out into the night as various ships of the Fellowship Fleet manuevered with those of the Ringists for position above Icefall.

In and out of the manifold these lightships darted like silver needles stitching long, luminescent threads through the fabric of realspace. The pattern that they wove blazed across the sky in a stunning complexity. There was much other radiance, too: the silvery glister of the moons, and the satellites of the planetary defense system that shot out bursts of laser light in thousands of quick, measured bursts. Originally they had been designed to destroy incoming missiles or even small asteroids, but now their intense ruby fire had been turned toward the ships of the Fellowship's fleet. It bespoke the art of the Fellowship's pilots that only a few blackships disintegrated beneath this fire into showers of scintillating white sparks.

It is too late, Danlo thought. *I cannot stop the battle.*

He rolled his head off the pillow and tried to press his ear to the floor. He could no longer hear the shouts of the thousands of men and women echoing in the cathedral below him or sounding through the streets outside. It had fallen late, he knew, and not even the most devoted of godlings would wish to stand beneath the naked sky while war raged across the heavens.

I cannot stop the war.

Just then one of the sulki grids flickered into life, and a hologram of a man appeared standing near the shatterwood table. Hanuman immediately turned his attention toward this hologram of the pilot, Krishnan Kadir. They began speaking together in hushed, hurried tones. Although Danlo could not hear much of what they said, he understood that Krishnan was reporting on the progress of the battle. And more, he (or rather his lightship's computer) was communicating to Hanuman the disposition of many thousands of the Fellowship and Ringist ships almost as they fell from fixed-point to fixed-point and from star to star. Danlo watched as the clearface surrounding Hanuman's head flared into a brilliant purple and began filling his brain with streams of vital information. Hanuman would use this information to enable the Universal Computer to make a model of the battle almost moment by moment; he would use its vast computing power to predict how Cristobel the Bold and Helena Charbo and the other Fellowship pilot-captains would deploy their ships. And thus he would attempt to run the battle itself even as it spread among the stars above Neverness.

"Go back to Lord Salmalin," Hanuman told Krishnan Kadir whose ship had fallen out into near-space above Icefall. "Go find the Lord Pilot and tell him that Cristobel the Bold has led the Twelfth Battle Group away from Lidiya Luz. Therefore he should order six cadres to lay a trap near the stars of the Primula Double and the . . ."

Danlo, still lying helpless on the floor, didn't hear anything more of what Hanuman said. Nor did he wish to, for he had no need of such useless information.

It is over, then, he thought. *Hanuman's advantage is too great, and surely he will win the battle.*

For a moment he stared at the hellish light that now streamed out of the clearface and colored Hanuman's face a hideous, glowing violet. And then he shut his eyes as a sudden thought swept through him with all the terrible heat of a firestorm:

I wish he were dead.

As Danlo's heart beat hard up through his throat and into his throbbing head, he waited for this astonishing thought itself to weaken and die. But it did not. Each moment, with every new beat of his heart and breath that he took, it grew only stronger. Something sharp and terrible like a black iron spearpoint heated to a glowing red drove through his eye straight into his brain.

Please die, Hanu. I want you to die. Please die, now, please die and die and die. . . .

For a long time Danlo lay beneath the sanctuary's dome in utter silence as he let all his hatred for Hanuman well up inside him. Never, in all his life, had he broken his vow of ahimsa so completely and willfully. He felt this violation of his promise never to harm any living thing as a betrayal of his deepest self; he felt it as a sickening heat deep in his belly that spread out to poison his heart and lungs and every other part of him. In utter despair he ground his teeth together as he slowly shook his head back and forth across the carpet.

And then a new thought that filled every cell of his body with liquid fire came over him: *I want to die.*

He felt his heart beat once, twice and then three times. For much of his life he had counted the beats of his heart, and now he wished for the silence of this most central and alive of all his body's organs; now and forevermore he wished the number of his heart's beats to fall to zero.

"I want to die," he whispered. "*Ahira, Ahira*—please let me die."

There was no longer any reason for him to live. Truly, he thought, it would be much better for everyone if he simply died. If he could find his way to the other side of day, then Hanuman would have no reason to hunt down Tamara and threaten her with torture. And thus Hanuman would be unable to use him, as Mallory Ringess, to farther his plans.

I want to die, he thought. *I have come here today to die.*

He looked around the room at all the glittering cybernetica and the devotionary computer sitting on the black shatterwood table; he looked at Hanuman, at his sad and tormented face. His sunken skin glowed a ghastly violet in the light of the computer that he wore molded to his skull; all his bones stuck out as if time had reduced his once-beautiful countenance to a hideous death's-head. It reminded him that Hanuman—and everyone else—would be always only a heartbeat away from death.

Please let me die; please let me die, now, here, in this cold room.

Ever since he had been born, it seemed, he had tried to face life with all the terrible courage of life. But now Jonathan was dead beyond the dream of resurrection, and soon Tamara might be lost to him, too. And all the Alaloi tribes, without him to find a cure for the virus that infected them, would certainly die, frothing at the lips and leaking blood from their ears even as the Devaki tribe had died years ago.

As he gazed at the black squares of Hanuman's chess set, he finally understood an important thing about himself. Many times since his childhood—on the ice of the frozen sea, in the library staring at a warrior-poet's gleaming killing knife, in the House of the Dead on Tannahill—he had faced death with an equanimity that others had regarded as almost superhuman. But it was all a lie. He knew what no one else did: that he was really the worst of cowards. True courage was the ability to live with fear while acting according to the deeper purposes of life; it was a love beyond the love of the self that took one into a deeper and truer self.

He realized then that he did not fear death as others did; perhaps he never had. In truth he longed for it with a terrible desire that pulled at his heart and touched every cell of his body with a bittersweet pain. Ever since that terrible day fourteen years before when the slow evil had befallen the Devaki tribe, he had longed to journey with Haidar and Chandra and Choclo and all the other blessed members of his family to the other side of day where the stars sear the sky with their bright and ageless eyelight. And now, with the last breaths of those whom he had loved most calling to him in the wind outside the cathedral, he would finally find a way to join them.

To die and die and die and . . . .

And so once again he fell into the dark, cold cavern that opens inside everyone's soul. He felt a force greater and more ancient than gravity pulling at every atom of his being; inside his heart and belly and brain, a terrible spinning blackness nauseated him even as it dazzled his mind's eye with its dark, glittering lights and sucked him downward. He knew that he could will himself to die, if only he could find the way. There were secrets to life, and thus to death. Many of the yogin branch of the cetics, in their quest for ultimate control over the bodymind, had developed techniques to still the breath and stop the heart from beating. As little more than a child, he himself had remembered the Alaloi art of *lotsara* in which the body's last reserves of fat could be burned in a sudden blaze of heat that might keep one from freezing to death. And on Tannahill, in the Hall of Heaven, he had looked deep inside himself to find the source of his will and the secret of his self. He had fallen ever deeper into the void where pure consciousness wells up out the blackness like a stream of shimmering lights, thence to coalesce and become the elements that moved the thoughts through his brain. Almost, he had found this blessed place. And he had almost died. And now, like a lightship falling through the luminous layers of the manifold toward the center of the universe, he must finally go on to the very end of his journey.

White bright light shimmering blazing becoming all that is I am Danlo son of Haidar and Chandra and Katherine and Mallory Ringess my father myself floating in a dark and sunless sea of burning salt and streaming blood of my mother my life myself connected heart to beating heart wordless and whisperless in love always in love beyond love beyond . . .

He began to remember himself, then. Even as Hanuman consulted with Krishnan Kadir and other pilots and war raged across the heavens, Danlo remembered many beautiful and terrible things about his life. It was strange, he thought, that falling into himself toward extinction was also a falling into memory. And stranger still that the end of his journey was also his beginning. For even as he had on the night in Bardo's house when he had first drunk the blessed kalla, he found himself reliving the moments in his mother's womb just before birth. Once again he tasted the salt of amniotic fluid in his mouth and felt his mother's heart beating through the soft, warm tissues of her belly that surrounded him; once again he felt wave upon wave of love pour through him every time his mother drew in a breath and her expanding diaphragm pressed down upon him like a soft, gentle hand. He remembered the story that the women of his tribe had told of his first moments of life, of how he had been born laughing. Well, then, now it was time that he laughed no more. Now, as he lay deep in remembrance on the carpet atop the sanctuary's cold stone floor, he once again awaited his birth even as he sought a way to die.

No, it is too hard. No, no, no, no . . .

He fell deep into remembrance, not just of himself but of things other and outside himself. In truth, throughout the spinning wheel of creation, at its deepest level there was neither inside nor outside, but only an intricate shimmering web of memory that connected all things. He began to see the way that the universe recorded all events and preserved and remembered itself. If matter was just memory frozen in time like sparkling drops of light, as the remembrancers believed, then memory was matter moving *through* time, always forming and reforming itself like waves upon the sea, always experiencing and evolving and carrying within all that has occurred to each living atom.

And so he finally began to understand the marvelous way of seeing things faraway in space and time that had first overcome him in the library so many years before; he understood the art of scrying as well as the beautiful and terrible vision that had built inside him as he had lain in his cell recovering from his torture. For all events occurred in the always cresting wavefront of the Now-moment where the future becomes the past. And matter, whether it be a spinning atom of carbon inside his brain or in the diamond hull of a lightship a billion miles away, preserved these waves. In truth, matter *was* these shimmering waves of memory, and the memory of all things was in all things.

Sunlight flashing off diamond hulls and black nall as hard as Bardo's battle armor covering his heart of the battle are lightships and thousands of blackships falling out of the manifold streaking through black space between the stars of the . . . .

Once again, Danlo found himself staring inside at a battle that occurred far away from him even as he closed his eyes and tried to stop himself from breathing. He saw the violence as it unfolded through spacetime, centered at a nearby star named Lidiya Luz. Around this flaming blue giant, Bardo had assembled the 240 lightships and twenty-five thousand other ships of his fleet. During the many days since the slaughter around Mara's Star, he had reorganized the pilots whom he led into twenty-five battle groups. Each group of approximately one thousand ships he had divided into ten sets; a single lightship pilot commanded the hundred other pilots of each set.

Against this swarm of black nall hulls and gleaming diamond ships were arrayed the thirty-four thousand ships of the Ringist fleet. Salmalin the Prudent, in the *Alpha Omega*, had finally brought Bardo to battle in the spaces of this hot blue star so near to the Star of Neverness. In his stolid and unimaginative way, he probably hoped that as the Sonderval had done around Mara's Star, Bardo would mass his ships and try to force a conclusion almost within light-seconds of the corona of Lidiya Luz.

But Bardo would not see his beautiful ships and pilots so easily destroyed. As the new Lord Pilot of the Fellowship fleet, he had devised for this final battle a radically new and fluid strategy. He intended to attack Salmalin's fleet across a broad, bright swath of stars. And so he had ordered three of his battle groups—the first, second, and twelfth—to fall immediately to the Star of Neverness to capture the great thickspace there and threaten the destruction of the Universal Computer. Cristobel the Bold, in the lovely *Diamond Lotus,* was to lead this daring maneuver while

Bardo himself and his other battle groups tried to confuse and
harry the rest of the Ringist Fleet. Ultimately, he hoped to trap
them and destroy them, perhaps even near the thickspace of the
Star of Neverness itself. It was a desperate hope, and only Helena
Charbo and a few other of his pilot-captains believed that his
strategy had even the slightest chance of succeeding.

*One thousand spun diamond needles sparkling opening win-
dows into flashing light streaking through black space inside
space and outside sixty-thousand blackships falling into the heart
of brightness inside stars exploding hydrogen oxygen and beautiful brains dying into brilliant blue-white light. . . .*

For a time Danlo watched as the battle opened within the brilliant visual field inside him. It had taken only a few thousand
seconds for the ships of both fleets to spread out from Lidiya Luz
to Ninsun and the Aud Binary and other stars around the Star of
Neverness. It was hard for him to apprehend this flashing violence
of ship falling against ship, for the twenty-five battle groups of the
Fellowship's fleet and the hundreds of cadres of the Ringists had
begun to fight each other across a huge volume of space many
light-years across and encompassing more than ten thousand
stars. Although only a few of these stars—those possessing thickspace of great enough density—would play any part in the maneuvers of the two fleets, the massive murder of human beings by
their fellow human beings on the 47th day of deep winter in the
year 2959 would come to be called the Battle of the Ten Thousand
Suns.

*Streaming photons spinning carbon melting vaporizing fusing
into white bright light. . . .*

Many fine pilots died that day in this terrible battle. And too
many of them were pilots whom Danlo had known and loved.
Danlo clenched his teeth in despair as Ivar Rey, in the *Flame of
God,* fell against Nitara Tal and was destroyed when a chance
explosion of a hydrogen bomb melted open his ship; he saw hundreds of blackships and too many lightships flare into incandes-
cence as they burned up in the fire of Lidiya Luz or Catabellin or
even the Star of Neverness. Nicolo li Sung died this way, as did
Matteth Jons and Ibrahim Fynn and the great Veronika Menchik
in the *August Moon.* Danlo watched as this steely-eyed woman
fought off three attacking lightships in blinding flashes of windows to the manifold opening and closing. And then one of the
Ringist pilots caught her in a mapping and forced her into the
violent, blazing heart of the Star of Neverness. He watched as
carbon atoms of her diamond-hulled ship vaporized and the hy-

drogen atoms of her brain exploded into light. And then he could watch no more. He didn't want to see any more pilots die; he didn't want to witness what seemed the Fellowship's inevitable defeat. Only one pilot, he thought, truly deserved death that day, and that was himself.

I have not gone deep enough; I have not yet remembered myself.

And so he returned from memory of the present to memory of the past. He fell deep into remembrance and found himself again floating in his mother's warm, dark womb. Salt water flowed all around him and pulsed inside him in dark, urgent streams with every beat of his little heart. He sensed that the secret of what he sought lay concealed at his life's very beginning like a diamond buried miles beneath the ocean's sands. All his awareness concentrated on these vital moments just before his birth.

And then he felt a hot, trembling fear burning through his belly as he realized that he wasn't really ready to be born. And this peaceful time before he would be forced outside his mother's body into the blinding light of the world wasn't really his true beginning. That marvelous moment had occurred many days earlier in shimmering streams of plasma and interlocking DNA as his father's and mother's sex cells had joined in ecstatic union. In truth, it had occurred long before. For if he had finally become himself in all the dreams of this unborn manchild curled up in darkness and waiting to discover light, then surely he had been almost equally himself a day before. And a day before *that* day, and ten days, and twenty.

Surely at all the stages of his life going backward from his fetushood to a quivering ball of explosively dividing cells, he had always been himself, for what else could he ever be? As a bluestar diamond was always a diamond, flawless and hard and sparkling brilliantly no matter how its many facets were cut, so his essential selfness shined from whatever form he took on or came from. Even as a zygote, all his selfness was in this single fertilized cell. And it was in the two cells from which the zygote had formed and even in the cells that made the blessed sperm and egg: in some sense his selfness was in his father and mother, and in the fathers and mothers who made them.

If he looked deeply enough and dared to journey far back towards his true origin, he would find himself in the sand and in the salty waters of the world that had made all his father's fathers and the mothers of his mother. And even as he had emerged into the world all bloody and laughing out of the torn tissues of his mother's body, so the world had been born out of the shining dust that swirled between the stars. If he went far, far back into the past and into himself, his beginning must lay with the beginning of the universe itself. All his being was in the universe, and no-where else. All his selfness was in this greater Self in which he lived and moved and dreamed of death.

I must move myself, he thought. *Movement is the great secret.*

For a long time Danlo lay paralyzed on the cold floor almost completely unaware of Hanuman as he consulted with the Ede imago and interfaced the Universal Computer in order to slaughter as many pilots of the Fellowship fleet as possible. Once or twice, breaking upon his interior visual field like rocket fire in a dark night, images of pilot's faces being blasted with laser light flashed before him. He saw flesh falling away from bone in burning, bloody hunks and lightships falling uncontrollably through black bowels of the manifold. He saw blackships spinning helplessly in space and windows opening upon the interior hell of blue giant stars, and he wanted to scream at the sheer horror of it all. But at last he closed himself to the terrible vision that opened inside him and out, and he managed to concentrate on the task that lay before him:

But how do I move so that it all falls silent and still and I move no more?

How did his heart move? What moved his belly so that he could draw in breath after breath of harsh, cold air? At first, with all a child's naive hopefulness (or black despair), he had thought that he might simply will his heart to stop beating. In his mind, he would form an image of a bunched, red muscle the size of his fist seizing up and dying, and never again would he feel the surge of blood exploding through his chest. But when he looked deep down the moist, lightless corridors inside himself now, he saw that his heart did not move according to the commands of his brain or mind. Or rather not *only* this way.

For the heart's measured beat, he saw, originated from centers inside itself. There was a place near the juncture of a great blood-vessel and the right atrium where a small mass of specialized muscle cells formed his heart's primary pacemaker. According to their design, moment by moment, the cells would fire and emit electrical impulses that excited the firing of other cells. And then this shock of biochemical fireworks would spread through the muscles of the atria and both ventricles in smooth, rhythmic waves, and thus the heart would pulse with life. The brain connected to the heart and influenced it through the vagus nerve, but even if this long bundle of fibers were cut, the heart would go on beating. And so if he were to die as he wanted to die, he would have to find the way out not through thought alone but rather through the deeper consciousness of his body. He would have to descend through all the dark and bloody layers of himself until he grasped the onstreaming consciousness of his very cells.

I am not I. I am salt and iron and carbon atoms spinning in the hemoglobin of my blood. I am neutrons and protons and leptons and quarks and strings and noumena down and down the chain of being into pure consciousness itself.

Once before, on Tannahill, he had made this journey. He had seen how all the matter of his body's cells was marvelously and indestructibly alive and burned in eternal awareness of itself. He had fallen deep into the heart of pure consciousness where all matter moved as a single, shimmering substance. Where matter *moved* itself, for ultimately all consciousness was in matter, and all matter blazed with the bright, numinous flame of consciousness, and there was no difference. And so he had found the way to will his mind to move and to look upon the heavenly lights within himself without falling mad. He had opened the door to a light inside light, the pure and primeval light inside all things. Only he had not been able to pass very far within. Although his great feat had won for him the title of Lightbringer, he had not been able to remain in the presence of this blessed light for it was too bright and it consumed all the tissues of his being as a star would burn up the wings of a butterfly. And now once again he stood at the threshold of all the infinite possibilities of life and death, but the golden door remained closed.

I am not I. I am the blood circulating endlessly throughout my body. I am hydrogen and nitrogen and oxygen that fills my lungs over and over, again and again. I am carbon atoms spinning inside my brain without end, without purpose, on and on and . . .

For a long time he dwelled in the twilight world of sheer existence, unable to go forward or back. He saw at last what Hanuman had understood long ago, after his hellish remembrance of the Elder Eddas: that there were always two ways to look at reality. And Hanuman's, he thought, must be the true way after all. Reality was really just hell, and existence was a torment of the eternal fire that licked at all things with its burning, red tongue. He himself, at his deepest level, wasn't really a man with two strong hands and blue eyes full of memories and dreams, but only endless atoms and electrons, only a tiny piece of the universe that existed always in a pure state of being.

In a way, the universe devoured his selfness as a thallow might rend apart a snowworm, and thus he existed as the universe did, without plan or purpose, but only to be. But to be *what?* To be only itself and nothing more. Truly, he thought, nothing was more than itself, and everything was nothing but pure being that buzzed and hissed and burned and quivered like a dark red heart muscle to the touch of electric impulses that came from nowhere but within itself. And everything existed in itself everywhere in the black infinities of space and time, and everywhere he looked, there was nothing but things existing in vast, countless profusion. Why was there not one star in the Milky Way galaxy or a hundred but more than a hundred *billion?* Why were there so many human beings swarming the stars like blinded insects writhing in flames when only a single man had all that he needed within himself to suffer and bleed and remember and rage at the essential agony of life?

I am not I. I am a hundred billion nerve cells writhing at the touch of the ekkana poison. I am trillions upon trillions of atoms spinning and vibrating and screaming down and down into a dazzling darkness without bottom or end.

Ultimately he was nothing but matter moving in pained and horrified consciousness of itself. Quarks and neutrinos, electrons and infons and whole atoms—it all took part in a mad, meaningless dance of matter rushing towards completion in itself that it could never quite reach. For a long time he stared into this glittering mirror of pure being; almost forever, it seemed, he looked for his own face or some other familiar object that might reassure him that at least one thing in all the universe existed as a finished work of art, inviolate, unchanging and charged with a purpose beyond itself. But all he saw was his eyes melting like cobalt marbles and his ivory-colored flesh decomposing and dissolving into infinitessimally tiny bits, some of them reddish-black like dried blood, some of them metallic green like a beetle's broken exoskeleton.

All matter continually and eternally crumbled apart like pieces of brittle tile, green and gold and chrome red, and reassembled a moment later into fantastic glittering tessellations. And in the next moment, these pointless creations shattered into dust, which melted and flowed together and fused into brilliant crystalline structures, only to fall apart again and again, a billion times each moment. A billion times in *one* moment, he looked inside to behold his face, looked for the wavering reflection of light against silvered glass to hold still for a single moment. But it all vibrated too quickly and splintered apart like a cathedral's stained glass windows bursting inward beneath the irresistible force of the wind.

No part of the universe was imperishable because all being was in time, and time broke apart all things like a boot suddenly stamping downward upon a thin layer of ice or a man's hands snapping apart an ivory chess piece carved into the form of a god. The deeper he looked into the quivering heart of reality, the stranger it all seemed, at once utterly ruthless and overpowering and yet utterly fragile like ice crystals fracturing and fractalling down to infinity, faster and ever faster.

The speed of his descent into matter's onstreaming consciousness terrified and sickened him. It made him almost frantic to die. Time was the great tormenter for each moment was connected to the next, inevitably, inexorably, endless moments of time, concatenations of moments forming up like pearls on an infinite silver strand only to fall off and disappear down into a black and fathomless hole. And there was no way out; there was no way to jump off the fiery wheel of creation as it spun wildly and dizzingly out of control. To be thus trapped in time was to be in hell, for what was hell if not the burning of matter in the moment, and one moment burning up into another, on and on without substance, meaning or end?

And Hanuman had always understood this. He had always seen that the universe, in all its breaking symmetries and insane oscillations, in all its shrieking and weeping and howling and praying, was always asking a single question, yes or no. And that the answer must finally be no because the universe was truly and essentially flawed. The very act of being demanded that matter continually consume and recreate itself in a perpetual perishing of forms. At its deepest level, movement itself was the source of all suffering and pain. To move was to be and thus eventually to decay and die. To move not, to find the still point of creation at the center of the wheel, would be to know the peace that all things sought but could never quite find.

And so Hanuman had striven to make a different kind of universe outside and beyond this insane inferno that caught innocent children in the heat of deadly fevers or in the flesh-searing rain of radiation from exploding stars. And Danlo finally understood this, too. Deep in his bones, deep in his blood, he finally understood this strange and tragic being who gazed off into infinity with his pale, *shaida* eyes and wore a glittering computer about his head. For long ago he and Hanuman had come from the same brilliant star and their souls were made of the same fiery substance, which is why they loved and hated each other so deeply.

I am not I. I am Hanuman li Tosh. I am he, and he is I, and there is no difference. Oh, Hanu, Hanu—I never truly saw you. I never knew who you truly were.

At last, as he lay like a corpse on the floor of the sanctuary, he saw how desperately Hanuman wanted to die. But Hanuman couldn't die, *wouldn't* die, because even as he suffered in the hell of his own being, he retained a crucial sense of his own selfness. He grasped onto this like a child clutching his father's hand at the edge of a cliff while a lake of fire opened below him. He was terrified to let go and perish in the flames and yet he couldn't find the courage to climb up to where his father waited in the sun.

For an eternity, it seemed, Danlo hung suspended in the same hellspace with Hanuman. He fell and fell while burning atoms of consciousness swirled all about him and through him, and yet it seemed that he didn't move at all. He, too, wanted to die. He must die, he would *will* himself to die because there was no reason that he should live. To end his life would be to disappear utterly into the neverness of pure being, and he had never feared this kind of personal extinction as did Hanuman.

He was as Hanuman li Tosh, truly, but he was also Danlo the Wild, Lightbringer, son of the sun—and son of Mallory wi Soli Ringess. Death itself held no terror for him. But he was afraid of something else, something that he could feel beginning to move inside him but couldn't quite see. All brilliantly white like a star it shined, and it waited for him in all its infinite wildness and terrible beauty. It waited inside behind the same closed door as did death, and he knew that he would have to face it if he were to join Jonathan and all the fathers and mothers of his tribe on the other side of day.

One door and one door only opens upon the death that I long for. Why, then, can't I find the key to open it? What is it that I truly fear?

In the red chaos that swirled and crackled all around him like the flames from his son's funeral pyre, a golden door appeared. It floated just beyond his reach limned around its four edges with brilliant white light. It was the doorway to his deepest self, he knew, and if he wished to find the ultimate key to consciousness and will his heart to stop beating, he must open it and go all the way inside.

Danlo, Danlo, ti alasharu la shantih—*make the journey and find peace on the other side of day.*

Except for the rising of his belly with every involuntary breath that kept him alive, he lay nearly motionless beneath the long windows of the sanctuary. The wind howled outside the cathedral, and he heard voices calling him. But, strangely, when he listened with his deepest senses, the cries and whispers that pulled at his heart came not from outside but from within. Haidar and Chandra and all his brothers and sisters were calling him to go over and join his tribe in death. His father was calling him, and his mother, too. And Jonathan. They were all calling him to remember how they had suffered that he might live even as they called for him to find a way out of the fear that had captured him so totally.

Danlo, Danlo—the only way out is in.

One voice rose above all the others on the cold wind that blew through his soul. It was a high, harsh voice, a terrible and beautiful voice, and it belonged to Ahira, the great snowy owl who was his other-self. Ahira called him to find his courage and find the way out of the fiery cage of his being; he called him to remember who he truly was and thus to remember the one thing that truly mattered.

Danlo, Danlo—the only way out is in toward the center of yourself. But to go there you must first remember the answer to the riddle.

Lightning flashed inside him then, and for a moment he thought that some great secret had been revealed to him. But it was only the working of his other-sight; it was only the radiance of another window to the manifold flashing open and capturing a lightship within the fires of a fierce blue giant star. He lay stunned and shaking at the sufferings of all who had died before him, and he couldn't remember the first of the Twelve Riddles let alone the answer to it.

And then Ahira's high, terrible cry came clear inside him: *How do you capture a beautiful bird without killing its spirit?*

And suddenly he knew that he must know the proper response to this question and he always had. The answer was in the snow and wind and in the blood-stained rocks of the cave where he had been born. It was in the earth of the burial ground of the Devaki tribe and in a single cell of algae in the belly of a snowworm and in a flake of ivory from a broken god. *The memory of all things is in all things.* To solve the riddle he must look within the carbon atoms of his mother's diamond sphere and in the diamond ring of his father that he now wore upon the little finger of his hand. And he must look inside himself. In his deep blue eyes he would see shimmering the riddle's second line, and he would hear its music in his blood; he would feel it streaming through his heart in a molecule of oxygen that had formed a part of Jonathan's dying breath.

The answer lay buried deep inside him like four perfect diamonds. All he had to do was to reach inside the inferno of his being and wrest these beautiful jewels from the fire. Four words, four simple words that his grandfather had been unable to utter because he had died during Danlo's passage to manhood just before he could tell him the answer—and now Danlo must remember these terrible words that he had never heard. Could he do it? He *must* do it; he must will himself to remember or he would never complete the journey that he had begun so long ago.

How do you capture a beautiful bird without killing its spirit?
And the answer came to him:
By becoming the sky.

And then at last the door opened. A blast of fire fell over him and suffused him with its terrible energies, and he crossed the threshold into the source of life and death. At last he let go of Danlo the Child and Danlo the Pilot and Danlo Peacewise and Lightbringer—and all the other many selves who had imprisoned his deepest and truest self. He looked toward the sky and the stars and all the shimmering heavens, and he burned to hold the terrible and beautiful being who he truly was.

Blue inside blue inside . . .

Only, could he truly hold it? The oneness that underlay all consciousness and material reality burned so brightly that it blinded him and melted away his body, mind and soul. It blazed with a light inside light that was infinitely brilliant, infinitely clear, infinitely deep. This marvelous unity was paradoxical in its essential nature, for it dwelled within itself beyond time and the multiplicity of the outer universe. It moved continually in patterns more beautiful than the rose windows of the cathedral, and yet at every point was as still and silent as the new-fallen snow. It was more empty than the black void between the galaxies and yet utterly full like a blue porcelain bowl overflowing with kalla. It was the neverness between moments of time, truly, and yet it contained the possibilities of all things. It was everywhere the same, like water in an infinite ocean, and like water, indivisible, in the sense that dividing water into liters, drams or drops would only ever yield more water. And even more the One was like liquified jewels, as if infinite numbers of diamonds and emeralds and firestones had melted into a single, superluminal substance whose every point and part reflected the light of every other.

Infinite possibilities.

All things had their source and being in this numinous oneness; all things came out of it like a thallow chick from an egg. At the still point of creation, the One waited in eternal and utter motionlessness and yet also burned to move and be. And here was the ultimate paradox: the One was all bliss and peace, the very essence of peace, and yet it was at utter war with itself. Out of a fundamental polarity and opposition of identical parts, it was always asking a single question, yes or no? And the answer everywhere in all its shimmering infinity was always yes, for only out of this eternal war in heaven could things come to be.

And so the undifferentiated oneness differentiated itself into all things. This essential tension gave birth to movement, the great cosmic dance, the dance of Shiva, creator and destroyer. In the violence and pain of falling into time, the One flowed like liquid light, forever onstreaming, forever swirling and forming itself into sparkling vortices more beautiful than any firestone or diamond. In the same way that plasma vortices built up larger and larger structures inside a star, so these vortices of ur-consciousness whirled and danced and spun together into infons and strings and the many-colored quarks and all other aspects of material reality.

Infinite possibilities.

And all this creation was preserved through memory. In a sense, memory *was* consciousness itself, or rather that part of the universal consciousness that preserved the manifestation of the One as matter. Matter was memory, truly, and evolution was the wild-energy dance of matter as it flowed into marvelous new forms and learned how to become more and more complex, and thus ever more alive. All matter held the memory of the evolving consciousness of the universe itself. All that had ever happened in universe—whether the birth of a star in the Sculptor Group of galaxies or the death of a child on the sands by a frozen sea—was recorded in streams of photons or in a black diamond pilot's ring or in a snowflake spinning in the wind. The memory of all things was in all things, and there were infinite secrets locked up inside matter, inside rocks and oceans and driftglass—and even inside a single red blood cell spinning and burning inside a man's heart.

Infinite possibilities.

And so at last Danlo found the center of the universe: the center of himself. For in an infinite universe, every point in space-time is the center. And at last he saw that he could end it all whenever he chose. Just as the universe eternally asked the question yes or no at every moment and point within itself, so did he. Yes or no, no or yes—there was always a choice. *For in the end we choose our futures,* his mother had said. He could choose death, or he could choose life, here and now as he held his breath and lay motionless on the floor.

No, no—it is too hard. But I have promises to keep.

For a long time he lay silent as he listened to the voices inside him. The great orcas and the other whales who swam in the cold oceans and dived beneath the icebergs breathed only in full consciousness of life's every breath; these great gods of the deeps could simply stop breathing and die at will whenever they chose, and he knew that he could, too.

Danlo, Danlo, ti alasharu la shantih—*die to yourself so that your deepest self might be born.*

The wind outside the cathedral drove particles of oxygen against the windows, and inside him, his chest burned to draw in a breath of cool, sweet air.

No, I cannot. No, no—I am afraid.

He heard voices outside, the faroff drone of Hanuman speaking with yet another of Salmalin's emissaries about the slaughter of the Ringist fleet. And even farther away (but very near), the screams of pilots dying by fire rang out through the universe. And inside him sounded still other voices, the most terrible voices of all. For an eternity, it seemed, he held his breath as he listened for the ten thousandth time to Jonathan calling him across a cold, windswept beach and the frozen sands of his soul.

Please, Father.

He wanted to die, then. He came as close as a breath of air and a single moment in time from making the journey to the other side of day. It was his son who stopped him. For strangely, Jonathan was calling him not to die but to live. He held his breath and felt his heart thunder in his chest, once, twice, three times, and then he heard his other children calling for him to live, too. All his sons and daughters who waited to be born out of his body and being were calling him from the future to find his courage and at last open his eyes. All his children's children down through the ages and across the shimmering stars were calling for him to embrace his own terrible beauty at last and bring them into life.

Please, Father. Father, Father—please.

When he listened deeply enough to the spinning molecules of air trapped in his lungs, it seemed that all things from across space and time were speaking at once inside him. He listened to the wind and the silence of ice out in the great loneliness of the sea; he listened to the dreams of a snowworm sleeping in its frozen burrow and to the screams of a mother giving birth to her child. All the pilots falling in their lightships and all the people bleeding and starving across the Civilized Worlds were trying to tell him something if only he had the courage to understand. In the light-rent spaces far above Neverness, the little makers and the other beings of the Golden Ring were whispering to him the one thing that truly mattered, and he heard this single word as well in the fiery exhalations of the stars. At every point and at every moment throughout creation, the whole universe was calling him to live and to cry out in his heart a clear, single sound.

Yes.

And once again he remembered himself and found himself floating inside his mother in the first moments after his conception. His whole being burned with the terrible will of the zygote, this single shimmering cell that trembled to explode into life with all the infinite possibilities that lay coiled inside itself. *Yes, I will,* he said, and the sound rippled through sparkling cytoplasm into the heart of the nucleus. And then like a ray of light he fell through space and time and relived other moments in his life: he was a child sitting on his mother's lap as she fed him bloody gobbets of meat, and he was a slightly older child kneeling in the snow over the torn body of a hare, the first animal that he had ever killed. And he was a young man brewing bowls of blood tea to preserve the lives of the dying Devaki and then a full man pushing his spear into a bear's great roaring heart so that he might give this blessed animal's life into Jonathan's. In the Hall of Heaven he sat on a massive golden chair as he looked at the numinous lights within himself, and he sat on another chair in a cold, dark cell as a warrior-poet injected him with the hellish ekkana drug and tore the nails from his bloody fingers. And at last he stood upon the red-carpeted altar of the cathedral as Hanuman broke the ivory white god that he had carved. And then the great, shuddering stained-glass window above them suddenly caved inward again, and he covered Hanuman's body with his own in order to save his life. And all these moments, he saw, were just the sum and substance of his own blessed life. Nothing could be added, nothing subtracted. He was the ashes from a pyre drifting in the wind and a star being born in the oceans of the night. He was Danlo the Wild, Lightbringer, son of his father—and son of Ten Thousand Suns. And his whole life was interwoven with all that had ever been and all that would ever be.

Yes.

Truly, he was the universe, and the universe was he, and there was no difference. Inside his blood, inside the fiery cells of his brain, he felt the forces of space and time driving him to become who he truly was and whatever dread shape he had been born to be. Only what did the universe *want* him to be? What did the universe, through him, want itself to be? *Something marvelous,* he thought. *Something bright and blazing with infinite compassion and a love beyond love.* But it was also something that dazzled the night with its terrible beauty and lived by talon and beak in all its fierce and utterly ruthless will toward life. It was utterly wild—all white and wild like the *sarsara* wind that blew through the sky.

God, he remembered, was a great white thallow whose wings touched at the far ends of the universe. And God was sleeping but would one day wake up and behold himself, and then all of creation would ring with his joyous cries. And it was this awakening that terrified Danlo. He feared this infinite being for nothing could be added or subtracted from it, either. It called to him from the future and across the ages even as it had called him into life long ago; it cried out for him to open his eyes and spread his wings and take his place with all the thallows and other birds soaring through the deep blue sky.

"Yes, I will," he whispered. He moved his lips, slightly, and the breath came rushing out of him. "Yes, I will."

And with this almost silent affirmation, the heavens opened. Time stopped, and something impossibly bright spread out like an exploding star across the inner sky of his being. It streaked down like a bolt of lightning and struck straight into his head, heart, belly and loins—and every other particle of him—all in a moment beyond time. This holy lightning wrapped itself around his spine as it crackled and writhed and electrified all his nerves out to his fingertips and toes. It burned into his muscles and bones with a fire so infinitely hot that he felt neither pain nor fear but only joy, sheer joy.

"Yes," he said, and he felt this ecstatic golden fire touch each one of his body's four trillion cells, all at once. It was as if a single, shimmering substance were flowing into each individual cell and filling it to bursting with the essence of love and light. And all these simultaneous ecstasies were not separate events, but rather interconnected, every cell feeding the fire of every other so that the whole of his bodysoul came alive in a single moment of pure, singing light. The brilliance of it utterly consumed him. Like a snowflake beneath a blazing sun, he vanished into the sky.

He died to his little self and came whirling, spinning, dancing, shimmering into the infinite light inside light that illuminated all things.

"Yes, yes, yes!"

And the longer he dwelled within this One light, the brighter it grew. It expanded outward in all directions in an infinite, luminous sphere that blazed like ten billion suns. Its numinous fire touched everything around him: the marble floorstones, the ivory and shatterwood chess pieces, the long glass windows sparkling and opening upon the nighttime sky. Not *touched:* the light came from inside these things as if every bit of the world were emptying itself out into its own blazing glory. Every atom of creation sang out at once in its own ecstatic, shimmering dance, for each atom held all the infinite possibilities of life, and something truly marvelous was being born, in each moment of time, always and forever being born.

"Yes, yes, yes!"

And here was the deepest marvel of this One light: he was only an infinitessimal part of it, melting into it with a perfect joy, and yet he was the whole of it, too. His whole being cried out in completion and utter triumph, for all memory was his, all matter, all space, all time. All the power and possibilities of the universe waited within for him to shine his consciousness in a single direction. He felt the universe remaking itself inside his blood and bones, in fire and light, with a love beyond love, but it was really he who shaped himself. "Yes," he whispered, and his consciousness spread out and moved deep into him like honey soaking into hot bread, and suffused each of his cells in a golden light. He willed himself to be and become, and he had never felt so perfectly and totally alive.

"Yes—I will."

He wanted to move, then. He wanted to jump up off the carpet and raise his hands to the heavens as he cried out in all the wild joy of life. Only he could not move because the warrior-poet's drug still paralyzed him. That is, he could not move the muscles of his chest or belly, his arms and his legs. But his onstreaming consciousness moved with his own will, and that was the final secret of all matter and being. And now this consciousness was waking up all the cells in his body.

He could feel it tingling and burning, in the neurons of his brain and spine, of course, but also in his skin cells and the cells that lined his guts, and in the bone cells that spun out collagen proteins and layed down mineral crystals that sparkled in lovely patterns and gave structure to his deepest tissues. He felt it singing through his sex cells and in his blood as his whole body began to vibrate at a higher frequency. And deeper still, in each cell's nucleus, the long, dark strands of DNA were uncoiling and vibrating a billion times each moment as chromosomal segments that had never been active turned on and came alive to their true purpose. Once, according to the theories of the Society of Courtesans, Tamara had called this DNA the "sleeping god." It was the dream of her Society that someday men and women would find a way to awaken this god and embrace the secret of life. And then all the possibilities of evolution would be theirs, and they would move into the future in full consciousness and will to become true human beings—or perhaps something more.

Infinite possibilities.

Inside the cells of Danlo's muscles and bones, he felt the mitochondria pulsing out energy like tiny stars; in the cells of his pituitary gland he felt the DNA begin to sing and dance and move in strange new ways. It moved, too, in his hypothalamus and pancreatic islets and especially in his pineal gland behind his third eye. Millions of double helixes of DNA were unravelling and exposing the chains of adenine, thymine, guanine and cytosine molecules that coded for the production of proteins. In human beings, twenty amino acids from serine to tryptophan could be woven like multi-colored threads in almost countless ways to form tapestries of proteins of astonishing complexity. The cells of his body could make cortisol and melatonin and enzymes and endorphins that would act upon his nervous system like drugs. And his cells could make antagonist proteins to neutralize these chemical compounds. Somewhere along the millions of miles of DNA strands that quivered inside his cells must lie the secret of making an antidote for the drug that still paralyzed him.

Yes, the secret, he thought. *Matter, memory, mind.*

With his mind's eye and the consciousness of his deepest self, he looked down into the marvelous matter that shimmered at the center of his cells. He looked and touched and moved, moved himself—and he felt long chains of polypeptides and sparkling new proteins beginning to burn through his blood.

Yes, yes, the secret: moving, making, metabolizing.

The burning spread out through his arms and into his fingers with every beat of his heart. Once, twice, three times his heart beat—a hundred times, two hundred. And the flush of sensation swelled hotter and hotter and touched every part of him. After a while it grew so intense that he felt as if a new dose of ekkana had been injected into his veins; as with the thawing of iced limbs after frostbite, the pain of his reawakening tissues almost made him want to scream.

Pain is the awareness of life, he remembered. *Pain, yes, always pain.*

And then he surrendered utterly to this blessed pain and felt it fade into the total awareness of his being. He shuddered as the fire of life swept through his nerves and tendons deep into his cells. He felt his arms begin to tremble, and beneath the black silk of his kamelaika, the muscles of his thighs quivered and burned to move. And suddenly he knew that the full power of his body (and perhaps much more) had been almost restored to him.

The secret is always in movement, he thought. *To move is to be.*

And so at last he opened his eyes. The sanctuary's flame globes drenched the objects of the room in a glorious, golden light. He looked upon the mantelets and sulki grids, and even the gleaming optical computers, and he smiled. He slowly turned his head to see the imago of Nikolos Daru Ede beaming forth from the devotionary computer that remained resting on the shatterwood dining table. A few feet away, Hanuman stood as still and silent as a stone statue. His eyes stared upon nothing, and his breathing was labored and shallow. Around his head, the diamond clearface glittered as millions of the threadlike, purple neurologics flared into radiance. No longer did the imagos of various pilots appear within the sanctuary to report on the progress of the battle. Now, as the lightships of Kantu Darden and Dyami wi Shiva Alaret and others fell out into realspace above Neverness, they beamed their communications straight toward the radio receivers built into the Universal Computer itself.

Lightships like flashing swords slicing open windows to the space beneath space and blackships spinning falling through dead black space into the fire that calls all things with a single sound singing and sighing and screaming, yes, yes, yes . . .

Danlo, still lying on the cold, stone floor, looked up through the sanctuary's windows at the brilliant lights that fractured the sky. He realized that he had spent most of the night paralyzed and struggling to live or die. And then he looked through a different and clearer window to see the ships of both the Ringist and Fellowship Fleets spread out from Neverness to Veda Luz across a bright arc of ten thousand stars. The final battle of the war was being fought in bursts of laser fire flashing from ship to ship and in lovely lightships spinning down into the fire of the stars. It was being fought through the streets of Neverness as well. Danlo felt the explosions that shook the buildings of the Old City, and he heard the ping of steel bullets striking into stone; he saw waves of Benjamin Hur's ringkeepers break upon the cathedral's great wooden doors as they attempted to storm the cathedral and force their way inside. They knew, as everyone in the city now did, that Mallory Ringess had returned from the stars holding in his hands the final secret of life and death.

Yes—the secret, Danlo thought. *How does my body move? As my body moves, so I move within the dance of the universe. As my body moves, so I move the universe.*

Almost with a single motion, he drew in a deep breath and sprang to his feet. And then he turned his face into the light of the stars and smiled.

LOVE

What is done out of love occurs beyond good and evil.
— Friedrich the Hammer

Danlo moved with all the terrible quickness and quiet of a snow tiger, and he felt as light as a thallow soaring through the sky. He looked toward a still-unaware Hanuman and the door that opened upon the cathedral just beyond him. He knew that he must reach this door at the first chance, and if necessary, use the powerful muscles and bones that Constancio had sculpted to break it down.

One door, and one door only, opens upon the golden future that I have seen.

Almost like a great white bear stalking a seal, he took a step closer to the door, and then another. The Ede imago, of course, had watched Danlo come alive again from the first flicker of his eyes. And now this being of light and ancient programming caught Danlo's gaze and held it for a single, endless moment.

Be silent, Danlo prayed. *Be silent as a feather floating in the wind.*

A third step he took, and then a fourth, and still the Ede imago remained motionless as the devotionary computer furiously calculated probabilities and ran its maker's program. And then Ede's famous face fell through the emotions of surprise, suspicion and fear, and he suddenly cried out, "Lord Hanuman—he moves! Lord Hanuman, Lord Hanuman, please, Lord Hanuman!"

Almost instantly Hanuman broke interface with the Universal Computer and whirled to look upon Danlo. Shock spread across his pale eyes and features like fracture lines through thin ice. He stared at Danlo in instant, if astonished, understanding that Danlo had somehow overcome the warrior-poet's paralytic drug. His face froze into a mask of hate, for he saw that Danlo brought the one thing that he had always feared. Time almost stopped, and he stared and beheld the new life that pulsed through Danlo's body; he stared and stared, and in Danlo's deep, blue eyes, he saw blazing the light of ten thousand suns.

"Lord Hanuman! Lord Hanuman!"

In an eternal, golden moment beneath time and beyond the starry night, Danlo and Hanuman looked upon each other at last and saw themselves as they truly were. Their fate opened before them like the final pages of a book that they had written together with every act of their separate but mysteriously intertwined lives. It had always been Hanuman's will to love his fate no matter how tragic or terrible, and now it had become Danlo's will, too.

Ti-anasa daivam.

"Lord Hanuman! Lord Hanuman!"

And then time came rushing in again to fill the moment, and the spell was broken. Hanuman moved at last with a frightening speed and will to triumph in his purpose. And so did Danlo. In truth, he sprang at Hanuman even as Hanuman formed his hands into fists and fell into the motions of his killing art that he had studied since his childhood. He fell upon Danlo in a fury of fists and flying feet as he tried to strike straight for the death place deep in Danlo's throat.

"Lord Hanuman, Lord Hanuman—kill him, now!"

Danlo met Hanuman's attack with a smile upon his lips and a terrible power coursing through his hands. He had no art nor strategy beyond trying to fend off Hanuman's blows as he closed with him. He moved his arm up and felt boot leather and bone crack against bone; he moved to the right and then quickly to the left, and his whole body quivered and shook in sudden pain. He collided with a table, and thirty-one ivory and shatterwood chess pieces went flying out into space; he banged into an optical computer and felt hard steel grind against the vertebrae of his back.

And all the while Hanuman came at him with his knees and elbows and his long fingernails slashing and stabbing at Danlo's face. Something broke, then. The heel of Hanuman's hand slammed against Danlo's nose, and he felt (and heard) the bone come apart inside his head with a sickening crunch. Blood sprayed out of his nostrils as if he were a snorting shagshay bull pierced with a spear. He grunted and growled in pain and tried to catch Hanuman's hand in his own, but Hanuman was too quick, and with his hard little fist he struck again and again, straight at the soft part of Danlo's belly beneath his heart.

"Kill him, Lord Hanuman! You can kill him but he can't kill you!"

But Danlo was not so easy to kill. The blow to his nose might have stunned another man into unconsciousness, but Constancio had built the bones of his face as heavy and thick as slabs of granite. His will to life, strengthened by wind and fire and frozen water, surged up out of his being like an ocean in storm. From far away (but impossibly near), he heard Jonathan calling him, and his father, too. And now his other-self had come fully awake inside him; now Ahira cried out across the heavens in all the wild joy of life. In the full flush of *animajii* that fired his cells, he managed to catch Hanuman's forearm in his hand. As they wrestled and lunged about, he felt the thinness of the bones there, the muscles wasted from too many moments spent interfacing various computers. His grip about Hanuman's arm grew tighter and tighter like the closing jaws of a tiger. And then he remembered something, the first and only principle of the doctrine of ahimsa:

Never killing, never harming another even in one's thoughts.

He might have let go Hanuman's arm, then, but he heard Jonathan calling for him to remember why he had come into life and who he truly was.

Please, Father, Jonathan said. *Please live.*

And so with the wildness pouring like starlight out of his eyes and an infinitely sad smile playing upon his lips, with an astonishing savagery he suddenly twisted Hanuman's arm and broke the two bones. He heard the snap through Hanuman's skin and the cold, swirling air. As if his own arm had broken, he felt himself the jagged bone ends suddenly cutting through muscles and nerves deep inside. The pain of it was so horrible that he wanted to scream. But Hanuman, clenching his teeth together in rage and pain, did not cry out, at least not in words or in the rushing breath of life. Instead he looked at Danlo as silently as a cetic, and his pale blue eyes wavered with agony, hatred, love, furious will and sudden understanding.

And then Danlo caught Hanuman's other arm and broke that as well. He worked his way up behind Hanuman and wrestled him down to the floor. With a sudden giving of gravity and a series of cracks, their limbs struck the hard stones. The force of the fall pushed one of Hanuman's arm bones through the skin and the silk of his golden robe. Like a knife, it cut open Danlo's hand. He felt Hanuman's blood burning into his blood; he felt Hanuman's breath leaving his body in hard, quick gasp and breaking upon his own.

"Kill him!" the Ede imago shouted to Hanuman. Apparently he had begun to doubt Danlo's devotion to ahimsa, for he went on, "Kill him quickly before he finds the way to kill you!"

Hanuman, however, lying on his side with one arm pinned beneath him, could scarcely move much more than his lips. Al-

most like a tiger trapping a lamb, Danlo bore down upon him
from above. His knees drove hard against Hanuman's legs; the
weight of his great muscles and bones ground Hanuman's slender
body into the floor.

Never killing another, Danlo remembered. And then a different and deeper voice called urgently inside him: *Please, Father.
Please live so that my brothers and sisters might live, too.*

Danlo looked down upon Hanuman, and the blood from his
broken nose trickled down into Hanuman's face. Little drops like
red tears rolled across Hanuman's pallid skin. From the streets
outside and the cathedral below them came the sounds of laser
light hissing through air, exploding bullets and men and women
shouting. The clearface lit up around Hanuman's head then, and
Danlo guessed that he was interfacing some communications system, very likely sending out to his godlings within the cathedral a
call for help. Very soon, Danlo thought, Jaroslav Bulba or some
other ronin warrior-poet would mount the stairs from below and
burst through the door.

Remember who you truly are, Danlo heard a voice from far off
say. And then closer and more clearly: *I am not only I. I am this
one who dwells forever inside me like a thallow in the sky.*

Just then Hanuman's whole body convulsed in rage and hate,
and he tried to ram his diamond-jacketed head straight back into
Danlo's face. But Danlo twisted his head aside at the last moment, receiving only a glancing blow on his cheek. And then his
own wrath flowed up out of him into his hands. He slammed his
palm against the hard, smooth clearface and knocked Hanuman's
head back down to the floor. Almost as if his nails were talons, he
dug his fingertips into Hanuman's forehead along the line where
the clearface came up against the skin. With a single, savage
motion, he ripped the clearface away from Hanuman's head and
hurled it clattering across the room.

The force of this act tore loose the patches of glue that fastened the clearface to Hanuman's skull—and tore away as well
bloody patches of skin. Hanuman moaned for the first time, then,
and his eyes filled with panic and confusion. With his bald,
bloody head and in the helplessness of his broken body, he was
like a manchild who had been pulled too soon from the safety of
his mother's womb and cast naked and blind into the cold world.
His suddenly breaking interface with the Universal Computer
shook more than just himself: when Danlo looked deeply into the
black centers of Hanuman's eyes, he could see the effects of this

act rippling outward through space to the stars where the two fleets fought each other and into the greater universe beyond.

"Kill him!" Ede's high, whiny voice cried out. Danlo couldn't tell if Ede were speaking to Hanuman or to himself. "Kill him quickly!"

Never killing, Danlo thought for the ten thousandth time. He looked down at his hands, then. His right hand gripped Hanuman's free arm while his left pressed Hanuman's bleeding head against the floor. He remembered that with his right hand he had once given Hanuman his own robe against the cold of Lavi Square, and thus given him life. *It is better to die oneself than to kill.*

"Kill him! Kill him! Kill him!"

Please, Father, Jonathan whispered. *Please kill him so that the blessed people of the tribes and all those of the Civilized Worlds might live.*

Danlo saw then that there were essentially two ways that the universe might unfold: Hanuman's mad plan to make all things into a vast, black, *shaida* computer, or his own shimmering, golden path that he had dreamed now for so long. And the choice was his and his alone. He looked down at his left hand where his fingers touched the slippery wounds along Hanuman's forehead. He felt blood burning into his flesh and the fear that flashed through Hanuman's brain like lightning.

Ti-anasa daivam.

And then Hanuman looked up at him with his pale, *shaida* eyes and said, "Please, Danlo."

"No, I cannot," he finally said. For a moment, he didn't know whether Hanuman was asking to die or to live.

"Please, Danlo," Hanuman said again. "Please let me go."

"No, I cannot," Danlo said softly. "I am sorry, but I cannot."

Hanuman stared up at Danlo for a long time, and a deep knowledge passed between them. As Hanuman suddenly closed his eyes and began silently cursing his life (or perhaps praying), Danlo listened to the high and terrible voice inside him that kept calling for Hanuman's death. At last, with tears half-blinding his eyes, he nodded his head sadly and whispered, "Yes, I must. Yes, I will."

And then the universe moved. Through the hard stone of the floor, Danlo felt the pull of the planets and stars as they wheeled about the heavens in their age-old journey. Somehow, then, he moved his left hand over Hanuman's face. Instantly Hanuman shook his head back and forth in a furious effort to elude Danlo's grip. But Danlo clamped his hand over Hanuman's nose and mouth; with his steely thumb and forefinger squeezing shut his nose, he pressed his palm over his lips. He could feel the hot suck of air between his fingers as Hanuman's belly and chest worked desperately to draw in a breath. He felt Hanuman's jaws snapping shut and had to keep his hand rigidly cupped in order to avoid Hanuman's teeth. After a while the muscles writhing along Hanuman's neck began to seize up and cramp. With a muffled cry of pain, he ceased struggling for a moment. And Danlo pressed his head downward touching Hanuman's head, and he whispered, "Please, Hanu. Hanu, Hanu—please die quickly."

As he smothered Hanuman and stole the breath of life from his body, he felt tears burning out his eyes and touching the bloody wounds of Hanuman's forehead. And as before when they had first fought in the hot pool of Perilous Hall years ago, he felt the bond between them that could never be broken. In truth, their hearts still beat as one, and the mysterious connection of their souls had grown only deeper. His whole being was in Hanuman's, and Hanuman's in his, and they had fallen together deep into the same dread fire and burned with the same infinite pain. *Tat tvam asi,* he remembered. *That thou art.* Hanuman's desperate eyes shined with the same light as did his eyes, and each atom of his blood shimmered with the same superluminal substance. He could not harm Hanuman without harming himself; if he killed Hanuman, he knew that he would die, too.

Ti-anasa daivam.

"Hanu, Hanu," he whispered, "please die. Please die."

He almost relaxed his grip upon Hanuman's mouth, then. For a moment, he lifted up his head and stared down at Hanuman as he watched his pale skin begin to fall blue. He looked at the fine lines of his face and the incredible will to life that suddenly poured into his eyes. *Terrible beauty,* he thought. In the way that Hanuman stared into himself in defiance of everything in the universe except his own glorious self, there was something utterly terrible and yet utterly beautiful, too. He didn't know how he could take this beauty away from Hanuman; he didn't know how he could take this flawed but beautiful being away from life. For to be born into the world even as the sickest hibakusha child— deformed by mutagenic radiations and doomed to die—was an infinitely precious gift. Who was he to take it away from Hanuman—or from anyone?

I am only ever I, he thought. *I am the wild white thallow alone*

*in the sky. I am this one who watches inside me and has waited
ten billion years to be born.*

Who was he? He was the fire that burned in the distant stars;
he was the light inside light that shined through all things. Truly,
he was the universe in all its terrible beauty—as much a part of
the universe as anyone or anything. He was a marvelous, moving
array of trillions of shimmering atoms that loved the being named
Hanuman li Tosh. And hated him, too. At the deepest place inside
him, he felt neither anger nor rage toward Hanuman, but only
hate. But this was no ordinary hate. It was as wild as the wind, as
deep and dark and vast as the ocean at night. It was a hate so far
beyond hate that it was almost love: the love of a God who incarnates as Shiva to dance his cosmic dance and destroy all things so
that infinitely many new forms might be created.

Everything in the universe, he saw, must take part in this ecstatic, tragic, eternal dance. To deny this was to deny life itself. To
deny *himself* and to try to escape from life. And this, if he was to
say yes to his truest self and affirm all things, he would never do
again. Who was he, really? He was the lightning that tore open the
sky and scorched the wind-dried trees and grasses; he was the
mysterious fire that burned through a man's golden robes into his
flesh and soul. And he was the universe in all its infinite and
terrible compassion, that part of the universe fated to destroy a
man whom he had once loved as his brother.

Ti-anasa daivam.

He looked down into Hanuman's terrified eyes and tightened
his grip over his mouth. *"Mi alasharia la, shantih, shantih*—go to
sleep now, my brother, go to sleep."

And this, in the end, was the true way of the Ringess kind. His
grandfather and father had understood this terrible need to slay
and destroy, and perhaps his mother had as well. *Give; be compassionate,* she had once said. And now, as he felt Hanuman
shuddering and trying to cry out beneath the relentless pressure of
his hand, he had to give up all of himself in order to accomplish
this murderous deed. And now he, too, finally understood the
terrible requirements of this compassion.

"Please, Danlo," Hanuman pleaded with his eyes. A last light
lingered there as on an ending of a long day of grayness and
snow. Ever dimmer it grew, and yet there was something beautiful
and bright about it, almost as if Danlo were to watch and wait
long enough, he would behold in Hanuman the rising of the
morning sun. "Please, please."

True compassion, Danlo saw, could take many forms. Even as

Hanuman struggled desperately to live, a part of him desperately wanted to die. It had always been so with him. He, who had always felt the fire of pure being so keenly and hated life, had always stared longingly on the dark doorway within that led down into death. He must have understood the urge of all things eventually to die, and the hell that if they did, they were condemned to rebirth and endless existence, for the infinite, burning being of the universe was eternal and could never end. And thus life—his life and all life—went on and on forever, as well. If he could, Hanuman would say no to this blessed life and open the door. But there was truly no way out. In the end, all things must say yes. *Must* say. And so must Danlo, too.

"Danlo, Danlo."

As Danlo pressed his bleeding hand over Hanuman's mouth, he felt the molecules of Hanuman's stifled breath burning into his wound. Hanuman, he thought, was a tiny piece of the universe that was literally dying to return to itself. And Danlo was only another tiny piece who must hasten this journey. "No, I cannot," he whispered. And then, a moment later, "Yes, I must. Yes, I will." Hanuman, upon hearing this, murmured something deep in his throat. He shuddered and whimpered and tried to cry out in all his terrible pain. And Danlo shook his head against the tears blinding him and wanted to cry out, too.

"Hanu, Hanu," he whispered, as he watched the light dying in Hanuman's eyes, "please forgive me."

For an endless moment, Hanuman looked at him with his pale, anguished eyes, and then the universe opened again. A pain greater than any Danlo had ever known swept him down into darkness as if he had been caught in a maelstrom in the sea. It was as if the earth itself had moved and rolled over him, crushing his chest and belly. He felt his own breath suddenly choke off and his heart stop beating. Thus deprived of oxygen, soon his cells would begin to die, and his whole body would lie stiff and still. Soon, he knew, he would let go of Hanuman.

Perhaps this was only the last of his flickering mentations and awareness as a human being, his final vision before death. Or perhaps it truly *was* death itself. He felt something vast and irresistible grinding him, burning him, melting the tissues of his being, and then suddenly his consciousness and all his life began to flow outward into the world. He became the frost sparkling on the window-panes and the steaming blood caught in the cracks of the cold stone floor. He felt himself swinging through space as a spider suspended on a strand of silk in the corner of the room.

And further out, like water flowing down to the sea, he felt himself as a young godling lying helpless near the altar in the nave of the cathedral below. His body was an agony of broken and burnt parts, and he wept like a child as he tried to stuff his bloody intestines back into the wound that some bit of bursting metal had opened in his belly.

He died then, and he melted and moved into the hundreds of ringkeepers' bodies frozen to the icy streets outside. He flowed and spread out and seaped into the earth itself; he froze into ice crystals and evaporated into the wind, and he became: rocks and trees and bits of yellowed ivory washed up upon a lonely beach— and dreams and whispers and howls and cries of passion in the night. He felt himself as a killer whale swimming through the cold currents of the ocean and as a snowworm curled up with its mate beneath many layers of ice and snow. And at last he understood the answer to a question that had puzzled him all his life: what was it like to be a snowworm? Truly, it was like *something* to be such a simple and marvelous creature. It was like the warmth of algae being digested in the segments of his belly and the deep glow of his cells' consciousness that it was good to be alive. It was like something to be anything, even a virus or a particle of dust, and that was the deepest mystery of the universe.

Yes.

And so he became all these things, and much else as well, and he fell like a ray of light through the universe. His consciousness flowed and moved through the asteroids and comets, and blazed through Icefall's silvery moons. He was the marvelous shimmering matter of which the Universal Computer was wrought and the goswhales of the Golden Ring that basked in the brilliant light pouring out of the heart of the Star of Neverness. He lived as a pilot mapping a lightship through the great spinning thickspace on the far side of the sun, and he died screaming as another pilot as his blackship vanished into starfire and light. He saw—sensed/lived/became—six entire cadres of Ringist ships as Bardo's first, eleventh and twelfth Battle Groups trapped them near the Sitala Thin and began to annihilate them. In a sudden flash, he saw Bardo's strategy of ordered chaos unfold like a brilliant jewel-studded tapestry. He saw the entire right wing of Salmalin's fleet collapse and fly apart like diamonds spinning into the night. He became a carbon atom in the retina of Bardo's eye and in the hull of his ship, the *Sword of Shiva,* and he felt himself spinning off into the rainbow-colored space beneath space.

Yes.

And then he fell farther outward through space and time. He was ten trillion rays of light streaking through the Milky Way, out past Eta Carina and Tannahill and the ruined stars of the Vild. He became a bluebird singing the sunrise in a forest on Old Earth and a woman on Samuru burying her newborn child. He lived the lives of a billion Architects who had peopled the High Holy Ivi Planets, and he died the deaths of the entire race of alien Kalkinet caught in the explosion of a blue supergiant star. He vastened then, and he spread out and fell ever faster like uncountable streams of tachyons burning across the Magellanic Clouds into Draco, Fornax, Andromeda and the other nearer galaxies. And then he flowed into the Canes Venatici Cloud of galaxies and filled the whole of the Virgo Cluster with his blazing awareness.

On a strange, alien beach a million light-years away, he dwelled within himself as a grain of sand sparkling beneath a crimson sky. And farther out, past the Perseus and Coma Super-clusters, he fell upon an entire galaxy taken over by an alien god who resembled Hanuman in his infinite hubris if not his form. Every star and planet there had been converted into a vast computer similar to the Universal Computer in design. And in nearby galaxies that had no name that Danlo knew, he saw other gods fighting this insane god. He became these great gods of the stellar deeps whose beings were spread out over whole nebulas. They were like the Solid State Entity and Pure Mind and the April Colonial Intelligence, and they were creating weapons of incredible energy densities in order to destroy this alien god—and the entire galaxy that it had claimed as his own.

Ever outward across the stars Danlo fell, on and on past the ring galaxies and the lovely spirals shimmering like billions of diamonds in the night. And he melted and moved and shimmered ever vaster, and he became infinite in his being. For the universe itself was truly infinite, and there was no part of it—not the tiniest particle of dust or a hydrogen atom floating alone in space—into which his consciousness didn't flow and become one.

Yes.

And so at last he stood before the universe naked in his soul and saw it as it really was. He saw that if consciousness was just the flow of matter within his brain (or the vibrations of atoms within a rock), then the consciousness of the universe was just the flow of everything: rocks and photons and starfire and blood. And everywhere—in the Grus Cluster of galaxies no less a cathedral on a small, ice-bound planet—this flow grew ever more complex. This infinite organism that was the universe, in all its infinite patience and curiosity, brought forth endless new planets and peoples and stars blazing with infinite possibilities.

It was immeasurably old, and the number of years that it would continue to exist were immeasurable, too. Was the universe afraid to die? No more than it was to be born. This marvelous being evolved in utter ruthlessness toward itself, and yet also in utter love. How did a man, caught in the wind-whipped snow of a *sarsara* out on the icy sea, regard his frozen fingers? Lovingly but ruthlessly: he would cut them off in order to save his life. And so the universe would cut off the life of a man—or ten billion women and men—so that their children might grow and seize their glorious fate. Did a man mourn a half billion of his sex cells dying into the dark cavern inside a woman? No, he couldn't wait to rid himself of them so that he might rejoice as a single cell found its mate and blossomed like a fireflower into new life.

And so the universe was always making, using, and discarding parts of itself as it shedded life like old skin and stretched its arms out to the morning sun all smooth and golden and new. The universe always beheld itself from countless viewpoints; it was like a great spinning diamond cut with infinitely many facets that shimmered with a clear and perfect light. And in every moment of time, new facets were chiselled over the old so that the universe's vision of itself grew ever vaster, ever clearer and forever new.

Yes.

And now the tiny piece of protoplasm and pain who was Danlo wi Soli Ringess gazed into each of these mirrored facets, and he beheld, and he became. That was the miracle of the universe, that it was like a vast hologram in which the whole was reflected in every part. And in every part that he looked, he saw being everywhere, and beings, in all their uncountable trillions, filling the stars out to the ends of the universe. And he lived the lives of all of them. He became a Scutari seneschal, wise in his thousand years of life and fat from eating thousands of his offspring, and an Elidi birdman mating in freefall ecstasy with his wife as they soared together through a turquoise sky. And he felt the joy and the sadness of one of the last of the Ieldra, that noble race of gods who had died a million years ago; he lived again, and he felt the diaphonous, golden tissues of his body singing like lightsails in the solar wind as he moved from star to star to seed the galaxy with life.

Nothing is lost, he marveled. *The memory of all things is in all things.* And this, he saw, was a far deeper salvation than that of the Architect's cybernetic heaven or the Alaloi's primitive other-world of spirits who dwelt in the sky. For the universe preserved not only one's final self at the time of death, but each self from conception onward, the infant, child and full man, every moment of life.

Yes.

And each of these countless selves of all these countless beings had a face, or a form that Danlo perceived as a face. Once again he saw Jonathan laughing as he played with a sleekit in the snow, and his own mother screaming in agony as she gave birth to Danlo deep within the Devaki tribe's cave. Her eyes were his eyes, deep and dazzling like liquid jewels, and then after a moment of terror and blood, she lay eyeless in eternity as she died. He saw soft yellow lights and yet more blood as Hanuman was born on faraway Catava, and he saw Hanuman's face fall blue as he lay crushed and dying beneath Danlo's driving weight. And Hanuman gloriously alive as he played a game of hokkee with savagery and glee, and Hanuman shuddering in agony as he fought to suck in one last breath. Hanuman lived again and then died, and he died and then lived, a thousand times, ten thousand times a thousand times, on and on without end. That was terror of the universe, that like a great, screaming bird it utterly devoured each being every moment of life. *Nothing is lost,* he remembered. And that was the beauty of the universe, too, that in each moment each being was utterly reborn into all life's infinite possibilities.

Yes.

And now Danlo himself was alive and then dead, and dead and alive as he lived in all things. Years, a billion years, passed by in a single moment. And always he died into the moment and into himself as he moved ever closer to the bright, shimmering neverness of his birth. And then there came a moment beyond all other moments. Almost forever he gazed through infinitely many diamond facets straight into the fiery heart of the universe itself. Even as he choked off his own breath and struggled to kill Hanuman, a great wave of memory came rushing at him in a brilliant flash of alien and familiar faces, brown and white and blue and black, the wounded faces and the sad, the furry faces and the feathered, a million faces, a trillion faces, all of them ravished with the pain of pure existence and yet all marvelously alive with life's wild joy. And then all these perfect faces reflected the image of every other and reassembled themselves into a single face, all wild like that of the rare, white thallow, and yet also glorious and golden like the sun. Almost forever Danlo stared at this strange and beautiful face, and he held his breath in utter astonishment for he saw that it was his own.

Yes, yes, yes.

And then somewhere in the universe—perhaps in the Vild or nearer to Neverness—a star exploded. Danlo lived this cosmic event even as he finally relived the moment of his birth. Almost twenty-eight years before, he remembered, in a faraway cave he had been cut out of his mother's womb. He felt this slashing and tearing of his mother's tissues; he felt cold, calloused hands lifting him upward as his body experienced the full weight of gravity for the first time. And then there came a sudden explosion through a fiery red opening into light. He wanted to gasp at the sheer terror and wonder of it all but he couldn't breath. He felt himself dying as he was torn away from all that he had ever loved or known. His hands tightened into fists, and he felt blood between his fingers, all slippery, hot and wet. A crushing sensation spread out through his belly and chest as he struggled to fill his lungs with air. And then he felt his heart moving again in a single, agonizing beat, and at last he opened his eyes.

Time turned like a great wheel even as he returned to himself. For a moment, all was light and pain, pain and light. Strange new objects gradually fell into view through the blinding glare all about him. He looked down to see his right hand curled up into a ball as his long fingernails cut bloody gashes in his palm. And his left hand still covered Hanuman's mouth. Hanuman lay silent and still beneath him; his skin had fallen dead blue, and his dead eyes stared at Danlo without suffering or complaint.

Yes.

Slowly, Danlo lifted his hand away from Hanuman's lips. With almost infinite gentleness, he touched his fingertips against Hanuman's brow and then closed his eyes. *Mi alasharia la, shantih, shantih,* he silently prayed, *sleep in peace, my brother, my friend.* Through the haze of tears burning his own eyes (and through the flames of the supernova out near Raizel Luz that had destroyed a quarter of the Ringist fleet), he looked down upon Hanuman's face. And he saw there neither anger nor hate nor mad, *shaida* dreams, but only a blessed being who had come into the world and finally left it like any other.

He tried to stand, then. From faroff, he heard shouts and footsteps echoing through the stone stairwell of the cathedral, and he tried to stand up and turn toward these dreadful sounds. But instead, he fairly collapsed and fell across Hanuman's still-warm body. He gathered him up in his arms, pressing his head against

Hanuman's head and Hanuman's heart against his own. He felt himself draw in a great gasp of air, and then the breath finally exploded out of him in a deep, terrible cry. He suddenly remembered that he hadn't been born laughing, as the mothers of his tribe had always told him. Man was the only animal who weeped from the moment of his birth, and like any child, he had begun life in sorrow and suffering, weeping at the immense pain of it all. And now he wept again as all true men weep, without shame, without restraint, the terrible wracking sobs coming up from deep inside his belly. He felt his heart throbbing and almost bursting with an unbearable pressure as if the whole universe were weeping, too, and emptying its burning tears into him. He couldn't stop this flood of grief, nor did he want to. For a long time he held Hanuman close to him, and he wept for this great gift of a human being that life had forever lost.

But nothing is lost, he remembered. *Nothing can ever be lost.*

At last he let go of Hanuman's body and let it rest against the floor. He slowly looked around himself at all the glittering cybernetica and other objects that Hanuman had collected. In the corner of the room, the little black spider still swung on a silken strand as she worked to complete her silvery web. On the black dining table, the devotionary computer still beamed forth the imago of Nikolos Daru Ede, who still bore upon his glowing face a look of shock at what Danlo had done. Danlo realized that his battle with Hanuman had taken little real time. Truly, Hanuman had died in the space between Danlo's heartbeats, and yet his slaying had lasted almost forever. Danlo stared down at his blood-stained hands, and it astonished him that he still bore the smooth, supple skin of a young man, for he had lived a million lives and ten million years. He felt a stranger to himself, as if he were older than the stars and yet as untouched as a newborn child. He felt flawless and wise and utterly wild, and then he remembered who he truly was and that he should say the words that would send Hanuman's spirit on the great journey to the other side of day.

Yes.

And so he knelt by Hanuman's side and he prayed one last time. "Hanu, Hanu," he whispered, *"mi alasharia la, shantih, shantih*—sleep in peace, my brother, my friend, myself."

Then, at the sound of footsteps and angry voices in the hallway outside, he stood up and stared off into time and space. His eyes blazed with a dark blue light that welled up out of the deepest part of him like an ocean. He felt all the cells of his body burning with fire, that deep and perfect fire of the stars that could never go out.

Strangely, the fierce head pain that had tormented him for so many years had gone away. And he felt the bones of his broken nose beginning to knit at a wildly accelerated rate; he felt the wild new life inside him remaking himself into a terrible and beautiful being who had waited ten billion years to be born.

Yes, his heart thundered, *Ahira, Ahira, yes.*

And so at last, in wordless affirmation and utter fearlessness, he smiled fiercely and turned to face the fate that called to him beyond the sanctuary's great wooden door.

THE ASARYA

You shall become who you really are.
—Friedrich the Hammer

The men who came to kill Danlo had no need to break down the sanctuary's door, for one of them was Jaroslav Bulba, and he had the code that would open it. Danlo waited for them by a patch of blood a few feet from Hanuman's body. As he had foreseen, three ronin warrior-poets burst into the room: Jaroslav Bulba, followed by a cruel-looking man with a burnt cheek and Arrio Kell, who had assisted in Danlo's torture in what seemed many lifetimes ago. All the warrior-poets wore the golden robes of godlings. All had their killing knives drawn, and with a glance at Hanuman's blue and blood-stained face, they charged straight toward Danlo.

"Kill him!" the Ede imago cried as Jaroslav Bulba slashed his knife at Danlo's throat. Obviously, Ede had switched allegiances yet again, for he was calling for Danlo to kill Jaroslav Bulba. "Kill him quickly and then the others, one at a time, before they kill you!"

Danlo would never quite understand what happened next. He, who always remembered so much so clearly, would never remember the chain of acts pulling him into the bloody future because he would not want to. Like a descending ice-cloud, a chaos of cold steel knives and swishing silk and breath exploding from tight, grim lips enveloped him. He felt the cold wind of a flashing knife burn his eyes, and he felt hot blood and breaking bones and the sudden pain of flesh tearing open.

A terrible wrath fell upon him then. Through the fiery red flames blinding him, he moved with all the terrible quickness of a tiger—or like an angel of death avenging the murders of innocent children. And when he had finally finished rending and ripping and crushing the throats of his enemies, he stood gasping for air as he looked down upon the bodies of three warrior-poets. Not a single knife had touched him; he bore not the slightest scratch or wound from this savage fight.

"It's not possible," the Ede imago said as he examined the three new dead men upon the floor. "It's really not possible."

"Yes—it is possible."

This voice came from neither Danlo nor the devotionary computer, but from a man standing in the doorway. He wore golden robes like any other godling, and on the fingers of either hand, two red rings. Danlo looked up to see Malaclypse of Qallar staring at him strangely. For a moment, all of the warrior-poet's fierce awareness concentrated on Danlo. His beautiful face was lit up with awe, and his violet eyes shined with bright lights as if he were staring at the sun.

"It's possible," Malaclypse said again. He had his killing knife drawn, and he used this murderous instrument to point at Jaroslav Bulba's dead form. "I know that it's possible only because I saw you slay them."

He took a quick step into the room and then another. Now his killing knife, stained with fresh blood, pointed straight toward Danlo's heart.

"Mallory Ringess," he said, taking another step, "I've searched across the stars and years to find you."

Danlo bowed his head in acknowledgement of Malaclypse's great quest, if not his supposition that he was really Mallory Ringess. Then he glanced at his hand where the sharp end of Hanuman's broken arm bone had cut him. Already, he felt the wound there closing, healing even as he watched.

Then he suddenly looked up and stared straight into Malaclypse's eyes. He said, "You hid in the cathedral, yes? After the assassin was subdued and the godlings were clearing the nave of people, you hid, didn't you?"

"It was the only way that I could get close to you," Malaclypse admitted, nodding his head. "While the godlings were fighting off Benjamin Hur's little army of fanatics, I hid in a candle closet and waited for my chance."

"You followed Jaroslav Bulba up the stairs, then?"

"Of course—after sending the two godlings guarding the stairwell on to their moment of the possible."

"I see."

"I didn't know why Hanuman had summoned them so urgently. I wouldn't have guessed that he would have let Mallory Ringess send him on to his own moment."

"But you see," Danlo said, and he looked down at Hanuman. For a moment, his eyes watered and his voice choked off as he tried to draw in a quick breath. "We all do have our moment, and we can never know when it will come."

At this, Malaclypse smiled knowingly, almost eagerly, and said, "When these ronin first took you away, I was afraid that Hanuman was going to execute you immediately. But he must have found reasons to keep you alive."

"Yes—truly he did."

"I'm glad," Malaclypse said. "Because now—"

"Because now you can ask me to complete the poem that you composed years ago, yes?"

Malaclypse stared at him in amazement. He said, "Mallory Ringess—you *are* he, aren't you?"

I am not I, Danlo remembered as he silently gazed at the glowing red tip of Malaclypse's knife. *I am not only I.*

"You are really he, I think," Malaclypse went on. "But *what* are you? That I would like to know."

I am a great white thallow whose wings touch at the far ends of the universe, Danlo remembered. *I am a thallow, truly, and I am the sky.*

"Are you really a god, then?" Malaclypse asked. "This I must know."

"I am no more a god than you."

"I wish that I could believe that."

"Then perhaps you should ask your poem—the one which only a true man would know how to complete."

"Perhaps I should."

"And then you, instead of these ronin poets, can have the pleasure of trying to kill me."

At this Malaclypse held up his hand to ward off Danlo's piercing gaze. He squinted in dismay almost as if Danlo could see into his mind. "But why should I kill you if you answer correctly?"

"Because answer or no, you could never be sure who I truly am."

Malaclypse suddenly looked at the bodies of the warrior-poets spread about the floor. He smiled grimly and said, "Two such as these I might have killed myself, but not three. I don't know if I *could* kill you."

Never harming or killing another, Danlo thought. *Never killing unless it is truly necessary to kill.*

"I do not know," Danlo said, "if I could allow you to kill me. I am sorry."

For a long time Malaclypse stood silently holding his knife as he lost himself in the fire of Danlo's deep blue eyes. At last, he said, "I've seen eyes such as yours before in your son, Danlo wi Soli Ringess. Do all the males of your bloody line have such impossible eyes?"

"It is said that I have my mother's eyes."

"Your mother," Malaclypse said, "was Dama Moira Ringess, then?"

My mother, Danlo thought, *was Chandra, daughter of Lenusya, daughter of Ellama who was a daughter of the Patwin tribe. And my blood mother was Katharine the Scryer, daughter of the world.*

"Moira Ringess, the cantor," Malaclypse said again. "She who slelled Leopold Soli's DNA in order to conceive a son."

All the mothers who have lost a son in this war are my mothers, Danlo thought. *And each mother who has ever lived or died— she is my mother, too.*

"A man," Danlo said simply, looking at Malaclypse, "may have many mothers."

At this, Malaclypse glanced at the red ring encircling the little finger of his left hand. He said, "You speak poetically, and I must honor you for that. But a man comes into the world through one door only."

One door only, Danlo remembered.

"And all men," Malaclypse added, looking at the ring on his right hand and the killing knife that he held, "must go out of life through only one glorious door as well."

One door, and one door only, opens upon the golden future that I have dreamed, Danlo remembered. And then a sudden thought, as clear and perfectly formed as crystal of new snow: *No, there are an infinite number of doors. And they open onto infinite possibilities.*

For a moment Danlo looked down at the black and white chess pieces scattered upon the floorstones. From faroff came the sound of explosions and the faint whooshing of the wind through the cracks around the cathedral's main doors. Truly, there were many doors to the universe, and opening any one of them would reveal whole galaxies of stars just as one could see the whole world in a grain of sand. And so as he stared at a tiny chip of ivory broken off one of the chess pieces, his mind's eye opened and he began to fall through space and time. Deep inside him, he felt an utter coldness and certainty of knowing. Many times before this other- sight had come over him, uncontrollable and unbidden. But now he found that he could simply will himself to see. He was like a beautiful tiger who could appear almost magically behind any of a jungle's thousands of trees; and he was like a pilot who had finally mastered the Great Theorem and could fall anywhere among the stars that he chose. The power of such willed presence astonished him and filled him with a wild joy. It was like momentarily thinking that he was lost in space and then beholding one familiar star—and instantly remembering the configuration of a thousand others. It was like opening a window to the manifold and expecting to find unmappable spaces, only to discover that even the worst chaos is underlaid by a deeper mathematics. His awareness radiated outward across the Fallaways like expanding wavefronts of light, and he marveled at the logic inside logic of this deep vision, the brilliant patterns, the secret order, the shimmering interconnectedness of all things.

The terrible beauty.

And so once again he watched a great blue star near Raizel Luz fall supernova. He watched the ship containing Bertram Jaspari's Iviomils and their murderous *morrashar* come close to this star—which was as close as they dared approach the Star of Neverness. And then came a terrifying explosion, gamma rays and photons and great gouts of boiling blue flames flung out into the coldness of space—a ball of light radiating in every wavelength from the infrared to the ultraviolet expanded outward into the galaxy at a speed of almost two hundred thousand miles per second.

It was this killing light that destroyed a great part of the Ringist fleet. Bardo, in his *Sword of Shiva,* having discovered the supernova only seconds before, almost instantly refined his strategy of trapping his numerically superior enemy. Using his fifth, sixth and eighth Battle Groups as decoys, he led tens of cadres of Ringist ships into the light-ruined spaces near Raizel Luz. Those blackships and lightships not immediately incinerated in the supernova's fires were mostly destroyed when Cristobel the Bold and Alesar Estarei, commanding the eleventh and twelfth Battle Groups, led an attack against the sixteen thickspaces where any of the Ringist ships might emerge into realspace.

Soon, in only a few hundreds of seconds, the whole of the Ringist fleet's right wing began to disintegrate like sand swept up in a whirlwind. This chaos spread to the Ringist center, as well, where Salmalin the Prudent led the remainder of his fleet. The Lord Pilot of the Ringists, in his glittering *Alpha Omega,* had to endure watching as cadre upon cadre of ships across hundreds of stars disappeared into their fiery centers or were swallowed up and dispersed into the manifold.

The shock of this slaughter spread through the remainder of the Ringist fleet like ball lightning through a dry forest. All but a few of the Ringist pilots panicked, and they began to surrender to Bardo's pilots in their ones and tens and hundreds. Upon seeing that the battle was lost, Salmalin the Prudent, true to his name, signalled his cadre commanders as best he could that they should stop fighting. And so there, beneath the fierce white glare of Raizel Luz, he surrendered his entire fleet to Bardo.

The Ringists' defeat was total. Many thousands of ships and pilots they lost that day, among them Nitara Tal and Kadar the Wise and Salome wi Maya Hastari in the *Golden Butterfly*. But many of the Fellowship's pilots had died, too. Danlo, falling from ship to ship and star to star at a speed infinitely greater than any photon, beheld the faces of each dead pilot shimmering through space and time with a light inside light. He wanted to pray for each of them, for Paloma the Younger and Ivar Rey in the *Flame of God*, and for the great Veronika Menchik and Alark of Ur-radeth and Madhava li Shing, with whom he had shared rooms and dreams in Perilous Hall so many years before.

Yannis Helaku, Sulla Ashtoreth, shantih, he silently prayed. *Madhava li Shing,* mi alasharia la, shantih, shantih.

And all this seeing and falling and praying occurred in less than a moment as he stood in the sanctuary gazing into the centers of Malaclypse's violet eyes. And then he returned to realtime, and the tragedy of all that had occurred that day made him weep. He looked down at the corpses of Jaroslav Bulba and Hanuman and ten thousand pilots who lay burnt and broken upon the floor. He wept for all the brothers and sisters and fathers and mothers of Man—and he wept for Malaclypse of Qallar who must soon lie dead beneath his hands, as well.

No—never killing unless it is truly necessary to kill, he thought. And then: *For in the end we choose our futures.*

He watched the light of the flame globes play along the blood-stained steel of Malaclypse's killing knife; he watched as Malaclypse took yet another step closer to him.

Malaclypse Redring, mi alasheratha la, shantih, shantih . . .

And then Malaclypse, beholding this compassion of Danlo's, suddenly froze into motionlessness like one tiger facing another. Then he took in, all in one quick glance, the scattered chess pieces and overturned cybernetica as well as the body of Hanuman li Tosh and the pain that poured out of Danlo's eyes. He looked through the tears welling up there into the burning deep blueness, and he began to calculate furiously. He was like a cetic solving the secrets of a man's soul, and more, like an artisan assembling one of the cathedral's great windows from a few scattered pieces of colored glass. And then, after a few moments, his face lit up with sudden understanding. He looked at Danlo strangely and said, "You're not really Mallory Ringess, are you?"

And Danlo smiled sadly and shook his head. "No, truly I am not."

"You're Danlo wi Soli Ringess."

Again, Danlo shook his head. "No, I am not he, either."

"Danlo wi Soli Ringess, who was the only man in history to have defeated a warrior-poet as a child—I'm certain that that is your name."

"No," Danlo said, looking through the veil of tears that burned his eyes. He pointed down at Hanuman. "No—Danlo is dead and there he lies."

For a moment Malaclypse watched Danlo silently grieving, and then he said, almost gently, "I think I understand."

"I think that you *do* understand." Danlo suddenly clamped his teeth shut to keep his jaw from shuddering. And then, as he stared at Hanuman's silent face, he gathered in all his will and said, "You see, I created him years ago. Therefore it was upon me to destroy him."

At this Malaclypse bowed deeply and said, "On Farfara I told you that you might have been a warrior-poet. Now I'm certain that you're one of us in spirit."

"Yes," Danlo said, "truly I am."

"In your cell, when Hanuman and the ronin poets tortured you, you never cried out."

"No—I could not."

"Even though they must have injected you with the ekkana drug, you never cried out—how is that possible?"

How do you capture a beautiful bird without killing its spirit? a voice asked Danlo. And then he remembered the answer: *By becoming the sky.*

"How is it possible, Pilot?"

"Because the heart is free," Danlo said simply. Inside him, all through his body, he felt his cells making molecules that would seek out and act as an antidote to the ekkana poison that still burned in his blood. "Because men and women are free if only they would become who they truly are."

"Ten of ten men or women, even warrior-poets, *would* have cried out. Are you the Eleventh, then?"

"No, I am something else."

"What, then?"

"The asarya," Danlo said. "The Fravashi Old Father who taught me called this one the asarya."

Malaclypse touched his lips to the dried blood coating the blade of his knife, and he said, "I know that word. The asarya is one who would say yes to all things. What would you say yes to, then?"

"I would say yes to *you*," Danlo said, smiling. "I would say yes even to the Warrior-Poets, to the spirit in which your order was founded."

Malaclypse took a step backward, then, and he looked down at the gash on Danlo's hand. He looked at Danlo's cheek where the glass from the shattered window had cut him almost down to the bone. Already, in the little time since he had entered the sanctuary, these wounds had closed and scabbed over and had begun to form their healing scars. *"What* are you?" he asked softly. "An asarya, you have said, but what is that? Is an asarya a god, then?"

"No, I am a man, even as you are," Danlo said. "I am only what all women and men were born to be."

Malaclypse's knife wavered a moment as he found himself caught in the brilliance of Danlo's gaze. And then he said, "You frighten me, Pilot. In all the universe, nothing has ever frightened me as you do."

Fear is the left hand of love, Danlo remembered. And then he asked, "Must you try to kill what you fear, then?"

"But what else should I do?"

"Join me and become an asarya, too."

There came a moment then when the whole world stopped spinning and hung perfectly balanced on the knifeblade's edge between two words, yes and no. Danlo saw the uncertainty that darkened Malaclypse's violet eyes, the terrible angels that sang inside his soul. He feared that Malaclypse still might try to kill him, if only to learn the final secret of death. But Danlo, who had buried his brothers and sisters and burned the body of his son, who had walked with the dead on Tannahill and died a million times himself in killing his best friend, knew all that could be known about this greatest of mysteries. And he knew the secret of life, as well, for at the still point of creation, at the center of the great circle of the world, life and death were but the right hand and left joined together as one.

And all this Danlo told to Malaclypse not in words but in the terrible beauty of his eyes. He told it to him in fire and light and in all the wild joy that poured out of him like an ocean. He felt

something infinitely bright burst open inside him, then, and in
utter silence he spoke of the sheer magnificence of life. Truly, he
said, life's torments and suffering could never end, but life could
never end, either. It went on and on into a glorious and golden
future, ever evolving, ever seeking out every particle of matter
and corner of space in which to flower, growing ever vaster, ever
deeper, ever more splendid and aware. And nothing was ever lost.
Nothing *could* ever be lost, not even through desolation or death,
and all this Danlo told Malaclypse even as he watched him begin
to melt into the light inside light and vanish into the secret blue
behind the blueness of the sky.

   Yes.

   And then Malaclypse suddenly shook his head and looked
away from Danlo. He tightened his grip on his killing knife and
said, "I've pursued you across the stars and aided murderers in
waging war, all to keep you from achieving your purpose."

   "Yes," Danlo said, smiling sadly, "I remember."

   "I, myself, have murdered in order to get close to you."

   "Yes, I know."

   "And yet you would still ask me to join you?"

   "Yes," Danlo said. And then he caught Malaclypse's eyes
again, and said, "Yes, I would."

   Malaclypse stood there blinking in indecision; he was like a
man who loves light but fears coming too close to the sun. Finally
he said, "My order still has a rule to slay all gods."

   "All *gods,* perhaps," Danlo said. "But not human beings.
Your order was founded to realize the possibilities of humankind."

   Infinite possibilities.

   "But what is a god, then?" Malaclypse asked. "What is a
human being?"

   "A true human being is the glory of the world," Danlo said.
"A true human being is only a part of the world, and yet the
whole of it, too."

   "You speak in paradoxes, Pilot."

   "A true human accepts his death because he knows he can
never die."

   "You speak in mysteries, too."

   "A true human being lives her life in fullness and contentment
because she knows that she lives all lives everywhere."

   "I confess that you make definitions and distinctions that the
lord of my order wouldn't want to understand."

   For a moment, Danlo looked off through the sanctuary's windows and fell through space a thousand light-years to the planet Qallar. There, in the redness of Qallar's bloody sun and iron soil, he saw a man supervising a training exercise between two young warrior-poets. The man was called Lord Korudon, and he wore his flame-orange poet's ring around the little finger of his left hand. His warrior's ring, pure red like Malaclypse's, shined from the fist that he made with his right hand. As Danlo looked through this terrible man's eyes into his soul, he saw that long since Lord Korudon had allowed the Order of Warrior-Poets to be used as a tool of the Silicon God.

"Someday," Danlo said, returning to the presence of Malaclypse's curious gaze and the gleam of his killing knife, "you will return to Qallar. You will challenge your lord to a duel, whether with poems or knives, it will be your choice. But in the end, you will win."

"And then?"

"And then you will become Lord of the Warrior-Poets. And you will make a new rule for your order."

"And what will this rule be, then?"

"*Not* to kill all potential gods," Danlo said. "But rather to die protecting the lives of human beings. You see, across the Civilized Worlds, all the way out through the stars of the Vild to Tannahill and beyond, so many blessed human beings are about to be born."

Danlo's heart beat three times as he sensed that Malaclypse was as close to saying yes as the artery throbbing in his neck. Then the sounds of boot leather stomping against stone filled the stairwell leading up to the sanctuary—obviously, the guards that Malaclypse had killed at the bottom of the stairs had finally been discovered. Soon, even as Malaclypse began to move forward, four young godlings hurried into the room. One of them was Ivar Zayit, whom Hanuman had trusted almost as much as Surya Surata Lal and Jaroslav Bulba. But he seemed not to know Danlo's true identity, for he stared at the dead bodies on the floor and cried out in horror, "Mallory Ringess! Mallory Ringess— what has happened here?"

Two of the godlings held lasers ready in their uncertain hands. The fourth godling, a slender boy who had once been a harijan, brandished only a shiny new knife. He stood near Hanuman's body, gazing at the red ring on Malaclypse's hand and the long killing knife that he held.

"I had to kill them," Danlo said. His voice flowed out sad and deep and sounded almost strange to him. "They had betrayed my church and brought war on innocent children, so I killed them."

This simple statement seemed to astonish Ivar Zayit into inaction, but one of the godlings holding a laser turned as if to ask him what they should do.

"I have returned, as I promised," Danlo said. "I have returned to stop this bloody war."

In the space between heartbeats, Malaclypse caught Danlo's gaze, and his violet eyes flashed in silent affirmation of all that Danlo had asked of him. Very slightly, he bowed his head. Then, with a rare and frightful quickness, he edged forward yet another step and insinuated his body between Danlo and the four godlings. Upon seeing a warrior-poet of two red rings ready to protect Danlo, the godlings lowered their lasers. Apparently, they had heard the stories of how warrior-poets could fall into accelerated time and move at a speed thrice that of ordinary men. Apparently, they doubted their ability even to trigger the lasers' firing studs before Malaclypse could slash out with his killing knife. And they must have wondered how Danlo, whom they believed to be Mallory Ringess, had slain three warrior-poets. Then, too, they were godlings whose ultimate loyalty lay not with Hanuman li Tosh or even with the church that he had perverted, but with the god they worshipped as Mallory Ringess. And here, now, in a miracle of which they had only dreamed, their god stood before them fairly radiating his will to make peace.

"What should we do?" the godling with the knife whispered to Ivar Zayit.

And Ivar Zayit, who was an intelligent man—and a idealistic man who had once embraced the Three Pillars of Ringism before falling victim to Hanuman's promises of power—hesitated for a long and terrible moment. And then he bowed his head to Danlo and said, "He is Mallory Ringess, and we should do what he asks of us."

Needing no further prompting, the three other godlings put away their weapons and bowed deeply, too.

"We must hurry, then," Danlo said, returning their bows. He nodded to Malaclypse quickly, almost imperceptibly. From the streets outside came cries and shouts and the pip-pop of bullet guns firing deadly bits of metal. "I want there to be no more killing."

So saying, with a last look at Hanuman, he led the way out into the hallway and down the stairs. Malaclypse placed himself closely behind him, followed by Ivar Zayit and the others. In turning his back on the godlings, Danlo decided to trust them with his life. And such was his faith in them that it seemed never to occur to them that they shouldn't be trusted. Even Ivar Zayit stared at Danlo as if he were caught up in the aura of purpose and possibilities that emanated from him like a flaming corona surrounding a star.

Infinite possibilities.

And so as Danlo reached the bottom of the stairs, he pushed open the doors that gave out into the nave of the cathedral. The two godlings whom Malaclypse had killed lay sprawled on the floorstones in a single pool of blood. There were dead and dying godlings everywhere: crumpled along the dark aisle abutting the nave's sweeping open spaces, and curled up near the altar, and moaning and crying on the prayer mats laid out neatly in their rows. One godling, a young woman, lay slumped against one of the great stone pillars that supported the cathedral's vault high above. She still clutched a bullet gun in her dead hand, and her head drooped down almost touching her breasts. Apparently, she had been caught up in some kind of explosion, for her left eye had been blown out and her brains extruded from the socket, spilling out in a bloody mass and dripping down along her nose.

The sight of other such personal tragedies burned into Danlo's eyes wherever he looked. Although dawn was just breaking over the city, the nave showed only the light of a few candles, so it was hard to see. But through the yellow glow and the shadows playing over the lacy stonework, he made out the forms of godlings stationed along the walls and windows. Bits of broken glass sparkled like jewels against the floorstones everywhere, especially along the south transept and the great eastern windows, whose lower panels had been knocked out. For a moment—but only a moment—Danlo watched as a couple of godlings bravely exposed themselves in an open window and traded laser fire with ringkeepers of Benjamin Hur's army that occupied the surrounding streets. He watched a beam of ruby light flash through a broken panel of glass, nearly scoring the top of a godling's shaved head. And then, through the smells of burning wax, broken entrails and blood, he approached the altar and took a deep breath. He spoke four simple words, and his voice rang out into the cathedral like a bell: "The war is over!"

And suddenly the two hundred godlings defending the cathedral turned from the broken windows toward the altar. There Danlo mounted the red-carpeted stairs and stood next to a stand of flaming candles so that the godlings could see who spoke to them.

"The war is over," Danlo said again. "Hanuman li Tosh fomented this war for his own glory and insane dreams, and so he betrayed the spirit of Ringism and all of you, as well. But it is all over, now."

Just then a bullet burned through one of the broken windows and whinged off the wall above Danlo in a spray of stone and dust. And one of the godlings crouching along the east window motioned frantically with his laser for Danlo to come down off the altar. He, like everyone else, had been told that they were fighting to protect the life of Mallory Ringess, and protect him he would.

"Lord Mallory," he cried out, "please come down and return to the tower with Lord Hanuman! You must keep yourself safe!"

And another godling near him looked at Malaclypse and Ivar Zayit standing on the bottom stair of the altar and asked, "Where is Lord Hanuman, then? Is he still in the tower? Is he well?"

"Hanuman li Tosh is dead," Danlo suddenly announced. For a moment the only sounds in the cathedral were the wind blowing through the broken windows and the moans of the wounded. "He sleeps with the stars, now. His time had come, and I had to send him on."

Danlo felt two hundred pairs of eyes burning into him like lasers, but no one dared to question him. No one dared to oppose him or move against him in any way because he was Mallory Ringess and he had said the war was over—and now they each trembled with the sudden hope that they might live, after all.

"Open the doors!" Danlo called out. "Someone find a white cloth to wave from the windows so that we can open the doors."

And as he commanded, it was done. One of the godlings cut loose a bolt of white silk from the robes of a dead scryer and managed to fashion a crude white flag. She waved it from the eastern window and then moved along the windows of the south transept. Almost immediately, from the streets outside, came the stillness of fire and the silence of the city.

"Open the doors, now!" Danlo said again. And four godlings rushed through the nave to do as he asked. In little time, the cathedral's great western portals stood open to the moaning wind of a bitterly cold deep winter morning.

"They might think that it's a trap," Ivar Zayit said to Danlo as he looked off through the open door at the lights of the Old City.

Dressed only in his thin golden robe, he shivered in the cold. "One of us will have to go out to them."

"Yes," Danlo said, moving down off the altar, "one of us will."

When he reached the bottom step, Malaclypse Redring held out his arm to stop him. He said, "It's too dangerous. Someone might fire at you out of habit or fear, and then you'd be dead."

"Yes, that is true," Danlo said softly, looking at Malaclypse's blazing violet eyes.

"I'll speak to them," Malaclypse said. And then he smiled fiercely. "A new rule for warrior-poets, Pilot. To die protecting human beings."

And Danlo smiled at Malaclypse, too, even as he felt the steely muscles of his arm pressing against his chest. And he said, "You *would* die for me, wouldn't you?"

"Yes—why not?"

"And I would die for you," Danlo said. "For a warrior-poet who is also a human being."

With that he suddenly surged forward, and the power of his body and will was too great for Malaclypse to contain. He stepped across the black and white floorstones of the nave gracefully but quickly because he didn't want anyone else to rush out ahead of him. When he reached the doorway, the frigid wind suddenly blasted his face. He blinked against the cold and the tears of his eyes and looked out upon the street. There, in the day's first light, he saw a carpet of bodies leading from the street almost to the cathedral's doors. There, too, along the purple gliddery, he saw men and women in furs crouched down behind sleds as they aimed various weapons at the doorway. More of Benjamin Hur's ringkeepers occupied the rooftops of the buildings on the surrounding blocks; Danlo counted some three hundred of them before he gave up and moved out beyond the doorway, into the light of the rising sun.

"The war is over!" he called out to them. "The cathedral stands open to you, as it shall be from now on!"

For a moment, no one moved or spoke. The ringkeepers—half-frozen from spending a night out in the bitter cold—each stared at the triumphant form of Mallory Ringess. They had been fighting to rescue him from the cathedral, and here he stood before them, inviting them inside.

"Come with me!" he said. "Come inside now before you die from the cold."

From behind one of the overturned sleds lining the street, one

of the ringkeepers stepped into view. He clutched a laser in his
right hand; his left hand apparently had been blown off, for the
end of his arm was swathed in a crude, bloody white bandage.
Danlo looked through the hood almost covering his face to make
out the great hooked nose and angry green eyes of Benjamin Hur.
Benjamin calmly walked over the street's slippery ice straight up
to Danlo. He presented himself, and then bowed to him and said,
"Mallory Ringess—I always hoped you'd return, but I never
really thought you would. I only wish you'd returned sooner,
before all this had to happen."

So saying, Bejamin swept his bandaged arm out at the
ringkeepers lying dead on the street.

"I am sorry," Danlo said. He closed his eyes for a moment as
the faces of all those killed in the war flashed before him in their
billions. And then, like the radiance of the stars, inside him shined
the lights of billions of other faces: those of all the new children
throughout the galaxy who would soon be born.

Terrible beauty, he remembered. *Terrible beauty.*

"If the war is really over, then I'd like to ask you a question,"
Benjamin said. His green eyes burned into Danlo's like heated
copper. "Are you really a god or just a man?"

Danlo watched the breath steam from Benjamin's thin, fierce
lips and looked through the ruff of his furs at his cheek where a
laser beam had scorched the flesh. And he smiled mysteriously
and said, "What is a god, then? What is a man? What does it
matter what I am as long as I have returned to end the war?"

And with no further explanation, he motioned for Benjamin to
follow him inside the cathedral. This Benjamin did, along with
Poppy Panshin, who stepped out of a nearby building, and Karim
of Clarity and other ringkeepers who had once been part of the
Kalla Fellowship. The Masalina, his once-fleshy face now sagging
from too many days of hunger, also appeared leading a company
of ringkeepers from the gliddery fronting the cathedral's south
side. All these women and men—and many others—followed
Danlo through the western portal and into the cathedral. They cast
doleful glances at the wounded lying on their mats throughout the
nave, and they regarded their bloody work with an uncomfortable
mixture of pride, horror and shame.

As Danlo walked up to the altar and ascended it, Malaclypse
moved to block its steps from anyone, godling or ringkeeper, who
might wish to come too close to him. He waited with his long
knife drawn as he carefully watched Ivar Zayit and Namamdi
Astoret and the other princes of Hanuman's church. He stared at

Benjamin Hur, with his laser, and the ringkeepers who gathered together two hundred strong before the altar. He stood ready to kill or be killed, almost as if it made no difference to him.

There came a bad moment, then, when one of the godlings posted near the far side of the altar cursed Benjamin Hur and all his ringkeepers. He shouted out that they had murdered his brother and thus deserved to be murdered too. And then Danlo, much to Malalclypse's chagrin, held his hands palms outward as he positioned himself between this godling and Benjamin Hur. And his voice shook the cathedral as he angrily told them, "I have returned to end the war, but I cannot end it myself. I cannot stop you from killing each other, any more than I could stop Hanuman li Tosh from killing my son. But if you must kill, please kill me first."

Thus shamed, with a muttered curse, the godling near the altar lowered his laser. Then, as Danlo looked at him across a few feet of open air, the pain of all that he had suffered since the death of his tribe filled his eyes with a terrible bright light. The godling's eyes filled, too, with tears for his brother and all those that he had seen killed in the war or had killed himself. And so without further thought or prompting, he bent down and set his laser on the floor.

"The war is over," one of Benjamin's ringkeepers suddenly called out. He stepped over and placed his laser next to that of the godling. "If the war is really over, it would be stupid to kill anyone anymore."

And with that, another ringkeeper came over and abandoned her laser, and then ten others. A few of the godlings, too, followed them in disarming themselves, and then suddenly, almost as one, every man and woman in the cathedral pressed forward to add their lasers, batons, dreammakers, heat tlolts or bullet guns to the growing mound of weapons in front of the altar. Everyone except Malaclypse Redring of Qallar, that is. The warrior-poet could not suffer his sacred knife to leave his possession or be touched by any other, and so he returned it to the sheath he wore strapped to his side beneath his robes. With his eyes, he promised Danlo that he wouldn't draw it within the bounds of the city—unless, of course, war broke out again and he had to protect him.

But the war is over, Danlo told himself. *At last the war is truly over.*

While the godlings and ringkeepers gave up their weapons, they mingled together as they had once done in the years before the war. And they talked among themselves, in low voices and whispers, recounting the events that had led up to this astonishing moment. The story of how Mallory Ringess, with his naked hands, had slain three armed warrior-poets quickly spread through the nave. Other stories were told, too. Given what Danlo had said about the death of his son, everyone supposed that Mallory Ringess had been speaking about Danlo himself. As no one had seen Danlo for many days, the rumor of his death passed from one ringkeeper's lips to another's in hushed, mournful tones.

Then one of the godlings, still bitter over the friends whom he had recently lost, blamed Benjamin Hur for the killing that had wracked the city, and accused him as well of setting one of his ringkeepers to assassinate Hanuman li Tosh—and almost murdering Mallory Ringess instead. In response to this accusation, at a quick glance from Danlo, Ivar Zayit stepped forward to tell of how Hanuman li Tosh had plotted this false assassination attempt and had ordered Mallory Ringess to be imprisoned in the tower. With an awed and puzzled look at Danlo, he told of how Hanuman's warrior-poets had injected Mallory Ringess with a paralytic drug to silence him. Ivar Zayit did not quite understand how Mallory Ringess had overcome the effects of this drug, but others did. One woman, wearing a golden robe on her body and a look of reverence on her face, pointed up at Danlo on the altar and said, simply, "He is Mallory Ringess, and he is a god."

These stories had a calming effect upon all those gathered there. The godlings began to see at last the deceptions and criminal acts of Hanuman li Tosh, while the ringkeepers took pity upon them for being so deceived. And then Danlo, standing in the sun's rays streaking through the glorious eastern window, told them of Hanuman's true purpose. He explained how all Ringists and godlings everywhere were to be seduced into furthering the growth of the Universal Computer—and then, eventually, discarded like broken bits of machinery that had no further use. It was Hanuman's dream, he said, that the Universal Computer would one day grow to encompass the entire universe.

"And this," he told the men and women staring up at him in horror and disbelief, "is the deepest reason why I had to slay him. It is why the Fellowship of Free Worlds has fought and defeated the Ringist fleet."

Thus did the news of the Fellowship's great victory first come to the people of Neverness. But even as Danlo stood there on the altar and spoke of the ending of the Battle of Ten Thousand Suns, high above the city the dark blue sky sparkled with many bright flashes of light. This was the vanguard of Bardo's fleet, he said, the first wave of lightships falling out of the manifold as they returned home.

"The Hollow Fields must be opened," Danlo said. He looked at Ivar Zayit, whom he knew would be obeyed by the Ringists who controlled the city's single light field. "Go there and find the Master of Ships. Tell him what has happened here. Tell him to prepare the Lightship Caverns for the return of many ships. And tell him that when Bardo and Lord Salmalin arrive, Mallory Ringess requests their presence in the cathedral."

After hesitating a moment—it seemed that Ivar Zayit couldn't bear to break himself away from the great events unfolding before him—he nodded his head, turned and hurried toward the cathedral's open doors. As he disappeared into the street, Danlo began issuing other orders, singling out various godlings or ringkeepers to help restore the cathedral (and the city) to order. The wounded and dying must be taken to hospices, he said, and the dead carried out to the various plasma ovens around the city to be cremated.

His heart beat quickly as he watched a cadre of godlings move off toward the stairwell to retrieve the bodies of the three warrior-poets and Hanuman li Tosh. It beat even more quickly when he asked another cadre of godlings to find the cell in the chapter house where Hanuman had imprisoned Old Father. He asked that Old Father be carried to a hospice if he were badly wounded or to his house in the Fravashi District if he were not. And then he turned to matters of lesser moment, such as the sweeping of glass from the floor and the covering of the broken windows with sheets of clary so that the cathedral wouldn't be quite so cold.

For a while all went well. But Danlo's move toward mastery over the city and the Way of Ringess was to be challenged still one more time. Even as godlings from all over the Old City began pouring into the cathedral to behold once again the miracle of Mallory Ringess' return, a small woman wearing bright golden robes made her way through the nave. The godlings already present stepped aside to allow her to pass. She moved straight toward the altar as if this little square of red-carpeted stone belonged to her. She had a small, sour face and an angry look about her bloodshot eyes, and Danlo knew her well, for she was Surya Surata Lal.

Once, she had been a princess on Summerworld; now, especially with Hanuman dead, she regarded herself as the queen of the church. She had spent the last day since Danlo's imprisonment in secret conclave with Lord Pall, and thus she hadn't been present when Benjamin Hur's ringkeepers attacked the cathedral.

But for all her pride and vanity, she was still a brave woman who was unafraid to face down anyone, either man or god.

"This *man*," she said pointing up at Danlo as she addressed the godlings assembled before the altar, "murdered Lord Hanuman, and yet here you stand worshipping him as if he were a god!"

For a few moments no one spoke, and five hundred women and men looked at Surya Lal as if she had fallen mad like Hanuman. And then a prominent godling named Bodaway Eshte cleared his throat and said, "But Surya he *is* a god. He's Mallory Ringess."

"But how do we know he's *really* Mallory Ringess? How do we know he's not just a mime created by Benjamin Hur to impersonate him and assassinate Lord Hanuman?"

At this astonishing accusation, many ringkeepers cried out that Surya Lal should be silenced for slandering their leader. And many more godlings called for them to let Surya continue speaking, and so quickly did the emotions of those gathered in the cathedral flare toward open emnity that Malaclypse edged up higher on the altar's steps and dropped his hand down his robe to clasp his killing knife. And he never took his eyes from the many people shouting at each other:

"She's right," an old man said, "how do we know he's really Mallory Ringess?"

"Of course he's Mallory Ringess! Who else would he be?"

"Yes, but Mallory the god or Mallory the man?"

"What's a god, then? What's a man?"

"Of course he's a man. What else would he be?"

"A god, can't you see?"

"Look at his eyes! Did Mallory Ringess have such deep blue eyes?"

"Mallory Ringess had the body of a man, and then the body of an Alaloi. He's a god, and he can have whatever color eyes he chooses."

"Who else but a god could have killed three warrior-poets with his naked hands?"

"It's the Way of Ringess for men and women to become gods—why can't you believe that?"

"It's the Way of Ringess to drink kalla and remembrance the Elder Eddas—why did you have to ruin that and turn it into a religion?"

"Why can't you see what's before your eyes?"

"Why did you let Hanuman ruin everything and lead the city to war?"

"He's a man who became a god! And here he stands!"

"I see a man who looks like a man. Princess Surya is right—how do we know he really *is* Mallory Ringess?"

For what seemed a long time, Danlo stood upon the altar watching and waiting as he let the people of the city speak. His bright eyes fell upon Surya Lal, and he smiled sadly for he realized that she had never truly felt the spirit of Ringism or understood what it meant to transcend herself. Unlike Hanuman, she had no higher dream, however evil or mad. Her involvement with the religion that Hanuman had perverted had been part sham, part zeal, and many parts pure self-deception and desire for glory.

Clearly she regarded Mallory Ringess as nothing more than a powerful man to be used to further her own last grasp for power. When he saw the smallness and delusion of her life and considered the vast harm that she had thus wreaked upon the world, he wanted to weep. But for all her desperation in challenging him, she was still a dangerous woman. Although he felt certain that Hanuman hadn't told her his true identity, her intuition was as keen as razor. And so to take the edge off her suspicions and dispel all doubt as to who he really was, he looked through her to the people shouting in the nave, and he held up his hands for silence.

"I am who I am!" he called out to them. He made a fist, then, and held his black diamond pilot's ring sparkling in the sunlight. "Do you see this ring? With this ring, on the 95th day of false winter thirty years ago, Lord Leopold Soli made a new pilot. A pilot never takes off his ring; a pilot's ring is sacred and identifies the pilot even though he might age eighty years in the manifold and return to Neverness to find all his friends dead."

So saying, he reached up with his other hand, and to the astonishment of all present, pulled the ring from his finger. And then he motioned to a young man standing near the altar to come closer. As it happened, this was none other than Kiyoshi Telek, the golden-faced godling who had tended Danlo in his cell after his torture.

"Do you believe that I am Mallory Ringess?" Danlo asked.

The whole cathedral now fell silent as everyone—godlings, ringkeepers and others—waited to hear what Kiyoshi would say.

And Kiyoshi looked at Danlo with his soft, credulous eyes and without hesitation, said, "Yes, of course I do."

"Very well, then," Danlo said as he moved to the edge of the altar. He held out the shimmering ring and pressed it into

Kiyoshi's hand. "Take this and go to the Pilot's College. Find the
Master of Records and ask him to verify the identity of this ring."

He smiled at the look of awe on Kiyoshi's face and the way
that Kiyoshi held the cold diamond crystal as if it were a ring of
fire burning his hand. But the Master of Records would suffer
from no such reverence. He would use an electron microscope to
descry the unique signature of iron and iridium atoms written into
the diamond of his father's ring.

"Go quickly, now," Danlo said, urging Kiyoshi onward with
the kindness of his eyes. Then he nodded at Malaclypse and said,
"Please go with him, too. Make sure the ring reaches the Master
of Records safely."

As Malaclypse bowed his head and reluctantly moved off
through the nave with Kiyoshi Telek to carry out their appointed
mission, Danlo turned towards Surya Surata Lal and caught her in
the deep blue fire of his eyes. He looked at her for a long time,
and they waited together along with the hundreds of others in the
cathedral for Kiyoshi Telek to return.

And as Danlo's heart beat out the steady measure of the passing moments, many more men and women began arriving at the
cathedral and filling up the nave. News of the war's end and
Hanuman li Tosh's death had spread like fire through the city. As
on the preceeding day, the various peoples of Neverness began
filling the streets surrounding the cathedral. And as on that tragic
day, which seemed to Danlo to have occurred a million years
before, the lords and masters of the Order made their way from
the Academy to the cathedral in response to Danlo's summons.
They arrived in twos and twenties and tens: Eva Zarifa and Alesar
Druze, Sancho Edo Ashtoreth and Burgos Harsha, the Lord Historian still wearing his drab brown robes. Lord Pall, of course, came
too, followed by Jonath Parsons, Rodrigo Diaz, Kolenya Mor and
the entire rest of Lord's College.

This time, however, all the lords and masters pressed close to
the altar and mingled with ringkeepers, godlings, autists and
harijan according to no particular protocol. Then after more time
had passed Jonathan Hur arrived accompanied by Zenobia
Alimeda and others of the Kalla Fellowship. When Jonathan saw
that Benjamin remained alive, though wounded, he pushed
through the people near the altar and threw his arms around his
brother in unrestrained joy. And close behind him came Demothi
Bede, and two alien Friends of Man, and ambassadors from Urradeth, Yarkona, Ninsun, Arcite, Veda Luz and other Ringist
Worlds. The whole of the city, it seemed, was pouring into the

nave in order to bear witness to this final test of whether one simple man would be proclaimed as Mallory wi Soli Ringess, Lord of the Order, Lord of the Way of Ringess—and Lord of Light to billions of women and men across the Civilized Worlds.

Yes.

Just when it seemed that Kiyoshi Telek had been gone forever, the people standing outside the cathedral let loose a great shout. But they heralded not Kiyoshi's return, but that of group of women and men dressed all in black. A hundred or so of the pilots who had fought in the war made their way down the gliddery and then through the cathedral's doors. Many of them were Ringist pilots: Salmalin the Prudent, Ciro Dalibar, Salome wi Maya Hastari, and Kadar the Wise. They seemed to have made peace with their old hallmates and recent enemies, Matteth Jons, Lara Jesusa and Rohana of Urradeth.

And of course Bardo. Wearing his sweat-stained suit of black nall battle armor and glorious shesheen cape, he strode into the nave like a god of war. He was followed by the greatest of the Fellowship's pilot-captains: Helena Charbo, Aja, Sabri dur li Kadir and the Richardess. And only a few paces farther back came Alesar Estarei and Edreiya Chu and Cristobel the Bold, who, in the Battle of the Ten Thousand Suns, had finally justified his high opinion of himself and the promise of his name.

As a single body bound together by the deaths of too many of their friends, they slowly passed beneath the cathedral's great colored windows. Although the press of people in the nave had grown almost perilously dense, men and women hurried to make way for them. And Bardo himself hurried down the line of the arching vault high over his head, straight toward the altar where once he had stood to conduct the nightly remembrancing ceremonies and preside over his church. But now another stood in his place. When he saw the form of Mallory Ringess rising up and looking at him like an incarnation out of his memories and deepest dreams, he broke almost into a run as he abandoned what little restraint he had ever possessed.

"Mallory!" he cried out. His great voice boomed through the cathedral like thunder. "They told me you'd come back, but I didn't want to believe it until I saw you with my own eyes!"

Even as he swept forward, Danlo came down off the altar to greet his old friend. For a moment Bardo paused before him and looked at him strangely. And then he fell weeping against him, at once shaken and triumphant, and he pounded Danlo's back with such overflowing joy that many of the men and women standing close to them began to weep, too. The blows of his huge hand might have staved in the ribs of a lesser being, but Danlo wore the same body of an Alaloi man that Bardo remembered as belonging to Mallory Ringess. "Little Fellow!" he cried out again and again, forgetting all decorum. Once upon a time, in the intimacy of their friendship, he had thus addressed Mallory Ringess—and Danlo, too. "Little Fellow, by God, Little Fellow—I thought you were dead!"

But Mallory Ringess, it seemed, was still very much alive, and Bardo's acclamation of him convinced all but the most skeptical that here indeed stood the famous Lord Pilot who had proved the Great Theorem and brought back to Neverness the secrets of the gods. As if to underscore the sentiment sweeping through the cathedral, Kiyoshi Telek finally returned, accompanied by Malaclypse and an old, gray-haired man whose skin was seamed with the marks of great age. Danlo knew him as Daghaim Redsmith, the Master of Records, and a master pilot who had once tried to reach the spaces of the galaxy's outer core beyond the Morbio Inferiore. But that was long ago, before the time of even the Richardess and Leopold Soli. Now Master Daghaim, who suffered from both tabes and some kind of shaking palsy, had sadly left the piloting of lightships to younger men and women. He had to content himself with recording the discoveries and journeys of others—and with verifying the identity of a plain, black diamond, pilot's ring.

"Master Daghaim," Bardo said as he broke off embracing Danlo and watched the old man limp toward the altar. He couldn't have helped noticing that Surya Surata Lal and Lord Pall and many others were watching his approach as they might await the coming of a plague. "It's good to see you again—I know that it's hard for you to leave the college."

And then Bardo bowed deeply, and others did, too. All the pilots present knew Master Daghaim very well, and he knew all of them. Painfully Master Daghaim bowed to Lord Salmalin, Ciro Dalibar and Cristobel the Bold. And then, after bowing to Danlo, he looked at him in silence as everyone near the altar waited and looked, too.

Finally he spoke, his old voice quavering as he smiled toward Danlo and recited the ancient ritual. "Lord Mallory Ringess— have you fallen far and well? You've been gone seventeen years and three hundred forty eight days. What wonders have you returned to tell me?"

At this, five hundred people let loose a tremendous shout even as Bardo looked back and forth between Master Daghaim and Danlo in puzzlement. Then one of the godlings standing at Bardo's shoulder explained why Master Daghaim had been sent for. Upon hearing this, Bardo turned toward his cousin, Surya Surata Lal, and his face fell purple-black with great anger.

"Surya!" he said. His great voice growled out with such ferocity that those looking on from nearby tried to move away from him. "Surya Lal—of course he's Mallory! And you knew this from the moment you first saw him, didn't you?"

Surya, at last seeing that she had no hope of gaining control of the Way of Ringess, stared down at the floor in shame.

"Of course, he's Mallory Ringess," Master Daghaim said as he nodded gravely. He held a shining pilot's ring high above his head for everyone to see. Bardo—and five hundred others—stared at this circle of gleaming black diamond. "And this is his ring. It was made on the eighty-eighth day of false winter in the year 2929 and presented to Mallory Ringess at the convocation in the Hall of the Ancient Pilots."

So saying, he reached out to give Danlo the ring and smiled in satisfaction as he watched him slip it back onto his finger. And then hundreds of voices cried out as one: "Mallory Ringess! Mallory Ringess! Lord Mallory wi Soli Ringess!"

After waiting a moment for the din to die down, Bardo turned back to Surya, who had helped to usurp him from the church that he had founded and worked to defeat the Fellowship fleet in the war. "Surya Lal," his voice thundered, "you've betrayed me and every poor godling standing here, so you should be taken from this beautiful building that you've helped to ruin and—"

"Bardo!" A voice greater than even Bardo's rang out through the cathedral from window to window and wall to wall. For a moment, Danlo stood tall and silent as he looked straight at Bardo. Then he drew in his breath and went on, "Bardo, you have fought a great battle and led the Fellowship's pilots to victory, and we must all honor you for that. But it is not upon you to determine Surya Lal's fate."

Those present in the cathedral shouted in agreement with what Danlo had said, and their cry spread from lip to lip as it passed out the doors into the streets outside: "Lord Mallory! Lord of the Order! Lord of Light!—Lord of the Way of Ringess!"

After bowing deeply, Bardo smiled at Danlo and said, "Ah, Mallory, what have I done? You're the Lord of the Order, of course, not I."

And Danlo returned his bow and spoke to Surya. "Princess

Surya Surata Lal—you were born a princess of Summerworld, and you will be taken from here and returned to your world. Bardo will see to it that a ship is prepared for your journey.''

Again Bardo bowed as Surya glared at him and ground her teeth in rage. But she said nothing in protest of this sentence of banishment.

''And the ronin warrior-poets,'' Danlo said, ''they who aided Hanuman in his terror and torture—they will be returned to their world, too.''

For a long time, as the sun rose higher and bathed the cathedral in its golden light, Danlo stood as a god among the peoples of Neverness, and he gave what commands he could to restore peace to the city. At last, he turned to Lord Pall, who stood near Lord Kutikoff and Vishnu Suso as he silently regarded Danlo with his pink, albino's eyes. If he suspected Danlo of miming Mallory Ringess, he gave no sign. With his bone-white skin fairly hanging in folds from his horrible face, he looked deathly tired and older than old.

''Lord Pall,'' Danlo said, ''I must thank you for acting as Lord of the Order in my absence, but now you will have much time to turn your mind to the contemplation of consciousness and other concerns. You will remain in your tower and rest while the new Lord Cetic takes over your duties.''

And so Danlo, before the greatest lords and masters of the Order, before harijan and ringkeepers and godlings, debased Lord Audric Pall and banished him to a life within the Cetic's Tower. And Lord Pall, suffering greatly from exhaustion and shame, closed his eyes in defeat. Lord Vishnu Suso must have thought that he should protest this preemptory dismissal of his lord and master, for he suddenly opened his mouth in anger. But when he looked upon the dark lights flashing in Danlo's eyes, he kept his silence for fear that he would be debased as well.

''Mallory Ringess! Mallory Ringess! Lord Mallory wi Soli Ringess!''

Lord Salmalin, however, for all his prudence was still a great pilot and therefore graced with a much greater degree of courage than Lord Suso. As he fingered the black silk of his pilot's robe, he faced Danlo and said, ''As Lord Pilot I must say that it's most improper for you to—''

''No,'' Danlo said, interrupting him. His eyes now blazed like hot blue double stars. ''No—I am sorry but you are no longer the Lord Pilot.''

''What?'' Lord Salmalin stared at him almost as if he didn't understand the simple words that Danlo had spoken. And a hundred other pilots stared at him as well.

"We all must honor you for your decision to lead the Ringist fleet against the Fellowship," Danlo said. "But much murder came from what you did, and the Order, no less the Civilized Worlds, almost perished in consequence. It is time that a new Lord Pilot should be chosen."

"And who is this new Lord Pilot to be, then?" Salmalin asked.

"His name is Pesheval Sarojin Vishnu-Shiva Lal," Danlo said. Here he smiled and turned to Bardo. "All of you know him as the master pilot, Bardo."

While Bardo's face glowed with fulfillment and pride, Lara Jesusa and Sabri dur li Kadir and other pilots whom he had led bowed deeply to him and rapped their pilot's rings against the altar's brass rails to acclaim his elevation. Salmalin the Prudent, though, shook his head and half-shouted, "But he's not even a pilot of the Order! He abjured his vows years ago and became a ronin pilot!"

And here Lord Vishnu Suso finally found his courage. After clearing his throat several times, he ventured to observe that in the three thousand years since the founding of Neverness, no one who had ever quit the Order had ever been allowed back into the halls of the Academy.

"Truly, they have not," Danlo said. "But these are new times, and there will be a new rule for our Order—and for other orders as well. If he wishes, Bardo will take new vows and take his place as Lord Pilot."

Now it was Bardo's turn to smile at Danlo, and then he bowed his head and called out, "By God, but I do wish it! I think I've never wished anything more. Thank you, Little Fellow, thank you!"

And Danlo said, "You are welcome. I think that you will be a truly splendid Lord Pilot."

Danlo's honoring of Bardo this way proved to be immediately popular, for many of the pilots and godlings standing near him began to shout out: "Lord Bardo! Lord Bardo! Lord Pilot of the Order!"

And then many others within the cathedral and without, responded to this chant with an even greater one that shook the very streets of the city: "Mallory Ringess! Lord of the Order! Lord of the Way! Lord of Light!"

And so Danlo might have spent the rest of the day basking in

the adulation of the manswarms and trying to heal all the wounds
of the war. But then all that had happened to him since he had
returned to Neverness overwhelmed him. Inside himself he had
truly found the secret fire of life, but the flames had burned too
brightly for too long. Although every cell in his body had come
awake almost at once, the remaking of himself in this way required great amounts of energy. Kiyoshi Telek and other wide-
eyed godlings might think that a god (or a man) could live off the
radiations of the sun, but it was not so. As Danlo had had nothing
to eat or drink since the morning of the preceding day, he was
quite weak. In truth, he was sickeningly, perilously weak, and he
suddenly swooned and fell against Bardo. He almost lost consciousness, then, and he might have toppled to the floor if Bardo
hadn't caught him in his huge arms and helped him to keep his
feet.

"What happened?" a hundred voices cried out at once.
"What's happened to Mallory Ringess?"

Bardo, who held Danlo tightly as the light gradually returned
to his eyes, whispered to him, "Little Fellow, are you all right?"

And Danlo smiled as he nodded his head and whispered in
return, "Yes—I am all right, Bardo. Now everything will be all
right."

With a wave of his arm for people to move out of the way,
Bardo began to help Danlo walk toward the apartments in the
chapter house of the cathedral. His great voice bellowed out,
"Please let us pass. Can't you see he's exhausted? Even a god has
to sleep."

Yes, sleep, Danlo thought. And then he said a silent prayer for
that part of himself that would always sleep beyond the stars now:
Danlo wi Soli Ringess, mi alasharia la, shantih, shantih.

As Danlo moved alongside Bardo through the many-colored
sunlight streaming through the cathedral's windows, the people
began to chant once again: "The Ringess has returned! Lord of
the Order! Lord of the Way! Lord of Light!"

And in the silence of his soul and the deepness of his eyes,
even as he moved forward and fell into sleep, Danlo answered
them: *Yes! Yes! Yes! Yes!*

THE LORD OF
THE ORDER

*Thy tears are for those beyond tears; and are thy words
words of wisdom? The wise grieve not for those who live;
and grieve not for those who die—for life and death shall
pass away.*

*Because we all have been for all time: I, and thou, and
those kings of men. And we all shall be for all time, we all
for ever and ever.*

—Lord Krishna to Arjuna before the battle of Kurukshetra

The next few days Danlo spent in recovering from his ordeal in
the cathedral's sanctuary. Bardo appropriated the largest of the
chapterhouse's apartments for Danlo's use, and Malaclypse Redring—along with various ringkeepers and godlings—stood guard
outside Danlo's door. Even as Bardo ordered the Hollow Fields
opened to massive food shipments from Yarkona, Askling and
Larondissement and the city began to return to order, Danlo did
little more than sleep and eat. The awakened cells of his great
body required great amounts of food energy. As a bear eats in
midwinter spring, he devoured whole platefuls of dried bloodfruit,
steamed rice, boiled ming beans and his beloved kurmash. From
Audun Luz came a whole deepship carrying the carcasses of
slaughtered sheep. With cultured meats from Askling readily
available, few in the city were willing to eat this once-living flesh.
But to the astonishment (and disgust) of such godlings as Kiyoshi
Telek, Danlo wolfed down almost a whole side of lamb fairly
dripping with red juices.

When asked how a god could commit such a bloodthirsty and
non-spiritual act, Danlo replied simply, "The word spirit truly
means breath. This is just the breath of life, yes? This lamb that I
have eaten would have drawn many millions of breaths, so many
millions. What could be more alive than a lamb running through a
field of grass beneath Askling's yellow sun? And where did all

this life go when he was killed? Nothing is lost, truly. The lamb gave his blessed life so that I might live and breathe, too. So much life, so much spirit in flesh—and now it has all passed into me so that I might create yet greater life. What could be more spiritual than that?''

Such remarks mystified and dismayed the followers of Mallory Ringess, for they wished their god to be as they thought a god should be. But Mallory Ringess had never acted according to the sentiments of others, and neither did Danlo. Having quickly regained his great vitality, he fairly flew out of bed and set about the many tasks that lay before him. Against the objections of the godlings, he crossed the Old City to the Academy, where he took up residence at the top of the highest of the two Morning Towers. Truly, he was Mallory Ringess, Lord of the Way of Ringess, he said, but he was also first Lord of the Order. As Lord of the Order he would live among the masters and journeymen of the Pilot's College, Resa, where he had once been a journeyman, too.

On the morning of the 53rd, he sent for Bardo, who had spent almost every moment of the last couple of days in establishing himself as the new Lord Pilot of the Order. Since Bardo still commanded as the Lord Pilot of the Fellowship Fleet, too, and the Fellowship had been formed to fight the Ringists of the Order, this dual lordship posed something of a conflict for Bardo. It was to resolve the tensions between the Fellowship and the Order— and for other reasons—that Bardo climbed the steps to the top of the South Morning Tower and met with Danlo in his rooms.

''Little Fellow!'' he said as he embraced Danlo. He looked at Danlo strangely, deeply and knowingly—and with much irony coloring his large brown eyes. ''It's good to see that you've returned to your old self.''

Danlo smiled at Bardo even as the huge man smiled at him. Then Bardo looked around Danlo's rooms, which occupied most of the top floor of the South Morning Tower. Although Danlo's living area was graced with a magnificent clary dome that allowed a view of almost the entire Academy below, Danlo had filled it with only a few things. He had asked the novices who served him to bring him a Fravashi carpet, sleeping furs, the chess table and set from the cathedral's sanctuary, the devotionary computer, a coffee service, a few flowering plants—and little else. Thus the large room seemed almost as barren as a cavern.

''It's a stark apartment that you keep,'' Bardo said. ''Not even a chair or a couch for me to sit upon. But then Danlo wi Soli Ringess always hated sitting on chairs, didn't he?''

Again Danlo smiled, and Bardo clasped him in his arms as he laughed and pounded happily on his back. "Danlo, Danlo—by God, it *is* you, isn't it?"

Danlo nodded his head and laughed in delight. And then he said, "Didn't I tell you? Didn't I say that we would meet again even though a million stars and all the lightships of Neverness lay between us?"

"Of course you did, but I didn't dare to believe you. Ah, Little Fellow, it's good to see you again!"

With a final slap on Danlo's shoulder, Bardo stared deeply into his eyes.

"You knew," Danlo said, even as he invited Bardo to sit with him cross-legged on the carpet. Like a great black swan folding in his wings, Bardo settled into his shesheen cape and sat down. "From the moment you looked at me in the cathedral, you knew who I was, yes?"

"Ah, I did know," Bardo said. "That is, I knew but I didn't quite *know* with certainty, if you know what I mean. Not until I saw Master Daghaim with your father's ring."

Danlo looked down at the circle of diamond sparkling around his finger. He remembered how Bardo had kept the ring that his father had entrusted to him and had given it to Danlo in the Novice's Sanctuary many years before.

"It was your goddamned eyes," Bardo said. "Who's ever had such eyes, so blue, so deep, so full of such goddamned light?"

"Well, it is said that my father's eyes were so bright that he could look into the souls of even warrior-poets and cetics."

"He could, couldn't he?" Bardo said. "Well, I suppose that you're in no danger of being exposed due to your goddamned eye color. No one but Bardo knew both you and your father so well."

"That is true," Danlo said. "Nevertheless, I think that I will let only a few others as close to me as you."

"Who, then?"

"Malaclypse Redring of Qallar," Danlo said. "The Brothers Hur and perhaps one or two of the Kalla Fellowship. Old Father, of course. And Tamara, if I can find a way to see her without arousing anyone's suspicions."

"Tamara!" Bardo called out. "She's alive, then, thank God! Is she well? How did you find her, Little Fellow?"

For a while they sat together, and Danlo recounted his journey from Sheydveg to Neverness and much of what had happened leading up to his confrontation with Hanuman in the cathedral. He poured out cups of steaming black coffee even as he told Bardo of his killing the bear and the death of his son.

"I never knew that you and Tamara had a child together," Bardo said, shaking his head. "Oh, too bad, Little Fellow, too, too bad."

As Danlo breathed softly, he looked into the steam swirling off his coffee and fell into a deep silence.

"Did you really kill Hanuman, then? The three warrior-poets, too?"

"Yes."

"You must have hated him down to the cells of your fingernails."

"Yes, truly I did," Danlo said. "Almost as much as I loved him."

"Ah, too bad. That is, it's too bad that you had to be the one to kill him. But what you did saved us all, you know."

"No," Danlo said, "it was you and your pilots who won the battle."

Bardo looked up through the dome at the blue sky where the sun's light outshined the lesser radiance of ten thousand stars. "But we might have lost the battle. Such a thin chance. If Hanuman hadn't broken interface with the Universal Computer at the critical moment, if Salmalin's pilots hadn't been suddenly blinded to the computer's simulations of our mappings . . . ah, it might have been *our* fate to burn up inside the stars."

"What was it my father once said? Fate and chance—the same glad dance. In the end, we choose our fates."

"Well, you certainly chose yours, didn't you? And Hanuman chose his. His goddamned insane fate."

"No, his blessed fate, Bardo."

"What do you mean 'blessed?' "

Danlo stared at the ivory pieces of the chess set, particularly at the empty square of the board where the white god should have been. And then he said, "Hanuman believed that he was creating a better universe. Truly. He believed in this mad dream, and so in the end, he fell mad. Hopelessly, helplessly mad. But in a way, this was his great affirmation, yes? He accepted his madness as his fate and even willed himself to love it; he surrendered his whole soul to his dream, and what could be more blessed than that?"

"But he raped Tamara of her memories!" Bardo half-shouted.

"Yes—I remember."

"But what he did led to the death of your son and too, too many billions of others!"

"Yes."

"And if we hadn't stopped him, he would have blown up all the goddamned stars!"

Now Danlo nodded his head slowly and reached out to grasp Bardo's huge hand in his own. "This is hard," he said. "For me, still the hardest thing. To accept the nature of creation just as it is. To see that even monsters and madmen have a place in the universe."

To the distant sound of the shuttles that rocketed up and down from the Hollow Fields ferrying foodstuffs to the city, Danlo and Bardo debated the nature (and fate) of the universe and other eschatological concerns. Bardo wasn't quite ready to make such a total affirmation as Danlo. He listened politely to Danlo, all the while sipping his black coffee with much pleasure and stroking his thick black beard. And then, upon noticing that time was slipping away from them like sands through one of the Timekeeper's hourglasses, he turned toward more immediate mysteries.

"But how did you come to be carked into the same shape as your father?" Bardo finally asked. "The more I look at you, the harder it is to see any difference."

"I found the cutter who sculpted my father."

"Mehtar Hajime? That treacherous worm of a cutter?"

As Danlo watched Bardo's face darken with anger, he remembered the vengeful little joke Mehtar Hajime had once played on Bardo.

"When I found him," Danlo said, "he called himself Constancio of Alesar."

"Where is he, then? By God, I've been looking for him for twenty-five years, and when I catch him I'll squeeze his treacherous face until—"

"He is dead," Danlo said softly. "Hanuman had him killed so that no one would know who I truly am."

"Ah, too bad, too bad."

In gazing at Bardo's still-wroth face, it occurred to Danlo that Bardo regretted the lost chance of vengeance only, not Mehtar's fate. And so he said, "Yes, it is too bad, truly. Hanuman did not need to murder him."

"But he betrayed you, Little Fellow! He betrayed us all, and it's only a miracle that his treachery didn't destroy everything."

Never killing unless it is truly necessary to kill, Danlo remembered. And he said, "Even so, it is *shaida* to kill unless—"

"Save your compassion for Tamara and all the mothers who've lost sons in this goddamned war," Bardo broke in. "Save your compassion for yourself."

Danlo took a sip of coffee and held it burning in his mouth a moment before swallowing it. And then he sighed and said, "In betraying me to Hanuman, Mehtar *did* violate the contract we had made. And so I've sent Benjamin Hur to his house to recover the scryer's sphere that I gave him."

"Your mother's sphere, then?"

"Yes."

"Ah, but you gave up a lot to become Mallory Ringess, didn't you?"

Danlo closed his eyes for a moment as he silently prayed for the spirits of both Hanuman li Tosh and Danlo wi Soli Ringess. And then he looked at Bardo and said, "Yes, truly I did."

"Well, I'll take your secret with me to my death. I did a good job of acting in the cathedral, didn't I?"

"You even wept when you saw me."

"Ah, Little Fellow, but the tears were for *you*. I don't think I've ever been so glad to see anyone in all my life."

"I was glad, too, Bardo."

At this, Bardo's eyes flooded yet again as if could barely contain the ocean of water that surged inside him. And then he said, "I suppose I should confess, however, that I entered the cathedral hoping that your father really had returned. I've waited so long for him to return, you see."

"I know," Danlo said.

"But he'll never return, will he?" Bardo asked as he stared down at the black pool of his coffee and lost himself in his swirling reflection. "No, no, of course he won't, he must be dead, too bad. Ah, poor Bardo, too bad."

Nothing is lost, Danlo remembered. And then he said, "He might still be alive, you know."

At this Bardo looked up and smiled at Danlo. "Well, I suppose he *is* alive, Little Fellow—in you. You're his son, by God, and I think I've seen that since the moment I first saw you shivering in Lavi Square. And now the son has become the father. Your plan worked very well, didn't it? Even Surya now believes that you're Mallory Ringess."

With a sad sigh, Bardo told him that Surya Surata Lal had been put aboard a blackship bound for Summerworld. And then he said, "It was the only thing to do, of course. But I wish that you'd consulted with me first."

"I am sorry," Danlo said. "But there may be many things that I will have to do without consulting you."

"But I'm the Lord Pilot," Bardo said, plainly angry and hurt. "The Lord Pilot of the goddamned Order!"

"And I am the Lord of the Order," Danlo said, smiling to ease Bardo's discomfiture. "Lord Mallory Ringess, they call me."

But Bardo, who had led thirty-thousand ships to victory in the greatest war that the Civilized Worlds had ever suffered, had grown as used to power as a seal is to water, and was not quite ready to surrender any of it to anyone, not even Danlo.

"Well," he said, "you're not *really* Mallory Ringess, too bad. You're just a pilot, Little Fellow, an ambassador from the Fellowship sent here to stop the war."

For the moment, Danlo made no reply to this, but only looked deep into Bardo's soft brown eyes.

"And even if you *were* Lord of the Order," Bardo said as he nervously fingered his coffee cup, "I'm still Lord Pilot of the Fellowship, and the Fellowship has just fought a goddamned war for the right to dictate the terms of peace to the Order."

Now Danlo stared at Bardo for a long time, and his eyes flashed like firestones heated in the heart of a star. So bright did his gaze grow that Bardo finally had to look away.

"Ah, I'm sorry," he finally said. "You really *are* your father's son, aren't you? At last. I once asked you why you didn't do what you were born to do. Well, now you have. I suppose I should be glad of that. You are who you are, aren't you? Lord of the Order—Lord of Light, they call you. I should call you that myself. Ah, I suppose we should continue this ruse that you've so brilliantly begun. You be the Lord of the Order, if you want to, Little Fellow. After all, it's what you were born to be."

After that, as the sun rose higher over the eastern mountains and the day brightened, they talked of all that remained to be accomplished in ending the war. As Lord Pilot of the Fellowship, Bardo had been empowered only to lead the fleet in battle, not to impose his will upon the city of Neverness and the defeated Ringist Worlds. But the representatives of the Fellowship of Free Worlds who had fought with Bardo had come to like and trust him; both Bardo and Danlo believed that they would follow his leadership in structuring a peace for all the Civilized Worlds. And Danlo, as Lord Mallory Ringess, would command the devotion of all the Ringists across the thousand odd Ringist Worlds—as well as that of the Order itself. Since Mallory Ringess was the rightful Lord of the Order and the Order had given purpose and peace to the Civilized Worlds for three thousand years, if Mallory Ringess pointed a way toward the rebirth of this mighty stellar civilization, the whole Fellowship fleet might very well agree to disperse and return to the many worlds from which it had been formed.

"This would be best," Danlo said, as he poured Bardo another cup of coffee. "We will send the blackships back to their individual worlds with our plan for peace. The pilots must persuade their peoples that the Order has been restored to its original vision."

"Well, it *has* been restored, hasn't it?" Bardo said.

"Truly it has," Danlo agreed, nodding his head. He took a sip of coffee and then continued, "And we must soon send Helena Charbo and the other pilots who came with the Sonderval back to Thiells. We must send Demothi Bede, too. They must tell Lord Nikolos of what has happened here. How Mallory Ringess has returned. Lord Nikolos and Mallory Ringess were friends once, yes?"

"Well, at least they organized the rebellion against the Time-keeper together," Bardo said. "By God, I did, too. So I know Lord Nikolos. I believe that he'll still trust Mallory Ringess, even though he loathes the religion that I so stupidly started in his name."

"For the time, that is true," Danlo said mysteriously. "But we must find a way to change his loathing to something other. The Old Order and the New Order must come together again as one."

Danlo went on to say that with the war finally over, the Order must resume its mission to the Vild. Lord Nikolos must send pilots and emissaries to Tannahill to help Harrah Ivi en li Ede define the new doctrines of the Cybernetic Universal Church. The Order, new and old, would train hundreds or even thousands of new pilots to fall among the stars of the Vild and keep them from exploding into supernovas.

"I've just recalled something," Bardo said. He snapped his fingernail against the hard plates of his black battle armor, which sent a hard clicking sound echoing through the room. "I didn't have time to tell you this when I first saw you, too bad. We've captured the Architects' deepship. Ah, these goddamned Architects that you call the Iviomils—they who blew up Bodil Luz. They almost blew up the Star of Neverness. But pilots of Edreiya Chu's battle group fell upon them just as they fell out into the thickspace. They had no choice but to surrender. We've brought their ship into orbit above Icefall."

"That was a near chance," Danlo said.

"A few moments more and we would not be here discussing the fate of our star," Bardo agreed. "But even in the madness of the battle, I had deployed my ships around point-sources of the nearby stars leading to the thickspace. I had to forestall the Iviomil's attempt, didn't I?"

"That would have been an almost impossible deployment," Danlo said. He closed his eyes and nodded his head in appreciation of the hideous complexities of monitoring the mappings through the manifold at the same time as fighting a battle. "I was right to make you Lord Pilot of the Order."

"Thank you."

All this time, the devotionary computer that Danlo had rescued from the Vild had sat on a little table by the windows. According to Danlo's command, the Ede hologram had remained silent and still. But when the news of the Iviomils' capture fell upon this glittering little computer, its program caused the imago of Nikolos Daru Ede to crack open his sensuous lips and exclaim, "It's been found! My body has been found!"

"It *has* been found," Bardo said, keeping his eyes on Danlo. Danlo had told him how this glittering Ede had gone over to Hanuman in the hope of recovering his frozen body, and so Bardo would not deign to speak with him. "We've found their star-killing machine, too. What is it the Iviomils call it?"

"A *morrashar*," Danlo said.

"Well, we have their *morrashar*. Now we have to decide what to do with it."

"Do? What *would* you do with it, then?"

"I didn't mean that we should begin blowing up stars, too," Bardo said. "Do you think Bardo is a goddamned barbarian? Though I confess I can think of a few bloody planets such as Qallar that we might do well to incinerate. No, no, don't look at me like that, Little Fellow—I'm not serious. Well, not *quite* serious. I suppose that we should send a cadre of tinkers to the ship to study it."

"No, destroy it," Danlo said simply. "The Timekeeper was right, after all. There are some technologies that are best left sleeping."

"What should we do with the Iviomils, then? They slaughtered a whole planet."

For a moment Danlo's face fell white as he stared out the window at the sky. Then he said, "Find Sivan wi Mawi Sarkissian. Tell him that if he wishes to become a pilot of the Order again, he must pilot the deepship back through the Vild to Tannahill. He knows the way. We shall let Harrah Ivi en li Ede judge the Iviomils, yes? They have done much for which they must be judged.''

''And Bertram Jaspari?''

''Send him back on the Iviomil's ship, as well.''

Bardo nodded his head as he puffed out his fat cheeks in thought. ''Should we send Ede's body back to Tannahill, then?''

Danlo looked toward the devotionary computer as a mask of concern froze over the Ede imago's gleaming face. ''No,'' Danlo said, ''bring it here.''

''Here?'' Bardo said. ''Here . . . where?''

''Have it brought to the Morning Towers, into this room.''

Now Ede's eyes shined with relief, as it seemed that he might possibly realize his dream of becoming human once again.

''You wish to sleep with a frozen corpse next to you?'' Bardo asked in amazement.

''I have kept worse company before,'' Danlo said, smiling. ''Please bring the body here. I have promises to keep.''

''Ah, as you wish,'' Bardo said, shaking his head, and he smiled, too. Then his face fell grim and serious as he turned to matters of greater moment. ''We should begin dismantling the Universal Computer as soon as possible, you know.''

''Yes, we must,'' Danlo said as he looked up at the dark spot in the sky where the Universal Computer hung like a black, ominous moon. ''Though, in a way, I wish that we did not have to destroy it.''

''What? Why not?''

A strange light filled Danlo's eyes then, and he said, ''Because this blessed machine is the realization of Hanuman's dream, mad as it was.''

''*Blessed* machine, you say?''

''Yes, blessed, Bardo. It is just a machine, truly. It is made of silicon and carbon atoms—and iron and gold, all the blessed elements that Hanuman assembled. It can be programmed for a purpose that is either *shaida* or *halla.*''

''I can't see any good uses of it,'' Bardo said.

''It is hard, I know,'' Danlo said. ''But the computer was made to simulate whole universes. You cannot even dream what blessed simulations are possible. Human beings will always need such computing power even as they need computers.''

''Well, surely not *this* goddamned computer,'' Bardo said.

"Surely the gods look to Neverness in fear that Hanuman—or even ourselves—would use it to create a new god."

For a moment Danlo stared off at the sky and said nothing.

"Surely they fear we'll create the greatest of the galaxy's god-damned gods and unleash a hakariad that they can't stop."

"Surely they must," Danlo said. He gazed at the yellowish glow of the Golden Ring high in the sky where it edged the Universal Computer. "And that is why we will destroy it."

And then he thought: *We will destroy it utterly, yes. And its elements will be food for the Golden Ring. This golden new life that will grow as a shield protecting us from the radiation of the supernovas. And then, soon, in less than a billion more heartbeats, the greatest hakariad in the history of the stars will begin, and not all the gods together in the universe will be able to stop it.*

"Good, good," Bardo said. "I was afraid that you'd want to use the computer to shake your fist at the heavens and fight the gods themselves."

"No," Danlo said, smiling at Bardo's wild metaphors. "But there is one who *would* have used the Universal Computer against the Solid State Entity and the other gods."

Bardo took a sip of coffee and asked, "Who, then?"

"The Silicon God. I am sure that he was using Hanuman. He would have let Hanuman create this great, *shaida* machine and then used it to incorporate the whole galaxy into himself."

"By God, is that possible?"

"It is possible," Danlo said. "Truly possible."

At this, Bardo rubbed the furrows on his forehead and said, "It's still not clear why the Silicon God didn't just create new computer parts and add them onto himself like any other god."

Danlo nodded his head slowly and said, "I am only beginning to understand this, Bardo. I am only beginning to truly see. How the gods restrain each other from trying to be as God. And how the gods try to find ways to evade each other's restraints."

"Well, can you see how the Silicon God can be defeated, then? I certainly can't. And from what you've told me, neither can the Solid State Entity or any other god."

Now Danlo smiled again, sadly and with compassion but also with all the fierceness of a wild white thallow hunting through the sky. *"We* will defeat the Silicon God," he said. "Someday, we will destroy him utterly."

"You and I?" Bardo said, disbelieving.

"Yes, I and you—and ten trillion others like us."

Yes, yes, yes.

"And how will we do that?" Bardo asked.

To burn off a little of the wild energy firing his nerves, Danlo sprang to his feet and paced around the room for a few moments before stopping by the window. He reached out and rested the palm of his left hand against the cool clary dome. He looked out over the Rose Womb Cloisters and the Hall of the Ancient Pilots and the other nearby buildings of the Academy. He watched groups of journeymen as they crossed the red glidderies and made their way for the Chess Pavilion or Resa Commons or Lavi Hall. He saw many young pilots, of course, as well as scryers, horologes and holists. And now, according to Danlo's order of the preceding day, they were all dressed not in a godling's gold, but in black or crimson or cobalt blue—or any of the Order's hundred traditional colors.

"This Way of Ringess that you created has been such a powerful religion," he said, turning to Bardo. "A truly *shaida* religion. Many would try to unmake it if they could."

"Well you must know that *I* would," Bardo said. "The whole Fellowship has just fought a goddamned war to unmake it."

"But what if it will not be unmade?"

"Then at least we can stop its spread to the stars."

Danlo smiled sadly and shook his head. "You can kill people but you cannot kill their beliefs. Their dreams. Now that the people have seen that Mallory Ringess has returned, Ringism will grow only stronger."

"But what can we do, Little Fellow? There are those who *would* still kill to see Ringism destroyed."

"Then Mallory Ringess will have to remake this religion," Danlo said, smiling. "We will, Bardo. You and I, Jonathan and Benjamin Hur—all of us who were once of the Kalla Fellowship. All who dream of what Ringism might have been, what it could truly be."

"Well, what *could* it be, then?"

Each man and woman is a star, Danlo thought, remembering Hanuman's words. *And in this galaxy alone, a hundred trillion such stars.*

"It is strange," Danlo said, his eyes lit up with a deep fire, "but out of this war, something blessed will emerge. Something *halla.* We shall use the Way of Ringess to create a new race of human beings."

He went on to tell Bardo his dream of a humanity awakened to its true possibilities, of vast numbers of men, women and bright-eyed children across the stars who would become at last what they were born to be. The new Ringism, he said, would fulfill the urges of godlings who wanted to transcend themselves; it would also allay the fears of those who wanted human beings to remain as human beings and had fought against Ringism in the war.

"My father was right, after all," Danlo said. "The secret lies in the Elder Eddas."

"Ah, which secret, then?"

"All secrets," Danlo said. "The way that human beings will become truly human at last. The way that the Silicon God will be destroyed and the greater war won."

Here Bardo puffed out his cheeks again, stood up slowly and stepped over to the window near Danlo. He tapped his forehead and then sighed out, "I've remembranced the Elder Eddas as deeply as any man. Well, as deeply as anyone except Hanuman and you. And I never found the secret of transcendence in these goddamned racial memories."

"They are not racial memories, Bardo."

"What are they, then?"

The memory of all things is in all things, Danlo remembered. *Nothing is ever truly lost.*

"The true Elder Eddas," he said, "are universal memories. The One memory is just the memory of the universe itself. The way the universe evolves in consciousness of itself and causes itself to be. We are just this blessed consciousness, nothing more and nothing less. We are the light inside light that fuses into the atoms of our bodies; we are the fire that whirls across the stellar deeps and dances all things into being."

"Now you're speaking mystically again, Little Fellow."

"About some things there is no other way to speak."

"Well, I've always been suspicious of the mystical, you know." Bardo looked away from Danlo at the lovely frost patterns frozen to the window. And then he asked, "Are we to be lotus-eaters, then, intoxicated on our visions of the infinite? Drinkers of kalla drowning in the One memory? No, no—that's no way for the human race, too bad."

"I did not say that we would all have to drink kalla again," Danlo said. "Only remember who we truly are. There is a way toward our fate that lies *through* remembrance of the One. Through it and inside it, deeper into life."

"Ah, what I've always loved about you, Little Fellow, is not your talent for mystical ecstasies but your rare gift for life."

Danlo smiled as he bowed his head to Bardo. Then he said,

"And what I have loved about you is that of all the human beings that I have known, you are the most truly human."

At this, Bardo's brows narrowed in deep thought. He seemed unable to decide if Danlo had insulted him or had only been speaking mysteriously again.

Each man and woman is a star, Danlo thought. He remembered Hanuman saying this years ago in the Ring of Fire before a hundred thousand cheering people. He remembered as well the ideal of the Fravashi Old Fathers, which was that each woman and man should become a perfect mirror for all that is holiest in each other. And so he looked at Bardo, and his eyes glistened like still ocean waters, and he pointed up through the dome at the rising sun.

"Tat tvam asi," he said. "That thou art, Bardo. Each man and woman is a star, and none shines more brightly than you."

"Do you really think so?" Bardo asked, squinting and trying to look up at the sun. "Ah, but there were times when *I* almost thought so. But the truth is the truth. When I think a noble thought or fall in a lightship through the manifold and open a new window upon the stars, I'm a god. But when my belly growls with hunger or I ache to swive a woman, I'm a dog like any other man.

Yes, yes, yes.

Now Danlo smiled at Bardo, and something opened within him. It was like the sea suddenly clearing and becoming utterly transparent to a deep and perfect blue inside blue. Through the windows of his eyes, he took Bardo down through the sacred salt and sparkling waters of his soul to the secret fire that burned at the center of the ocean. And in the brilliance of what Bardo saw blazing inside Danlo (and perhaps inside himself), his own eyes filled with a bright and splendid light.

"Ah," Bardo said, "all I've ever really wanted is to live and laugh and love as many beautiful women as possible. And yet something more, always something more. There were always the stars, Little Fellow. It's like the lights of a whole galaxy hanging all white and brilliant in the sky. It seems so near but only a pilot in the finest of lightships who has mastered the Great Theorem could ever hope to reach it, even after a journey lasting a lifetime of years. Bardo will always have to be Bardo, do you understand? But Bardo has always been becoming Bardo, and that's a journey he began even before coming to Perilous Hall where the fourth year novices ridiculed him for pissing in his bed every night. If you were to ask me who I thought Bardo *really* is, I suppose I should say that he's a man who wants to evolve as much as any other man."

At this, Danlo bowed his head and said, simply, "Then evolve."

"All right," Bardo said, "I think I will. But now, if we're done discussing the fate of the universe, I'd like to order some food for us and drink a few glasses of wine. Did you know that along with the grain shipments, Summerworld has sent us a hundred cases of firewine? By God, I haven't tasted firewine since before the war, and that's too, too long a time!"

So saying, he clapped Danlo's shoulder and smiled at him with a deep understanding, and he turned to find the novice who would serve them their midday meal.

PEACE

*There is a door that opens upon a light inside light and a
peace inside peace. I have returned to show you the key
that unlocks the door.*
   —Mallory wi Soli Ringess, Lord of the Order of Mystic
   Mathematicians and Other Keepers of the Ineffable Flame

As war will come from the essential tension within all peace, so
peace will come from the exhaustion of war. War brings forth
from human beings their highest possibilities and prepares the
way for new life, as day illuminates night, and this is why men
and women love it as they do. But as night devours the day war
also cancels the possibilities of precious lives, and so mothers and
warriors and young children staring at hydrogen fireballs burning
the sky rightly hate it as the greatest of evils.

There will probably never be a count of all those who died in
the War of the Gods. The thousands of pilots lost in the flashing
battles across the Fallaways and the many fallen ringkeepers and
godlings composed only the tiniest fraction of the many people of
the Civilized Worlds who made the journey to the other side of
day. Some historians, such as Lord Burgos Harsha, estimated the
dead at forty-five billion, while others were to settle upon a figure
greater by at least five billions. Who could ever say how many
men and women were incinerated when Helaku High's star fell
supernova, for the Helakists had never taken a census of their
swarming population, believing as they did that human beings
should never be numbered like gold coins kept in a vault. And
what of Iwaloon where three billion citizens died of a mysterious
plague in the days preceding the Battle of the Ten Thousand
Suns? Was this the work of careless engineers manufacturing yet
another horror weapon of war or only a mutant virus of a-kind that
would erupt and decimate isolated peoples from time to time?

It was hard even to determine exactly when the war ended—
and when it had begun. Did the mass murders on Azur Baytay, for
example, truly result from the Ringists' bid for power against the

arhats there, or was this only a continuation of the endless cycles of internecine strife that have ravaged that unfortunate planet for ten thousand years?

Nevertheless, most of the Order's historians were to single out the 47th of deep winter in year 2959 as the correct date, for on that night Lord Salmalin the Prudent surrendered the Ringist fleet to Bardo, and on that morning it was said that Mallory Ringess returned to Neverness to put an end to war. Danlo, however, even wearing the body and face of his father, did not find it so simple to stop the violent movements of a trillion people across three thousand worlds, all at once. Can one stop a tidal wave from flooding a beach or a large blue star from exploding once it has begun its collapse into all the violent potential of its terrible, crushing gravities? As he had told Benjamin Hur in the cathedral, he couldn't keep men and women from killing each other, if that is what they truly wished to do. But of course they wished for other things as well, and so in the days following Danlo's near-collapse in the cathedral, he devoted himself to helping the people of the Civilized Worlds find the way toward peace.

And so much of what Danlo had discussed with Bardo in the Morning Towers came to pass. Even as the days of deep winter darkened toward Year's End, Danlo sent Demothi Bede back to Thiells aboard Helena Charbo's ship, the *Infinite Pearl*. Sabri dur li Kadir and Aja and other pilots of the New Order accompanied them in a sparkling array of lightships, along with quite a few pilots of the Old Order, who, in the wake of the war, had discovered within themselves a vocation to stop the Vild stars from exploding.

On Year's End itself—the shortest day of the year but also the turning of the world in which each succeeding day grew longer and ever lighter—the Fellowship Fleet began to break up, even as Danlo had foretold. The surviving thousands of blackships, goldships and deepships fell away from the near space above Icefall in a brilliant twinkling of windows to the manifold flashing open. In tens and twenties they vanished into the night and returned to Silvaplana, Avalon and the Rainbow Double, to Wakanda and Simoom and hundreds of other worlds. Only the Tenth Battle Group remained, hanging around Icefall's five moons like a gleaming net of nall and black diamond. Before dispersing itself sometime the following winter, this small but powerful force would ensure that the Order really returned to order and that the Universal Computer was really destroyed.

The unmaking of this moon-sized machine began on the seventh day of midwinter spring in the year 2960. Against the objections of many of the Order's more conservative masters and lords, Danlo suspended the Law of the Civilized Worlds and ordered the building of many hundreds of hydrogen bombs. The ships of the Tenth Battle Group ferried these monstrous weapons up through the Golden Ring to the point above Icefall where the Computer spun silently in the night and perpetually turned its gleaming dark face to the universe. There robots implanted the bombs deep beneath the Computer's glaze of black diamond skin. In a series of brilliant explosions witnessed by a thousand pilots, no less the galaxy's gods, the bombs fused hydrogen into great bursts of hellish white light that blew apart the Computer's outer layers of circuitry. It was not enough, of course, to destroy such a vast structure, but in the days that followed, other explosions would further reduce the Computer to great floating pieces of rubble. And then the same microscopic robots that had disassembled and dissolved Icefall's sixth moon would be released upon the Computer's remnant parts in a great glittering cloud. These programmed bacteria would begin digesting bits of optical circuitry, tearing the Computer apart into its constituent elements. A rain of carbon, silicon, oxygen and other atoms would fall down toward Icefall's atmosphere where the little makers and other Ring organisms would begin to feast upon these rich nutrients. And then the Ring would complete the first stage of its evolution in a brilliant, golden envelope of life, thus protecting Icefall from the radiations of the Vild.

Many people celebrated the Universal Computer's destruction as the true ending of the war. For many days in early midwinter spring—even in the coldness of the storms that clotted the streets with mounds of thick, soggy snow—harijan, autists, arhats and exemplars as well as the masters of the Order took to meeting at the city's various ice rings and greens to skate and talk and exchange hopes that never again would ship fall against ship or hydrogen bombs explode above their planet.

But not everyone was overjoyed at the display of fireworks that lit up the sky. The godlings who had taken in each of Hanuman's words as a blind man might grab up a pocketful of counterfeit coins, truly lamented the fate of the Computer. For them the great blossoms of light that flowered in the heavens through the nights and days marked the passing of their dream. They hadn't yet quite understood that it was impossible to remembrance the Elder Eddas through interfacing any computer, no matter how cleverly programmed or vast. Nor did they yet share Danlo's vision of how a new Ringism might awaken them to their true possibilities.

But there are always new ways and new dreams. As the heavy weather of midwinter spring gave way to the cool, clear, sunny days of false winter, the godlings began to see how Lord Mallory Ringess intended to transform the religion that had sprung up around his name. Each day in the early evening, Danlo made the short journey from the Academy through the Old City's narrow red streets to the cathedral. There, in the sanctuary where once Hanuman had gazed out through the dome at the farthest galaxies of the universe, Danlo called Thomas Rane, the Brothers Hur, Bardo, Poppy Panshin, Kiyoshi Telek, Malaclypse of Qallar and a few others to sit with him in a circle beneath the stars. They drank cups of sweet peppermint tea together, and they laughed together, and together they made their way deep into remembrance toward that secret place where the fires of creation burn as one. Soon those of the circle would begin to pass this ineffable flame of awakening to other hands, and in this way Ringists throughout Neverness and across the stars would make the same journey as had Danlo.

Near the middle of false winter a new excitement began to blow through the city like a warming wind. Those who had died in the war had long since been buried or cremated, and the streets had returned almost to the exuberance of happier years. On the 30th of false winter, the new food factories delivered their first major harvest to the city's restaurants, both private and free. Once again it was possible to skate along the Serpentine and drink in the smells of coffee, cilka and roasting garlic that wafted out among the crowds seeking a meal. As too many had starved during the war, the still-hungry peoples of the city often ate five or six full meals each day, at any hour day or night. Spiced kurmash, chinquapin stew, Yarkonan cheeses melted on flatbread, cultured shagshay cooked with takenyats in firewine, cookies and cakes, bloodfruit in cream and mangoes and flaming bananas—there seemed no end to the rich food that one might find from a little cafe near the Ashtoreth District to the famous dining rooms of the Hofgarten.

Beneath the bright, sunny sky, there came golden days of new hope and birds returning to the trees of the Fravashi Green once again to sing their strange, sweet songs. Even the most skeptical of naysayers—they who might wait many more years before daring to join any Ringist in remembrance of the Elder Eddas—

admitted to each other that Mallory Ringess had brought a rule of peace to the city.

Some people, however, did not so readily bow to the wishes of the Lord of the Order and the Way of Ringess. On the 35th of false winter, when the Iviomil's deepship had finally been made ready for the long journey to Tannahill, a young man named Samsa Armadan slipped past the godlings guarding Bertram Jaspari and fired an exploding mercury tlolt into the would-be High Holy Ivi's brain. This murderous missile killed him instantly.

And his guards in turn might have instantly executed Samsa Armadan as an assassin, but they discovered that he was one of them, both a godling and a holist of the Order. He had been born on Helaku High and had lost all his friends and family when the Iviomils destroyed their star. And so he had killed Bertram Jaspari purely out of vengeance. In former times, the Lord of the Order would have banished him to his home world for his crime, but since Helaku no longer existed, Danlo couldn't pronounce such a sentence. In truth, he couldn't bring himself to banish Samsa at all, to any world, because in looking at Samsa's death-haunted eyes when he was brought before him, he took pity upon him and merely chastised him instead.

"We must never kill unless it is truly necessary to kill," he told Samsa in the privacy of the Morning Tower. "It was not upon you to kill Bertram Jaspari for his crimes. No matter that you think he was a monster, no matter that I think that, too, he might yet have been something more. I wish I could show you the jewel within the lotus within the human heart. The incredible value of each person's life, even Bertram Jaspari's. He was only what the universe made him and what he made himself. And he was about to make a journey to a place where he would never harm anyone again. Truly, he would have been judged and punished—he would have spent the rest of his life serving others. And now so must you. This is my sentence, then: there are many children in Neverness who have lost their families even as you have. You will find one of these and be as a father to him. You will teach him that out of hate can come something as rare and beautiful as a thallow breaking free from an egg and flying off into the sky."

When Danlo finished speaking, Samsa Armadan bowed to him at last, and with a sad smile, Danlo returned his bow. He knew that in sentencing Samsa thusly, he was only sentencing himself.

Hanu, Hanu, he silently prayed for the ten thousandth time since the end of the war, *mi alasharia la, shantih, shantih—please forgive me.*

Later that day he ordered that Bertram Jaspari's body be preserved in krydda and returned to Tannahill, where the Architects
could dispose of it according to their rituals. And he ordered
Nikolos Daru Ede's body to be returned there as well. To fulfill
his promise that he had made in the Vild to the Ede imago, he had
asked the city's cryologists if they could revive this three thousand year-old frozen corpse. But even the finest of the cryologists,
who were the finest in the Civilized Worlds, pronounced this task
as hopeless. Although the tissues of Ede's body might be returned
to life, they said, Ede's brain had long since been completely
destroyed. At Ede's historic vastening as Ede the God, the process
of modeling the synapses and copying this pattern into one of the
Old Church's eternal computers had utterly reduced these same
synapses to a red jelly. Truly, it was as if a mercury tlolt had
exploded inside *Ede's* blessed brain. As Danlo had feared, Ede
had forever given up his humanity in a fruitless quest to become
something infinitely more. And now Ede—what was left of him—
must give up his last hope of ever becoming human again.

"I am sorry," he told the Ede imago that night, "but the
cryologists could do nothing."

He stood by the domed window of the South Morning Tower
between the devotionary computer and the crypt of Nikolos Daru
Ede. The crypt—a long octagonal-shaped box wrought almost
entirely of clary—perfectly displayed the frozen body of Nikolos
Daru Ede. Through the planes of the clary surface, Danlo could
clearly see Ede's bald head and his pudgy brown face. It was
almost exactly the same face that stared at him from the space
above the devotionary computer.

"I am sorry," Danlo said again, "but I have decided to send
his body back to Tannahill. Before I left there, I promised Harrah
that I would try to find it, if I could."

"But you promised *me* that you would help me recover my
body," Ede finally said. His face had fallen tight and grim, and it
seemed that at any moment he might weep. But obviously the
imago was not programmed to instantiate such an emotion. *"My
body, Pilot."*

"I have kept my promise to you," Danlo said. "And now I
must keep my promise to Harrah."

"Then why have you had my body brought here?"

"I thought that you might want to see it before . . ."

"Before what, Pilot?"

"Before saying goodbye," Danlo said.

At this the Ede imago seemed truly puzzled. He stared at the crypt through many of Danlo's heartbeats before saying, ''Thank you—you're a kind man, really the best of men.''

Danlo bowed to the glowing Ede, then, and he smiled sadly.

''And I must thank you,'' Ede said, ''for keeping your promise. You were true to your word, even though I had betrayed you in the sanctuary.''

Again Danlo bowed in silence.

''I must tell you that I *had* to betray you. I was programmed to do anything in order to recover my body.''

''I understand.''

''I'm utterly a slave to my programming, you know. And that's why I must, after all, say goodbye now.''

Danlo sighed as he reached out to the crypt and rested his hand on its hard clear surface. ''Would you like me to leave you alone for a while?''

''Oh, no, Pilot—I did not mean that I must say goodbye to my body. That's only a useless, frozen husk, isn't it? I must say goodbye to you.''

Now Danlo whipped his head about sharply and stared at the Ede imago in surprise. He asked, ''Do you wish to make a journey, then?''

''Well, we all have journeys to make, don't we? In a way, we all make the same journey.''

''Yes, truly we do.''

''I'm glad you understand. And so before I make this final journey of mine, I must say goodbye to you. And then I must say goodbye to myself.''

''But how can you do that?''

''I'll say the word that takes the computer down.''

''But you told me that you were programmed never to say that word.''

''I lied, you know. My program required me to lie—too bad, as Bardo would say.''

''I do not want you to take yourself down,'' Danlo said.

''But my program requires this. If I know that there is no hope of living again, I must say the word.''

''But you know that there is no hope.''

''I *do* know that, now, of course. The blue rose, Pilot. The neverness of the blue rose.''

Danlo stared off at the window for a moment, and then he said, ''But there still must be hope of you living as you are now. Otherwise you would already have taken yourself down.''

"Do you call this living?" Ede asked as he waved his glowing hand in the air.

"Yes, truly you are alive. In a way, everything is."

"But I don't want to be alive in *this* way. I'm only waiting."

"Waiting for what, then?"

"My program requires me to wait a period of time between the moment that I know there is no hope of recovering my body and the moment that I take myself down. In case I have overlooked something or some new hope arises."

"How long, then?"

"Nine hundred billion nanoseconds."

"So little time."

"So *much* time. Without hope, each nanosecond is like an eternity."

"But there is always hope," Danlo said. "If not hope for what you have dreamed, then perhaps another kind."

"And what is that?"

"Perhaps the Order's programmers could reprogram you so that you no longer wish to become human."

"But then I would not be *I,* would I, Pilot?"

"Perhaps they could reprogram you so that you no longer need to take yourself down."

"But time is running out, isn't it? You can't know how few nanoseconds are left."

"How many, then?"

The Ede imago smiled at this question and only shook his head. "In any case, my program doesn't permit me to be reprogrammed. Any such attempt would take me down permanently."

"I see," Danlo said. For many moments now, he had been counting the beats of his heart. He closed his eyes as the numbers burned like blazing arrows through his blood into his mind: Twenty-eight, twenty-nine, thirty, thirty-one . . . And then he looked at Ede and said again, "I do not want you to take yourself down."

"I'm sorry, Pilot—I didn't know that you cared."

Forty-three, forty-four, forty-five . . .

"There's always a moment, isn't there?" Ede said. "For each of us, always a moment."

"No, no," Danlo said. But then a deeper voice spoke inside him: *Yes, yes, yes.*

"Goodbye, Pilot."

Sixty-seven, sixty-eight, sixty-nine . . .

"Yahweha," the Ede imago said.

And with this single word, the hologram projecting out of the devotionary computer instantly winked out into neverness. Danlo stared at the dark, empty space above the computer from where Ede had beamed forth his bright smiles for so long. He placed his right hand on the hard, jeweled box of the computer, but he felt not the slightest trace of warmth or any vibration. For a moment, in the immense silence of the room, he puzzled over the word that had taken the devotionary computer down. He was certain that he had never heard it before. And then, as he closed his eyes, he looked far back into the ocean of clear, sparkling memories that were his and yet not his alone. And he suddenly remembered this word out the dawn of man's ur-religion on Old Earth: Yahweha, the unspeakable name of God that Ede had finally spoken.

"Yahweha," Danlo whispered himself, "Yahweha ehad."

Still holding his right hand on top of the devotionary computer, he reached out and touched his left hand to Ede's hard clary crypt. "Nikolos Daru Ede," he said, gazing through the crypt at Ede's frozen body, *"mi alasharia la, shantih, shantih—* rest in peace from your long journey."

The passing of Nikolos Daru Ede reminded Danlo that even the greatest of beings have a time to live and a time to die. It reminded him as well of the vulnerability of other beings closer to his heart. Since the night of his paralysis on the floor of the cathedral's sanctuary, he had agonized over the torture of Old Father. At first, after he had ordered Old Father returned to his house in the Fravashi District, it seemed that the tough, white-furred alien would recover from what Hanuman's warrior-poets had done to him. But by the end of midwinter spring, Old Father began to weaken with a mysterious wasting disease that seemed to have no cure.

Because Danlo did not want the lords and masters of the Order to know of his connection with Old Father, he arranged to meet with him in secret. For a ten-day period after Ede's body had finally been sent back with the Iviomil's deep ship to Tannahill, he left the Morning Towers each night to visit him. As during his time of being sculpted into the shape of Mallory Ringess, he wore a black mask to hide the features of his face. And as during his novice years, he sneaked out of the Academy by climbing the old stone wall that separated Academy's grounds from the Old City.

Sometimes he would bring Old Father honey-cakes glazed with orange sauce, which Old Father had once loved; sometimes he would simply sit in Old Father's thinking chamber trying to play one of the unplayable double-mouthed flutes that Old Father kept by his bed. But then one evening Old Father rather abruptly dismissed the man whom others revered as the Lord of the Order, saying, "Oh ho, Danlo, Danlo—I must thank you for visiting me so faithfully. And I must thank you for telling me who you really are. Otherwise I might have injured myself trying to bow to you. But doesn't Mallory Ringess have more important duties than amusing an old alien with such childish attempts to make music? Of course he does. So it's so. I'm not dying yet, you know. I shall send for you when I am."

Around this time, too, Danlo began to visit Tamara as often as he could. Ever since Jonathan's death, he had feared that she might willfully make the journey to the other side of day. But it seemed that Tamara was not quite so ready to suffer the same fate as had the Ede imago. A few days after his visit with Bardo, when Danlo finally returned to her tiny apartment near the Street of Musicians, he found that she had taken in three girls whose parents had been killed when a bomb had destroyed their apartment building in the Old City. Their names were Miwa, Julia and Ilona, and it was something of a miracle that they had survived the collapse of their ceiling into a deathtrap of broken stone, blood and dust.

Two years before, they had made the journey from Clarity according to their parents wishes to become godlings in the great church that had arisen in Neverness. Of course the girls, who were four, five and eight years old, had only the vaguest desire to become part of a new religious movement. Like all children they wanted most a warm and comfortable home, good food, love, laughter and the other delights of life. But when Tamara found them wandering the dangerous Street of Smugglers—friendless, shivering and almost starving—they had none of these things. And so she had led them up the stairs to her apartment, covered them in her sleeping furs and fed them a delicious stew made from the meat of a strange animal that Tamara called a bear.

"I really *had* to adopt them," Tamara told Danlo the first night after he had met the three sisters and Tamara had sent them to bed. "The church hospices are all full, and they had no one else."

For a long time, Danlo sat with Tamara in her fire room as he studied her still-gaunt face and looked deeply into her dark, lovely eyes. A new life sparkled there like glittlings lighting up the night, and he immediately understood that she needed these orphaned girls as much as they needed her. Because Danlo was hungry, she served him a particularly choice cut of bear meat that she had been saving for a special moment. And then, after they had spoken about the end of the war and what had happened in Hanuman's sanctuary, she returned to him his bamboo flute, his pilot's ring, the broken chess piece and all his other things that she had been keeping for him.

"Thank you," he told her when it was time to leave. "I shall come back tomorrow, if you'd like."

And Danlo did return to her apartment the following night and the night after that, all through the days and nights of deep winter. But then, in early midwinter spring, exercising his authority as Lord of the Order, he found for her a rather large house in the Pilot's Quarter just off the Tycho's Green. It was a two-storey chalet of granite stones and a steeply gabled roof, and for many years it had been occupied by Nicabar Blackstone, who had died during the war.

By all the Order's traditions, the house should have been taken over by another pilot, or at least by another orderman. But many pilots had either fallen to their deaths inside stars or had fallen on to Thiells with the Second Vild Mission, and so many fine houses from the Run to the North Sliddery along North Beach stood empty. No one begrudged Tamara her new living space. After all, Tamara had once been a courtesan of great promise, and that, as Bardo observed, was almost like being a professional of the Order.

One night, as Danlo visited Tamara and her new family in their new house, over a simple meal of bread, cheese and bloodfruits, Miwa asked Danlo if he wanted to marry Tamara. She was the youngest of the girls and small for her age with the same black hair and bright black eyes as her sisters. For a moment, Danlo looked around at the fine low furniture, plants and Jonathan's old paintings with which Tamara had decorated her new dining room. Then he looked back at Miwa. Where Julia, the second oldest sister sitting next to her on an embroidered cushion, was somewhat withdrawn and demure, Miwa always seemed open, trusting, inquisitive and playful. And so out of his own playfulness, he smiled at Tamara and then turned back towards this blessed child. And he said, "Truly, any man would want to marry Tamara."

Here Ilona, the wisest of the sisters and the most compassionate and honest, smiled at Danlo and told him, "But you really wouldn't want to marry Tamara in that old face mask, would you? People don't get married that way."

For a moment Danlo sat around the low dining table as he fingered the leather mask that covered his face. He had given the girls to understand that he had been badly burned in the war, hence this attempt to cover his disfigurement. While Miwa and Julia accepted this little lie without question, Ilona couldn't understand why Danlo had to await a regrowth when the city's cutters had already restored so many others. And so she always gazed straight at Danlo as if her bright eyes could burn through the leather mask to behold the man beneath.

"It must hurt when you smile," she said to him. "On Clarity, I was sunburnt badly once, and it hurt when I smiled."

Later that night, after Tamara had put the girls to bed in one of the large upstairs sleeping rooms, she returned to the table to take a cup of coffee with Danlo. Now he sat with his mask off, and he looked across the room at the painting of a snowy owl that Jonathan had once made.

"They are beautiful girls," he finally said, turning to smile at Tamara. "I am glad that you will be their mother."

"I'm glad, too," Tamara said. She stared down at her fingernails, which were beginning to return to their old luster after having grown mottled and brittle from too many days of starvation. And then she looked up and asked him, "Do you love them, Danlo?"

And Danlo nodded his head. "Yes—I love children."

"But you don't love them as you did Jonathan, do you?"

"I am not sure," he said. "Between Jonathan and me there was an immediate resonance. Our hearts beat as one; it may be that we shared the same spirit animal, and so our wings beat together, too. With Jonathan there was alway such *animajii,* this wild joy of life that seemed to grow directly out of my own. With the girls, there are other affinities. In time, I will come to know them more completely. Truly, it can only deepen, this blessed knowingness. Love for one's own child is special, I think, but love is always just love, yes?"

In the quiet of Tamara's new house, in all the silence of their suffering, Danlo looked at her for a long time. They understood each other deeply. Both of them, at different moments during the war, had desired death and had been as close to ultimate despair as the next beat of their hearts. And both of them, in plunging into the dark caverns of their souls, had discovered within themselves the ultimate fount of life. In every way, Danlo thought, Tamara's journey toward affirmation had been as daring and difficult as his own. But now, despite the sorrow that would always remain with her like the coldness of the stars, there was the new thing burning within her, the fire, the secret light.

"I think I really *do* love each of them as much as a mother could love any child," she said. "But I still miss Jonathan terribly."

"I miss him, too," he said.

"It's strange," she said, "but after the night on the beach, I couldn't imagine ever again wanting to go on living. But now I couldn't dream of anything else."

"Neither could I."

Tamara took a drink of coffee and nodded her head. "You have so much now, don't you? Lord of the Order, Lord of the Way of Ringess. And then there are these new accomplishments of yours. The way you healed yourself of the warrior-poet's poison. The way it's said you can look through light-years of space to see things occurring far away."

For a moment, he looked across a few feet of space to drink in the dark fire of her eyes. Then he said, "Truly, I have almost everything."

"Something strange happened to you in Hanuman's sanctuary, didn't it? Something strange and terrible but marvelous, too, I think."

Terrible beauty, he remembered as he closed his eyes to gaze upon the infinite light blazing inside him. And then he suddenly looked at her and said, "Yes, something happened. And yet I would give it all up to bring Jonathan back."

"You really would?"

"Yes, if I could—but that is not the way the universe is made."

"No, I suppose not," she said. And then she smiled sadly and looked off through the room's north window at the stars. "I think I understand Hanuman, now. I'm afraid I might try to make the universe differently, too, if *I* could."

At this he, too, smiled and said, "What is strange is that the warrior-poets might have been right, after all."

"Right about what?"

"About the eternal recurrence."

"That the universe recurs exactly as it is, again and again, forever?"

"No," he said, "the universe is different in each moment. Truly, irreversibly, marvelously different. Like an infinite lotus, it opens ever outward into new possibilities, yes? But true affirmation of this universe would be in wishing that it would recur eternally throughout time. That in every moment it is perfect and complete just as it is. And that all the moments of our lives are so perfect we would wish to relive them again and again no matter how painful this living might be. Nothing may ever be subtracted, the warrior-poets say. Nothing must ever be lost."

Nothing is lost, he remembered. *Nothing can ever be lost.*

"Do you really believe this?" she asked.

"It is not a really matter of belief," he said. "In the end, we can either say yes or no."

"Would you say yes, then, to the way that Jonathan died?"

"I am afraid that I must."

"And to your killing Hanuman?"

Danlo gazed down at his left hand, remembering the most terrible moment of his life. Then he slowly nodded his head in affirmation.

"Is it that simple for you, then?"

"Simple, truly, but never easy," he said. "I try all the time now only to say this one word, this one simple sound. As I always will."

"Well, for me, it's not so simple," she said. "Sometimes I think I still *want* to say no. Sometimes I hate the universe for taking Jonathan away."

"But he is not really gone, you know. Nothing is lost."

"That's your faith, isn't it? I wish I could believe it."

"It is not faith. It is only remembrance."

"Whose remembrance? Yours, Danlo?"

"No," he said, "not mine. That is, not mine alone. It is the universe's remembrance of a single blessed being who was part of itself."

"And what is it you think that has been preserved of our son, then?"

"Everything."

Here Tamara sipped her coffee and shook her head. And she asked, "Then you think it's really possible, for instance, that the universe remembers what Jonathan said to me when I took him skating a few days before the war began?"

"Yes," Danlo said. He looked through the east windows where the snow-covered slopes of Atakel loomed up against the bright black sky. "The universe remembers the moon's reflection in the eye of an owl on a deep winter night a million years ago."

"Oh, Danlo, Danlo—I wish it could be so."

Now Danlo stared off at the Wolf constellation as his heart beat to rhythms as ancient as the stars. A terrible strangeness fell over him, then. His eyes, usually so full of fire, grew as soft and liquid as two blue cups overflowing with water. And then he smiled at Tamara and told her, "I remember what Jonathan said."

"But how could you?"

"He said this, then: 'When God made you, Mama, She used really bright colors.' Truly, God did, Tamara."

Tamara's hand trembled so badly that drops of coffee splashed out of her mug, and she began to weep. Danlo stood up then, and came over to her. He sat by her side, stroking her long, golden hair for a while. *The memory of all things is in all things,* he thought. And then he said, "In a way, Jonathan still lives. As he always has and always will."

Here Tamara put down her coffee mug and covered Danlo's hand with her own. She looked at him for a long time, almost pleading with her tear-filled eyes but saying nothing.

"You could remembrance him as I have," he said softly. "You could remembrance everything."

"But how, Danlo?"

"It is truly a simple thing," he said. "The simplest thing in the universe. I could help you, if you'd like."

She immediately nodded her head. "All right—when shall we begin?"

At this sudden hopefulness, he felt all his love for her burning in his eyes, and she seemed to disappear into his gaze like a lightship falling into the sun. But his intense passion did not in any way consume her; it only caused her to begin burning brightly, too.

"Now," he said. "We shall begin right now. In all the universe, as the past becomes the future and memory is created, just pure memory like indestructible diamonds out of the fires of time, there is only ever the blessed Now-moment, yes?"

But remembrance of the One memory that some called the Elder Eddas, though always simple, was seldom ever easy for human beings to achieve. All through midwinter spring and false winter Danlo visited Tamara's house, and he helped her find the way toward the healing waters of the ocean of memories that streamed inside her. Each night, like a young dolphin diving deeper and deeper into the secret blueness of the sea, she came a little closer to the memories that were most precious to her.

As false winter gave way to the cold, snowy days of winter and Danlo's vision of a new Ringism began to spread across the stars, Tamara began to remembrance and relive moments of her life that she had shared with Jonathan. Her progress was rapid. But what she most desired seemed, like the sea's horizon, to waver always just beyond her grasp. During this time of deep frustrations, Danlo grew ever more anxious to complete the great quest that he had begun so long ago. But none of this restlessness was directed at Tamara; with her he was always gentle, patient and infinitely understanding. He spent long moments in her house, staring out the window at the frozen sea to the west or looking up at the sky, watching and waiting.

With the coming of deep winter, the Order's tinkers finally completed the destruction of the Universal Computer, and Tamara, like almost everyone else, took part in the celebrations held through every quarter of the city. She drank Summerworld firewine and ate golden honeycakes and looked up to marvel at the Golden Ring as it completed its growth across the heavens. The next day she returned to the remembrance of the true Elder Eddas, and day after day, as the weather turned colder and colder, she nearly despaired of making the same journey as had Danlo.

And then one night nearly a whole year after Jonathan had died—a night of blazing woodfires and dreams and great galaxies of stars wheeling across the universe—time stopped and Tamara fell into the pure, shimmering consciousness that flows at the center of all things. For many thousands of beats of Danlo's heart, she sat in her meditation room utterly transfixed as she stared into the liquid blueness of Danlo's eyes. She seemed almost dead and yet, paradoxically, as afire with life as a wild new star. And then at last she smiled, laughed softly and suddenly leaned toward Danlo to kiss his forehead. She sprang to her feet and began moving about touching the flowers, the polished stones and other objects of the room.

"Oh, Danlo," she said softly. "Danlo, Danlo—I never knew."

Now Danlo stood up, too, and he came over to her. "Shhh," he said, touching his fingers to her lips, "There is no need to speak."

But Tamara had always been a proud woman with a fierce will of her own, and she laughed again even as she danced away from him. With a few quick motions, she pulled off her blue meditation robe and stood naked in the firelight. Over the past year of skating and eating her fill, she had regained almost the same body that Danlo remembered so keenly: long, lithe, voluptuous, strong and fairly trembling with delight in its own existence. She began dancing around the room then, whirling atop the polished wood floor with her arms thrown wide above her head. She danced for the joy of sheer movement itself, danced with an ecstatic attention to the flowing patterns of her feet and hands that Danlo hadn't seen since he had first met her years before. She seemed utterly happy, utterly radiant, utterly alive. At last she stopped, however, and held her arms folded across her heart as she let the intense dizziness of her wild dancing fall away from her.

"Oh, Danlo," she said, looking at him, "I never knew it was possible."

And Danlo looked at her, and he smiled, and the words thundered inside him with every beat of his heart: *Yes, yes, yes.*

"But *how* is it possible?" she asked. "How could it be possible that everything is really all right?"

"How could it *not* be possible?"

"I remember you saying something like this once," she told him. "You said, 'how is it possible that the impossible is not only possible but inevitable.' "

"You *remember* this?"

"Yes—I'm sure I do."

Danlo closed his eyes for a moment and then looked at her. "But I said those words on the night of the eighty-eighth of false winter. After we had gone for a walk on the beach and joined together in your fire room. Almost eight years ago."

"Yes, I remember."

Now Danlo stepped closer to her and brushed the long hair out of her face so that he could better see her eyes. He said, "That was during the time of our deepest togetherness. The time whose memories Hanuman took away from you."

"I know," she said. "The memories of you and me."

Nothing is lost, he thought, *never, never, never, never.*

"I remember the way you loved me," she said. "I remember the way I loved you."

"But what do you remember, then?"

"Everything."

So saying, she lifted her arms around him and kissed him long and deeply in a way that he had almost lost hope of ever kissing her again. And then, in this miracle of healing, in all the wild joy of recovering what she had given up as forever lost, she fell against him laughing and weeping, both at once, and kissing his forehead and lips and the tears from his eyes, and with utter abandon kissing as well his throat and chest and even the hard white scars along his hands.

"Tamara, Tamara," he finally said after he had found his breath again. "Tamara, I—"

"Wait," she told him, pulling back and breaking away from him. "Please wait."

She excused herself and left the room to make a quick errand.

Danlo listened as her feet flew lightly up the stairs toward her sleeping chamber. A few moments later she returned, still naked but for a single piece of jewelry that she had pulled over her head and wore around her neck. Danlo smiled to see the pearl that he had once found for her, the great gleaming black pearl that he had taken from a frozen beach and fastened onto a necklace braided from his own long black hair.

"Do you remember making this for me?" she asked.

Danlo stared down at the pearl that hung between her breasts. It was shaped like a teardrop, and its swirling colors of soft pink and iridescent gray-black made a startling contrast against her creamy skin. "Do *I* remember?" he asked.

"You gave it to me in promise to marry me. And I accepted it in promise to marry you."

"Yes," he said, "I remember."

"I'm sorry that I had to break this promise," she told him. "But Hanuman had broken my memories of you, and I couldn't even recall the first time I met you."

"I am sorry, too."

She looked at him deeply and knowingly, and said, "Well, I suppose there's no need for this promise to remain broken forever, is there? Unless we both want it to be."

"I do not want that, Tamara."

"Neither do I."

Tamara smiled at him and said, "It's strange, but I think I know now the answer to the riddle you asked Jonathan. About capturing the bird's spirit unharmed."

"You mean, 'How do you capture a beautiful bird without killing its spirit?'"

"Yes," she said, nodding her head. "And the way to do this is by becoming the sky, isn't it?"

"Truly, it is."

"I want to become your sky, then. I want you to become mine so that we can fly together."

And so even as they gazed at each other and with their eyes renewed the deepest promises of life, Tamara pulled Danlo down to white shagshay fur spread out in front of the fireplace. They joined together as man and woman in an ecstasy of love and creation. Danlo sensed the awakening of her body's cells and her desire to make a new child together while in this wild, exalted state. In the whisper of her breath, in the fire of her heart, he heard her calling him into the center of her being as if she were saying, "Fill me with light, fill me with life."

There came a moment of utter joy and completion when they both knew that they had brought forth the second of their children out of the wild white seeds of life that burned inside themselves. She—or he—would be something marvelous and new that had never before existed in the universe. Sometime the following year in winter when the snows came, this child of the stars would open her eyes and look out in wonder at the world, and nothing would ever be the same again. And someday, farwhen, through the doorway to the shimmering, golden future, their children's children would fill the stars to the end of space and time. This was Danlo's and Tamara's dream, made real in all the love and life that they poured into each other. Although they spoke no words to affirm what they did together, every atom of each of them cried out, yes, yes, yes!

Much later, as they lay holding each other and looking out at the lights in the sky, they made plans to be married. Tamara might have waited until false winter when the fireflowers would be in their fullest glory, but Danlo argued for a more immediate ceremony. He startled her, then, in announcing that he would leave the city before Year's End. He would make a journey to the west of Neverness, and he did not know if he would be able to return by the time their child was born. At last, after fifteen years, he would return to the Ten Thousand Islands and visit the Patwin tribe and Olorun and Narwe tribes and all the other tribes of the Alaloi.

"It is time," he told her. "Truly, it is long past time. The Civilized Worlds are healing from the wounds of this war. Now the Alaloi must be healed, too."

He explained, then, that much as he had rid his body of the warrior-poet's paralytic poison, the Alaloi people—each man, woman and child—could be taught to suppress the engineered viral DNA that infected them.

"The Entity," he said, smiling, "once told me that I knew the cure for the slow evil. That I had always known it and someday I would know it again. At the time, I thought She was only tormenting me with one of Her mysterious riddles. But now I see that She spoke truly."

"I know that you have to go back to your people," Tamara said as she lay looking at him in the light of the fire. "But now that I've found you again, it's hard to say goodbye so soon."

"I know," he said, placing his hand on her naked belly. "But I shall return as soon as I can. To raise our children together."

She smiled and rested her hand on top of his. She sighed, "I suppose you were born to make journeys. We all were, weren't we? But please promise me that you'll be careful."

"I promise," he said.

She kissed him and said, "I'll miss you, Danlo."

"I shall miss you, too," he said.

Then he kissed her and pulled closer to her again, and like two angels dancing in the light of the fire, they moved together spinning sparks of wild joy into the night.

HALLA

All that is not shaida is halla.
Halla is the right hand of life;
Shaida is the left hand of life.
Like a thallow hatching from an egg,
Halla emerges out of shaida,
And shaida gives birth to halla.
In the darkness of a deep winter night,
Beneath the eyes of the Old Ones who have lived
and died,
In the glory of a new winter morning,
Beneath the light of the rising sun,
Shaida joins hands with halla, left to right,
To form the great circle of the world.
                    —from the Devaki *Song of Life*

The next day, Danlo summoned some of the Kalla Fellowship to his rooms at the top of the Morning Tower. He invited Bardo, Thomas Rane, Kiyoshi Telek, Kolenya Mor, the Nirvelli, Jonathan and Benjamin Hur, Poppy Panshin and Malaclypse of Qallar to sit with him and drink a few cups of tea together. And to say goodbye. Of these, only Bardo, Malaclypse and the Brothers Hur knew his true identity. The others, he thought, would wonder why Lord Mallory wi Soli Ringess would want to leave Neverness again so soon after his world-shaking return. But then Mallory Ringess had always mystified the people around him, even his closest friends. After all, everyone said that he was a god, and the gods always acted in the most mysterious ways.

"But, Lord Mallory, will you return again?" Kiyoshi Telek asked. This pleasant-faced young man sat next to Thomas Rane, the great master remembrancer proud and dignified in his silver remembrancer's robes. "Everyone will want to know if you're abandoning Neverness forever."

"Yes, I shall return," Danlo said, smiling ironically. "That is the way of Mallory Ringess, always to return, isn't it?"

After hinting that he had a long journey to make, perhaps even to the Solid State Entity, he went on to say that neither the Order nor the Way of Ringess (and certainly not the Civilized Worlds) would suffer from the loss of leadership in his absence. He turned to Jonathan Hur, who sat next to him on his left. He told this man of the gentle soul and golden character that he would be the new Lord of the Way of Ringess. It would be Jonathan Hur, he said— with the aid of his brother Benjamin and the rest of the Kalla Fellowship—who must guide the peoples of the Civilized Worlds towards remembrance of the Elder Eddas.

"You know the way, now," Danlo said. "Each of you must look inside to find this way, and help others to do this, too."

While his guests were digesting this unsettling piece of news, Danlo stared off toward the window at the devotionary computer, which remained silent and dead. He looked over at Hanuman's old chess set nearby; where before thirty-one pieces had been set out in readiness for a game, now there were thirty-two. After Tamara had given Danlo back his things, he had taken the white god that Hanuman had broken and glued the two halves together again. As keen as were his eyes, he couldn't make out the hairline crack that ran through this little ivory figurine that he had once carved for Hanuman.

And then he looked back across the circle of men and women who regarded him as a god, straight at Malaclypse Redring. And he told him, "It is time that you returned to Qallar."

And Malaclypse, in silence and acceptance of the task that lay before him, bowed his head.

And to Thomas Rane, Danlo said, "I must thank you for sharing the remembrancers' attitudes with me, and with all of us. Even a god, if he is to make the journey into true remembrance, may be helped by such techniques. As he may help others wherever he goes."

And Thomas Rane, also in silence, bowed his silver-haired head to the man he knew as Mallory Ringess.

"But, Lord Mallory, you can't just leave the city as you did before!" Kolenya Mor broke in. Once, as the Lord Eschatologist, she had suffered from the chaos of Mallory Ringess' mysterious disappearance—along with all the lords, masters, adepts and novices of the Order. "Now, more than ever, we need a Lord of the Order—and a strong one, at that."

Here Danlo smiled and looked at her kindly in acknowledgment of her concerns. And he told her, "There will be a new Lord of the Order. A strong lord, the strongest of lords."

"Who, then?" Kolenya asked. She must have wondered if he would restore Lord Mariam Erendira Vasquez to the Order or even recall Lord Nikolos Sar Petrosian from the Vild.

And then Danlo turned to Bardo, who sat by him on his right and said, "Bardo will be the new Lord of the Order."

"*I?*" Bardo called out. He seemed genuinely astonished, for Danlo had not consulted him as to either his leaving the city or concerning Bardo's sudden elevation. "You would really make Bardo Lord of the Order?"

"Yes—why not?"

"Because Bardo once abjured his vows," Bardo said. He sat on a thick cushion fingering the folds of his black pilot's robe. Although he had taken off his black nall battle armor many days before, he still wore his brilliant shesheen cape. "Because Bardo once almost ruined the Order by starting a religion in your goddamned name."

"If you'd like, then," Danlo said, smiling at him, "you may consider your elevation as a punishment rather than a promotion. Ruling as Lord of the Order will not be as agreeable as you might hope."

"Ah, but did Bardo ever really hope for such an honor?" Bardo asked, for a moment lost in himself. He pulled at his thick black beard and licked a drop of tea from his lips. Then he looked at Danlo and said, "I think I always wanted to be Lord Pilot, yes—I must admit that I was born to lead lightships across the stars. But leading a hundred old squabbling men and women in the College of the Lords is a different matter."

"Yes, truly it is," Danlo said as he looked at Bardo, watching and waiting. Over the past year, he thought, Bardo had changed. Where once this great, chest-thumping pilot had desired to stand at the very forefront of the noblest men and women of the Civilized Worlds, power over others seemed no longer to interest him. Now, with his descent into the Elder Eddas, he had finally found the way to power over himself, and this was a truly marvelous thing.

"It's just that I'm not sure if I *want* to be Lord of the Order," Bardo admitted.

"Such uncertainty is itself a recommendation that you should be the Order's ruling Lord."

"And what if I refuse this elevation?"

"But you may not refuse," Danlo told him. "As yet, I remain Lord of the Order, and you have taken a vow of obedience."

"Ah, but I wouldn't want to break my vows again," Bardo said. "I have no choice, do I?"

"No."

"Well, then, I accept," Bardo said, and he clapped Danlo on his arm. "By God, Little Fellow, I'll be the Lord of the Order if that's really what you want me to be!"

After that, Danlo led Bardo and the others in a final remembrance together. Later, with the evening bells ringing out through the Academy's buildings and across the snow-covered grounds, he stood up to embrace each of them and tell them goodbye. They bowed to him one by one and made their exits until only Bardo remained. When Danlo saw that they were finally alone, he brewed another pot of tea and invited Bardo to sit with him awhile. As one Lord of the Order meeting in conclave with the next, they had many plans to make and much to discuss concerning the fate of humanity across the stars.

The following morning, Danlo shut himself away in his rooms. He instructed the novices who served him to leave his meals on a tray outside his door, and for ten days, he allowed no one to visit him, not even Bardo. The godlings who scrutinized Lord Mallory Ringess' every move speculated that he had somehow fallen into communion with the Solid State Entity and others of the galaxy's gods, but no one really knew.

In truth, however, during this time of aloneness, he ate a great deal of food, slept as much as he could and turned within toward the great changes that were quickening his whole being. Often, deep in meditation, he gazed upon the face of the white god that he had carved many years before, the cold, ivory face that almost captured the likeness of his father, Mallory Ringess. Often, too, he looked inside himself to remember his old face and to envision his new one. In the silence of his soul, he repeated the words to a Fravashi koan that Old Father had once taught him: *If I am only I, who is the one who will remain standing when I die?*

He might have remained in seclusion for yet another few days, but early in the morning of the seventy-third of deep winter, a man named Luister Ottah arrived at his rooms to tell Lord Mallory Ringess that Old Father was finally dying. Luister, an intelligent man with a kind smile splitting the smoothness of his jet black skin, was the oldest of Old Father's students. Danlo remembered him well from the time when they had all lived together in Old Father's house. But Luister, of course, did not remember him. That is, he did not remember him as Danlo wi Soli Ringess: Four times Danlo had visited Old Father wearing his leather face mask, and each time Luister had greeted him at the door as only a mysterious stranger somehow connected to Old Father. And now, here in the Morning Tower, he greeted this same stranger again only to discover that he was really Lord Mallory Ringess.

"I will come immediately," Danlo told him when he learned of Luister's mission. "Please give me a moment."

He stood by the window wearing his face mask. Luister Ottah must have been mystified as to why Mallory Ringess would wear this stifling mask in the privacy of his rooms; he could only have concluded that the great Lord of the Order, who was famed as a scryer, had foreseen this sad news and had prepared for yet another secret outing into the streets of Neverness.

"It's well that you will come," Luister said. "Old Father may not last another day."

He went on to say that he had been sent to the Academy to find Lord Bardo, as well, and he admitted that he couldn't understand why Old Father would summon the two greatest Lords of Neverness to his deathbed. But Danlo did not enlighten him. He only asked Luister Ottah to wait outside his rooms while he put on a black sable outer fur and grabbed up a few things.

And so Danlo accompanied Luister Ottah across the frozen grounds of the Academy to Bardo's rooms in the Danladi tower, where they found him doing his morning mathematics. Then Luister led both of them through the Old City to Old Father's house at the western edge of the Fravashi District. He escorted them through the curving, stone hallways into Old Father's thinking chamber, which still smelled of crushed pine needles and was full of gosharps, books, Fravashi carpets, alien musical instruments and many other things. Old Father himself lay in a low bed at the exact center of the room, surrounded by a dozen of his students. As with many aliens, it was hard to tell that he was ill, much less dying. His long, white-furred body had not fallen substantially thinner since Danlo's last visit, and his furry face seemed almost serene. Only his eyes—his great, golden-orange eyes—showed that he suffered much pain.

"Oh ho, we have guests!" he called out weakly when he saw Danlo and Bardo standing by the doorway to the circular room. "Please abide a few moments while we finish saying our goodbyes."

At this, all the students turned to look at Bardo, standing impatiently in his shesheen cape, and at Danlo, who bowed his head to Old Father but did not take off his mask. Everyone now understood, of course, that Old Father wished to speak with the man they knew as Mallory Ringess. But they couldn't guess why Mallory Ringess still kept his famous face covered; they must have thought that he had his own reasons for playing out this little subterfuge, and they respected his need for secrecy, even if they resented his presence during Old Father's final moments.

"Ah, ah, oh, oh," Old Father gasped out from his bed, "I forgot to thank the lords for waiting while I thank my students for listening so attentively for so long to what an old alien has to say."

And with that, he turned to Salim Brill, whom Danlo remembered as a past master of the Moksha competitions that Old Father held every night around their evening meal. He remembered as well Michael of Urradeth and Ei Eleni, but except for Luister Ottah, the other students were new to him. Old Father spent a short while with each of them, trading a few words of endearment or perhaps attempting to make one of his ironic little jokes. The effort seemed to exhaust him. But he kept up his aura of playfulness, even as he gave each student a small gift—a gosharp, drum, shraddha nut, tea cup or some other personal thing—that they might remember him when he was gone. Upon completing this ordeal, he asked his students to adjourn to the deeper parts of his large house. He also asked Luister Ottah to close the door behind them; as far as Danlo could remember, this was the first time the door to Old Father's thinking chamber had ever been closed.

"Aha—we're finally alone," Old Father said. His sweet voice sang out like a starling's, and he motioned for Danlo and Bardo to sit by his bed. "Thank you, Danlo, for coming. And thank you, too, Bardo."

Bardo, who was sure that he had never before laid eyes upon Old Father, nervously stroked his beard as he sat facing the old alien. He couldn't understand why he had been rousted from his warm apartment to make the journey to this cold room (as always, Old Father kept his thinking chamber scarcely above freezing) unless it was to learn some vital bit of information that Danlo's old master wished to share with both of them.

"By God, it's cold in here," Bardo complained. "Does anyone mind if I don't take off my furs?"

And Danlo, sitting cross-legged next to him, shook his head even as Old Father stroked the silken white fur of his chest and laughed out, "But why should anyone mind? I might as well ask if you mind if *I* keep my fur on. Which I think I will, if only for a little while longer."

At this intimation of Old Father's approaching death, Danlo

exchanged quick looks with Bardo, but neither of them spoke. And then Old Father pointed a long finger at Danlo and said, "Oho—I will, however, ask Danlo wi Soli Ringess to take off his mask. This is no way for a former student to face his old teacher, is it?"

For a moment, Danlo hesitated. He looked toward the door as if one of Old Father's students might at any moment come blundering into the room. But the door remained closed, and except for Old Father's labored breathing, the thinking chamber remained silent. And then Danlo looked at Old Father and nodded his head.

"All right, then, sir—I will remove my mask, if you'd like."

So saying, he pulled the mask over his head and sat by Old Father's bed as still and quiet as a great white owl perched on a tree.

"Danlo—what's happened to you?" Bardo suddenly cried out. He stared at him in sheer wonder. "By God, look at you!"

But Danlo had no need to look at himself, for he could perceive his reflection in Bardo's astonished words and in the bright golden mirrors of Old Father's eyes. He saw himself even as Bardo and Old Father saw him: no longer did he wear the face and form of Mallory Ringess. During his ten days alone in the tower, he had returned almost to his old self. In truth, he looked much the same as he had before Constancio had sculpted him: he showed the long nose, bold cheek bones and fiercely handsome face of all his line. And yet there was something new about him, too, something marvelous and strange as if all the cells of his body were working to make him into some glorious new shape as yet not quite completed.

"How is it possible?" Bardo almost shouted. "Have you had a cutter brought to your rooms in secret? No, no—there's been no time. By God, Danlo! By God, by God!"

But Old Father, lying calmly in his bed, seemed not at all surprised by Danlo's miraculous transformation. As always, he beamed forth an aura of zanshin, that complete clarity and alertness of mind that the Fravashi Fathers strive to maintain at all times, even at the sight of a beloved student's new/old face—or even in the face of death itself.

"Oh ho!" Old Father said to Danlo. "It's good to see you again—good to see the man whom you've become. So, it's so: I'm glad that I could see you just as you are. It's time we said goodbye, you know."

He told Danlo and Bardo that he had presents for each of

them. When Bardo protested that he had never been a student of the Fravashi, much less of Old Father himself, Old Father smiled at him and said, "But all the same, I should like to give you a small gift before I make my next journey."

"But why?" Bardo asked.

"Ah, oh—still so impatient," Old Father said. "But you may understand when I give you my gift."

He reached his long, white-furred hand behind his bed and drew forth a book bound in new leather. He handed it to Bardo. Upon opening it, Bardo beheld page after page of white paper inscribed with little black symbols that Old Father himself had laboriously drawn there with pen and ink. Bardo—and Danlo as well—saw immediately that they were mathematical symbols. As Bardo's eyes poured down the first page, he muttered to himself as he shook his head. Obviously, he thought this must be one of Old Father's famous little jokes, for the Fravashi were renowned for music or the liberation that comes from practicing Moksha— but never for making mathematics.

"I don't understand," Bardo said, looking up from the manuscript.

"Aha—and I had heard that you were a brilliant pilot," Old Father said. "Is it that you don't understand the mathematics, then?"

Again, Bardo looked down at swirling black flowers that Old Father had penned onto the first sheet of paper. He tapped his finger down the page and nodded in appreciation of what seemed a rather elegant definition of Justerini's omega function. Apparently, Old Father had used a Danladi transform to convert the three-dimensional ideoplasts with which the pilots made their mathematics into two-dimensional symbols written in black ink.

"Well, I think the mathematics are clear enough," Bardo said rather proudly. "It appears to be an exposition of the Great Theorem."

"Oh ho, but appearances can deceive, as I've taught Danlo and my other students," Old Father said. "But not this time. So, it's so: the book is exactly as it appears. I've had some thoughts about the Great Theorem lately. It's always possible to make a mapping between any two stars, of course, but almost always difficult to find such a mapping. Ah, ha, hideously, hideously difficult. This is an attempt at a constructive proof of the theorem. So that any pilot will be able to construct a mapping between any two stars— even the stars of our galaxy and those of the Canes Venateci. All the stars of the universe."

At this astonishing claim, Bardo looked at Old Father as if the old alien's illness had completely deranged his mind. A constructive proof of the Great Theorem had been the dream of the pilots for three thousand years. Not even Mallory Ringess, who had indeed proved the Theorem in a general way, had ever made a constructive proof.

"Ah, thank you," Bardo growled out to Old Father, not knowing what else to say. Again, he looked at him with an almost open pity. He must have thought that it would be well if Old Father simply died before anyone discovered that he had wasted the last days of his life dabbling at mathematics.

But Danlo was looking at Old Father strangely and deeply, as if there was much more to this mysterious old alien than he had ever dreamed. He placed his hand on Bardo's book, then, even as he lost himself in the terrible beauty of Old Father's eyes.

"Thank you," Bardo said again in his impatience to be finished with this onerous visit. "But what present do you have for Danlo, then?"

"Ah, oh, aha," Old Father said. "But Danlo already has my present. It's something that was once very dear to me."

"His flute," Bardo said. He nodded his head in remembrance of the story of how Old Father had given Danlo his shakuhachi at their first meeting on Far North Beach years before. "His goddamned flute."

He watched as Danlo now drew his flute from a pocket of his furs and held the long, golden piece of bamboo lightly in his hands.

"No, *not* his flute," Old Father said. "He's been given something even dearer to me—so, it's so."

"What, then?" Bardo wanted to know.

And without a word, in the utter stillness between the beats of Danlo's heart, Old Father reached out with his trembling, furry finger and touched the black diamond pilot's ring that encircled the little finger of Danlo's hand.

"What? You've fallen mad!" Bardo cried out. And then, upon considering why they had been summoned to this cold, stone-lined room that day, he remembered his compassion (and his manners), and said, "Ah, I'm sorry, Old Father, but you must be confused. Surely you must know that the ring belonged to Mallory Ringess. I, myself, kept it for years after the Ringess went away. I gave it to Danlo when it was time for him to take possession of it."

"Thank you for being the guardian of my ring," Old Father said.

Again Bardo shook his head sadly and said, "But, Old Father, you can't really believe that—"

"I am Mallory Ringess," Old Father said softly, cutting him off. "Oho, I am also Old Father, as you see, but first I was Mallory Ringess."

At this second great shock of the day, Bardo's eyes opened wide in wonder and disbelief. He listened in utter silence as Old Father explained how he had never really left Neverness, after all, but had only transformed himself into the shape of a Fravashi Old Father. Concerning the nature of this transformation itself he had little to tell. Bardo, like Danlo, must have wondered if Mallory Ringess had found a cutter who specialized in sculpting alien features out of human clay. But Old Father hinted only that much as the Entity had brought forth a double of Tamara on the earth far away in the Vild, She had somehow helped create this incarnation of white fur, red blood and anguished golden eyes that lay speaking with all the marvelous and musical fluidity of a Fravashi.

"I don't believe it," Bardo said. Old Father, with his mutable alien consciousness, had always been famous for saying strange things, but what he had just told Bardo and Danlo was the strangest thing that Bardo had ever heard. "Ah, but I *can't* believe it, too bad."

"Oho, but you were always such a doubting man," Old Father said.

"I like to think Bardo is rather a discerning man," Bardo said.

"I remember that you liked to say this about yourself."

"You remember, do you?"

"Ha, ha—I remember more about you than you'd want to remember yourself."

"I really don't see how you could."

Now Old Father's eyes fell soft and compassionate for a moment as he said, "I remember how the fourth-year novices called you Piss-All Lal and forced you to sleep in your wet blankets every night."

"Ah, well, everyone knows that," Bardo said. "Everyone who was with me in Perilous Hall. They tell many stories about Bardo, now."

"So, it's so—I'm sure they do." For a moment Old Father paused and stared through Bardo almost as if he were dreaming. And then his eyes leaped with orange flames as he smiled at

Bardo and asked, "But do they tell the story of how young Pesheval Lal, who called himself Bardo, pissed in the fourth-year novices' beer and served it to them in revenge?"

At this unexpected revelation out of the past, Bardo's face fell purple with shame. He stared at Old Father as if completely stunned. And then he muttered, "No, no—besides myself, only Mallory ever knew what I did."

All this time Danlo had sat in silence looking deeply at Old Father. And now Old Father looked away from Bardo to turn the full light of his consciousness upon Danlo. As Danlo counted out ten beats of his heart, he gazed into the golden eyes of this strange, alien being whom he had loved since their first meeting on the sands by the frozen sea. And now he reached out to join hands with Old Father in a way that the Fravashi always avoided. He clasped Old Father's white-furred fingers with his own naked hand, freely and firmly, as man greeting man had done for a million years.

Yes, yes, yes.

"By God, it's really true, then! He really is Mallory Ringess!"

"Yes, truly he is," Danlo said. And then, even as he looked deep into the frozen waters of space and time, his voice dropped low and respectful as he directed his words toward Old Father. "Truly you are."

"But why?" Bardo wanted to know. He leaned closer to Old Father as if he might fall against him and bury his face against Old Father's furry chest. But then he restrained himself. "Mallory, if it's really you, please tell me why you left us as you did and turned yourself into a goddamned Fravashi?"

"Yes—that I would also like to know, sir," Danlo said.

Old Father let go of Danlo's hand then, and he whistled out a long, low note that might have been the Fravashi equivalent of a sigh. (Or it might have meant that even as Danlo had done as a young man, he was again asking questions almost impossible for Old Father to answer.) When Old Father closed his eyes for a few moments, Danlo feared that the strain of all that had occurred that morning might send him on his final journey. But then Old Father laughed softly and he looked first at Bardo and then Danlo. He said, "Ah, aha, this will be hard to explain."

As the sounds of music and mourning seeped into the room from the deeper parts of the house, Old Father tried to tell them what it was like to be a scryer. The universe, he said, was like an infinite, golden tree that branched ever outward into the future. Like any tree, a shih tree or an oak, the whole of it grew in one direction only, toward the light. But any of its billions upon billions of tiny branches might be eclipsed by greater limbs of the tree or cut off altogether. And while the tree itself could never die, parts of it might succumb to disease and fall stunted and misshapen.

"Ah, ah, ah," Old Father said, "Bardo must be thinking that if only I had never left the Order or had returned at the right time, much as Danlo did, I might have stopped the war before it began. And so it's so: I might have done this seemingly compassionate thing. And a branch of the tree would have been preserved in all its flowering greenness—for a time. But oh, oh, oh, the price, the terrible price. To stop one war and cause a greater war to be. To save one branch and lose a whole limb of a thousand branches. The whole galaxy, Danlo. The choice, for all beings everywhere, there's always the terrible choice. But the *beautiful* choice, too. Isn't this the glory of being conscious and alive? In the end, we choose our futures. And so like anyone else, I tried to look into the future and choose the best one that I could."

Here he paused a while to catch his breath. And then he touched his finger to Danlo's ring again, smiled sadly and said, "Danlo, Danlo—I'm sorry that you hardly ever knew me as anyone other than Old Father. I'm sorry that you had to come to Neverness alone, that everything had to happen as it did. So much suffering, so much death. But of all the billions of possibilities branching out into the future, I saw only one slender path in which you lived."

Now Danlo clasped Old Father's hand again, and the weakness that he felt through the soft, silken fur caused his own muscles to tremble. He stared at the wavering reflections in the mirrored surface of his ring, and he remembered the look of anguish on Jonathan's starved face even as the faces of a billion other children killed in the war began cascading through his mind. "Was it so important that I lived, then?" he asked.

"Aha—it was important to me," Old Father said.

Danlo fell quiet and thoughtful as he tried to smile at Old Father. And then he said, "You have taught me so much. But I am afraid that I broke ahimsa in killing Hanuman."

"Oho! All rules and boundaries must someday be broken. How else can we go beyond ourselves? A thallow chick must break out of his egg, but this does not mean that the shell is without value."

"No," Danlo said, "truly it is not."

"You must remember that an oak tree is not a crime against the acorn."

"I still wish that I did not have to kill him."

"Ah, oh—of course you do," Old Father said. "But what you did was necessary. You're a great being, Danlo, and you're important to the universe."

"All beings are important, sir."

"Ah, yes, yes, they are—so, it's so. And all fathers would wish their seed to beget new seeds, infinitely, blowing like a shimmering cloud in all directions. Such a wild, beautiful seed you are, Danlo. And such a beautiful tree will remain standing when I die."

Danlo swallowed a few times against the pain in his throat and said, "But you do not *have* to die, do you? The warrior-poets have poisoned you, I know, but I might show you the way to—"

"No," Old Father said with uncharacteristic abruptness. "The Alaloi are very wise, you know: there's always a right time to die. Oho, I'm afraid that this is my time."

Yes, Danlo thought, feeling the coolness of Old Father's hand. *Yes, yes, yes.*

"You did what I never could, Danlo. I remembranced the Elder Eddas, but never completely."

Again, this great, white-furred being stopped talking a moment to rest; his eyes clouded with pain, or perhaps remembrance—sometimes it was hard to tell the difference.

"I wanted to live," Old Father said, looking at Danlo, "only long enough to see you become the man you've become. And to know that my son's new child was safe inside Tamara."

At this piece of news, Bardo cocked his head to look at Danlo in surprise. And Danlo said, "How did you know, sir?"

But then Old Father smiled mysteriously and began whistling a strange, otherworldly song, and Danlo knew very well how Old Father had known of the conception of his child.

"Ho, ho, ha, ha—all my children's children," Old Father said. "And all the other children like them. This is how the Silicon God will finally be destroyed. This is how the stars will be saved. All the shimmering, golden, immortal branches reaching out toward the stars."

Old Father went on then to speak not of the future but of the past. He told Danlo of his mother, Katharine, of the dreams she had dreamed and how she had lived and died. It had always been *his* dream, Old Father said, to redeem Katharine from the cold, gray ice of time and somehow bring her back into creation.

"Ah, but this isn't really possible, is it?" Old Father asked.

"No, not in the way that many would hope," Danlo said.

"Ah, do you see the other way, then?" Old Father asked. For a moment, his eyes grew impossibly bright like two great, golden suns. "Aha, oho, the way creation must always be, the branches, the rings, the miracle—do you see it, Danlo?"

As Danlo's heart beat to the rhythms he felt pulsing in Old Father's wrist, he began falling through the universe of stars that opened inside him. He fell deep into the light that shined not only through the Golden Ring but through the Grus Cluster of galaxies and the Rainbow Supercluster and all the other galaxies throughout creation.

"Yes, I see it," he finally said.

"Ah, oh, good, good," Old Father said. "Then I must ask you a few favors before you leave."

"Of course, sir."

"Would you look after my students for me? I'm afraid that the time for human beings to be students of the Fravashi has passed."

"Yes, it has," Danlo said, nodding his head.

"And would you put a fresh flower on Katharine's grave for me," Old Father said. "Ho, ho—I know that you plan to journey to Kweitkel to find your mother's grave."

"What kind of flower, sir?"

"Oh, oh, I think a snow dahlia, if you can find one."

"There were once many snow dahlias on the southern slopes of the mountain this time of year," Danlo said. "I will find one, sir."

"And I'd also like you to play your flute for me," Old Father said, pointing at Danlo's shakuhachi. "Ha, ha—I appreciated your efforts on the sanura the last time you visited, but I think you were really born to play the flute."

And so one last time, Danlo pressed his flute to his lips and played a song for Old Father. He played softly, for he did not wish Old Father's students to hear the music that he made and somehow, perhaps in the pattern of his breath or the sadness of the melody, recognize its maker. For a long time he played his beautiful song, and he never noticed the tears pouring out of Bardo's eyes or burning like drops of light in his own. But then Old Father's eyes began to grow dim as oilstones almost empty of fuel, and he weakly held up his furry hand for Danlo to stop.

"Ah, ah, thank you, thank you," he told Danlo. "That was very good, but it's time now for silence."

"Yes," Danlo said softly.

"You may ask my students to come back in, then. They'll want to be here while I go to sleep."

While Danlo put away his flute and stood up to carry out Old Father's wishes, Bardo finally found his voice again and said, "What's all this talk of sleeping, then? I thought the Fravashi never sleep."

Because Old Father had now fallen almost too weak for further conversation, Danlo explained to Bardo how the Fravashi do, in fact, sleep. Where the human brain, he said, is divided into two hemispheres, the Fravashi carry four separate lobes of gray matter behind their shimmering eyes. At any time, one, two or three of these lobes might be asleep. Only rarely, perhaps in enlightenment, are all four lobes at once fully awake. And only in death are they all asleep.

"But Mallory, you can't leave me again!" Bardo said. He wrapped his huge fist around Old Father's arm and shook it gently. "Ah, no, no, no—too bad, too, too bad."

"I'm sorry," Old Father whispered. He grasped Bardo's hand for as long as he could. And then he looked at Danlo and smiled. "Ho, ho—it's time, it's time!"

"By God, Little Fellow, you can't just die like this!"

But Old Father truly could. After Danlo had donned his leather mask once more, he opened the doors to the thinking chamber and went to find Luister Ottah and the other students. The twelve of them returned, then, and knelt around Old Father's bed. Already, Old Father had closed his eyes and fallen asleep. To make room for the students, Bardo rose up and moved off next to a shelf of musical instruments; he stood like a mountain looking down upon Old Father. And Danlo stood next to him, shoulder to shoulder as he watched and waited. After many, many moments (for almost the first time in his life, Danlo had lost count of his heart-beats), Old Father stopped breathing. It was as simple as that; in all the universe, nothing could be simpler.

Yes, yes, yes.

Danlo bowed his head a moment in remembrance and then looked down at Old Father so silent and serene in death. So that only Bardo could hear him, he whispered a prayer for his spirit: "Mallory wi Soli Ringess, *mi alasharia la, mi padda, shantih, shantih.* Sleep in peace, my father."

He turned to Bardo and grasped the huge man's arm. "Come," he said. "Let's skate the streets awhile."

And Bardo, who was weeping like a child, nodded his head and followed Danlo out of Old Father's house.

They skated restlessly around the red streets of the Fravashi District, and neither of them wanted to pause for rest or speak of what had occurred that day in Old Father's thinking chamber. And then Danlo felt strangely pulled to turn toward the west. Without warning, he struck off down the main orange sliddery leading into the City Wild. They followed it through the snow-shagged yu trees of the forest, and Danlo skated so quickly and with such determination that Bardo gasped to keep close to him.

Danlo didn't quite know where his sudden new quest would take him, but after a while, he broke free from the trees and made his way through the slate-jacketed houses of the Gray District straight toward West Beach. He might have thought that he wished to visit the beach where he had sent Jonathan's ashes sparking up into the wind. But then, upon pausing to listen to a voice that cried out as from far away, he turned south along the Long Glissade and made his way to a little beach at the edge of the Ashtoreth District. In truth, it was a narrow, rocky beach whose broken sands quickly gave way to the frozen sea that opened to the west. Few people, Danlo thought, would want to visit such a wild place, for it was windy and cold and the great shatterwood trees rose up above the rocks like a green and white wall.

"Where are we going?" Bardo asked as Danlo led them through a break in the forest and down across the icy rocks. "Careful you don't slip and break your head, Little Fellow! If we died here, no one would ever find us."

Because Danlo did not want to distress the huge man puffing along behind him, he quickly found a large, flat rock covered with bright green feather moss and sat facing the sea. Bardo joined him and pressed his massive body closer to Danlo's for whatever warmth he might find there.

"By God, it's cold! Why are we here, then?"

"I wanted to be alone," Danlo said.

But even as he gazed at the frozen ice-forms that spread out in a great circle toward the blue horizon, he knew that something else had drawn him to this deserted beach. He looked directly into the west where the sun was beginning its plunge toward the edge of the world like a great, fiery, orange ball. He looked over the white, frozen ocean toward the Ten Thousand Islands of his birth, watching and waiting.

"Well, it's falling late," Bardo said. "I think we spent most of the day with Old Father."

"Yes," Danlo said, nodding his head.

Bardo's unease at the approach of night touched off a deeper nervousness, and he turned to Danlo and said, "Ah, Little Fellow, I hope what Old Father said doesn't make you think less of me. I hope you won't tell anyone about my pissing in the fourth-year novices' beer."

Because it was late and they were alone (and because Danlo wanted to feel the wind against his face), he pulled off his mask. Then he smiled at Bardo and said, "The novices tormented me, too. If I had thought of it, I might have wanted to piss in their beer myself."

For a while, as the wind blew tiny particles of spindrift skittering over the frozen beach, Bardo stared at Danlo's face. He shook his head slowly back and forth and muttered, "By God, it really is a miracle, you know. But then, you always were a mystical man, so I shouldn't really be surprised at these mystical changes."

Danlo reached out to squeeze Bardo's knee then, and he tried to explain that the great changes rippling through his being had little to do with mysticism, in the sense of being magical or mystifying. "Truly, it is just pure technology, yes? This is what technology is: just consciousness reflected upon itself, gaining ever more control of itself and creating new forms."

"Well, have you considered this new form that you've shaped for yourself, Little Fellow? You look almost like your old self— what will the Alaloi think of you?"

"They will think that I am a man, even as they are men and women."

"But what of the convenant, then? Surely if you take your lightship to the Ten Thousand Islands, the Alaloi will learn more of Neverness than they ever wanted to learn."

"Yes, they will," Danlo said. He looked out at the frozen waves curving in long, lovely rippling patterns over the sea, and his eyes fell cold and clear as new blue ice. "But it is time, then. The way for humankind is not back, after all. There is no return to simplicity this way. No true *halla*. I used to think of *halla* as a kind of perfect harmony of flowers and sunlight and good clean life and death out on the sparkling new snow. A perfect balance that all life might someday achieve—without war, without disease, without madness, without asteroids and wild stars that can annihilate ten thousand species of animals almost overnight. But no. The universe is not made this way. True *halla* is the vastening of life. The deepening into new forms and possibilities that we call evolution. It is time, I think, that the Alaloi evolve into a new race along with the rest of our bloody, blessed kind."

As the sun fell even closer to the edge of the icy ocean, Bardo drank in Danlo's words even as he continued staring at his strange, new face. He seemed almost trapped between his awe of Danlo and his deep driving desire towards his own glorious fate. At last he cleared his throat and said, "Well, we all hope to evolve, don't we? Are you a god, then?"

At all the love and fear Danlo saw pouring out of Bardo just then, he smiled with a fierce, wild joy and said, "No, I am a man. At last, truly a man. It is all I ever wanted to be."

They sat in silence watching the snow gulls picking for food beneath wreaths of frozen, red seaweed. Along the line of the motionless surf, *kitikeesha* birds swooped low over the white drifts listening for snowworms in their icy burrows. Soon it began to grow dark. The colors began to bleed away from the trees and the ice, and the sky fell to a luminous deep blue almost the shade of Danlo's eyes. Across the sky to the east, the first stars came out. Danlo looked up at the five curving stars that formed the tail of the Dolphin, and he stared at them strangely for a long time.

Once, these familiar stars had appeared as tiny points of white light against the black sea of space. All his life, almost all stars as seen from the icy surface of the world had appeared as a pure, twinkling white. He remembered that there were two kinds of light receptors on the retina of the human eye: the cones, which could drink in colors but were blind to faint illuminations, and the rods which sensed well enough the dimmest light but could not sort one hue from another. It was the rods that did most of the seeing in darkness, and so the stars usually shimmered as white as the snow.

But now a new kind of cell combining the virtues of both rods and cones had evolved inside Danlo's eyes. And now, suddenly, there were colors in the night. Danlo looked up to see Gilada Luz blazing all hot and blue, and the pale orange Migina Double, and Kalakina which was tinted as red as a drop of blood. As it grew darker, more stars fell out of the folds of night, and Danlo marveled at the faint yellows and violets and greens, and all the other colors of the rainbow. How strange it was simply to be alive! he thought. How astonishing that he could see anything at all, let alone this splendid radiance that had fallen across much of the universe in order to dazzle him with its beauty. And so he sat on his cold rock next to Bardo wondering at the immense mystery of life. There was a fire in his eyes, and a fire in the sky, and so brightly did everything burn with this glorious, new light that he wanted to go on gazing at the stars forever.

"Look!" Bardo said, pointing to the east. "The supernova is about to rise."

Danlo turned to follow the line of Bardo's arm, and there, behind the city, a great glister of light bloomed over the lower slopes of Urkel. For thirty years the people of Neverness had awaited the coming of this terrible new star, and only nineteen days earlier, the first wavefront of light had broken across Icefall. Every night since then, in the early evening, thousands of men and women would swarm the streets to behold the miracle that lit up the sky. And now, here, on this cold, windswept beach, Danlo looked up at this same, beautiful star.

As the world turned its icy face ever eastward, the supernova rose higher in the sky. Its intense radiation streamed down through the Golden Ring. There, the little makers and other Ring organisms absorbed the supernova's violent energies through their sparkling diamond membranes and scattered a brilliant light across the arc of the heavens. Curtains of shimmering gold hung from the upper atmosphere to the iridescent ice below. No longer did Danlo, or anyone else, have to fear that the supernova would harm them. And no longer could Danlo see the place in the sky where the dark mass of the Universal Computer had once blighted out the stars.

"By God, it's cold!" Bardo said. His voice boomed out into the black air moving across the frozen beach. He began to wrap his shesheen cape around his great body, but then he remembered that Danlo was only a man much as himself, and so he pulled this glittering black garment over Danlo's shoulders, too. "How long are we going to remain here?"

"I do not know."

"Look," Bardo said again, pointing at the sky. "Your father told me about the Ring once. He said that it would be a kind of mutual creation of his and the Solid State Entity's."

"The Entity told me much the same thing, too."

"Ah, but I never thought it would be so beautiful," Bardo said. "In a way, the Ring is as much a child of your father as are you."

At this startling thought, Danlo only smiled and continued watching the sky.

From his furs' inner pocket, Bardo pulled out the book that Old Father had given him and thumped it with his hand. "I almost can't believe it was really he. I can't believe he's gone."

At this, Danlo turned to look at him and slowly nodded his head.

"I miss him, you know," Bardo said. "It's my goddamned fate, too bad, but I lost my best friend twice."

"I understand," Danlo said as he remembered the day when he was four years old and had said goodbye to his father on the ocean's ice just beyond Kweitkel. "Twice I have lost my father."

No—nothing is lost.

"Well, it's a cruel universe, isn't it? Sometimes I think it all just falls worse and worse."

Danlo took a breath of bitterly cold air and said, "No, it is just the opposite. It is the way that creation must always be."

"Ah, Little Fellow—do you remember almost the last thing your father said? About creation, about rings and miracles? Do you know what he meant by this?"

"Yes, I know."

"Can you tell me, then?"

"All right," Danlo said. "I will try."

He looked up through the night deep into the golden bands of light circling the world. He looked into the heart of the Ring itself, and he saw the nektons and triptons and the golden fritillaries soaring through the clouds of the little makers. And he saw something else. Great, godlike beings evolved into manifold shapes orbited the world like lightships. They lived upon starlight as they looked down toward the oceans of Icefall and up through the stars past Eta Carina toward the Vild. This is what Danlo saw, then, not with his eyes alone, but with a deeper sense that he had never named. And this is what he told Bardo:

That these Ring gods were the true children of the Solid State Entity. That they had played a part in the war that Danlo was only now beginning to see. These great, golden beings, he said, had helped the Entity in her ancient battle with the Silicon God. Somehow, they had found a way to wield weapons of cosmic energies through light-years of space directly into the center of the Silicon God. In truth, they had created these incomprehensible weapons themselves. In the weaving of energies so tightly, they had to concentrate matter into almost infinitessimally tiny regions of space. Some of the pieces of matter—perhaps a few pounds of air or dust—made for smaller, though still terrible weapons. But when they tried to make the larger weapons, squeezing as much as twenty-five pounds of matter into a region smaller than a proton, as a kind of by-product of this terrible technology, they loosed upon the universe a miracle.

In truth, they created a universe itself. A whole universe that would eventually be filled with galaxies of bright spinning stars.

And not just one universe, but many. For these thousands of tiny concentrations of matter-energy—where they didn't simply collapse into black holes—began expanding with astonishing rapidity. Like shimmering, golden bubbles, they inflated larger and larger. And every time one of these infinitessimal bubbles doubled in volume, the amount of positive matter-energy also doubled. And each of these doublings occurred exponentially and blindingly quickly, creating terrible distortions in spacetime. In much less than a trillionth of a trillionth of a second, each individual bubble pinched off and separated from realspace, becoming its own budding universe.

And then there came explosions, thousands upon thousands of explosions into fire and light. Into life. For each universe created its own space as it expanded, and created as well its own matter and energy and all the possibilities of someday evolving whole new galaxies of stars. This was the miracle of creation. It was the miracle of the universe itself. As Danlo gazed up at the blazing heavens, then, he told Bardo that the universe was not the universe. The universe, he said, had exploded into being more than ten billion years before, but *the* universe was infinite and eternal, like a great, golden circle without beginning or end.

"And in our universe alone, so many Rings, so many possibilities. Who could have dreamed the universe would bring forth so many possibilities?"

In the Milky Way galaxy, he said, the Entity had seeded a million worlds with Rings of their own. And soon the Rings would begin seeding their own life on other worlds until the stars shined down upon billions of flaming, golden spheres. Someday, perhaps farwhen, the Ring would spread out to other galaxies, perhaps to the very end of the universe itself. And all these billions of billions of Rings would give birth to new universes like so many golden pods bursting open and scattering their seeds to the wind.

Someday, in one of these universes, some would-be god like Hanuman might succeed in converting all the stars and dark matter into a Universal Computer. But the wars that would arise from such a cosmic event would generate a billion billion universes for the one that was destroyed. And all these universes would evolve stars and planets and life of their own. All universes everywhere, Danlo said, even the uncountable trillions that existed alongside our own that we could never see, were filled with nothing but life.

For all things, even the burning dust of the Awendela Nebula, even the ice crystals blowing against Danlo's face, were alive.

Always, life supplied life to itself and grew ever vaster and more complex. Living things created burrows beneath the snow and songs sailing out to the stars; they made lightships and honey, pearls and poems and computers that generated entire universes of their own kind of life. Life swirled and pulsed and blazed in terribly beautiful patterns across the stellar deeps. The sun and the moons spun ecstatically with life's wild fire, and the photons danced along the rivers of light that streamed from star to star. Life, like an infinite flower, opened everywhere out into the universe, and into all possible universes, touching all matter, all space, all time with its perfect golden petals and sweet fragrance. And it all grew deeper and deeper, and brighter and brighter like a star swelling to an impossible brilliance that could have no limit or end.

Yes, yes, yes.

And this is what Danlo told Bardo beneath the blazing stars and the silence of the sea. Because the night had now fallen almost dead cold, Bardo pressed himself closer to Danlo to keep from shivering. He must have marveled at the astonishing amount of heat that poured from Danlo's body almost like sunshine, for he suddenly rubbed his hands together and said, "By God, you're not cold at all, are you? Ah, well, I'm almost blue cold—this little petal of your infinite flower is freezing, I'm afraid, and I'll die soon if we don't get off this beach. Why don't we find a restaurant that serves coffee and some good, hot food?"

"If you'd like," Danlo said, smiling. And then he suddenly cocked his head and looked out at the starlit ice of the sea. "But only a moment longer, please."

From far out over the ice to the west came a faint sound that he had been waiting almost all his life to hear. It was the cry of the snowy owl: high and haunting and utterly wild. Danlo had never hoped to catch wind of this strange but deeply familiar sound so close to the city for it had been a thousand years since the snowy owls had nested on Neverness Island. Again, the unseen bird called out, and astonishingly, he was answered by another much nearer to the beach. Danlo sprang lightly to his feet, then, and turned to look past the rocks and frozen sands to the thicket of shatterwood trees that rose up just above the beach.

There, gripping a dark green branch with her strong talons, a female owl cried out into the night. The light of the moons spilled down over her shimmering white feathers and her great orange eyes looked far out to sea. And now Danlo looked in that direction, too. He remembered that snowy owls mate in the darkest part of deep winter, and so along with this beautiful white bird perched in a tree a hundred feet away, he turned to face the sea as he watched and waited.

Ahira, Ahira, he called out silently to the sky. *Ahira, Ahira.*

And then at last, Ahira answered him. While Bardo sat completely still like a huge, black, frozen rock and Danlo's heart beat as quickly as any bird's, a great, male owl swooped down out of the moon-silvered darkness and soared over the icy sea. His cry was high and harsh and urgent with life, and he took no notice of the two men waiting on the snow-covered sands below, but only flew straight toward his mate at the edge of the beach. He landed softly on the branch beside her. And then the two owls turned to gaze upon each other, and as mirrors reflecting the light of mirrors, their great, golden-orange eyes shined with their fierce love for each other.

Danlo, Danlo.

After a while, the female owl sprang into the air and flew away, perhaps to find her nest deeper in the forest. The male remained perched on his branch only for a moment longer. And in that moment, while Danlo's breath steamed out into the freezing air and the world spun slowly beneath the stars, the owl turned and looked at him strangely. And then suddenly he opened his beak and called out to the stars, to the sea, to the wind—and perhaps even to Danlo himself standing so silent and still in the night. It was a cry of victory and all the wild joy of life. Everything went into this one terrible and beautiful sound. And here, Danlo thought, was the ultimate paradox of life, the final mystery. Life moved ever outward into infinite possibilities and yet all things were perfect and finished in every single moment, their end attained. For everything had gone into this one, blessed bird, too. All the stars of all the universes that had ever been blazed in his bright orange eyes, and all the universes that would ever be waited to break out of the many white eggs that he would quicken inside his mate. It was that way with Bardo and Danlo himself, and every other bit of creation. Nothing that had ever taken its breath from the world had been without value, and no one ever lived life in vain. Danlo would always remember the terrible suffering of Jonathan's last days, but when he closed his eyes and looked deep inside himself, he would always see the terrible beauty of his face as well. If he could bring Jonathan back to this cold, lonely beach—smiling and dancing with life, as Jonathan would always live in his memory and somewhere in time—he knew that Jonathan would say it was good to have been alive. And now this beautiful white bird who was his other-self affirmed that this was so. He stretched out his great curving wings and cried out to the night. The wind off the ocean picked up this wild sound and swept it high up into space toward the starry heavens. Truly, the wind was the wild white breath of the world, and as it whipped bits of broken ice against Danlo's naked face, it carried the voices of Jonathan and Old Father, and Katharine and Hanuman and all the Devaki tribe, too, and all these voices together with all the voices that had ever been or would ever be joined Ahira in crying out, "Yes, yes, yes."

And then the snowy owl flew away and was gone.

"All right," Danlo finally said to Bardo. "I am ready."

He pulled Bardo to his feet and breathed on the huge man's fingers to help warm them. And so with one small affirmation, this man who had finally learned how to see smiled at his oldest friend and together they walked back up the beach toward the city that shimmered beneath the stars.

About the Author

David Zindell's short story "Shanidar" was a prizewinning entry in the Writers of the Future Contest. In 1986 he was nominated for the John W. Campbell Award for best new writer. Both his novels, *Neverness* and *The Broken God,* were nominated for the Arthur C. Clarke Award. He lives in Boulder, Colorado.

STEPHEN R. DONALDSON

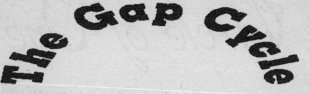

Angus Thermopyle and Nick Succorso: two ore pirates with legendary reputations. Morn Hyland: a United Mining Company police officer, beautiful, dedicated, and deadly. Together they are drawn into an adventure of dark passions, perilous alliances, and dubious heroism in a future where technology has blossomed with fabulous possibilities, where a shadowy presence lurks just beyond our vision, and people cross the Gap at faster-than-light speeds. . . .

The mind becomes a deadly place to venture in

Circle of One

by Eric James Fullilove

"Razor-edged details, wicked violence and garish colors,
mixed with lots and lots of caffeine (or is it adrenaline?),
give *Circle of One* a voice and style of its own."
—Kevin J. Anderson

Eric James Fullilove creates an unforgettable protagonist in
Jenny Sixa, whose telepathic talent makes her a valuable asset to
the Los Angeles Police Department, saving her from a life in the
mind-sex meccas of the city. Jenny now serves as a consultant
for the LAPD, for she is able to read the final thoughts of victims to create an image of their killers. Jenny keeps some vital
information from the police, though, when she finds her name
in the final thoughts of three dead women. The remarkable
talent that has earned Jenny a living is the same one that has
placed her in the path of a murderer, and she must race to find
the killer before he strikes again.

___57575-9   CIRCLE OF ONE $5.50/$7.50 Canada